The Romance Collection

*Three very different,
complete love stories.
Something for every mood...*

I'm Having Your Baby?!—Linda Turner
Sensation: passionate, dramatic and thrilling

Who's the Boss?—Barbara Boswell
Desire: intense, provocative and sensual

Part-Time Wife—Susan Mallery
Special Edition: vivid, satisfying, full of family, life and love

LINDA TURNER

began reading romances in school and began writing them one night when she had nothing else to read. She's been writing ever since. Single and living in Texas, she travels every chance she gets, scouting locales for her books.

BARBARA BOSWELL

loves writing about families. 'I guess family has been a big influence on my writing,' she says. 'I particularly enjoy writing about how my characters' family relationships affect them.'

When Barbara isn't writing or reading, she's spending time with her *own* family—her husband, three daughters and three cats, whom she concedes are the true bosses of their home! She has lived in Europe, but now makes her home in Pennsylvania.

SUSAN MALLERY

makes her home in the Lone Star state, where the people are charming and the weather is always interesting. She lives with her hero-material husband and her two attractive-but-not-very-bright cats. When she's not hard at work writing romances she can be found exploring the wilds of Texas and shopping for the perfect pair of cowboy boots. Susan writes historical romances under the names Susan Macias.

The Romance
Collection

LINDA TURNER
BARBARA BOSWELL
SUSAN MALLERY

SILHOUETTE®

DID YOU PURCHASE THIS BOOK WITHOUT A COVER?
If you did, you should be aware it is **stolen property** as it was reported *unsold and destroyed* by a retailer. Neither the author nor the publisher has received any payment for this book.

All the characters in this book have no existence outside the imagination of the author, and have no relation whatsoever to anyone bearing the same name or names. They are not even distantly inspired by any individual known or unknown to the author, and all the incidents are pure invention.

All Rights Reserved including the right of reproduction in whole or in part in any form. This edition is published by arrangement with Harlequin Enterprises II B.V. The text of this publication or any part thereof may not be reproduced or transmitted in any form or by any means, electronic or mechanical, including photocopying, recording, storage in an information retrieval system, or otherwise, without the written permission of the publisher.

This book is sold subject to the condition that it shall not, by way of trade or otherwise, be lent, resold, hired out or otherwise circulated without the prior consent of the publisher in any form of binding or cover other than that in which it is published and without a similar condition including this condition being imposed on the subsequent purchaser.

Silhouette and Colophon are registered trademarks of Harlequin Books S.A., used under licence.

*First published in Great Britain 2002
Silhouette Books, Eton House, 18-24 Paradise Road,
Richmond, Surrey TW9 1SR*

THE ROMANCE COLLECTION © Harlequin Books S.A. 2002

The publisher acknowledges the copyright holders of the individual works as follows:

I'm Having Your Baby?! © Linda Turner 1997
Who's The Boss? © Barbara Boswell 1997
Part-Time Wife © Susan W. Macias 1996

I'm Having Your Baby?!, *Who's The Boss* and *Part-Time Wife* were first published in Great Britain in separate, single volumes.

ISBN 0 373 04773 8

55-0102

*Printed and bound in Spain
by Litografia Rosés S.A., Barcelona*

CONTENTS

I'M HAVING YOUR BABY?!
Linda Turner

WHO'S THE BOSS?
Barbara Boswell

PART-TIME WIFE
Susan Mallery

Dear Reader,

It's an absolute delight to be able to offer you three wonderful books by three terrific and successful Silhouette® authors, all gathered together in this very special collection.

These three books represent the kind of stories that you would find in our Sensation™, Desire™ and Special Edition™ series, and offer the perfect opportunity to sample lines you might not have tried before.

Susan Mallery has a three-book set of linked books out in Special Edition from now until March, Barbara Boswell will have a Christmas story out in December, and Linda Turner's *Nighthawk's Child* and *The Enemy's Daughter* are on the shelves in March in our Montana Brides and Sensation series. So as you can see, there are plenty of chances to pick up something new from one of these writers over the next few months now that you've discovered them!

All the best,

The Editors

I'm Having Your Baby?!

LINDA TURNER

SILHOUETTE®
SENSATION™

Prologue

Gasping, her lungs straining, she ran through the dark, deserted alleys of downtown like a wild thing, her face as colorless as the pale moon that played hide-and-seek with the clouds overhead. The night was chilly, the black asphalt of the streets damp from the recent rain, but she never noticed the cold or the still-dripping eaves and dirty puddles that had collected in potholes. Blindly, she ran on, granting herself no mercy despite the stitch that burned like a fire in her side. Only one thought hammered in her brain. Home. She had to get home. She would be safe there.

Somewhere in the stygian darkness behind her, the terror she couldn't put a name to hunted her. She'd lost him for now, but she knew he was back there somewhere in the maze of shadowy streets and alleys, cursing her, damning her, chasing her. She could feel him, smell him on her skin. If he got his hands on her again, he wouldn't make the mistake of letting her fight free a second time. Sobbing, she cut through another dark passageway, her long hair streaming out behind her.

Suddenly, a large Victorian house loomed before her, looking as out of place among the towering buildings of downtown as a well-preserved but shrunken old woman among giants. Frantic, she tried to punch in the security code that opened the front door, but her fingers were trembling so badly she couldn't manage it. Her blue eyes wide with fright, she dared to look over her shoulder. It was three in the morning and the street behind her was empty and still. Too still. Whimpering, she whirled back to the keypad and wildly stabbed in numbers. When she finally hit the right combination three tries later, she was through the door in a flash.

She didn't remember running through the deserted foyer or darting up the central staircase that looked like it had come straight out of *Gone with the Wind*. Suddenly, she was stumbling to a stop in front of her own apartment, and somewhere deep inside, the control that had gotten her this far started to crack.

Shaking with reaction, she fumbled for the spare key on the ledge above the door and practically fell inside. The second the door shut behind her, darkness engulfed her. Then the tears started. Hot, endless, racking tears that slid soundlessly down her cheeks. Wrapping her arms around herself, she wanted to collapse boneless to the floor, but she couldn't. Not yet. Not when she could still smell the monster's sweat on her, still feel his hands on her, hurting her, marking her skin. Bile rising in her throat, she tore at her clothes and stumbled to the bathroom without bothering to turn on a light.

Dazed, aching, desperate to be clean again, she stood under the shower lathering herself with hands that felt like they would never be steady again. Her arms grew heavy, her movements stiff and jerky. The hot water turned lukewarm, then finally cold. Roused from the numbness that engulfed her like a fog, she blindly shut off the shower and grabbed a towel. Tired. God, she was so tired! Exhaustion pulling at her, she made her way down the dark hall to the bedroom and slipped into bed. Before her head hit the pillow, her mind shut down and she was spiraling down into the black, protective folds of sleep.

Chapter 1

It rained again just after dawn, the slow, soaking, drizzly kind of rain that made it impossible to crawl out of bed in the morning. Snuggling deeper under the covers, she buried her face in her pillow and fought wakefulness with everything she had in her. It was early yet, she thought drowsily, refusing to open her eyes to check the clock. And she was still so tired—she felt like she'd just gone to bed. Just two more hours. That was all she needed. Maybe then she'd wake up with enough energy to get her through the day.

But even as her mind drifted and sleep beckoned, the murmur of the rain called softly, insistently, to her. Outside the bedroom window, the city was beginning to wake up. Traffic was already starting to pick up, and somewhere nearby, the steady warning beep of a delivery truck backing up shattered the peace of the morning. Groaning, she gave up in defeat and pushed up on her elbows to check the clock on the nightstand. Her eyes never made it past the dark head on the pillow next to her.

Linda Turner

A man. There was a man in bed with her.

Horrified, she stared at him in confusion. She was hallucinating. She had to be. Who was he? What did he want? The answers her dazed mind supplied sent sick panic skittering through her. Dear God, what had he done to her? With bile rising in her throat, she searched her blurred memory for answers, but before she could come up with any, he stirred, and her heart stopped in midbeat. Scrambling backward on the bed, her only thought to get away, she screamed.

Sound asleep, Joe Taylor jerked awake. "What the hell!"

Bolting up and still groggy, he instinctively grabbed for the gun he kept in the nightstand drawer. It wasn't until his fingers closed around the cold, hard butt of the revolver that he recognized the sharp, feminine cry and realized that the only threat was the unexpected visitor in his bed.

And just as quickly, he was furious. What the hell was she doing here? Did she think she could leave him for two months without a word, then crawl back into his bed whenever the mood struck her? Like hell!

Shoving the gun back in the drawer, he turned toward her, angry words already rising to his tongue, only to freeze, shocked, at the sight of her. With her stubborn chin, wide mouth, and too large eyes, she'd never fit the traditional definition of beauty, but there had always been something about her that had stolen the breath right out of his lungs. This time was no different, but not for the usual reasons. Looking thinner, more petite than he remembered, she was pale as a ghost, her oval face scratched and bruised, her sapphire eyes wide and terrified.

"What the hell happened to you?" he demanded. "You look like you've been in a fight."

When she cringed like a trapped animal, Joe scowled.

What the devil was wrong with her? Why was she looking at him like that? He started to ask her, but she never gave him a chance. Her eyes darting around the room, she felt blindly behind her for the edge of the mattress. When she found it, she whirled and flew from the bed...only to take two steps and suddenly seem to realize she was naked.

"Oh, God!" she gasped.

Blushing scarlet, she swallowed a sob and looked frantically around for something to cover herself with. All she found was a towel on the floor. In the time it took to blink, she had it wrapped around her and was running for the door.

There'd been a time when Joe would have laughed at her modesty, snatched the towel from her, and dragged her back into bed for some serious loving. But not now. Not after she'd completely cut herself off from him for two months. And not after he'd caught sight of the bruises covering her. Spitting out a curse, he rolled from the bed and moved, lightning-quick, to cut her off.

"Dammit, quit running from me!" he snapped, uncaring that he was standing stark naked before her. "You're hurt. Let me see."

"No!" Her eyes wide and desperate and dark with terror, she backed away from him as if he was a rapist. "Stay a-away from m-me!" she stuttered in rising hysteria. "You even think about hurting me, and I swear I'll claw your eyes out! If you don't believe me, you just try it!"

Shocked, Joe stopped in his tracks. "Hurt you?" he repeated incredulously. "You think I would *hurt* you?"

"I don't know!" she cried, looking anywhere but at him. "How am I supposed to know what you're capable of? I've never seen you before in my life!"

Unable to believe he'd heard her correctly, Joe blinked in confusion. Was this some kind of joke, or what? She had to be pulling his leg. But Annie had never been much of an actress—her feelings were always right there on her face for the whole world to read. And right now, there was nothing but terror there. And a total lack of recognition in her eyes.

Dear God, she wasn't faking. She really didn't know who he was!

Staggered, he frowned at her in bewilderment. What the hell was going on here? How could she not know him? He was her husband, for God's sake!

Not thinking—needing some answers, dammit!—he started to reach for her, only to have her shrink back in horror. He stiffened, a muscle clenching in his jaw. He'd thought she no longer had the power to hurt him. He was wrong. His expression grim, he carefully reached past her for the robe hanging on the hook on the back of the bedroom door.

Any hope that she would feel less threatened when he was decently covered died the second he belted the robe and lifted his eyes to hers. Her arms crossed protectively across her breasts to hold the thick bath sheet in place, she bumped up against the door, wariness etched in every line of her slender body.

"I'm Joe Taylor," he said quietly. "Your husband."

Whatever reaction he had been expecting, it wasn't the sudden flash of temper in her sapphire eyes. "Don't be ridiculous. If you were my husband, don't you think I'd remember you?"

For an answer, he strode over to the dresser, snatched up a silver-framed photo, and thrust it into her hands. "Then how do you explain this?"

The smiling man and woman who stared up at her from the picture were decked out in their wedding finery and obviously very much in love. And while there was no doubt that the groom had the same square-jawed, rugged good looks, brown eyes, and coal-black hair as the man standing before her wearing nothing but a robe, the woman was a total stranger to her.

Puzzled, she tried to shove the picture back into his hand, but he wouldn't take it. "If this is supposed to prove something, I missed the point. That's not me."

"The hell it isn't! If you don't believe me, look in the mirror."

She should have, but something held her back. Something that gripped at her heart with cold fingers. "No."

"Why?" he asked softly. "Because you're afraid I'm right? Then tell me what you look like."

Goaded, she opened her mouth to do just that, but no words came out. Nothing. She didn't have a clue if she was a redhead or a bleached blonde, pretty or plain. Fear, like a snake slithering through high grass, slipped through her blood, and the only way she could fight it was to look in the mirror. Without a word, she jerked around to face the dresser.

And came face-to-face with the woman in the picture.

"No!"

She thought she screamed, but her cry was hardly more than a hoarse, strangled whisper. The reflected image was bruised and scratched, but there was no question that the woman in the mirror and the one in the wedding picture were one and the same. They were both her, and she didn't recognize either one of them.

"No!" she cried again, her voice strong with fear as she shoved the picture back into the hands of the tall, lean man who watched her like a hawk. Her husband. Oh, God! "This is some kind of a trick," she said desperately. "I don't know who you are or how you managed to make that picture, but I want you out of here. Do you hear me? Get out!"

Joe had no intention of going anywhere, but he knew if he made one wrong move, she was going to shatter. "Calm down," he said soothingly, taking a step back and giving her room. "Nobody's going to hurt you, especially me. Just take it easy. There's nothing to worry about—people have trouble with their memories all the time. Just relax and it'll probably all come back to you. Do you remember your name?"

She automatically opened her mouth to answer, only to hesitate, the arrested look of surprise that washed over her face changing abruptly to horror. Stricken, she stared up at him helplessly.

She couldn't remember her own name.

Something twisted in Joe's heart. "It's Annie," he told her gruffly. "Annie Taylor. Sit down, honey, and let's talk about this. Tell me what you do remember. What'd you do yesterday?"

Hot tears slowly gathering in her eyes, she just looked at him blankly. "I don't know. I—I don't remember."

"Then how about last night?" he tried. "You weren't here when I went to bed, so you must have come in sometime after that. How did you get in? Did you have your key with you? Where's your purse?"

He kept the questions simple, but she didn't have any answers. She couldn't even tell him what day it was, and she was scared out of her mind. He couldn't say he blamed her. More worried than he dared let her see, he said, "Maybe you left it in the living room. Let's check it out."

With her trailing behind him, he strode out of the bedroom and looked around for her purse. But there was no purse, no luggage, nothing but a single key lying on the table in the entrance hall. "Well, this explains how you got in," he said, holding up the key. "You used the spare that's usually kept over the doorjamb. Now, what about your clothes?"

They found them in a heap on the bathroom floor, torn,

dirty and bloody. Joe swore at the sight of them and turned to find her staring at them without the slightest sign of recognition. Her face was expressionless, as if the bloody clothes themselves had nothing to do with her, and it was that, more than anything, that told him something was very, very wrong.

"I think you need to see a doctor," he told her. "Today."

"No!"

The panic was back in her eyes, and she looked ready to bolt.

Moving to reassure her, he said quickly, "I'm not talking about going to a hospital or anything like that. Just to a friend. Grant Alexander. I know you don't remember him, but he was best man at our wedding, and he's a damn good internist. All I have to do is give him a call and he'll fit you in this morning."

"But I don't have any clothes—"

"There are some things in the closet in the bedroom," he cut in, his mouth flattening as he thought of the things she'd left behind in her haste to leave. "Why don't you get dressed while I give Grant a call?"

She didn't want to—he could see the doubts clearly in her eyes—but she couldn't seem to come up with another excuse. Nodding reluctantly, she headed for the bedroom.

"What do you mean, you woke up and she was in bed with you?" Grant demanded the second Joe called him and told him Annie was back. "Just like that? After she disappeared for months?"

"I always knew where she was, Grant. She called me the day after she left and gave me the address of the apartment she'd rented," Joe reminded him. "And Phoebe kept in touch." In fact, if it hadn't been for Annie's best friend and partner in the real estate office they ran together, he wouldn't have known if his wife was alive or dead.

"But Annie was the one who should have been talking to you. Not that I'm criticizing," he added quickly. "You know I'm crazy about her, buddy. I think you two were made for each other—I just don't know how you kept from going after her. I know, I know—you promised her you wouldn't, but I'd have been over there ten minutes after she told you where she was. So is she back for good or what?"

"I wish to God I knew," Joe said flatly. "There's a problem. I think she's got amnesia."

"Yeah, right. Tell me another one."

"I'm serious, Grant." He told him everything then, from the second he'd awakened to find her naked in his bed to the moment he found her bloody clothes on the bathroom floor. "I'm telling you, something's seriously wrong. She didn't even remember her name until I told her what it was."

"That sounds pretty damn convenient, don't you think?"

Joe stared at the locked bathroom door that Annie was hiding behind and had to admit that there was a cynical side of him that had wondered the same thing. But the look of panic on her face when she'd looked at their wedding picture was something that would go with him to his grave. Not even an Academy Award–winning actress could fake that kind of fear.

"You wouldn't ask that if you could see her," he said. "She's got some nasty bruises on her. In fact, she's banged up pretty bad. I don't know if she's been in an accident or car wreck or what, but every time I get anywhere near her, she starts shaking like a leaf."

"Then what was she doing in bed with you this morning?"

"To tell you the truth, I don't even think she knew I was

there. And I was dead to the world. It seems like I've been putting in twenty-hour days ever since she left, and last night I guess it just caught up with me. I never heard her come in. Then, this morning, she woke up screaming. I'm telling you, Grant, she's really got me worried."

He didn't ask his friend if he could take a look at her, but he didn't have to. All business, he said, "I'll meet you at the office within the hour."

"We'll be there," Joe said with a quiet sigh of relief. "Thanks, pal. I owe you one."

Dressed in a faded yellow blouse and old jeans that apparently should have been familiar to her but weren't, Annie followed the grim-faced, enigmatic man who claimed to be her husband into the parking garage where he kept his car. He, too, had changed, and looked much less threatening in black slacks and a white shirt than he had naked. Still, as she walked from the sunny street into the darkened interior of the garage, she felt as if someone had stepped on her grave. Shivering, she stopped cold, unable to make herself go any farther.

Don't be a ninny, an irritated voice muttered in her head. *You can do this.*

She had to. Her past, her very identity, had somehow been stolen from her, and the cold black hole in her memory scared her to death. She didn't know who she was or what she was, and if she was ever going to find out, she had to go with him to his doctor friend and find out what was wrong with her.

But when Joe stopped next to a green Regal that was apparently his, then unlocked and opened the passenger door for her, a soul-destroying fear came out of nowhere to clutch her by the throat. "No!" she said hoarsely. "I can't do it!"

Surprised, Joe glanced over his shoulder to find that she'd

stopped six feet back. "Can't do what? You said you'd go to the doctor."

"I know. I'm sorry. I thought I could, but I can't." Her gaze slipped from him to the car, and right before his eyes, she turned a sickly shade of green. "I can't," she choked. "I can't get in that car with you."

A muscle bunched in his jaw. "So it's me."

"No. Yes! I don't know!" she cried.

In the dark, quiet shadows that surrounded them, she thought she heard him swear, but she couldn't be sure. He was so quick at hiding what he was thinking—she couldn't read his eyes at all. Was he going to insist she get in his car? The coppery taste of fear pooled on her tongue. What if he tried to force her? Was he the type of man who would do that? God, why couldn't she remember?

Frustrated, furious with herself for not remembering, she knew she'd fight him if he so much as laid a finger on her. But the struggle she braced for never materialized. Instead, even as she watched, the tension slowly drained out of him. "Okay," he sighed, "if you can't, you can't. It's no big deal. The important thing is to get you to the doctor. Would you feel more comfortable if I called a cab? *I'll* follow you in my car," he quickly assured her, "so you don't have to worry about anyone crowding you. How's that sound?"

Grateful, she nodded stiffly. "I think that might be better."

Joe had the foresight to request a woman driver when he called for a cab, and forty minutes later they reached the medical complex Grant Alexander shared with five other doctors. His office was on the second floor, and Joe gently nudged Annie in the direction of the stairs without sparing a glance at the elevator. If she panicked at the thought of getting in a car with him, he didn't even want to think about what she would do if he followed her into the close confines of an elevator.

The reception area was fairly crowded, but they didn't have to wait. Within seconds, they were shown into Grant's private office, and moments later, the doctor himself was rushing in. As tall as Joe, but stockier, with Ivy League good looks, he greeted Joe, then turned to Annie, his sharp, intelligent eyes narrowing slightly at the sight of her battered face.

"Hello, Annie," he said. "It's been a while. How are you?"

He didn't rush her, didn't try to touch her or do anything that would spook her. Relieved, Annie smiled weakly. "I'd like to think I've been better, but I can't be sure of that. I'm sorry. I know I should know you, but I don't."

"There's no need to apologize," he said easily. "You look like you've had a rough time of it lately."

She shrugged, unable to tell him any more than she'd been able to tell Joe. "I guess so. I don't remember."

"Anything?"

Mutely, she shook her head. His gaze, missing nothing, traveled over the vivid bruises that marred her tender skin. Frowning, he said, "Let me get my nurse to show you into an examining room, and I'll see if I can find out what the problem is. Okay?"

Logically, she knew she had no reason to fear him. He was a friend of Joe's and a doctor, no less. Still, her heart lurched with a panic that was becoming all too familiar. "Your nurse will be there?" she blurted, before she could stop herself.

Surprised, he couldn't miss her sudden wariness or the defensive way she wrapped her arms around herself. Exchanging a look with Joe, he nodded. "She'll be right there the entire time. Even then, if you feel uncomfortable or scared at any time, I want you to tell me. Would you feel more at ease if Joe sat in on the exam?"

Her eyes flew to Joe's, the pounding of her heart turning erratic. It wasn't a completely unexpected question. Although she still found it hard to believe that the dark, silent man at her side was her husband, he apparently had been for some time and it was perfectly natural for the doctor to assume that she would feel safer with him at her side.

Nothing, however, could have been further from the truth. She had no reason to believe that he'd hurt her, but there was something about him that made her knees weak and her pulse jump. Something that made her want to trust him, yet run from him at one and the same time. And God help her, she didn't know why.

"N-no, that's not necessary," she said shakily, and missed the sudden tightening of her husband's granite jaw as she forced herself to drop her arms from around herself. "I know I'm being paranoid, but I can't seem to help it. I feel like someone dropped me into an episode of 'The Twilight Zone' when my back was turned. Nothing makes sense."

"So you remember 'The Twilight Zone,'" Grant said with a smile as he opened the door at his nurse's knock. "That's a start, anyway. Let's go take a look at you, then see what else you remember."

It didn't take Annie long to discover why Grant Alexander's waiting room was full. He was a kind man with a gentle touch who took the time to talk to his patients. He didn't rush her into the exam once his nurse had helped her change into a gown, telling her instead about his friendship with Joe and the wild times they had had together over the years. He made her laugh...and relax. Then the examination started.

Because she didn't know exactly what had happened to her, Grant recommended a complete physical, and she endured it as best she could. But it wasn't easy. Dressed in a gown that tied in the back, she felt horribly naked and vulnerable. She tried to convince herself that there was no reason to tense up, but the knotting muscles of her stomach didn't seem to get the message. When he touched her, it took all her self-control not to cringe.

She thought she'd hidden her distaste for the whole procedure pretty well, but when he finished the pelvic exam and his nurse helped her sit up, she quickly discovered she wasn't fooling anyone, least of all him. Taking a step back, he gave her some space and said quietly, "You don't have to hide what you're feeling, Annie. It's okay to be scared."

Flushed, she looked away. "And I thought I was hiding it so well. How'd you know?"

"Your breath catches in your throat every time I start to touch you." His gray eyes discerning, he examined the bruises on her face. "Why do you think that is?" he asked. "Because you don't remember me, or because I'm a man and some man hurt you?"

She wanted to say that it was because he was a stranger, but everyone she'd encountered today—from her husband to the taxi driver to Grant and his nurse—were strangers. It was only the men who sent fear backing up in her throat.

"I d-don't know," she stuttered. "Just the thought of being touched by a man—*any* man—makes me... I can't explain it.... I just—" Unable to find the words, she shrugged, tears welling in her eyes. "I'm sorry," she choked. "This is so *stupid!*"

He handed her a tissue, his eyes kind as they met hers. "Don't be so hard on yourself. You've obviously suffered some kind of a trauma. You have a bruise on your temple, but no concussion, so I don't think it's a head injury that's causing your amnesia." Patting her hand, he pulled up a stool and sat. "Tell me what you do remember."

Despite his full waiting room, he looked as if he was prepared to hear her life story—if she could recall it, but in the end, there was nothing to tell. She had a vague memory of taking a shower the previous night, then going to bed. Before that, her mind was a blank.

"What about last week? Last year? Your childhood? Where did you go to high school?"

She couldn't tell him how many brothers or sisters she had, her favorite color, if her parents were even alive. Nothing. For all practical purposes, her mind was as empty as a newborn baby's. Except for the fear that had lingered there like a black shadow ever since she looked in the mirror, saw a stranger's face, and realized that something terrible must have happened to her.

Suddenly cold all the way to the bone, she asked bluntly, "Was I raped?"

He opened his mouth, then hesitated, and she went pale. "Oh, God!"

"No, no," he said quickly, swearing. "There's no evidence that you were molested recently—"

"*Recently?*"

Cursing himself, he nodded for his nurse to leave them alone. As soon as the door shut, he turned back to her. "Annie, I think Joe should be in on this conversation."

"If I wasn't raped, then something else must be wrong. What is it?"

"Annie—"

"*Tell me!*"

"You're pregnant, okay? Dammit, you're pregnant!"

The news hit her hard, like a freight train that came out of nowhere. Pregnant, she thought, dazed. She was pregnant, and her husband's best friend was waiting expectantly for a response from her. Hysterical laughter threatened to choke her. How was she supposed to know how to react when she didn't remember anything? Had she planned this pregnancy? Did she even want a baby? How would Joe, a husband she didn't know, feel about becoming a father?

Instinctively, her hand slid down to the faint bulge of her stomach. "When?"

"I was hoping you could tell me that. You don't remember getting pregnant?"

Something in his tone warned her that the question was a loaded one. "No," she said cautiously, "but Joe should. Shouldn't he?"

He winced, then quietly dropped the bomb she unconsciously braced for. "It's hard to pinpoint how far along you are since you're barely showing and you can't remember when you had your last period. And Joe might not be much help. You left him two months ago, and he hasn't seen you since. Which means the baby might or might not be his."

Each word hit her like a blow, sucking the air from her lungs. Stunned, she heard a roaring in her ears and realized it must be the rush of her blood. This couldn't be happening, she thought. It was all just some horrible nightmare that would be over any second.

But the sympathy in his gray eyes was too real, the regret he couldn't hide too personal, and she knew he wouldn't lie to her. Not about something like this.

"Oh, God," she whispered, "he didn't tell me. I woke up screaming in his bed and he never once told me that I had no right to be there. Why? Why didn't he tell me?"

"I can't speak for him," Grant said, "but my guess is that there wasn't time. You were hysterical and scared to death of him, and getting you to a doctor was more important than giving you a play-by-play of your marriage. He's a good man, Annie. Seeing you like this couldn't have been easy for him."

"But I left him. Why?"

"That's something you'll have to discuss with him," he said, patting her hand as he pushed to his feet. "Why don't you get dressed now, then come back to my office when you're ready? I'm going to talk to Joe, then see about getting you in to see someone else about your amnesia."

He left before she could call him back, shutting the door quietly behind him. Alone with the questions that stumbled around in her head in search of answers that weren't there, Annie didn't move for a long time. What kind of woman could be pregnant and not know who the father of her baby was? Dear God, what had she done?

Restless, Joe prowled around Grant's office like a man who had just missed the last bus out of town. What the hell was taking so long? Had Grant found something? Something serious? Dammit, he should have insisted on sitting in on the examination! Whether she remembered it or not, Annie was still his wife, and he had a right to know if something was seriously wrong with her.

The door behind him opened then, and he whirled to see Grant step across the threshold, his aristocratic face set in grim lines. "What is it?" he asked sharply. "And don't try to put me off by claiming nothing's wrong," he warned his friend tersely. "I can see by your face there's a problem."

"Not one I was expecting," Grant retorted somberly, as he moved to the tufted leather chair behind his desk and sank into it. "Sit down, Joe. We need to talk, and I don't think you're going to like what I have to say."

He didn't want to sit, but something in his friend's expression had him reaching for a chair. "I don't see how it could be any worse than what I've been imagining for the last thirty minutes, so just lay it on the line. I can take it."

From the hard, searching look Grant gave him, it was obvious that he wasn't so sure of that, but he finally nodded. "First off, I could find no physical cause of Annie's amnesia, so I've got to believe that it's a result of some trauma she suffered and doesn't want to remember. She's terrified of men, and while I was examining her, she voiced a fear that she'd been raped. She wasn't," he said quickly, when Joe seemed to turn to stone. "But deep down in her subconscious, she was aware of the possibility that she could have been. I think it's safe to say she was attacked."

Joe had come to the same conclusion, but hearing his own fears put into words turned his stomach. A muscle jumped along his tight jaw. "That might explain why she refused to remember what happened to her, but why would she block out the rest of her memory?"

"The mind is a funny thing," Grant replied, "and we're a long way from understanding it. Just to be sure, I'd like you to take her to Preston Ziggler for a second opinion. Amnesia is not something you run into every day of the week, and he's had more experience with it than anyone else in the city. I'll give him a call and see if he can fit her in sometime this afternoon."

Joe nodded. "Fine. Whatever you say. Whatever it takes to get her memory back. She might hate my guts, but I'd rather see recognition and hate in her eyes than this godawful wariness. You are saying that she'll get her memory back, aren't you?"

"Probably," Grant agreed, "though there's no saying how long it will take." He hated like hell to tell him the rest, but there was no way to avoid the truth. "There's something else you should know. God knows, I wish I didn't have to be the one to tell you this, but you're going to have to know eventually anyway. And I'll tell you right now, there's no use asking Annie about it because she can't tell you a damn thing—at least not yet. So don't hassle her for answers she can't give you. That's the last thing she needs right now."

"Hassle her about what?" Joe growled, scowling. "Dammit, what the devil are you talking about?"

It wasn't the kind of news you wanted to tell your best friend, but the Fates hadn't given him a choice. Cursing the powers that be, he sighed heavily and gave it to him straight, with no sugarcoating. "She's pregnant, man. And she hasn't got a clue who the daddy is."

Chapter 2

Annie was pregnant.

Nothing else registered. Caught off guard, Joe stared at Grant like a man who suddenly didn't understand English. How? When? Questions slapped at him, stunning him. A baby. They were going to have a baby, ready or not. From out of nowhere, a laugh bubbled up in his chest and almost choked him. Of all the things he'd imagined, this was the last. Lord, how was a man supposed to react when he found out he was going to be a father for the first time? A crooked grin started to tilt up the corner of his mouth.

Then the rest of Grant's announcement slapped him in the face.

She hasn't got a clue who the daddy is.

He stiffened even as he told himself not to be a fool. This was Annie they were talking about. She'd been a virgin when he met her. He'd courted her for months, wooing her and earning her trust and love before she'd allowed him any kind of true intimacy. There was no way she'd have let a stranger touch her, let alone get her pregnant, just weeks after she'd left him. She just wasn't capable of that kind of behavior. The baby had to be his.

If you won't give me a baby, then I'll find someone who will.

From the cold ashes of their last bitter argument, the threat she'd made right before she left him echoed cruelly in his mind, taunting him. Things hadn't been good between them for a while—mainly because of work. In the months before she left him, he'd had nothing but one problem after another with the staff at Joe's Place, the restaurant he owned on the Riverwalk. He was losing money and customers, and all his attention had been focused on finding new people to replace the troublemakers, then getting the business back on its feet financially. At the same time, Annie and Phoebe had just opened their real estate office the previous spring and were having to hustle just to break even.

In all the chaos, Annie had wanted to have a baby. Her timing couldn't have been worse.

He'd tried to reason with her, to convince her to wait, but every discussion had ended in an argument. She'd accused him of not wanting children at all when nothing could have been further from the truth. Six months to a year—that's all he'd wanted. Six months to get their lives back on track. Then they could start talking about babies.

But Annie hadn't been willing to wait. She'd given him an ultimatum, and they'd both said some things they shouldn't have. She'd ended up sleeping in the guest room, and when he woke up in the morning, she was gone. When she'd called later, it was to announce that she needed some serious time to herself to think about their future—*if* they had one. So she'd rented an apartment on the north side. She'd contact him when she was ready to talk.

Respecting her wishes and giving her the time she wanted

was the hardest thing he'd ever done, but he hadn't had much choice. She'd been so upset that if he'd come after her, he would have lost her for sure.

And now she was back. And expecting a baby. There was a possibility that she could have been pregnant when she left him and not known it. But if that was the case, why hadn't she let him know when she discovered her condition? She'd been gone for two months, for God's sake! Surely sometime during that time, she could have found a few minutes to pick up the phone and let him know he was going to be a father.

Unless the baby wasn't his.

The thought slipped like a dagger between his ribs. He immediately tried to reject the idea. But she'd been hurt and furious and in a reckless mood when she'd left him, desperate for a baby. And as much as he hated to admit it, she hadn't been the same Annie he'd married for some time. She'd been on edge, unhappy, and nothing he'd done had seemed to please her. She'd complained about the hours he worked and the attention she claimed he didn't give her. She might very well have gotten that attention from another man.

"Joe?" Grant said worriedly, when he just sat there. "I know this has to be a shock—"

"Shock?" he laughed harshly, his face set in bitter lines as he looked up from his grim thoughts. "Yeah, it's a shock, all right, when you find out your wife might be carrying another man's baby. And the hell of the thing about it is that she doesn't have any more of a clue how she got in that condition than I do. Dammit, Grant, I need some answers, and I need them now! When is she going to get her memory back?"

Helpless, the other man could only shrug. "There's no way to predict that."

"Then try narrowing it down. Are we talking about a couple of days? A week? What?"

"It all hinges on the severity of the trauma she suffered," he replied. "If I were you, I'd take her home, take care of her, and make her feel safe. She'll remember when she's ready."

"And if the baby's not mine?"

"Then you've got some decisions to make," his friend said somberly. "Either way, that's something you can't discuss with her now. The less pressure she has to deal with, the faster her memory should come back."

"What do you mean...her memory *should* come back? Is there a possibility that it won't?"

Grant hesitated. "I don't like to say never, especially when this isn't my field of expertise. I think that with time, she will remember her past. Recalling whatever or whoever terrorized her, however, is another matter. Something scared her enough to make her forget her own name, and she may block that for the rest of her life."

All too easily, Joe could see the stark terror in her eyes when she'd thought he was going to hurt her. He wasn't a violent man, but at that moment he would have given everything he had to put his hands around the throat of the man who had put that look in Annie's eyes. "That may be for the best," he said grimly. "Some things are better off forgotten."

Grant agreed. "Whatever happened, at least she followed her instincts and came home. I know it's not much consolation, but deep down inside, she has to trust you, man, or she never would have run to you."

Long after they left his friend's office, Joe tried to find some comfort in that thought, but trust was the last thing he saw in Annie's eyes when she looked at him. The sapphire blue depths that had once gazed up at him with such love were leery and full of apprehension. As cautious as a lone woman on a deserted highway who had no choice but to accept the help of the first stranger who came along, she finally let him talk her into his car, but she clung to the passenger door, ready to bolt if he so much as looked at her wrong.

And as much as he hated to admit it, it hurt. The Annie he knew, the only woman he'd ever loved, had been full of fun and sass and unafraid of the devil himself. Seeing her like this—pale and nervous and clearly frightened—of him, dammit!—tore him apart. What the hell had happened to her? Who had hurt her and why?

As Grant had predicted, it was determined after a battery of tests that Annie's amnesia was psychological rather than physical. She would remember her past when she was ready and not until then. As for her pregnancy, Annie's gynecologist, Dr. Sawyer, couldn't tell them. When she was further along, a sonogram would help determine how developed the baby was, but at this stage, it was impossible to pinpoint exactly how far along she was. Yes, Dr. Sawyer admitted, Annie could be less than two months pregnant. But then again, the doctor had seen women who were three or four months along and didn't look much bigger than Annie. Joe was told to take her home, make sure she took her prenatal vitamins, and let her rest. For now, there was nothing anyone else could do.

So eight hours after they left the old Victorian house where they lived, they returned, knowing no more than they had when they'd set out...except that Annie was carrying Joe's or somebody else's baby. Every time he thought about it, it was all he could do not to grab her and demand some answers. Answers that she couldn't give him, he reminded himself bitterly as she gazed up at the house like a first-time visitor.

Anticipating her questions, he said, "It's called the Lone Star Social Club. Back in the trail-riding days, cowboys used to come here on Saturday nights to meet decent women."

Earlier, Annie had been too upset to even notice where she was, let alone appreciate the old mansion's turrets and gingerbread architecture, but now she couldn't help smiling. Painted cream and trimmed in rose and robin's-egg blue, with stained glass in every window and wide porches upstairs and down that wrapped all the way around it, it looked like something out of a fairy tale. "It's gorgeous! How in the world did it survive all these years?"

"Actually, it almost didn't. Ten years ago, the city was on the verge on condemning it when somebody stepped in and saved it. It was divided into apartments and restored, and it's been the talk of the Riverwalk ever since. In case you don't know, it's located on pretty prime property, so whoever saved it must have had some major bucks."

Surprised, she said, "What do you mean, *whoever saved it?* Don't you know? Whoever owns it is your landlord."

"Technically," he agreed. "But he must be some kind of recluse because he's never revealed his identity to anyone."

Trailing her hand along the porch railing, Annie marveled at the wonder of the workmanship. "If I owned this, I think I'd tell the whole world. It's beautiful. Is it haunted?"

He smiled, not surprised by the question. She might not know who she was, but she was still the same romantic she'd always been. "That depends on who you talk to. Some say that on still summer nights, you can hear the sound of music coming from the old ballroom in the attic. But it could just be coming from the nightclubs farther upriver."

Her eyes wistful, Annie shook her head. "No, I like the ballroom version better."

"I know," he said ruefully, and punched in the security code on the keypad to the left of the mansion's front door.

There was no elevator, only the grand staircase that led to the second floor. As they started up it and Annie marveled over the wainscoting and sweep of the stairs, it suddenly hit Joe that while she might be home again, he was a long way from having his wife back. If he even wanted her back. He was a stranger to her, and she was scared of men. To make matters worse, she had not only walked out on their marriage without trying to save it, she might have also betrayed him in the worst way a woman can betray a man. And she didn't even remember it. How were they supposed to live together under those circumstances?

Wishing he could feel nothing but indifference when he looked at her, he couldn't help noticing as they stepped into their apartment that whatever hell had sent her running blindly back there for protection was beginning to exact its toll. The bruises on her face stood out in sharp relief against her colorless skin, and she'd looked as if she had hardly enough energy to put one foot in front of the other.

Something shifted in his heart then, a damnable tenderness he seemed to have no control over. Silently cursing himself for the weakness, he said tersely, "You look bushed. Why don't you go lie down while I fix us something to eat? I'll call you when it's ready."

She wanted to argue—except for the brief history he'd given her about the house, he'd barely said two words to her since they'd left Grant Alexander's office that morning. And over the course of the afternoon, his expression had grown more and more forbidding. They needed to talk, but she was so tired she could barely see straight.

"Maybe you're right," she admitted. "I am a little wiped

out. Just give me a few minutes to put my feet up and I'll be good as new."

Five minutes. That was all she thought she needed, but the second she sank down on the couch and stretched out, what was left of her energy drained out of her. Her eyelids grew heavy, and within ten seconds flat she was out like a light. Forty minutes later, when Joe came into the living room to wake her, she hadn't a clue that he was there until his hand settled lightly on her shoulder and he called her name.

Her eyes flew open, and before she was even awake, she found herself staring up into the face of a man as he bent over her, his dark, shuttered brown eyes much too close for comfort. Her breath lodged painfully in her throat, and for a split second, she was caught in the claws of a nightmare. The feel of a stranger's hands on her, hurting her, was all too real.

A blind man couldn't have missed the terror in her eyes. Swallowing a curse, Joe jerked his hand back. "I didn't mean to startle you. Are you all right?"

A scream already working its way up her throat, she blinked, and just as quickly, recognition rushed through her. Limp, she pressed a shaking hand to her pounding heart. "J-Joe!"

"I called your name," he said in that rough voice she knew would follow her into her dreams. "I thought you heard me."

"No. I must have died away—"

"The food's ready when you are—"

They both spoke at once, their words tumbling over each other as they sought to bridge the sudden awkwardness between them. Quickly sitting up, Annie swung her legs over the side of the couch. "I'll be right there. Just give me a second to wash my face."

"Take your time," he said stiffly as he turned toward the door. "Just come on in the kitchen when you're ready." He was gone before she could say another word and never saw her wrap her arms around herself as the door swung shut behind him.

When she left the bathroom a few minutes later, her face was freshly washed and she was sure she was ready to face her husband. After all, he wasn't a threat to her. She didn't know why she had left him, but every instinct she had told her it wasn't because he'd physically or mentally abused her. He just didn't seem the type, so there was no reason to jump when he touched her. She was home. And safe.

Yet nothing seemed familiar. Not the antique iron bed in the master bedroom where she'd slept last night, or the living room with its rose-colored camelback sofa, or the gourmet kitchen, complete with a commercial stove large enough to feed an army. And most especially not the man she'd apparently shared the apartment with for the past five years.

Stopping in the kitchen doorway, she watched as Joe turned from the stove, two heaping plates of something that smelled wonderful in his hands. He'd been personable and charming with everyone they'd encountered over the course of the day, everyone, that is, except her. With her, he'd been reserved, watchful, his thoughts and feelings well hidden behind those dark brown eyes of his. He hadn't said a word about the baby other than to inquire about how she was feeling, and she didn't have a clue if he was glad or mad that she was back in his life. Which was something she could definitely identify with. She didn't know why she'd come back to him when she was scared or where, if anywhere, they were going from here. Questions. God, she had so many questions!

"There you are," he said, spying her in the doorway.

"You want to eat outside or in? There's a harvest moon tonight, and it's not too cold."

Confused, she followed his gaze from the dining alcove, where a Duncan Phyfe table large enough to easily accommodate eight sat, to the French doors at the far end of the kitchen that opened onto an outdoor balcony that overlooked the San Antonio River two stories below. There, in the gathering twilight, an antique wicker table and two chairs offered an enticing view of the Riverwalk.

"Oh, outside," she said, a delighted smile spreading across her face. "I had no idea we had a view of the river. It's beautiful!"

If Joe had needed any further proof that she had blocked out everything about their life together, she'd just given it to him. She loved that balcony—in happier times, they'd eaten every meal out there when the weather permitted—yet there was no doubting her surprise at the sight of it. She honestly didn't remember it.

"That balcony and this apartment is why we haven't bought a house yet," he informed her as he crossed to the patio table and set their plates on it. "You loved this old place from the moment you moved in and refused to even consider leaving it unless we found something similar. So far, we haven't. I'm beginning to think it doesn't exist. Have a seat and I'll get us something to drink."

Joe wasn't surprised when she didn't have to be told twice. Captivated, she stepped onto the balcony, which was hardly big enough to hold the table and two matching chairs, and stared down at the sights below. Framed on both sides by a forest of tropical plants and flowers, the river lazily meandered through skyscrapers and under arched bridges, creating a colorful, inviting oasis right in the middle of downtown.

She was still there, watching the activity below like a

tourist, when he returned a few minutes later with glasses of iced tea. Taking the seat across from her, he couldn't help smiling when she hardly spared him a glance. "Your food's getting cold," he pointed out dryly. "And it's one of your favorites."

That got her attention. Glancing down at the concoction on her plate, she frowned and lifted a doubtful eyebrow at him. "Are you sure? It doesn't look like something I would like."

Considering the fact that she didn't remember her middle name, let alone her favorite brand of soda, he wondered how she could possibly know what she did and didn't like. But he only said, "Trust me. You'll love it."

"What is it?"

"Fajita chicken spaghetti. You helped me come up with it on a rainy Saturday afternoon, and I've been serving it at the restaurant ever since. It's one of the most popular items on the menu."

"Restaurant?" she echoed, surprised. "You own a restaurant?"

"Right down there, around the bend," he said, nodding downstream. Watching her closely, he said, "It's called Joe's Place. Don't you remember?"

Mutely, she shook her head and took a bite of the spaghetti. "Oh, this is delicious! And this is something we came up with together? When? How?"

She was full of questions, and as they both dug into their food, she asked about everything from the restaurant to how they'd met. "Actually, you have the house to thank for that," he told her ruefully. "I tempted fate the day I moved in here."

"How?"

"Apparently, a lot of cowboys met their downfall here when this place was still a social club. I don't know if the ghost of the lady who ran the place is still wandering around working her magic or what, but according to legend, when anyone single moves in here, they end up falling in love within one year."

"And you lived here when you met me? How long?"

"Two weeks."

Her eyes dancing, Annie clearly didn't believe him. "You're kidding."

"Ask Mrs. Truelove if you don't believe me. The old lady who manages the place," he explained when she looked at him inquiringly. "I don't know if it's true or not, but supposedly she's the granddaughter of the lady who originally ran the place after the Civil War. I'll introduce you to her tomorrow."

Remembering the doctor's suggestion that she be allowed to remember in her own way at her own speed, Joe turned the conversation to their neighbors and life on the river, avoiding more personal topics...like how she'd turned his bachelor pad into a home soon after he'd married her and brought her home with him for good. They'd been so happy then, neither one of them had thought anything could ever come between them.

Then she asked about their separation. Leaning back in her chair, she frowned. "Why did I leave you? What happened? Was there another woman or what?"

She could have been asking about the marriage of a stranger on the street for all the emotion she showed. "No," he said flatly. "It was nothing like that. I never cheated on you, Annie. When I make a vow, I stand by it. I thought you were the same way."

He didn't make any accusations, but he didn't have to. She was the one who'd left him and come back pregnant, without a clue as to who the father of her baby was. And there wasn't a single thing she could say to defend herself.

The easy, lighthearted mood shattered, and what was left of her appetite evaporated. Suddenly she found herself fighting the need to cry and was horrified. It was just the baby, she rationalized. Pregnant women cried over everything, didn't they? Especially when they were tired. She needed sleep, some time to herself to think, to try to figure out who she was. Tomorrow, she promised herself dispiritedly, would be better. It had to be. How could it get any worse?

Carefully setting down her fork, she dropped her napkin next to her half-full plate. "I wish I could tell you that my vows were just as important to me," she said with quiet dignity. "Obviously, I can't. No one regrets that more than I do. Now if you'll excuse me, I think I'll go to bed. It's been a long day."

She pushed to her feet, but he was there, blocking her path, before she could step back into the kitchen. "I know you're exhausted and I promise I'll let you go to bed in just a second, but first there's someone I need you to talk to—"

The doorbell rang then, cutting him off, and there was something in his sudden inability to quite meet her eye that set Annie's heart thumping in her chest. Warily, she looked past his broad shoulders toward the entrance hall. "What have you done, Joe? Who is that?"

"It's just Sam Kelly. I called him while you were sleeping and asked him to come over after supper. He's a friend, Annie. He won't hurt you."

"If he's another doctor—"

"He's not. He's a detective with the San Antonio Police Department."

Alarmed, she took a quick step back and came up hard against the patio table. "He's a cop? No! I don't care if he is a friend of yours, I won't speak to him. I haven't done anything wrong."

Cursing himself for not telling her sooner and giving her

time to prepare herself, he tried to calm her without touching her, as he instinctively wanted to. He might as well have asked himself not to breathe. He could do it for a while, but not forever.

"It isn't a question of you doing anything wrong," he told her, hooking his thumbs in the back pockets of his jeans to keep from reaching for her. "Something happened to you, and we need to find out what it was. Sam can help. He's not just a friend—he's our neighbor. He lives right next door. I called him because I thought you'd be more comfortable talking to him than some rookie you don't know from Adam."

If panic hadn't been churning in her stomach like boiling acid, she might have been amused. How did she make him understand that she didn't know *anyone* from Adam? "There's nothing to talk about," she argued. "I don't remember anything."

"He still needs to be aware of the situation. Sam's a damn good detective. If anyone can find out what happened to you, it's him." When the doorbell rang again, he lifted an eyebrow at her. "It's your call. If you really don't want to talk to him, I'll explain the situation to him. Considering the circumstances, I'm sure he'll understand."

She hesitated, wanting nothing so much as to escape to the bedroom. But whatever she was, she didn't like to think that she might be a coward. She needed to know what she was running from. If this Sam character could help, then she had to talk to him. Even if her knees did shake at the thought.

Straightening her spine, she sighed. "No. You're right. Maybe he can help me find some answers."

The man Joe let into the apartment was tall and lean, with an angular face and dark brown hair that was cropped close and still somehow managed to curl. His smile appeared the second he spied Annie sitting on the couch, his eyes kind but watchful as he approached her. He looked like someone she could trust, but that didn't do a lot to settle her nerves.

"You don't remember me, do you?"

His tone was wry, his stance nonthreatening, and Annie found herself liking him. "No, I'm sorry, I don't. But don't take it personally. I don't remember me, either."

"Or me," Joe added as he shut the front door and joined them in the living room. "Since there's no sign of any head injuries, the doctors think she's suffering from some sort of trauma-induced amnesia. She showed up here last night, took a shower, and went to bed. That's all she remembers."

"So you have no memory of how you got here?" Sam asked, turning to Annie, his forehead knit in a frown. "Did you drive?"

She shrugged. "If I did, I don't know where I left the car. What kind of car do I have, anyway?"

"A '62 Volvo sedan," Joe said, rattling off the license plate number for Sam. "It's your pride and joy. There's no way you'd voluntarily walk off and leave it even if you ran the damn thing into a tree."

Pulling a small notebook from his pocket, Sam noted the information in his own particular brand of shorthand. "I'll call it in and see if there're any reports on it." Watching every nuance of Annie's expression, he said, "How do you feel when you try to remember? Or do you feel anything at all? What's going on in your head, Annie?"

That was something she didn't even have to think about. Her arms stealing around herself, she stared off into the blackness that had once been her past and felt again that sinister wickedness that lingered just out of sight in the shadows, stalking her every waking moment. "Fear," she said hoarsely. "I'm scared to death and I don't know why."

"Did someone hurt you?"

"I don't know."

"How do you think you got the bruises?"

Her gaze dropped to the sickly yellow discolorations that marred her wrists below the sleeves of her blouse. There were others under her clothes, on her throat and breasts and thighs. She didn't have to remember how she had gotten them to know that they weren't the result of any kind of accident. The outline of gripping fingers was clearly visible on her skin.

Rubbing at them as if she could rub them away, she could only shrug. "I can't imagine."

His jaw rigid, Joe retrieved a brown grocery sack from the entrance-hall closet and gave it to Sam. "Those are the clothes she was wearing when she came home. I found them on the bathroom floor this morning. You'd better take a look at them."

The long-sleeved white blouse, black slacks and tapestry vest that Sam dumped out on the coffee table were caked with dried mud. One sleeve of the blouse was nearly torn off, but it was the large rust-brown stains on the garments that drew both men's eyes.

Careful not to touch them any more than necessary, Sam scowled. "Someone lost a hell of a lot of blood, and it obviously wasn't Annie. I'm going to take these into the lab and have them analyzed."

Annie hardly heard him. She'd seen the clothes before. She knew how terrible they looked. But seeing them now, in the old-fashioned prettiness of the living room, she just felt sick. "I think I-I need t-to lie down. I d-don't feel..." she swallowed thickly and jerked to her feet "...very well."

Joe swore and hastily moved to her side, cursing himself for his thoughtlessness. "C'mon, honey, why don't you go to bed? It's been a rough day, and you're worn out. Excuse us a second, Sam. I'll be right back."

He didn't give her time to protest but simply ushered her into the master bedroom and quickly found her one of his old T-shirts to sleep in. He would have helped her change, but one look at her face and he knew that was never going to happen. Which was probably for the best.

"Can I get you anything else?" he asked stiffly. "Something to drink? Another pillow?"

"No, nothing. I'll be fine. Really."

If she was fine, he was Rip van Winkle. With his T-shirt clutched to her breast and her blue eyes large and haunted, she looked small and vulnerable and needed somebody to hold her. But it wasn't going to be him or any other man. Turning away, he headed for the door before he gave in to the temptation to reach for her anyway. "Then I'll leave you alone. Good night."

Her soft, husky good-night followed him across the room, but he didn't look back. He didn't dare.

"Is she okay?" Sam asked worriedly as soon as he rejoined him in the living room. "I know amnesia must be a hell of a shock to the system, and she didn't get those bruises from a walk in the park, but I don't think I've ever seen her look so breakable."

"She's pregnant," Joe said, and saw by the quickly concealed surprise on the other man's face that he didn't need to elaborate. Sam, like most of their friends, knew that Annie had left him months ago. It didn't take an Einstein to figure out that her condition, in all likelihood, had nothing to do with her husband. "She's scared to death of being touched. She wasn't raped, but it might not have been from lack of trying on some bastard's part. Until she regains her memory—which could be months, if ever—the only clue we've got to what happened to her is her clothes. I want whoever hurt her caught, Sam."

Sam nodded, understanding perfectly the need for revenge. Whatever their problems were, Annie was still Joe's wife, and Joe was the type of man who protected what was his. "I'll get back to you as soon as I get a report from the lab. If nothing else, we should be able to find out something about the blood on her clothes and where she might have picked up that mud. Unfortunately, that's not a hell of a lot to go on. Finding her car would help. Do you know where she's been living since she left here?"

"In an apartment on Mockingbird Lane," Joe replied tersely and gave him the address.

Wishing he didn't have to ask the next few questions, Sam knew there was no way around them. "I hate like hell to ask you this, Joe, but I've got to. Was she living by herself? Dating anyone? What about her neighbors? Do you know anything about them?"

His mouth pressed flat into a thin white line, he shook his head. "No. Nothing. She's been working with Phoebe at their real estate office, but other than that, she could have taken up with the Dalai Lama and been living with a lover from a past life for all I know. She wanted privacy and I gave it to her."

Surprised, Sam glanced up from his note-taking. "Do you really think she'd do something like that?"

"I don't know," he replied, and silently cursed the bitterness he heard in his voice. "At this point, I don't know anything except that she's not going to be able to handle any more questions. You saw the way she reacted to the sight of her clothes. She can't take the stress right now."

"Then my best bet would probably be to start at the real estate office," Sam said as he pushed to his feet and headed for the door with the bag that held Annie's ruined clothes in his hand. "I'll nose around her apartment, too, and see what I can find out. I'll get back to you when I have something to report.''

With Sam's leaving, silence descended over the apartment, but it was a far from peaceful quiet. Left alone with his thoughts, Joe found his gaze drifting down the hall to the closed door of their bedroom. Was she asleep? he wondered broodingly. Or staring up at the ceiling and dreading the moment he came to bed? Dammit, what was he going to do with her? They were still married, but in her mind, she'd known him all of one day. Considering the circumstances, only a monster would insist on his marital right.

Not that he was looking for or expecting sex with the lady, he hastily assured himself. They made a fine pair. She didn't want him to touch her, and he, dear God, didn't trust her as far as he could throw her. Even if her memory came sweeping back tomorrow, what possible chance at a future did they have?

Long after the rest of the world was asleep, he was still pondering the question, the answer as elusive as ever.

He didn't sleep with her.

The thought hit Annie the moment she opened her eyes the following morning. Staring at the empty side of the bed, she didn't have to see the unrumpled pillow to know that she had had the bed to herself all night. She seemed to have a sixth sense where Joe Taylor was concerned, and if he'd been anywhere within touching distance over the course of the last eight hours, the thumping of her heart would have awakened her immediately. Instead, he'd chosen to sleep elsewhere rather than share a bed with her.

She should have been relieved. The last thing she needed right now was a husband she didn't remember crowding her. He'd done the gentlemanly thing and given her space, and she should have been thanking him for it. Instead, something that felt an awful lot like hurt wrapped around her heart, confusing her. Had she actually *wanted* him to sleep with her?

You're pregnant, Annie, a voice in her head snapped, *and you can't even assure the man that the baby is his. How else do you expect him to react? A lesser man might have told you to come back when you had the answers he was entitled to. Be thankful he's letting you stay because you've got nowhere else to go.*

Flinching at the lonely thought, she threw back the covers and rolled out of bed, only to be presented with another problem when her eyes fell on the jeans and faded shirt she'd worn yesterday. She had no other clothes. What was she supposed to wear?

"Annie? You awake?"

The tap that followed the hushed whisper was the only warning she got. The door flew open and she was caught flat-footed in her panties and the T-shirt she'd borrowed from Joe as he swept into the room. His arms loaded with clothes, he hardly spared her a glance. "Good, you're awake. I brought you some things—"

In the act of dumping the clothes on the bed, he looked up...and stopped short. In one all-encompassing look, he took in her bare legs, her tousled hair and the shadowy nipples that she knew were barely concealed by the thin material of his T-shirt. He didn't move so much as a muscle, but he didn't have to. His eyes turned hot and molten, and she would have sworn he touched her. Her breath hitched in her throat, her body quickened, confusing her.

She wanted to run, to bolt for the door, but she couldn't and didn't know why. He was her husband; he must have seen her like this a thousand times before. There was no reason to act like a virgin caught stepping from her bath. She was safe.

But the look in his brown eyes was dark and dangerous and intimate, touching her deep inside. She felt heat bloom in her cheeks and wanted to hide. All she could do was wrap her arms around herself to cover her breasts and drag her eyes away from his to the colorful garments that slid from his hands to the bed. "You went shopping this early in the morning?"

"Actually, I went over to your apartment and bullied the manager into letting me in," he replied stiffly. "I thought you'd feel more comfortable in your own things, and there was no use buying anything since you had a whole closet full of clothes right across town. I hope you don't mind."

Touched, Annie didn't know what to say. Going to her apartment, seeing where she'd lived when she'd left him, where she'd possibly betrayed him with another man, couldn't have been easy for him. But he'd done it for her...to help her feel more like herself. Did he have any idea what that did to her? She wanted to cross to him, to touch him, to ease the rigidness of his jaw and assure him that he had no reason to doubt her. But how could she know that for sure?

So she stayed where she was and said, "No, of course I don't mind. In fact, I was just wondering what I was going to wear. I'll have to buy maternity clothes eventually, but for now, I can wear my old clothes. Thanks."

It was the wrong thing to say. At the first reminder of her pregnancy, the heat in his eyes cooled. "I'll leave you to sort through them," he said curtly. "We usually eat breakfast at the restaurant, so come on out when you're ready."

Striding out of the bedroom that they'd once shared as man and wife, he shut the door behind him with a snap that made her wince. Was this the way he was going to react every time the baby was mentioned? she wondered, staring after him. If he did, it was going to be an awfully long pregnancy.

Chapter 3

Annie expected Joe's Place to be one of those elegant, high-dollar restaurants where the local in-crowd could be seen sipping champagne over brunch on the river. The second she stepped through the river-level entrance, however, she saw that it was anything but that. Instead of crystal, white tablecloths and fancy chandeliers, it was strictly blue-collar. The decor was straight out of the fifties, complete with black-and-white linoleum floors, red chrome tables and chairs, and a soda bar, in perfect condition, that looked as if it had been salvaged from an old drugstore. Annie took one look and loved it.

The Saturday-morning breakfast crowd was loud, relaxed and boisterous, and when customers called out to Joe—and to her, too—she couldn't help smiling. Fascinated, she watched waitresses in old-fashioned uniforms wind their way through the crowded tables with hurried grace, trays loaded with plates of ham and eggs and hash browns balanced one-handed over their heads. Cholesterol was obviously not a major concern here, and no one seemed to care. The place was packed.

The tantalizing smell of coffee filled the air, as well as that of freshly baked cinnamon rolls, and Annie felt her mouth water. It seemed like days since she had eaten. Closing her eyes, she dragged in a deep breath, savoring the combination of scents. Pancakes and sausage, she thought, smiling. She'd get a short stack and all the coffee she could drink.

The nausea came out of nowhere. One second she was anticipating the sweetness of syrup on her tongue, and the next, her stomach roiled sickeningly. Caught off guard, she stiffened, horrified. No! This couldn't be happening! Not here. But even as she told herself that she probably just needed to eat, her stomach had other ideas. Nausea rose with sickening swiftness in her throat, and she knew that if she didn't do something fast, she was going to disgrace herself right there in front of a restaurant full of people. Her hand pressed to her mouth, she looked frantically around for a rest room.

She didn't remember making a sound, but Joe was suddenly there, immediately taking charge as he slipped an arm around her waist. "Hang on, honey," he said quietly, and quickly urged her to the rear of the restaurant, where the rest rooms were concealed by a large screen painted with palm trees. Without batting an eye, he whisked her into the ladies' room.

Before Annie realized that he had followed her inside, she ran out of time. Groaning, she lost the meager contents of her stomach while Joe held her head. Mortified, she wanted to crawl in a hole. "Just shoot me right here and get it over with," she moaned. "Then I can die in peace. I can't believe I did that!"

A smile tugging at the corners of his mouth, he chided,

"Don't be ridiculous. You don't remember it, but right after our honeymoon, I got the flu and was sick as a dog for twelve hours straight. You never left my side." His hands incredibly gentle, he brushed her hair back from her colorless face, gave her a cup of water to rinse her mouth, then helped her over to a chair in front of the vanity mirrors that lined one wall. "Just sit here a minute and get your breath. You'll be good as new in no time."

If she'd had the energy, Annie would have laughed at that. He couldn't be serious! She was a whipped puppy, so embarrassed she didn't think she'd ever be able to look him in the eye again. "You shouldn't be in here," she murmured, turning her face away. "What if someone came in and saw you?"

"They'd just see a man taking care of his nauseated wife," he said simply, wiping her hot face with a paper towel he wet at the sink. "How's that feel? Better?"

It felt like heaven. He had big, strong hands, the kind that could, no doubt, break a man in two if he was angry enough. But he was so gentle with her, so careful, she found herself fighting the need to lean into him and give herself over to his caring.

Disturbed, she caught his hand before it could make another cooling swipe down her face. "If this is an example of what the mornings are going to be like for the next couple of months, I'd better not go out in public for a while," she said with a rueful grimace. "Why don't you go get us a table and I'll be out as soon as I wash up? I just need a few moments to get myself together."

His fingers trapped in hers, Joe stared down at her and felt as if he'd just been kicked in the head by a mule. Morning sickness. When he'd seen the blood drain from her face and her hand flutter to her mouth, his only thought had been that she was in trouble. She'd looked up at him with desperation in her eyes, and he hadn't known if she was scared of the crowd or what—he'd just known he had to help her. And all the time, the baby was just making its presence known, refusing to be ignored even though it would be months before it would be here. Like it or not, he was going to have to deal with that. But how, dammit? How the hell could he?

Pulling his hand from hers, he straightened, the agitation churning in his gut locked inside where no one could see. "Take your time—there's no hurry. I have a table by the kitchen reserved for our use at all times."

No one so much as lifted an eyebrow when he walked out of the women's rest room, but Joe knew his staff. The second he'd walked through the front door with Annie, the news had spread like wildfire. By the time he took a seat at his table, he wasn't surprised to see Drake Gallagher, his manager, striding toward him with a frown etching his chiseled face.

He and Drake went way back, back to the days they'd first worked together as busboys when they were just sixteen. Drake had eventually gone on to manage a place in Austin, but when Joe's Place had been in trouble, he'd ditched that job to come back to San Antonio and help Joe get the restaurant back on its feet. Annie had always been a favorite with him and, like the rest of the crew, he'd had a hard time accepting her leaving.

Never one to mince words or worry about taking advantage of their friendship, Drake signaled a waitress to bring them both a cup of coffee, grabbed a chair across the table from him, and said without preamble, "It's about time you two came to your senses. I'd about given up hope on you. So what's wrong with Annie? She looked a little green around the gills."

Joe opened his mouth to tell him that she was pregnant, only to shut it with a snap. The news would be out soon enough—there was no sense fueling speculation any sooner than he had to, and he didn't want to talk about it in front of half the restaurant. "Her stomach's kind of jittery this morning. We've got a problem, Drake."

"Oh, God. What is it this time?"

His lips twitching at his groan, Joe understood how he felt. In the last few months, they'd done nothing but put out fires. Pouring cream into his coffee, he told him of Annie's return home and amnesia. "She's not going to know you or any of the rest of the staff, so spread the word, okay? And make sure none of the guys corner her. She's pretty skittish right now."

Stunned, Drake nodded. "Of course. She's probably scared to death. What do you think happened to her?"

"I don't know, and neither does she. The police are checking into the situation, but unless she remembers something or the lab finds something on her clothes, they won't even know where to start an investigation. In the meantime, I don't want to leave her alone, so you're going to have to take over most of the load here until things get back to normal."

"Hey, no problem," Drake assured him. "You just take care of Annie and don't worry about this place. I can handle things for as long as you need me to. It's not like I've got a family to rush home to, and Annie needs you. Maybe you should get her out of town for a while, take a vacation or something. A complete change of scene might do you both good."

If they'd really been back together, Joe would have jumped at the chance to be alone with her on some secluded beach a million miles from their nearest neighbor. But although she was back, they weren't even close to being reconciled and there was a possibility that they never would be. Regretfully, he shook his head. "The doctors said she has a better shot at remembering if she has the security of familiar things around her. And I don't think we should be away from town right now. The builders are coming along fine on the new place, but I want to be here if there're any glitches. And Annie needs to be near her doctors just in case she starts to remember."

The conversation turned to business then—a booking for a private party, problems with a supplier, the previous day's receipts, which were up—and neither man noticed the woman who rushed across the restaurant until she was practically upon them. "Joe! Thank God, I found you! I'm sorry to interrupt, but I've really got to talk to you."

Surprised, Joe lifted a brow at Phoebe Duncan, Annie's best friend and partner. A small woman with a shock of red hair and impish green eyes, she was one of those unflappable women who usually roll with the punches. She almost always kept her head when everyone else was losing theirs. But not today. Her freckles stood out in sharp relief across her pale cheeks, her eyes were wild, her curly hair disheveled. She'd been maid of honor at his and Annie's wedding, and in all the years since, Joe didn't think he'd ever seen her so frazzled.

Quickly rising to his feet, as Drake excused himself to check things in the kitchen, Joe pulled a chair out for her. "Sit down, Phoeb. You look like you're stuck on fast-forward. What's going on?"

She sat, but only to pop up again like a jack-in-the-box. "It's Annie. God, you must think I'm some kind of nutcase to come rushing in here like this, but I didn't know what else to do. Have you heard from her? I know you guys haven't been talking, but I was hoping she called you. No one's seen her at the office—"

"She's okay, Phoeb—"

"She didn't even check in yesterday to let me know she wasn't coming in," she continued, not even hearing him. "Of course, she could have gone to Kerrville. She mentioned she had to meet with a lady there who wanted to list her property with us, but she didn't say when she was going. And I don't know the woman's name, so I can't check with her." Chewing on her bottom lip, she said, "Something's wrong, Joe. I can feel it in my bones. She's not answering her phone and her car's gone. Maybe you should call the police."

"She's fine, Phoebe," he tried again, smiling. "She showed up at—"

That was as far as he got. Annie stepped out of the rest room then, drawing her friend's gaze, and with a cry of relief, Phoebe was out of her chair and hugging her as if she hadn't seen her in years. "Thank God! Do you know how worried I've been? Where have you been? I've been going crazy picturing you in all sorts of trouble and all the while you were with Joe. You dog, why didn't you call me and tell me you were back together?"

Taken aback, Annie looked wildly to Joe for help. "I'm sorry, but I don't know who—"

"How did the renter turn out the other night?" Phoebe asked eagerly as she released her and sank back into her chair at the table. "Did he take the entire tenth floor? At the price he was getting, he would have been a fool not to. So did he sign the contract? Tell me everything."

"What night?" Joe demanded sharply before Annie could so much as open her mouth. "You're not talking about Thursday night, are you?"

"Yeah. Why?"

"Annie had a meeting that night? With who? Where?"

He threw the questions at her like darts, not giving her

time to answer one before he thought of another. Surprised, she started to tease him about his fierceness, only to notice just then that Annie was waiting for her to answer as expectantly as Joe was.

Her brows drawing together in a frown, Phoebe glanced back and forth between the two of them in confusion. "Is someone going to tell me what's going on here or do I have to guess? Annie?" she asked when her friend hesitated and looked to Joe for an answer. "Why are you looking at Joe like that? What's wrong?"

"She has amnesia," Joe answered for her. "That's why she didn't call in yesterday—she didn't even know you existed."

"Oh, c'mon!"

Amused, she clearly didn't believe him, but Joe was dead serious. "I talked to Sam Kelly about it last night, and if you'd waited a little while, he would have showed up at your office some time today to tell you all about it. Annie came home Thursday night after I'd gone to bed and I didn't know she was there until the next morning. I should have called you myself, but yesterday was so wild, frankly, I didn't even think about it. We spent the day going from one doctor to the next trying to find out what happened to her."

The blood slowly draining from her face, Phoebe glanced uncertainly at Annie. "This is a joke, isn't it? Like that time you tried to convince me that George Strait listed his house with us?"

Liking her immediately, Annie wished she could have given her the answer she wanted, but she had no memory of that or any other joke she might have played on her. "I'm sorry, but it's true. I know we must be friends, but I don't even know your name. Have we known each other long?"

The other woman winced as if she'd struck her, tears welling in her eyes. "Oh, God, Annie, you really don't remember! I'm Phoebe. Phoebe Duncan. We've been best friends since first grade. How can you not know me?"

"That's what we're trying to find out," Joe interjected. "Let's order breakfast, then you can tell us about this meeting Thursday night."

After her earlier bout of nausea, Annie was sure she was crazy to even think about eating breakfast, but the second the waitress set her order of pancakes and sausage in front of her, her mouth watered hungrily. Suddenly starving, she dug into her food like a field hand who'd been hard at work for hours and immediately discovered why Joe's Place was packed to the gills with customers. The food was out of this world.

While they were eating, Phoebe told Annie about how they had met in first grade, their instant friendship, and the mischief they'd just naturally fallen into over the years. Unable to stop grinning, Annie was sure her friend was stretching the truth, but Joe assured her she wasn't. When she and Phoebe got together, there was no telling what would happen.

Polishing off the last of her French toast, Phoebe sighed in contentment and pushed her plate away. "Well, there's another inch to the hips, but it was worth it. I don't know how you do it, Joe. Every time I eat here, the food gets better. So when are you going to give me some of your recipes?"

"I'm not," he retorted, chuckling as he leaned back in his chair. "Flattery will get you nowhere, Phoeb. You know that."

Undaunted, she only shrugged, her green eyes twinkling. "You can't blame a girl for trying. Nothing ventured, nothing gained."

"True enough. Now what about Annie's meeting Thursday night? Who was it with and where?"

"A Mr. Sal Larkin," she answered, abruptly somber, "at the Transit Tower. He was coming from Houston and wouldn't be able to meet with her until around eight o'clock. Normally, I would have gone with her, but it was my grandfather's eighty-fifth birthday and the family was having a party I couldn't get out of."

"So you went to the party, and Annie met the renter alone. And that's the last time you saw or heard from her?"

She nodded miserably. "I had no idea she was in any kind of trouble. By the time I got in Thursday night, it was too late to call her, so I figured I'd check in with her the next morning before I left for a seminar in Austin for the day. But I missed her again. She never showed up at the office at all yesterday, and when I couldn't reach her at home this morning, I really started to worry."

"What about this Sal Larkin character?" Joe asked with a frown. "What do you know about him? Is he someone you've dealt with before?"

"No. We got the leasing contract with the Transit Tower and ran our first ad at the beginning of the week. Mr. Larkin called on Wednesday and spoke to Annie about needing an entire floor of the building. Apparently he wanted to get out of Houston and move his telecommunications company to San Antonio."

"Have you heard from him? Did he actually show up for the appointment?"

"I don't know. He didn't call, so I assume he showed up." Glancing at Annie, she said, "Does any of this ring a bell, girlfriend? What happened after you left the office that night?"

Annie would have given anything to remember, but her

mind was a clean slate. "No, nothing. I can't even tell you where our office is, let alone what happened after I left it."

"You can't, but maybe someone can at the Transit Tower," Joe said. "I'm going to check it out. Phoebe, will you stay with Annie until I get back? I don't like leaving her alone."

Annie, already rising to her feet, had no intention of being baby-sat like a two-year-old. "I'm going with you. If something happened there, I have a right to know what it was."

"I'll tell you everything when I get back," Joe promised. "Here are the keys to the apartment—"

"I'm going, Joe," she cut in firmly. "Just because I lost my memory doesn't mean you have to treat me like a little girl. I can handle this."

Exasperated, he demanded, "How do you know? You don't even know what *this* is!"

"Then I'll find out at the same time you do," she said stubbornly, lifting her chin. "You're coming, aren't you, Phoebe? I'd like for you to be there."

"You're damn right I'm coming! Somebody hurt you, and I want to find him as much as you do. Besides," she added, grinning, "after watching you two avoid each other like the plague for months, just seeing you talk to each other again is the best surprise I've had all year. I wouldn't miss this for the world. Let's go."

Mumbling under his breath about stubborn women, Joe knew when he was beaten. Giving in, he escorted them both outside.

The Transit Tower was one of the city's oldest office buildings and one of the most distinctive landmarks on the San Antonio skyline. With its steep pointed roof and radio antennae that seemed to climb straight up into the clouds, it stood out among the other skyscrapers like an old oak among saplings.

Circling the building and the surrounding blocks twice, Joe finally gave up the idea of parking on the street and headed for the large parking garage next door. With all his attention focused on the traffic, which was surprisingly thick for a Saturday morning, he never noticed Annie's agitation until he started to turn into the garage's entrance bay. Still leery of getting in a car with him, she'd chosen to sit in the back seat, leaving the front for Phoebe, but her comfort zone ran out before he even knew anything was wrong. He'd barely stopped to take the ticket at the automatic entrance gate when she fumbled for her door handle.

Startled, he glanced over his shoulder at her and frowned at the sight of her ashen cheeks. "Annie? What is it? What's wrong? Dammit, honey, you can't get out here! Let me park first."

In a panic, she hardly heard him as she clawed at her seat belt and finally found the release. "No! I can't go in there! I just can't. Please..."

She had the same look of terror on her face that she'd had when she woke up and found herself in bed with him the previous morning, the one that ripped his heart right out of his chest. Alarmed, cursing the fact that she was out of reach in the back seat, Joe turned and stretched out his arm to her, needing to touch her. "Calm down, sweetheart. It's all right. There's nothing to be afraid of—I'm not going to let anyone hurt you—"

The impatient blaring of a horn sounded from right behind them, cutting him off. Swearing, Joe shot the other driver a furious glare in his rearview mirror and saw that three other cars had lined up behind him and were waiting to enter the garage. "Damn! I'm holding up traffic—"

"Annie and I don't need to go into the garage with you,"

Phoebe said quickly, as she released her own seat belt. "Why don't we get out here and wait for you at the front door? C'mon, Annie, let's take a walk."

Annie didn't have to be told twice. She was out of the car as if the devil himself was after her, hurrying away from the garage entrance just as fast as her legs would carry her.

Frowning after her in concern, Joe almost got out to follow her. Then the driver behind him blared his horn again. "Take care of her," he told Phoebe as she hurriedly climbed out of the car. "I'll just be a second." Pushing the button for a gate ticket, he drove into the garage, but not before he caught a last glimpse of Annie standing on the sidewalk with Phoebe, her eyes huge in her pale face as she stared in revulsion at the building.

What was going on inside that head of hers? he wondered as he cruised the first floor, then the second, for an available parking spot. She wasn't a woman who scared easily. In fact, she didn't blink an eye at showing property in parts of the city that most people wouldn't be caught dead in. But she'd definitely been in a panic the second he approached the garage. Had something happened to her here?

Anxious to get back to her, he shot up the ramp to the third floor and sighed in relief when he saw that there were plenty of spaces there. Finally! Turning into the first empty spot, he quickly parked and locked the car and was halfway to the elevators when he stopped short at the sight of the car parked all by itself at the far end of the floor. Even in the shadows that engulfed the garage, there was no mistaking that it was Annie's. As far as he knew, there wasn't another '62 Volvo that distinctive shade of yellow in the city.

He reached it in ten long strides, his brow furrowed as he tried the door. It was locked. Peering in the driver's-side window, he could see her day planner lying on the front seat, apparently right where she'd left it. Nothing looked out of place or the least unusual.

"Dammit, why would she just walk off and leave her car here?" he muttered to himself. "She loves the damn thing. She wouldn't just leave it."

Scowling, he walked completely around the vehicle, looking for something, *anything*, that might tell him what had happened there two nights ago. But if she'd run into any kind of trouble there, there was no sign of it. The car was untouched, everything just as it should be.

Then he saw it. A brownish stain on the pavement a few spaces over from the one where her car was parked. Even as he started toward it, he tried to convince himself it was probably just an oil stain. But as he drew closer and went down on one knee to examine it, a sick feeling spilled into his stomach. Unless he was mistaken, it was dried blood.

For a long time, he didn't move. He was going to have to tell Annie. Clenching his teeth on an oath, he would have given just about anything to keep it from her, but she had a right to know. First, he had to call the police. Returning to his car for his cellular, he quickly called Sam Kelly.

Watching her friend pace restlessly as they waited for Joe, Phoebe said, "Maybe this wasn't such a good idea, Annie. Are you sure you're okay? You're as white as a sheet. Why don't you wait here and I'll go back inside and get Joe and tell him you've changed your mind? We can do this another day."

As her gaze darted to the garage entrance, Annie would have liked nothing better than to jump at the suggestion, but she couldn't. Not when the fear gripping her threatened to render her powerless. It was a feeling, she was discovering, that she hated.

Glancing at the other woman, wishing she could remember her and the good times they'd had over the years, she asked quizzically, "What kind of woman was I before? You've known me all my life. Right now, you know me better than I do. What was I like? Was I a wimp or what? I can't believe I was one of those women who looked over her shoulder every time she went out of the house, but I can't deny that I'm scared. And I don't know why. God, this is so hard!"

Tears welled in Phoebe's green eyes. Impulsively, she reached over to give her a fierce hug. "You, a wimp?" she laughed shakily. "Are you kidding? You're the gutsiest person I ever knew. Why do you think we've been friends for so long? We're partners in crime, kid. We always have been. So you quit worrying about what kind of person you are. You've got amnesia, for God's sake! Who wouldn't be scared?"

She would have said more, but Joe stepped out of the parking garage then. Annie took one look at the granite set of his jaw and braced for bad news. "What is it? What's wrong?"

"I found your car," he told her.

"And?" Phoebe asked, obviously waiting for the other shoe to drop.

"And it's fine. It's on the third floor and appears to be untouched."

His tone was matter-of-fact and not the least bit alarming. Annie should have been relieved, but she was starting to figure Joe Taylor out. When his eyes were shuttered, his face blank, he was hiding something. Her eyes searching his, she said, "But there's something else, isn't there? Something you're holding back because of me. Just spit it out, Joe. If it concerns whatever happened to me, I have a right to know."

She was right, but that didn't make telling her any easier.

He'd seen her fear yesterday morning when she thought he was going to hurt her, and then again just moments ago. He didn't need to know what she'd been through to know that it must have been pure hell. Given the opportunity, he would have made sure she never remembered it at all, but there were some things he couldn't protect her from. This was one of them.

"There's a stain two spaces over from your car," he said flatly. "I can't be sure what it is, but it looks like dried blood, so I called Sam. He should be here any moment."

"Show me. Maybe it'll jog my memory."

"The hell I will!" he growled. "The doctor said you'd remember when you were ready, and not until then. Forcing the issue won't do you or the baby any good."

Watching the interplay between the two of them, Phoebe sucked in a sharp breath. "Baby? What baby?"

"She's pregnant," Joe said curtly. "She didn't tell you?"

"No! My God, a baby! That's wonderful!" Joy lighting her face, she turned to Annie to hug her, only to freeze at the despair in her eyes. "What is it? What's wrong? You've been wanting a baby for years—"

Realization hit her then, widening her eyes. "Oh, my God, you don't remember!"

Miserable, Annie shook her head. "No. Nothing." At her side, she could feel Joe growing colder and colder, but there was nothing she could do about the awkward situation. If anyone knew what she'd been doing the last few months, it was Phoebe, and there were questions that needed to be asked. Joe was entitled to hear the answers.

"Did I..." She glanced away, heat climbing in her cheeks. "Was I seeing anyone that you know of?"

Phoebe, clearly as uncomfortable as she, cast a quick look at Joe's stony face and could do nothing but shrug. "I don't know. I'm sorry, but the only time we ever argued in our lives was when you left Joe. I thought you were making a big mistake and told you so. You didn't want to hear that, of course, so we made a pact not to discuss your love life. If you were dating anyone, I didn't know about it, but then again, I made it clear I didn't want to. And you never whispered a word about possibly being pregnant."

Annie wanted desperately to believe that she hadn't said anything about the baby because she'd been so stressed about the possible breakup of her marriage that she hadn't even realized that she was pregnant. But she only had to look at Joe's set face to know that he'd jumped to a completely different conclusion—if she hadn't even told her best friend about the pregnancy, it was probably because the baby wasn't her husband's.

No! she wanted to cry. She wasn't that kind of woman! But even as the words hovered on her tongue, she couldn't say them. Not when she didn't know for sure who or what Annie Taylor was.

Silence fell after that, a thick, uncomfortable silence that no one seemed inclined to break. Then Sam Kelly arrived with an evidence team. "I'm going in with you," she told Sam, and shot Joe a challenging look that just dared him to try and stop her. "I need to see whatever's in there."

The tension in the air was thick enough to cut with a knife, and Sam obviously didn't have to be hit in the head to know that he had just stepped into the middle of a disagreement. Glancing from Annie to Joe and back again, he didn't take sides either way. "That's your choice," he said diplomatically. "I can't tell you if that's wise or not—you'll have to use your own judgment. Joe said when he called that your car looked untouched, but we're going to dust it for prints anyway, so don't touch it until we've had a chance to go over it."

They all headed for the two parking-garage elevators,

where they split up, with the evidence team taking one and Annie, Joe, Phoebe and Sam the other. At the most, it was a forty-second ride to the third floor—it should have been easy. But the second the doors slid shut, closing them in, Annie knew she wanted nothing to do with whatever was on the third floor.

Trapped at the back of the elevator, however, she had left it too late to change her mind. Breaking out in a cold sweat in spite of the fact that it was a warm autumn day, she rubbed her chilled arms and tried to focus on positive thoughts as they rose slowly toward the third floor. She was perfectly safe. Joe and the police were here, and there was no reason to be afraid.

But when the elevator doors finally slid open and everyone else filed out, she stood flat-footed where she was.

Her gaze trained on the shadowy confines of the garage that stretched out in front of the open doors, she didn't see Joe stop when she didn't follow. "Annie?"

He didn't say anything else, just her name, but he told her without words that she didn't have to do this. All she had to do was push the button for the first floor and turn her back on whatever was out there waiting to terrify her. He and Sam would handle this for her, and no one would condemn her for it.

No one but herself. She could turn tail and run and all it would cost her was her self-respect.

Dragging her tortured eyes from the shadows, she lifted them to Joe. "When you were a kid, were you ever afraid of monsters under your bed at night?"

He nodded. "Sometimes."

"Everyone told you there was no such thing and there was no reason to be afraid, and you wanted to believe them more than anything. But every time you got anywhere near that bed once the sun went down, you got this big lump in your throat. Do you remember?"

"I remember, honey."

"This garage is where my monsters live." She couldn't tell him how she knew—she didn't know. She just knew she had a lump in her throat the size of the Alamo and she wanted out of there. But running wouldn't accomplish anything. The nightmare went with her wherever she went.

"I have to face this monster, Joe." She barely spoke above a whisper, but she was already stepping out from the corner of the elevator, her shoulders square and the glint of determination in her eyes.

From his scowl, he clearly didn't agree, but all he said was, "Just remember, you don't have to prove anything to anyone."

She didn't agree, but she only nodded and forced herself to walk to his side. At the far end of the floor, the bright yellow Volvo drew her like a magnet.

This was her car? she wondered in surprise as she slowly walked toward it. According to Joe, it was her baby, her pride and joy, a member of the family that she'd polished and waxed and changed the oil in as often as you wiped an infant's bottom. It had been beautifully restored and no doubt drew looks from everyone who passed it on the street. And it didn't look the least bit familiar to her.

Watching her carefully, Joe asked, "Do you remember it?"

She shook her head numbly. "No. How long have I owned it?"

"Eight years. You bought it right after your twenty-first birthday."

He could have told her she'd bought it last week, and she wouldn't have known any different. Joe handed Sam his set of keys, then joined her and Phoebe off to the side as the evidence team dusted the vehicle for fingerprints inside and out. And she felt nothing, absolutely nothing.

"There are quite a few prints," Sam told them a few minutes later. "But considering the condition of the car, I don't think we're going to find anything out of the ordinary. It looks like Annie just locked it up and walked away."

Squatting down on his haunches, he examined the rust-brown stain on the concrete fifteen feet from the car. "It's blood, all right," he said curtly as he pushed to his feet and stepped out of the way so his men could collect what evidence they could. "And a hell of a lot of it." His sharp eyes meeting Annie's, he arched a brow at her. "Are you getting any flashbacks? Anything that might tell you what happened here?"

"Besides fear?" she replied, shivering. "No. Nothing."

She was trembling and from the looks of the green cast to her complexion, on the verge of nausea. Wanting to take her in his arms and reassure her, Joe reminded himself that he couldn't lose his head over her just because she was in trouble. "Why don't you and Phoebe wait for us downstairs, then?" he suggested. "There's nothing more you can do, and you're only torturing yourself by hanging around here."

"I agree," Phoebe said, adding her two cents. "This place gives me the willies. Let's get out of here."

This time, Annie didn't have to be told twice. Leaving the men to finish investigating the scene, she hurried toward the elevator with Phoebe on her heels.

As soon as they were out of earshot, Sam said, "I didn't want to say anything in front of Annie, Joe, but I wouldn't be surprised if these bloodstains turn out to match the ones on her clothes. What the hell was she doing here?"

Joe explained about Annie's meeting with the potential renter from Houston. "We don't know if the guy ever showed or not. Phoebe's going to call him as soon as she gets back to the office and find out."

"I'll get his name and number from her and do it for her," he said. "If I can't get him, I've got a friend on the Houston force who owes me a favor. He'll track him down and see what he knows about what went down here on Thursday night."

If he was still alive.

Sam didn't say the words, but they were both thinking them. If the dried blood on the floor matched that on Annie's torn clothes, someone had lost an awful lot of blood. And if that someone was the renter from Houston, he could not only be missing and hurting right now. He could be dead.

Chapter 4

From the garage, they walked over to the Transit Tower and checked out the tenth floor. To Annie's relief, the enervating fear that had gripped her in the parking garage was noticeably absent in the office building, and she was able to look around with interest. The rental space was empty of furniture and similar to that found all over the city. If she'd ever been there before, she had no memory of it.

Sam, however, was taking no chances. He had the evidence team check for fingerprints while he questioned the building security guard. The place was covered with hundreds of different prints that could have belonged to anyone, however, and the security guard was little help. He recognized Annie from a previous visit but didn't remember seeing her or anyone else on Thursday night.

At a dead end, there was little more anyone could do for now. One after the other, they drove out of the parking garage, with Joe following Sam in the Regal and Annie and Phoebe bringing up the rear in the Volvo. Since Annie's purse and driver's license were still missing, Phoebe drove, cracking jokes all the while to tease Annie out of the somber mood she'd fallen into.

They didn't see him. But he saw them. Especially *her*. Sitting in the passenger seat of the familiar yellow Volvo, she looked him right in the eye and didn't even blink. Stunned, he almost ran off the road.

Had she seen him? She must have—she couldn't have missed him! But if she'd seen him, she sure as hell hadn't acted like she'd known him, which didn't make any sense. The lighting had been poor the other night, but he wasn't stupid enough to think that she hadn't gotten a good look at him. He'd been right in her face, for God's sake! Given the chance, she should have been able to pick him out of a lineup at fifty yards.

If it hadn't been for her, he'd have been in Mexico by now, damn her to hell! It was what he'd worked and planned and risked everything for. But after she'd gotten away from him, he'd been afraid to chance it. He was well known to the police, and once the tricky little bitch went to them with a description of him and his van, his butt was fried. So he'd laid low and waited for them to come for him, sweating like a pig. But there'd been no knock at his door, nothing.

He'd waited for a day and a half, wasting precious time, and with every passing hour his fury had grown until he'd known he couldn't afford to wait any longer. She was a loose end, one that he'd left dangling long enough. She knew more than enough to send him to the chair, and unless he found a way to shut her up for good, he'd spend the rest of his life looking over his shoulder.

So he'd come back to the parking garage in the hopes that in the struggle between them, she might have dropped something that would tell him who she was. Instead, there she was, driving right past him. God, he had to be living right! She might as well have delivered herself to him on a platter. All he had to do was follow her, find out where she lived, and take care of her when the timing was right. She'd never know what hit her.

A feral gleam burning in his close-set blue eyes, he executed a quick U-turn and threw a rude hand gesture at the other drivers who dared to honk at him. Seconds later, he was a half block behind the Volvo and slowly closing.

A derisive smile curling his thin lips, he marveled at the stupidity of his quarry as the two women in the Volvo drove ten blocks to a parking garage on the river without ever realizing that they were being followed. Talk about a bunch of dumb idiots, he thought. He boldly drove into the garage behind them and found a space just five spaces away from theirs on the first floor, and they never noticed.

He didn't intend to let them out of his sight, but he'd hardly climbed out of his van and started after them when they were joined by a tall, lean, dark-haired dude who looked like trouble. Swearing under his breath, he quickly stepped back behind his van and reached for the knife hidden in his boot. But he didn't need it. The trio headed for the stairs that led to the Riverwalk and never glanced back.

Following them after that was a piece of cake. Blending in with weekend tourists, he drew nearer without them being aware of it. Then, before he quite realized where they were headed, they stepped through the doors of Joe's Place. By the time he followed them inside, the three of them were stepping through the swinging doors of the kitchen like they owned the place.

"Damn!"

Muttering a curse, he hesitated and was wondering what to do next when the restaurant hostess approached and shot him a friendly smile. "A table for one, sir? Smoking or non?"

He should have split right then and gotten out while he still could without being recognized. But he was desperate. Unless he found out who the curly-haired chick was, he was a condemned man. Glancing around, he spied an empty table that gave a clear view of the kitchen door and nodded toward it. "I'll take that one. You sell beer in this joint?"

"Yes, sir, we do." If she thought it was too early to be hitting the bottle, she kept the thought to herself. Her smile firmly in place, she handed him a menu. "I'll send your waitress right over. Enjoy your meal."

Not sparing the menu a glance, he kept his eyes on the kitchen door and waited for the waitress. Ten minutes later, she still hadn't showed and he was getting impatient. He started to grab a busboy and demand some service, but just then, a fresh-faced waitress hurried over to him, her cheeks flushed with excitement.

All smiles, she said charmingly, "I'm *so* sorry! I didn't mean to keep you waiting, but the place is a madhouse today. The owner's wife came in today after being gone for months and everybody's talking about her. She's got amnesia! Can you believe it? At first I thought she was just playing around, but it's true. Every time she sees me, she usually asks about my baby, but this time, she didn't even know who I was. It was the strangest thing. What are you supposed to say to a person who hasn't got a clue who you are?"

Stunned, the man just looked at her. Was she for real? Had the bitch really lost her memory? Was that why she'd looked right through him? Elated, it was all he could do not to grin like an idiot. All this time, he'd been worrying for nothing. She wasn't going to send the cops after him—she wasn't going to do jack squat. Because she didn't have a clue about what happened to her Thursday night. If he was lucky, she never would.

"Amnesia, hmm?" he said, schooling his features to casual interest. "I never knew anyone who had that before. And you say this is the owner's wife?"

"Yeah. Annie Taylor. Joe—that's the owner—" she explained helpfully, "was hoping that she might remember the restaurant since they used to eat most of their meals here, but so far, nothing's clicked. It's like she was just born yesterday or something."

"She doesn't know *anybody?*"

"No, not even Joe. Isn't that the wildest thing you ever heard?"

"Yeah, wild," he muttered. Trying not to look too excited, he leaned casually back in his chair. "So is this permanent or what? There must be something the doctors can do."

"You'd think so, wouldn't you?" the girl said chattily. "But apparently she has to remember on her own. And poor Joe can't push her too much or she might never get her memory back."

"No kidding? Man, that's rough." An idea already forming in his head, he had to fight back a smug smile of anticipation. So he'd scared her witless, had he? If the little witch thought she was terrified now, wait till she found out that he was just warming up. By the time he got through with her, she'd be lucky if he didn't turn her into a blubbering idiot.

Suddenly realizing how much she'd been talking, the waitress laughed. "I didn't mean to talk your ear off—I just find this kind of stuff so interesting. So what can I get you?"

He almost told her to forget it—she'd just given him everything he needed, including the broad's husband's name—but what the hell? He felt like celebrating. "How 'bout your biggest chicken-fried steak and a beer?'' he suggested. ''I just got some good news.''

"I'm going with Phoebe for a couple of hours," Annie announced as she and Phoebe followed Joe into his office. "She's showing a house at two and I'd like to see it."

Phoebe had made the suggestion as they'd followed Joe through the downtown traffic, and Annie had jumped at the chance to do something that would get her mind off what might have happened to her Thursday night. She'd expected Joe to agree that it would be better for her to get out for a while than sit around worrying about what Sam's lab tests were going to turn up, but now, seeing his sudden scowl, she wasn't so sure.

"You want to go back to work? I don't think so."

Taken aback, she blinked. "Excuse me?"

"You're in no condition to even think about working yet," he said in the patient voice a father might use with a young daughter when explaining why she couldn't go out and play on the road. "As soon as I get some work together to take home with me, we'll go back to the apartment."

A meek, obedient wife might have taken that sitting down, but Annie had a feeling that was something she'd never been. Amusement warring with the first faint stirrings of temper in her eyes, she cocked her head and openly studied him. "I'll be the first to admit that I don't remember a thing about our marriage," she said dryly, "but I can't believe that I married a dictator. It just doesn't feel like something I'd do. Are you sure you're my husband?"

Watching the beginning of the fireworks from well out of the line of fire, Phoebe laughed. "He's all yours, girlfriend. I know—I was a witness."

Joe's lips twitched, but his jaw remained as unyielding

as the Rock of Gibraltar. "Grant said you were supposed to rest," he told Annie. "And so did Dr. Sawyer."

"I did," she argued. "I slept ten hours last night. And it wasn't like I was planning to run a marathon or anything," she added. "Phoebe's going to be doing all the work. I'm just going along for the ride. Maybe I'll remember something."

Unmoved, he shook his head. "Forget it. You're not supposed to force your memory."

Exasperated, Annie turned to her friend for help. "Is he always this stubborn?"

"From where I'm sitting, I'd say you two were pretty even," Phoebe said with a grin. "God help the baby."

Annie gave her a withering look. "That's not quite the endorsement I was hoping for, Phoeb. I'm trying to win an argument here, in case you hadn't noticed."

"Just for the record," Joe pointed out, "you were the one who always had the tenacity of a bulldog. So I'd watch who I was calling stubborn if I were you."

"But this is ridiculous! You can't expect me to sit around here and the apartment for the next six to eight months and twiddle my thumbs waiting to have the baby. I'll go crazy."

She had a point. She had amnesia, not a deadly disease, and he couldn't keep her pinned up for the entire length of her pregnancy. But just the thought of letting her go anywhere without him made him want to bar the door. Because he was concerned, he told himself. That was all. Right now, she was as vulnerable as a child and had no one to protect her but him.

Yeah, you keep on telling yourself that and you just might start to believe it in another hundred years or so, a caustic voice drawled in his head. *You know you never got over her. Why don't you just admit it and put yourself out of your misery?*

Muttering a curse under his breath, he growled, "I have no intention of keeping you locked up like some kind of prisoner. I was concerned about you being stressed out from this morning, but you know better than I do how you feel. Go ahead and go if you want. Just call if you're going to be late getting back. Okay?"

When her face lit up like a Christmas tree and she nodded, he tried not to take it personally. She wasn't thrilled at the thought of getting away from him—she just needed a break. Considering the circumstances, he supposed he couldn't really blame her.

"We'll only be gone a couple of hours," Phoebe assured him. "After the showing, I thought I'd take her by the office and see if anything looks familiar. I'll have her back by two-thirty or three, tops."

He nodded, resigned to the inevitable. He didn't have to worry that Phoebe would let anything happen to her. She was as protective as an older sister and wouldn't let her out of her sight. Still, he knew he would be watching the clock every second that they would be gone, and there wasn't a damn thing he could do about it. Pushing to his feet, he forced a smile. "Then you'd better get out of here or you'll be late for your appointment."

Within ten minutes of leaving with Phoebe, Annie knew why they had been friends for most of their lives. Carefree and irreverent, Phoebe told one outrageous story after another, swearing they were all true, not stopping until Annie cried with laughter. And for the first time since she'd awakened naked in a strange man's bed, Annie was able to forget the horror of not remembering who or what she was. With Phoebe, it didn't matter that she couldn't remember having been maid of honor at her wedding when she married right out of college, or being there for her when her husband beat her and she kicked him out. The bond between them was deeper than memories, and they seemed to have a zillion things to talk and laugh about. It was wonderful.

Wiping at her streaming eyes as they headed for the Dominion, an exclusive gated community on the outskirts of town where the rich and beautiful lived, she laughed, "Stop it! You're killing me. You're making that up!"

Her eyes twinkling, Phoebe held up her hand and swore solemnly, "As God as my witness, I'm not. We were on our way to Dallas and had *three* flats in one day! And not one man stopped to help us. You changed the last one, and when a carful of college boys flew by and honked, you threw the tire iron after them."

"I did not!"

"Yes, you did. I swear! It took us twenty minutes to find it in the tall grass on the side of the road."

Grinning, Annie said, "God, I wish I could remember that. We must have had some fun times together."

"Oh, we did! Lord, we were something. Do you remember the time we…"

She didn't remember anything, of course, but that didn't stop Phoebe from reminiscing. Listening, Annie felt as if she was eavesdropping on another woman's life, a woman she still didn't know but was beginning to realize she liked a great deal. Was she really that daring? That adventurous? She and Phoebe must have given their parents fits growing up…and a lot of reasons to laugh.

Soaking up the stories like a sponge, she couldn't seem to stop smiling. "It's a wonder we didn't spend all our time in detention when we were in school. I bet the principal was crazy about us."

"Old Cue Ball?" she retorted with a chuckle. "Why do you think he lost all his hair?"

They were still chuckling when they met with the prospective buyer at the entrance to the Dominion and showed him a mansion that overlooked the golf course. It was a breathtaking place, and watching Phoebe in action, Annie could see why she'd gone into business with her. She was good. Damn good. All joking forgotten once the buyer showed up, she was gracious and professional and able to answer all the man's questions without once consulting her notes. Singing the property's praises without being too pushy, she dropped subtle hints that the place wouldn't be on the market for long considering how reasonable the asking price was.

Listening to her, Annie almost choked on a laugh at that. How could Phoebe say that with a straight face, when the asking price was nearly a million dollars?

Behind the man's back, Phoebe winked at her. "We've got a live one here," she whispered when the buyer stepped out onto the patio to inspect the pool. "What do you want to bet he doesn't walk away from here without signing a contract?"

"Are you kidding?" she hissed, casting a quick look toward the open patio doors. "All he's done since we got here is point out everything that's wrong with the place."

Practically rubbing her hands with glee, Phoebe grinned. "Don't you just love it when a man plays hard to get?"

Annie laughed—she couldn't help it—and before it was all said and done, she had to give Phoebe credit. The man followed them back to their office, filled out the necessary paperwork, and signed on the dotted line. Annie would never have believed it if she hadn't seen it with her own two eyes.

Laughing, Phoebe gave her a high five as soon as they had the office to themselves. "God, I love this business! It's days like this that make it all worthwhile. C'mon, let's celebrate!"

Considering the size of the commission she'd just made, Annie expected her to suggest they go out for champagne or something, but her friend reached into the bottom drawer of her desk and drew out a cookie tin instead. Popping the lid, she held it out to Annie with a smile. "It doesn't get any better than this, girlfriend. Try one."

Amused, Annie reached into the tin and pulled out something that seemed to be a combination of a cookie and a brownie and was dark with rich chocolate. Taking a bite, she groaned with pleasure. "Oh, that's wonderful! Did you make these?"

Phoebe nodded. "It's your mother's recipe. When we were kids, we used to drive her crazy eating the dough before she could bake it. I was hoping you'd remember."

Her smile fading, Annie tried, but as before, all she came up with was a black wall that blocked her memory and wouldn't let anything through. "I want to," she said huskily, "but I can't. There's just nothing there. Tell me about my mother...my parents. Where are they? Do I see them often?"

"They died in a car accident when you were twenty," her friend said softly. "Your father was never around much when we were growing up—he was always working—but your mom was great. She taught us both to drive a stick shift and water-ski. And man, could she cook! She was always trying something new. It's too bad she didn't live long enough to meet Joe. She would have loved talking shop with him."

She sounded like a wonderful mother, but nothing Phoebe said stirred a memory. Regret darkening her eyes and squeezing her heart, she said, "I wish I remembered her. Maybe then I wouldn't feel so alone."

"You have Joe, Annie. I know he still seems like a

stranger to you, but you can count on him," she said earnestly. "Just give it some time."

Since time was all she had, Annie could do nothing else. But no one seemed to realize how difficult that was. She was living with a man she didn't know, sleeping in his bed at night, while the two of them circled each other during the day like two adversaries in some kind of contest. She could see the emotions in his eyes every time he looked at her, feel the jerky beat of her heart whenever he inadvertently touched her, and couldn't for the life of her explain any of it.

"Tell me about him," she said impulsively. "I have so many questions that I can't ask him to his face."

For a minute, Phoebe almost told her, but then she shook her head, a crooked smile tilting up one corner of her mouth. "Oh, no, you don't. The doctor wants you to remember on your own. If you want to talk about Joe, you tell me about him. For all practical purposes, he was a stranger to you until a couple of days ago. Now that you've spent some time with him, what do you think of him?"

That was something she didn't even have to think about. "He's strong and protective—the kind of man who naturally takes charge in a crisis. And gentle," she added, remembering the way he had taken care of her when she was sick. "He's a good man."

"Yes, he is," Phoebe agreed. "Make sure you remember that in the days and weeks to come."

The opening of the second Joe's Place was still two months away, but Joe knew he was quickly running out of time. The entire staff, including a chef and manager, had to be hired, the menu had to be decided on and the work on the building itself wrapped up. While Annie was out with Phoebe, he spent the afternoon going over résumés for potential managers. Determined to avoid the type of problems he'd had before he brought Drake into the operation, he went over one after another.

Nothing, however, registered, and he had no one to blame but himself. Every time he let his guard down, his thoughts wandered to Annie. What was she doing? Had the office she shared with Phoebe brought back any memories? And if it had, were they good ones or bad ones? How long would it take her to remember their marriage?

He had to believe that eventually it would all come back to her. It had to. She needed her past, needed the security of knowing who and what she was, and he wouldn't deny her that even though he knew those selfsame memories would cause problems for them. He *was* the workaholic she'd accused him of being before she'd walked out—he couldn't deny it. But he had to draw the line when she compared him to her father, who, according to both Annie and Phoebe, had loved making money more than he'd ever loved his wife and child.

The money had never been an issue, dammit! He hadn't come from an upper-middle-class background like hers. His father had never kept a job for longer than a month or two without finding an excuse to quit. While her mother had stayed home with her when she was a child, his mother worked just to keep food on the table. He didn't want that for his wife and child if something happened to him. He'd tried to explain to her how important it was to him to build a nest egg so that when they did have children, their future would be secure, but she hadn't listened. She'd wanted a baby and nothing else mattered, least of all his own hopes and dreams for her and his children.

And he still resented that, he discovered as he stared blankly down at the résumé of a wanna-be manager. She tore his life up when she left him, and now she'd torn it up again by coming back the way she had. If, God help them, she didn't get her memory back, only a blood test would tell them if the baby was his when it was born. How the hell was a man supposed to concentrate when he had a thing like that hanging over his head for months to come?

Frustrated, angry with her and himself and the entire situation, he reached for the next résumé. It went without saying that he might as well have saved himself the trouble. His eyes kept drifting to his watch. Where the devil was she?

Finally giving up in defeat, he abruptly pushed to his feet, put the résumés away, then wandered out into the restaurant to greet customers and make sure they were enjoying their meals. It was that personal touch and his true interest in the customers' wants and needs that had made Joe's Place a success over the years. But when his eyes kept drifting to the restaurant's front doors, he knew he wasn't fooling anyone, least of all himself. Keeping the customers happy was important, but he was prowling around for only one reason. He was waiting for Annie.

It wasn't, however, until she stepped through the main doors an hour later that he realized that he hadn't really expected her to come back to him at all. Relief hit him then, the force of it stunning him, infuriating him. What the hell was wrong with him? He had no problem with watching over her, protecting her, seeing to her needs until she got her memory back. But he wouldn't, by God, care. Because if he did and she left him a second time, he didn't think he could endure it.

The restaurant was packed that night, the crowd lively. Deciding that he wasn't ready for another intimate dinner on the balcony like the one they'd shared the night before in their apartment, Joe suggested they eat supper at the restaurant instead, and Annie readily agreed. He thought he'd be able to keep his distance more easily in a crowd, but he hadn't reckoned on Annie. She'd had a wonderful afternoon with Phoebe and was thankful to have made a new friend, even though it was one she'd had for years. Her eyes sparkling, her smile as quick as her laughter as they waited for their food to be brought to their table, she retold some of the stories that Phoebe had told her and had no idea that Joe had heard them all before. And he didn't tell her. This was the Annie he had first met and fallen in love with, the one who had been gone for too long.

Watching her, captivated in spite of all his best intentions, he fought the pull of her smile and the sparkle in her eyes, but she didn't make it easy for him. In spite of the other diners who sat at tables all around them, the world was reduced to just their table. And Annie. He couldn't take his eyes off her.

She ate her steak and baked potato and part of his, eating with a ladylike grace and truck-driver appetite that he couldn't help but appreciate. Amused in spite of himself, he said, "How about dessert?"

"Oh, I shouldn't," she protested, then made him laugh when she said wistfully, "but strawberry shortcake does sound good."

"Hey, don't stop on my account," he said dryly, and signaled for the waiter.

Afterward, when she laughingly claimed she was starting to waddle, he walked her home. There were two ways home—they could walk along the river or take the stairs to street level and cut through the next block—but with no conscious decision on his part, Joe took the Riverwalk.

It was a mistake—he realized it immediately. The moon was out, music spilled from the nearby restaurants and clubs, and lovers strolled hand in hand everywhere he looked. Keeping his hands strictly to himself, he should have looked for the nearest flight of stairs and gotten the hell out of there, but he didn't. Memories played in his head, haunting him, seducing him. How many times had he and Annie walked this same way, touching each other all the way home, teasing each other until they were both hot and breathless and couldn't wait to fall into bed? They'd driven each other crazy more nights than he could remember, and he'd loved it.

If she hadn't left him, if she hadn't come back to him just because she was pregnant and in trouble, they could even now be going home to bed.

But she had, and he'd never been one to play what if. His mouth compressed in a flat line, he hurried her along. "C'mon, it's getting late. You must be tired."

Annie opened her mouth to tell him she was fine, but he didn't give her a chance. Jostling through the festive crowd, he pulled her after him and extended his stride, until she almost had to run to keep up with him. Then they reached the arched gate that opened onto the private back gardens of the Lone Star Social Club. Quickly unlocking it, he hustled her inside, into the house, and up the stairs before she could even think about catching her breath.

"Joe! What in the world! What's wrong?"

"I've got some paperwork to catch up on," he retorted as he unlocked their apartment door and pushed it open. "Will you be okay here by yourself if I go back to the office for a while?"

He didn't step into the apartment, but waited in the hall like a man who had a train to catch. Confused, she stared up at him searchingly. The charming man she'd just had dinner with was gone, and in his place was the cold stranger who kept his emotions safely hidden and treated her like an unwanted relative who had suddenly turned up on his doorstep without warning. He had to deal with her, but he really didn't want to, and for that, she felt the constant need to apologize.

She told herself she had no right to feel hurt—you had to care about someone before you gave them the power to hurt you. And in spite of the fact that they'd been married for five years, Joe Taylor was a virtual stranger to her. But still, there was an ache deep within her chest that was as raw as an open wound, and he had put it there. She would have died, however, before she let him know it.

Forcing a smile that never reached her eyes, she said airily, "Of course. I probably should go to bed anyway—it's been a long day. So go on. I'll be fine."

Her tone was just right, her smile breezy. She gave every appearance of being strong and independent, and there was no reason to linger. He stayed, however, right where he was and frowned down at her. "Are you sure? Maybe you shouldn't be alone right now—"

"I'll be fine," she insisted. "Will you just go? If I need you, I'll call. Okay?"

He should have gone then—he told himself he wanted to. But the memories that had dogged his quickened footsteps all the way home were there in the dark depths of her sapphire eyes, and he couldn't look away, couldn't turn away. He saw his hands settle heavily on her shoulders and would have sworn they belonged to someone else. Then he was dragging her up on her toes and he couldn't stop. He just couldn't stop.

He crushed his mouth to hers, his tongue already plundering, savoring. He didn't give her time to think, to object, but took like a man who hadn't tasted any kind of sweetness in ages. Hungry, greedy for more, he couldn't get his breath, couldn't get a handle on his self-control and didn't care. His blood was hot, boiling, his head spinning. And still he wanted more.

Lost to everything but the fury of his own needs, he didn't realize that she'd stiffened like a poker until he wrapped his arms around her and tried to draw her flush against him. Her arms wedged between them, she didn't give so much as an inch. Between one frantic heartbeat and the next, his head cleared.

He'd damn near taken her right there in the hall like a madman!

Swearing, cursing himself, he released her, but it was too late. The second he stepped back, he saw her eyes were wide with shock, her cheeks bright with color. "I'm sorry! That was a stupid thing to do! I know you didn't want that— I don't know what came over me." Stumbling for an acceptable explanation when there wasn't one, he backed away. "It won't happen again," he promised. "You don't have to be afraid."

Desperate for a way out, he finally remembered why they were standing in the hall. "I'm going back to the restaurant now. The number's in the book by the phone. I'll be back by eleven. Lock the door."

Dazed, she stumbled across the threshold and shut the door, only to lean weakly against it, conflicting emotions hitting her from all sides. He'd kissed her. Why? What did he want from her? She'd been so sure that he was only tolerating her presence because of the possibility that she was carrying his baby, but the hot emotions she'd seen in his eyes when he reached for her had nothing to do with anything as bland as tolerance. Lord, who would have thought the man could kiss like that? She must have kissed him a million times before, but this was the only time she remembered, and she couldn't seem to get her breath.

It won't happen again. You don't have to be afraid.

Wincing, she hugged herself. She hadn't been afraid...exactly. If her life had depended on it, she couldn't have said what she was. Except confused. And restless. He, on the other hand, hadn't been able to get away from her fast enough.

Pressing her ear against the door, she listened to the dying sound of his footsteps as he headed for the stairs halfway down the hall and told herself that he wasn't running from her, only the situation. She wasn't the Annie Taylor he'd married and separated from. It wasn't *her* he was rejecting.

An hour ago, she might have taken comfort from that, but it didn't help now. Because *she* was the Annie Taylor he'd kissed.

When the phone rang ten minutes later, she was in the master bedroom turning down the bedspread. Figuring it was Joe, checking to make sure she was okay, she stretched out on the bed and reached for the extension. He must have called the second he got back to the restaurant. "You don't have to worry about me," she said huskily, by way of a greeting. "I'm fine. Really."

She wouldn't have been surprised if he'd apologized again, but her only answer was silence. Frowning, she unconsciously tightened her fingers around the receiver. "Joe? Is that you?"

There was no answer, just a silence that hummed in her ear, and for no reason she could explain, her heart started to knock against her ribs. It was just a wrong number, she told herself. Just some ignorant person who didn't know how rude it was to not admit that he'd dialed wrong, then apologize. There was no reason to be afraid.

But when she hung up, she was shaking.

Five seconds later, she was in the living room, fumbling with Joe's address book for the number to the restaurant. It had to be here somewhere, she told herself frantically. He'd told her it was. All she had to do was calm down and think. *Think,* Annie! What would he list it under?

She was near tears when she found it and quickly reached for the phone. She had three numbers punched in when she suddenly froze. What was she doing?

Disgusted with herself, she slammed down the phone. "Don't be such a baby!" she muttered. "It's just a stupid wrong number, for heaven's sake! There's no reason to get all bent out of shape. Or call Joe! He's busy and won't appreciate you calling him away from work just because you're paranoid."

There was absolutely nothing to be afraid of. In her head, she knew that, but her body wasn't listening. Her pulse was pounding, her palms damp, her mouth dry as dust. She wanted to hide, which was ridiculous. This was her home. Closing her eyes, she dragged in a shuddering breath and willed herself to calm down.

How long she sat there, she couldn't have said. Her breathing gradually returned to normal, her heart rate steadied. Finally thinking more clearly, she double-checked the lock on the front door and found it secure. Her tight nerves eased, but she knew there was no way she was going to be able to sleep. Not now. The apartment was too quiet, too empty.

For the sake of her sanity, she switched on the TV just to break the heavy silence that engulfed her, then went looking for a book to read. She was just reaching for one on the top shelf of the bookcase in the living room when the phone rang again.

She froze, she couldn't help it, her heart in her throat. She wouldn't answer it. It was probably just another wrong number, anyway. She'd just let it ring and whoever was on the other end would eventually get disgusted and hang up. All she had to do was wait him out.

But it could be Joe.

The thought slipped up on her from behind, nagging at her. He'd been reluctant to leave her there alone—he could be calling to make sure she was all right. If she didn't answer, he'd be worried....

She made no conscious decision to move, but suddenly she was across the living room and reaching for the phone. "Hello?"

For a split second, she thought it was going to be another wrong number. Then a rough, male voice on the other end of the line said, "Annie."

That was it—just her name in a matter-of-fact voice that was more of a statement than an inquiry. There was nothing threatening about it, nothing the least bit sinister. But between one heartbeat and the next, she was terrified, and she couldn't explain why. Sobbing, her skin crawling, she slammed down the receiver. Feeling dirty, she ran for the bathroom.

Chapter 5

The water pounding down on her head had long since grown cold, but Annie never noticed. Huddled in the corner of the shower stall, her brow furrowed with fierce concentration, she soaped a washcloth, then ran it over her breasts, hips, legs and arms, missing nothing in between. Then she numbly repeated the process. Once, then twice, then again. In the bedroom, the phone rang, but she didn't hear it. Time, the world, ceased to exist. There was just her, the water and the soap.

Clean, she thought dully. She had to get clean. She had to get the dirt out from under her skin.

Down in the restaurant, Joe frowned and hung up the phone in his office. There was nothing wrong, he assured himself. Annie had probably unplugged the phone in the bedroom when she'd gone to bed. And once she was asleep, she'd never hear the one in the living room. There was no reason to go running up to the apartment, as if she was some sort of maiden in distress. He'd heard her lock the dead bolt himself, and she'd promised to call if she needed him. The fact that she hadn't could only mean one thing—she was perfectly safe and he was being paranoid.

Deliberately, he tried to bring his attention back to his paperwork, but he couldn't shake Annie from his thoughts. Just because she hadn't called didn't mean she wasn't in trouble. What if she hadn't been able to get to the phone?

"Damn!" Pushing back his chair from his desk, he muttered curses, chastising himself for worrying like an old woman. But there was no getting around it—he wasn't going to get any more work done tonight until he knew for sure that she was all right. Gathering up his paperwork, he headed for the door.

"I'm going to check on Annie," he told Drake. "I probably won't be back tonight."

"Sure thing, boss," Drake responded, with a mock salute. "Don't worry about anything here. I'll hold down the fort."

It normally took him five minutes to walk home, but this time he made it in two. Worry etching his brow, he unlocked the front door to the apartment and stepped inside. The TV was on in the living room, tuned to an old John Wayne movie. Annie had always been crazy about the Duke—the sound of his familiar drawl should have been comforting, but wasn't. A quick glance around assured him that everything was as it should be, but he couldn't shake the feeling that something wasn't right. Then he heard it. The shower.

Relief flooded him, and he groaned aloud at his own stupidity. He'd had this image of her struggling with some unknown intruder and all the time she'd just been taking a shower. With the water pounding down on her head, she couldn't possibly have heard the phone ringing. God, what an idiot he was! Thankfully, he hadn't called Sam like he'd wanted to. He'd never have heard the end of it.

Promising himself that he'd have a phone installed in the

damn shower stall tomorrow, he sank down on the couch to watch the end of *True Grit*. Ten minutes passed, then another five, and the water continued to run in the bathroom. Wondering what was taking Annie so long, he glanced at his watch and frowned. Nearly twenty minutes had passed since he'd stepped into the apartment, and he didn't know how long she'd been in there before that. What the hell was she doing?

His frown deepening with concern, he crossed to the bathroom door and knocked sharply. "Annie? What's going on in there? Are you all right?"

His only answer was the continued running of the water.

You go charging in there like some sort of knight in search of the Holy Grail and you're going to scare her to death, a caustic voice warned in his ear. *Especially since you've already grabbed her and kissed her once tonight. Hold your horses and let her have her privacy. She'll be out when she's done.*

But another ten minutes passed and Annie showed no sign of cutting off the water. Struggling for patience, Joe paced and cursed and tried to ignore the worry squeezing his heart. But he was fighting a losing battle, and with a muttered curse, he knocked on the bathroom door, then pushed it open before she could say yea or nay. Like it or not, he was going in.

He half expected her to scream, but with the shower door closed, she didn't even see him. "Annie? Are you all right?" he called over the steady drone of the shower. "You've been in there an awful long time."

She'd heard him—she had to. But silence was his only answer. Truly worried now, he strode over to the shower stall. Later, he couldn't have said what he expected to see when he jerked open the door, but it wasn't the sight of Annie standing under a cold spray of water, her face as pale as death, her arms heavy with exhaustion as she dragged a washcloth over herself again and again. In some spots on her breasts and thighs, her skin was red and nearly rubbed raw.

Alarmed, he didn't even stop to think, but stepped into the shower fully clothed. "Annie? Honey? What is it? What's wrong?"

She glanced up at the first sound of her name, her hands stilling, and it was then that Joe's heart stopped in his chest. He'd never seen such stark terror in anyone's eyes before and it scared the hell out of him. He wanted to reach for her, to wrap her close and demand to know what had happened, but he was afraid to touch her.

She blinked, her gaze locked and focused on his, and suddenly her blue eyes were swimming in tears. "J-Joe...help m-me. I—I c-can't g-get clean."

He'd sworn when she left him that he'd never let her break his heart again, but he felt it crack then, and it didn't matter. Nothing mattered but Annie. "Oh, baby," he rasped, his own eyes stinging as he reached to take the washcloth from her, "you're so clean, you're squeaky. Here, let's turn the water off and get you out of here."

With a savage twist of his hands, he shut off the cold spray, plunging the bathroom into a thick, heavy silence. Her arms climbing up her body to hug herself, Annie tried to say something, but suddenly her teeth were chattering and she was shaking with cold and shock. Joe ached to hold her, but he wasn't sure how she'd react and he didn't want to upset her any more than she already was.

"Don't try to talk," he murmured soothingly as he pulled towels from the linen closet and wrapped them around her as tenderly as if she were a child. "Whatever the problem is, I'll handle it. Just stand there and let me take care of you, honey. Everything's going to be okay."

Biting her bottom lip to still its trembling, she nodded and docilely did as he said, not uttering so much as a whimper as Joe gently patted the water from her breasts and hips and legs. His emotions fiercely held in check, he told himself to get a grip.

But a muscle jumped in his jaw every time he touched her poor chafed skin. Lord, she had to be hurting—it hurt him just to look at her.

What happened while he was gone? he wondered furiously. Why had she done this to herself? Questions tore at him, but she was in no shape to give him any answers. Not now. She could barely stand and words were beyond her as goose bumps rippled across her skin. Wrapping a towel around her dripping hair and another around her shivering body, he urged her into the bedroom. "C'mon, sweetheart. Let me find you a nightgown and then I'll put you to bed. Once you warm up, you'll feel better. Okay?"

Only able to manage a jerky nod, she stumbled over to the bed and perched hesitantly on the side of the mattress. By the time Joe finally found her a gown and robe, some color had seeped back into her face, but her knuckles were white with strain as she clutched at the towel that covered her. And when her gaze lifted to his, awareness of her own nakedness was there in her eyes.

Hesitating, Joe unconsciously curled his fingers into the softness of her nightclothes. "Can you dress yourself?" he asked huskily.

Heat climbing in her cheeks, she swallowed thickly. "Y-yes. I—I think s-so."

He didn't want to leave her by herself, but she couldn't have made it plainer that she needed a few minutes to herself. Crossing to her, he laid her clothes next to her on the bed. "I'll just be in the living room," he told her quietly. "If you need some help, just holler."

Walking away from her when he knew she still needed him was one of the hardest things he'd ever done, but he didn't intend to be gone for long. Grabbing some dry clothes for himself from their closet, he hurried into the guest bathroom to dry off and change, then headed for the kitchen to make her a cup of hot cocoa. Within minutes, he was back, knocking at the bedroom door.

"You okay, honey? I brought you some cocoa. I thought it might steady your nerves. Are you decent?"

Cold all the way to her soul in spite of the gown and robe that now covered her from her ankles to her throat, Annie hugged herself and had to swallow twice before she could answer. "Yes. You can c-come in."

The words were hardly out of her mouth, and he was there in front of her, studying her with eyes that were dark with worry. And, just as quickly, the tears that she'd thought she'd cried out in the shower were back, spilling over her lashes. He was being so sweet to her, and she was acting like a basket case. God, what must he think of her?

"I'm sorry," she sniffed.

"Don't be ridiculous," he chided. "After everything you've been through, I imagine you're entitled to a few tears." He held the steaming mug out to her and smiled coaxingly. "I made it just the way you like it—with an obscene amount of whipped cream."

Sure her stomach would revolt if she dared to put so much as a swallow in it, she took the cup to warm her hands. The scent of chocolate, dark and sinful, drifted to her nose, tempting her. Staring down at the mound of whipped cream floating in the chocolate, she hesitated.

"Go ahead," Joe urged softly. "It'll make you feel better."

She didn't think she would ever feel better again, but she took a sip, then another, and felt heat spread through her like liquid sunshine. She sighed and held the mug to her chest. For the first time in what seemed like hours, she had some body heat to fight the cold that invaded her very soul.

When she glanced up, Joe was watching her with eyes that were as fierce as a hawk's. "What happened while I was gone?"

She didn't want to tell him, but one look at his set face and she knew he would never be satisfied with anything less than the truth. But God, how did she tell him without sounding like a baby who was afraid of her own shadow? "This is so stupid," she blurted out, dashing impatiently at the tears that slid down her cheeks as she stepped past him to pace the length of the bedroom. "I don't know what's the matter with me. Nothing really happened. It was just a phone call—"

"Someone called? Who? When?"

She nodded. "About five minutes after you went back to the restaurant. Actually, it was two phone calls. I thought the first one was a wrong number because no one said anything, so I hung up. Then a few minutes later, the phone rang again. I almost didn't answer it, but I knew you'd be worried if it was you...."

"And?"

"A man said my name—"

"And?"

"And that was it." A strangled laugh, verging on hysteria, forced its way through her tight throat. "I know—it sounds ridiculous. There was nothing to be afraid of, but the second he said my name, I was terrified. And I don't even know why! He didn't threaten me or anything. For all I know, he could have been an old friend of yours who's wondering right now why I hung up on him. God, I feel like such an idiot!"

"Why? Because you're afraid? Honey, if we could explain away fear, nobody would be scared of anything.'' Moving to her side, he slung a brotherly arm around her shoulders. "You don't have to apologize for being scared. You were, and now we have to figure out why. Did you recognize the caller's voice? Did it sound familiar at all? Maybe you knew him."

For a second, just a second, the weight of his arm across her shoulders felt like heaven, and she allowed herself the luxury of melting against him. But then she could hear the caller's voice in her ear, saying her name, and suddenly she couldn't bear to be touched.

Shrugging out from under his arm, she was halfway across the room before he even realized there was a problem. She saw his surprise, the slight tightening of his jaw, but there was nothing she could say, no explanation she could give, that would make sense. He would think it was because of the kiss—that she didn't trust him—but the wariness he'd stirred in her then was nothing compared to this.

Regret darkening her eyes, she turned away. "No. At least I don't think so," she amended. "I don't remember ever having heard it before, but I guess that doesn't mean much, does it?"

She couldn't have made it clearer that she didn't want his touch if she'd screamed and fought her way free of him. His expression carefully shuttered, Joe didn't so much as flinch. "Okay, so you don't remember his voice, but he had to know you since he called you by name. What did he do after that?"

"I—I don't know. I hung up." Emotions skittered across her face, as easy to read as a Dr. Seuss book. Fear, trepidation, revulsion. Her gaze unfocused, directed toward something Joe couldn't see, she swallowed and dazedly rubbed her hands up and down her arms just as she'd done when he'd found her in the shower. "I felt so dirty, I couldn't stand it,'' she whispered half to herself. She blinked then, her eyes lifting to his with painful, helpless bewilderment. "I couldn't get clean, Joe. I tried, but it didn't matter how much soap I used, I still felt dirty. And I don't know why."

He went to her then because he couldn't help himself, because she needed him, whether she knew it or not. And he, God help him, needed her. "You're not dirty, honey." Taking a chance, he lifted his hand and lightly ran a finger down her smooth cheek. "You're clean and beautiful, and if someone made you feel otherwise, they're the one with the problem, not you."

He was so close he could see the doubts in her eyes. He knew he was crowding her, but God, he ached to just hold her, dammit! To feel her against him and forget for a moment they'd ever been apart. But he hadn't forgotten the shock in her eyes when he'd kissed her. And a man could only watch his wife cringe from his touch so much before he learned to keep his hands to himself.

Stepping back, he gave her the room she needed. "Now that we've got that straightened out," he began, "why don't I—"

The sudden knock on the front door was sharp and demanding. Startled, Annie stiffened, every line of her body tight with apprehension as her eyes flew to Joe's. Swearing, he growled, "Who the hell is that at this time of night? Stay here, honey, while I check it out."

The last person he expected to find knocking on his front door at ten o'clock at night was Sam Kelly. Jerking the door wide, he motioned him inside. "You don't usually come calling this time of night. What's up?"

"I probably should have waited until tomorrow for this, but I've got some news and I thought you'd want to hear it as soon as possible." Stepping into the living room, he glanced around. "Where's Annie?"

"Here," she said from the short hallway that led to the bedrooms. "What's wrong? Did you find out what happened to me?"

"Not to you, no," he said regretfully. "But I did find out what happened to Sal Larkin." At her blank look, he said, "You know, the renter you were supposed to meet with at the Transit Tower the other night. He never showed because he was in a car accident on the way in from Houston. He's been in the hospital ever since."

"Oh, no!"

"I know it's not much consolation, but at least we know he wasn't involved in what happened to you," he said. "He was in emergency surgery at the time and couldn't have possibly had anything to do with whatever went down in the Transit Tower parking garage. That means someone else is involved. All we've got to do is figure out who."

"That may be simpler than you think," Joe told him gravely. "Annie got a couple of strange phone calls tonight when I was at the restaurant."

"What kind of phone calls?"

Pale, she grimaced. "One was a hang-up. The next one was a man. He called me by n-name—"

"And scared her out of her mind," Joe finished for her angrily.

He told him then about Annie's reaction to the call. "Whoever he was, he had to have something to do with her amnesia," he said grimly. "She was terrified of him. And I'm telling you right now, Sam, if I ever get my hands on him, the miserable piece of scum is going to wish he'd never been born."

Sam understood exactly how he felt—in his shoes, he'd have been as outraged as Joe, but the last thing this case needed right now was an outraged husband muddying the water. "Hold your horses, Kemosabe," he warned, shooting him a hard look. "For all we know, this could be just a case of a simple wrong number—"

"The hell it is! He called her by name!"

"Her name's in the phone book, isn't it? She's a licensed Realtor, Joe. Doesn't she have both her home and business numbers listed? It could have been a business call that scared her for some reason."

It could have, but Joe wasn't buying that for a second. "You didn't see her in that shower, Sam. She was freaked, and you know Annie's not the type to freak easily."

"Which is all the more reason for you to take care of her and let us handle whoever made that call," he replied. "Annie's shaky enough over this without you trying to take the law into your own hands." Turning back to Annie, he motioned for her to join him on the couch. "Why don't you come over here and tell me about this call, Annie—"

"All he said was my name."

"I know," he said patiently, as she reluctantly crossed to the couch, "but what did he sound like? Did he have an accent? Were there any noises that you could pick up in the background? Any strange sounds that might tell us where he was calling from? Close your eyes and just think a minute. Maybe there was a train whistle or some music..."

Obediently, Annie did as he asked, praying that in her terror, she might have missed something, anything. But all she could hear when she replayed the call in her head was that voice...flat, totally without emotion, yet somehow horribly frightening at the same time. Who was this man who could terrify her with just the sound of his voice? What did he want with her? And when would he call again?

Her eyes flew open, the new fear draining the last of the color from cheeks that were already lily-white. "There was nothing," she rasped hoarsely. "Nothing. He called me by name, and then there was this long silence. Do you think he'll call back? I can't talk to him again. I won't!"

"You're damn right you won't," Joe growled. There was no way he was standing back and letting some sick joker terrorize her this way. "From now on, I'll answer the damn phone, or we'll let the machine get it." And she wasn't going to be left alone again either. When he couldn't be with her, he'd make sure someone else was.

Turning to Sam, he arched a dark brow. "Well?" he demanded. "You still think this was a simple wrong number?"

He didn't, but it didn't matter what he thought. He had to go by the law. "At this point, it doesn't matter, Joe. It's not against the law to call someone by their name over the phone. If we could prove he knew what he was doing to her when he did it, we might have a slim case of harassment, but he'd have to call a heck of a lot more than twice. If I were you, I'd get caller ID on your phone just in case this joker calls back. At least then we'd know where he was calling from and we might be able to find out who the devil he is."

It was a long shot, but the only one they had. Joe nodded. "I'll make the arrangements the first thing Monday morning."

By ten o'clock Monday morning, Joe had someone from the telephone company installing caller ID at the apartment and, to the amusement of the telephone repairman, a new phone in both bathrooms. Over the next few days, however, the new service turned out to be unnecessary. Whoever had called Saturday night and scared the living daylights out of Annie hadn't called back. Not taking any chances, though, Joe made sure she wasn't left alone again. If she wasn't with him at the restaurant, she was with Phoebe, or he brought work home with him.

As promised, Sam got back to them with the results of the lab tests on Annie's clothes and the stain in the parking garage, and the news wasn't anything they hadn't expected. The bloodstains matched each other, but not Annie. As for the fingerprints on her car, they all turned out to be hers.

With the case at a standstill, they seldom discussed it, but settled into a routine that seemed to take the anxiety from Annie's eyes. Her memory still persisted in eluding her, but she was more relaxed…as long as they remained in the apartment. The second they stepped outside, however, the fear was back, the tension gripping her visibly—a thing that was difficult to watch. Realizing that she didn't know friend from foe, Joe took immediate steps to remedy the situation.

"C'mon," he told her after breakfast one morning. "I'm going to introduce you around so if someone speaks to you in the hall, you'll know if it's someone you can trust."

He didn't have to think twice about who to introduce her to first—he took her straight downstairs to Alice Truelove, who lived in the smaller of the two apartments at the back of the mansion. And as he'd hoped, Alice beamed in delight at the sight of Annie by his side and snatched her into her arms for a fierce hug. "I wondered when you were going to get down here and tell me you were back! I saw you and Joe go out to dinner the other night, but I didn't want to intrude. Lordy, lordy, look at you! I knew this old house would work its magic if you two would just give it enough time. Joe, isn't she a sight for sore eyes?"

"Yes, ma'am, she is," he replied, grinning when Annie couldn't help returning the small, spry woman's enthusiastic hug. "I thought it was time I got her down here—she needs a friend she can trust."

Quickly and efficiently, he told her the whole story and

wasn't the least surprised when Alice's faded blue eyes took on a hard gleam. With her plump figure, beautifully lined face, and cloud of stark white hair that she invariably wore twisted up in a bun, she might look a soft pushover of a granny, but she could be tough as nails when she wanted to be.

"You visit me whenever you want, sweetie," she told Annie. "I just dare anyone to try and bother you. I've got my Colt .45 that my daddy gave me in my bedroom, and you can bet the bank that I know how to use it."

"I don't think you'll need the peashooter," Joe drawled, grinning, "but Annie might drop by sometime when I have to take care of some things at the restaurant. Thanks, Alice."

"For what?" she sniffed. "You two are like family. You call on me whenever you need me. Since Annie doesn't remember the stories about the mansion, I can tell them to her all over again."

"Later," Joe laughed, tugging Annie down the hall to the next apartment. "She'll get back to you later."

Over the course of the next few days, he took her around to all their neighbors in the mansion and reintroduced her to them.

Not surprisingly, it was the women she was most at ease with. She chatted every morning with Mrs. Sanchez across the hall and asked Susan Lucas, a renter who lived downstairs and had just had her second baby two months ago, everything she could think of about pregnancy and babies and parenting. But it was Alice she kept going back to. And true to her word, the old lady spent hours entertaining her with stories about the Lone Star Social Club.

After one particularly entertaining afternoon, Annie's eyes were sparkling when she and Joe went to the restaurant for dinner. "How old do you think Alice is?" she asked him after they'd given their orders to the waiter. "I know you said she's supposed to be the original owner's granddaughter, but if I didn't know better, I'd swear she was the original owner herself. She knows the names of everyone who ever met and fell in love there all the way back to the turn of the century. But she couldn't be that old, could she?"

Joe grinned. "God only knows. From what I hear, she was here long before the Riverwalk was ever thought of."

"Do you think that old legend about unmarried renters falling in love is for real? How could it be? It's just a house."

"With a heck of a wallop," he replied, chuckling. "I can't explain how it works, but I've lived there for nearly six years, and nobody remains single for long. Even Bob Jackson bit the dust, and he was the most hardened bachelor I ever met. He swore when he moved in that the *curse* wasn't going to get him, but I'll be damned if he didn't elope with his new secretary five months later. Talk about shaking up a few people. One of Jackson's best friends lived on the first floor and moved out immediately."

"So he's still a bachelor?"

"Are you kidding? His sister introduced him to her roommate and he found himself walking down the aisle three months later. Last I heard, they had three kids and were expecting another one on Valentine's Day. And then there was you, of course," he added. "I took one look at you and knew my days as a bachelor were numbered."

He said it teasingly, with a twinkle in his eye, but there was nothing funny about what she'd done to him. She'd turned his life upside down and filled a void that he hadn't even known was there, and he'd loved her for it. He hadn't realized how much until she walked out and he'd found himself faced with the emptiness of his own lonely existence.

He wanted her back, dammit. Wanted back what they'd once had together. Needed back what he'd carelessly let slip through his fingers. But she wasn't the same woman who married him or even the same one who'd walked out on him. Staring soul deep into her sapphire eyes, he didn't see how they could ever find their way back to what they had once had. Not if she'd betrayed him with another man.

"Joe? Are you okay?"

Lost in his thoughts, he blinked and brought her back into focus to find her frowning at him in concern. "Yeah, I'm fine," he said in a gravelly voice, then deliberately changed the subject. "So what are you and Phoebe doing tomorrow?"

"Showing a ranch up by Kerrville," she said promptly. "A couple from Corpus is driving up to look at it and another one west of Bandera, so we should be gone most of the day. What about you? You going to be at the new place all day?"

"Probably," he said, fighting a smile as their food was set before them and the waiter automatically set a bottle of ketchup on the table. Over the last few days, she had developed a fondness for the red stuff that bordered on a craving. Most of the restaurant staff had learned that it didn't matter what she ordered to eat, she was going to ask for ketchup before the meal was over. "The opening's just around the corner and there's still a lot to do. The painters are finishing up in the morning in the dining area, and the kitchen appliances are supposed to be delivered Thursday. The printer's also delivering the invitations sometime tomorrow, but they still have to be addressed."

"I'll help you if you'll bring the guest list home," she

promised, digging into her food with gusto. "Why don't we eat at home tomorrow night and order in a pizza?"

That was an offer she wouldn't have made three months ago, not when she was so dead set against him opening another restaurant. Remembering the times she'd accused him of being more concerned with the shape of his business than the condition of their marriage, Joe knew he should tell her about the day she'd left him. If he didn't, he would be giving her just one more reason to resent him when she got her memory back.

But he was damned either way, and he hated to ruin the mood when there hadn't been a tense moment between them in days. The decision made, he said, "Good idea," and damned the consequences. "Have Phoebe drop you by here when you get back tomorrow and we'll walk home together."

The florist's box was propped against their front door, but Annie never noticed it. She and Phoebe had driven away from the ranch in Kerrville with a huge contract in hand and should have celebrated, but all Annie had wanted to do was get back to Joe and tell him about her day. She'd missed him. She hadn't expected that, and she had to admit that the idea shook her. After all, it wasn't as if she spent every waking moment with him. He had a business to run, not to mention a second restaurant to open, and over the course of the last few days, she'd spent hours at a time with Phoebe and other friends and neighbors while he worked. He couldn't devote all his time to her, and she didn't expect him to.

But today had been different. She'd been gone since morning, and in spite of the fun she'd had with Phoebe, she'd found herself wondering what he was doing, where he was, if he'd given her so much as a second thought since she'd left. Then, when Phoebe had dropped her off at the restaurant and she walked in to discover him in conversation with Drake near the riverfront entrance, her eyes met his and her heart just seemed to stumble.

A fanciful woman might have thought he was waiting for her, especially when a slow smile quirked up one corner of his mouth the second he saw her. Trapped in the heat of his gaze, she didn't have a clue if she was fanciful or not. She just knew that for the first time that she remembered, she was having dinner with her husband alone. There would be no waiters to interrupt them, no old friends to wander in and greet them. It would just be the two of them, like any other married couple, spending a night in at home. Her mouth went dry just at the thought of it.

He greeted her with a kiss on the cheek that set her skin tingling and her mind jumping forward to the moment when he shut their front door and they were alone. She hardly heard Drake greet her or wish her good-night after Joe collected the invitations for the grand opening to the new restaurant from his office. They started home, and before she was ready for it, they were walking down the second-floor hall to their apartment.

Struggling to get control of the smile that kept breaking out on her face, she told herself that the only reason she was looking forward to spending time alone with him was that this man who called himself her husband was still such a mystery to her. But her wildly thumping heart wasn't buying that, and she didn't care. They were only going home, but it felt like a date, and she intended to enjoy herself.

Turning to face him as they reached their front door, she grinned. "So what do you want on your pizza? Or maybe I should ask what do *I* want? I do like pizza, don't I?"

"Are you kidding?" he chuckled. "You can eat your weight in the stuff. And just for the record, you like sausage and pepperoni...just like I do." He started to insert the key in the dead bolt, only to stop in surprise as his gaze dropped to the florist's box propped against the door. "Hey, what's this?"

"I don't know," she said, eyeing the white box curiously as he bent down to pick it up. "I didn't order anything. Did you?"

"No, but it's got your name on it. Have you got a secret admirer you haven't told me about?"

It was, to say the least, an unfortunate choice of words.

Suddenly realizing what he'd said, he unconsciously dropped his gaze to her slightly rounded stomach, which was barely concealed by her long, thigh-length sweater. In the damning silence that fell between them, they both knew there was a good possibility that over the last few months she'd had not only an admirer, but a lover as well.

"If I do, I seriously doubt he would be sending me presents here," she replied quietly. "There must be some mistake."

"Maybe," he agreed, frowning. "Let's go inside and see what's in it."

He set the invitations on the entrance-hall table as soon as they were inside, then carried the box into the living room and set it on the coffee table. It was harmless-looking cardboard, the kind of box roses came in, but tied with twine. And the card with Annie's name on it was unsigned. With no florist's stamp on it there was no way to tell where it had come from.

"Maybe we should call Sam," Annie suggested worriedly, chewing on her bottom lip as she sank down onto the couch next to him. "He'd probably want to know about this."

"Let's see what's in it first," Joe said, and cut the twine with his pocketknife. "For all we know, it could be a welcome-home present from one of the neighbors who didn't want you to make a fuss."

Knowing what a matchmaker Alice Truelove was, Annie had to admit that it would be just like the old lady to send flowers without signing the card in the hopes that she would mistakenly think they were from her husband. Her mouth softened into a smile. "You're talking about Alice, aren't you?"

He nodded, but it wasn't flowers in the box. Instead, it was a single piece of cedar, and a dead one at that. The needles on it had long since turned brown. Confused, Joe frowned. "What the hell!"

Her blood roaring in her ears, Annie stared at the small branch in puzzlement. It was harmless; it couldn't hurt her. But then Joe picked it up and the scent drifted under her nose, and suddenly her stomach turned over. "Oh, God!"

"Annie? Honey? What's wrong?"

Her eyes wide, her hand pressed to her mouth, she couldn't answer him. With a muffled moan, she ran for the bathroom. Swearing, Joe threw down the cedar branch and rushed after her.

She'd been sick every morning, losing the contents of her stomach almost as soon as she crawled out of bed, but even when the nausea was at its worst, it had never been like this. She was violently ill and there wasn't a damn thing Joe could do but hold her head and curse with worry.

Murmuring to her when she was finally spent, he jerked down the toilet lid, helped her sit down, and quickly wet a washcloth. "Just close your eyes and ride it out, sweetheart," he murmured as he gently wiped her face with the cool cloth. "You're going to be fine."

She should have been—she always had been before. But as a faint bit of color came back into her cheeks, the fine trembling that hit her told her this wasn't going to be like the other times. "I'm s-sorry," she stuttered, winding her arms around herself. "I—I don't know what's the m-matter with m-me. The s-second I smelled the c-cedar, I j-just got s-so scared I felt l-like someone had p-punched me in the stomach."

Swearing, Joe didn't stop to think, he just scooped her up in his arms and sat back down with her on his lap. When she automatically froze, he knew she was going to fight her way out of his hold any second, but then something in her just seemed to give. With a sob, she collapsed against him and let him hold her, really hold her, for the first time since she'd come home. And in her misery, she had no idea how close she came to destroying him.

Softly cooing to her, he soothed her with endearments and caresses, and all the while the voice of reason cautioned him to be careful. She was scared and vulnerable, and he was setting himself up for a fall, big-time. Any warm body would do when you were scared, but once she calmed down, she'd shy away from his touch just as she always did.

But he ached for her, dammit! He didn't want to. He didn't like it, but there it was, like it or not. And there was no way he was letting her go as long as she needed him. For now, he found to his surprise, that was enough.

Chapter 6

The dream crept out of the darkness like something wicked that only dared to expose itself in the blackest hours of the night. Sweeping over Annie's defenseless, sleeping body, it swallowed her whole with no warning whatsoever. One second her breathing was slow and steady, her sleep deep and restful, and the next she was being hurtled into the middle of a horrifying nightmare. Her throat clenched tight, she tried to scream, to move, to escape, but fear paralyzed her. Helpless, all she could do was shrink into herself and ride out a terror that had no beginning or end.

It was dark. God, it was so dark! There were no city lights, no moon, no houses close by, no one to see her. And no one to help her. She wanted to run, to hide, but it was too late for that. Staring down at the shovel in her hands, she started to tremble. How could she do this? How could she not? Swallowing a sob, she drew in a deep breath and deliberately made her mind go blank. Then she began to dig.

The ground was soft from the rain that had fallen earlier in the evening, the air tangy-sweet with the scent of cedars that surrounded her like a forest. Another time, she might have enjoyed toiling in the earth after an autumn rain. But not now. Not here. This was no garden that she dug; and the deeper and longer the hole got, the sicker she felt. Her fingers wouldn't stop shaking, and the handle of the shovel kept slipping from her grip, scraping the soft skin of her palm. Once, she almost pitched headlong into the pit and felt her stomach roil. Sweat broke out on her brow, and she wiped it away with a hand that felt as if it would never be steady again.

Time slowed, then stopped altogether, and torture took on a whole new meaning. With the coppery taste of fear on her tongue, she didn't allow her attention to wander from the shovel and the dirt. And an ever-deepening hole that yawned like the entrance of Hell at her feet. Then, before she was ready, it was long enough, wide enough, deep enough.

She stared at it and almost gagged. Merciful God, she couldn't do this! But she wasn't given a choice. The cold form lying on the ground next to her rolled into the shallow grave with a soft, sickening thud and landed face up. Glazed, sightless eyes stared unblinkingly up at the night sky.

A sob lodged in her throat. Her eyes shied violently away, but not before her gaze locked in fascinated horror on the small, fatal bullet hole in the middle of the dead man's forehead. Inanely, she wondered where all the blood was. There should have been blood.

Images stirred in her head. Terrible, tormenting images that made her heart stumble in her breast and her throat constrict on a frozen scream. She slammed her eyes shut, but still she could see him, this same man, standing before her, his startled gaze locked on the gun, the sure knowledge in his pale blue eyes that he was looking at his executioner. The gun exploded, and in the next instant, he was flat on his back, much as he was now, his life force draining out of him onto the pavement before he could even ask God to have mercy on his soul.

And now she had to bury him.

Oh, God, oh, God. The shovel fell numbly from her fingers, and she couldn't make herself move to catch it. Her tongue thickened; bile pooled in her mouth. Her flesh crawling, she sank to her knees and cupped her trembling hands in the loose dirt piled next to the grave.

Don't look at its face! It's not real. It's not a man if you don't look at his eyes. Think about the dirt, the grittiness of it under your nails and covering your skin. When this is all over, you're going to go home and scrub it off. Then you'll be clean and all of this will go away like a bad dream.

Her movements stiff and jerky, she scooped up dirt and tossed it, scooped it and tossed it, and never once looked to see where it landed. Instead, her gaze was fixed, and in her mind, she was already in that shower. She could feel the soap against her bare skin, the water beating down on her, pounding the tension out of her tight shoulders, relaxing her, cleansing her. Just the thought of it brought tears to her eyes.

But the face. She had to cover the face.

There was a roaring in her ears. Her fingers curled into the dirt, and the scent of cedar needles and fresh dirt rose to her nose.

No! a frantic voice in her head cried out in protest. *Don't do this! Please don't do this.*

But her hands took on a life of their own. In slow motion, they lifted the dirt and carried it up the long length of the still, half-buried form before her. And then, before she was ready for it, her hands were hovering right over the dead man's face.

She tried not to look, but she couldn't stop herself. His skin was pasty white, the mouth frozen in a silent scream. With his square-cut jaw, chiseled bone structure and thick cloud of black hair, he might once have been a handsome man in spite of the small scar that marred one corner of his mouth. But not now. Not in death. Death had robbed him of life, of spark, and left behind a bloodless, macabre monster that she knew would haunt her nightmares the rest of her life.

Frozen, so close she could smell the death that rose from him, she felt the trembling of her fingers worsen and could do nothing to stop it. In what seemed like slow motion, the dirt cupped in her hands trickled into his eyes and mouth and nose.

"No!"

Her unholy scream echoed through the apartment like the screech of a banshee. Slumped against the headboard of their bed, where they'd both fallen asleep while he'd held her after she was sick, Joe bolted up, his heart in his throat and his eyes wild and confused. "What the hell! Annie? My God, what's wrong?"

She didn't hear him. Devastated, tears streaming down her bloodless face, she bent over, her arms wrapped around her middle, and rocked in misery. "What have I done? Oh, God, what have I done?"

She sounded so horrified, so revolted with herself, he reached for her without thinking. "Honey, you haven't done anything. What makes you think you have? You were just dreaming—"

"No!" Already shaking her head, she didn't let him finish...or touch her. Scrambling out of bed, she backed out of reach until she stood all alone, her face etched in despair.

"You don't understand!" she cried. "It wasn't a dream. It was a memory. I think I killed a man."

Joe paced the confines of the kitchen like an innocent man who had just been convicted of a felony, more frustrated than he'd ever been in his life. *I think I killed a man.* Dear God, she'd meant it! She actually thought she'd killed a man. And no amount of talking on his part had changed her mind. She didn't know how or why or even who the man was, but there was no other explanation for her burying a dead man in a stand of cedars. It all fit, she'd claimed. The blood on her clothes and on the pavement in the parking garage, her desperate need to get clean, the sick despair that had spilled into her stomach at the sight of that cedar branch. She'd killed a man—and someone out there knew it.

She'd been so serious, so *sure,* that she'd scared the hell out of him. Shaken, he'd immediately hustled her into the kitchen, warmed her some cocoa, then spent the next fifteen minutes trying to convince her that she'd just had a night terror. Granted, it had been a particularly nasty one and horrifyingly real, but it was still a far cry from a memory.

He might as well have saved his breath. Her chin took on that stubborn set he'd come to know too well over the course of their marriage, and nothing he'd said so far had persuaded her that there was no need to call Sam.

"Dammit, this is ridiculous!" Quelling the small niggling doubt that whispered in his ear—dear God, was it possible that she'd done such a thing?—he pushed back from the kitchen table and rose to glower down at her. "I know you—better than you know yourself right now, I might add—and you just haven't got what it takes to kill anyone. You're a soft touch, Annie Taylor. If I'd let you, you'd pull every bum off the street into the restaurant kitchen and feed them. You could no more shoot someone between the eyes than you could fly."

Even to his own ears, his tone was desperate and edged on panic. He couldn't tell who he was trying to convince—her or himself—and she knew it.

"No one wants to believe that more than I do," she said hollowly, "but I can't. The evidence is too damning."

"A dream isn't evidence!" he snapped. "Your mind's just playing tricks on you. You got that damn package with the cedar in it this afternoon and it scared you. So tonight your subconscious came up with a way to explain your fear. That's all it was."

It was a logical explanation, and more than anything else in the world, Annie wanted to believe it. But she couldn't. Not when she could still feel the grit of the dirt on her skin and smell that damn cedar. Just thinking about it made her want to gag. She'd buried a dead man—she knew it.

Her cocoa turning cold in her hands, she pushed it away. "We have to call Sam, Joe. He needs to know about this."

"No."

"If you won't call him, I'll do it myself."

"The hell you will!"

She flinched at his roar but her stubborn jaw only lifted a notch higher. "Raising your voice isn't going to change my mind. Sam said to call him if I remembered anything, and that's what I'm going to do."

He wanted to shake her. He wanted to lock her up in their bedroom and not let her go anywhere near Sam or any other cop who might take her ridiculous story seriously. But she'd fight him on that, so all he could do was pretend to go along with her, and in the process, appeal to her maternal instincts.

"All right," he said flatly. "If you really want to call him, I can't stop you. But in case you hadn't noticed, it's three o'clock in the morning. If you call him tonight, you probably won't get any sleep the rest of the night. Do you think that's good for the baby?"

He saw the answer in her eyes and pressed the advantage. "If you really shot someone and buried him, which I strongly doubt, he's not going anywhere tonight. Waiting another few hours to notify the authorities isn't going to hurt anything."

He was right, but she was afraid to close her eyes again, afraid that she'd get caught up in that nightmare again and never find her way home. Swallowing a sob, she shivered and wished Joe would hold her. But she couldn't ask, and he didn't take the initiative. Considering the circumstances, she really couldn't say she blamed him. She'd killed a man. When Joe had vowed to love and cherish her for better or for worse, she doubted that he'd expected *worse* to include murder.

Jerking to her feet abruptly, she needed to walk, to pace, to work this out in her head, but there was no place to go. No place but back to bed, and she couldn't do that. Turning away, she stared blindly out onto the balcony. "All right, I'll wait until the morning to call him, but I can't go back to bed. I just can't."

"You're not going to dream, honey," he said softly from behind her.

"You can't be sure of that."

"Yes, I can. I'll sit by the bed and wake you the second I think you're dreaming."

Surprised, touched that he would even suggest such a thing, she whirled to face him. "I can't ask you to sit up the rest of the night. You've got to work tomorrow."

"I don't need much sleep," he fibbed easily. "Don't you remember? Give me a two- or three-hour catnap and I can go for another twenty hours easy. I'm wide-awake, so while you're sleeping, I'll just sit by the bed and address the invitations. We never got around to that, remember?''

She should have said no—she couldn't take advantage of him that way. But she was punch-drunk, she was so tired. She desperately needed to get horizontal, but if she closed her eyes even for a second, the dream would be on her, and she might not be able to fight it off a second time.

"All right," she agreed. "But only if you promise to go to bed if you get tired. I'd feel terribly guilty if you stayed awake just because of me."

His fingers crossed behind his back, he nodded solemnly. "On my honor as a Boy Scout. Now will you go to bed before you fall on your face? You can barely keep your eyes open as it is."

Another time, Annie would have quizzed him about being a Boy Scout, but the last of her energy was spent and she couldn't manage any more protests. Sighing as he slipped a supporting arm around her waist, she let him lead her to the bedroom.

She didn't dream, but she didn't sleep very well, either, and she woke the next morning with sandy eyes and a headache. For once her stomach wasn't acting up, but she found little comfort in that. Before she even opened her eyes, the events of the previous evening came flooding back. The cedar branch left on their doorstep, the dream, the face of a dead man that was indelibly sketched in her memory. "Oh, God!"

She would have bolted right out of bed, but before she could even think about throwing back the covers, her gaze landed on Joe. He was seated in the chair next to the bed, just as he had been last night when she'd closed her eyes for the last time and drifted back to sleep, only he wasn't working on the invitations for the restaurant opening as he had been then. Instead, he was slumped in the chair, asleep, his chin resting on his chest and his pen still clutched in his hand, the invitations spread out around his feet on the floor.

Something shifted in her heart, a barrier that she hadn't even known was there, giving way to a rush of emotions that pulled at her heartstrings and made it impossible for her to drag her gaze away from him. Settling back against her pillow, she studied him quietly, noting the night's growth of beard that darkened his shadowed jaw, the enticing curve of his sensuous mouth, the sweep of dark lashes that any woman would have killed for. He was, she couldn't help noticing, an incredibly sexy man. And he was her husband.

That knowledge no longer shook her as it had at first. She'd come to accept the fact that he was a part of her life. She didn't remember loving him, but at one time, he must have loved her fiercely. She could still see the lingering traces of it in the dark secret depths of his eyes, still feel it in the gentleness of his touch and the way her own heart leapt at the sight of him.

What kind of lover was this man who was her husband? she wondered, her eyes searching as they traveled the lines of his sleeping face. Was he generous and caring and as interested in pleasuring her as he was himself, or were his own needs his only concern? Did he hold her afterward or just roll away and go to sleep? He seemed to be a toucher, but that could be wishful thinking on her part. She couldn't remember, but she thought she must be the kind of woman who needed the man she loved to keep her close after the loving. Would Joe know that without having to be told? Was he that sensitive to his lover's needs? Would the time ever come when she would find that out for herself?

Images stole into her mind, hot, intimate imaginings that fired her cheeks and stole her breath. With an ease that shocked her, she could picture herself stroking him, loving him, giving herself totally and completely to him. Just him. Until they were both spent, replete, sated. Just thinking about it left her weak. And hot on a chilly autumn morning.

He shifted slightly, and her heart jerked in alarm. *What are you doing, Annie?* a voice cried in her head. *Get out of that bed before he wakes up and finds you staring at him like a sex-starved spinster just waiting for the chance to jump his bones!*

But even as she moved to throw off the covers, it was too late. The pen slipped from his fingers and fell to the floor, barely making a sound. But it was enough to wake him. Wincing, he stirred, rubbing at the back of his neck, and she watched in fascination as he slowly came awake. As rested as if he'd lain on the bed beside her all night, he stretched and yawned with an animal grace that did funny things to her stomach. Then his eyes opened and settled on her as if he'd known all along that she was watching him, and she could do nothing to stop the damning blush that slowly stole into her cheeks.

A sleepy smile tugged up the corners of his mouth, then, before she could even begin to guess his intentions, he leaned over and kissed her. Startled, her heart missed a beat, and she couldn't for the life of her raise her hands to push him away. He was still half-asleep, she told herself weakly. He'd forgotten that he'd promised not to kiss her again. He didn't know what he was doing. He couldn't. But the second his lips settled gently on hers, he showed her in two seconds flat that he was a man who knew exactly what he was doing.

His mouth moved on hers, as soft as a summer breeze, gently wooing, seducing, so different from the heat and flash and hunger of that other time, when he'd caught her so completely off guard. Captivated, she trembled, her eyes closing on a sigh. Her heart murmuring a languid rhythm that seemed to echo in her blood, she wanted to reach for him, to wrap her arms around him and never let go. But she was afraid that if she did, this would all turn into a dream. So she curled her fingers into the covers and focused all her attention on just his mouth. The taste, the feel, the heat of it. How could she have forgotten him? she wondered dizzily. Forgotten *this?*

Need crawling through him, raking him with silken claws, Joe fought to keep the kiss light and easy. But damn, it was hard! He'd been dreaming about making love with her when he woke up to find her staring up at him from their bed, and it had seemed the most natural thing in the world to lean over and kiss her. Just a simple good-morning kiss— that was all it had started out to be. But he'd still been caught up in that damn dream and his defenses had been down, his body hot for her. The second his mouth had touched hers, he was lost.

Dear God, he ached for her! It had been too long since he'd kissed her, too long since he held her close and loved her until they were both so weak they could hardly move. She was his wife, dammit, and he wanted her! She might not remember anything about their life together, but she wasn't indifferent to him—not if those soft little whimpers she made at the back of her throat were anything to go by. He could crawl into bed with her and love her like there was no tomorrow, and she'd never utter a word of protest.

But there was a tomorrow. And a yesterday, one where she might have gotten pregnant by another man. And as much as he wanted to forget that, he couldn't.

Cursing his raging hormones, calling himself seven kinds of a fool, he reluctantly lifted his head. And nearly kissed her again when he saw the glazed desire in her eyes. Swallowing a silent groan, he forced a crooked smile and told himself to keep it light. "Good morning, sleepyhead. I guess

I don't have to ask you if you slept all right. You were rattling the windows."

Surprised, her pulse still skipping madly, she gasped, "I was not!"

"You were snoring a beat you could dance to halfway down the Riverwalk," he claimed outrageously. "I spent most of the night waiting for Alice to break into song downstairs."

He was so solemn, she might have believed him if it hadn't been for the twinkle dancing in his eyes. The need humming in her veins giving way to amusement, she laughed. "You're making that up! Anyway, you're a fine one to be talking. *I don't need much sleep,*" she mimicked. *"Give me a two- or three-hour catnap and I can go for another twenty hours easy."*

His grin unrepentant, he shrugged lazily. "So I exaggerated a little." When she lifted an eyebrow at that, he laughed. "Okay, so make that a lot. My intentions were good. You needed to sleep and you did. Mission accomplished. Now, how about breakfast?" he asked, deliberately changing the subject. "Is the baby up to ham and eggs this morning, or are we sticking with dry toast?"

She knew what he was doing—deliberately mentioning the baby in order to distract her about last night—and for that, she wanted to kiss him. But she'd already done that, and he'd been the one to pull back.

Her pride battered slightly, she forced a smile, determined to keep things as light as he. "I don't know about the baby," she said easily, "but if you're talking scrambled, with hash browns and plenty of ketchup, you've got a deal."

"Somehow I had a feeling you'd say that," he said dryly. "So I had a whole case of the stuff delivered yesterday. You want ketchup, sweetheart, you've got ketchup." Playfully swatting her on the thigh, he grinned. "So up and at 'em, lazybones. It's your turn to cook."

She wasn't, by any stretch of the imagination, a gourmet cook, but she had discovered over the last few mornings that she could handle breakfast quite well, thank you very much. So as soon as she was dressed, she set to work at the stove while Joe made the toast and orange juice. The kitchen was large enough to hold a small army, but every time she turned around, she seemed to find Joe in her path. He teasingly accused her of throwing herself at him, but he was the one who was always brushing up against her, making her laugh and her heart skip. By the time they finally sat down to eat, the last thing she was interested in was food. Breathless and flushed, she was hungry for something a lot hotter than ham and eggs.

But she'd been so upset last night over the package left on their doorstep that they'd never gotten around to ordering pizza. She took one bite of the eggs she'd scrambled, and her stomach reminded her that it had been nearly twenty hours since she'd eaten. With a murmur of pleasure, she dug in.

Given a choice, she would have lingered over the meal for most of the morning, enjoying the food and coffee and Joe's company. But she couldn't. Not when last night's nightmare was still so fresh in her mind. As soon as they were both finished eating, she rose to carry their dishes to the sink. When she turned back to face Joe, her jaw was set. "I want to go to the police station and talk to Sam this morning. He needs to know what I've remembered."

"Honey, that was just a dream—"

"No, it wasn't," she insisted stubbornly. "It happened, Joe. I remember."

Startled, he followed her to the sink, his dark eyebrows

snapping together into a straight line over his narrowed brown eyes. "What do you mean, you remember? Are you saying you've got your memory back?"

"No. Not much of it, anyway. But I remember kneeling on the ground covering a dead man with dirt." Haunting bits and pieces of too real images rose before her eyes, sickening her. "I can still see his face," she said faintly, shuddering. "I didn't imagine it."

"You didn't kill him," he said flatly. "I don't care what you dreamed, you didn't kill anyone."

His belief in her warmed her heart, but nothing he could say could erase the doubts that were lodged like a fist in her throat. "I need to find that out for myself. Please, Joe."

He wanted to argue. Dammit, he wanted to grab her and shake some sense into her! But there was a pain in her eyes that stabbed him right in the heart and as much as he wanted to believe she was being paranoid, he couldn't dismiss her fears nearly as easily as he would have liked. "All right," he sighed. "We'll go talk to Sam. But I still don't think it's necessary."

Thirty minutes later when Sam escorted them into a small interview room at the police station where they could talk in private, Joe hadn't changed his mind. "I told her she just had a vivid dream," he told his friend as they each took a chair at the table in the middle of the room, "but she insists it was real."

"It was real," Annie retorted. "I think I killed someone, Sam."

Unlike Joe, Sam didn't automatically dismiss her claim as just a trick of her overactive imagination. Instead, he sat back in his chair and regarded her steadily, his thoughts well hidden behind his steady gaze. "Tell me about it," he suggested.

She started at the beginning, with the delivery of the cedar branch to the apartment, and told him how the sight and smell of it sickened her. Just thinking about it made her fingers tremble and she quickly locked them together in her lap, then began to recount the memories that had assaulted her in the middle of the night. "It wasn't just a dream," she said finally. "The details were too exact. I could feel the dirt, smell the cedar, everything."

"But you don't remember shooting him? Or even holding a gun?"

"Well, no, but—"

"Then how do you know you killed him? Just because you buried the man doesn't mean you're the one who murdered him," he pointed out logically.

"But there was no one else there," she argued.

"Maybe not in your dream, no. But dreams aren't always reliable. How big was the dead man?"

Caught off guard, she blinked. "I don't know. Six-one or so, maybe a hundred and ninety pounds."

"And you think you not only killed him in that parking garage, but somehow managed to get him in your car, then drive him out in the sticks somewhere and bury him? All by yourself? C'mon, Annie, I know you're tough, but there's just no way you could have done that. There had to be somebody else."

"Which would explain a hell of a lot," Joe said promptly. "Like why someone keeps trying to terrorize her with phone calls and this damn thing…" he motioned to the cedar branch, which lay brown and stiff in the box it had been delivered in. "If she really did bury a corpse in a bunch of cedars, that damn branch wouldn't mean anything to anyone but Annie and whoever was with her."

"But why would this person want to terrorize me?" she cried. "I don't even remember him."

"Exactly," Sam replied. "As long as you have amnesia, he's safe. You can't identify him."

His brown eyes black with rage, Joe swore. "He scared her out of remembering her own name once. Now he's trying to do it again, only this time he wants to make sure she doesn't remember him."

"Because as long as she hasn't got a clue who he is, all we have to work with is a body that could be buried anywhere in the state of Texas," Sam concluded. "So that's where we'll start." Turning back to Annie, he said, "I know this isn't pleasant for you, but can you describe the dead man for me? I'm going to check missing persons and anything you remember might help identify him."

Her mouth cotton-dry, she could see the corpse as clearly as if it lay stretched out before her on the table. "He was a white man, with thick black hair, a square jaw and chiseled face. I—I don't know how o-old he w-was. It was kinda hard to tell."

"You're doing fine," he assured her. "Just take your time and try to remember everything you can. Was there anything odd about him? Any identifying marks like a mole or something that would make him stand out in a crowd?"

"A scar!" she blurted out, suddenly remembering. "Right by the left side of his mouth. I remember thinking that he must have been handsome even with the scar."

Frowning at the description, Sam rose abruptly to his feet. "That sounds familiar. Hold it a second and let me check something. I'll be right back."

He was back almost immediately with an eight-by-ten photo he held out to Annie. "Have you ever seen this guy before?"

It was the picture of a man in a business suit. Lean and rugged, his black hair conservatively cut and styled, he had the kind of good looks that would inevitably draw women's eyes wherever he went...in spite of the small scar that marred the left side of his mouth.

Annie took one look and blanched. "Oh, God, that's him!"

"Easy, honey," Joe said soothingly. "Whoever the hell he is, he can't hurt you."

"He's Robert Freeman," Sam informed them, tossing the picture onto the table. "The president of Brackenridge State Bank. He's been missing for over a week. And so has a hell of a lot of money from the bank. Up until now, we had reason to believe that Mr. Freeman had embezzled the money, then skipped the country. Apparently, we were wrong...at least about him skipping the country."

"You think Annie stumbled across someone killing him in the Transit Tower parking garage?" Joe asked shrewdly.

Sam nodded grimly. "That makes more sense than her shooting Freeman between the eyes. She was probably just in the wrong place at the wrong time and got dragged into a murder. In all likelihood, the murderer planned to kill her, too, but somehow she managed to get away."

His jaw rigid, Joe would have given anything to have five minutes alone with the bastard who had terrorized her. No wonder she'd blocked it from her memory! Frowning at her pale face, he reached over to cover her clenched fingers with his. "Does any of this sound familiar, sweetheart?"

"Not really," she said with a regretful shake of her head. "I know I buried him. That's all. Whenever I try to remember anything else, I just run into this black wall."

And it was that black wall of forgetfulness that could get her killed. Somehow the killer had found out who she was and where she lived and was doing a good job of scaring her. But as long as she lived, there was a possibility that she could remember him at any time. Eventually, he would have to come after her. And when he did, he would have a distinct advantage. Because he could pass her on the street and look her right in the eye, and she probably wouldn't know him.

Joe glanced at Sam and saw the same knowledge in his friend's eyes. "I think this would be a good time to get Annie out of town for a while," he told Sam. "We've got a cabin in the Davis Mountains that we used to get away to when we were first married, but we haven't been there in a few years. She'll be safe there. It's forty miles from town and out of sight of the road. No one will even know we're there."

"But what about the restaurant?" Annie protested. "And the opening for the new place? It's just a couple of weeks away, isn't it? I can't ask you to drop all that and run away to the mountains with me. You need to be here to handle things."

If he hadn't been so worried about her safety, Joe would have laughed at the irony of the situation. In the months before she'd left him, she'd done nothing but complain about how little time they spent together because he was always working. And now she was finding excuses for him to stay in town and work.

"Your safety is more important than the damn restaurant," he said. "Anyway, Drake can handle a lot of things for me. And it's not like I'll be completely out of touch. If something crops up that I need to handle personally, he can call me on my cellular. Anything else will just have to wait until we get back."

"But when will that be?"

"When you get your memory back or Sam catches the bastard who did this to you—whichever happens first."

"But that could be months!"

"You're already starting to remember things," Sam pointed out. "Granted, there are still a lot of pieces missing, but knowing that you're safe at the cabin may be just what you need to let your guard down and remember the rest. And while you're gone, we've got some new leads to follow," he added. "Knowing Freeman is dead changes things. We've been looking for him in Canada and Mexico, not in a grave in the country. We'll find him, Annie. Then we'll find his killer."

"But he could be buried anywhere. There's cedar all over Texas. You could look for years and never find his body."

"True, but you've given us more information about that night than you realize. We know that you had an eight-o'clock meeting at the Transit Tower and that you showed up at your and Joe's apartment sometime around two or three in the morning. You didn't have a car or any money to catch a cab or bus, so you must have walked all the way home once you got away from the killer. That means he couldn't have taken you too far out in the country to bury Freeman. That narrows our search considerably."

"So you see? It won't be that long," Joe said. "Just a couple of weeks. And getting away will be good for you and the baby. You need the rest."

And they needed this time together. *He* needed it. He didn't know if he'd ever be able to trust her again, and when she got her memory back, she could hurt him all over again, but that was just a chance he would have to take. There were still feelings between them, and he had to see if there was any chance of a future between them.

Her eyes searching his, she hesitated, but he saw in a glance that he'd already won. Giving in, she grumbled, "I still feel guilty about taking you away from your work, but if the two of you think this is for the best, who am I to argue?"

Elated, he only nodded. "Good. We'll leave at dawn."

Chapter 7

When Joe had first started looking for property to buy, six years ago, he'd wanted someplace completely isolated from the rest of the world, a retreat from phones and faxes and temperamental chefs, not to mention a never-ending stream of customers it was his responsibility to please. He worked long, hard hours and seldom took any time off for himself, and when he did, he wanted to look out his front door and see nothing but a wide expanse of uninhabited land that stretched all the way to the horizon. He'd had to go all the way to West Texas, but he'd finally found what he was looking for in the Davis Mountains.

There, the air was clean and dry, the population minimal. His neighbors were hard-working ranchers who minded their own business and didn't have time to come calling, which was just fine with him. He didn't want to be rude, but he didn't want to be bothered, either. Not here. And he wasn't. With his cabin located at the end of a private road halfway up the side of a mountain, his only visitors were mule deer and skunks and an occasional mountain lion.

He'd brought Annie there for the first time on their honeymoon, and now, as they drove up the drive to the cabin, memories came sweeping back. God, it seemed like yesterday! The night had been clear, the stars brighter than anywhere else in the country, but not nearly as bright as the love shining in Annie's eyes. She'd spied a falling star and tried to get him to wish on it, but he hadn't been able to look away from her. She was everything he'd ever wanted, and that week they'd spent there—and the getaways they'd managed over the next few years after that—had been the happiest of his life.

Wondering if the simple frame structure would strike a spark in her memory, he braked to a stop next to the front porch and cut the engine. Silence, soul deep, immediately engulfed them. Watching her in the starlight, he waited for recognition to flare in her eyes, but there was nothing there but natural curiosity. She didn't remember.

Not sure if he was disappointed or relieved, he reminded himself he was going to have to be careful not to rush her into something that either one of them might not be ready for. He shouldn't have needed the reminder—he hadn't forgotten that she could be carrying someone else's baby—but lately, he found it harder and harder to believe that she'd walked into another man's arms and bed so quickly after leaving him. For the sake of his own bruised heart, he needed to keep his distance until he knew if he could live with that or not if she had, but with every passing day, that became more and more difficult. He wanted her close, skin to skin, without the past between them. He dreamed of her, ached for her, longed for what they had once had, even though he knew what they'd once had could be gone forever.

Another man might have hated her for that, for the doubts that he was now forced to live with because of her, for the limbo that there was no way out of until she got her memory back, but he couldn't. He still loved her. He'd suspected it the first time she'd had morning sickness, and he'd known it for sure when she'd opened that damn florist's box and seen that cedar branch. The terror in her eyes was something he never hoped to see again, and given the chance, he would have gladly turned back the clock and been the one in the parking garage that Thursday night when she stumbled across a murder and changed their lives forever.

He was a one-woman man—he knew that now and accepted it. And she'd been his woman from the first time he laid eyes on her. They didn't, however, live in a fairy tale, and he had some serious thinking to do. If the baby turned out not to be his, could he raise another man's child without seeing Annie's betrayal every time he looked at it? Because it was a part of her, he wouldn't be able to stop himself from loving it if he tried. But a dagger of jealousy twisted in his heart at the thought of her loving another man. Until he could get past that, he had no business touching her.

It was, he thought, clenching his jaw, going to be a long couple of weeks.

"Well, this is it," he said, shattering the silence. "Does anything look familiar?"

Annie stared at the rustic cabin that sat like a hulking shadow in the darkness and shook her head. She was sure that it was probably charming by the light of day, but right now, it was hard to tell. During the long drive from San Antonio, Joe had told her that the place had all the comforts of home, including hot and cold running water and electricity, not to mention a view that was out of this world. And gazing at the stars that twinkled overhead like a brilliant, glittering canopy, she had to admit that the promised view, at least, was spectacular. But the cabin looked awfully small.

"No," she said regretfully, "but things might look different in the morning. Did we spend a lot of time here?"

"As much as we could when we were first married. Not so much over the last couple of years." Pulling the keys from the ignition, he pushed open his door. "Why don't you stay here while I open up and check for uninvited visitors?"

Surprised, she lifted an eyebrow at him. "I beg your pardon?"

"Snakes," he said succinctly. "They have a way of finding a way inside since the place sits empty for so long."

"Oh, God," she whispered faintly. "And this is where you come to *relax?*"

"Yeah," he laughed. "I guess I'm a glutton for punishment. Hold on, and I'll be right back."

He was out of the car and striding up the porch steps before she could warn him to be careful, and a split second later, a light flared on as he unlocked the cabin door and stepped inside. He disappeared from view. Suddenly cold, she shivered. She didn't have to search her nonexistent memory to know that she didn't like snakes.

He was back almost immediately and pulling open her door for her. "All clear," he announced. "Let's get this stuff inside and then we'll see about supper. You're probably starving."

She'd passed that state about fifty miles back, but she hadn't wanted to suggest that they stop because it was getting so late and he'd seemed in a hurry to reach the cabin. Now, at the mere mention of food, her stomach growled with embarrassing enthusiasm. Laughing, she admitted, "I guess it wouldn't do any good to deny it, would it? What can I carry?"

Chuckling, he handed her a grocery bag of fruit. "Maybe you'd better start with something edible. I know how you are when you haven't eaten in a while. Even the furniture starts to look good."

"I'm not that bad." She gave him a withering look, only to ruin the effect by reaching into the bag for an apple.

Grinning, he said, "I rest my case. Get the screen door, will you?"

He hefted a large ice chest filled with perishable items and started up the porch steps. Hurrying around him, Annie quickly pulled open the screen door for him to pass through, then followed him inside. Two steps past the threshold, she stopped abruptly and swallowed, her heart knocking against her ribs as she got her first good look at where they would be spending the next few weeks, possibly the next few months.

Except for the small partitioned area that jutted out of a corner, which she presumed was a bathroom, the cabin consisted of one room. One very *small* room when compared to the apartment they'd left behind in San Antonio. There were no other walls or partitions, nothing but pockets of living space and no privacy whatsoever. The kitchen, with its apartment-size stove, refrigerator, and tiny table took up one corner, while an overstuffed couch sat before a corner fireplace in what served as the living room. It was the last remaining corner, however, that drew her gaze and made her heart stumble in her chest.

A bed. There was one bed, a double, that looked like it had come right out of a bordello in an old western movie. Made of iron and painted white, the headboard and footboard were shaped like hearts and delicately decorated with iron roses. Annie took one look at it and knew somehow that this was where she and Joe had spent their honeymoon.

Her knees weak and her pulse wild, she stared at it, transfixed, and wondered why he'd brought her there. Was this his way of telling her that he didn't care whose baby she was carrying—he was ready to resume their marriage? Or was he so completely over her that it truly didn't bother him to bring her there because the place had no meaning for him?

No! What about the kisses they'd shared? she wanted to cry, and knew she was in trouble. She had no right to ask him to explain himself, no right to expect him to feel anything for her but possibly lust and a whole lot of distrust. She was the one who had left him. She was the one who'd returned pregnant, with no idea of who the father of her baby was. And she was the one who'd buried a dead man, a man she still wasn't convinced she hadn't killed. Considering all that, she was lucky that he even spoke to her, let alone went out of his way to see to her welfare.

But, God, she hated this! She hated not knowing who she was, what she was capable of. Thinking that she might have killed a man was bad enough, but not being able to recall the circumstances of her baby's conception tore her up. What kind of woman was she? Why couldn't she remember? She wanted to believe that it was because her mind had chosen to forget everything rather than remember whatever violence she'd faced in the Transit Tower parking garage. But what if that was just wishful thinking on her part? What if it was the truth about herself and the choices she'd made in her life that she really couldn't face?

"Well, that's it," Joe said as he unloaded the contents of the ice chest into the refrigerator. "I'll get the luggage after we eat. Since it's so late, how about soup and sandwiches for supper?"

Thankful for the distraction, Annie pushed back her troubled thoughts and forced a smile. "That sounds great. I'll set the table."

* * *

By nine-thirty, they had finished eating, done the dishes, and brought in their luggage from the car. There was no television, no paperwork to catch up on, nothing to do but go to bed. And though they'd both managed to look anywhere but at the sleeping alcove while they were eating, there was no avoiding it now.

Annie told herself there was nothing to be concerned about. It was a bed just like any other bed—nothing was going to happen in it that she didn't want to. And it wasn't as if this was the first time they'd slept together. Whenever she'd cried out in the night, he'd been there to hold her until she fell back asleep, and most mornings, he was still there when she woke up. Another man might have already pushed for his husbandly rights by now, but if she'd learned anything about Joe in the last week, it was that he would never insist on any kind of intimacy between them that she wasn't ready for. Even if they shared a bed, he wouldn't lay a finger on her if she didn't want him to.

She knew that, accepted that, was thankful that he was such a patient, caring man. So why was her heart pounding like a hammer? They'd chatted like old friends all through supper, but suddenly the cabin was filled with a silence that seemed to throb with expectation. Her gaze clashed with his, then quickly skittered away. Swallowing, she snatched up her overnight bag and hugged it to her breast like a shield. She knew she was acting like a nervous virgin, but she couldn't seem to help herself.

"I'll take the bathroom first, if you don't mind," she said huskily, and swept past him with a speed that was embarrassingly close to a run.

"Smooth, Annie," she muttered under her breath as she shut the bathroom door and leaned back against it. "Real smooth. What do you think you accomplished by running in here? Unless you plan on sleeping in the tub, you're going to have to face him eventually. Why don't you just do it now and get it over with?"

She should have, but she couldn't. So she hastily pulled off her clothes and eased down into a tub of warm water. Twenty minutes later, her skin pink and clean, her hair a riot of dark curls, she pulled on her flannel gown and robe and knee socks. The coward in her hoped that Joe had already gone to bed, but the chances of that were slim. Left with no choice but to deal with the situation, she drew in a fortifying breath and pulled open the bathroom door.

The first thing she saw was the bed. Joe had pulled back the patchwork quilt that covered it and turned on the bedside lamp, leaving the rest of the cabin bathed in shadows. The pillows were plumped, and even from halfway across the room, she could see that the sheets were fresh and clean. In spite of the ruggedness of its surroundings, with nothing more than the addition of a rose on the pillow and a bottle of champagne on the nightstand, it could have been as elegant as the honeymoon suite at the Hilton.

All it needed to be complete was the bridegroom.

Automatically, her eyes went looking for him. She found him on the couch. He sat slouched low on his spine, his legs stretched out before him and crossed at the ankles, watching her with dark, enigmatic eyes. A pillow and a neatly folded blanket sat on the cushions next to him.

When her eyes widened at the sight of the bedding, he pushed to his feet and started toward her like a lion on the prowl. Caught in the trap of his heated gaze, she stood rooted to the spot, horribly afraid that the granny gown she'd been so sure only moments before was hardly appealing was now far too revealing.

She expected him to walk past her to the bathroom, but he stopped right in front of her instead, so close that when she drew in a sharp breath, the tips of her breasts brushed his chest. "I'm going to sleep on the couch," he said in a low growl that stroked over her like a caress. "Because if I don't, I won't be able to keep my hands to myself. Unless, of course, you don't want to sleep alone."

He arched an eyebrow at her, time rolling to a stop while he waited for her answer. When she mutely shook her head, a wry smile twisted his mouth. "I had a feeling you'd say that. And you're probably right. If you weren't, I just might try to change your mind. But not tonight. You look tired, sweetheart. Go to bed. It's been a long day."

Leaning down, he pressed a fleeting kiss to her mouth, then stepped around her into the bathroom and quietly shut the door behind him. Dazed, her blood humming in her veins, it was a full two minutes before Annie moved to the bed.

When she slipped between the sheets and snapped off the bedside light, she was sure she'd never be able to sleep. But she'd been up before dawn, and the sound of the shower running in the bathroom was a steady, hypnotic lull. Settling against the pillows, she closed her eyes and sighed. Long before Joe stepped out of the bathroom, she was asleep.

Lost in her dreams, she never saw him move to the side of the bed and stand there in the dark, staring down at her. Her breathing slow and easy in sleep, she never saw his expression soften, never saw him lift his hand to her hair and caress a wayward curl. If she'd opened her eyes, just for a second, she would have seen him hesitate, would have seen the pain and regret that registered in every line of his body. But she didn't, and when he turned away, she was none the wiser.

It was the steady thud of an ax hitting wood that woke her late the next morning. Stirring, she frowned, then jolted awake, startled, when something hit the side of the cabin, hard. Blinking the sleep from her eyes, she was still trying to figure out what woke her when another loud thunk reverberated through the cabin. Frowning, she pushed her tangled hair from her eyes. "What the devil's going on?"

She spoke to an empty cabin. In a single, all-encompassing glance, she saw that the couch where Joe had slept was just as it had been when she'd gone to bed last night. The blanket and sheets were neatly folded and piled in a stack, with the pillow on top. She might have thought he hadn't slept there at all if she hadn't gotten up during the night to go to the bathroom a zillion times. Every time she'd passed the couch, he'd been lying in exactly the same position, dead to the world.

So where was he? Throwing back the antique quilt that had kept her as warm as toast all night in the cool mountain air, she rushed over to the window and pulled back the curtain to find Joe chopping firewood right by the cabin's back porch. He'd already worked up a sweat and pulled off his shirt, and in the morning light, his skin gleamed like bronze as he brought the well-sharpened ax down with gratifying force on the wood. Without breaking rhythm, he lifted the ax again and swung with all his might.

The wood split without so much as a groan, but Annie couldn't take her eyes from Joe. Lord, the man was put together well! He wasn't one of those muscle-bound jocks who liked to work out and lift weights, but he managed to keep fit nevertheless. He had a lean, rangy body, with strength evident in every clean line of his broad shoulders and slim hips. With no effort whatsoever, he split the length of wood into kindling, then tossed the pieces into a pile at one end of the porch. One of them missed and hit the wall of the cabin instead, causing a thump like the one that woke her.

Leaning against the window frame, Annie felt something

warm spill into her stomach. She could have stood there for hours, but then he turned unexpectedly toward the window where she stood, and her heart jumped in her throat. Hastily stepping back out of sight, she grinned at her own foolishness. He was her husband; they'd been married for over five years—she should be able to look at him without self-consciousness, she chided herself.

But she had no memory of the past, only of the last week and a half. She knew she could trust him with her life, but her heart was another matter. He made her weak at the knees with a touch, breathless with a fleeting kiss. She didn't know what had driven her to leave him, but there was no doubt that there was still something between them. Something strong and exhilarating and scary in the kind of way that had her constantly fighting the need to smile.

They both knew that it was just a matter of time before they did something about it. But not yet, she thought as she grabbed jeans and a blouse from her suitcase and stepped into the bathroom. She wanted time. Time to get to know him better. Time to remember not what had driven them apart two months ago, but what had brought them together five years ago. Because she had a feeling that when she did remember why she'd left him, she was going to need the memory of her love for him to hold on to and ease the hurt she wasn't ready to remember.

Lost in her thoughts, she washed her face and brushed her teeth, then automatically tugged on her clothes, hardly paying any attention to what she was doing. Until she tried to snap her jeans and couldn't. Surprised, she adjusted the fit and tried again, with the same results. Frowning, she glanced down to see what the problem was and found her stomach in the way.

Only then did it hit her. The baby. She was really starting to show and her jeans no longer fit.

Stunned, she felt a silly grin curl around her mouth and almost laughed out loud. Every time she'd had to deal with morning sickness, she was reminded of the changes taking place in her body, but up until then, she'd only associated her pregnancy with discomforts she had no control over. Nausea, backaches, tiredness that seemed to zap all her energy. But now she only had to look at her rounded stomach to see the baby safely cradled inside her.

A baby, she thought, smiling tenderly. She really was going to have a baby. A sweet tide of love flooded her, a rush of warmth that melted her bones and brought the sting of tears to her eyes. Turning, she pulled open the bathroom door. She had to tell Joe!

He was in the process of straightening the woodpile on the porch when Annie rushed outside with a funny look on her face and tears streaming down her cheeks. Her hair was wild, the smile that flirted with her mouth tremulous. Stopping short at the sight of him, she hesitated, a wealth of emotions he couldn't begin to identify flickering in her eyes.

Straightening, he frowned. "You okay? What's going on?"

She laughed, a shaky sound that he'd never heard from her before. "Nothing. I'm fine. I was just getting dressed..."

When she stopped and pressed a hand to the smile that kept turning up the corners of her mouth, he arched a brow. "And?"

"And I can't snap my jeans," she admitted, grinning.

Joe's gaze automatically dropped to her belly, which was concealed by the loose-fitting gingham blouse she wore. From her happy expression, he was obviously missing something, but he couldn't for the life of him say what it was. "So?"

"So they don't fit," she laughed. "Look."

She held up her blouse, revealing her slim hips and barely zipped, unsnapped jeans. His gaze drawn like a magnet, Joe could no more have dragged his eyes away than he could have chopped wood with an ice pick. He told himself there was nothing the least bit seductive about the way she lifted her shirt. In fact, she was so damn pleased with her condition that it obviously hadn't occurred to her that he might be affected by her pose one way or the other.

But he was. God, was he! He took one look and felt like all the air had been sucked from his lungs.

Her jeans didn't gap open much, but through the narrow V, Joe could see pink panties trimmed in lace and the soft white skin of her rounding belly. Her still small, but blatantly pregnant, belly. Fascinated, he stared at her long and hard, his fingers itching to touch her, to skim across her bare skin and chart the changes occurring almost before his eyes in her body.

That was his baby she could be carrying, his child. He'd always known one day that they would have children, but he'd never given much thought to what pregnancy would do to Annie. Oh, he'd known she'd gain a hefty amount of weight and, like all expectant mothers, she'd walk around with her stomach leading the way. What he hadn't expected was the beautiful glow of her skin or the way she seemed to grow softer, more vulnerable, with every passing day.

And then there were the changes in himself. She'd always been a woman who could take care of herself, and he'd loved that about her. But now, seeing the remains of her tears clinging to her cheeks, protectiveness raged like a storm inside him. All he could think of was wrapping her close in his arms so that nothing and no one could ever hurt her or the baby again. She was his. *They* were his....

Even as he tried to convince himself, his mind taunted

him with images of Annie in the arms of another man. No! he wanted to roar. She wouldn't have done that to him, to *them.* She couldn't have.

But then again, he'd never thought she'd leave him, either.

His blood running cold at the thought, he jerked his eyes back up to hers. "We'll have to get you some maternity clothes the next time we go into town," he said woodenly. "Until then, just leave your jeans unsnapped. There's no one out here to see anything."

That wasn't the response she'd expected—he knew that the minute the words left his mouth. The light died in her eyes; her happy smile dropped from her mouth. Not a word of reproach passed her lips, but guilt still stabbed him in the heart. He felt like the lowest form of heel, but he couldn't give her the enthusiasm she seemed to need from him. Not yet. Turning away before he said something he would regret, he picked up the ax and returned to the woodpile.

Letting him go, Annie stared after him, more encouraged than her common sense told her she had any right to be. Another woman might have been hurt by what appeared to be his total lack of interest in her pregnancy, but he hadn't fooled her for a second. He wasn't a cold or indifferent man, and she'd seen the flash of heated emotion that had flared in his eyes when she'd lifted her shirt and shown him her belly. He'd wanted to touch her as badly as she'd needed him to, and for a moment there, she'd half expected him to sweep her up into his arms and carry her to bed. When he hadn't, she'd known to the second when he'd remembered the baby might not be his.

Oh, he'd hidden it well, but she hadn't missed the clenching of his jaw or the green-eyed monster that had glared at her through his eyes when he thought that she might have betrayed him. He was jealous, and she was thrilled. Because a man who didn't care wouldn't have blinked an eye at the thought of her leaving him for another man.

After sitting empty for over a year, the cabin and yard were in desperate need of maintenance. The gutters were in terrible shape, sunlight peeked through some of the roof tiles on the porch, and the inside of the structure needed a thorough scrubbing and dusting. So, after breakfast, Joe attacked the porch roof and Annie went to work inside.

It was hot, dirty work. Annie couldn't remember the last time she'd done any physical work around a house, and she thoroughly enjoyed herself in spite of the fact that there was no dishwasher or vacuum cleaner or even a radio to break the silence while she worked. Humming to herself, she washed not only the breakfast dishes by hand, but every dish and skillet in the cabinets.

While they were draining, she pulled the dusty curtains from the windows and tossed them in the washing machine, then made up a solution of water and vinegar to clean the windows. Outside, she could hear Joe hammering on the roof, then his muttered curse when he accidentally hit a finger. When the curtains finished washing and she stepped outside to hang them on the clothesline strung between two cedar posts just yards from the back porch, she couldn't stop her eyes from lifting to the roof. There in the bright sun, Joe was down on his knees and bent over the leaky tiles of the roof, frowning with concentration as he hammered a crooked cedar tile back into place.

It was a sight that was to become very familiar to her over the course of the day. When he finished the roof, he turned his attention to the gutters, then the porch railing. He never seemed to run out of things to do, and every time Annie stepped outside, she found herself looking for him. A couple of times, he caught her watching, and the looks that passed between them all but sizzled. Then he turned his attention back to his work, and her breathing slowly returned to normal. Until she stepped outside again. And she found a lot of reasons to step outside.

Just a week ago, she hadn't wanted him to come anywhere near her, but there was something about him that she couldn't resist. And their situation didn't help matters any. Only Drake, Phoebe, and Sam knew where they were, and for all practical purposes, they were completely alone in the world. He couldn't make a move, a sound, without her being aware of it. And when they sat down at the table for lunch and supper, it was his dark, watchful eyes she found herself looking into, his deep, sexy voice that she silently sighed over.

But it was the nights, she was to discover, that were the worst. Her body was exhausted, but when she crawled into bed later that evening and he stretched out on the couch in the dark, sleep was a thousand miles away. Restless, she shifted, trying to get more comfortable, only to freeze as the darkness seemed to amplify every single sound. Could he hear the thunder of her heart? The way her breath hitched in her throat?

A nervous giggle bubbled in her throat at the thought and was hastily swallowed. She had to stop this! After five years of marriage, she was supposed to be well past the stage of mooning over her husband. But he made her want things she couldn't remember and yearn for a closeness that they'd lost somewhere along the way. Why? What had happened to them? How could they have let what they'd once had slip through their fingers without a fight?

She fell asleep, wondering and worrying in her dreams, knowing that if she didn't remember soon, it was going to be too late. She cared for him so much more than she should, and they could be here, alone together, for who knew how long. How was she supposed to protect her heart, when the pull he had on her grew stronger with every passing hour?

The next day, she was still asking herself the same questions, and the answers were as elusive as ever. And that was when the panic started. She was falling in love with him for the second time in her life, but the knowledge brought her little peace. They were on a collision course with heartache and quickly running out of time. There was no way to avoid the inevitable disaster unless she somehow got her memory back.

So while he spent the day recaulking the cabin windows and trimming the trees that brushed against the eaves, she tried her damnedest to remember not only the day she'd first fallen in love with him, but the exact moment she'd turned her back on him and walked away. In doing so, she knew she might get more than she bargained for. Not only could she turn out to be a woman she didn't like at all, but by trying to force one memory, she could be opening herself up to a whole flood of bad ones. Either way, she was probably going to get hurt, but at least she'd have some answers.

All she got for her efforts, however, was a low-grade headache that stayed with her all day. By the time they'd finished supper and retired to opposite ends of the couch to relax in front of the fire before going to bed, it had progressed to a constant pain that pounded at her temples. Unable to concentrate on one of the paperback novels they'd brought along to pass the time, she let it fall to her lap and squeezed her eyes shut. It didn't help.

"Problems?"

Her eyes still closed against the light that only seemed to intensify the pain, she nodded and rubbed tiredly at her temples. "It's just a stupid headache."

"Have you taken anything?"

"No. The baby..."

She didn't have to say anything more—he knew she would never chance doing anything that might hurt the baby. Silence stretched between them, but she couldn't bring herself to find some tidbit of conversation to break it. Then she heard him move, and before she could begin to guess his intentions, he slid across the couch, not stopping until he was sitting right next to her, his thigh firm against hers. Startled, she tensed and her eyes flew open. "What—"

"Shhh," he murmured, resting his hands on her shoulders. "Don't go getting all skittish on me. I'm just trying to make you feel better."

"Said the spider to the fly," she drawled. Drawing back slightly, she eyed him warily. "What *are* you doing?"

"Just giving you a massage," he retorted, grinning. "Why? What'd you think I was doing?"

Her mind drifted to hot, slow-moving images of the two of them touching, kissing, loving. And an ache that had nothing to do with the one in her head settled low in her abdomen.

"Annie? Are you in there? Where'd you go?"

She blinked and looked up to find him staring into her eyes, trying to follow her into her thoughts. Mortified, she felt a hot blush steal into her cheeks, and wanted to die right there on the spot. "Sorry," she said in a rough voice she hardly recognized as her own. "I guess my mind just wandered for a second. Maybe I should go to bed."

"Not yet. Turn around and let me give you a back rub. It'll make you feel better."

She shouldn't have, but when his hands urged her to scoot around and present her back to him, she couldn't summon the will to resist. Without a word of protest, she settled sideways on the couch with him right behind her. Then his hands worked their way down her spine and back up to her neck, massaging the tension out of her tight muscles, and she melted like a candle in the sun. By the time his fingers slid into her hair and found the throbbing in her temples, she was boneless. Groaning, her eyes still closed and a soft smile curving her mouth, she leaned back into his touch.

She was falling asleep in his hands and seemed to have no idea what she was doing to him. *Don't!* he wanted to warn her. *Don't trust me that much. I want you too badly.*

But he couldn't say the words any more than he could push her from him. Unable to resist temptation, he leaned down and kissed the side of her neck. Under his mouth, her skin was soft and warm and far too tempting. His teeth hurt, he wanted her so badly. And there wasn't a damn thing he could do about it. Not when her head was hurting and she was so tired she could barely string two words together.

"That's it, sweetheart," he whispered. "Just relax. You were probably out in the sun too much today. Tomorrow I'm going to make sure you stay inside with your feet up."

"No," she muttered, leaning more heavily against him. "It wasn't that. I was trying to remember."

His fingers stilled at her temples. "Grant said you were supposed to just take it easy and let everything come back at its own pace."

"I tried that. It isn't working."

"What about your dream?" he reminded her. "You described that dead banker to a T, so he must have had something to do with whatever happened in the garage. Give yourself time. The rest will come when you're ready to deal with it."

"But what if it doesn't?" Voicing her worst fear, she turned to face him, her eyes troubled and dark with worry. "What if I never remember anything?"

His gaze locked with hers, Joe didn't pretend to misunderstand. She wanted to know about them. What was going to happen to them if she couldn't tell him where she'd been for the last two months? Who she'd been seeing? Who she might have been sleeping with when she still had a husband at home? Did they even have a prayer of a chance with so many unanswered questions between them?

She needed reassurance—he could see it in her eyes, hear it in her voice—but he couldn't give it to her. "I don't know," he said, letting her go. "I guess we'll have to wait and cross that bridge when we come to it, won't we?"

Chapter 8

By unspoken agreement, they strictly avoided discussing the future after that. And all physical contact, including massages. Knowing it was for the best didn't make it easy on either one of them, but somehow they managed. The work that still needed to be done around the cabin was a welcome distraction, but it was a small place, and by the end of the third day, they had it in tip-top shape. Then the real torture began.

When Annie left him back in the summer, Joe thought he knew what hell was all about, but as the days dragged, he realized he was only just beginning to know the meaning of the word. They were literally living in each other's pocket and bumping into each other every time they turned around. There was no privacy, no space, no *room* to get away from each other. When she took a bath every night, he found himself listening for the sound of the running water and waiting for the subtle, enticing scent of her shampoo to drift under the bathroom door to tease his senses. By the time she finished and left the bathroom in a cloud of fragrant steam, he was hard and aroused and frustrated. Every damn night.

Considering that, it was little wonder that he dreaded the setting of the sun. The nights were impossibly long, and when he did manage to fall asleep, which was only for short stretches at a time, Annie was waiting for him in his dreams.

He wasn't, he discovered, a man who handled celibacy well. He was short-tempered and edgy, with too much time on his hands. And the only distraction was Annie herself. Through half-closed eyes, he watched her every move and didn't care that she knew it. If Sam didn't call soon about a break in the case, they were going to have to go into Marathon or El Paso and see about getting Annie some maternity clothes, but for now, she still wore her jeans unsnapped. Just knowing her pants were only partially zipped under the long tail of her shirt drove him quietly out of his mind.

Once he might have found comfort in the fact that she was just as miserable as he was, but that only made him want her more. They were both waiting, fighting the inevitable, and the tension in the cabin was as sharp as shattered glass. By the morning of the fifth day, Joe couldn't take it anymore. He was going to blow the lid right off the place if he didn't do something about the hot energy crawling under his skin.

"Let's go for a walk," he said curtly as soon as they finished breakfast. "The doctor said you needed exercise, and we haven't been out of sight of the cabin since we got here."

"I'll pack some sandwiches," she said eagerly, as anxious as he to get out. "We can have a picnic."

At that point, Joe would have agreed to a full-scale barbecue cooked over an open campfire if it would get them out of the forced intimacy of the cabin. "Take whatever you want. I've got a backpack in the closet. I'll get it while you're getting the food together."

They were ready in five minutes and out the door in five and a half. It was a cool morning, but crystal clear, with the scent of pine heavy in the air. Wearing lightweight jackets they could later tie around their waists as the temperature rose, they took a path that meandered north of the cabin, walking single file at a leisurely rate as they struck off through the trees.

The forest was hushed and cool and bathed in shadows, the atmosphere almost churchlike, and neither felt the need to break the companionable silence. So, for long stretches at a time, the only sound was the whisper of the wind through the trees and the crunch of pine needles under their feet as they hiked farther and farther from the cabin. For the first time in days, they were both at peace.

They might not have spoken for hours, but, just as they stopped for a break, Annie spied a young deer standing fifty yards away in a small clearing off to their right. Still as a statue, it stood poised for flight and watched them with dark, liquid eyes. Instinctively, she reached for Joe's hand.

"Look," she whispered, and nodded toward the clearing.

His fingers closing around hers, he stood with his shoulder brushing hers, hardly daring to breathe. Then, just when it seemed as if time itself had stopped, the deer turned and bounded off into the trees, its white tail waving like a flag before it disappeared in the shadows.

That should have broken the hushed silence and the spell that had fallen over them. But when Joe looked down at Annie and found her looking up at him with shiny eyes, the intimacy that had pulled them together in the cabin was nothing compared to what they'd just shared there in the forest. He had to order himself to let her go, but even then, his fingers tightened around hers before he could bring himself to release her and step back.

"That was a surprise," he said in a voice as rough as a gravel road. "You don't see too many deer around here this time of year. Hunting season's right around the corner, so they're usually pretty skittish once the weather starts to cool off."

Her heart thumping in her chest, Annie could understand how the deer felt. Nothing had happened, but something in his gaze made her feel as if she'd just had a brush with a kind of danger that had nothing to do with fear. She wanted to run for the hills...and turn into his arms. Torn, she did neither, but followed his lead and acted instead as if nothing had happened. With her pulse skipping and her stomach jumping crazily, it wasn't easy.

"I could never shoot anything so beautiful," she said huskily, only to realize she didn't know if she'd ever done such a thing or not. "At least, I don't think I could. I'm not a hunter, am I?"

His lips twitched but didn't quite curl into a smile. "You? Hardly. Grant tried to give us some venison once, and you accused him of shooting Bambi."

She laughed, relieved. "Serves him right. If we need meat, that's what the grocery stores are for."

This time, he grinned, his brown eyes crinkling with amusement. "That's what you told him. He never made the mistake of doing that again." Still grinning, he said, "C'mon. Let's see if we can find Bambi's mother."

They hiked for the rest of the morning, then had lunch in a meadow that offered a breathtaking view. It was a quiet, tranquil spot, and though they were both more talkative than they had been all morning, Annie knew Joe wasn't any more relaxed than she was. In spite of the leisurely lunch they'd eaten, her heart rate hadn't slowed one iota from the moment she'd taken his hand when they'd spied the deer. And she doubted that his had, either. Though he was much better at concealing his emotions than she was, there was a tension in his jaw and a heat in his eyes that stirred a restlessness in her that made it nearly impossible for her to sit still.

So as soon as the remains of their lunch were repacked in the backpack, she jumped to her feet, eager to put some distance between the two of them before she did something stupid and reached for him again. If it happened a second time, she was afraid she might not be able to let him go. "Can we climb to the top?" she asked him as he, too, rose to his feet. "It doesn't look like it's that far."

"It's not," he replied, frowning. "But it's pretty rough."

"But the doctor said to get some exercise."

"Somehow I don't think he had mountain climbing in mind," he replied dryly. "And you're going to be sore enough tomorrow as it is. We haven't exactly been taking a walk in the park, you know. We're at least two miles from the cabin, and we've been climbing ever since we left."

"But it's such a wonderful day and I feel fine. We don't have to go all the way to the top if you don't want to. Just a little way up. Please? It'll be a downhill walk all the way home."

She wouldn't have figured herself for a finagler, but she looked up at him pleadingly and shamelessly batted her lashes and he never stood a chance. Oh, he knew she was blatantly working her wiles on him, but he laughed, and instead of teaching her a badly needed lesson about the dangers of flirting with her husband, he was willing to be amused.

"Okay," he chuckled, "but I don't want to hear a single word of complaint out of you tonight when you're as stiff as a zombie and can't even get in bed without help."

"Not a word," she promised solemnly, her blue eyes

twinkling. "I swear. Let's go check out that rock. I bet it's got a great view of the valley."

The *rock* she pointed to was actually a limestone outcropping that formed half the side of the mountain three hundred feet above them. As far as distance went, it wasn't all that far, but the path wasn't the most stable one. A fire had taken out all the trees and vegetation several years ago, and since then, the path had been washed out by storms. Steep and rugged, there was nothing to hold on to but the crumbling rock itself. One wrong step and it was a long way to the bottom.

"If it does," he retorted, "you won't be seeing it today. It's too dangerous."

"There must be another way to the top," she argued. "Look! There's a path that cuts through the trees. C'mon, let's check it out."

She started around him before he could stop her, and in the process, stepped in a hole that was hidden from view by a layer of pine needles. Her ankle twisted, and with a startled cry, she pitched awkwardly to the side. Lightning quick, Joe reached for her, his curses ringing in her ears as he caught her just before she could hit the ground.

"Dammit, Annie, what the hell are you trying to do? Hurt yourself? If you fall up here, we're a long way from a doctor!"

"I know. I'm sorry. It was my mistake. I wasn't watching where I was going."

It happened so fast, neither one of them had a chance to catch their breath or protect their hearts. One moment she was falling, and the next she was in his arms. Startled, she lifted her gaze to his, and all she could see was a need in his eyes that was as fierce as her own. Somewhere in the back of her head, the thought registered that she should move, slip free of his touch, laugh off the moment while she still could. But it was already too late for that. It had been from the moment his hands had caught her close.

"Joe..."

She couldn't manage more than that, just his name, but even she could hear the longing that turned her voice husky and deep. He stiffened, a muscle ticking along his hard jaw, and she almost cried out in protest. But then something in him seemed to snap, and with a muttered curse, his arms tightened around her. "Dammit, woman, I didn't bring you out here for this," he growled. "I swore I wasn't going to touch you again until you got your memory back. It's the only sane thing to do. We could both get hurt—"

"But I already hurt," she replied softly. Taking his hand, she pressed his fingers to her mouth. "Here. And here." Daringly, she moved his hand down to cover her wildly beating heart. "All I want you to do is kiss it and make it feel better. Just this once."

He shouldn't have. One of them had to keep a cool head, and if it wasn't going to be her, then it had to be him. But her breast was soft and warm in his palm, her heart hammering out an erotic rhythm that echoed in the throbbing of his own blood. He wanted her more than he wanted his next breath, and with a groan that came from the depth of his being, he knew he could no more resist her than a wolf could resist the call of the wild.

"Damn you, Annie," he muttered, drawing her closer, against his heart, "you don't play fair."

Covering her mouth with his, he gave in to the hunger that was knotted like a fist in his gut. His arms locked around her, his tongue dove deep, taking, wooing, seducing. Struggling to hang on to what was left of his control, he tried to give her tenderness, but he was too needy, too hard. His blood was hot in his veins, his arousal pressed against her belly, his mouth rough.

Intoxicated by the taste of her, he blindly fought at the buttons of her jacket, his fingers fumbling in his haste. He wanted, *needed,* to touch her—everywhere—to feel the softness of her skin, the delicateness of her bones under his hands, the sighs that rippled through her as he kissed his way down her body. Now. Right here on the side of the mountain.

Dizzy, delighted, Annie felt the rub of his tongue along hers, the touch of his fingers as he tugged her jacket from her and moved to help him. Reaching for the hem of the oversize sweatshirt she wore, her hands bumped into his. He cursed softly in frustration and she couldn't help but smile against his mouth. This was what she'd longed for since the last time he'd kissed her, what she'd dreamed of in the night and fantasized about during the day, this heat that jumped from his skin to hers, this fire that burned without a flame, deep inside her. Her heart quickened, and his answered. Seduced, she murmured his name and crowded closer.

Lost in the taste and feel and heat of each other, neither of them noticed that dark, angry clouds were gathering overhead and the temperature had started to drop until a cold wind danced across the exposed skin of Annie's chest and stomach as they fought to rid her of her sweatshirt.

Suddenly cold where only seconds before she'd been burning, she gasped. And only just then noticed the sky. "Oh, God! Look!"

Abruptly brought back to earth, his breathing ragged, Joe looked up and swore at the sight of the ominous clouds directly over their heads. "Damn, it looks like a norther's blowing in. We've got to get out of here!" The words came out harshly, but he couldn't help it. Not when his blood was boiling and he was so close to howling like a madman. Jerking her sweatshirt back down, he snatched up her jacket from where it had fallen to the ground and quickly helped her into it, as an icy wind picked up and started to swirl around them. Another glance at the sky had him reaching for her hand. "C'mon, honey," he shouted over the wind. "Just hang on to my hand."

The wind caught her hair, tugging it around her, blinding her. Muttering a curse, she grabbed it with her free hand and anchored it at the back of her neck. "Don't worry, you couldn't pry loose of me with a crowbar," she cried. "What's the shortest way back?"

"Straight down that path." They'd taken a circuitous route up the mountain, but now he nodded toward a rocky trail that didn't zigzag as most mountain trails did, but headed sharply down the hill in a straight line. "Just stay behind me and step everywhere I do." The words were hardly out of his mouth when it started to drizzle. Glaring at the sky, he cursed. "Damn, I should have seen this coming. C'mon. Let's go."

Anchoring her close, he plunged down the side of the mountain as fast as he dared, but they'd only gone a hundred yards when the skies just opened up and dropped an icy deluge on them. They were soaked to the skin in the time it took to gasp.

Annie's fingers caught tight in his, Joe slid on the wet ground and caught himself just seconds before he could drag them both down into the mud. "Dammit to hell! Hang on!" he yelled at her over the roar of the wind. "Once we get past these rocks, the going'll get a lot easier."

Annie didn't see anything that looked the least bit easy. In fact, the path he pulled her down looked like something out of her worst nightmare. Her heart in her throat, it took all her concentration just to nod and keep her feet. Then they reached the end of the rocks, the footing improved, and Joe picked up the pace just when she thought they couldn't possibly go any faster. Her wet hair streaming out behind her in the rain, she held on for dear life as they dodged trees and boulders in their mad rush down the mountain.

By the time they reached the cabin, the rain had the sting of sleet mixed in with it and an early darkness had fallen. Chilled to the bone, her tired muscles stiff from strain and the cold, Annie stumbled inside behind Joe and couldn't make herself go any farther. Shivering, she just stood there, hugging herself, right inside the door.

"Get your clothes off and get in the tub while I light a fire," Joe told her as he tore off his jacket and strode quickly to the fireplace. "Damn, I'm going to need more kindling. Hang on, while I get some from the porch."

Not bothering with his wet jacket, he hurried outside in his shirtsleeves and returned almost immediately with an armload of wood to find Annie standing right where he'd left her. Frowning, he stopped short. "Annie? C'mon, you need to get warm. Do you need some help getting out of your clothes?"

"N-no," she stuttered, shaking her head. "I don't think s-so. I'm just so c-cold." But as much as she needed to warm up, she couldn't make her arms unlock from around her body.

Joe waited, watching her through worried eyes, cursing himself for ever suggesting that damn walk in the first place. He should have checked the weather on the car radio—he knew how quickly fronts blew in out here—but all he'd been able to think about was getting out of the cabin and putting some space between them. If she got sick because of him—

He dismissed the thought before it could take hold and quickly turned to deposit the wood by the front door. Grabbing some towels from the bathroom, he took time only to light the gas wall heater in there before he returned to where Annie stood by the front door.

"All right, I've got the bathroom warming up. Now let's see about you."

Dropping a towel over her head, he rubbed her sodden hair briskly, then wrapped the towel turban-style around her head. Her teeth were still chattering, however, and his fingers quickly moved to the buttons of her jacket. "Okay, honey, drop your arms. That's it. No wonder you're freezing. This damn jacket's nearly frozen solid."

Without bothering to take his eyes from her, he threw the offending garment in the direction of the kitchen sink. "How's that? Think you can make it into the bathroom now and handle the rest while I start a bath for you? You really need to get in a warm tub and soak for a while."

"I may s-stay in there all n-night. Just give m-me a push in the right direction to get m-my legs going."

He did more than that. He swept her up in his arms, carried her into the now toasty bathroom, and set her on a stool next to the old-fashioned claw-foot tub so he could remove her shoes for her. Once he was sure she could manage her sweatshirt, he ran the water in the tub for her, adjusting it so that it wouldn't burn her chilled skin.

"Okay, it's all yours," he said finally. "Don't come out until you're good and warm."

"But you need to get out of your wet clothes, too," she protested.

"I'll change by the fire," he assured her, heading for the door. "Holler if you need anything."

He left her to her bath, shutting the door behind him as he stepped out into the main living area of the cabin. It was totally dark now and colder than the devil. Stripping off his shirt, he retrieved the firewood from where he'd left it by the front door and set about warming the place up.

* * *

After the fiery kisses they'd exchanged on the side of the mountain, the evening didn't end anywhere near the way Annie had thought it would. In spite of the chill that permeated her every pore, the desire Joe had stirred in her lingered in her system long after they returned to the cabin, rumbling like a thunderstorm that had moved out to sea and was still making its presence known. But for the first time, her mind was willing, but her body wasn't.

As Joe had predicted, their little hike, not to mention their dash through the rain, quickly caught up with her, and by the time she dragged herself out of the tub, she was a whipped puppy. Stiff and sore in spite of her long soak in the tub, she didn't have the energy to swat a fly, let alone think about making love to her husband.

Miserable, she tried to hide it and swore she didn't so much as wince when she joined Joe in front of the roaring fire he'd built in the fireplace. But he had eyes like an eagle and merely gave her an *I told you so* look that had her lifting her chin and claiming, "I'm fine."

"Sure you are," he snorted when she eased down onto the couch in slow motion. "I hate to tell you this, sweetheart, but if it came to a race between you and a snail, I'm not sure who'd win."

"That goes to show how much you know," she sniffed. "I could run a marathon if I wanted to."

"And maybe finish by the next millennium," he teased. Walking over to the stove, he dished her up a bowl of stew from the pot he had warming on the stove. "Here. It's just canned, but it should warm you up some. Tomorrow I'll make us some chili."

Dressed in dry jeans and a red cable-knit sweater he'd changed into while she was bathing, he took the seat next to her on the couch and made sure she ate every bite. As soon as she was finished, he scooped her up in his arms. "Okay, beddy-bye time for you."

"Joe! I can walk."

Flashing a grin at her, he strode over to the bed. "No kidding? Is that what you call it? It looked to me like you were just shuffling along." He already had the covers pulled back, and an instant later, he plopped her down right in the middle of the mattress.

Her heart thumping crazily, she expected him to join her, but he only pulled the comforter up to her neck and started tucking her in tight. Disappointed, she reached for his hand to stop him. "Aren't you—"

"No," he said quietly. A crooked grin tilting one corner of his mouth, he leaned down and kissed her on the cheek. "When I have you moaning in my arms, honey, I want it to be from pleasure, not pain. So go to sleep," he said gruffly. "You'll feel better tomorrow."

She didn't want to, but the down comforter and patchwork quilt he'd piled on the bed for her trapped in the heat, warming her all the way to her toes. By the time he doused the lights and stretched out on the couch with the one remaining cover he'd saved for himself, she was softly snoring.

The sleet stopped sometime before midnight, but the wind howled for hours, rattling the screens on the windows and causing the old cabin to moan and groan. Gradually, the logs in the fireplace burned down, slowly turning to embers that offered only marginal warmth against the cold that crept through every available crack and crevice.

Still asleep, Annie frowned and tugged the covers higher over her shoulders, unconsciously shifting to avoid the chill air that nipped at the back of her neck. The cold, however, followed her under the blankets that surrounded her like a cocoon, brushing at her exposed skin, refusing to be ignored as it cooled the sheets and persistently pulled her toward wakefulness.

Moaning softly, she pressed her face into her pillow, but then a log fell in the fireplace, sending a shower of sparks shooting up into the chimney. Startled, she came awake just in time to hear Joe damning the cold. "Joe? What's wrong?"

"Nothing," he said in a voice raspy with sleep. "The fire just died down and I'm putting more wood on it. Go back to sleep. It'll warm up in here in a few minutes."

He sounded more than a little put out. Frowning, Annie pulled the covers down just far enough to clear her nose and found him at the hearth, adding logs to the fire. Silhouetted by the flames, he was wearing the same jeans and sweater he'd changed into after their day in the great outdoors. As she watched, he tossed in another log, and in the flare of sparks that followed, she could see that his dark hair was tousled and his jaw was rough with the shadow of his beard. And he was shivering with cold in spite of the fact that he was standing so close to the fire.

Alarmed, she bolted up. "Why are you shivering? Did you catch a chill in the rain? Here, let me do that while you get under the covers. You look like you're freezing."

She started to throw off her own covers, but he stopped her with a hard look. "If you know what's good for you, you'll stay right there. I'll be fine once the fire catches good."

"But you've only got one quilt," she argued, suddenly realizing that he'd given her most of the covers when he'd tucked her into bed. "Dammit, Joe, why didn't you say something? No wonder you're cold. Here, take a couple of these—"

"No. I'm fine. And the couch is closer to the fire than the bed is. Just go back to sleep, will you? I'm fine."

"While you stand there shivering?" she retorted indignantly. "I don't think so. You never should have taken the couch on a night like tonight anyway," she scolded. "It must be thirty degrees in here. We should be sharing our body heat—"

The words died on her tongue when he shot her a glare hot enough to melt lead. "We'll be sharing a lot more than that if I crawl into bed with you, and you're in no shape for that tonight. So just leave it."

She should have. He was right. Her sore muscles had only tightened with sleep, and she had to be crazy to even think about inviting him into her bed. But helplessly caught in the heat of his eyes, she couldn't look away. He wanted her. She could see the need in the taut lines of his face, hear it in the rasp of his voice, feel it in her own body, in the steam that seeped through her like liquid heat. Making love would only complicate things between them, but logic had nothing to do with the need running rampant through her body. From the moment she'd awakened to find herself naked in his bed, it seemed they'd been circling each other in an elaborate dance of desire that had finally brought them to this moment in time. Yes, he could hurt her. But could anything hurt worse than denying them this one chance to love each other in spite of whatever the future might bring?

The decision made, she curled her shaking fingers into the covers and lifted them invitingly. "Come to bed and let me warm you," she whispered huskily. "The fire's hot enough."

Something flashed in his eyes, something dark and dangerous that made her heart trip over itself, and without a word he came to her, his tread slow and measured, his eyes trained unblinkingly on hers. She expected him to crawl right under the covers with her, clothes and all, but he stopped two feet from the bed and stripped his sweater over his head. In the firelight, his powerful shoulders and arms were sculpted and hard.

Deliberately, his hands dropped to the fastening of his jeans. "If you get scared or want me to stop, all you have to do is tell me," he said in a voice gritty with need. "I would never do anything to hurt you."

Her eyes locked on his fingers, she nodded mutely and suddenly felt as if there wasn't enough air in the room. Not sure if her reaction was a result of anticipation or fear, she told herself there was no need to be nervous. He was her husband—they'd made love countless times in the past. Just because she didn't remember a single one of those times didn't mean she had to tremble like a schoolgirl about to see a naked man for the first time. She was a grown woman, for heaven's sake!

Over the clamor of her own frantic thoughts, the rasp of his zipper being lowered was like a growl in the silence. Unable to stop herself, she glanced down…and promptly slammed her eyes shut.

He laughed, and she wanted to die. But then she heard his jeans hit the floor, and suddenly she ran out of time. A second later, the bed dipped as he slid in beside her. "You can open your eyes now," he said dryly. "I'm all covered up."

Mortified, she peeked through her lashes to find him lying on his side facing her, his head propped in his hand and his brown eyes glinting with amusement as he studied the red-hot tide of color that washed into her cheeks. "I'm sorry," she blurted out. "You must think I'm an idiot. It doesn't seem to matter that we've been married for five years or that I'm pregnant—I can't remember doing this before. I guess I'm a little nervous."

That was an understatement of gargantuan proportions, but he thankfully didn't tease her about it. "Then I'll just have to show you there's nothing to be nervous about," he said softly, smiling down into her eyes. "Just relax and leave everything to me."

She wanted to—God, how she needed to!—but her nerves were wound tight, her heart threatening to beat its way right out of her chest. She felt that she would shatter if he touched her, she desperately needed his hands on her, but she couldn't ask for that. Not yet. Her eyes swimming, she smiled tremulously. "Would you kiss me first? I always feel better when you kiss me."

With just that one simple admission, she destroyed him. He felt something crack, something near his heart, something that he would have sworn was stone hard. He lifted a hand to her hair and was stunned to find his fingers weren't quite steady. "So do I, sweetheart," he said thickly. "So do I."

He kissed her then the way he'd longed to, the way he'd dreamed of for longer than he could remember. Like it was the first time, the last time, and he only had one shot at it. With the patience of a man who knew exactly what he wanted and how to get it, he nibbled at her lips, then slowly deepened the kiss, easing her into it, until the only thought in her head was him and the magic he brought to her.

Seduced, she moaned and clutched at him, her fingers sinking into his shoulders and telling him without words that she wanted more. With a murmur of agreement, he made the kiss hotter, while his hands began a quiet, devastating seduction of their own. He never touched bare skin, but he didn't have to. With a skill that left her breathless, he rubbed the flannel of her gown over her breasts, her hips, until her sensitive skin all but cried out for the feel of his flesh against hers.

Gasping, she arched against him, her restless legs tangling with his. "Joe, please..."

She expected him to reach for the buttons of her gown then, but it was *her* hands he lifted to the buttons. "Take the gown off for me," he whispered. His brown eyes, glinting with playful humor, met hers. "I'll even close my eyes if you want me to."

She laughed, the sound hardly more than a gurgle of amusement. "Sure you will."

He pretended to look hurt. "Would I lie to you?"

He was teasing, but her expression was never more serious as she searched the rugged lines of his face in the light from the fire. "No, I don't think you would." Without another word, she started unbuttoning her gown.

Heat flashed in his eyes, warming her inside and out as his hand covered hers, and a grin propped up one corner of his mouth. "Does that mean I have to close my eyes? We're just getting to the good stuff, you know."

She grinned and pulled him down for a lingering kiss. When he finally eased back, they were both breathless and needy. "No, you don't have to close your eyes." With an easy, incredibly seductive movement of her thumb, she slipped the buttons free.

"There are already enough secrets between us as it is—I don't want any more. And it's not as if you haven't seen me before."

She was right, but as she sat up and slowly pulled the gown over her head, a pretty blush firing her cheeks, Joe felt as if time was spiraling backwards to when they were first married, when she was shy and eager and sweet and they couldn't get enough of each other. They'd laughed a lot in bed back then and thoroughly enjoyed each other. The shyness couldn't last, of course, but she'd never lost her modesty, and somewhere along the way, he'd failed to even notice, let alone appreciate it. They'd both gotten caught up in their own careers, in life itself, and the laughter had died.

Linda Turner

He wanted it back, he thought fiercely. He wanted back that wonderful something that they'd once had and let slip away. The Sunday mornings in bed with the comics. The shared bubble baths that had ended up flooding the bathroom floor. The strawberries and champagne at midnight. It was here now, so close it was almost in his grasp. All he had to do was find a way to hang on to it. And her.

Her gown landed on the floor beside his clothes, and his breath hissed out between his teeth. It always amazed him that she'd never thought of herself as pretty when she'd stopped him in his tracks the first time he'd laid eyes on her. Beauty had nothing to do with the world's definition of classical good looks, but with what came from the soul. And Annie's every emotion had always been right there in her face. She had a smile that was filled with warmth and laughter and eyes that spoke straight from the heart. She could sass with the best of them and cry over a lost puppy. If she was hurting, you knew it, and if she loved you, you knew that, too. And when she was at her most vulnerable, as she was now, she was breathtaking.

Her skin had always been flawless, but never more so than now, with pregnancy. She didn't try to hide herself from him, but the blush that slowly stole up from her breasts told him that she was fighting the need to cover herself. Needing to touch her, to hold her, he gently enfolded her in his arms, only to clench his teeth on a moan as her breasts, fuller now than they had been just days ago, settled against the hard wall of his chest.

"Honey, if you had a clue what you did to me, you could make me do anything you wanted," he groaned. "You're killing me. You know that, don't you?"

Her bare hip nudging his, she moved against him, mischief dancing in her eyes. "Are your muscles hurting, too?"

"Witch," he laughed. "I believe you mentioned something earlier about me warming you up."

"No, *I* said I'd warm you," she corrected, grinning. "I believe I've done that."

"Oh, yeah, baby. I'm hot." And with no more warning than that, he rolled with her in his arms, dragging her under him.

At first, he thought he had gone too far, too fast. She stiffened instantly, her hands gripping at him as if to push him away, and he silently cursed himself for rushing her. But then she dragged in a shuddering breath, and he could almost feel the tension gradually drain out of her.

In the sudden stillness, her eyes lifted to his. "Okay?" he asked huskily.

She nodded, forcing her hands to release him, but only so she could loop her arms around his neck. "Make love to me," she whispered. "That's the only memory I want to have when you hold me like this."

She didn't have to ask him twice. Gathering her close, he kissed her hungrily, the patience he'd been so determined to give her quickly unraveling. "You want memories, sweetheart, I'll give you memories."

Giving in to the need that burned like a fire in his belly, he trailed his hands over her bare skin, warming her breasts, her stomach, the inside of her thighs, the very heart of her. Startled, she cried out and bucked against him, but he only recharted the same course with his mouth. She was still shuddering when he worked his way up her body to capture a pouting nipple in his mouth. Suckling her, he nearly lost it when she whimpered and clamped her hands around his head to hold him close.

"Joe!"

"I know, honey," he said raggedly, blowing softly on her sensitive nipple. "But it gets better." And to prove it, he twirled his tongue around that same damp nipple as if he was licking an ice-cream cone. Clutching at him, she nearly came up off the bed.

Fantasies. He gave her every fantasy she'd ever had and some she'd never dreamed of, teaching her things about her body that would have shocked her by the light of day. He loved every inch of her and she loved it. She sobbed and cried and wept with the beauty of it, and more often than not, she didn't know where her body ended and his began. And when she came apart in his arms for the third time before he took his own pleasure, the only memories in her head were those of Joe and his loving.

Chapter 9

Cuddled close in his arms, her head against his chest and the reassuring cadence of his heart pulsing in her ear, Annie stared dreamily out the cabin window and watched dawn slowly crack the darkness of the night. The blue norther that had raced through the previous afternoon was halfway to San Antonio by now and still blowing strong. The rain and sleet were gone, taking the clouds with them, and as she watched the morning sunshine creep across the land, the sky turned a beautiful deep blue.

The fire had long since burned itself out, and the air had a definite chill to it, but with Joe warming her like a blast furnace, she didn't need any other heat but his. Snuggling against him, she felt his arms tighten around her and smiled. He'd been awake nearly as long as she had and had been content to just hold her.

Dropping a soft kiss to his chest, she could have lain in his arms all morning, but after the night—and the loving—

they had shared, she knew they could no longer pretend that the rest of the world didn't exist.

"Joe?"

Nuzzling her neck, he buried his face in her hair. "Hmm?"

"We need to talk."

She felt him smile, then his hands began a slow exploration under the covers, warming her, making her muscles go weak one by one. "You talk and I'll listen," he growled. "Damn, you feel good in the morning, sweetheart. I've missed waking up with you like this."

The admission distracted her as nothing else could, and with a murmur of pleasure, she found his mouth and kissed him sweetly. When she would have pulled back, however, he groaned a protest and took the kiss deeper, his mouth avid and hungry on hers. Melting, she clung to him and tried to remember what was so important that she had to talk about it now.

She was breathless when he finally let her up for air, her blood warm in her veins. Her head slowly clearing, she stroked her hand down his back under the covers and said softly, "We have to talk about the baby, Joe."

He stiffened immediately. "No, we don't."

"But we can't ignore the situation. Not after last night—"

"Do you remember who the father is?"

"No, but—"

"Then there's nothing to talk about." Untangling himself from her arms, he slipped out of bed and drew the covers back over her before reaching for his clothes, his jaw rigid. "Stay in bed until I get a fire lit. I've got to get more wood."

He was gone before she could protest, shutting the front door sharply behind him as he stepped out on the porch.

When he returned a few minutes later, he didn't spare her a glance, but strode straight to the fireplace and knelt to rekindle the fire that had burned down to nothing but glowing ashes. His movements stiff and jerky, the set of his broad shoulders unyielding, he shut her out without saying a word.

Huddled against the headboard, her knees drawn up to her chest and the covers just barely reaching her bare shoulders, she shivered, but not from the cold. *Don't!* she wanted to cry. *We have to find a way to work this out. To decide what we're going to do if the baby turns out not to be yours. If last night meant anything at all—*

But no words of love had been spoken in the dark. No undying vows of everlasting devotion had been whispered in her ear. He'd promised her memories, nothing else, and he'd delivered. Until she remembered the past, they were likely to be the only ones she had.

In no time at all, he had the fire blazing again, with enough firewood neatly stacked at one end of the hearth to keep it burning for hours. There was no reason for him to go back outside, but when he turned away from the fireplace, he headed for the front door.

Surprised, Annie sat up straighter, clutching the covers to her breasts. "Where are you going?"

"For a walk," he retorted, jerking open the door. "Don't wait breakfast for me. I don't know when I'll be back."

He didn't ask her if she wanted to go with him, or give her time to make the suggestion herself. The door shut with a snap behind him and he was gone. Staring after him, her eyes stinging with unexpected tears, Annie told herself that he just needed some time to himself. And who could blame him? She wasn't the only one who suffered because of her amnesia. He didn't know if he was going to be a father or a duped husband, and there was no answer she could give him, nothing she could say that would end the turmoil he had to be feeling. All she could do was leave him alone and let him come to grips with it in his own way.

Determinedly dragging her gaze away from the door, she grabbed her clothes and escaped to the bathroom for a shower. Twenty minutes later, she still had the cabin to herself. Tempted to glance out one of the front windows to see if she could spot Joe, she did no such thing, but started breakfast instead in the hope that he would back any minute. And when he walked through the front door, she didn't want him to find her pacing the floor and worrying just because they'd had a little disagreement. She did, after all, have some pride.

Whistling with a forced cheerfulness, she laid slab bacon in an iron skillet and set it on the front burner of the stove, then pulled a carton of eggs from the refrigerator. She'd cooked the same breakfast any number of times since she'd come home—the simple chore should have been a snap.

But she was distracted, and twenty minutes later, she had a disaster on her hands. She burned the bacon and kept breaking yolks when she tried to fry eggs over easy, the way Joe liked them. By the time she finally admitted to herself that she was having a bad day, she'd gone through half a dozen eggs and had to end up scrambling them. If Joe had been there, he would have teased her unmercifully. But he was nowhere in sight—she checked.

Frustrated, not sure if she was going to laugh or cry, she set the cooked food on the table and shook her head in disgust. It was a pretty sorry sight. The toast was cold and the eggs runny, but it was all edible, nonetheless. And there was enough for an army. The only problem was there was no one there to eat it but her, and she only had to feel her stomach rumble once to know that she wasn't going to be able to force down a single bite.

Tossing down a pot holder, she grabbed an old sweater from the closet and headed for the door. She wasn't chasing after the man, she assured herself. She was just going to tell him breakfast was ready. Then she'd leave him alone.

Calling his name, she struck off into the trees, following his footsteps in the damp ground. Within seconds she'd left the cabin behind, but his tracks were still clear, and she forged ahead. Then his tracks just gave out. Frowning, she was searching the pine needles underfoot for some sign that he had been that way when suddenly the images underfoot and those in her head shifted and changed....

The trees were thick as thieves in the night, surrounding her, hiding her from view, and if she hadn't known better, she would have sworn she was miles from civilization. But there was a small shopping center a mile down the road and Interstate 10 just beyond that. Holding her breath, she listened for the sound of a motor, a car, but it was late—most people were at home in bed by now. And those that weren't wouldn't come anywhere near where she was. There was a creek at her back, and it was raging with water from the storm that had flooded the city earlier in the evening.

"Oh, God!"

Recognition hit her then, draining every drop of blood from her face as broken images flashed before her eyes and the pieces fell together like a child's puzzle. And just that easily, she could see the spot where she'd buried Robert Freeman. It was on the Driscoe Ranch, just north of the city limits, where the new Forest Park subdivision was scheduled to be built next spring.

"No," she whimpered, burying her face in her hands. But terror, as fresh as when she'd knelt beside the open grave *she* had dug and covered that poor man's face with dirt, clawed at her, ripping away chunks of the darkness that shrouded her memory, giving her no choice but to remember. "No!" She didn't want to remember that—it was just a dream! But the image persisted, as real as her hands in front of her face, and suddenly she was running, screaming for Joe.

Locked in her worst nightmare, her eyes wide and desperate, the thunder of her heart loud in her ears, she never heard him frantically call her name as he searched the woods for her. She burst through the trees into the cabin clearing, and suddenly he was there, reaching for her, and with a sob, she went into his arms. "We have to go back!" she cried, clinging to him as tears streamed down her face. "I remember where I buried the banker."

Joe took the news like a blow to the chin. No, dammit! They needed more time together before they went back to the real world. Before she remembered everything and he lost her again. Just a few more days, another week, just long enough for her to fall in love with him again, so she wouldn't just walk out the door when she remembered that he hadn't wanted her to have a baby right now.

But they'd just run out of time and there wasn't a damn thing he could do about it. She was right. They had to go back.

Swearing silently, damning the Fates, he murmured soothingly, "It's okay, honey. Everything's going to be all right. Nothing's going to hurt you."

"You have to call Sam."

"I know. I will," he promised. "Just as soon as you're calmer. You're still shaking like a leaf."

Her eyes welling with tears all over again, she buried her face against his chest. "It w-was horrible," she said thickly. "I could see m-myself b-burying him, and suddenly I—I knew where I dug the grave. It wasn't a dream, Joe. I really did it."

He winced at the horror in her voice and knew there was

nothing he could do to take away her fear. And he hated it. He hated his own helplessness, his inability to do anything when she needed him most.

Tightening his arms around her, wishing he could draw her right inside him and protect her from the world, he said, "We're not going to jump to any conclusions until we get back to town and get some answers. You hear me? Promise me, Annie. Just because we haven't thought of a logical explanation for this doesn't mean there isn't one."

"But—"

"No buts. Promise me."

He was whistling in the dark and they both knew it, but she gave him the promise he needed. "All right. I'll try not to jump to any conclusions."

"Good." Turning her toward the cabin, he urged her up on the porch. "Why don't you start packing while I call Sam? It looks like we're going home."

They drove all day, stopping only for gas, a quick bite to eat, and bathroom breaks, but an hour after the sun had set, they were still on the road. It had been a long, exhausting day and it wasn't even close to being over with. Each dreading what was to come, they stared straight ahead at the dark ribbon of the highway and hardly spoke.

Twenty minutes before they reached the outskirts of San Antonio, Joe called Sam on his cellular to give him their estimated time of arrival. Casting a quick frown of concern at Annie, who sat stiffly at his side, her hands tightly gripped in her lap, he told his friend, "We'll meet you at the entrance to the ranch."

"I'm already there," Sam told him. "The evidence boys have been there most of the day, ever since you called. We set up lights when it got dark, but we haven't found anything yet. I had to bring in the dogs, Joe," he warned him.

"I hate like hell for Annie to see them, but this old ranch is at least three thousand acres and covered with cedar. One part of it looks pretty much like another, and Annie was scared and probably confused the night she buried the body. If she can just get us close to where she thinks she dug the grave, the dogs'll find it."

"You're just doing your job, Sam," he replied grimly. "Nobody can find fault with you for that. We'll be there as quick as we can."

Pushing the end button, he set down the phone and reached over to cover Annie's hands in the dark. "I know this isn't going to be easy for you," he said quietly, "but there's nothing for you to be frightened of. I'm not leaving your side, and knowing Sam, half the police department will be there to make sure you're safe and nothing goes wrong. Whatever happens, just remember that you're the victim in this. You haven't done anything wrong, honey."

"Not unless you count burying a dead man without notifying the police." Her hand turning in his, she grasped at his fingers. "I'm trying to be objective, Joe, but I've got to tell you that right now, I'm not getting anything but bad vibes about this."

"Just hang in there, honey. It will be over soon, and you'll be fine."

She wanted desperately to believe him, but as they drew closer and closer to the turnoff that would take them to the old Driscoe Ranch, tension knotted in her stomach like a hot, hard ball. Then they were exiting the interstate, and she thought she was going to be sick. The feeling only got worse when they reached the ranch entrance, where Sam was waiting for them, as promised.

His expression more somber than she'd ever seen it, he greeted her with a nod as she and Joe stepped from the car. "I hate like hell that you have to be a part of this," he told her, "but we've searched the area that matched the description you gave us and haven't found anything."

"He's there," she said hoarsely, hunching her shoulders against a cold that had nothing to do with the chilly weather. "I know he's there. Did you check along the creek?"

He nodded, grimacing. "There are creeks all over this damn ranch, but they're seasonal and it hasn't rained in weeks. They're all dry."

Staring past him at the lights that flickered in the darkness among the trees, signaling where the police were concentrating the search, Annie could see the grave again as clearly as if she stood before it. "It's way back in the back," she said hollowly. "In the northwest corner. I'll have to show you."

No! Joe almost roared. He didn't want her to so much as set foot on the property, let alone hunt down a shallow grave, but the nightmare would never be over until she did. His face carved in harsh lines, he slipped his arm around her waist. "Why don't you drive, Sam? We'll ride with you."

There was nothing to mark where the grave was, not even a pile of fresh dirt, but Annie gave Sam directions to it without making a single mistake. When he braked to a stop facing a dry creek bed, she pointed to where his headlights cut through a thin stand of cedars. "There," she said flatly. "I buried him at the base of that big cedar."

Not convinced, Sam frowned. "Are you sure you've got the right place? There are a million cedar trees around here, and that dirt doesn't look like it's been moved in a hundred years."

"That's it," she retorted. "Trust me."

"All right, then," he sighed. "Let's check it out."

Within ten minutes, he had the lights and a portable generator there, as well as the evidence team. Then the dogs were brought in. If Sam needed proof that Annie had the right spot, he got it. The second one of the handlers led a bloodhound to the spot where Annie had indicated, the dog let out a howl that could have curdled blood.

Standing next to one of the powerful lights that stripped away the night for fifty yards in every direction, Joe's arm a comforting weight around her shoulders, Annie shivered as a second, then a third dog took up the howl, like some kind of eerie twilight bark. Fighting the need to squeeze her eyes shut like a frightened child, she stood straight as an arrow and faced what was to come.

The dogs were taken away, and for the sake of preserving evidence, the grave was exhumed by four officers with shovels rather than heavy machinery. In the tense silence that had fallen with the silencing of the dogs, the sound of the first shovel striking dirt was like the blow of a hammer. Annie flinched, then forced herself to stand still, waiting, like the others, for the first sign of the body. It seemed to take forever.

Although she'd only dreamed of the dead man once, his image was so fixed in her mind that she could have picked him out of a crowd of thousands. She'd thought she'd known what to expect, but the body the four policemen finally uncovered was discolored and cold and starting to decompose. Covered in dirt, the shock of dark hair and the banker's pinstripe suit clearly visible in the bright light, it was and wasn't the man she'd buried. The features looked different, like something out of a horror movie. If it hadn't been for the telltale scar near the mouth, she might not have recognized it at all.

"Oh, God, the scar!" Gagging, she pressed her hand to her mouth and, for the first time, turned away. Shaking, she pressed her face into Joe's shoulder. "It's him. It's him!"

Standing next to her and Joe, Sam motioned for one of the men to bag the body. "Come on," he told Joe. "Let's get her away from this circus and back to the car. It's colder than hell out here."

Murmuring to her, Joe steered her toward the car, and within seconds, the three of them were headed back to the ranch entrance. Numb with cold, Annie sat in the back seat with Joe and couldn't get warm in spite of the fact that Sam had the heater turned up to high. She could feel the warmth wrapping around her ankles, but it didn't seem to help.

His angular face harsh in the meager light that came from the lit dash, Sam parked next to Joe's car and left the motor running. His arm resting against the top of the back seat, he turned sideways in the seat to face his passengers. "I've got to ask you some questions, Annie," he said carefully, quietly. "I know you probably wish I'd do this another time, but your memories are probably never going to be fresher than they are right now."

He looked so miserable that she couldn't help leaning forward to pat his arm. "It's okay, Sam. I know you're just doing your job."

His mouth quirked into a rueful smile. "Yeah. But sometimes it's the pits. So tell me about that night and how you remembered where the body was."

"I was walking in the woods looking for Joe and it just came to me," she replied. "I could see the creek and knew there was a strip center down the road, close to Interstate 10. And suddenly, I just knew."

"You knew what?"

"That the land I was seeing was on the old Driscoe Ranch. It was like a veil lifted for just a second and everything fell into place."

"Do you remember how you got here that night? Who you were with? What kind of vehicle you transported the body in? We know someone else had to be with you, Annie. Who was it? Give me a name, a description, anything."

Closing her eyes, she tried to force the memory past the wall that was once again in place, but all she remembered was the fear. "I was scared," she said shakily. "Terrified. That's all I remember—just being scared out of my wits the whole time I was digging the grave."

"Scared of what?" Joe asked. "Of who?"

"I don't know. I don't remember anyone else being there." Suddenly realizing what she had just said, she blanched. "Oh, God, maybe I really did kill him and was afraid of getting caught—"

"Stop it!" Joe ordered harshly. "Do you hear me? We've already been through all this, and I don't want to hear another word about you killing anyone. For God's sake, we left town because someone was trying to terrorize you! He's the son of a bitch who probably did this. He's the one you should be looking for," he told Sam angrily. "He's been to our apartment, dammit! Surely someone must have seen him."

"We're working on that," Sam said. "We still don't know how he got inside the mansion to leave that delivery on your doorstep, but we think someone visiting one of the tenants was probably on the way out and let him in. With so little to go on, it hasn't been easy. But we got a break tonight, thanks to Annie. We won't know how big a one until the lab boys do their thing."

That was all Joe needed to hear. "Then you don't need us any more. I'm taking her home."

"Not without a uniform, you're not," he said, and reached for his radio. "From now on, you're under twenty-four-hour surveillance until whoever's after Annie is safely under lock and key."

Nothing could have pleased Joe more. "You won't hear

any complaint out of me. Let us know if you find out anything." Opening his door, he pulled Annie out after him. "C'mon, honey, let's go home."

News of the discovery of Robert Freeman's body hit the streets the next morning, and Annie awoke from a troubled sleep to find her face, along with that of the dead man's, splashed across the front page of the paper. Horrified, she stared down at the picture of herself and told herself this couldn't be happening, but the constant ringing of the telephone told her the nightmare was all too real. Newspaper and television reporters from as far away as Houston and Dallas called, wanting exclusive interviews. And those who didn't call were camped out on the front porch of the Lone Star Social Club, just waiting for her to stick her nose out the door so they could bombard her with questions.

Agitated, her stomach clenching with nerves, she hated being the focus of their attention. A man had died a horrible death, and she had buried him. There was nothing else she could tell them. Why couldn't they leave it at that? Didn't they know that if she remembered *anything,* she'd go to the police immediately?

Feeling as if she were trapped in a dark, bottomless prison with no way out, she forced down breakfast because the baby needed her to eat, but the French toast tasted like cardboard and tended to stick in her throat. Halfway through, she pushed it away and rose to her feet to prowl around the kitchen.

Joe didn't say a word, but she felt his eyes on her and turned to find him watching her in concern. "I'm sorry," she said, waving helplessly at her abandoned plate. "That's all I can manage."

The phone rang—again. Unable to stop herself, she flinched. After the first five or six calls, Joe had let the answering machine take over, but it was the constant ringing that grated against her nerve endings. Would it never stop?

Watching her jump like a startled cat when the phone rang for the third time in as many minutes, Joe swore viciously. She was pale as a ghost, with dark circles under her eyes, and she had to be exhausted. He'd held her in his arms all night long, and he knew better than anyone just how little she'd slept. She was on the edge, dammit, and too damn thin! She needed to eat, to rest, but as long as reporters were hounding her and she thought she was somehow responsible for Robert Freeman's death, he knew there was little chance of her doing either.

Making a snap decision, he pushed back from the table. "I don't know about you, but if I have to listen to that damn phone ring all day, I'm going to go crazy," he said tersely. "Get dressed, honey. We're getting out of here for a while."

He took her out the back way so that the reporters camped out on the front porch of the old Victorian wouldn't see them, then spirited her down to the Riverwalk. Turning the opposite way from Joe's Place, he strolled hand in hand with her like they were lovers on a holiday and made her laugh at least a half-dozen times. And although there was a plainclothes policeman only three steps behind them every step of the way, they were, for a little while at least, able to forget last night and the decomposing face of a man Annie had apparently been the last one to see alive.

Even on the Riverwalk, however, they couldn't escape the real world for too long. With Annie's picture boldly splashed across the front page of every paper in the city, it wasn't long before she was recognized. Joe caught more than one startled glance thrown their way and knew if he had seen them, Annie had, too. He felt her stiffen beside him, her steps falter, as a bald-headed man with a beer belly hanging over his belt openly stared at her with a suspicion he made no attempt to hide. For two cents, Joe would have decked him. But that would only have caused a scene, and that was the last thing Annie needed. So he just shot the jerk a go-to-hell look and turned Annie back the way they had come.

"I need to check in with Drake at the restaurant," he told her when she gave him a puzzled look. "And you need to put your feet up for a while. If you want, you can even take a nap in my office."

It was a good idea, but the second they stepped into the restaurant, Joe knew he'd made a mistake. The place was unusually packed for a weekday morning, and it wasn't hard to figure out why. There was a friend or business acquaintance at just about every table, all of them no doubt wanting to reassure themselves that Annie was okay since they hadn't been able to get her on the phone. And she didn't know any of them from a stranger in the street.

When she got her memory back, she was going to be overwhelmed. Now, however, she had to greet and chat with people she didn't remember, which was bound to be stressful for her. But there wasn't much he could do about it. When friends went out of their way to check on you, you couldn't just brush them off.

Forcing a smile, he nodded in greeting and tightened his fingers around hers. "I hate to tell you this, sweetheart," he said in an aside that carried no farther than her ears, "but it looks like all our friends have shown up at the same time to make sure you're okay."

Startled, she looked around. "Friends? Where?"

"At every table. Lord, it looks like our wedding reception." Grinning ruefully, his eyes met hers. "I know this is the last thing you want to do today, but I don't think that we've got much choice. They're here because they're concerned about you, sweetheart. You're going to have to talk to them."

After all that she had been through, he wouldn't have blamed her if she balked, but she had always had class. Squaring her shoulders, she dragged on a smile that wasn't just for show but actually reached her eyes. "Then you'll have to introduce me," she said simply. "Let's start with the couple at the table by the fountain. They look really worried."

"They're my godparents," he told her. "And they're crazy about you."

The next two hours were a blur that Annie never quite remembered later. Feeling as if she and Joe had stumbled upon a surprise party in their honor, she smiled and laughed and charmingly apologized for her faulty memory just about every time she turned around. People whose faces didn't look the least bit familiar hugged her and kissed her, and she could do nothing but return the affection and wonder who they were. Joe, bless him, stayed faithfully by her side and, when he got the chance, tried to drop hints in her ear about who everyone was so she could keep track. After the twentieth introduction, she stopped trying to keep the names straight and struggled instead just to keep smiling. When everyone was satisfied that she was okay, she promised herself, she was going to go home and go to bed.

But just when part of the crowd left, others, including Phoebe and Alice Truelove, arrived, and the process started all over again. Exhausted, her head throbbing and her back starting to ache, she reinforced her smile and thought of the nap she was going to take when this was all over. Then she started to cramp.

At first, she told herself it was her imagination. She was just tired and had been on her feet too long as she and Joe circulated among their friends. But the small twinge that caught her in mid-sentence quickly turned into a very real cramp that ripped through her abdomen like a rusty knife. Ashen, she gasped and clutched at Joe's arm with one hand while the other protectively covered her belly.

Caught in mid-sentence, he glanced down at her with a distracted smile that vanished the second he saw her distress. "What is it? You're pale as a ghost."

"The baby," she said faintly, only to wince as another cramp caught her. "Oh, Joe, I think something's wrong!"

"Excuse us," he said curtly to a restaurant-supply buddy, who had stopped by just to offer them his support. Without another word, he swept Annie up in his arms and quickly carried her to his office. Setting her down in his big office chair, he knelt next to her and cupped her face in his hand. "Are you in pain? Where does it hurt? Should I take you to the hospital? Dammit, sweetheart, talk to me! What do you want me to do?"

Helpless tears welled in her eyes. "I don't know," she cried, clinging to his hand. "I'm so scared! I know you can't be as happy about it as I am—not yet, anyway—but I don't think I could take losing it. Not on top of everything else. Please..."

"Hush," he ordered with gruff sternness and pressed a quick kiss to her mouth. "You're not going to lose the baby. Just hang on while I call Dr. Sawyer."

His hands were steady as he turned to his desk and quickly found the phone book, his voice even as he called Annie's obstetrician to relay the problem to her. But on the inside, his gut was churning, and he silently admitted to himself that he was scared out of his mind. Could a woman die these days from a miscarriage? God, he couldn't lose her! Not now. Not when he was just finding her again.

The doctor wanted to talk to Annie directly, so Joe

quickly put her on the line, then stood at her side and listened to her end of the conversation with growing misgivings. He didn't know much about the aches and pains of a normal pregnancy, but even he could tell that things didn't sound good.

When she finally handed him back the phone to hang it up, she was paler than before, her eyes stricken. "She said to get to the hospital as fast as we can. She'll meet us there."

Two hours later, Joe was prowling the hospital corridor outside the emergency room, ready to tear the place apart if he didn't get some answers soon. When Annie's doctor stepped out in the hall, he reached her in two long strides. "How is she?" he demanded. "Is she okay? She hasn't lost the baby, has she? When can I see her?"

The older woman smiled and patted him on the shoulder. "She's going to be fine, Joe. And so is the baby. You can see her just as soon as we get her transferred upstairs to a room."

"A room? You're keeping her?"

"Just overnight," she assured him. "Just to make sure." Her smile fading, she warned, "You're going to have to see that she takes better care of herself. She's not eating right or getting enough rest. I know there's not a lot anyone can do about her memory, but all this stress isn't good for the baby, Joe. Or Annie. She's too thin. But it's her blood pressure I'm really worried about."

Joe stiffened, alarmed. "Her blood pressure! What's wrong with it?"

"It's through the roof, that's what's wrong with it! And that's nothing for a pregnant woman to play around with, Joe. If something isn't done to get it down, she and the baby could be in real trouble."

Staggered, he took the news like a blow to the head. "It's this damn murder! I guess you saw this morning's paper?"

Elizabeth Sawyer nodded. "It must have been hell for her."

"It was. She hardly slept last night, and today, we haven't been able to turn around without running into a reporter or friend. She's trying to rest, but how can she when the only thing people in this town are talking about is her?"

"Then a short stay in the hospital will at least get her away from the gossip and notoriety for a while. Maybe things'll die down by tomorrow."

Joe hoped so, but he wasn't holding his breath. "Can I stay with her awhile?"

"A half hour now and another half hour tonight," the doctor replied. "I'm sorry, Joe, but it's the only way she's going to get some rest." Glancing at her watch, she smiled. "Why don't you go on up to the fourth floor? She should be in her room by now. Someone at the nurses' station will tell you which one."

She was lying in bed, trying to keep her eyes open, when Joe finally found her room and walked in. She was still pale, but the color was starting to seep back into her cheeks, and the panic had faded from her eyes. When she smiled sleepily at the sight of him, he felt his heart expand like it had taken a breath.

Crossing to the bed, he took her hand and pressed a kiss to the back of it. "Hi, sleepyhead," he said huskily. "The doc said I could stay for a little while, but you look like you're out on your feet."

He started to pull his hand back, but she stopped him simply by tightening her fingers around his. Her heavy eyelids drifting down, she murmured, "Don't go yet. I want to know what Dr. Sawyer said. Just let me rest my eyes for a moment."

"Rest them as long as you want, sweetheart. That's why you're in here. To rest and take it easy." His hand still held in hers, he pulled up a chair next to the bed and sat down to wait for her to open her eyes again. But her breathing slowed, the grip of her fingers relaxed, and he suddenly realized that she was asleep.

He should have left then, but he stayed the full thirty minutes, sitting by her bed, holding her hand while she slept. A nurse peeked in once, then left them alone, and still he sat there. He could have lost her. And the baby. All this time, he'd thought he was doing so well keeping his heart on a leash. Determined not to let himself care too much until he knew who the baby's father was, he would have sworn that the concern he'd felt was nothing more than what he would have felt for any other unborn child. He'd been wrong.

Chapter 10

"I'm going to let her go home," Dr. Sawyer told him the next morning when she caught up with him right outside Annie's hospital room. "Her blood pressure's much better, but she's not out of the woods. She just can't take any more stress."

"I know," Joe said, guilt stabbing him. He should never have let her stand around talking to people yesterday. She hadn't had enough time to recover from the long drive from the mountains, let alone the nightmare at the Driscoe Ranch. When he'd walked into the restaurant and seen the crowd waiting for them, he should have thanked everyone for coming, then insisted that Annie get the nap she needed. That wouldn't happen again.

"I'm going to unplug the phone and TV and discontinue the paper for a while," he promised. "I should have done it already, but it all happened so fast."

The doctor nodded approvingly. "Good, but you can't stop there. I'm talking no arguments, no discussions that'll push her blood pressure up or start her stomach churning, no situations that'll strain her already frazzled nerves. If she's going to carry the baby to term and deliver it safely, she has to be kept happy and calm. So if you're having any marital problems," she warned sternly, "you're going to have to wait until both Annie and the baby are out of danger to work them out. Do I make myself clear?"

Joe nodded. "Perfectly. But just for the record, the only problem we're having right now is Annie's memory. It's coming back in bits and pieces, and none of it's been pleasant for her."

"No, I don't imagine it has," Elizabeth Sawyer said sympathetically. "But knowing you're there for her has to be a comfort to her. Just stay close, Joe."

He planned to do just that, but as he stepped into her room as she was finishing her breakfast, Annie's lost memories chafed him more than she could possibly know. She looked up at him with a bright smile of welcome and all he could think about was taking her in his arms and telling her everything. She needed to know about the argument that they had had the night before she'd left him, how much he'd regretted it ever since. They'd both been unhappy and upset and the situation had just blown up in their faces. He needed to tell her that he hadn't meant any of it, and if he could go back and unsay the words, he would, in a heartbeat. She might not remember any of it, but he did, and the things they'd said were festering like a boil under the skin. Until they could discuss it and clear the air between them, they were never going to be able to put the past behind them and go on with their marriage.

But he couldn't tell her that. Frustrated, wishing he could whisk her back to the cabin and have her all to himself again, he could do nothing but growl, "Good morning, Mrs.

Taylor,'' then lean down and brush a tender kiss across her mouth.

He'd meant to keep it light and teasing, just a playful nip that would make her laugh and her eyes sparkle. But the second his lips touched hers, he felt her start of surprise, the way her breath hitched in her throat and her mouth opened shyly to his, and the desire that was never far from the surface whenever she was near flooded through him in a hot rush. With a murmur of pleasure, he gathered her close and kissed her with a sweet tenderness that left them both weak with need.

Her heart thundering a thousand beats a second, Annie stared up at him with dazed eyes as he slowly, reluctantly, raised his head. "Well," she laughed shakily, "I guess I don't have to ask if you missed me. That was some kiss, Mr. Taylor."

Trailing a finger over the blush stealing into her cheek, he drawled, "I aim to please, Mrs. Taylor. How's my favorite wife this morning?"

"Excuse me, but did you say your *favorite* wife?" Her blue eyes, bright with mischief, sparkled up at him. "I know I've forgotten a lot of things, but surely I would have remembered if you were a bigamist."

He chuckled, grinning. "No, I haven't been holding out on you—you're the one and only Mrs. in my life. So how are you and that baby of mine feeling? Dr. Sawyer said you had a good night."

Caught off guard, she blinked, sure she must have misunderstood him. But his steady gaze met hers head-on, and there was no doubt that he'd just claimed the baby as his. Confused, she stared up at him searchingly. "We did. *I* did. But Joe, I still don't know who the baby's father is. Did Dr. Sawyer say something that led you to believe—"

"Shh." He cut her off simply by pressing his fingers

gently to her lips. "We didn't even discuss the baby's paternity, sweetheart. As far as I'm concerned, there's nothing to discuss. The baby's mine."

He meant it. She looked in his eyes and felt as if he'd reached right inside her and touched her heart. He really didn't care if she remembered later that someone else had fathered her baby—he was claiming it as his. He would love it and care for it and give it his name, no questions asked.

"Oh, Joe."

She started to cry, she couldn't help it, but before she could do much more than sniff, he replaced his fingers with his mouth, gave her a quick kiss, then straightened, grinning, and presented her with a sack he'd been hiding behind his back. "No tears, honey—you'll get your new clothes all wet. And then what will you wear home?"

Distracted, she glanced down at the plastic shopping bag he'd shoved into her hands, then back up again to where he stood watching her expectantly. "You bought me clothes? Maternity clothes?"

"Well, I could hardly let you parade around town with your jeans unsnapped, could I?" he teased.

"But it's barely nine o'clock in the morning. How—"

"I went shopping after I left here last night," he explained. "The maternity shop in the mall was already closing, but when I told the lady I needed to buy you a complete wardrobe, she opened right up. I hope I got the right size."

He'd bought her a red corduroy jumper and a long-sleeved white cotton blouse that she could also wear with pants, and she loved them on sight. Rushing into the bathroom to try them on, she emerged a few minutes later, dressed in her new clothes and barefooted, a pretty blush tinging her cheeks and a smile stretching from ear to ear.

Spreading her arms wide, she twirled in front of him. "What do you think? Is it me?"

Joe took one look and felt the punch of desire all the way to his toes. She gave the old saying *barefoot and pregnant* a whole new meaning. There was nothing the least bit fancy or seductive about the outfit, but somehow, she made it look like silk. He'd always liked her best in red, and that hadn't changed. With her dark hair and creamy complexion, her skin took on a rosy glow and her eyes a sparkle that was bewitchingly lovely. She looked the way she had when they were first married...happy and carefree and in love...and all he wanted to do was sweep her into his arms and carry her home to bed.

But as much as he wanted to, he couldn't. She needed to rest, and that's the last thing he would let her do if he got his hands on her anytime soon. "Oh, it's you, darlin'," he drawled, grinning. "If I'd known I was going to get a private fashion show, I wouldn't have had the rest of the stuff delivered to the apartment. Why don't we go home and you can try it all on for me?"

"Go home?" she echoed, startled. "I can go home?"

"Just as soon as you get your shoes and jacket on and I sign a few forms for insurance. Of course, I guess I could arrange with Dr. Sawyer for you to stay a few more days if you like," he added teasingly. "You do look more rested—"

"Oh, no, you don't, Joe Taylor!" she warned as she hurriedly stepped into her loafers and grabbed her jacket from the small closet near the bed. "You're not leaving me here a second longer than you already have. See? I'm ready. I'll meet you at the car."

She didn't even know where he'd parked, but she was already out the door and heading toward the elevators. Laughing, Joe hurried to catch up with her. "Slow down, sweetheart. You're not going anywhere without me, remember? I've got the keys."

* * *

Over the course of the next three days, Joe totally abandoned the restaurant, leaving it and the arrangements for the grand opening of the new one in Drake's capable hands while he stayed home with Annie and took care of her. Hardly letting her out of bed except to go to the bathroom or lie on the couch with her feet up, he took Dr. Sawyer's order literally and saw that she rested around the clock and ate like it was going out of style. He cooked tempting dishes for her, all but hand-fed her, and made sure she cleaned her plate. When she grew tired of lying around reading, he entertained her with funny stories and even brushed her hair for her until she fell asleep. If she'd been the least bit self-centered, she would have been spoiled rotten.

Instead, she was enchanted.

For three days and nights, he made it impossible for her to think of anything but him. He babied her and pampered her, and made her heart sing every time he stepped into the room where she was. And she couldn't keep her eyes off him. She watched him because she couldn't help herself, because she longed for the feeling of his arms around her again, because there was no question that she was falling in love with him all over again. And she no longer had the strength to fight it.

By the afternoon of the third day, she only had to look at him to know that it was his baby that she carried. She couldn't remember its conception or prove anything until she got her memory back or the baby was born, but she knew, she just knew, that it was his child she carried. It had to be. Even if they had been having problems before she'd left him, she couldn't imagine herself letting any other man touch her, let alone make love to her. Not after loving Joe.

Knowing that she hadn't been unfaithful to him lifted a load from her shoulders she hadn't even known was there until it was gone. And just that easily, she was free. Free of the pain of self-doubt, of questioning her own integrity. She still didn't know why she had left him or what she had done during the two months they were separated, but at least she hadn't crawled into bed with another man while she still had her husband's wedding ring on her finger.

She had to tell him, of course. Whether he believed her or not, he had to know that *she* believed that she'd never turned her back on their marriage vows.

So that night after supper when she insisted on helping him with the dishes, she struggled to find the words. Rinsing dishes for him to load in the dishwasher, she cleared her throat, searching for an easy way to begin, but there wasn't one. He'd never once mentioned the future or voiced an opinion on whether he thought their marriage had a ghost of a chance after everything that had happened, and she didn't want him to think that she was bringing up the subject because she expected anything from him. But he had to know that she'd never given him any right not to trust her.

And there was no way to say it but just blurt it out. "I didn't fool around on you when I was gone, Joe," she said with quiet confidence, shattering the comfortable silence between them. "There was no other man. The baby really is yours."

In the process of reaching for the plate she held out to him, he sent her a sharp look. "You remembered something?"

"No," she said with quiet dignity. "I just know."

Staring down at her, he wished like hell he could believe her, but unlike her, he remembered every moment of that last month before she'd left him. And they'd only made love once. And while it wasn't impossible that she could have gotten pregnant then, the chances were slim. And no one regretted that more than he did.

Taking the plate from her, he turned to add it to those

already in the dishwasher. "It doesn't matter. I'll love it no matter whose it is."

He meant to reassure her, but when he turned back to her, her eyes were swimming in tears that, even as he watched, spilled over her lashes and slid silently down her face. Alarmed, he reached for her. "What is it, honey? I thought you'd be pleased."

"I am!" she sniffed. "But I want you to believe me."

Did she think he didn't want that, too? In spite of everything that had happened, he still loved her. But love and trust, he was discovering, didn't necessarily go hand in hand. Once, she could have told him the moon was turning cartwheels in the sky and he would have found a way to believe her, but those days were gone, apparently forever. And no one regretted that more than he did.

"I didn't say I didn't believe you," he pointed out huskily. "Just that I would love the baby no matter what. I'm trying, Annie. The last couple of weeks haven't been easy on either one of us, and all we can do is take things slow and give ourselves some time. Everything will work out the way it's supposed to."

"I know. It's just so hard sometimes." Giving him a watery smile, she dashed impatiently at her wet cheeks. "I'm sorry. I didn't mean to cry all over you, but I don't seem to have any control over it. I guess it's because I'm pregnant. It's supposed to make you weepy or something."

He laughed and gathered her back against his chest. "Are you kidding? Sweetheart, you've been able to cry at the least little thing every since I've known you. We went to a Super Bowl party at Grant's house on our first date, and you cried when the Cowboys won—and when the losers congratulated them. You get teary-eyed over 'The Star-Spangled Banner,' for God's sake! Why do you think I carry a handkerchief with me everywhere we go? Nine times out of ten, you're going to get sentimental about something before we get home."

"Stop!" she cried, laughing. "I couldn't possibly be that bad!"

"Wanna bet? I can have you in tears—and I don't mean unhappy ones—in about thirty seconds flat, and I don't even have to turn on a sappy movie to do it."

"You can not!"

"Watch me," he growled, and swept her up in his arms.

"Joe! What are you doing? Where are you taking me? Put me down. You don't have to carry me like I'm some kind of invalid."

Chuckling, he ignored her and carried her into the living room, where, one by one, he turned out all the lights until only one was left burning. Sinking down onto the couch, he settled her comfortably on his lap. "Now," he said with a wicked grin, "watch the clock."

He just meant to tease her, to nuzzle her neck and tell her how she knocked him out of his shoes with just her smile the first time he laid eyes on her, but she felt so good in his arms, so trusting, that it wasn't that first meeting he found himself remembering, but the night they'd first made love. His heart did a slow, lazy turn, and suddenly it was vitally important that she remember, too.

With fingers that were suddenly unsteady, he captured her face in his hands and stared down at her with eyes that were dark with emotion. "The first time we made love, you were still a virgin," he told her in a low, rumbling voice that had turned as deep as the night. "You were so beautiful, so sweet, and I was terrified of hurting you. We'd waited so long, and I wanted it to be perfect for you, but I felt like a raw kid who'd never been alone with a woman before. My hands were shaking," he admitted ruefully. "Do you remember?"

Mutely she shook her head, and just that easily, he won their bet. Tears welled in her eyes, but he took no joy in the victory. He wanted, *needed,* her to remember. Not just their first time together, but their love. *Him,* dammit! They'd had something that should have transcended decades, lifetimes, and they'd foolishly let it slip through their fingers. Somehow, they had to get it back.

"Then you smiled at me and kissed me," he said softly, "and I knew that I'd move heaven and hell before I'd hurt you. If you remember nothing else, remember that, sweetheart."

A single tear spilled over her lashes. "Oh, Joe, I want to. I want to remember everything!"

"You will, honey. Just give yourself time."

He kissed her then because he couldn't help himself, because it seemed like weeks instead of days since he'd held her like this, because he didn't want to think about the things she might remember that could take her away from him. As long as he was holding her, kissing her, loving her, he couldn't lose her. Not again.

But he hadn't forgotten Dr. Sawyer's warning. Reluctantly, he dragged his mouth from hers, but only to trail slow kisses over the curve of her cheek. "We've got to stop this, sweetheart," he breathed into her ear. "It's getting late and you need to go to bed. The doctor said you were supposed to rest, remember? That means eight hours of uninterrupted sleep a night."

She moaned softly and clung to him. "Only if you come with me." Turning her head to capture his mouth with hers, she kissed him sweetly, hotly. "I don't like sleeping without you. I keep reaching for you."

He groaned at that admission and tried to remember all the reasons he'd stubbornly slept in the guest room ever since he'd brought her home from the hospital. But she was so soft in his arms, so damn seductive, that he could hardly think straight. He was already hard for her, his body crying out for the feel of her under him, surrounding him. And the doctor hadn't specifically said no sex.

He never remembered making a decision, but suddenly he was pushing up from the couch with her in his arms and heading for their bedroom. The lights were still on, the stereo softly playing, the dishwasher grumbling as it went through its cycles. He didn't care. The rest of the world could have been racing past their front door like a herd of elephants, and he never would have noticed. Not with Annie in his arms.

He walked straight to their bedroom and laid her in a patch of moonlight on their bed, then came down beside her without ever taking his mouth from hers. Somewhere down on the Riverwalk, music drifted faintly on the cool night air, but he never heard anything but Annie. The whisper of her clothes, then his, as he undressed them both, the music of her sighs, the thunder of her heart. Her skin was like marble in the moonlight, her hair a dark tempting cloud across the pillow. Impossibly moved, he murmured to her, kissing his way down her body and back up again. Under his mouth, he felt her breathing change, her heart quicken. Smiling against her belly, he pressed his ear to her rounding belly and wondered if he imagined the slight murmur that could have been his child's heart. Sweetness rippling through him, he traveled up to her breasts and knew that he wasn't imagining the increased fullness there. Or her sensitivity. He kissed a tightly puckered nipple, and she moaned, arching into his mouth as her hands blindly flew to his head to cradle him close.

Tenderness. She'd never known such tenderness. Tears rose to her eyes, horrifying her because she was afraid he would misunderstand, but before she could blink them away, he was rising above her to kiss them away. His voice rough in the darkness, he told her how she delighted him, the pleasure that she brought him with just the light in her eyes. With every word, every touch, he slowly, inexorably drove her from one sensual peak to another. And all the while, tears streamed silently down her cheeks.

She knew he must have loved her a thousand times before, but she couldn't believe that any of those times had been like this. So sweet. So overwhelming. So incredibly beautiful. He knew just where to touch her to make her shudder, just how to kiss her to make her melt. He made her throb; and God help her, with maddening patience, he made her want until she burned.

And that was when she turned into a woman she didn't know. Sobbing, aching for release, she clutched at him, scratched at him, demanding everything. And he laughed. The monster laughed!

"Yes," he growled, kissing her fiercely as his fingers twined with hers and trapped them against the mattress. "I want you wild, sweetheart. Hungry for me. Show me what you want."

Loving her, urging her on, he destroyed her inhibitions and taught her that she was a sensuous woman who knew how to get what she wanted. She teased, she seduced, she rubbed and flirted and drove him crazy with fingers that were quick as lightning at one moment and slow as a winter dawn the next. And he never stood a chance. She had the satisfaction of making him groan and thought she had him right where she wanted him. He was hers and she meant to claim him. She was still contemplating ways she could drive him out of his mind with pleasure when he parted her thighs and surged into her. Before she could even gasp, she shattered, his name a startled cry upon her lips.

* * *

Long after she'd drifted off to sleep in his arms, Joe held her close, his body sated and exhausted, bittersweet emotions churning in his gut, keeping him awake. He hadn't lied when he'd told her that he would love the baby no matter what, but looking back with a clearer head than he'd had in months, he knew now that if the baby turned out not to be his, he had no one to blame but himself. He'd wanted security for them in a world where there really was none and had ended up sacrificing the most important person in the world to him to get it. God, what a fool he'd been!

He'd been so focused on what he wanted that he hadn't been able to see what she needed. All she'd wanted was more of his time and attention, a baby, the type of home life that she'd always dreamed of. Hardly unreasonable requests of a wife from her husband. But at the end of an eighteen-hour day that had held nothing but one headache after another, he hadn't been happy about coming home to what had sounded like demands, just because he was tired. They'd fought and argued and grown further and further apart. Instead of giving their marriage first priority, he'd given all his attention to the restaurant, and they had come apart at the seams. Over and over again, she'd tried to tell him how unhappy she was, but the words just hadn't registered. And now that he was listening, it might be too late. She slept contentedly enough in his arms tonight, but how long would that last once she remembered that for the last six months of their marriage, he'd seldom been there for her when she needed him?

He could lose her again, he thought, shaken. At any moment of the day or night, time could run out and the shadows clouding her memory could lift. He'd hurt her once; she might not want to chance that kind of heartache again, especially now that there was a baby to protect. She could walk out the door, and it would all be over. Forever. Because if she left him a second time, she wouldn't be back.

No, dammit! he thought fiercely. He wouldn't lose her. Not again. Instinctively, he tightened his arms around her, only to have her murmur in protest. Easing his hold, he quietly soothed her with his hands and voice until she drifted back to sleep, but deep in his gut, worry gnawed at him. It was a long time before he slept.

The man standing in the shadow of the building across the street watched the last of the lights in Apartment 2B of the old Victorian mansion go out, his expression as cold and bitter as the night. The bitch was starting to remember. She'd already led the police to the body—it was only a matter of time before she remembered the rest and had the cops hunting him down like some kind of rabid dog.

Damn her, he should have gotten rid of her when he had the chance! he thought furiously. But the conniving little witch had tricked him. She'd acted like she was half out of her mind with fear and had all but crawled to do his bidding. Then, when he'd dropped his guard, she'd brained him with the shovel. By the time he'd come to his senses, she'd been halfway back to town. If he could have gotten his hands on her then, he would have taught her just what real fear was.

But her time was coming, he promised himself. Oh, yes! And then he was going to make her suffer for all the hell she'd put him through. He just had to get to her before she remembered and eliminate her. Ten minutes, that's all he needed. Ten minutes alone with her and Annie Taylor would never bother him or anyone else again.

He knew it wasn't going to be easy. He'd been tailing her ever since she'd come out of hiding to lead the police to Freeman's body, laying back out of sight, watching her, studying her. But that damn husband of hers hadn't let her out of his sight for a second, let alone ten minutes. He'd watched her like a hawk protecting its own, and the few times he hadn't been hovering close, the pig in street clothes hovering outside their apartment was always there, always watching. It was damn frustrating.

A lesser man might have given up and run for Mexico while he still could. But trouble was what he was good at. And he wanted Mrs. Taylor. He wanted her bad. And he was going to get her. He already had it all worked out.

Far back in his subconscious, Joe heard the sirens echoing through the canyons of downtown, but it was the shrill ringing of the phone that woke him just before dawn. Mumbling a sleepy curse, he kept one arm snug around Annie and fumbled for the phone on the nightstand with the other.

"'Lo?"

"Mr. Taylor?"

"Yeah?"

"This is the 911 operator, sir. I'm sorry to disturb you at this hour, but we just got a call that your restaurant at 3257 Navarro is on fire."

"What!" Coming abruptly awake, he bolted straight up in the bed. "Has anyone called the fire department? What started it? How bad's the damage?"

Already reaching for his pants, he barked the questions into the phone, but the operator was as cool as a cucumber. Her voice professional and steady, she replied, "We have no way of knowing that at this time, but two fire trucks have been sent to the scene. They should be arriving shortly."

Only then did the sirens that seemed to be screaming to a halt right outside their bedroom window register. "I hear them now. Thanks for calling. I'll be right there."

He slammed down the phone and quickly strode over to the closet for a shirt. When he turned back to the bed, it was to find Annie pulling on a forest green sweater and jeans, her face pale in the predawn light. "It's the restaurant," he told her grimly. "There's a fire. I've got to get over there."

Annie didn't bother asking questions that would be answered soon enough. She simply sat on the side of the bed and quickly tugged on thick socks and her shoes. "I'm going with you."

"The hell you are," he growled. "It's too dangerous."

"I'll stay out of the way," she promised, "but I'm not letting you go down there alone." The matter settled as far as she was concerned, she tied her shoes and pushed to her feet. "Let's go."

"Dammit, Annie, will you listen to me?" Hurrying after her, he caught up with her just as she pulled her jacket from the closet by the front door. Grabbing her arm, he whirled her to face him. "You are *not* going with me! You got that?"

It was the wrong tone to use with her. Her chin came up, her blue eyes flashing fire as she stood nose to nose with him. "I don't remember asking your permission."

He swore, but he couldn't get angry with her when she was ready to fight him and anyone else for what she believed in. His Annie was coming back to him slowly but surely, and even though there was a chance that all their newfound closeness would vanish with the return of her memory, he couldn't regret it.

Sighing, he released her, but only for a moment. Before she could even begin to sputter a protest, he leaned down to give her a quick, hard kiss. "You're right," he said, surprising her. "I can't stop you from going. But it's probably already a madhouse down there, and a fire's no place for a pregnant woman. I don't want you to get hurt, honey," he said bluntly. "I know you don't want me to face this alone, but I'd much rather do that than take a chance on something happening to you or the baby. If you stay here, at least I'll know you're safe."

He had a point, the dog, one that she didn't have a single argument for. But everything inside her rebelled at the thought of letting him walk out the door alone. For all they knew, the restaurant could even now be burning to the ground. She wanted to be with him, to be at his side and offer what comfort she could. But he was right. She had to think of what was best for the baby.

"Promise you'll call me as soon as you see how bad it is," she insisted. "If I don't hear from you within fifteen minutes after you walk out the door, I'm coming down there. I mean it, Joe—"

"I'll call," he promised, giving her another quick kiss, "just as soon as I see what's going on."

He was gone before she could tell him to be careful, leaving behind a silence that was thick and heavy and cloying. The sirens had finally stopped wailing outside, but she could hear the broken, staticky transmission of the fire trucks' radios on the morning air, the sound of shouting a hundred yards downstream where Joe's Place sat nestled in the bend of the river, the wicked crackle of flames burning white-hot.

Chilled, sick to her stomach, she slipped on her jacket and hurried out onto the balcony off the kitchen. The restaurant was blocked from her view by a thick stand of magnolia trees, but nothing could block the smoke that rose from the fire. Thick and black, it lifted into the morning sky like a thunderhead until it dwarfed the surrounding skyscrapers of downtown.

"Oh, God." Hugging herself, she stared at it and felt her heart sink. She'd hoped that the fire was nothing more than a simple kitchen fire, smoldering grease that put out a lot of smoke and not much else. But that kind of smoke didn't come from anything minor.

She should have gone with him, she thought, stricken. Even if he didn't want her to. Joe's Place was more than just a business to him—he'd put his heart and soul into every inch of that restaurant—and losing it would devastate him. She could just see him, standing back out of the way of the firemen, watching it burn and knowing there was nothing he could do to stop it.

Restless, her heart breaking for him, she went back inside so she wouldn't miss his call and anxiously paced the confines of the living room. She knew he had to be there by now—it only took a matter of minutes, and he'd been running when he went out the door. But five minutes passed, then ten, and she grew more and more agitated. Why didn't he call? He knew she was worried—

She jumped at the sudden, sharp jangling of the phone and snatched it up before the first ring was completed. "Joe? What took so long—"

"Mrs. Taylor?"

The male voice at the other end of the line wasn't Joe's but it sounded vaguely familiar. Wondering if it was someone from the restaurant, she clenched the phone tighter. "Yes? Who is this? Please, I can't tie up the line. I'm waiting for a call from my husband—"

"I know," the caller cut in grimly. "I'm sorry to be the one to inform you of this, but Mr. Taylor was injured in the fire."

"What! How? Is he all right? Where is he? I'm coming down there—"

"No! He's not at the fire. He's already being transported to the hospital."

"What hospital? I'll meet him there."

"The Methodist."

Tears welling in her eyes, she choked, "Thank you so much for calling me! I'm leaving right now."

Before she even slammed the phone down, she was running for the door, her feet barely touching the floor. He was hurt. Fear squeezed her heart. What could have happened? she wondered wildly. Was he burned? She whimpered, tears gathering in her eyes at the thought. No! He couldn't be! The firemen wouldn't have let him get anywhere near the flames.

She was halfway down the stairs when she remembered that she hadn't driven since the morning she woke up in his bed with no memory of who she was. Joe had had her car moved to the parking garage down the street from the apartment, but she hadn't a clue where her keys were and there wasn't time to look for them. The morning shift had to be arriving at the restaurant by now—they couldn't have heard of the fire yet. If she couldn't grab a cab, she'd get one of the waitresses to drive her to the hospital.

Her thoughts already jumping ahead to what she would find when she got there, she never saw the man waiting for her on the mansion's wraparound porch until she came running out the front door and almost ran over him. "Oh! I'm sorry! I didn't see—"

She glanced up, intending to offer an explanation for nearly flattening him, but the words died on a strangled gasp. Recognition slapped her in the face, and between one frantic heartbeat and the next, she remembered. Everything. "Oh, God!"

"Well, well, well," he sneered, watching in satisfaction as horror flared in her eyes. "I see you remember me. That'll make things easier, won't it?"

"No!" she lied. "I don't remember anything. I swear!"

"Then maybe I should remind you," he taunted, his smile

ugly. "The last time we saw each other, you brained me with a shovel right before I was about to—"

She clamped her hands over her ears, horror rippling through her as one terrible memory after another slapped at her. The murder in the garage she'd stumbled across just by dumb luck. The dead man's blood soaking her clothes as she was forced to help lift the corpse into the murderer's van. And the grave. The smell of dirt and death and fear. And then that awful moment when this monster had her down in the dirt, his breath hot and foul on her face as he fumbled with his zipper.

He'd tried to rape her.

"No!" she screamed, and turned to run.

One step. That's all she was able to take before he grabbed her with the speed of a striking rattler and sank his fingers into the tender skin of her arm. "Oh, no, you don't. You're not going anywhere but with me. We've got a little unfinished business, lady."

Frantic, she looked around for the policeman that she only just then noticed was nowhere in sight. Smug, her tormentor only laughed. "Don't bother searching for your watchdog. He's taking a nice long nap thanks to a little konk on the head. C'mon, let's get out of here."

"I can't. My husband's hurt—"

He laughed, the sinister sound sliding over her nerve endings like ground glass on an open wound. "Stupid bitch! *I'm sorry to be the one to inform you of this, but Mr. Taylor was injured in the fire,*" he mocked.

Horrified, she gasped. "You made that call?!"

Grinning evilly, he nodded. "I thought about setting that fire while he was cooking in that fancy restaurant of his, but this is better. He's off putting out fires, and I've got you. He won't know anything's wrong until it's too late."

"I'll scream!" she cried, tugging wildly against his hold.

"Let me go or I swear I'll scream so loud they'll hear me all the way down at the restaurant!"

"Over the sound of those damn sirens?" he taunted as another fire truck, sirens screaming, rushed right past them on the street. "I don't think so. Anyway, I've got this."

Moving in what seemed like slow motion, he pulled a small, deadly pistol from behind his back and pointed it right between her eyes. Frozen, her heart stopping dead in her chest, Annie didn't have to ask him what his intentions were. She could see the murder in his eyes. He was going to kill her.

Chapter 11

"Now that we have that settled," he snarled, "I suggest you get in the van." Nodding toward the faded red van that was illegally parked at the curb, he smiled evilly. "We're going for a little ride."

"No! Please—"

"Oh, you're going to please me, all right. This time I'm going to make sure of it. You shouldn't have gone to the cops." His eyes dark and flat and cold as hell, he tightened his grip on the gun. "You know what I do to people who don't know how to keep their mouths shut? I put a bullet between their eyes and it takes care of the problem every time. And just think—you even know where you'll be spending eternity. Thanks to your loose tongue, you've already got your own grave dug. Oh, the cops filled it in, but you shouldn't have any trouble digging it out again. I've got the shovel all ready for you in the back of the van."

Her eyes locked in revulsion on the gun, Annie felt a whimper squeeze its way through her tight throat and hastily, painfully, swallowed it. No! she thought furiously, stiffening. She wouldn't show this monster weakness—he thrived on it. And she damn well wouldn't drive herself to her own execution without putting up a hell of a fight. He was going to kill her anyway. Why should she make it easy for him?

Standing her ground, praying he couldn't hear the knocking of her knees, she said flatly, "If you're going to kill me, you're going to have to do it here. I'm not going anywhere."

It was the wrong thing to say to a man who had nothing to lose. His eyes narrowing dangerously, he edged closer and snapped the gun under her chin, grinding it into the hollow below her ear. "Don't tempt me, lady," he ground out softly between his teeth. "Killing gets easier every time you do it, and with all the sirens around here, I can take care of you and anyone else who gets in my way and be halfway to Mexico before anyone finds the bodies. You want to do it here? Fine. I'm ready when you are."

"Annie! Hello, dear. I just heard the fire engines and came outside to see what was going on. Did you see all the smoke coming from the Riverwalk? It looks like it's coming from the bend of the river—"

Stiffening at the first sound of Alice Truelove's worried voice, Annie whirled just in time to see the Lone Star Social Club's elderly manager hurrying up the steps to the porch. Her heart stopping in her breast, she wanted to cry out at her to run, but she never had a chance. In the blink of an eye, the man at her side stepped close and jabbed the gun in her ribs so the old woman couldn't see it. One look at the hard glint in his eyes and Annie knew that if she so much as breathed wrong, he'd kill them both.

Forcing a stiff smile, she said, "Hi, Alice. I saw the smoke, too, but I don't think we have anything to worry about." The fib stuck in her throat and she had to swallow before she could go on. "You haven't met my...brother, have you? This is...Mike. Mike, this is Alice Truelove. She manages the Lone Star."

"Great," he muttered, pushing the gun harder against her side. "Now let's get out of here."

Startled, Alice looked back and forth between the two of them. A blind woman couldn't have missed the tension between them, and Alice Truelove had the eyes of a twenty-year-old. Her gaze narrowing slightly, she greeted the man at Annie's side cautiously, then turned to Annie. "You're leaving? But what if the fire's near Joe's Place? Maybe you should wait—"

"I can't." Stumbling for an explanation, she blurted out the first bald-faced lie she could come up with. "I'm sure it's coming from farther downriver—Joe's down there and he would have called if there was a problem. And M-Mike and I h-have plans. He's in town for just a short time and wanted to visit our father's grave."

Bewildered, the older woman blinked in confusion. "And you're going there *now?*"

"I have to," she said quickly when the devil at her side nudged her toward the steps. "When Joe gets back, will you tell him that I had to go but I'll be back as soon as I can? I didn't have time to leave him a note."

"Of course, dear. I'll watch for him and catch him the second he walks through the front door." Trailing after them, she frowned worriedly at the top of the steps as they hurried down the sidewalk. "It was nice meeting you, Mike!" she called after them. "Drive carefully."

Not sparing her a glance, he only muttered nasty curses in Annie's ear and hustled her around to the passenger door of his van. Jerking it open, he pushed her across the seat so he could follow her inside. "You drive," he told her coldly, and forced her into the driver's seat. "And don't even think of trying anything funny or I'll come back later and pop off granny and your old man just for the hell of it."

Annie shuddered, not doubting him for a second. She'd already seen him kill once, and he hadn't even blinked. Nausea swelling in her throat, her heart thudding, she started the van and slowly pulled away from the curb. Joe would come for her. He had to. Clinging to the thought, she scanned the rearview mirror for him expectantly. But the only person in sight was Alice. Still standing on the porch, a frown etching her brow, she watched them drive all the way down the street until they turned the corner and they disappeared from view.

Alice Truelove considered herself a discreet woman who knew how to mind her own business. Oh, she enjoyed playing matchmaker now and again, but she wasn't one of those nosy landladies who was always pushing her nose into the lives of her tenants. That just wasn't her way. The Lone Star Social Club was more like a boardinghouse than an apartment building and while the eight apartments were spacious, they were all within what had once been a single home. And when you were living right on top of people, all you had to do was stand back and listen to find out what was going on.

Unlike most of the other tenants, she'd known Annie and Joe Taylor were in trouble long before most of their other neighbors had. For months, they'd spent too much time apart, and whenever Alice had seen the two of them together, their smiles had been forced, the unhappiness in their eyes plainly visible. As much as she'd hated it, Alice hadn't really been surprised when Annie had left.

But, Lord, she'd been sad for them. And the longer Annie had been gone, the more Alice had worried. No one knew better than she how the Lone Star could draw lovers together, but no amount of charm had seemed to help Annie and Joe.

But she was back now, and Alice had only had to see them together to know that the Taylors were well on their way to finding each other again. She couldn't have been happier for them if they'd been her own kin, but as she stared down the street where Annie had disappeared in a van that Alice had never seen before, she couldn't shake the feeling that something wasn't quite right. If that fire wasn't at Joe's Place, it was too close for comfort, and Annie should have been down there with Joe. And what was the all-fired hurry to get to the cemetery, anyway? Surely they could have waited until later to do that?

Troubled, she started to turn back into the house, telling herself that it was none of her business if Annie and her brother chose to run off when her husband's restaurant could be burning to the ground. She wasn't a busybody and if she wanted to steer clear of earning that tacky title, she would go into her own apartment and not worry about what the Taylors were doing.

But she hadn't known that Annie even had a brother. And she really hadn't liked the looks of him. Or the look of fear in Annie's eyes. If Mike really was her brother as she'd claimed, what could Annie possibly be scared of? And if he wasn't, then who was he and why had Annie gone with him? Busybody or not, Alice knew a bad smell when she smelled one, and she was going to get some answers. Hurrying inside, she headed for the phone.

When she dialed the restaurant, however, all she got was a stilted, recorded message from the phone company that said the number was not in working order. And outside, another fire engine screamed down the street. Worried, she hung up the phone, grabbed the key to her front door, and headed for the Riverwalk and Joe's Place.

Ashes. What had once been one of the most popular restaurants on the Riverwalk was now nothing but a burned-out shell. A black skeleton of charred, still-smoking beams that looked like they would fall in on themselves any second. The last of the flames had been put out, but the firemen who had been called to the scene were taking no chances. Decked out in yellow rubber coats and boots, they kept the water coming, soaking everything in sight.

It was still early yet, but the sound of sirens had brought people running. They stood on both banks of the river, silent, solemn spectators, tourists and locals alike, and watched the scene as grimly as if the loss were their own. Only a few knew that the gray-faced man who stood alone on the fringes of the crowd was the one who had really just lost his life's work.

The smell of burned wood sharp in his nostrils, Joe felt nothing but numbness. Gone, he thought dully. In the time it took to strike a match, it was all gone.

"It looks like it was arson, Mr. Taylor," the fire inspector said grimly as he stomped through the ashes to join him. "It went up too fast and was too hot to be an electrical fire. If I had to guess, I'd say it was gasoline, but it'll be a while before we can pin down what accelerant was used. I've already notified the police. They're going to want to talk to you."

Nodding, Joe stared blindly at the disaster before him and tried to make sense of it. But how could anyone explain an arsonist? He readily admitted he wasn't a saint—he hadn't gone through life without making an enemy or two. But this wasn't the act of a business competitor who might be hacked at him for lowering the price of his lunch special.

Oh, no. This was vicious, without conscience, the work of a bastard who had wanted to strike a low blow. He had.

And Joe didn't know a soul who fit that description. Not one. Anyone who knew him knew that he was a reasonable man—if they had a beef with him, all they had to do was discuss the problem with him. Not burn his restaurant to the ground.

"We also have a witness who claims he saw the arsonist," the fire inspector continued. "The only problem is, we don't know how reliable he is. He's a homeless man, a laid-off construction worker who promised to tell us everything we wanted to hear if we'd just buy him breakfast. He might just be looking for a free meal."

Only half listening at first, Joe snapped to attention. "He saw the bastard set the fire? Where is he? I want to talk to him."

"I thought you might," the other man replied, his mouth curling in a tight smile. "C'mon, he's over here."

Joe followed him over to the spot that had been the Riverwalk entrance of the restaurant. Now it was nothing but a pile of blackened bricks. Beside it waited a gaunt, middle-aged man with a grizzled jaw and bloodshot eyes. His clothes were wrinkled but clean, his canvas tennis shoes worn and holey. Not the least bit intimidated, he held out his hand to Joe and introduced himself. "How do you do, sir? I'm Seth Bishop. You're the owner?"

Joe nodded and gave his hand a firm shake. "Joe Taylor. I understand that you saw the slime who did this. Can you describe him for me?"

"It was right before sunup," the older man replied, "so the light wasn't real good, but I could tell he was a tall fella—at least six-two or three. But he wasn't real heavy, maybe around two hundred at the most. He was dressed all in black, so he sort of blended in with the shadows."

There was a commotion by the barriers the police had put up to keep the crowd back, and Joe looked up to see Alice Truelove hurrying over to him. "Joe! Thank God," she sighed. "I've been worried sick—"

"I'm fine, Alice," he assured her quickly. "Just a minute and I'll be right with you." Turning back to Seth Bishop, he asked, "What about this jerk's face? Would you recognize him again if you saw him?"

"Oh, yeah. He was an ugly son of a bitch...." Suddenly aware of what he'd said, he cast a quick look at Alice and mumbled, "Sorry, ma'am. I didn't mean no disrespect," before turning his attention back to Joe. "He was sort of shifty-looking, Mr. Taylor, with a square jaw and a big nose, and one of those marine haircuts. I think his hair was brown, but it was so short, it was hard to tell. And he had one of those little red cans of gasoline with him. That's why I noticed him in the first place. He kept looking around real nervous-like, then disappeared into the bushes on the side of your building. Next thing I knew, the place was going up like a bonfire and he was racing up the stairs to street level down there by the Commerce Street Bridge."

Startled, Alice gasped. "Why, that sounds like Annie's brother!"

Distracted, Joe frowned in confusion. "What are you talking about? Annie doesn't have a brother."

Her worst fears confirmed, the old lady blanched. "Oh, dear, I was afraid of that. But Annie insisted he was her brother and they were going to their father's grave. I thought it was odd. The fire trucks were screaming and the smoke was coming from this direction, but she insisted that she and her brother had to go to the cemetery right away—"

"Cemetery? What cemetery?" Alarmed, Joe grabbed her by the arm. "Start at the beginning, Alice. Where did you see Annie and this man?"

"On the front porch of the house." Her beautifully lined cheeks as pale as parchment, she told him everything she could remember about the odd conversation with Annie and the man she'd introduced as her brother. "She said his name was Mike and he was only in town for a short while," she concluded. "They were going to their father's grave, but they wouldn't be gone long. Since you were gone, she wanted me to be sure and tell you where she'd gone when you got back. Then they left in a red van. Annie was driving." Distressed, she looked up at him with tears in her eyes. "She's in trouble, isn't she? I shouldn't have let her go. If something happens to her because of me..."

She couldn't finish the thought. His face carved in harsh lines, Joe told himself there was no reason to panic. Annie was still leery of men she didn't know—she never would have gone off with anyone she wasn't comfortable with. Alice must have misunderstood. After all, she was pushing eighty, and sometimes her hearing wasn't very good. Annie could have said this Mike character was a friend's brother or something like that, and Alice just missed it.

It was the only logical explanation, but it did nothing to ease the jumble of nerves that coiled in his gut. No one knew better than he did just how sharp Alice Truelove was. She'd been managing the Lone Star Social Club for longer than anyone could remember and could tell you the name of every tenant who had ever lived there. She didn't make mistakes about anything to do with her renters.

So who had Annie gone off with? And why was she driving some strange man's van? She hadn't driven since she'd lost her memory, and in the past, she'd never liked to drive other people's vehicles. What the hell was going on?

Questions pulling at him, doubts churning like acid in his stomach, he slipped an arm around Alice's shoulders and gave her a reassuring squeeze. "Let's don't go jumping to any conclusions. We don't actually know that she's in trouble. What about the cop that was assigned to watch over her?"

"He was nowhere in sight," she said worriedly. "And she looked scared, Joe. She tried to pretend that everything was okay, but she had that same look in her eyes that she had when she first came back to you. You know—that terrified, hurt look that just made you want to wrap your arms around her and promise her she was safe."

His jaw clenching, Joe nodded stiffly. Oh, yes, he remembered, all right. It was a look he'd hoped to never see in her eyes again. Dropping his arm from her shoulders, he dug in his pocket for his wallet and pulled out a twenty dollar bill. "This doesn't come close to showing my appreciation, Mr. Bishop," he said quietly as he pressed it into the other man's hands. "But it should get you a good meal. If I can ever do anything for you, you'll find me right here, rebuilding this place. Now, if you'll excuse me, I've got to see about my wife."

With Alice at his side, he hurried back to the apartment, hoping against hope that Annie had returned while he was gone. But the apartment was empty and looked perfectly normal. She'd even locked the door when she'd left. There was no note, nothing to show why she had walked out of their apartment with a stranger looking scared to death.

The silence and a worry he couldn't control tearing at him, he turned back from a quick inspection of the apartment to find Alice standing just inside the front door, twisting her hands. "I think we need to talk to Sam," he said flatly, and headed next door.

Sam had a rare day off, but that only meant one thing. Instead of working down at the police station, he worked at home. A cup of coffee growing cold at his side, he grabbed one of the unsolved case files he'd brought home from the office with him and spread it out on the kitchen table in front of him. Concentrating on its contents, he didn't hear the knock at the door. Then the doorbell rang.

He almost ignored it. He had a hell of a lot of work to do, and if that was Alice, she'd want to chat, and he just didn't have the time. She was a sweet old lady, but she didn't like to see anyone unhappy, and she'd been trying to find him a nice woman ever since he and his wife had divorced a month and a half ago. So far, he hadn't had the heart to tell her she was wasting her time.

The doorbell rang again and he gave up in defeat. "Hold your horses. I'm coming."

He strode into the living room, promising himself he was going to get rid of his visitor just as soon as he could. But the second he jerked open the front door and saw Joe and Alice standing there, their faces drawn and grave, he immediately motioned them inside. "What is it? What's wrong?"

"We're not sure anything is," Joe told him as Alice preceded him into the apartment. "The restaurant burned to the ground this morning—"

"What! I heard the sirens, but I didn't realize it was the restaurant."

"It was set," he said flatly. "But that's not the worst of it. While I was down there taking care of things, Annie left the apartment with a man she introduced to Alice as her brother. Supposedly, they were going to visit their father's grave."

Surprised, Sam frowned. "I didn't know Annie had a brother."

"She doesn't. Whoever this jerk was, he matched a witness's description of the man who set the fire at the restaurant."

Swearing, Sam shut the door and motioned them both to sit down. "What the hell happened to the uniform I had assigned to your place?"

"I don't know. He was there when I left—that's the last time I saw him. Maybe he got called away because of the fire. Things were pretty intense there for a while. The fire department was afraid the fire was going to spread to the buildings on either side of the restaurant, and they were calling in all the help they could get to evacuate everyone."

"That's no excuse," Sam growled. "He was ordered not to leave his post no matter what. He should have known the fire was a possible distraction. Damn rookies!"

"Don't blame him," Joe said bitterly. "I should have seen it, too, but I got a call that it was the restaurant, and I never even thought that Annie was the real target."

"We'll get her back, Joe. How long as she been gone? Give me a description of this man she was with. Did anyone see what kind of vehicle they were in?"

"I did." Her mouth twisting with distaste, Alice gave him a detailed description of Annie's companion. "They left in a faded red GMC van and turned west onto Commerce. Annie was driving. I'm not sure what year the van was, but it wasn't one of those fancy new ones."

"Did you get a glance at the license plate?"

Regretfully, she shook her head. "I was so upset that Annie would go off with that man when Joe's restaurant might be burning that I didn't notice." Worried, she said, "You are going to catch him, aren't you?"

"We're damn sure going to try," he growled. "But I can tell you right now, folks, we haven't got a hell of a lot to go on. Why would Annie say they were going to her father's grave? Is he buried here in town?"

"No, he's buried in Oklahoma." A thought hit Joe then and chilled his blood. His eyes flew to Sam's. "A grave.

She said she was going to a grave. Do you think she was trying to tell me the bastard was taking her to where she buried Freeman?"

The words were hardly out of his mouth before Sam was quickly striding to the phone. "You may be right. It would be a smart move on his part since we've already exhumed the body and investigated the scene. He wouldn't be expecting us to go back there and probably figures he's a regular Einstein for thinking of it."

Snatching up the phone, he called the police station and spoke to another detective. Quickly and concisely, he gave him a description of the van and Annie's companion. "When last seen, the van was going west on Commerce. The suspect had Annie Taylor with him, and I believe they're headed north on I10 to the Driscoe Ranch. No weapons were seen, but we have to assume that Mrs. Taylor is with him under duress and the suspect is armed and dangerous. Get backup out there to where Freeman's body was found. I'll meet them there."

When he hung up, his only thought was to grab his gun and car keys and run for the door. The only problem was Joe was standing right in front of the front door, blocking it. "I'm going with you."

His tone was hard and curt and would brook no argument. Sam gave him one anyone. "You know you can't go, Joe. This is a police matter. Let us handle it."

"She's my wife."

"You could get hurt."

"She's my wife."

It was an argument Sam had no response for. Swearing, he scowled at his friend and gave serious consideration to cuffing him to the nearest solid piece of furniture. But if it was his wife in the hands of a piece of scum, he wouldn't be able to stand on the sidelines and watch someone else try to save her, either.

"Dammit, Joe, I know that and I don't blame you for being worried. But you can't help Annie now. If anything, you'll be in the way…" Seeing the granite set of Joe's chin, he gave up with a muttered curse. "I could arrest you for interfering with a police investigation. You know that, don't you?"

Joe only shrugged. "Do what you have to do, but hurry up and make up your mind. Annie needs me."

"For all we know, she could come back any second. You should be here."

Eager to help, Alice said, "I'll watch for her. If she comes in, I'll call the station and they'll notify you."

Trapped, Sam could do nothing but give in. Sighing in defeat, he scribbled his cellular number on a pad by the phone. "Just call me direct, Alice, if you see Annie or hear from her. C'mon, Joe. Let's go."

She couldn't lose control now. Joe was coming for her.

Annie knew it as surely as she knew that she had never been more miserable in her life than she had in the two months that they'd been separated. Tears threatened then, hot, scalding tears that thickened in her throat and burned her eyes, making it nearly impossible to see, let alone drive. No, she told herself fiercely. She couldn't think about that right now, couldn't remember the things they'd said to each other, the way they'd hurt each other. If she did, she'd fall apart, and she'd be damned if she'd give her captor the satisfaction. She'd rather eat worms.

Dashing at her wet cheeks, she forced down the lump of emotion in her throat and stiffened her spine. Her heart slamming against her ribs, her voice carefully expressionless, she asked, "Where do you want me to go?"

Smug now that he had her right where he wanted her, he leaned back in his seat and eyed her with cool deliberation, the gun he still held on her not wavering so much as a centimeter. "Turn right at the next intersection and stay on San Pedro until I tell you to turn."

Following his instructions, Annie almost wilted in relief. He hadn't been serious about taking her back to the Driscoe Ranch. He'd just been pulling her chain, trying to frighten her to death. But that was okay because this was better. Much better. San Pedro was one of the city's major thoroughfares and ran for miles through one neighborhood after another. It went right past San Antonio College, where there were almost always people about. If she kept her eyes open and she was lucky, she just might be able to spot someone, *anyone,* she could signal to for help.

Her hands damp on the steering wheel, she checked the rearview mirror and the side ones, then glanced ahead, her eyes constantly searching for the light bars of a patrol car. But the traffic was disappointingly normal, and as they drove past the college, there wasn't so much as a security guard in sight.

Watching her through narrow, beady eyes that missed little, her companion warned coldly, "Don't even think about trying something, you little bitch. You hear me? I've got no reason to keep you alive, so don't push me." Signaling with the gun, he motioned for her to change to the left lane. "Get over. We're turning left on Hildebrand."

Her heart froze in her breast. If they drove far enough west, Hildebrand led right to Interstate 10. From there, it was only ten miles to the Driscoe Ranch. No! she cried silently. This was all just a cruel joke. He couldn't really be taking her back there. He wouldn't! He couldn't be that sadistic.

But this was the same man who had looked Robert Freeman right in the eyes and put a bullet in his head.

Nausea curling into her stomach, she slowed down for the turn onto Hildebrand and silently ordered herself to get a grip. Panicking now wasn't going to do anything but get her killed. She had to stay calm and keep her wits about her and stall as long as she could to give Joe and the police a chance to find her. Because they would come for her. Going as slow as she dared, she turned at the next intersection like an old woman who had a carton of eggs on the front seat and was afraid of jostling them.

"Get on with it," he ordered tersely. "Now!"

"There's a school zone—"

"The hell there is!" Uncaring that someone in a passing car might see, he held the gun so she could see him caress the trigger. "I said drive and I meant it."

Her heart in her throat, she had no choice but to pick up her speed to the posted speed limit. Then, all too soon, she could see the interstate in the distance. Her fingers gripped the wheel until her knuckles turned white. *Act normal,* a voice whispered in her ear. *Don't let him see that you're afraid.*

But the monster thrived on fear—he could smell it in the air. His mouth curling into a sinister smile, he said, "Go north on I10."

"No!"

Wicked laughter whispered over her, making her skin crawl. "Oh, yes," he purred. "You know the way."

She turned because she didn't have any choice. Because he was going to kill her no matter what she did, and the longer she could put it off, the more time she had to think up some kind of way out of this nightmare. She had a baby to think of, to protect, a husband who would blame himself the rest of his life if something happened to her. She had to do something!

But short of running the van into another car and chance hurting herself and the baby, not to mention a total innocent in the other vehicle, there was nothing she could do while she was driving. So she drove, reluctantly following his roughly growled directions, every muscle in her body slowly, painfully, tightening as they drew closer and closer to the spot where he'd forced her to bury Freeman after he'd killed him in cold blood in the Transit Tower parking garage.

Then, before she was ready for it, she was leaving the road behind and taking the van over a rough path carved out of ranch land that was thick with cedar and cactus. Within minutes, the city, civilization, *help,* was left behind. She braked to a stop and felt her breath lock in her throat as her eyes fell on the mound of dirt under a cedar tree fifty yards in front of the van.

It looked like exactly what it was—a grave. Once Freeman's body had been removed, the police had pushed the dirt back over the shallow pit, but she didn't fool herself into thinking it would be empty for long. Once before, he'd intended this to be her final resting place, and she'd outsmarted him. He wouldn't let her do it again.

"Get out," he said coldly, shattering the silence. "You've got some work to do."

Her hands starting to shake, she climbed out of the van and looked around wildly for a way out. But she was trapped as surely as if he had her backed up against the wrong end of a dead-end alley. Last time, after she'd knocked him cold with the shovel, the dark shadows of the night had covered her like a shroud and he hadn't been able to follow her. But it was broad daylight now, and there was nowhere to run, nowhere to hide. The second she tried to make a break for it, he'd shoot her.

Trapped, she stood quivering by the van, her heart jerking out a frantic rhythm as he came around to join her. Now, she thought, swallowing a sob. He would do it now. And there was nothing she could do to stop him!

But instead of shooting her, he grabbed her by the arm, startling a gasp from her, and hauled her over to the pile of dirt. Forcing her down on her knees, he aimed the gun right at her head. "Dig!"

Stunned, she stuttered, "I—I can't. I h-haven't got a shovel."

He laughed, truly amused, but there was nothing funny about the hate that glistened in his eyes. "You think I'm stupid enough to give you a shovel after what you did the last time? Not on your life, bitch. Use your hands."

She couldn't. She couldn't put her hands in the same dirt she'd dropped by shovelfuls on Robert Freeman's pasty face. Not without gagging. With no amnesia to protect her now, time spiraled backward in a dizzying rush, and all too easily she was sucked back into the nightmare of the fateful night she'd watched the banker die. She could feel the chilly slap of the wind against her skin, the terror that burned her throat and stomach, the bile that rose to her mouth every time her eyes inadvertently found the small, deadly bullet hole in the center of his forehead.

And now it was her own grave she had to dig.

Trembling, her fingers curled into fists. This wasn't the end. She couldn't let it be. She'd always been an optimist, the one who fought against all odds when people all around her were giving up and wimping out. Even when she'd left Joe, she hadn't given up on their marriage, though there'd been a lot of people who had been quick to accuse her of doing just that. She'd just loved him so much that she'd had to resort to drastic measures or risk losing him forever.

She had to do the same thing now. She couldn't give up just because things had gotten a little sticky. The fiend standing over her had made a mistake with her the night he'd killed Freeman—there was a good chance he would do so again. All she had to do was be ready.

But it was hard. God, it was hard! She couldn't seem to stop shaking or draw a deep breath. Dizzy, the gun like an obscenity just inches from her head, she raised up on her knees and bent over the pile of dirt, forcing herself not to cringe. Scooping it up in her trembling hands, she turned and tossed it aside, then bent to the task again. And again. Time ceased to exist. There was only the feel of the dirt on her hands, the smell of it and cedar in her nose, and the bitter taste of fear on her tongue.

Working in rhythm to the frantic pounding of her heart, she zoned out and couldn't have said when she first noticed that the man at her side had become almost hypnotized by the repetition of her movements. The hand pointing the gun at her head was steady as a rock, but the finger that had mockingly played with the trigger when she'd first started to dig had relaxed and now barely touched it. Slanting a look at her tormentor beneath her lashes without once breaking her rhythm, she caught a quick glimpse of slightly glazed eyes and bored features.

For the first time in what seemed like hours, hope stirred in her breast. She was more than halfway through hollowing out the grave. Whenever he decided it was deep enough, he wouldn't say a word—he'd just pull the trigger. If she was ever going to do anything, she had to do it now.

There was no time to plan, no time to do anything but act. Her fingers scooping up two handfuls of dirt, she turned just as she had every other time...and tossed it in his face.

Chapter 12

"You bitch!"

Snarling, he dropped the gun and grabbed at his eyes, and that was all the opening Annie needed. She whirled, a sob lodging into her throat, and darted into the trees.

"Damn you, come back here! Do you hear me?" he screamed as he dropped to his knees and scrambled for the gun. "You come back here or I swear to God you'll beg me to kill you when I finally catch up with you!"

He cursed her to hell and back, but she never looked back. She didn't dare. Her lungs straining, the pounding of her heart booming like thunder in her head, she ran, dodging trees and bushes, whimpering as cedar branches slapped at her face and grabbed at her clothes. From nowhere, a vine reached out to snag at her foot. She stumbled, crying out in surprise.

And her tormentor heard her. Lifting his head like the devil scenting a sinner, he blinked the last of the dirt from his eyes and spied her thirty feet to his right, half hidden among the trees. A nasty grin stretched across his thin-lipped mouth as his fingers closed around the gun. Straightening, he took aim.

The roar of the gun going off sounded like an exploding cannon amid the thick stand of cedars. Annie screamed and dived for cover, knowing as she did so that it was too late. He'd had a clear shot and she'd been a sitting duck. Her breathing ragged, she cowered in the dirt, waiting for the pain to register.

But the only place she hurt was where she'd scraped her knee against a rock and ripped the skin away. Not questioning her good fortune, she was up and running in a heartbeat, tearing through the trees like a madwoman, her only thought to get away.

Caught up in the terror that shrouded her brain, she never saw her kidnapper curse and take aim again, never saw Sam Kelly step out of the trees and shoot the gun from his hand. All she heard was the report of the gun. Sobbing, her lungs burning, she ran blindly, without a thought to where she was going, tripping over rocks and cacti, hurting herself and too scared to care.

Sweat trickling into her eyes, she didn't see the man who stepped out of the bushes in front of her until it was too late. She plowed into him, and, lightning quick, his arms closed around her like a trap.

"No!" Screaming, she pounded at him with her fists, striking out at his head and shoulders and connecting with every blow. "Let go, damn you!"

Joe flinched and tightened his hold on her. "It's all right, honey. You're okay. I've got you now. You're safe."

Panic choking her, she didn't hear. She fought him

wildly, scratching and biting at him, fear for her unborn baby giving her added strength. "No! I won't let you hurt me again! Do you hear me, you slimeball? I'll kill you—"

Joe grunted at a particularly well-aimed blow to his middle and grabbed her hands, trapping them against his chest. "Annie, it's me. Joe. I'm not going to hurt you, sweetheart. *Look at me!*"

The softly grated words penetrated the terror gripping her, and with a start of surprise, she glanced up. Her eyes, wide and unfocused, abruptly cleared. "J-Joe?"

If he lived to be a hundred, Joe didn't think he would ever forget the broken sound of his name on her lips. His throat tight, tenderness flooding his heart, he had to swallow twice before he could say thickly, "Sam got him, honey. He's never going to hurt you again."

Dazed, she glanced around. "Sam? Sam's here? Where—"

"Over there in the trees," he said, nodding back behind her where Sam and a half dozen uniformed officers already had her kidnapper in cuffs. "Alice rushed down to the restaurant just as soon as you left and gave me your message. Thank God, she ran into you or we never would have figured out where he'd taken you."

Emotion clutching his heart, the need to touch her almost more than he could bear, he gently swept her hair back from her face with fingers that were still far from steady. Close, he thought, shaken. They'd come so damn close to not reaching her in time. With backup behind him, Sam had broken every speed limit, but then as they neared the Driscoe Ranch, he'd had to cut the sirens and slow to a crawl as they made their way through the cedars to the creek at the back of the property. To do anything else would have tipped Annie's kidnapper off to their presence and probably have gotten her killed, but the silent, careful drive through the ranch had taken ten years off Joe's life.

Then, as they'd approached on foot the site where Freeman's body had been found, he'd seen Annie running through the trees like a wild woman, falling, and a bastard with a gun take aim. At her, the woman he loved more than life itself. His heart had literally stopped in his chest.

He could have lost her right there. Just that easily, he could have lost her forever. Sick to his soul at the thought, he couldn't stop touching her and assuring himself that she was really all right. "It's over, sweetheart. The son of a bitch is in custody and we all saw him try to kill you. Even if you never remember what he did to you that night in the parking garage, he's going to jail. He'll never come near you again."

Desperate to believe him, she stared up at him searchingly. Behind her, she heard Sam reading her tormentor his rights, but it was the rock-solid steadiness in Joe's eyes and the feel of his hands on her that convinced her more than anything that the nightmare was finally over. She was safe.

Terror drained from her in a rush. Light-headed, her knees threatening to buckle, she started to tremble and couldn't stop. She felt Joe stiffen in alarm and tried to tell him she was okay, but her throat was hot and tight. "Oh, J-Joe," she choked, and threw herself into his arms. Bursting into tears, she clung to him as if she would never let him go.

Later, she never knew how long she cried. It seemed like forever. Her eyes burning, her throat raw, she cried because she was safe, because nothing could hurt her while Joe had his arms around her, because she'd been so afraid that she would die and he would never know what had happened to her. But most of all, she cried because she remembered. And it hurt.

Sweeping her up off her feet, Joe carried her to Sam's car, murmuring to her all the time. "Go ahead and cry, sweetheart. That's it, let it all out. After everything you've been through, you're entitled."

"I remember," she cried, pressing her face against his throat, soaking his shirt. "I finally remembered."

Joe's heart constricted, missed a beat, then stumbled back into rhythm. Instinctively, his arms tightened around her, denial instantly rising to his tongue. He knew she needed to remember—he wanted her to—but not yet, dammit! Not until they'd had more time together. Not until he'd won her love back and she'd at least give him a chance to work things out between them before she walked out on him again.

"We'll deal with that later, honey," he said, shushing her. "Right now it's more important that you're okay. Did he hurt you? You're white as a sheet. Maybe we should have a doctor take a look at you…"

She sniffed, wiping at her cheeks. "No, I'm all right. Really. I'm just a little shaky. I'll be fine once I get away from here."

The sound of a siren drowned out the last of her words, and they both looked up in time to see an ambulance race through the cedars and brake to a stop in a cloud of dust. A shout from Sam drew the paramedics, who burst from the vehicle to the spot where his men had the suspect handcuffed and surrounded. Sitting on a fallen log, his mouth twisted with bitterness and blood dripping from the makeshift bandage wrapped around his forearm, the wounded man stared stonily ahead, ignoring them all.

Leaving the suspect to the uniformed officers and the paramedics, Sam strode over to Annie and Joe, his eyes narrowing as they took in Annie's pale face and tearful eyes. "What did he do to you, Annie? If he so much as laid a finger on you, I need to know."

"Nothing...this time," she assured him. "But on the night Freeman was killed, he tried to rape me."

The scowl darkening his brow didn't ease so much as a fraction, but there was a definite glint of satisfaction in his eyes. "You got your memory back."

She nodded. "After Joe left to check out the fire at the restaurant, I got a call that he'd been hurt in the fire—"

"What?!"

"That's how he got me out of the apartment," she told Joe, wincing at his roar. "I thought his voice sounded familiar, but as soon as he said you were hurt, all I could think about was getting to you. I rushed out of the house, and there he was, waiting for me on the front porch. The second I saw him, it all just came rushing back."

Her mouth flattening into a grim line, she turned hard eyes on the man who had put her through hell twice. "He and Freeman were partners and were supposed to skip the country that night that I came across them by accident in the Transit Tower parking garage."

Remembering, she felt her blood run cold and buried her hands in her jacket pockets. "When Mr. Larkin didn't make our appointment at eight, I figured he'd had some trouble coming in from Houston. So I waited another hour just in case, then headed back to the parking garage."

Disgust, self-directed, twisted her mouth. "I should have been paying more attention—I know that now—but I was ticked that Larkin hadn't had the courtesy to at least call me and cancel, and I didn't even notice how deserted the garage was. Then when I was almost back to my car, I heard Freeman and that scumbag over there arguing about how they were going to split up the money. That's when I realized they'd robbed the bank. Freeman claimed he'd taken most of the risk, so he should get a larger percentage. That's when he shot him," she said, distaste twisting her mouth as she stared at her kidnapper. "He didn't even try to reason with him. He just pulled out a gun and shot him."

Her eyes stark with the horror of it, she blinked up at Joe and Sam. "It all happened so fast, I didn't have time to try to hide. Not that it would have done any good," she added. "There were only two cars on that floor—my Volvo and the van—so there was no place to hide. I don't remember making any noise, but the next thing I knew, he was holding the gun on me."

"He made you help him load the body in the van, didn't he?" Sam guessed. "That's why you had blood all over your clothes."

She nodded, shivering. "He told me if I didn't do what he said, he was going to kill me right there. I had no reason not to believe him."

Joe swore long and hard. "Goddamn his filthy soul, I hope he burns in hell."

"After the body was in the van, he forced me in the back with it and drove out here," she continued. "The whole time I dug the grave, he was holding the gun on me, just daring me to give him a reason to pull the trigger." Her voice cracked then, and she had to swallow before she could continue. "I kept telling myself that if I just went along with him, he wouldn't hurt me. But then after I finished burying the body, he...h-he grabbed me a-and—"

"That's enough," Joe growled. "Dammit, Sam, she's pregnant! She's been through enough. I'm taking her home!"

She would have liked nothing better, but the truth had been locked up inside her for too long, and she had to get it out. "No, I have to finish this now," she insisted. Lifting her chin, her eyes met his unflinchingly. "He didn't rape me, but it wasn't from lack of trying. When I fought him, he told me he was going to put a bullet in my head when he was through with me, then bury me on top of Freeman. That's when I hit him in the head with the shovel."

"You should have aimed a hell of a lot lower and cut him off at the...knees," Sam amended grimly. "Knocking him senseless was a good start, though. So how'd you get home?"

"I walked," she said simply. "All night."

"Why didn't you call me?" Joe demanded. "You know I would have come for you."

He didn't so much as mention their separation, but she heard the hurt in his voice and knew what he was really asking. Even though they'd been separated, surely she must have known that she could call on him for help. Why hadn't she?

"I was terrified." Just thinking about it again made her want to fold in on herself and cry. "There are some houses a couple of miles down the road, but I was so scared, I wouldn't go anywhere near them. All I could think about was getting away. And getting home."

To him.

At the time, she hadn't realized that she was instinctively making her way to him. Her brain had been on automatic pilot; her feet had had a will of their own. But deep down inside, her heart had led her to the one person who could make her feel safe.

"I was so afraid that he was following me that I didn't even turn on a light once I got in the apartment," she continued huskily. "I took a shower in the dark, then went to bed. When I woke up in the morning, I didn't remember anything."

"Did he say anything about the money?" Sam asked. "Freeman took half a million from the bank. That's not exactly the kind of change you carry around in your pocket."

"They packaged it up and sent it to an apartment they'd already rented in Acapulco," she said promptly. "The son of a bitch was real smug about that, especially after he killed Freeman. The whole time he made me dig the grave, he kept bragging about how he'd get to keep all the cash now. All he had to do was fly down there and pick it up, and he could live the rest of his life like a king."

Sam snorted. "Now I guess he's going to have to eat those words, huh? Idiot. If he'd run for the border instead of trying to scare you to death, he might have gotten away with it. Now, all he's got to look forward to is a nice long stretch in Huntsville with the rest of the pond scum." Relieved, he shot Annie a broad grin. "You just made my job a whole lot simpler. If he was stupid enough to put that money in the mail, then we can bring the feds in. They can find out where he sent it, and when, and get it back."

Turning to Joe, he tossed him his keys. "Take her home, man. I'm going to be tied up at the station for a while, so you might as well take the Jeep. If I need a ride later, I'll give you a call."

Joe didn't have to be told twice. Bundling her into the

Wagoneer, he climbed behind the wheel and headed home. He tried to tell himself they could relax now—it was over—but he only had to look at Annie's face to know that it was a long way from that. Pale and silent, her eyes not quite meeting his, she sat beside him, well within touching distance but somehow out of his reach.

Had she remembered the baby wasn't his? he wondered, only to immediately reject the idea. No! She was his and so was the baby. He loved her, dammit, and somehow he had to find a way to convince her that they belonged together, no matter what. Because he wasn't going to lose her. Not after they'd just found each other again. Somehow they'd find a way to work it out. But first he had to show her how much she meant to him.

He hadn't forgotten how she'd reacted when she'd first started to remember the nightmare she'd been through, and the second they got back to the apartment, he walked her straight back to their bathroom and turned on the shower. Without a word, he turned back to her and reached for the hem of her sweater.

"Joe!"

"Shh," he soothed. "I smell like smoke and I know you want to get the feel of that bastard's hands off you. Let me take care of you. We'll both feel better after a nice hot shower."

He needed to pamper her, to wrap her close and take the shadows from her eyes. They would have to talk—he knew that as well as she did—but not yet. Not until he had a chance to touch her and hold her. If he lost her after that, at least he would have these minutes—and the last few weeks—to remember.

Slowly, piece by piece, he gently peeled her clothes from

her, then tore off his own and urged her under the warm spray of the shower. In the time it took to draw in a sharp breath, they were both soaked. Without a word, he reached for the soap and worked up a thick, cleansing lather between his hands.

Steam swirled around them, encasing them in a world of misty heat and tenderness. The pounding of his heart slow and heavy in his chest, he washed her gently, running his hands over her long after the soap had slid from her body and washed down the drain. A sigh rippled through her; her breathing changed ever so slightly—he heard it, felt it. And still he stroked her, warming her, heating her until her eyes grew languorous, the muscles of her neck weak. With a soundless moan, she leaned her head against his chest and groaned.

A smile pulled at the corners of his mouth. "That's it, baby," he rasped softly. "Just relax."

He washed her all over, until she was flushed and boneless and came apart in his hands. Her knees had long since deserted her, and with a murmur for her to hang on, he shut off the water, propped her against the wall, and reached for a towel. His body hard and tight with need, he dried them both, then scooped her up and carried her to bed.

He ached to make love to her, but he only settled her against him and pulled the covers over them. When he had her where he wanted her, her head against his shoulder, her body snug against his, he sighed. Now, with nothing between them, they could talk.

"Before you say anything," he said quietly, "I want you to know that I love you. I fell in love with you the first time I ever laid eyes on you and that hasn't changed. It never will. The whole time you were gone, I was miserable."

"Joe—"

Taking the hand she pressed to his mouth to stop his confession, he dropped a kiss to her knuckles, then trapped her fingers against his heart and held them there. "No, I need to say this," he insisted. "Now that you've got your memory back, you know who the baby's father is. If you were so unhappy when you left me that you turned to somebody else like you threatened to, then I've got to take the blame for part of that. I should have listened to you."

Tears pooled in her eyes. "Oh, Joe, there wasn't another man," she was finally able to tell him without a doubt. "I just said that to shake you up. I was pregnant when I left you."

The announcement fell between them like a lit firecracker. She saw shock, then hurt flare in his eyes and would have given anything to take the admission back, but she couldn't. For too long, they had avoided talking to each other about anything important, and on the rare occasions when they hadn't been able to sidestep a discussion about the pitiful state of their marriage, they'd done nothing but argue and cast blame. But now they had a baby to consider, and it had to stop.

"You knew you were pregnant when you left?"

"That's *why* I left."

He took the news like a slap to the face, and she ached for him. God, they'd made each other so unhappy! "I didn't know what else to do," she confessed huskily. Scrambling up, the sheet pressed to her breasts, she sat facing him and tried to make him understand. "You weren't ready to be a father—you kept finding excuses to put it off—but we were going to have a baby, anyway. All your time was wrapped up in the restaurant, and then when I found out you were going to open a second one without even discussing it with me, it just seemed like we were going in two different directions."

His shoulders propped against the headboard, he had to admit she was right. "That was my fault. I should have told you. I was going to, but I knew you'd hate the idea, and I kept putting it off, hoping to find the perfect time. But it just never came up. You were always so touchy about the time I spent working—"

"Because you were spending seventy hours a week at the restaurant and I never saw you! I was afraid you were turning into my father right before my eyes, and I was turning into my mother. I could see myself raising our child alone while you made more and more money, and it scared me to death."

Still afraid of that, she said soberly, "I can count on the fingers of one hand the times my father did things with me and my mother when I was growing up. For most of my childhood, he was a stranger to me. I didn't—I *don't*—want that for our baby. So I left." She tried to smile, but could only manage a weak grimace of pain. "Looking back now, I can see it was a stupid thing to do, but I thought I could shake you up and make you realize that I was more important to you than your restaurant. But you worked harder than ever while I was gone. I checked."

He didn't deny it—he couldn't. It was true. He'd spent every waking moment at the restaurant during the two months she was gone. And there'd been a lot of nights he'd slept on his office couch rather than go home to an empty apartment, an empty bed.

"I couldn't face this apartment without you," he said bluntly. "So I buried myself in work. I had to or I would have come after you even though I promised to give you some space."

When she only looked at him, unconvinced, it was all he could do not to snatch her back into his arms. They'd always communicated better in bed than anywhere else, and all he had to do was hold her, kiss her, and they'd both forget that there'd ever been a cross word between them.

But making love wouldn't solve this problem. Their whole future lay in the balance, and unless he could find a way to convince her that he was nothing like her father, he was going to lose her. This time for good.

Taking her hand, he rubbed his thumb in slow circles across her knuckles. "I understand your fears, honey, but put yourself in my shoes for a minute. You know what my childhood was like. While your daddy was devoting all his time to working, mine couldn't keep a job. Half the time, birthdays and Christmas were just another day of the week. Oh, he always had an excuse, and according to him, it was never his fault. But it was, dammit!" he said resentfully. "He was just flat out irresponsible. I swore when I had a wife and kids, I would never do to them what my old man did to me and my mother. That's why I worked like a fiend. It was never just about making money. You wanted a baby and so did I, but it was important to me to make sure we were financially secure first. Anything else would have been unacceptable."

Her eyes, dark with despair, lifted to his. "But no one ever thinks they're really financially secure. Especially when they have children. You'll want to make sure you have enough put away to take care of me and the baby if something happens to you. Then if we have another baby, you'll need to put more away. Don't you see? It's a vicious circle that never ends. The next thing you know, our children will be grown and you won't even know them. Or me."

"You really think I would let that happen? Where was I when Sam thought you needed to get out of town for a while?"

"With me at the cabin, but—"

"That right," he cut in. "And we weren't just there a day or two, either. I was prepared to stay weeks, even months, if that's what it took to keep you safe. And then today, when the restaurant went up in flames, I didn't even think twice about it once Alice told me you were in trouble. Yes, the restaurant is important to me, but I *love* you. None of it means a damn without you."

He saw the doubt in her eyes, the desperate need to believe.

Aching to kiss her, to draw her into his arms and show her that the trials they had been through had only strengthened their love, he couldn't do anything but tighten his hold on her hand. If she didn't know in her heart that he was sincere, all the kisses in the world wouldn't do any good.

"If I learned anything over the last couple of months, honey, it's how precious our time is together," he said huskily. "We don't know when it's going to be snatched away from us, and I don't want to lose any more of it than we already have. If that means compromise, then I'm all for doing whatever's necessary. We'll work it out together. Because I want to be there to hold you when you're sick and rub your back when it hurts. Our baby's going to need a brother and a sister and a full-time daddy who's crazy about her mother. Nobody else can do that like I can. Give me a chance, sweetheart. Give *us* a chance."

Her blue eyes searching his earnest brown ones, Annie

didn't doubt that he meant every word. Deep inside, her heart expanded. God, she loved this man! More now than the day she'd married him. She'd known when she left him that she was gambling everything. A successful, married man, alone and lonely, was an easy mark for any number of unscrupulous women with dollar signs in their eyes. But he was and always had been a chance worth taking.

She could trust him, she realized as a slow smile broke out on her face. With her heart, with their baby, with a future that looked more beautiful with every passing second. Her eyes shining with love, she lifted an impish eyebrow at him. "A brother *and* a sister, hmm? Three kids? You think you're ready for that?"

His own grin wicked, he drawled, "Honey, as long as you're their mama, I'm ready when you are. So are you giving us a chance or what?"

Surprised that he even had to ask, she laughed happily and launched herself into his arms. "What do you think?"

Epilogue

Five and a half months later

Twins. They had twins.

Standing at the side of his daughters' crib on their first night home from the hospital, Joe gazed down at the impossibly small babies and couldn't seem to stop smiling. Lord, they were so tiny! And unbelievably beautiful. Just like their mother. And they were all his. He still couldn't believe it. How could he have known that this was what it was like to be a daddy?

Glancing toward the bed, his heart turned over at the sight of Annie sound asleep on his pillow. Her labor hadn't been easy, but she'd pulled through it without a word of complaint. He'd been so proud of her. She'd been in so much pain, but her only concern had been for the babies. And him. He'd been a basket case. Every time a pain had ripped through her, he was the one who'd winced. By the time he'd held his daughters for the first time, he knew why they called it labor. He'd felt like he'd been caught in the wringer of an old washing machine. Annie, on the other hand, had been as fresh as a daisy once the hard part was over with.

God, he loved her! He didn't know if he'd ever be able to show her how much. The last six months had been like something out of a dream, but if he was dreaming, he didn't want to ever wake up. While they'd waited for the birth of their babies, they'd made some drastic, but much needed, changes in their life. They'd opened the second Joe's Place as planned, then rebuilt the original, but only after some structural changes in the original design. It was larger now, and included not only a nursery, but a real estate office for Annie and Phoebe. He only had to walk across the non-smoking area to see his wife whenever he wanted. A man couldn't ask for much more than that.

Annie was on maternity leave right now, of course, but later, she intended to put in ten or so hours a week, just to keep her hand in things until the kids were older. When she did, Joe would keep the babies. He couldn't wait.

Providing financial security for Annie and their children would always be important to him, and doing so in a way that both he and Annie could live with had been his one big concern. But things had a way of working out in the most unexpected ways, and no one had been more surprised than he when Drake had approached him soon after the restaurant had burned about buying into the business. He'd already proven himself to be a great manager, but he wanted something more permanent than that, more lasting, something he could help build and have the satisfaction of knowing that at least a piece of it was his.

After discussing it with Annie, they'd agreed to sell Drake twenty percent, and that had turned out to be the smartest business move he and Annie had ever made. With the money that Drake brought into the business, they were able to set up trust funds for the kids that would be worth a fortune by the time they reached adulthood. A second manager had been hired, freeing Joe from the hands-on running of either restaurant, so he spent his days overseeing everything and his evenings and nights at home. Just that easily, he and Annie had everything they'd ever wanted.

Satisfied that his children were safe and sleeping soundly, he made his way across the room in the dark and carefully climbed into bed, trying not to wake Annie as he lifted her slightly and settled her against his chest. But the second he was horizontal and holding her close to his heart, she stirred against him and pressed a kiss to his chest. "Hi, daddy," she murmured teasingly. "How're the kids?"

"Sleeping like angels," he replied softly. "Which is what their mama should be doing."

"Later," she promised. "Right now, I'm too happy. How about you?"

"Oh, I'll sleep later, too. Right now, there's this beautiful woman in my arms who's keeping me awake."

Chuckling softly, she playfully punched him in the shoulder. "You know what I mean. Are you happy?"

The old Joe would have given her a quick, positive answer without thinking about it, but he was a far cry from the Joe Taylor who had once taken happiness and love for granted. He'd been blessed and he knew it. "I've got you and the kids and this funny feeling in my heart whenever I think about the three of you," he murmured, tightening his arms around her. "I walk around with a goofy smile on my face all the time and I can't seem to stop humming. If that's not happiness, then I don't know what it is."

Love flooded Annie's heart and brought the sting of tears to her eyes. Drawing back just far enough to see his beloved face, she gave him a watery smile. "Me, either, but I'm suffering from the same thing and it feels wonderful. Do you think it could possibly get any better than this?"

"I don't know," he said with a grin, tenderly wiping the tears from her cheeks. "But we've got the next forty or fifty years to find out. Ask me again, then."

"You can count on it," she promised, laughing, and kissed him like there was no tomorrow. They had decades ahead of them, where once she wouldn't have given them weeks. Just thinking about it made her light-headed with joy. How had she gotten so lucky?

* * * * *

Look for Linda Turner's The Enemy's Daughter *and* Nighthawk's Child *in March.*

Who's the Boss?

BARBARA BOSWELL

**SILHOUETTE®
DESIRE™**

One

Though he knew they were first cousins and shared the Brennan gene pool, Cade Austin had never seen such a dissimilar pair. From his vantage point at the end of the corridor, he watched Kylie Brennan and her younger cousin Bridget walking toward him. Conversation between the cousins appeared minimal and a bit strained.

He saw Kylie slant a covert glance at Bridget, and a slight smile tilted the corners of Cade's mouth. He was willing to bet his fifteen percent stock ownership in BrenCo that Kylie had never worn a tight, tiny, belly-button-exposing, black ribbed T-shirt, like the one Bridget was wearing now. Bridget had matched it with a brilliant lime-colored faux leather skirt that scarcely covered her behind, black stockings and little-girl style shoes with thick black straps and jarring lug soles. Bridget was one of BrenCo's receptionists, but rarely dressed like one. Cade had seen movie hookers whose outfits were more conservative than some of Bridget's.

Kylie's light gray suit, white silk blouse and traditional pumps looked professional and classy. *She* dressed like the attorney Cade knew she was.

However, as president, Cade enforced no company dress code, though he was somewhat relieved that the rest of the staff chose more traditional attire for the workplace. Employees could wear whatever they liked at BrenCo as long as they showed up on time and got the job done. Which Bridget did. She was both reliable and competent. The old "never judge a book by its cover" adage definitely applied to Bridget Brennan.

Cade reminded himself not to make that mistake with her cousin Kylie, either. She may or may not be what she seemed; he needed time for a thorough assessment.

His eyes focused more intently on her. The last time he'd seen Kylie Brennan had also been the first time, exactly fourteen months ago at her uncle Gene's funeral, right here in Port McClain, Ohio. She had flown in shortly before the service and been unable to stay for the post-funeral festivities. Her parents explained she was in the middle of a trial and had only that day off before court resumed.

The other Brennans hadn't been pleased by Kylie's abrupt arrival and departure. "She inherits controlling interest in the company from Gene and she can't even stick around long enough to eat some corned beef and cabbage at his wake?" complained Lauretta Brennan.

"Kylie must have been Uncle Gene's favorite, and I don't understand why." Ian Brennan sulked. "She didn't grow up in Port McClain, and she saw the old man only once a year at most."

"Ever hear the one about familiarity and contempt? Mystery solved, Ian," replied his cousin Bridget.

Ian had shot her a killing glance, the one he reserved for most of his relatives.

Cade smiled at the memory. Twenty-two-year-old Bridget often said what he was thinking himself but was too polite to share. At least *some* of the time he was too polite. Other times he, too, just said what he thought, a trait that hadn't endeared him to most Brennans.

He didn't care because he'd had the approval, confidence and full backing of the one Brennan who counted, Gene Brennan. Gene, the man who had hired him eight years ago and eventually made him president of BrenCo, who had given him the job opportunity of a lifetime and all the challenges and privileges that went with it.

Until fourteen months ago, he'd had only to answer to Gene Brennan, but the older man's sudden death had changed everything. Gene had left fifty-one percent of BrenCo stock—controlling interest—to his niece Kylie, the daughter of his favorite brother Wayne. Since Cade already owned fifteen percent due to the generous stock options afforded him as CEO of BrenCo, the remaining thirty-four percent of the company's stock had been equally divided between Gene's two younger brothers, Artie and Guy, lifelong residents of Port McClain. Gene's house and personal effects had been willed to brother Wayne, a retired navy captain.

The local Brennans—Artie and his ex-wife Bobbie and their kids Brenda, Brent and Bridget; Guy and his wife Lauretta and their kids Ian, Todd and Polly—hadn't been shy about vocalizing their displeasure with the terms of the will. It was one of the very few things they all agreed upon.

The out-of-town Brennans—Wayne, wife Connie, son Devlin and daughter Kylie—remained apart from the grousing and the grumbling, separated from the rest of the clan by more than mere geographical distance. Of course, one could argue that branch of the family had done very well by Gene Brennan's last will and testament. The other Brennans often argued that point.

For the past fourteen months, Cade had continued to run BrenCo as before, the only difference being the absence of Gene Brennan himself. Cade sometimes wondered if he were the only one to miss the man. Certainly, Gene's relatives here in Port McClain didn't even pretend to. As for his niece-heiress, financial statements were regularly sent to Kylie Brennan at her address in Philadelphia along with Cade's written offers to discuss company business with her at any time, but she'd displayed no interest in either his offer or the business.

Until two weeks ago. Two weeks ago, Cade had received a note from Kylie Brennan stating her intent to come to Port

McClain. She would be staying in her uncle Gene's house for the duration of her visit, but she hadn't specified why she was coming or how long she intended to stay. That bothered Cade. An open-ended visit? He didn't like the sound of it.

Even more ominous was Artie Brennan's phone call, announcing that he and Guy had already talked with Kylie about the possibility of selling the company. "Kylie is the majority stockholder and that makes her the boss, *your* boss, Cade." Artie had reminded him with gleeful malice. "If she votes to sell BrenCo, it gets sold."

His boss. Cade clenched his jaw as *his boss* approached him. She was twenty-seven years old and she was his boss! The situation was ridiculous, it was unthinkable, untenable. But true.

Gene, how could you do this to me? Cade's eyes flicked heavenward as he silently invoked his departed mentor. Of course, Gene's death at sixty-two had been completely unexpected. Given his parents' longevity—Ma and Pa Brennan had lived well into their eighties—Gene had probably intended to alter his will at some later date, after Cade had bought enough stock to own controlling interest in BrenCo as planned.

But time had run out and they were stuck with the one and only will he'd written, naming Kylie Marie Brennan his major heir. Making her Cade Austin's boss.

"Hey, Cade!" Bridget greeted the company president the same way she greeted her peers at Club Reek, her favorite night spot along the banks of McClain Creek.

"Hey, Bridget," he replied gamely. He saw the glimmer of humor in Kylie's eyes, saw the sudden smile cross her face. Cade inhaled sharply.

Kylie Brennan was blessed with natural beauty: high cheekbones, wide-set china blue eyes, and a heart-shaped face framed by her thick, dark slightly-below-the-chin-length bob. But that smile of hers transformed her classic good looks into something more compelling, more intriguing. She had a wide, generous mouth and a dimple on her left cheek, and when she smiled she appeared both sultry and sweet, wholesome yet enticingly sexy. All in all, a fascinating contrast that evoked an immediate and tangible response from Cade.

He felt the stirrings deep in his groin and was appalled. The woman was his boss! The last thing he—or BrenCo—needed was for him to be turned on by this alluring young woman who had the power to sell the company out from under him. Who could single-handedly wreck his future plans and take BrenCo from him with one crucial decision. Sell.

Damn, why did she have to be so attractive? He studied her soft full lips and imagined...

"So I guess you two know each other, huh?" Bridget's voice jerked him from the erotic fantasy he'd been drifting into.

Cade was grateful for the reality check. What was happening to him? He never daydreamed while he was working, not unless the subject had to do with environmental engineering, and then it was called brainstorming. Nor was he prone to sexual fantasizing in his spare time; he'd outgrown that puerile pastime long ago. Yet here he stood, conjuring up what was definitely a sexual fantasy. During office hours. Starring his could-be-trouble beautiful young boss! *Was he losing his mind?*

"Cade Austin," he said, briskly extending his hand to Kylie. Hopefully, his inner turmoil wasn't evident. "We haven't been formally introduced but I saw you at Gene's funeral."

"Kylie Brennan." She put her hand in Cade's and was immediately struck by the size of it. His fingers were long and strong and closed around hers. "I'm sorry I haven't kept in touch. I received all your company updates but I've been very busy..." Her voice trailed off.

It was a lame excuse and she knew it. Cade Austin was a busy man, but he had taken the time and effort to send those business communiqués to her. Reflexively, she lifted her eyes to his. Their gazes met and he raised his dark brows in a gesture she couldn't quite interpret. Was he merely acknowledging her explanation? Or silently berating or mocking her for it? She couldn't tell.

And then it occurred to her that he was still holding her hand, that their handshake had lasted longer than the conventional introductory shake, which elevated it to an altogether different realm. When she felt his thumb glide lazily over her knuckles, she felt a sharp thrust in her abdomen, stunning and swift, as if she'd been kicked. Except the sensations jolting through her were pleasurable not painful. Alarmingly pleasurable.

Kylie felt a hot flush of color spread upward, heating a path from her belly to her suddenly very pink cheeks. She quickly removed her hand from his.

What on earth was the matter with her? she wondered, a little frantically. She was twenty-seven years old, not a schoolgirl who hadn't yet tamed the swirling rush of hormones in her system. Yet she was reacting to Cade with a wild surge of awareness, appallingly similar to her teenage crushes on certain cute boys all those years ago.

There was nothing cute or boyish about Cade Austin, far from it. He was thirty-five years old and six feet four inches of solid masculinity, with a muscular frame and well-defined features. Kylie's gaze took in his strong jaw and square chin, the sharp blade of a nose and firm, hard mouth.

She was standing close enough to see that his eyes were hazel, flecked with green, and watched her with an alert, assessing intelligence. What if he knew the turmoil he was so effortlessly evoking within her? The possibility made her cringe.

Her mouth felt dry, and Kylie quickly flicked the tip of her tongue over her lips. She felt Cade's eyes follow the small movement. Kylie took a step backward, then another. Hopefully, putting some physical distance between them would enable her to put an end to her distraction and his domination.

And he was dominating her, with his greater height and strength and sheer virility. Kylie understood body language; she'd made good use of it in court but never before had she been so personally affected by it.

"What brings you to Port McClain at this particular time, Miss Brennan?" Cade asked, his tone impeccably polite.

And yet...Kylie swore she heard a mocking note in his tone, subtle enough to be indiscernible if one wasn't paying close attention. She met Cade's eyes again and set her mouth in a determined line. She always paid attention.

"I wanted to visit my relatives and to be brought up-to-date on BrenCo. This month seemed like the perfect time to come here to—"

"The perfect time to come here," Cade echoed. There was no mistaking the taunt in his tone this time. "Yeah, sure. March in Ohio is a veritable paradise, especially when a place is as close to Lake Erie as Port McClain. We've got the notorious lake-effect winds, temperature *and* record snowfalls. Port McClain, the perfect place, the perfect time. Wonder if the Chamber of Commerce could pitch the town as the newest winter vacation destination?"

"We get enough snow in Port McClain to be a ski resort," Bridget stated. "Except it's totally flat here. We don't even have a hill. But it would be cool to have a ski lodge anyway, wouldn't it, Cade?" She completely ignored Kylie.

"What's the point of a ski lodge without any skiing?" Cade was clearly not taken with Bridget's idea.

"It could be like a Club Reek with a fireplace," Bridget explained. "Sort of an antiski lodge."

"An antiski lodge, hmm?" Cade echoed, smiling.

Or was he grimacing? Kylie found it difficult to differentiate. "Let me rephrase from a perfect time to visit to a convenient time to visit," she suggested quickly, before Bridget went off on another tangent.

"And has your visit been convenient so far?" Cade asked.

He sounded so unctuously solicitous that Kylie guessed he was aware that so far her visit had been anything but convenient. "No," she admitted grimly. "No, it hasn't."

"You arrived in Port McClain last night, I believe? And planned to stay in Gene's house," Cade prompted.

"Uncle Gene's house is currently uninhabitable." Kylie was sure she wasn't telling him anything he didn't already know. "I'd written to both Uncle Guy and Uncle Artie two weeks ago and asked them to have the electricity, water, gas and phone service turned on in the house and to hire a cleaning service to prepare the place for occupancy."

"Let me guess, nothing had been done," Cade surmised. "Your first mistake was asking both Artie *and* Guy, and then letting them know you'd asked them both. You unwittingly set up a Brennan double play. Artie and Guy could each claim that he thought the other was taking care of the house, while each did nothing. Meanwhile, both your uncles could enjoy a hearty laugh imagining you showing up at Gene's place, which has been vacant since his funeral."

Kylie thought of her phone calls last night to her two uncles who had each claimed he thought the other was handling her requests. It had seemed a logical, albeit annoying, slipup. But to think it was premeditated, that they'd relished the idea of her standing in the creepily dark, cold, damp and musty old house...

"That's an awful thing to say," Kylie scolded, rejecting his premise.

She glanced at Bridget, expecting her to second the objection. After all, Cade had insulted her father and their mutual uncle Guy.

Bridget merely shrugged. "So where'd you stay last night? Not at Uncle Gene's Haunted Mansion, I'm sure."

"I stayed at the Port McClain Hotel."

Cade and Bridget looked at each other and laughed.

"That place has all the ambience of the House of Usher. And you must've been one of the few guests who rented a room for the night, instead of by the hour." Cade's eyes gleamed. "You'd have done better to stay at one of the motels off the interstate exit."

Kylie thought of the sounds she'd heard last night in the room above her, the steady traffic through the halls. Cade's remarks explained a lot. She shuddered. "When I talked to Aunt Lauretta last night and asked her where to stay, she said the Port McClain Hotel."

"Wow! She deliberately sent you there?" Bridget laughed harder. "Chalk one up for Aunt Lauretta."

"You should have contacted me about the house," said Cade. "I would've taken care of all the arrangements and the place would have been ready for you. I suggest that you rely upon me, not the Brennans, while you're here in Port McClain. Now, would you like me to have my secretary Donna make those calls to the utilities and a cleaning service for you?"

"I've already done all that from my hotel room this morning." Kylie was irked by his condescending, paternalistic attitude. Did he think she was incapable of making a few phone calls? "And

I intend to rely on myself while I'm here in Port McClain," she added coolly.

"Is it true you lost your job, Kylie?" Bridget suddenly interjected. "That's what my brother, Brent, heard from my dad who heard it from Uncle Guy. They all think you'll be glad to sell the company 'cause if you're out of work, you'll need money, right? That's what they're hoping for. *They* want to sell real bad and get big bucks for their shares. Aunt Lauretta and Ian are really pushing for it, too, and—"

"Bridget, this is company time and you're wasting it." Cade interrupted her, his tone stern, all signs of friendliness gone. "Get back to work right now."

Bridget smoothed her hands over her short, spiky black hair. "I didn't say anything that everybody doesn't already know," she said defensively. "Why would Kylie be here if she didn't want to—"

"Bridget, if you're not gone by the time I count to three, your pay will be docked, one hour for each number I reach." Cade's voice was calm but steely enough to send Bridget heading down the corridor before he even uttered "one."

Kylie shifted uncomfortably. "I've never found bullying to be an effective tactic to use in dealing with—"

"You've obviously never had to deal with your relatives. I've found it effective in dealing with some Brennans, at times the *only* effective method of dealing with them." He folded his arms in front of his chest and stared down at her.

It was as if he were looming over her, a most unfamiliar sensation. Kylie felt her stomach tighten. At five foot eight, she wasn't used to feeling small and powerless in a man's presence, but Cade Austin's big muscular frame seemed to dwarf her. It was a disconcerting sensation. No wonder Bridget had taken off. At a petite five-two, she was like a mouse facing a lion.

Cade's face was hard and still, and his hazel eyes watched Kylie with the same concentration said lion might focus on his intended prey. She swallowed and willed herself to maintain her composure. She was no scurrying little mouse.

"I know what you're doing and it's not going to work," she said, summoning up the necessary bravado. A useful trick of the legal trade. How many times had she faked a bold confidence she was far from feeling in the courtroom?

"What am I trying to do, Kylie?"

It didn't escape her notice that he'd used her first name for the first time. Big deal. Everybody called everybody by their first names these days; formality had gone the way of the TV antenna. So why did Cade's use of her given name seem to create an aura of intimacy between them?

"You're trying to physically intimidate me, Cade." She used *his* first name in an attempt to counter his effect on her. To turn the disturbing intimacy into everyday, meaningless informality.

"If that's what you think, I apologize. Physical intimidation isn't my style." Even as he spoke the words, his fingers closed around her upper arm. "Come into my office. We have a lot to discuss."

"May I suggest making your invitations sound less like orders?"

A grin slashed his face. "Now why would I want to do that? There are times when one must be persuasive, Kylie." He led her into his office, his fingers still encircling her arm.

"I believe you mean coercive. And I don't appreciate it. Cade."

She was excruciatingly aware of his hand on her arm, of his nearness as he walked closely alongside her. If he wasn't physically intimidating, he was certainly physical, and she was reacting to him with a primal feminine awareness.

Inside his office, Cade dropped his hand and closed the door. "Is it true you lost your job?" he asked, as frankly as Bridget had blurted it out.

Kylie winced. "Unfortunately, yes. There were budget cuts—" She paused to see his dark brows arch, his glance unmistakably skeptical.

"It's true!" she exclaimed, stung. "What did you think, that I'd been fired for—"

"Incompetence? Such a possibility never crossed my mind."

Right words, wrong tone. He was deliberately baiting her. Kylie resolved not to rise to it. "I don't know what, if anything, you knew about my job. But I was with the Public Defender's office in Philadelphia. The new governor made big cuts in the state budget and left the counties to decide where and how to downsize services."

"I'm going to take a wild guess that your department was downsized and your job along with it?"

Kylie nodded glumly. "The Philadelphia Public Defender's office staff was one of the agencies to feel the budget ax. They cut nine full-time investigators and twelve attorneys, on the basis of seniority. I was one of the newest hires, I'd been working there since I graduated from law school two years ago."

She gazed out the window. Cade's big corner office had a spectacular view of Lake Erie, which lay in the distance. The rippling waters almost seemed to blend into the cloudy gray skyline. "I don't know how the people left in the PD's office will ever get the job done now. Even at full staff, we were shorthanded and had too many cases. Our clients will have to bear the brunt of—"

"I'd better warn you that I'm not a bleeding heart who cries over the rights of all those unfortunate, misunderstood criminals. My sympathies lie with the victims of crimes who are usually forgotten while the legal eagles enjoy their competitive courtroom jousts."

Kylie stifled a groan. She'd heard that rhetoric before, too many times to count. She'd given up trying to defend herself against those who had no use for defense attorneys, especially ones paid for by state tax dollars. She stood silently, staring at the lake.

"Don't I even rate a rebuttal?" Cade was unaccustomed to the silent treatment. He stared at her profile, his eyes lingering on the porcelain texture of her skin, the graceful curve of her neck. He couldn't keep his eyes off her, he acknowledged resentfully, while she couldn't seem to tear her eyes away from Lake Erie.

She appeared so aloof and unreachable, very much in control. He felt an inexplicable urge to shatter her poise. To get under her skin, the way she'd so effortlessly gotten under his.

"I'm waiting for your righteous 'even-the-most-heinous-criminal-has the-right-to-a-lawyer-who'll-try-to-get-him-off' spiel." His tone and stance were as challenging as an opposing counsel's. "So what if a homicidal psychopath walks on a technicality? It's all in a day's work, and then you lawyers go off and have a drink together afterward."

But he didn't succeed in putting even a minor dent in Kylie's composure.

"It's not like your views toward defense lawyers are unique, you know," she said dryly. "Even my parents and my brother hated that I wasn't on the prosecution team. You haven't said anything I haven't already heard a few thousand times."

"I think you just called me a repetitive, predictable bore. Ouch."

Now what? For the first time in his memory, Cade wasn't certain what to say or do next. He was floundering and unfocused, just like this meeting. An unheard of lapse in the professional history of Cade Austin. If only she weren't so attractive, if only she were less verbally adept. If only...

Stalling for time, Cade pressed a button on the intercom. "Donna, bring Miss Brennan and me some coffee," he ordered. Donna's coffee was strong enough to power a space shuttle. Hopefully, a dose of it would jolt him out of this uncharacteristic mental morass.

A few moments later Donna entered, carrying a tray with a coffeepot, two cups and containers of cream and sugar. She placed the tray on the wide square table that stood between a charcoal gray leather sofa and two matching armchairs.

"Can I get you anything else?" Donna hovered, solicitous.

"This is fine." Cade motioned her away, and Donna obediently headed for the door.

"Thank you very much, Donna," Kylie said, smiling warmly. She did not approve of Cade's cavalier manner toward his secretary and hoped that she sounded gracious enough to make up for it. He'd ordered Donna around and hadn't even asked or thanked her properly for the favor she'd done for them!

Cade sat down on the sofa with his coffee. Across the office, Kylie stood stiffly beside his desk, making no move to join him.

He sighed. It was obvious she was displeased. Well, that was par for the course. Brennans were invariably ticked off about something. There was nothing too trivial to escape their wrath. Gene excepted, of course.

"I know you're upset about something." He'd decided long ago that the best way to deal with the ever-edgy clan was to be up-front with them. Kylie was one of them; he better follow his usual procedure. "Are you offended by my opinion of the criminal justice system?"

"Hardly. You're certainly entitled to your own opinion."

"I agree. But if that isn't it, what is? I'm not a mind reader so unless you tell me what's wrong, we're at a standstill."

"I'll be happy to tell you." Kylie's eyes flashed. "It bothers me the way you autocratically make assumptions and then imperiously act on them. For instance, you didn't ask me if I wanted coffee, you simply demanded that Donna bring it. And when she did, you never even thanked her, you simply flicked her off like she was a—a gnat."

"I did no such thing!" Cade jumped to his feet, indignant. The hot coffee spilled over the sides of the cup onto his fingers. He muttered a curse under his breath.

"Are you all right? Did you burn yourself?"

"I'm fine!" His fingers felt as if they were on fire as he set the cup on the table, though he would've rather faced amputation than to admit pain to *her!* "As for your accusation, it's ridiculous and unfair. I treat Donna and everyone else at the company with respect."

"Of course, you're denying your dictatorial behavior because it is so ingrained that you aren't even aware of how you're perceived."

"Donna has worked for me for the past six years and I can assure you that she does *not* perceive me as brushing her off like a gnat!"

"Maybe not." Kylie shrugged. "Because she's grown accustomed to such treatment. Just as my cousin Bridget accepted your threat to dock her pay if she didn't instantly obey your command. It's obvious to me that your management style is of the 'when you say jump, the employees must reply how high' school."

"My management style is what made this company the success it is today, *Miss Brennan*. BrenCo is thriving. We're not only prosperous, we're the biggest employer in this town. Your uncle certainly had no complaints when I refocused and expanded BrenCo from a small household waste disposal firm to a regional environmental cleanup leader in its field. This past year has been BrenCo's most lucrative yet, and within the next five to ten years we'll—"

He abruptly broke off. "Damn, I see where you're headed. Typical attorney trick, create a smoke screen to obscure the facts. You're complaining about Donna when what you're really trying to do is to set up a—"

"Let me set the record straight. I was not using a smoke screen to obscure any facts, *Mr. Austin*. I was criticizing your management style and being quite forthright about it."

"Don't bother to equivocate. I read your agenda loud and clear, lady. You're in cahoots with your uncles to sell BrenCo," Cade said harshly. "You know that Gene's will set up provisions for BrenCo's management to remain the same until one year after his death. Now the time is up. And here you are."

Kylie guessed that health workers learning the Ebola virus was in their midst looked a lot like Cade Austin did at this moment, faced with her presence. And he seemed to be waiting for her to say something.

"Here I am," she agreed, noncommittally.

Her simple statement seemed to further infuriate him. "That this year happened to be the most productive one in the company's history has only whetted your family's urge to sell." Cade glared at her accusingly. "They have delusions of striking it rich when in reality selling the company is akin to killing the goose who laid the golden eggs. Not that I expect the Brennans to grasp the implications of something as intricate as an allegory."

"I'm a Brennan and I have no trouble understanding allegories," Kylie countered.

Cade might know her relatives better than she, but they were *her* relatives and she was getting a little tired of listening to him take verbal swipes at them. "And I'm not in cahoots with anybody. I don't have a hidden agenda. Are you one of those paranoid types who sees a conspiracy lurking behind every remark and every action? Your motto is Trust No One?"

"If I have a motto, it would be Trust No Brennan." Cade glowered at her. "Gene excepted, of course."

"Of course." Kylie was exasperated. "Sounds like you and Uncle Gene had yourselves a merry old time, sitting around trashing the rest of the Brennans. You delighted in taking offense at perceived slights and misinterpreting everything that was said and done. Yes, I'm beginning to get a very clear picture of things now."

"Oh, are you?"

She nodded. "Look at the way you misinterpreted this coffee incident. How you overreacted. I prefer tea, but you never bothered to ask, you ordered coffee for me and expected me to drink it. Naturally, I was annoyed by such high-handedness. Furthermore, I'm not used to being waited on. In the PD's office, everybody served themselves. But did you give me a chance to explain anything? No! You instantly assumed that I'm a conniving, greedy witch looking for a reason to fire you and sell this company. Didn't you?"

She advanced toward him in full cross-examination mode, her gaze piercing and intense. "Didn't you?" The sound of her own voice startled her. She'd used this tone in challenging murder suspects. It occurred to her that perhaps she was also overreacting.

"You drink tea." Cade stared at her. "You're in a snit because I didn't offer you a choice between coffee or tea?" His tone was as incredulous as his expression. "No doubt about it, you've taken the Brennan family irritability to new heights."

"I'm not in a snit. I'm trying to make a point that you don't seem to be getting. Whether it's intentional or not, I'm not quite sure. Is it?"

"Is it what? Is what it?" Cade ran his hand through his hair, tousling it. His head was spinning. "This is crazy." Or maybe he was headed that way.

He felt frazzled, completely befuddled. The Brennans had always driven Gene nuts. His late boss had long ago delegated dealing with them to Cade, who merely found them annoying, not insanity-inducing. But *this* Brennan...Kylie Brennan...

The two of them were practically standing toe-to-toe. Her aggressive advance had fallen into the category of physical intimidation—which she'd accused him of using!—and brought them very close. Not that Cade was feeling the least bit intimidated. He was feeling...aroused.

Everytime he inhaled, the scent of her perfume filled his nostrils. It was a subtle, spicy, sexy aroma, just like her, and it further clouded his thoughts. The urge to touch her was so overpowering that he would've given in to it had he not beaten a purposeful retreat to the window. A tactical victory for her, but at this point he was too disconcerted to care.

"I can't stress how strongly I disapprove of you treating Donna like a servant," Kylie scolded his back, which he'd turned toward her. "It's pure classism. I am also opposed to sexism, racism and ageism," she felt compelled to add, just for the record.

"Well, so am I!" Cade exclaimed. She was the defense attorney, but she had him on the defensive for sure. "BrenCo is an equal opportunity employer. We've won citations for our fair hiring practices."

"I'm very glad to hear that." Kylie was genuinely relieved. "It would be awkward to have to report BrenCo to the EEOC, although I wouldn't hesitate to do so if the situation warranted."

Cade turned to gape at her. "How did we get from you preferring tea to the EEOC?"

"Actually, I'm not sure." Kylie's blue eyes were troubled. She'd always prided herself on her talent for presenting her points in a coherent and lucid form in the courtroom. "My clients would've been toast if I made the sort of irrational leaps I seem to be making today. You—confuse me," she admitted, averting her gaze from him to Lake Erie on the horizon.

"Glad to hear it. The feeling happens to be mutual." Cade began to pace the office, back and forth, on edge and ready for action.

Kylie remembered a *National Geographic* special on TV featuring a leopard pacing his territory in a remarkably similar prowl. Keeping in mind the unlucky mammal who'd wandered into the leopard's line of vision, she took a few prudent steps out of Cade's path, just to be on the safe side.

"You confound me in a way I never thought a Brennan could," he growled. "Or anybody else, for that matter." The admission did not please him.

They stared uneasily at each other for a few long moments.

"We've gotten off to a bad start." Kylie was the first to speak.

"A perceptive observation," muttered Cade. He grabbed his coffee and took a large gulp. And nearly choked. The brew was so ghastly it made airline coffee taste like a gourmet specialty brand.

Kylie was watching him. "I think I'll definitely stick to tea," she murmured.

Their eyes met. Kylie caught her lower lip between her teeth in a nervous gesture she rarely resorted to anymore. But Cade Austin made her nervous, and in a way that was exciting, not threatening. Which made him all the more dangerous.

She drew a sharp breath. "Do you think we could start over?"

"We can do whatever you want, Kylie."

His sudden suggestive smile made her heart jump. She knew instinctively that he was quite aware of his own masculine appeal and wielded it when necessary. He'd decided to use it now, as an alternative maneuver.

Kylie realized just how susceptible she could be when he chose to disarm her with his charm. "I'm speaking professionally," she said quickly. "As a public defender, I'm accustomed to seeking common ground in my clients' best interests and in this case—"

"You're not a public defender anymore, Kylie. Thanks to the terms of Gene's will, you're a businesswoman and an important figure in this community. I don't know if you're fully aware of how dependent Port McClain is on BrenCo or the economic impact the company has on this town."

"You mean like in 'if BrenCo sneezes, Port McClain catches a cold'?" She paraphrased the old General Motors maxim.

His smile widened, and this time it was reflected in his eyes. "Exactly like that."

Kylie reminded herself to breathe. Maybe starting over on friendly terms wasn't such a good idea, after all. It was easier to keep her composure and her imagination in check if she was feeling hostile toward him. When he smiled at her in that particular way, she could feel herself melting inside. She wanted to please him, to do whatever it took to keep him smiling...A dangerous notion, indeed.

Get a grip, Kylie, she ordered herself. She was not here to please Cade Austin, and she was on a lot safer ground when he was scowling at her.

"I know it's my responsibility to learn everything about the company and its impact on the town. I was stunned when I heard that Uncle Gene had left controlling interest in BrenCo to me. No more than you were, probably," she added with a wry grimace.

"The contents of Gene's will turned out to be a surprise to a lot of people."

"The understatement of the year, no doubt. Well, I don't want to sound ungrateful, but owning any part of a toxic waste plant wasn't exactly my idea of a dream come true."

"BrenCo isn't simply a toxic waste plant, Kylie. We take environmental waste from all over the state—and other states, too—and properly dispose of it in a way that is not only safe but beneficial to the environment." Cade's hazel eyes gleamed. "I expect all your liberal cohorts in the Public Defender's office would deny such technology even exists. That crowd believes *no* waste is the only safe waste, a ridiculous, hopeless point of view. Even the fires of our cave ancestors released waste products into the air."

"I know. I—haven't mentioned my inheritance to anyone," she confessed, a little sheepishly.

"Afraid of being dubbed the Princess of Toxic Waste by all your green friends?"

Kylie tilted her head and gazed at him from under her lashes, the feminine signals elemental and unconscious. "Why do you assume that my cohorts and friends are all wild-eyed liberals?"

"It's a natural assumption. If there is such a thing as a conservative public defender, I'd bet my shares in BrenCo that he has a multiple personality disorder with each alter unaware of what the others are doing. You can imagine the mayhem that will ensue when the conflicting personalities finally collide in the poor sap's conscious mind."

Kylie laughed. "You surprise me," she admitted. "I wouldn't have thought you were capable of appreciating the absurd."

"I wouldn't have lasted eight minutes, let alone eight years, in this town filled with Brennans if I didn't have a healthy appreciation of the absurd."

"Brennans. You talk about them as if they're a separate species."

"Now you're catching on. Brennans fall somewhere between vampires and parasites, though precise classification has yet to be established."

He was kidding, displaying an even greater, healthier appreciation of the absurd. Wasn't he? "Gene excepted, of course," she interjected his usual disclaimer.

"Gene excepted, of course. And according to Gene, your dad would have to be excepted, too. Gene admired your father, he was very proud of him. He often boasted about his brother Wayne, the navy captain who commanded a battleship and lived all over the world. He was a fan of your big brother, too. Gene always referred to him as 'my-favorite-nephew-Devlin-the-doctor.'"

"Devlin is finishing his orthopedic surgical residency at the University of Michigan Medical Center in Ann Arbor," Kylie lapsed naturally into her role of proud sister and daughter. "Dad is retired now. He and Mom are living in Florida and still aren't sure how they'll adjust to staying in the same place for more than a few years."

"If they're like my folks, who are retired army, they'll end up buying an RV and trolling the interstates on endless trips. Occasionally, they swing by Port McClain to see me."

"In March, no doubt. After all, it's the perfect time to visit here. The lake-effect wind and all that snow are big draws."

"Touché." Cade raised his brows again in that particular way of his.

Kylie raised her eyebrows right back. "Maybe Bridget's antiski lodge will be packing in crowds on their next visit."

"You're really on a roll here, aren't you?" Cade's voice was deceptively mild as he studied her.

She was flirting with him. Or was she? Given their volatile interaction since she'd set foot in his office, there was always the chance she was expressing her antipathy to him. What a blunder it would be to mistake aversion for flirtation!

But Cade was a risk-taker by nature. He took one now and moved closer to her. Close enough to cup her chin in one hand and tilt her head a little.

Kylie felt the world careen. He was going to kiss her; she could read the hot sensual intent in his eyes. And she was going to let him. She wanted him to kiss her, she wanted it very much.

The realization stunned her. This kind of behavior was completely unlike her. She'd never been driven by sexual urges. She was too cerebral, governed by her head, not her body's impulses.

Yet here she was, melting against Cade Austin as he pulled her into his arms. Closing her eyes as his mouth lowered to hers. Parting her lips for the breathlessly anticipated impact of his...

Two

"Cade, I'm sorry to interrupt but Bobbie Brennan is on the phone," Donna's voice, loud and clear, sounded over the intercom.

Startled, Kylie and Cade jumped away from each other as if they'd been blasted apart by a bomb.

Kylie's heartbeat thundered in her ears. She'd come so close to kissing Cade Austin that she had felt the warmth of his breath on her face. She'd been in his arms, his body pressing into hers, the formidable length of him, hard and strong, revealing the force of his own desire. The intimate recall made her shake. Heat scorched her from the top of her head to the tips of her toes.

From the corner of her eye, she saw Cade sink into his desk chair. She walked unsteadily to the window and touched her forehead to the cool glass.

"Bobbie says it's an emergency and she must speak to you immediately," Donna stated.

"An emergency?" Kylie snapped to attention. She turned around, her eyes widened with alarm.

"Don't worry, it's probably nothing serious. Everything is an emergency to Bobbie." Cade heaved a groan. "The cornerstones of her personality are hysterics and vengeance, and one fuels the other."

"I told Bobbie you were in an important conference and couldn't be interrupted but needless to say, she refuses to take 'no' for an answer," Donna continued. "She threatened to come down and break into your office with a hatchet if she had to. I decided we'd better not risk it."

"We've learned the hard way that ignoring Bobbie is not the way to go," Cade said tightly.

"Do you really think Aunt Bobbie would hatchet her way into your office?" Kylie was incredulous.

"There is already a long list of outrageous things Bobbie has done, when thwarted. Taking a hatchet to my office door would not be a stretch for her."

"Get ready, Cade," Donna warned. She sounded like a pilot announcing an emergency landing. "I'm putting her call through on speaker phone right now."

"Cade!" Bobbie Brennan's shriek filled the office.

Nails on a chalkboard sounded euphonious in comparison. Kylie flinched.

"Brent is in jail!" Bobbie screamed. "They set bail at twenty-five thousand dollars! A fortune!"

"Remember that you pay a bail bondsman ten percent which is twenty-five hundred dollars, Bobbie," Cade reminded her.

"I don't have that kind of money for a bail bondsman. It may as well be twenty-five million! What are we going to do, Cade? Oh, this couldn't have come at a worse time! I'm all out of patience with Brent, this time he's gone too far!" Bobbie's tone grew even more vitriolic. "It's all Artie's fault, damn him! He's a terrible father, he's the cause of all Brent's problems."

"Tell me why Brent is in jail, Bobbie. What are the charges against him?" Cade had to ask three times before she stopped yelling long enough to hear him

"I wrote down what the cop said, but I'm crying too hard to read my writing." Bobbie sobbed noisily.

"Shall I call Artie and ask him?" Cade asked.

"No! That loser is the reason Brent is in jail." Bobbie's sobs instantly ceased. "Brent has been charged with second degree burglary. You see, Artie rented out the basement of his house to this nasty young couple—I *told* him not to do it!—and Brent put a video camera behind a two-way mirror with a hole in it so he could tape that couple in their bedroom."

"Tape them without their consent?" interrupted Cade.

"So they say." Bobbie gave a very audible sniff. "They claimed they noticed a light in the mirror and investigated it and found the hidden camera, then called the police."

"Did Brent say why he was taping this couple?" Cade asked, grimacing.

"He—Brent—said he was going to turn the tape into a movie." Bobbie's voice grew lower. "You know, like one of those art films."

"An art film," Cade echoed flatly. "Just a minute, Bobbie." He switched off the phone. "Well, this is a new one. Brent, with art film aspirations."

"More than likely, he planned to sell the tapes to one of those places that pays for privately made porn videos," Kylie murmured. "In Philadelphia, a copy could go for as high as five hundred dollars."

"Does Bobbie have her facts straight? Granted, what Brent did is sleazy and illegal but is it really *burglary?*"

"It sure is." Kylie nodded her assent. "We've tried similar cases. Second-degree burglary covers unauthorized filming of individuals."

"That sleazy little jerk has outdone himself this time." Cade's expression was equal parts disgust and impatience. He switched Bobbie back on. "Have you called an attorney for Brent, Bobbie?"

"Of course not!" she howled. "I called *you!* We have to get Brent out of jail right away, Cade. You know what can happen to a good-looking boy like him in a place like that!"

"You've seen too many prison movies, Bobbie. Nothing is going to happen to Brent in the Port McClain lockup." Cade's tone was both firm and reassuring. "Besides, he's spent time there before. Remember the last time he was arrested? We decided that sitting in that cell would be a good lesson for him. He spent a week there and it didn't hurt him a bit. In fact, he's stayed out of trouble until now, nearly two years later, and that's a record for him.''

"I hoped he was finally growing up. I was going to ask you to give him another chance at BrenCo." Bobbie began weeping again.

"Bobbie, you know what Gene said. No more chances for Brent at BrenCo. It was even written in his will. I won't hire Brent for a job here, no matter what," Cade added with absolute finality.

"Maybe you would if Brent got himself together," countered Bobbie, ignoring Cade's absolute finality. "Damn Artie! He had to go and rent out the basement! You can be sure we didn't see a dime of that couple's rent money, Artie kept it all for himself. Cade, I can't afford to bail out Brent and I don't know if Artie will do it or not."

"Then Brent can stay in jail till his hearing, Bobbie. He's not a child, and he shouldn't expect his parents to bail him out—literally—every time he gets into trouble." Cade caught Kylie's eye. She nodded her agreement.

"Whose side are you on?" Bobbie swung from sorrow to rage. "Artie's? He doesn't care if Brent rots in jail, either!" In the next breath, her tone turned whiney. "Did you remember that Brenda and I have to take Starr Lynn to the regional novice competition in Detroit next week? We'll have expenses—food and gas and the motel. And Starr Lynn needs an extra special skating costume. We found one that is absolutely perfect for her. It costs six hundred fifty dollars, plus tax."

"Six hundred fifty dollars for an ice-skating costume for a twelve-year-old is ridiculous, Bobbie," Cade said calmly.

"It's not unreasonable, some of the girls have costumes that cost nine hundred fifty. Are you going to help us or not, Cade?" demanded Bobbie. "I can always send Brenda over to your place tonight to—"

"No, not Brenda!" Cade said so fervently that Kylie was instantly on alert. She studied him even more closely. "Look, Bobbie, let me make a few phone calls about Brent. Meanwhile, promise me you'll at least look for another costume for Starr Lynn. You have a week till the competition."

"We'll look, but I doubt that we'll find anything else so perfect for Starr Lynn. And she deserves the best, Cade. Even *you* know that. Call me tonight about Brent." Bobbie hung up abruptly and with such force that the sound of the receiver slamming echoed throughout the office.

"Good Lord!" breathed Kylie.

"Don't drag Him into it," Cade said dryly. "Well, Ms. Public Defender, feel like taking your cousin's case?"

"I'm not a member of the Ohio Bar. I can't practice law in this state unless I'm granted reciprocity."

"Which you haven't even applied for?" guessed Cade. "Smart move on your part. Defending your cousin Brent would be as thankless a job as your last one."

Kylie ignored the dig. "Why did Aunt Bobbie dump Brent's arrest on you?" she asked curiously. "What are you supposed to do about it? And what's all this about a six-hundred-dollar skating costume?"

"Six-fifty, plus tax." Cade rubbed the back of his neck, then heaved a resigned sigh. "Even though you aren't licensed to practice here, you fire questions like a professional inquisitor."

"Maybe you wouldn't mind answering them?" she prompted.

"Let me tell you a little about the Brennans of Port McClain, Kylie. At any given time, one of them is either feuding with another or feels miffed or snubbed or cheated in some way. They've made a life-style of backstabbing and bickering."

"And being thrown in jail?"

"So far, jail has been the sole province of your cousin Brent, a fact for which we can all be grateful. The reason I'm so knowledgeable about the Brennans and why my number is programmed into Bobbie's phone is because your uncle Gene annointed me Alpha Male of the clan. Gene's brothers and their wives and kids were always trying to drag him into their civil wars, and it bothered him so much that he delegated his patriarch position to me. Gene was very good at delegating," he added wryly.

"So you not only run BrenCo, you also mediate family feuds?"

"I've had far more success managing the company than I've had trying to keep peace among the Brennans. Reaching a consensus among that group is harder than getting a unanimous vote in the UN General Assembly."

"I know that Uncle Artie and Aunt Bobbie's divorce was very bitter," Kylie murmured. "That's really all I know about it."

The Brennan extended family had played only a minor role in the lives of her very mobile, very nuclear family—which made it both strange *and* awkward that she was now involved via Uncle Gene's will.

"Wish I could say the same," growled Cade. "Well, let me bring you up to date. Artie and Bobbie have been divorced fifteen—or is it sixteen?—years but are still deeply entrenched in each other's lives. They are one of those tiresome couples who are eternally obsessed with each other."

"Obsessed with making each other miserable?"

Cade nodded. "They're masters of the art. I suppose you could say that Brent's problems are the result of his dysfunctional family but he's no longer a troubled teen, he's twenty-seven years old. I consider him to be fully responsible for his own actions."

"I agree," said Kylie.

He looked surprised. "I thought a bleeding heart type like you would drag out the crying towel and use Brent's unhappy childhood and his battling parents to excuse him."

"Maybe I would, if I were defending him in court. But since I'm not..." Kylie's voice trailed off, leaving the obvious unsaid. "I haven't seen Brent in years. But I do have an indelible memory of him from when we were kids. He lured me into the attic of Uncle Gene's house by telling me that our grandmother had a trunk filled with dolls there. When I looked into the trunk, he shoved me in and locked it. I don't think he had any intention of ever letting me out."

"Ah, Brennan family fun." Cade smiled sardonically. "See what you missed by not growing up here in Port McClain with the rest of the tribe? How did you get out of the trunk, by the way?"

"Lucky for me, my brother noticed I wasn't around and figured that Brent had something to do with it. Devlin *persuaded* Brent to admit it and lead him to me."

"Dare I ask how Devlin persuaded Brent?"

"He, uh, punched Brent in the nose," Kylie confessed sheepishly. "And broke it."

"Ah, bullying. As I mentioned earlier, it works well with certain Brennans. And I like the irony of Devlin's progression from breaking bones to setting bones as his life's work. That little bit of family history does explain why both Artie and Bobbie refer to your brother as 'that thug.' It's one of the few things they agree on."

"My mom and dad refer to Brent as 'that monster.' After the trunk incident, whenever we came to visit in Port McClain our parents kept Dev and me away from Brent. And after Uncle Artie and Aunt Bobbie's divorce, we didn't see much of Brenda or Bridget, either."

"What about your other cousins, Guy and Lauretta's kids? Did you spend much time with them?"

"No. Todd and Polly were a lot younger than Dev and me. And Ian—"

"Was an obnoxious creep?" suggested Cade. "He still is. Surprisingly enough, Todd and Polly are okay. Even likable, a fact that continually takes me by surprise."

"Maybe they were somehow switched at birth?" Kylie suggested drolly.

"Maybe they were." Cade grinned, then grew serious once again. "Your cousin Todd is in his junior year at Ohio State, majoring in business and Polly will graduate from Port McClain High in June. She has a scholarship to OSU and wants to study engineering. Both kids want to work for BrenCo someday and I think they'll be assets to the company. BrenCo should be here for them to return to, Kylie. It is Gene's legacy to his family and to this town," he added, willing her to meet his gaze.

Kylie averted her eyes from the pull of his. She'd been warned by her uncles that Cade would apply strong pressure to sway her to his point of view—which was to keep BrenCo a privately held company with him at the head. Asking her to consider the future of the younger Brennans seemed to be yet another strategy.

She couldn't immediately choose sides, Kylie reminded herself. She had to be like a judge and listen to all the arguments, to weigh all the evidence and information before rendering a decision. Keep the company in its current state or sell it to one of the giant firms that would merge BrenCo into their conglomerate? Her uncles, aided by cousin Ian, had invited an industry agent to town to explain the advantages of a sale and merger. She had to hear him out. Her decision was too vital to be rushed.

"Tell me why Aunt Bobbie wants to buy Starr Lynn a six-hundred-fifty-dollar ice-skating costume," she asked lightly, in a deliberate change of subject. "Plus tax."

She could tell by Cade's expression that he wasn't pleased with her blatant stall. She watched him assessing her—perhaps debating what tactic to take with this latest backstabbing, bickering Brennan who'd been inflicted upon him? Bullying, maybe? Kylie braced herself, prepared to fight back.

Instead, Cade returned to the coffee table and this time drained his cup of the dark murky brew.

"Your cousin Brenda's daughter Starr Lynn wants to be a figure skater. I guess you could say she already is one. She's been taking ice-skating lessons since she was four. The kid is definitely talented. She's won a number of novice competitions—that is the level just below the juniors which is just below the seniors—and she's being considered for admission to one of the top programs in the country at the Winterhurst Ice Rink in Lakewood. Bobbie and Brenda see Olympic gold in her future, and given Starr Lynn's talent and drive, it's not a totally unwarranted dream."

"You sound vaguely fond of Starr Lynn." Kylie settled into the charcoal gray leather chair across from Cade's, her thoughts centering on Starr Lynn Brennan, aged twelve.

She hadn't seen Brenda's child in years, though she remembered when Starr Lynn had been born. Vividly. Brenda, seventeen at the time, hadn't been married and it had been something of a family scandal, even for the Wayne Brennans living on a naval base in Europe, far from Port McClain.

"Starr Lynn *is* amazing out there on the ice." Cade's voice tore Kylie from her reverie. "She works so hard, getting up at dawn to practice, going to school and then putting in more hours of practice. Then there's her skating and dancing lessons and all the competitions. The kid is a real trouper,'' he added gruffly.

"You *are* fond of her!" Kylie marveled. Her eyes narrowed a bit. "What about her mother? I haven't seen much of Brenda in the past several years but she's always been pretty...and sexy."

She was horrified by the acerbic note that had slipped into her voice and hoped that Cade wouldn't notice.

A vain hope. He smiled, a smug cat-who'd-chowed-down-the-canary grin. "Brenda is still pretty and still sexy in that flashy bad girl way of hers." He leaned back in his chair and met Kylie's eyes. "Every now and then, Brenda decides that I would be a good match for her. I have never agreed. You can believe it when I say that Brenda Brennan holds all the appeal of a rattlesnake for me. Make that a rattlesnake about to strike and me without an antivenom kit."

"So that's why you panicked when Aunt Bobbie suggested sending Brenda over to your place tonight?"

"I did not panic!"

"Yes, you did." Kylie was aware that she was entirely too elated by his rejection of her cousin Brenda.

The feeling disconcerted her. How petty, how unlike her. She was not jealous of Brenda! Yet she couldn't deny the relief—the thrill?—of listening to Cade compare her cousin to a rattlesnake. Did she possess some long dormant Brennan vs. Brennan tendencies, which suddenly had been activated?

Cade Austin would undoubtedly think so. She saw the way he was watching her and blushed. Suddenly, an escape from his probing hazel eyes was essential.

"I've taken up enough of your time." Kylie jumped to her feet and headed toward the door. "I should have called first and made an appointment. I—I'm sure you have things to do and I'm keeping you from them."

"As president of BrenCo, I always have things to do." Cade followed her to the door, then moved in front of it. "But I always have time for our major stockholder, of course. You don't need to make an appointment, you have a standing one with me, Kylie. Whenever you want it."

His back was against the door, blocking it. "Would you like a tour of the plant? Perhaps an overview of company policy? A look at our financial records and written long-range goals?" While his words were strictly business, his tone and his expression conveyed an entirely different message.

Kylie interpreted the subtext, but not quickly enough. Before she could speak, move or even breathe, Cade's hands were on her waist, pulling her to him.

No one had ever been so physical with her. The men in her world were talkers who used words, not actions. Kylie could match any man verbally—even best them—but dealing on a tactile level was a very different playing field for her. Just as Cade Austin was very different from the men she knew. He acted first, without explanation or warning or eloquent discourse.

Kylie felt the warmth of his hard frame suffuse her. His big hands slid to her hips and settled her against his masculine strength. Instinctively her legs parted, letting her feel the full burgeoning force of his manhood.

The effect on Kylie was electrifying. The rampant sexuality of their position abruptly short-circuited the rational workings of her brain. Instead of thinking things through and behaving rationally, she ceded to the elemental craving he'd elicited deep within her. For the first time in her careful, well-organized life, she impulsively acted on what she was feeling—and that was a powerful, hungry need that demanded to be assuaged.

His mouth came down on hers, taking her lips and parting them in a kiss that was unlike any she'd ever known. This was no idle or tentative getting-to-know-you kiss. Cade kissed her as if he already knew her very well, as if he knew all about her secret yearnings and would fulfill them whenever he chose.

His kiss was hard and deep and intimate, demanding and receiving her body's most primitive, passionate response. It was a kiss outside the realm of her experience, beyond the constraints her mind persisted in placing on her emotions.

But there were no constraints now, not with Cade. He'd somehow slipped past her usual defenses and circumvented her control.

Her arms were around his neck and she was clinging to him, her anchor in the wild unfamiliar sea of sensuality. She gasped a shuddering breath when he boldly covered her breast with his hand. It was too much too fast, Kylie knew it. She'd spent years fending off unwanted intimacies, usually more bored than angered by such attempts.

But she was neither bored nor angry now. And the too-soon intimacy that Cade was taking was not unwanted. Far from it. Kylie felt the heat of his palm cupping her, felt his long fingers begin a slow massage, and she loved it. A little whimper escaped from her throat and she quivered with sensual pleasure.

Through the soft silk of her blouse, through the lace of her bra, he rubbed her nipple with his thumb. The tight bud was achingly sensitive, and she pressed against his hand, encouraging him, needing more. An erotic barrage of hot little sparks burned in the most secret, feminine part of her.

He was hard and virile and continued to press boldly against her, evoking a syrupy warmth that flowed through her. She felt soft and weak and pliant. When his hands cupped her buttocks to lift her higher and harder against him, Kylie clung tighter to him, moist and swollen with desire.

The intensity of her response shocked and excited her. She'd never experienced such fiery sensuality before, she had begun to believe she was one of those strictly analytical types whose passion could only be expressed in her work. A cool, methodical woman whose thrills came from the mental gymnastics required in preparing or presenting a case in a courtroom, not from a man's kisses and caresses.

Cade Austin was proving her very wrong. He wasn't simply a man, he was *the* man, and he was shattering all those myths she'd held about herself. In his arms, she'd become a passionate woman. The wild and wanton thoughts tumbling through her mind were as new and as stimulating as the feelings surging through her. And it seemed that Cade could read them all...

He scooped her up in his arms. Another first for her. She

couldn't remember ever being carried, though presumably it was her mode of transport before she'd learned to walk.

She was totally unprepared for and completely defenseless against the tantalizing sensation of being lifted in a man's arms and held against his chest as he strode across the office.

Kylie—the stable, dependable defender of the less fortunate—suddenly felt seductive and intensely feminine, like a character out of one of those romance novels she never had the time or inclination to read. Cade was so big, so strong. He handled her with ease, laying her down on the charcoal gray leather sofa and then coming down on top of her.

Her head was spinning, her eyelids felt extraordinarily heavy. It took too much energy and effort to keep them open so she allowed them to close, plunging her into a dark world of pure sensation.

He kissed her again, and she wrapped her arms around him, savoring the hard warm weight of him. The taste of him, the feel of him was exactly what she wanted, what she needed. She slipped her hands under the jacket of his suit to knead the muscular length of his back. The cloth barrier of his shirt frustrated her; she wanted to feel his bare skin beneath her fingers. She tugged at the material tucked into the waistband of his trousers, trying to get it out of her way.

Before she could succeed, Cade pushed aside her jacket and opened her blouse. Kylie felt his fingers deftly unfasten the front clasp of her bra. She knew she was exposed to him but instead of trying to cover herself, she arched upward, yielding greater access to him.

The touch of his hands on her bare breasts unleased piercing shards of desire deeply within her, too pleasurable to even consider ending. He fondled her, stroking and caressing, making her desperate for more.

"Cade, please!" She hardly recognized that desperate, husky cry as her own voice.

"I know, sweetie, I know." His voice was thick and raspy. "Me, too."

Kylie reached up to touch the hard, shaven skin of his cheek. She was charmed by his inarticulate mutter. She needed no translation, she knew exactly what he was saying. That he was as wonderfully out of control as she was. That he wanted her in the same fierce way that she wanted him.

Then his mouth was on the soft skin of her breast, kissing a sensuous path to its taut center that was tingling with arousal. She held her breath as his lips closed over her nipple to gently suckle her, then moaned as flames of desire licked through her. She hadn't known that a man's mouth on her breasts could affect her like this. The sensation was so intense, it was exquisite pleasure bordering on acute need.

His fingers slipped beneath the layers of her panty hose and white cotton panties to caress the soft, bare flesh of her belly. She felt him trace her navel, and she reflexively sucked in her stomach to provide him easier access. He dipped his thumb into the small hollow and kindled a wildfire that streaked directly to the pulsing heart of her femininity.

Kylie squirmed, trying to clench her legs together to ease the consuming ache there. Cade moved his thigh higher between hers, pressing against her. It helped but not enough. She wanted, she needed...

"Yes?" Cade murmured.

Through the dizzying fog of sensuality, Kylie realized that he was seeking her permission to continue. She wondered why he'd bothered; he didn't have to ask. Stopping him was the farthest thing from her mind. She wanted him with an urgency that bordered on desperation.

"Yes," she whispered.

She had no sooner spoken the word when Donna's voice boomed into the office once again, irrevocably shattering their private sensual cocoon. "Cade, Noah is here for your lunch meeting with the mayor."

Cade muttered an oath. Kylie's eyes flew open.

He was kneeling on one knee above her, in the process of sliding her panties and panty hose over her hips. Kylie gasped as the reality of the situation struck her with the force of an anvil. *She was on the verge of having sex with a man she hardly knew!*

"Kylie, I know this interruption isn't what either of us wanted to happen, but—"

"Get away from me!" she ordered, her voice little more than a raspy whisper.

She was horrified. *Sex on the sofa in Cade Austin's office?* What had she been thinking?

The answer, of course, was that she hadn't been thinking at all.

"I completely forgot that Noah and I are to have lunch with the mayor today. That's Noah Wyckoff, our senior vice president of operations." Cade caressed her midriff, seemingly mesmerized by the contrast of his tanned fingers against the snowy whiteness of her skin.

"I don't care who he is or who you're having lunch with." Kylie slapped his hands away and tried to sit up, a difficult feat with him hovering over her. "Let me go right now!"

Instead, he stunned her by picking her up again and carrying her toward a door at the far end of his office. His movements were so sudden, so unexpected that Kylie had no time to rally a protest. He'd opened the door and put her on her feet before she could utter a sound.

Kylie glanced around her. She was standing in a well-appointed bathroom—the executive washroom?—and Cade had reclosed the door, leaving her alone to repair her hair, makeup and clothing.

"Kylie, you'll need this." Cade rapped lightly on the door, then handed her purse to her.

Kylie snatched it with shaking fingers and swiftly slammed the door shut. He was so cool, so self-possessed! How had he recovered his wits and his composure so quickly, while she was still a shivering, quivering, unable-to-think-straight mess?

She forced herself to face the painful truth. Obviously, Cade hadn't been as sensually enthralled as she'd been. It was a devastating conclusion, both insulting and humiliating, but Kylie had never been one to hide behind the walls of denial.

One quick glance in the mirror made her groan aloud. Her mouth was moist and swollen and looked well-kissed, her lipstick was missing in action. And her hair...Kylie winced. It was in tousled disarray. She looked like she'd been doing exactly what she had been doing—indulging in a hot sexual tryst on the office sofa!

Moments later, she heard voices in the office, Cade's and another man's, presumably Noah Wyckoff, whose untimely appearance had interrupted the most impassioned episode in her life. The *stupidest* episode in her life, Kylie silently amended, reassessing the encounter through a critical, analytical eye.

Though she had been swept away, Cade had not been overpowered by that same wild abandon. And now, viewed in retrospect, his passionate advances seemed calculated, his recovery too quick and complete.

Kylie trembled. It hurt that his seemingly spontaneous burst of passion had actually been premeditated, a means of controlling her. He had seen her attraction to him and decided to use it to his advantage. Seducing BrenCo's major stockholder would be a real coup for the company president, bent on using her to further his own aims.

Her cheeks flamed. It was difficult enough to admit that she had lost her self-control and been ready to surrender—*aching to surrender!*—to a man she'd known less than an hour. But acknowledging that he had been playing sexual games with her, that she had been alone on that passion-drugged cloud, carried her to new heights of mortification. And outrage.

Her uncles had warned her that Cade Austin was ruthless and would stop at nothing to get his own way. It seemed that they were telling the truth.

Determinedly, Kylie worked on putting herself together until the mirror showed the reflection of an immaculately groomed woman, as cool and untouched by passion as she'd always believed herself to be. She pulled open the bathroom door and entered Cade's office.

The tall, wiry, bearded man talking to Cade started visibly at the sight of her. "I—didn't realize you had company, Cade," Noah Wyckoff murmured, glancing from Cade to Kylie, then back again.

"Ms. Brennan isn't company, Noah. She owns the company," Cade said. "I'd like you to meet—our boss." He completed the introductions.

Kylie noted sourly that unlike herself, Cade hadn't required a sojourn in the bathroom to eliminate any telltale evidence of their hot little interlude. She had needed a mirror, makeup, a comb and a vital rearrangement of her clothing to look as unruffled and undisturbed as he did—after no ablutions at all!

"Noah and I go back a long way," Cade said smoothly, filling in what could have been an awkward silence. "We were college roommates at MIT, three years in the dorms, one in an apartment that almost got condemned by the health department."

Noah chuckled at the memory. "Those were the days."

"How very interesting," Kylie managed to choke. She was seething. Cade spoke with the easy assurance of a host making small talk at a cocktail party. Another strike against him, for she was still too rattled to carry off a semblance of conversational patter.

She decided Cade Austin was as slick as an oil spill, which brought her to the unhappy conclusion that she had almost succumbed to the practiced charms of a smooth operator. Another appalling realization in a day that seemed to be filled with them. And it was only lunchtime!

The tension in the office was palpable. Noah cleared his throat. "Will you be joining us for lunch, Ms. Brennan?" he asked politely.

"No," Kylie said, more sharply than she'd intended. She had nothing against Noah Wyckoff but the prospect of spending another moment in Cade's company was intolerable.

"I have an appointment." She swept from the office without looking back.

"I'll be in touch, Kylie." Cade's voice followed her into the corridor.

A promise or a threat? Kylie mused cynically, deciding it must be the latter. Well, he was in for a surprise the next time he got *in touch* with her because she was prepared for him now. She knew the lengths to which he'd go to influence her, to control her. All her defenses were on alert and ready for their next encounter.

She could hardly wait.

Three

"That one is an entirely new Brennan prototype, one we haven't seen before," Noah remarked after Kylie's departure. "The Ice Queen. I swear the room temperature in here rose twenty degrees the moment she walked out."

"You think she's cold?" Cade gritted through his teeth, staring at the door through which Kylie had just exited.

"You think she's not?" Noah gave a short laugh. "With her around we won't need to build an autoclave to dispose of medical waste, she can freeze it with a single glance." He flopped down onto the sofa and sighed. "Of course, we won't be building anything if she sells BrenCo."

"Which Artie and Guy Brennan are desperate for her to do."

"She won't listen to *them*, will she?"

"I have no idea what Kylie Brennan will do." Cade stared sightlessly at the intricate patterns of the Oriental carpet at his feet. He felt disoriented, as if he'd been flung from a whirling carousel. Yet he was supposed to stand here, still and steady, without displaying a trace of the disequilibrium that had him reeling.

Though Kylie had left the office, she remained so firmly ensconced in his head that the images running before his mind's eye seemed more real than Noah's actual presence. Cade pictured her face, softened with passion. He could taste the sweetness of her mouth and feel the sultry heat of her body pressed to his.

He couldn't remember the last time he'd been so affected, so *consumed* by a kiss. He had learned early on that a kiss was simply a preliminary, a means to the climactic end. But kissing Kylie had been so exciting, so arousing, it was an end in itself.

And then he pictured her breasts, so round and full and milky white, the nipples a dark dusky rose. He remembered the way she had responded to him, how she'd clung to him, moaning her pleasure as his mouth closed over those sensitive little buds.

It had been so good and he wanted more, much more. They had barely begun when they'd had to stop, and now his body was tense and throbbing with all those unmet needs she'd aroused in him.

Cade groaned.

"We have to think positively," Noah said, misinterpreting the cause, though not the source, of his old friend's apparent agony. "Gene named her his heir, so he must've seen something in her that set her apart from the rest of the clan. I mean, imagine what we'd be facing if he'd left Guy those shares! BrenCo would be sold as fast as you can say 'Lauretta wants an in-ground swimming pool, a fur coat and a fancy vacation to brag about.'"

"She said she had an appointment." Cade began to pace the office. "Who with? One of the uncles?"

"I got the impression she just said that to blow us off," Noah said frankly. "She seemed like she was in a big hurry to get out of here."

"Yeah," Cade agreed, frowning. "She couldn't wait to get away."

From him. That rankled. He remembered the way Kylie had looked at him when she'd emerged from the bathroom, appearing as perfect and untouched as a porcelain doll that had never been removed from its box. He'd had to exert considerable willpower to keep from snatching her into his arms and transforming her back into that passion-mussed creature who had lain beneath him, warm and soft and hungry for him.

But the cold disdain in her blue eyes had served as an effective restraint. She'd glared at him as if he were some kind of unspeakable substance she'd accidentally stepped in. Cade read her loud and clear...she didn't want him to come anywhere near her.

He knew if they had been alone, he would have handled things differently. He would've tried to convince her that not only did she want him near, but she wanted him deep inside her. And judging by her explosive response to him earlier, he could have succeeded.

But Noah's presence halted any such attempt. What had gone on between Kylie and himself was intensely private; Cade wanted no third-party involvement, not even his best friend's. So he'd allowed Kylie to sweep out like the Ice Queen Noah believed her to be, rather than acting on those primitive possessive urges rushing through him. They were still rushing through him.

"Did you hear the latest breaking news on the Brennan front?" Noah asked, drawing a pensive Cade's attention. "Brent has been arrested and is in jail. Get this, he'd set up a videocam—"

"I heard. Bobbie called in full-blown hysterics. Did you know that unauthorized filming of individuals is a burglary charge?"

"I do now."

"How did you hear about Brent so quickly? From Bridget? I guess Bobbie must've called her here and—"

"Actually, it was Brenda who called and told me, a short while ago."

"Brenda?" Cade gaped at him. "Why would Brenda call you?"

"It seems I'm her new best friend." Noah shrugged nonchalantly, but Cade noticed that the other man did not meet his eyes.

He felt an ominous stirring. "How did that happen? And when?"

Noah shrugged again and gazed intently at the lake view, as if bent on observing every rise and swell of the water. "I saw her at The Corner Grill about three weeks ago and we ended up having coffee there after her shift ended. I've heard from her almost every day since. She either phones or drops by my place with a question or with something she's whipped up in the kitchen. She's, uh, a pretty good cook.''

"You've been seeing her every day for nearly a month?" Cade's voice rose in apprehension.

"Nothing's happened between us. As I said, we're just friends."

"You sound sorry about that. Does that mean you're thinking about—taking things further with her? God, man, be careful!"

"You sound so alarmed, like I'm about to take a dive into a vat of Agent Orange." Noah grinned, clearly amused. "What are you worried about, that Brenda is set on having her wicked way with me?"

"I'm worried because she is Brenda Brennan, who is manipulative and conniving and the first woman I've heard you mention since Janice left Port McClain two and a half years ago."

"I've spent the past two and a half years exactly the way you have, working sixteen-hour days to implement our ideas and bring this company to the industry's cutting edge." Noah was defensive. "I haven't been pining over Janice or avoiding women, I've been focusing all my attention and energy on BrenCo."

Cade laid a hand on Noah's shoulder. "Look, I know how hard you took the divorce and I don't want to see you get mixed up with a—"

"I appreciate your concern, but we're not nineteen anymore, Cade, you don't have to look out for me. I've been married and divorced, remember? You've done neither. Doesn't that make me the more experienced one? The one who should be giving the advice?"

"No. Not when Brenda Brennan is involved." Or any other woman, Cade added silently.

Despite Noah's marriage and divorce, Cade believed his friend to be as naive about women as he'd been during their college years. Back then Cade, a worldly army brat with a wealth of experience, had felt protective toward the shy, brilliant Noah who'd led a quiet sheltered life of privilege and private schools. He still felt that way.

Cade decided that now was not the time to remind Noah how he'd advised him against marrying Janice in the first place, that he had seen the divorce coming on their wedding day when he'd been cast as best man and had to pretend to be happy for the woefully mismatched pair.

"Cade, I know you're the expert on the Brennans but you're wrong about Brenda," Noah exclaimed earnestly. "I've gotten to know her pretty well these past few weeks. She is bright and sensitive and vulnerable."

"I've never seen that side of her," Cade muttered sardonically.

Lord, what a day this was turning into! First, he'd been blindsided by his attraction to Kylie Brennan, now he was faced with the alarming revelation that his best friend and the number two man at BrenCo was on the verge of being bamboozled by Brenda Brennan.

His eyes flicked to his desk calendar and he noted the date for the first time that day. March 15. "Beware the Ides of March," he quoted grimly. "An applicable bit of advice."

"Don't let the mayor hear you say that. Not on the day we're to convince him that supporting our zoning permit to build an infectious waste autoclave is a great idea." Chuckling, Noah glanced at his watch. "And speaking of the mayor, if we don't leave now, we'll be late for our meeting with him. A bad move. You know how His Honor reveres punctuality."

Cade stifled the urge to issue one more warning about the insidious wiles of Brenda Brennan. Noah didn't want to hear it, he'd made that clear. Worse, Cade found himself challenging his own expertise in matters dealing with the opposite sex. His previously resolute confidence was not quite so resolute.

This morning's encounter with Kylie Brennan had done that to him. He'd always considered himself to be unshakable, but she shook him up, all right. She just might be the most dangerous Brennan of all—smart and alluring and a completely unknown entity. He vowed to be on his guard—on full-alert status!—during their next encounter.

It worried him that he was already looking forward to it.

The old Brennan homestead was a stately though dilapidated Victorian-style house built in the late 1800s in Port McClain's oldest neighborhood. The spacious lots were landscaped with towering trees, tall hedges and flower gardens. Gene had bought the house for his parents years ago and lived there with them until they died, then stayed on alone until his own death last year.

Wearing jeans, boots and a thick cerulean blue sweater, Kylie sat on a weather-beaten wooden glider on the deep front porch. She'd driven her rental car to the house to oversee the flurry of activity initiated by her morning phone calls.

She stared out at the long, spacious front yard extending to the deserted tree-lined street and remembered summer visits when her grandparents were alive, when the yard was green and bright with color from Grandma's prized gardens. Now it looked as desolate and untended as the inside of the house, where currently a trio of maids from the cleaning service were working hard to make the place livable once again.

A crumpled paper bag held the remains of her lunch, a takeout order from The Corner Grill, a short walk from BrenCo headquarters. Kylie shivered as a chilly breeze rustled the bare branches of the trees. She debated whether to go inside or stay out here. The electricity and water had been turned on, but she didn't want to get in the way of the busy cleaning crew. Unfortunately, she couldn't leave yet, she was still awaiting gas, telephone and cable TV service.

Kylie swung back and forth on the glider, bored and growing colder by the minute. An old-fashioned front porch like this conjured up images of warm summer nights, gentle breezes and tall glasses of lemonade. Instead, the wind was picking up and the sky was darkening. Before long, she wouldn't have to swing herself on the glider, the force of the wind would provide the necessary momentum all on its own.

A tan-colored minivan, filthy and streaked with road salt, pulled into the long gravel driveway and drove right up to the stone path leading to the porch. Kylie tensed as her cousin Brenda climbed out and headed toward her.

She was struck by Brenda's resemblance to her. While they

weren't the "identical cousins" of TV sitcom land, they looked enough alike to be easily identified as family members.

There were some differences, of course. Brenda's hair was longer and pulled high on her head in a ponytail. She wore darker, heavier eyeliner and a dramatic shade of red lipstick, contrasting sharply to Kylie's muted, natural-look makeup. Brenda was several inches shorter than Kylie, and her figure was more voluptuous, her curves lushly revealed by her short tight black sweater and even tighter black jeans. She wore a black leather jacket, which couldn't have provided much protection against the cold wind.

Kylie pulled the zipper of her fleecy blue coat higher as she walked to meet her cousin. "Hello, Brenda. It's nice to see you again." The good manners her mother had instilled in her down through the years automatically kicked in.

"I figured you'd be here," Brenda greeted her without preamble. "I heard you bought lunch-to-go at The Corner Grill. I'm a waitress there, but I'm off today," she added.

Kylie nodded, for lack of a better response. She tried to remember the last time she'd had a conversation with Brenda and couldn't. The few times she had seen her cousin in the past years they'd been surrounded by other Brennans and barely had the time or opportunity to exchange hellos.

Well, there was nobody around now. Perhaps for the first time ever, the two cousins were alone together. They stood on the wide flat stone just below the three wooden stairs leading to the porch.

"How long are you planning to stay here?" Brenda asked bluntly.

"I'm not really sure," murmured Kylie with a small smile. No one could accuse Brenda of not coming immediately to the point.

"Are you here to sell the company and Uncle Gene's house like my father and Uncle Guy said?" Before Kylie had a chance to say a word, Brenda forged ahead. "They brought this big shot to town from Cleveland to convince you to sell BrenCo. His name is Axel Dodge. Have you met him yet? Ian was the one who hooked him up with Dad and Uncle Guy. A bad sign, right there. Ian is nastier than air pollution...he's human toxic waste. Too bad BrenCo can't dispose of *him* through one of their environmentally friendly processes."

"Axel Dodge?" Kylie chose to ignore the slur to their mutual cousin and tried for a tactful diversion. "That sounds more like a car dealership than a person's name."

Brenda's lips twitched, as if she were on the verge of a smile. She immediately suppressed the urge and scowled instead. "If you're as smart as Uncle Gene seemed to think, you'll tell Axel Dodge to get lost. Then you'll tell Ian, Uncle Guy and my father to butt out of BrenCo for good. They're greedy, and it's made them stupid. So are you if you listen to them."

Kylie thought of Cade's comment about the bickering, backstabbing Brennans. Now here was Brenda, bashing three members of the clan and indirectly Kylie herself, right to her face.

Nor had Brenda finished her tirade. "Dad and Ian and Uncle Guy don't care about the business, they don't care about the people in town who'll lose their jobs if the company is sold. All they want is to get their hands on some quick easy money to throw around."

"You sound exactly like Cade," Kylie blurted out.

"I heard you saw him today." Brenda's deep blue eyes seemed to bore into her. "Bridget told me you showed up at BrenCo and Cade took you into his office. She said he was looking at you the way our cat watches the fish in Starr Lynn's aquarium."

Every now and then, Brenda decides that I would be a good match for her. Cade's voice seemed to be echoing in Kylie's head. The intensity of her cousin's stare unnerved her. Was Brenda jealous of the time she'd spent with Cade? She couldn't tell, but remembering her own ignoble reaction to the thought of a Cade and Brenda coupling brought a rush of color to Kylie's cheeks.

Brenda noticed. "Did Cade put the moves on you?"

"Brenda!" Kylie made a strangled protest.

"You're actually blushing! He did hit on you, just like Bridget said he would!" Brenda exclaimed gleefully. "How far did you get? Did you do The Nasty right there in his office?"

"Certainly not!" Kylie was aghast. She remembered the way Cade had kissed her, had touched her, had carried her in his arms. Her blush deepened. "I—I'd really rather not discuss this, Brenda."

"Are you mad at Cade? Did he come on too strong? You can't blame him for trying to get next to you, Kylie. Why, he'd be crazy not to," Brenda stated baldly. "You're the major stockholder and Cade wants full control of the company. He should've had it, too. Everybody knows that Cade intended to buy out Uncle Gene's shares."

"Why didn't Uncle Gene leave the shares to Cade or make some arrangement in the will for him to buy them?" Kylie quizzed, hoping to divert her.

"My mama says Uncle Gene was so arrogant he thought he was immortal. He lived his life like he was gonna live forever but he didn't, and now BrenCo is at risk. Which would kill him if he weren't dead already," Brenda added with relish. "Uncle Gene loved the company more than anything or anybody in the whole world. I bet the threat of BrenCo being sold has that nasty old grouch spinning like a top in his fancy mausoleum."

Her outspoken cousin did not hold back when it came to other Brennans, Kylie noted, which fit Cade's description of the inner workings of the family. However, Brenda's staunch defense of Cade took her completely by surprise.

"You seem to be very loyal to Cade Austin," Kylie murmured, trying to sound casual.

"And you're wondering why." This time Brenda did smile. "No, you're way past wondering, you're *dying* to know why."

Kylie stared at her, transfixed. There was a sweetness about Brenda when she smiled. She looked younger, the hard weariness erased from her face.

"I think Cade's hot, I admit it." Brenda's smile widened and her blue eyes sparkled, making her very pretty indeed. "I mean, what's not to like? He's big and strong and good-looking, not to mention single. He's got that macho, take-charge attitude that women find irresistible, even fem-lib types like you, I'll bet. He has lots of admirers in town but he usually goes into Cleveland for his, uh, social life. It's less than an hour down the interstate and there's a lot more to do there than here."

"So he leaves town to play swinging bachelor in the city?" Kylie's heartbeat was pounding in her ears.

"I heard he's dating a lady dentist there. Can you imagine dating a *dentist?* They put their hands in peoples' mouths!" Brenda shuddered her distaste. "Anyway, I made it pretty obvious to Cade that I was interested in him but he never took me up on it. Mama says that's why she trusts him, because he could've used me but he didn't. Plus, he's been very good to Starr Lynn. BrenCo has this special fund to support local athletics—the high school teams and Little League and Girls Softball—and Cade put Starr Lynn on the list. Uncle Gene was opposed, he said figure skating was too individualistic and elitist to qualify for his community sports aid. That mean old coot didn't want to give my baby a cent, but Cade made sure Starr Lynn gets money for her training every year from that fund."

A lady dentist? Kylie didn't hear a word about Cade's valiant support of young Starr Lynn's endeavors. A slow burn kindled within her. *He was involved with a lady dentist from Cleveland?* Yet he'd made a heavy pass at her this morning anyway.

Well, as Brenda had so succinctly stated, why wouldn't he? Seducing a woman in order to control her was a course of action dating back to the last millennium, probably even before. Nor were Cade's intentions anything she hadn't already figured out herself, but hearing Brenda announce it, learning about the existence of another woman...

Kylie swallowed and found it painful. There was a hard lump lodged in her throat.

"You can have him if you want him, you know."

Brenda's voice sounded above the cacophony going on in her head. Kylie looked up to meet her cousin's gaze. She was disconcerted to find Brenda studying her, practically dissecting her with those glittering Brennan-blue eyes of hers.

"Why would I want a man who has no qualms about using me, despite his involvement with another woman? Who is only interested in my shares of BrenCo?"

"My guess is that your BrenCo shares aren't the only thing

about you that interests him," Brenda said, giving her another embarrassingly thorough once-over. "You're beautiful. Classy. And smart. I bet you could beat out any dentist with a flick of your pinky."

Kylie smiled in spite of herself. "Maybe Cade doesn't share your aversion to dentists, Brenda."

"Lady Drill-bit hasn't landed him yet," Brenda pointed out. "I think it would be cool if you and Cade got together, Kylie. In fact, I'll help you nail him if you want."

Having heard Cade rant against the Brennans, Kylie doubted that Brenda's assistance would be of much use, even if she wanted help *nailing* Cade. Which she most certainly did not because she didn't want any man who was unscrupulous and avaricious, qualities Cade Austin possessed in spades! Still, she was oddly touched by Brenda's offer. Her display of cousinly solidarity was heartwarming. According to Cade, that self-appointed Brennan-ologist, her cousin should have been venal and vengeful toward her.

"Thank you, Brenda," Kylie said quietly. "I appreciate your offer, but I don't want Cade Austin."

Brenda mulled this over. "Are you interested in another man? Some guy back in Philadelphia?"

Kylie shook her head.

"Would you help me?" Brenda asked suddenly.

Kylie was back on her guard. "Help you to, er, nail Cade? To lure him away from Madame Root Canal in Cleveland?" she tried to make a joke, though she didn't feel at all like laughing.

"No, I've given up on Cade. There is somebody else, a man who's different from any other man I've ever known." Brenda's voice filled with emotion. "He doesn't treat me like I'm some kind of cheap, stupid nobody. He—acts as if he actually likes talking to me." She paused, seemingly staggered by the notion.

Kylie watched and listened carefully. At this particular moment, Brenda put her in mind of countless clients she'd defended, women who had no faith in their own abilities or appeal. Women who had been used by men and who considered themselves worthless. Most of those women weren't lucky enough to find a man different from any others they had known, a man who actually considered what they had to say to be worth listening to. But it seemed her cousin had.

Kylie made her decision on the spot. "I'll be glad to help you any way I can, Brenda."

"Do you really mean it?" Brenda's face lit up. "I can hardly believe it! Who would've ever thought that *you* would help me?"

"I can imagine the kinds of things you've heard about me," Kylie said dryly. Especially after Uncle Gene's will was read. "But, truly, I'm neither a fiend nor a demon."

"We thought you were a—well, never mind. When I came out here today to warn you about Axel Dodge, Mama said it was hopeless, that you'd never listen to me. But I thought I had to try, for BrenCo's sake."

Kylie pondered the alliances within the family and the company. And politics was supposed to make strange bedfellows! "I haven't met Axel Dodge but—"

"You will," Brenda cut in, frowning. "We heard that Dad and Uncle Guy are going to call you tonight and set up a meeting for tomorrow. Axel Dodge will be there. Probably Aunt Lauretta, too." Brenda's voice lowered, becoming hushed and confidential in tone. "I can't stand her! She puts on phony airs, just because she's married to the editor of the *Port McClain Post*—as if that crummy little rag is the *New York Times* or something! Anyway, everybody knows Uncle Gene bought Uncle Guy that position of editor with all the money he gave to the paper."

"I hadn't heard that," Kylie murmured, both drawn in and repelled by the family gossip.

"Oh, there's lots you haven't heard, but I'll fill you in. For instance, did you know that Aunt Lauretta calls herself a *socialite?* Can you believe it, a Port McClain socialite? That's good for a laugh."

"It does seem like something of an oxymoron," Kylie murmured.

"Yeah!" Brenda exclaimed so fervently that Kylie wondered how her cousin had interpreted her remark. She didn't want to stir up a Brennan vs. Brennan feud with herself in the middle and felt obliged to add, "Aunt Lauretta has always been very nice to me, every time I've seen her."

"Don't be fooled, she hates you," Brenda warned, her eyes flashing. "She hates your mother and dad and brother, too. She says the four of you think you're superior to everybody here and that you turned Uncle Gene against the rest of the family so he'd leave you the most in his will. Uncle Guy and Ian feel the same way. You should hear the awful things they say about you and your family!"

Kylie felt a blind rush of anger surge through her. If it was Brenda's intention to turn her against the Guy Brennan branch of the family, her salvo had been quite effective. Kylie caught herself right before she retaliated with a crack about small town snobs and their petty jealousies. She took a deep breath, willing herself to remain rational and in control.

"You know, Bridget and I have always loved your mom and dad!" Brenda exclaimed enthusiastically. "They're our favorite aunt and uncle. We treasure the dolls Uncle Wayne and Aunt Connie sent us from all over the world when we were kids. And now Starr Lynn loves to look at them. She knows they'll be hers someday."

Kylie's sense of humor asserted itself. Brenda was laying it on awfully thick. It appeared she was attempting, without a trace of subtlety, to claim most-favored Brennan status. If nothing else, Cade had made a legitimate point about the family backstabbing. This was an anecdote she might've shared with him—if she didn't despise him as a conniving user.

The cousins' attention was drawn to the street, where a dark green Buick was turning into the driveway.

"That's Cade's car," Brenda announced. "Bridget, Brent and me think Cade should drive something sexy and super-expensive, like a Porsche or a Ferrari. I mean, a Buick seems so staid and no fun. So very Port McClain. Uncle Gene drove a Buick, so did Grandpa Brennan."

"Maybe Cade keeps a flashy sports car stashed in Cleveland to use when he's playing smooth operator," Kylie said cattily.

"You think so?" Brenda suddenly clasped her hands to her face, her blue eyes huge. "Oh, Kylie, Noah is in the car with him!"

"Noah Wyckoff?"

"You know him?" Brenda seemed to be having trouble breathing. "How?"

"I met him today in Cade's office." Kylie noticed her cousin's loss of composure and reached an immediate conclusion. "Brenda, is Noah Wyckoff the man you told me about?"

Brenda nodded her head. "He's such a nice guy. But he's shy. I've been encouraging him—Mama says I'm chasing him—but he hasn't made a single move on me. He hasn't even held my hand yet! I know he likes me but I'm getting desperate."

Cade parked his maligned Buick directly behind Brenda's minivan, which was behind Kylie's car, a sparkling clean white compact. One of her stops this morning had been to the car wash to remove the grime from her long drive from Philadelphia.

The two men walked toward the cousins, their stride leisurely and unhurried—as if they were merely paying a casual visit, as if they were not on a mission of pressure and manipulation. But Kylie wasn't fooled. She seethed.

"Mama says I should play it cool," Brenda whispered urgently. "She says I'm acting too available and Noah will lose interest in me if I keep it up. But he *needs* encouragement, Kylie. If I play hard to get, he might decide not to try to get me."

Kylie watched Cade and Noah approach them, her heart beating far faster than it should. Not from nervous excitement, she insisted. From anger. From sheer disgust. She would not be used by that snake Cade Austin again!

She wanted to order him off the premises and would have done so, but for her promise to help Brenda *nail* Noah Wyckoff. As one who hadn't conspired in a female entrapment plot since junior high, Kylie wondered how useful she would be to her cousin's cause. But she had promised to try. She cast a quick glance at the visibly nervous Brenda.

"One thing I've learned is that mothers often have a way of being right," Kylie murmured. "It came as a distinct surprise to me because as a teenager, I thought my mom was fairly clueless. But the older I get, the more I realize that mothers usually know what they're talking about."

"Meaning I should play it cool like Mama says?" Brenda was skeptical.

"If Noah is shy, you don't want to scare him off by coming on too strong." Kylie had a feeling that Brenda unleashed might fall into the category of downright unnerving.

"Then *you'll* have to do something to keep him around. Like—like ask us to have dinner with you tonight," Brenda whispered urgently. "Insist on it!"

Cade and Noah came to a halt a foot or two away from them.

"Well, this is a surprise." Brenda's voice lowered to a sultry purr and she shot Noah the hottest come-hither look Kylie had ever seen directed at anyone. So much for playing it cool.

A dull flush spread from Noah's neck to his forehead. "Hello, Brenda," he mumbled, then glanced uneasily at Cade.

"We didn't expect to see you two here, especially during working hours. That's very unBrenCo of you." Brenda took a few steps closer to Noah. "But we're thrilled you're here, aren't we, Kyle?"

"Incredibly thrilled," Kylie echoed, deadpan.

She saw Cade clench his jaw as he observed Brenda's come-on and Noah's reaction. Kylie instantly intuited his disapproval. Cade did not like the idea of a Brenda-Noah match, not at all. She watched as his frown became a full-fledged glower, and a naughty thrill shot through her. Why, Cade positively *hated* Brenda's fledgling relationship with his friend.

All of a sudden, her promise to her cousin became a pleasure to fulfill.

"What are you doing here, Brenda?" Cade demanded, in a parole-officer-to-recalcitrant-parolee tone of voice.

"Brenda and I have been catching up on family gossip," Kylie replied breezily. "In fact, we have so much to talk about we're having dinner together tonight." She turned to Noah. "I'm sorry I had to rush off this morning, I hope I didn't seem rude."

Noah shifted uneasily. "Er, not at all, Miss Brennan."

"Kylie," she corrected with a dazzling smile. "You're kind to overlook it, Noah, but I'm afraid I really was rude. As a way of making amends, I'd like to invite you to join Bren and me for dinner tonight."

"Kyle and Bren?" Cade gritted through his teeth.

"I—I would very much like to have dinner with you. Both."

Noah's eyes were locked with Brenda's and his breathing had accelerated.

"That's wonderful!" Brenda cooed. She moved so close to Noah that their bodies were a hairsbreadth from touching.

Cade scowled. "What time and where are we eating?"

"You're not invited," Kylie snapped. "It's just the three of us."

She'd already formulated her plan, which included pleading a migraine headache, ideally before the soup was served, and then going home, leaving the couple to finish the meal and the evening alone.

"Kylie's mad at you, she thinks you're a two-timing pig," Brenda said succinctly.

"What?" Cade gasped.

"Well, what do you expect her to think?" Brenda demanded. "You made a big play for her in your office this morning and you already have a girlfriend, um, stashed in Cleveland. With your sports car."

"Brenda!" Kylie groaned. As an ally, her cousin had a long way to go.

"What kind of tales have you been telling?" Cade was outraged.

Kylie wasn't sure if the question was directed at her or Brenda, or maybe both of them.

Noah stared at the ground, his shoulders shaking oddly. Cade realized he was laughing. "This isn't funny!" he snarled.

"Probably not," Noah agreed. But he didn't stop laughing.

Brenda laughed, too. "Did you know his girlfriend is a *dentist*? Who knows what kind of kinky stuff they do with all that weird dental equip—"

"Shut up, Brenda!" Cade's eyes smoldered. "Kylie, I want to talk to you. Right now."

He caught her arm and dragged her up the stairs and onto the porch, out of earshot of Brenda and Noah who were now chatting easily together. Their shared laughter had proven an effective icebreaker.

Kylie did not go quietly, she protested all the way. "Stop

manhandling me! I don't want to talk to you. Unless we're discussing BrenCo, we have nothing to say to each other."

She tried to pull away from him but he had an iron grip on her arm and propelled her alongside him. It was a strange sensation, having her feet move when she didn't want to walk. Once again, Cade's size and strength had proven superior to her will. Kylie fumed. Despite Brenda's assumption, she did not find his macho, take-charge attitude irresistible. More like infuriating.

"Let me go!" she ordered.

Cade responded by ignoring her command and reinforcing his grasp, taking hold of her shoulders with both hands. He held her firmly in place, mere inches in front of him. "Just to set the record straight, I do not have a girlfriend stashed in Cleveland. Or a sports car."

"You're claiming that Brenda invented the lady dentist?" Kylie instantly regretted her reply.

She shouldn't have said a word, she should have frozen him out with icy silence. But she was curious. Would he lie about the woman in Cleveland? She half hoped he would, then she could brand him a liar and be done with him forever. There was nothing she despised more than a calculating liar.

"I assume Brenda is referring to Anne Woodley," Cade said tightly. "Anne is a dentist in Cleveland and we dated a while, but stopped seeing each other well over a year ago. To be more accurate, it was several months before Gene's death and no, there wasn't a big dramatic breakup scene. We didn't have that kind of relationship. Anne and I mutually decided to end it and we've remained on good terms."

"How civilized. And how convenient to remain on good terms with your dentist friend. Does that mean you commute to Cleveland for regular checkups?" The words were out before she could think not to say them. Kylie was horrified with herself. She seemed to be acquiring the Brennan cousin habit of blurting out whatever crossed her mind.

"You don't owe me any explanations," she added quickly, striving for damage control. "I don't care if—"

"Telling Brenda that I'm a two-timing pig implies that you do care." Cade's temper was dissolving, his angry expression swiftly transforming into one of dawning male satisfaction. A slow smile crossed his face.

Kylie was determined to wipe it off. "I never said that. The words—and the sentiment behind them—are strictly Brenda's own."

His smile widened. "Well, just to set the record straight and to keep the facts current, John Paul Vukovich here in Port McClain is my dentist. He's first-rate. I highly recommend him if you're in need of any dental work while you're in town."

Kylie swallowed. This was definitely an area to avoid. Sometimes in court an inflammatory loser of a topic was introduced. With disaster pending, the smartest course was to drop it quickly and move onto something else.

"What are you doing here?" she demanded brusquely. The old tried-and-true adage "the best defense is a good offense" was tried-and-true because it worked.

"Noah and I wanted to fill you in on our plans for BrenCo's future. We had a very rewarding lunch meeting with the mayor and thought you should be informed." Cade was still holding her and his fingers began to knead her shoulders. "And I wanted to see how things were going out here at Gene's place. If you've had any problems, I'll—"

"I haven't had any problems. Everything is progressing very well here." Kylie knew she should step away from him. There was no reason for her to stand here, letting him hold her.

Except she liked his touch too much to make him stop. Alarm bells sounded in her head. The lady dentist might've been relegated to footnote status in his personal history but there were other reasons for keeping Cade Austin at arm's length. First and foremost was her fifty-one percent stock ownership in BrenCo. *That* was what Cade Austin found most appealing about her. Not her body or her mind. She could look like a troglodyte and have the personality of a stone and it wouldn't matter, he would still attempt to seduce her.

He wanted to control her, to sweet-talk her into doing his bidding so he could retain control of BrenCo. Her pride demanded that she resist him. What woman wanted to be wanted for her shares in a toxic waste plant?

You can't blame him for trying to get next to you, Kylie. Why, he'd be crazy not to. You're the major stockholder and Cade wants full control of the company. Brenda had neatly summed up the situation.

Kylie lifted her eyes and met his. He was watching her, his gaze piercing. Assessing. Planning his next move? He considered himself an expert in the art of dealing with Brennans, and she was one of them.

The wind whistled around them and she shivered. Cade rubbed his hands up and down her arms to warm her. "It's too cold to stand around out here," he said softly. "Why don't we go inside and—"

The sound of car doors slamming, immediately followed by the roar of a car engine broke the silence. Cade and Kylie both turned to see Brenda drive her minivan over the frozen yard, going around Cade's car, which was blocking the driveway. Noah was in the front seat beside her.

"Hey!" Cade shouted and bolted down the porch stairs. "Brenda! Noah! Come back here!"

Brenda gave the horn a jaunty honk, then steered the van back onto the driveway. Within seconds, she'd peeled out and was on the street, heading away from the house.

You go, girl. Kylie grinned as she offered her silent support to her cousin. Mother's wisdom aside, playing it cool simply wasn't Brenda's style. Wasn't it better to simply be yourself in a relationship, without resorting to wiles and games?

She watched Cade standing at the foot of the stairs, his arms folded in front of his chest. She wondered what he was thinking; she could guess, but wondering and guessing weren't enough. Kylie left the porch to go stand beside him. For a few moments, the two of them stared at the trail of exhaust lingering in the air, the last traces of the getaway van and its occupants.

"I forgot all about them." Cade appeared stunned by his memory lapse.

"Poor Cade. So much to do, so little time," Kylie mocked. "You were concentrating so hard on trying to charm me on behalf of my BrenCo stock that you couldn't properly chaperone

Brenda and Noah. Personally, I'm glad they escaped,'' she added tartly.

"Escape, ha! It's more like a kidnapping. Brenda lured poor Noah into—"

"You're lying to yourself, if you believe that. Noah looked thrilled to see Brenda. He was practically breathless with excitement. No, this was definitely a mutual escape from the condemning eyes of Big Brother. That's you," she stated, just in case he chose not to get her point.

"You're enjoying this immensely, aren't you?" Cade asked, his expression as dry as his tone.

That surprised Kylie. She'd expected him to be jumping up and down shrieking his frustration, à la Rumpelstiltskin. Well, perhaps her next statement would drive him over the edge. "I think Noah is good for Brenda. I've gotten the impression that she hasn't been very well treated by men. He seems to be a wonderful change for her. I'm going to do whatever I can to help them get together."

"That save-the-world streak of yours is rearing its ugly head, I see." Cade rolled his eyes. "You've been in Port McClain less than twenty-four hours and you're already on a crusade."

Still, he wasn't ranting and raving. Kylie's eyes narrowed. "You're not angry?"

He shrugged. "I don't waste my energy on something I can do nothing about, and right now there is nothing I can do about Brenda and Noah." He smiled at her, that heart-stopping smile that had wreaked havoc on her self-control and her common sense earlier that day. "I'd rather concentrate on you."

Four

"**D**on't you have a company to run?" Kylie took a step away from him, then another. Cade surprised her by dropping his hands and letting her move out of his reach. She hadn't expected him to acquiesce, and she was aware of a vague disappointment, which unsettled her. Had she wanted him to turn caveman and yank her against him?

Definitely not, Kylie assured herself. Reflexively, her eyes flew to his face to find him watching her, his mouth curved into an enigmatic smile.

"Are you telling me to get back to work, Boss Lady?"

"Of course not. It's just—I just— There is really no need for you to be wasting your valuable time here. I have everything under control." Everything except herself. She felt edgy and off balance, not to mention maddeningly conflicted. Kylie admitted the unholy truth to herself—she wanted him to stay as much as she wanted him to leave.

"I'm sure you do. And I'll give you a reprieve from me...but only on one condition." His smile had changed and this time it wasn't hard to read—it was elemental and pure male and stirred Kylie's already heightened senses.

"What condition would that be? Turning over my BrenCo shares to you?"

She hoped that she looked and sounded sufficiently cool and cynical. She certainly didn't feel it. Inside, she was as nervous as a schoolgirl, churning with a dangerous mix of confusion and excitement.

"If and when I buy those shares from you, there will be no conditions attached." Cade was serious now, the glimmer of humor in his eyes completely gone. "The decision to keep or to sell your shares in BrenCo is yours alone to make, Kylie. But it must be an informed decision."

"And you just happen to be the one to inform me?" she suggested wryly.

She suspected the facts he presented would lead to only one inevitable choice: to maintain the status quo at BrenCo. No doubt her uncles had facts to support the opposite decision, to sell BrenCo. Kylie stifled a sigh, and wished she were back in a courtroom in Philadelphia with a judge and a jury to make the informed decisions.

"Yes, I'm going to *inform* you, Kylie." He flashed a wicked pirate's grin.

How had he managed to make that innocuous verb sound titillating and filled with lusty promise? A veiled substitute for a specific, vigorous act. Kylie felt her cheeks flush with heat, even though the icy wind was whipping around them.

"If you have time now, I brought all the necessary information with me for a full presentation." Cade's voice, once more firm and serious, broke into the chaos swirling in her head.

Kylie stared at him. He was all business, not a trace of the seductive grin or the suggestive note evident in his voice. He could've been addressing the State Chamber of Commerce, so sober and professional was his mien. Had her fevered imagination conjured up that sexual innuendo? she wondered nervously. It was so unlike her. Why, her imagination had never before come close to being fevered!

'We can go inside the house or return to my office, if you prefer,'' Cade continued in his BrenCo chief executive tone.

"And, um, is that the condition you mentioned? To listen to your presentation?" She was guiltily aware that her mind had been drifting too far and too fast.

Worse, she was flooded with images of this morning's sojourn in Cade's office. The big gray leather sofa...his mouth, hard and demanding on hers...herself flushed and breathless and out of control as she writhed against him.

Kylie swallowed. If his presentation included a repeat of this morning's sensual blitz, she would do well to remain on her own turf where she was in command.

"I prefer to go into the house," she said decisively. "We'll have to keep out of the cleaning crew's way, which might mean moving from room to room, but that shouldn't be more than a minor inconvenience."

The trio's presence would also serve to deflect any possible physical encounters between her and Cade—not that she was encouraging any such thing! After this morning's embarrassing, too-revealing fiasco, she was determined to relegate the relationship between her and Cade Austin to a strictly professional basis.

"Whatever." Cade accepted her declaration with a shrug of nonchalance. "I'll get my briefcase from the car."

Kylie waited for him in the foyer of the front hall. The kitchen, living room and dining room each had a cleaning crew member hard at work so the pair chose the only unoccupied downstairs room. They entered Gene Brennan's study, which already had been vacuumed, polished, dusted and scrubbed.

Cade walked around the room, glancing at the books that lined the shelves, at the vast walnut desktop that was gleaming and bare except for a Lucite pen holder containing an assortment of ballpoint pens, the kind sold in packs at discount drugstores.

He sat down in Gene's chair behind the desk. When he leaned back, it creaked and bobbed precariously. "Same rickety old chair. Gene refused to get it fixed or buy himself a new one. He hated spending money on himself. He wanted almost every penny to go back into the business."

Kylie walked to the window and looked out. From the broken

desk chair, the view was of four dented old metal garbage cans lined against the side of the house surrounded by the remains of frozen weeds. In the immediate foreground was the rotting wooden door that opened into the old-fashioned, unused coal bin in the cellar. The visual effect was that of a seedy back alley.

"This must've been a particularly unappealing sight right before garbage pickup day, with the cans overflowing and all," Kylie mused aloud. "And in warm weather if the window was open, the incomparable aroma of rotting garbage would fill the air."

She shook her head, puzzled. "Of all the rooms in this house, with so many of them overlooking the front or backyards with those big beautiful trees and flower beds, why did Uncle Gene choose this one for his office at home? Let's face it, it's hardly a room with a view."

"A nice view didn't matter to him. I doubt that Gene ever glanced out the window. Your uncle was very single-minded, Kylie. If he was doing his paperwork in here, that would be his sole focus. Period. And keep in mind that Gene didn't find garbage offensive. BrenCo started out as a household waste disposal firm, remember?"

"Please don't make that awful 'garbage was his bread and butter' joke!" Kylie held up her hand, as if to ward it off. "I remember my grandfather and my uncles each saying it about ten times every time we visited. And my mom would always nudge me to remind me to be polite and laugh."

"Bad jokes aren't part of my presentation," Cade promised. "I want to tell you how—"

"I know the basic facts," Kylie cut in. Cade Austin's wildly successful stewardship at BrenCo was a familiar part of Brennan lore. "Uncle Gene hired you away from the SaniTech Corporation eight years ago and gave you free rein at the company. You have an environmental engineering degree and an M.B.A., and you built BrenCo into a leading industry giant in the field of universal waste disposal."

"Gene allowed me to implement my ideas and choose my own team," agreed Cade. "I brought in Noah Wyckoff, among others.

We built up BrenCo and you inherited it. That makes you a player in the field, too, Kylie.''

Kylie winced. Her friends tended to equate waste disposal with Chernobyl, and she well remembered the jokes she and her brother used to make about BrenCo—that the color of the waters flowing in McClain Creek was an unnatural neon chartreuse, that workers at the plant glowed in the dark. Not true, of course. Just jokes.

But now she was a player in the field she'd mocked for years.

"Don't flinch." Cade was scowling. Since he couldn't keep his eyes off her, he observed her every reaction, no matter how brief or subtle. "Come on, Kylie, as a public defender you've dealt with all kinds of felonies but you don't flinch and wince or shudder at murder, grand larceny, armed robbery or assault, do you? Well, BrenCo's disposal of toxic waste is both safe and legal yet you seem determined to cast it as a repulsive and unseemly crime against—"

"That is sophistry, and if we were in court, I'd be all over you for it."

"I think it's a pretty good point," he drawled. "And even though we're not in court, I wouldn't mind having you all over me."

"Now there's a line worthy of either Beavis or Butthead." Kylie turned away from him to stare out the window again.

Once again, Cade read her loud and clear. She would rather contemplate the ugly view of the garbage cans than waste her eyesight looking at a crude, regressed adolescent like him.

He frowned. What a lousy time for her to shift into humorless feminist gear! Was she expecting an apology from him? He railed against it. Apologize for what? He'd made a little joke, and being the prickly Brennan that she was, she had been quick and eager to take offense.

For a few long minutes, neither of them spoke.

"Gene's office here at his home looks exactly like it did when he was alive. It's as if he just stepped out for a minute or two." Cade was the first to break the silence. After all, he was used to dealing with Brennans, and she was merely another one.

He stared moodily at Kylie as she gazed out the window. Who

was he kidding? She was so much more than a troublesome Brennan and his pursuit of her was not solely motivated by BrenCo. Cade faced the uneasy truth. She was the woman who'd seized his imagination—and other more tangible parts of him—as no other woman before her.

He studied her profile, the smooth ivory skin and the soft pink of her cheeks, the graceful curve of her neck. He watched her tuck several loose strands of her dark brown hair behind her ear, drawing his attention to her delicately shaped earlobes, pierced with small gold studs. Out of her professional garb, wearing jeans and a sweater, she looked very young, relaxed and informal...but twice as lovely and sexy as hell.

As if on cue, he felt his sex stir, growing heavier and thicker as he continued his perusal of her. Though her sweater was comfortably oversize—certainly nothing like the second skin garments favored by her cousins Brenda and Bridget—he could see the outlined curves of her breasts. The subtlety, the private secrets of what lay beneath the thick fabric both teased and tantalized him because he *knew* what was so discreetly concealed.

The sensual memory of Kylie Brennan lying on his couch, her eyes closed, her lips parted, her lush, naked breasts in his hands struck him hard. Literally. Cade leaned forward in the broken chair and nearly groaned aloud.

"Nothing has been taken out of Uncle Gene's study since he died?" Kylie's voice drifted through the erotic haze encompassing him. "It's always looked like this, so sparse and impersonal?"

She turned to gaze around the office. "There are no pictures or certificates on the walls, not even a diploma. Nothing to break up the plain old beige wallpaper. And the desk and the tabletops are bare. There is almost a kind of monastic feel to the place."

Cade, who was far from feeling remotely monastic, merely grunted a nonreply.

"This is the first time I've ever been in Uncle Gene's office," Kylie continued softly, walking along the length of the bookshelves, glancing at the titles stored there. Engineering textbooks by the dozens. Bound thick copies of environmental studies. A dictionary. Several biographies, all of military officers. It appeared that light reading to Gene Brennan meant the voluminous editions chronicling the lives of Pershing, MacArthur and Patton, among others.

"When we visited here as kids, this door was always closed and I used to wonder what was inside," Kylie confessed. "Dad told Devlin and me that Uncle Gene's office was strictly off-limits." She smiled at the memory. "As born-and-bred military offspring, we knew that meant to keep out, no questions asked."

"So you never even tried to sneak in here? Not once?" Cade recalled his own days as a born-and-bred military offspring. He knew he would've made it inside the off-limits territory at least once or been busted trying.

The difference between officers' kids and noncoms' kids? Between navy and army brats? Or simply the basic differences between rule-conscious Kylie and risk-taking Cade?

"Never, not once," Kylie affirmed earnestly.

"Such obedient angels!" Cade laughed. "No wonder Gene preferred you and your brother to his hometown nieces and nephews. Apparently, that gang had no respect for the rule not to enter his Holy of Holies. Right up until he died, Gene would become irate telling how Brenda, Brent and Ian would sneak into his office whenever they were at the house visiting their grandparents."

"Weren't they just children at the time?"

"Of course. But Gene was convinced they were treacherous little connivers and he never changed his view of them. After your grandparents died, he wouldn't let them into the house. He said there was no reason for them to be there, that he'd only tolerated their presence in his house because his mother and father insisted on inviting their grandchildren over."

"That's awfully cold." Kylie thought of the way Brenda had referred to their uncle Gene. Mean old coot. Nasty old grouch. Apparently, she had some justifiable grounds for those sentiments. "He—he didn't have a very strong sense of family, did he?"

But Uncle Gene had supported his parents, he'd adored her dad and he'd left controlling interest in his successful company to her. Kylie felt both guilty and disloyal for judging him harshly.

"Gene wasn't a doting uncle and he never pretended to be. Your younger cousins didn't irritate him as much as the older ones, but at best he was indifferent to them." Cade shrugged. "As for Gene's sense of family—he felt he couldn't escape his family. He considered them to be the proverbial millstone around his neck."

Kylie eyed him shrewdly. "And now the Brennans are *your* proverbial millstone?"

"Millstone? Ha! Try concrete abutment."

He had a flat, droll way of delivering certain lines that made her unsure if he was kidding or not. Kylie gave an uncertain little laugh. "I guess you must've gone ballistic when the will was read. I inherited the shares in BrenCo and you got the concrete abutment. Makes you wonder if Uncle Gene was of sound mind."

Their eyes met.

"He was," Cade affirmed. "And as Noah often reminds me, things could've been a lot worse. If Artie and Guy had those shares, BrenCo would already be on the block."

"I just don't know why Uncle Gene left them to me." Kylie stared at Cade, bewildered. "Why not my father or my brother?"

"I admit I've wondered that myself," he murmured.

He didn't mention that he'd also lamented the fact that Gene had bypassed Wayne and Devlin Brennan in favor of Kylie. He'd talked to both men by telephone and knew that either of them would've left all decisions regarding BrenCo to him. Neither one would have allowed any other Brennan to make a pitch at selling the company because Cade would've nixed it first. But Kylie "let's-give-all-sides-a-fair-hearing-just-like-we-do-in-court" Brennan was a wild card.

And the wild card happened to be the heiress.

He gave her a brooding stare. What a helluva dilemma Gene had set up for him! He resented Kylie but he wanted her, too. And the balance was perpetually shifting. When he was in her presence desire won out, but apart from her the scales tipped in favor of resentment.

Kylie felt his eyes on her. "I—I know this can't be easy for you, but I hope you understand my position. I have to be fair. And I'd like to weigh all the—''

"What was Brenda really doing here this afternoon?" Cade broke in, frowning. "Skip the catching-up-with-family-news excuse, we both know it's bogus. Was she trying to turn you against me? Telling you that I was involved with—"

"You have Brenda all wrong." It was Kylie's turn to interrupt. She did *not* care to delve into another rehash of Cade's relationship with the lady dentist from Cleveland. Imagining him with another woman—kissing her, caressing her, smiling into her eyes—made her stomach churn with flulike intensity. Best to get this discussion back to BrenCo.

"The reason Brenda came by was to warn me that her father and Uncle Guy would be calling me today to set up a meeting with them and their consultant, a man named Axel Dodge. Brenda and Bobbie are solidly behind you, Cade. Or else they're solidly against Artie and Guy, I'm not quite sure which cause is stronger."

"Axel Dodge?" Cade didn't look at all pleased. "So Guy and Artie are conspiring with that weasel?" He heaved a sigh of disgust. "It figures."

"You know him?"

"His reputation—and it's not a good one—precedes him. Dodge is based in Cleveland and acts as something of an independent agent, a business headhunter of sorts, pointing out the acquisition value of smaller companies to larger ones. Then, if there is a successful buyout or takeover, Dodge gets a commission fee."

"Sort of like a real estate agent?"

"More like a remora." Cade stood up and crossed the office to stand in front of her. "Don't listen to him, Kylie. Dodge will attempt to snow you with half-truths and bits and pieces of information taken out of context and if that doesn't work, he'll throw in some blatant lies. And your uncles will be willing dupes, going along with whatever he says so they can get some quick money for their BrenCo shares. I'm telling you now, Kylie, I won't let that happen."

He moved closer, and the purposeful sexual intent burning in his eyes told her something else. That he was going to make something happen right now. That he was going to touch her again, to kiss her again. Because he really wanted her or because he knew his lovemaking successfully blocked out her capacity for reasoning and judgment?

Kylie backed away from him. Cade's agenda and his fierce opposition to the possible sale of BrenCo was well-known to her, but she still hadn't heard the other side. Should she assume that Cade was also willing to snow her with half-truths, with bits and pieces of information taken out of context or even blatant lies? And Cade had a powerful advantage that she feared he wouldn't hesitate to use—her explosive attraction to him.

She wanted him badly and he had to know it. She was afraid of the lengths to which she might go because she'd never been in a comparable situation before. She had never ached to be in a man's arms the way she was aching to be held by Cade right now. She'd never hungered for a man's kiss the way she desperately longed for Cade's mouth to open over hers this very minute.

Shaken by the force of her emotions, Kylie scurried from the study. She'd taken two steps into the hall when his arm snaked out and pulled her back inside, closing the door behind her. He pressed her back against it and leaned heavily into her.

Before she could say a word, he bent his head and kissed her, long and slow and deep. Kylie felt herself sinking luxuriously into the dark seas of sensuality as he moved his hands over her, caressing her breasts and hips and thighs. As if he had every right to do it, as if she already belonged to him. As if he were irrevocably branding her with his touch.

Trembling, Kylie raised her hands to his shoulders to cling to him and kissed him back with a sweet, searing fire all her own. She couldn't believe this was happening to her, she'd never dreamed desire and need could burn so hotly within her. He was making her want him in a way she'd never wanted a man before, and the urgency, the desperation, was staggering.

Their tongues met and teased in a seductive mating ritual, an erotic simulation of what was to come. Kylie felt the heaviness of his arousal against her, she smoothed her hands over the broad expanse of his back and combed her fingers through the springy thickness of his hair.

She'd never been the possessive type; she had always considered herself to be too fair-minded and egalitarian for that, but as she caressed him, as she kissed him, Kylie knew a primal yearning to make Cade Austin completely her own. To mark him off-limits to every other woman forever.

At long last, they simultaneously broke the kiss, though their lips remained only centimeters apart as they held each other, gasping and light-headed from the twin forces of passion and lack of air.

Her eyes closed, Kylie rested her head against Cade's shoulder as he rubbed her nape. "Let's go to bed." His voice was a raspy growl that sent shivers of longing rippling through her.

She wanted to, Kylie admitted achingly to herself. Right now, in the middle of the afternoon with the cleaning crew very much present in Uncle Gene's mausoleum of a house, she wanted to slip upstairs to one of the dusty old bedrooms and make love with a man she'd known for far too short a time. A man who might very well be using her sexually for his own ends... And according to her own cousin, who could blame him?

Kylie knew the answer to that. To her, the act of physical love was an act of commitment based on trust and emotional intimacy. It was what she'd been taught, what she firmly believed.

And even though she was in Cade's arms shaking with desire for him, she wasn't sure if she trusted him. As for emotional intimacy, how could it exist between two people who barely knew each other?

"We can't, Cade." Her voice seemed to be reverberating in her head. It sounded more like a miserable wail than the firm statement of intent she'd meant to deliver.

And Cade misinterpreted her completely. "I know, baby. Not here. We'll go to my place. Come on." He hooked his arm around her waist and pulled open the door, moving into the hall with her.

Kylie remembered how easily he'd swept her onto the porch earlier, how she'd walked right along with him though her mind was issuing the opposite orders to her legs. She knew a repeat performance was about to occur—this time with her ending up in his Buick on the way to his bed—unless she made herself unmistakably clear.

"Cade!" she cried desperately, her voice almost beseeching.

Cade didn't even slow down. That breathless little whimper was less a protest, more a plea. He couldn't be faulted for not knowing what she was pleading for, Kylie acknowledged grimly. Try again.

"Cade, no. I'm not going with you. You are leaving and I'm staying here." This time she sounded as if she meant it.

Cade stopped in his tracks, bringing her to a halt as well. This time he had heard what she'd said. Perhaps the appearance of a maid at the same time that the heavy brass door knocker sounded served to aid his comprehension.

He stared down at Kylie, watching her lovely face transpose into a mask of determination. "Don't say no, Kylie," he growled.

"You know it's too soon, Cade."

"I know you think it's too soon." He arched his dark brows in the way that already had become so familiar to her. "But waiting isn't going to change anything and you know it. We want each other—hell, we're *burning* for each other—and we are going to—"

"The cable man is here, Miss Brennan," the maid announced.

Kylie and Cade started visibly. They'd been so absorbed in their sexually-charged exchange, they had forgotten both the maid and the rapping at the door. But the maid hadn't been distracted; she'd answered the knock and admitted a uniformed cable installer.

"First time in Port McClain history that the cable guy shows up when he's supposed to, and it has to be today," Cade grumbled. His eyes narrowed, and he caught Kylie's wrist, halting her. "You must be planning to stay around for a while if you're getting cable."

Having the house cleaned and the utilities turned on were basic necessities for even the shortest stay. But having cable TV installed...that was not a short-term necessity—it was an action that implied longevity.

"I haven't decided how long I'm staying in Port McClain," Kylie murmured. She used her other hand to pry his fingers from her wrist. "I told you that in the note I sent."

"Where's your TV set, sir?" asked the cable installer. He'd grown impatient waiting for the couple to acknowledge him and had taken matters in his own hands, addressing Cade.

"It's her TV set," said Cade. "It's her house."

And *her* company, added a devil's voice in his head. For an eerie moment, he almost felt Gene Brennan's presence right there in the hall, and his old boss was laughing uproariously at the perverse joke.

"Right this way." Kylie headed down the hall toward the kitchen, where she knew one of the two TV sets in the house was located. The installer followed her.

Cade debated whether to stay or leave. Traipsing after Kylie struck him as a tactical error. She'd already said no to him, and he didn't want to play stalker. Nor did he wish to appear overeager, pathetically hanging around for whatever crumbs of attention she might bestow on him. Better to withdraw and establish his—

"It's gone!" Kylie's cry of dismay echoed throughout the first floor.

Automatically, Cade rushed to the kitchen, his strategic planning session forgotten.

Kylie, the cable man and one of the cleaning crew were standing there, looking at the empty space where Gene's twenty-inch-screen television set had been.

"There was no TV here when I came in," the maid stated unequivocally.

Kylie's eyes met Cade's, then flicked to the cable installer. "I guess I should've checked first. I didn't think that Uncle Gene might've given the set away," she murmured apologetically.

"Gene didn't give it away," said Cade. "Your father inherited this house and everything in it and when your folks left after the funeral, they took only some books and photographs with them. Everything else was left intact and the place was locked up. It's supposedly been locked ever since."

"Maybe there's been a burglary," suggested the maid, her interest piqued. "Is there anything else missing?"

"Like maybe another TV?" prompted the cable man. "Because if there aren't any sets here, I'm wasting my time. I do have some other stops to make, you know."

"Gene kept a smaller TV set in his bedroom," said Cade. "We may as well go up and see if it's still there."

He and Kylie, accompanied by the entire cleaning crew and the cable installer trooped upstairs to Gene Brennan's bedroom. Where there was no TV set.

"Well, I'm outta here." The cable installer departed in a flash.

"Maybe you'd better see what else is missing," suggested one of the cleaning crew. "None of us has cleaned upstairs and we don't want to go into a room and be blamed for—"

"Nobody is blaming you," Cade interrupted. "I have a very good idea who has been helping himself around here. Go on back to work, and Kylie and I will go through the rooms and see what else he's taken."

The crew headed back downstairs, leaving Kylie and Cade alone.

"He?" Kylie repeated as they walked around her uncle's bedroom. She had no idea what to look for, which belongings might be gone. Uncle Gene's bedroom had not been declared off-limits during her childhood visits but she couldn't remember ever setting foot in this room. "Who do you have in mind?"

"Your light-fingered cousin Brent, who else? I should've guessed he would pull something like this. I *would've* guessed if I'd given it any thought, but I haven't been out here since your folks left."

"Cade, you really have no evidence to support your accusations."

"Oh, please! Spare me the innocent-until-proven-guilty rhetoric. I'm not the district attorney and I don't need evidence to build a case, and you're not Brent's attorney so you don't have to mount a defense. Let's just use logic and common sense. Brent has a track record as a thief and things are missing from his relatives' house. He took those two TV sets and probably more.

I'd bet the zoning permit to build our new infectious waste autoclave on that."

Kylie grimaced at the imagery. "Whatever happened to betting the farm? And what on earth is an infectious waste autoclave? Not that I really want to know."

"You ought to know, boss. It's your business to know." Cade sat down on Gene's bed. The ancient box spring and frame squeaked ominously, as if protesting the unwelcome burden. "BrenCo has a zoning permit to build a two-million-dollar autoclave, which is like an industrial-size pressure cooker. By the end of the year, we'll be handling ninety tons of medical waste a day."

"Does that means BrenCo will be importing medical waste into Port McClain?" Kylie was incredulous.

"Correct. BrenCo will be taking medical waste from in and out of state, drawing from hospitals and clinics, veterinarians' offices, dentists' offices and mortuaries."

Cade's face was alight with an enthusiasm Kylie couldn't comprehend. Had her parents and brother felt this way when she had tried to explain why she'd defended the criminals she had been assigned?

"Medical waste consists of gowns and needles exposed to infectious patients as well as blood and body tissues," Cade continued, eager to school her in what appeared to be a favorite subject of his. "Since an autoclave sterilizes infectious waste with heat and pressure instead of burning, it doesn't produce air or water pollution like regular hospital incinerators. They spew large amounts of dioxin and mercury into the air. After treatment in our autoclave, the sterilized waste will be able to be sent to a municipal landfill."

"And that's good?"

"Of course. It's good for everybody, especially Port McClain."

"Does the community know how very lucky it is?" Kylie asked sardonically. Tons of imported medical waste did not strike her as good fortune, even if it was slated to be sterilized. "Or have you kept your plans a secret, to be sprung on an unsuspecting town after the dirty deal has already been signed, sealed and delivered?"

"You sound as if you're making a closing argument to the jury." Cade lay back on Gene's bed. At least three springs in the mattress stabbed him and he switched positions, trying to avoid being impaled. How had Gene managed to sleep on this lumpy torture rack night after night?

"There is no nefarious secret deal, Kylie." He raised himself on his elbow and propped his head on his hand. "BrenCo presented the plans in a town meeting shortly before Gene's death and explained all about the autoclave and its functions, just like I explained it to you. We had a videotape presentation and a question and answer session, we encouraged citizen participation, then scheduled another meeting for a vote on the project."

"You did?" Kylie was taken by surprise. She didn't expect corporations to invite citizen input.

Cade nodded. Her obvious amazement amused him. "I minored in industrial psychology, Kylie. I know about the importance of maintaining excellent community relations. BrenCo's PR department is a model for others in the field. Anyway, the bottom line is that the autoclave will bring at least a hundred new jobs into Port McClain, the process is superior to any existing ones, and we even received a recommendation from the EPA. The town's support for the project was overwhelming. We have the zoning permit and building will begin—"

He broke off abruptly. If BrenCo were sold, he didn't know when or if the autoclave would be built, or if he would even be part of the company. Cade rejected the possibility outright. It was definitely time to take another tack.

"When will building begin?" asked Kylie.

"Come over here and I'll tell you."

She shot him a quick glance. He was smiling the kind of smugly arrogant male smile that made a woman itch to erase it. Challenge glittered in his eyes. Kylie heaved an exasperated sigh. So they were back to playing those games again?

"Do you honestly believe that the sight of you lying on a bed is so irresistible that if I come any closer, I won't be able to stop myself from jumping you?"

"Well, I wouldn't recommend jumping on this bed. It's liable to collapse. Just sit down on the edge. Slowly and carefully."

"No, Cade. I told you that I will not—"

"We have a lot to talk about, Kylie. Our autoclave discussion sidetracked us from the problem of Brent who's undoubtedly been robbing this place blind since Gene's funeral." Cade lay flat on his back and raised his hands behind his head, to pillow it. "We may as well be comfortable during our little chat, hmm? Really, *really* comfortable."

She recognized at that moment that he was kidding. He'd been teasing her and by taking him seriously she had not only leaped at the bait, but she'd also swallowed it whole.

"Congratulations. You tricked me into sounding like a testy old prude. I hope you have a good laugh over it."

Cade swung his legs over the side of the bed, then stood up. "Actually, I was hoping things would go the other way—that the sight of me on the bed would prove to be so irresistible that you wouldn't be able to stop yourself from jumping me."

"Don't bother, Cade." She tilted her head, looking up at him from beneath her lashes. "It won't work twice."

"That's the trouble with smart women," Cade pretended to complain. "They're always one step ahead."

She folded her arms and eyed him assessingly. "I have a feeling that the day *anyone* gets one step ahead of you has yet to dawn."

"If that's a compliment, thank you. If it's an insult, consider it duly noted."

She left her uncle's bedroom and walked down the hall, Cade at her side. He reached for her hand. She swung it away from him, tucking both into the front pockets of her jeans.

"Okay, I get it. You don't want to hold hands. Am I allowed to put my arm around you?"

This time she didn't miss the needling note in his voice. "No," she said sweetly.

"Too soon for that, huh?"

She caught his reference to their little scene downstairs, and an embarrassing flood of color heated her cheeks. "As far as I'm concerned, forever is too soon for—"

"Careful, sweetie. You're on the verge of sounding like a testy old prude again."

"I know you're trying to provoke me, Cade, but it's not going to work."

"If I really wanted to provoke you, you'd be provoked, Kylie. Instantly."

"You're that irritating? That obnoxious? That confident of your ability to be infuriating?"

"All of that and more."

"No doubt you honed your talents by associating with the Brennan family for the past eight years?"

"No doubt," he agreed.

He sounded the way her brother used to, back in those days when teasing her was their sibling way of life. Kylie cast a quick covert glance at Cade. What was it about him that made her feel so off balance? How could she feel like his kid sister one minute, then feel like she could fall madly in love with him the next, only to want to smack him the moment after that?

"Where are we going now?" Cade asked, sauntering alongside her, close enough to touch her if he chose.

Kylie waited for him to do it, but he chose not to. She told herself that she was relieved. Perhaps, he'd finally gotten her hands-off message. "I'm going to my grandparents' room."

She swerved to the right, accidentally brushing against him. Every erogenous zone in her body clamored for her to do it again—and to prolong the contact. She restrained herself. "Although I can't remember if there was anything worth stealing in their room."

"Well, if there was, Brent has already swiped it, you can count on that."

"Cade, it really isn't fair to—"

"Wearing your public defender hat again? All right, counselor, I'll keep my unsubstantiated speculations to myself—for now." He paused on the threshold of her grandparents' bedroom. "Were you really planning on having dinner tonight with Brenda and Noah?"

She stepped inside the room. "Yes, but I think that's off now.

It seems unlikely they'll come back for me. In fact, I hope they don't. I've never relished being the third wheel."

"You won't be. You're having dinner with me tonight. I'll pick you up here at seven...unless you're planning to stay another night at the Port McClain Hotel? If that's the case, I'll pick you up there."

"I checked out of the hotel but—"

"Good. I'll be here then. Seven o'clock." He took off down the hall, breaking into a run.

Kylie hurried to the wooden railing that lined the upstairs hall, overlooking the staircase. Cade was already bounding down the steps, two at a time. "I didn't agree to have dinner with you," she called as he reached the bottom step.

He didn't look up, he didn't stop, he left the house without responding to her protest. She didn't know if he'd pretended not to hear her or if he really couldn't—after all, two vacuum cleaners were whirring loudly downstairs.

As things now stood, he would be arriving back here at seven o'clock to take her to dinner.

Kylie decided she was annoyed at his high-handedness. She had never appreciated macho displays of dominance...not that she'd been subjected to many. There was something about her— her no-nonsense demeanor? her ability to argue?—that caused males to treat her as a genderless equal. Professionally, that worked to her advantage. On a personal level, being genderless did not garner a whole lot of dates.

Kylie hadn't really minded. She was very much the captain of her own ship and always had been, to use one of her father's favorite navy metaphors.

But to use another one...Cade Austin was the admiral of the entire fleet.

Five

The Creek View restaurant was aptly named because it was built along the banks of Port McClain Creek, and a wall of windows provided a panoramic view. The decor of the place provided an odd contrast, the stone fireplace and wood-paneled walls suggesting the rustic atmosphere of a cabin, while the snowy white linen tablecloths, three-taper candelabras and gold-edged china place settings on each table were distinctly formal.

As a hostess seated Kylie and Cade in a private little alcove beside the window, rain began to fall, hitting the glass with increasing force. Kylie glanced outside at the fast-moving waters. It wouldn't take much more water for the rough wide creek to overflow its banks.

Cade followed her gaze. "Worrying about the possibilities of a flood?"

"Not quite worrying. Wondering," she amended. "Does it happen often?"

"Too often. But none of the businesses along the creek want to move. They claim that a waterfront location is too valuable to leave, so they simply clean up after every flood and persevere.

Your cousin Bridget's favorite hangout, Club Reek, got its name because certain flood aromas lingered.''

"And nobody minds?"

"Nobody minds."

"Just the sort of hardy, undaunted souls to welcome infectious waste with genuine enthusiasm," Kylie murmured. "You knew what you were doing when you chose to expand BrenCo here in Port McClain."

"I sense a backhanded compliment, but thank you all the same. And in case you're wondering why I brought you to a restaurant on a flood plain in the middle of a rainstorm, you mentioned earlier that you liked fish. This place serves the best in Port McClain."

"Along with everything else, it seems." Kylie leafed through the thick menu. "Italian, Mexican, Chinese, French, Thai, Greek and good old American dishes, too. Kind of an international extravaganza."

"I recommend the trout," Cade said dryly. "It's fresh, grilled or broiled, and always good. A wholesale place that sells frozen entrées to restaurants provides the international extravaganza. The microwave does the rest."

"Still, the thought of traveling the world frozen course by course is kind of intriguing." Kylie smiled across the table at him. "Think of the possibilities—an appetizer from Italy, a salad from Mexico, the vegetable course from China, the meat course from—"

"Sounds like one of the dinners my mother used to make. She picked up new recipes from every country we lived in and saw no reason not to mix them up. We had some harrowing meals."

"One of the hazards of being a military brat," Kylie agreed with a laugh. "What countries did you live in?"

"We were stationed at posts in Japan, Germany, and Italy, plus in five different states. We sometimes mixed with air force kids because there were air bases in the vicinity, but there were no navy families around."

"Dad had a tour of duty in Italy, but not near the army. We also lived in Spain, England, the Philippines and four states."

Military kids had their own versions of war stories about living in foreign places and transferring to school after school, and Kylie and Cade swapped them, laughing.

"And your dad was a high ranking officer, a captain." Cade studied her. "The army's equivalent of a colonel, am I right?"

"Something like that," she agreed.

He couldn't seem to drag his eyes away from her. She looked cool and lovely and serene. Her simple navy blue dress might have appeared plain—even severe—on anyone else, but on her it was as classy and elegant as the pearl necklace encircling her neck. He guessed she could wear torn dirty rags and make them look tasteful. And sexy.

He noticed that the top two buttons of her dress were undone—a casually stylish touch, not meant to be titillating—but he was aroused by the modest exposure of her skin. He wished she would unfasten another button so he could see more; he wanted to undo each and every button on her proper little dress...

With great effort, Cade dragged his mind from *that* path. He cleared his throat. "I bet you were the model navy captain's daughter. Good manners, good grades, good looks. The perfect little princess."

"No, the highest ranking officer's daughter would be the princess. That's an admiral's daughter in the navy. In the army, she'd be the general's daughter."

"Hmm. I used to know one of those."

"Was she a perfect little princess?" Kylie was curious. She'd never known a general's daughter, though she'd met admirals' daughters from time to time. They did tend to be princesses of perfection.

"Leslie was neither perfect nor princesslike." Cade chuckled, as if he was enjoying a private joke. "She was—how can I describe her? Born to be Wild. Always looking for adventure."

"And you were happy to accommodate her, uh, quest?" Kylie asked drolly.

"Sure. Wasn't there some restless son of a seaman eager to seek adventure with Captain Brennan's darling daughter?"

"I don't have an adventurous streak. I still don't. I was Born to be Dull, I guess."

"Oh, I don't know about that. Defending criminals for a lousy state paycheck could be interpreted as rebellious by some."

"My mom and dad did consider my work in the Public Defender's office to be a phase, one I would hopefully outgrow."

"I bet your folks felt like writing the governor a thank-you note for making those budget cuts. To be honest, I don't like the idea of you associating with felons and prisoners, either."

"You'd rather that I be here, associating with BrenCo and my relatives?" she countered archly.

"I don't mind having you here associating with me, Kylie. I think we're going to be very, very close."

He gave her a slow sexy smile as he stretched his legs under the table, inadvertently brushing against hers. Well, not quite inadvertently, he admitted. Quite deliberately, in fact. He positioned his calves on either side of hers and left them there.

Frissons of heat emanated from their point of contact and shot through Kylie's entire body, centralizing in her deepest most secret part. "Behave, Cade," she warned.

Her voice was embarrassingly shaky. Why, she'd sounded more commanding and in control as a first year law student nervously arguing her first moot court competition!

"Do I have to?" Cade reached across the table and laid his hand over hers.

"Yes." She knew that taking action—withdrawing her hand from his and tucking her legs tightly beneath her chair out of his reach—would add more credibility to her order. But a sensual lethargy was fast suffusing her. Her legs felt too weak to move, her hand felt too good in the firm clasp of his. Kylie left them exactly where they were.

However, in case he misread her body language she felt obliged to inform him, "And to avoid any misunderstandings right from the start, after dinner we're going our separate ways. I'm going back to Uncle Gene's house and you're going to your own home."

He lifted her hand to his lips and gently nibbled on her fingertips. "Consider me forewarned."

She watched him through a fast-blinding haze of sensuality. Her body felt languid and limp. If he could affect her so profoundly with such a simple caress, her declaration of how this evening must end might have to be revised...

Kylie gave her head a shake, as if to dislodge that traitorous thought. Though she knew Cade Austin better than she had this morning when they'd ended up on his sofa together, she still didn't know him well enough to sleep with him tonight, she reminded herself sternly. It was time for her to set limits, to redirect the course of action.

"Where do you live? Near Uncle Gene's place?" she asked crisply as she yanked her hand away from him. She nearly knocked over the candelabra in the process.

Cade was quick to steady it. His smile told her he knew all about the riot going on inside her, but he politely answered her question. "I have a house on the outskirts of town, in the McClain Woods development. A nice neighborhood, fairly new compared to Gene's part of town. Your uncle Guy and aunt Lauretta bought a house there about seven years ago."

"So you're neighbors?" Her heart was still racing. Was it possible to will it back to its regular rate?

"Not exactly. They live about eight blocks from me, too far to walk to borrow a cup of sugar or to drop in for a cup of coffee. Thank God."

"You're not the neighborly type? Or just not neighborly to anyone named Brennan?"

"My neighbors seem to think I'm okay. Draw your own conclusions."

"Oh, I will. I am."

She gave a sudden gasp. Cade had reached under the table and lifted her foot onto his lap. She felt his fingers caress her ankle then slip inside the soft navy leather of her pumps to begin a sensuous massage of her instep.

Kylie was shocked. No one had ever touched her foot like this. She'd never imagined such a thing! Yet she was feeling the effects of his provocative caress all through her body, in every intimate place...

She jerked upright in her chair, dragging her foot away from his exquisitely pleasurable, wicked touch. "Don't, Cade." Her breath caught in her throat. "We decided to forgo the seduction, remember?"

"No, I have no recollection of that." He pretended to look puzzled. "Was this a mutual decision or one of your unilateral decrees?"

"I don't issue decrees. I—strive for consensus whenever it's humanly possible."

"Maybe back in Philly you do, but not here. I think you're on a Port McClain power trip, relishing your position as BrenCo's biggest cheese."

He was clearly teasing her but his words stung anyway. What was that old saw about there being truth in jest? Troubled, Kylie pondered her behavior. "Have I really been acting that way?"

"I've been hearing a lot of 'Cade, no' and 'Cade, don't' and 'Cade, we can't' and 'Cade, we shouldn't.' Very repressive, boss. Definitely symptoms of a power trip."

"That isn't what I meant. I was discussing business, not sex, and you know it." She was turning out to be an incredibly easy target, she acknowledged wryly; Cade got her every time he took aim.

A waiter arrived and Cade gave their orders. Trout for both of them. The moment he left, Cade turned his attention back to Kylie. "Was I being chauvinistic and overbearing again, ordering for you?" His eyes gleamed.

She knew he was trying to rile her, expecting a repeat of her earlier coffee-tea fuss. Kylie balked at playing the sour straight man to his comic foil; she was neither prim nor humorless.

"I don't object to a man ordering for me although I do think the concept is more than a little retro." She settled back in her chair and folded her arms, unconsciously assuming a classic defensive posture. And went on the offensive. "Did your lady dentist friend from Cleveland enjoy such quaint—"

"Remind me to thank Brenda for spreading irrelevant gossip and pointless speculation," Cade growled. "I repeat what I said earlier, I have not seen Anne Woodley in nearly a year and a half and I have no plans to see her in the future. Case closed."

"I thought you said you two remained on good terms." Kylie was enjoying the cross examination. If they were in court, she'd be the one scoring the points with the jury. "Is no contact at all your idea of good terms?"

Cade shifted uncomfortably. "Look, it's not like we were in love or anything ridiculous like that. Anne kept talking about her biological clock running out. She made it quite clear that she wanted a sperm donor, not a relationship. I have to admit the whole scenario gave me the creeps and I bailed out."

"I can relate to that. There's something very unappealing about being used, whether it's for your sperm or your shares in BrenCo."

Their eyes met. "I could deny that I'm not using you but you wouldn't believe me, so what's the point?"

Kylie was disheartened. She'd never heard such a lackluster denial. Even so, she knew she was susceptible to him, to being used by him. Her mind clouded when he looked at her in that particular way and her senses rioted at his simplest touch. It was a humbling admission, and one that stirred her ire.

Reflexively, Kylie struck back and she knew exactly where to aim. "Did I tell you that I finally have phone service? Guess who was my first caller?"

"It was either Guy or Artie," Cade surmised grimly. "Calling for the purpose of setting up your meeting with Axel Dodge."

She nodded.

"Are you going to tell me where and when it will be held?"

"They specifically asked that you not be included in the meeting, Cade. And that I not reveal any information about it."

"I expected that of them. I suppose I was foolish to expect something more from you."

Was that *hurt* resonating in his voice? Kylie was taken aback. Or was he merely acting, and doing a stellar job of it?

But suppose he was genuinely disappointed in her? Kylie hated letting people down. She'd set out to needle Cade not to crush him. Remorse flooded her. "Cade, I want you to understand that I can't—"

"You don't owe me any explanations, Kylie," he interrupted coldly. Tension seemed to visibly emanate from him. "You're free to do as you please, to see whoever you want, whenever you want. I have no intention of interfering."

The waiter arrived with a basket of rolls and Cade examined the contents, taking a long time to select his choice. Kylie stirred uneasily, watching him. He seemed so remote and withdrawn. And though she had halted his attempted seduction and tried to squelch his teasing, she found herself missing the camaraderie between them. If that's what it was.

"Cade?" Whatever it was, she wanted it back. She didn't like the cool distance between them and sought to end it. "I—You—" she faltered a little when he made no response whatsoever. "You know all about my family but I don't know a thing about yours, except that your folks are retired army who still like to travel. Do—do you have any sisters or brothers?"

Cade, who was meticulously buttering a piece of his chosen hard roll, looked up and grimaced. "Oh God, this sounds suspiciously like banal first date conversational filler. What's next, trading astrological signs?"

Kylie was undeterred. "I'm a Libra. You know, the scales. Weighing both sides."

"That certainly fits. Of course, you take it to extremes."

She let that one pass. "And you are?" she prompted.

"Tired of this conversation."

"All right. We can sit here in silence while you sulk, if that's what you prefer." Kylie took her turn delving into the breadbasket. "It won't bother me."

Cade said nothing. He continued to spread the butter on his roll with a concentration that set her nerves on edge. Surely Michelangelo hadn't put as much effort into painting the Sistine Chapel as Cade was expending on buttering that damn roll!

She looked around her. The restaurant was filling up, nearly every table was taken. And at every table, the diners were talking and laughing and looking convivial. Except at theirs, of course, where dour silence reigned supreme. The sound of the rain against the window seemed to magnify, and she watched it for a while.

When she finally glanced back at Cade, she found him staring at her.

Kylie met his gaze, only to find that she couldn't look away. The flames from the candles seemed to blaze in his eyes, accentuating the green flecks there. Hazel eyes flecked with green. They were the most captivating, fascinating eyes she'd ever seen.

Her mouth felt dry and she grasped her water glass. Cade reached across the table and took it from her, replacing it with a glass of chilled red wine.

"Try this," he instructed. "It's a vintage catawba wine from the Meiers Wine Cellars in Sandusky, Ohio. I know fish is supposed to be served with white wine but we'll disregard that decree. You ought to try a local product while you're here."

"I didn't know there were any vineyards in Ohio." Bemused, Kylie looked at the wine bottle. She couldn't remember the waiter placing it on the table, she had no recollection of him opening it. It was unnerving to realize that when she was in Cade's presence, she seemed to focus solely on him, vitally attuned to his every move, look and nuance. Anything or anyone else hovered on the periphery of her awareness.

Cade touched his own wineglass against hers. "To the future of BrenCo," he proposed the toast. "I think we can agree to drink to that, can't we?"

Kylie took a sip of the wine, then another. "It's not bad," she admitted. "In fact, it's pretty good."

He smiled. "It's only a matter of time before Sandusky takes its rightful place among the wine capitals of the world."

"And deservedly so." The more wine Kylie sipped, the more she appreciated its flavor and bouquet. She drained her glass before Cade was half-finished with his, and he quickly gave her a refill.

"You're not planning on getting me drunk, are you?" She frowned her disapproval at the very idea.

"Give me credit for some style, Kylie. Getting a woman drunk is sleazy and obvious, and I've never aspired to either."

"If I did get drunk, would you take advantage of my diminished capacity?"

"Not even if you begged me to." A flash of humor shone in his eyes. "Oh, before I forget—my sign is Taurus."

She knew it was his version of the peace-seeking olive branch and accepted it gratefully. "That would be the bull. Stubborn, single-minded, aggressive. A description of you?"

"Possibly," he conceded. "You're really into this astrology stuff, hmm?"

"No, but my grandmother—my mom's mother—is. I picked up a lot of information from her without even trying."

"Sort of absorbed it through osmosis? That happened to me with dog breeds. My sister raises weimaraners and talks about dogs incessantly. After spending an hour with her, I was able to hold my own in a detailed discussion about the declining popularity of poodles."

"The popularity of poodles is declining?"

"You don't want to know."

"So you do have a sister?" Kylie latched onto the nugget of personal information. She didn't really want to discuss poodles, anyway.

"I have four sisters—one thirteen months older than me, she's the weimaraner nut—and three younger. I also have two younger brothers."

"Wow! Seven kids!" Kylie's eyes widened. Having just one sibling, she found the number of Austins staggering. "Was it fun growing up with all those sisters and brothers? Moving around so often from army post to post must've really been a challenge with—"

"Fun and challenging doesn't quite describe it," Cade interjected. "It was really hard on my mother because my father was gone so much of the time. Dad always volunteered for unaccompanied assignments—it meant more money for the family, but sometimes I think he just wanted to escape from the nonstop commotion at home. My mother was overwhelmed by all the responsibility, she was dependent and passive and needed someone around to take charge and make decisions..."

His voice trailed off. "I don't know why I'm boring you with ancient history. All the Austin kids managed to grow up and are on their own, and my mother is thrilled to have my dad retired and with her full-time. End of story."

Kylie eyed him thoughtfully. "Would I be wrong in assuming that the someone who was in charge and made the decisions while your dad was away on all those remote tours of duty was you?"

"It was me," he confirmed her hunch. "And there were many times when I wasn't a patient, understanding John-Boy Walton type of big brother. My sisters and brothers claim I was a tyrant, although they're becoming more forgiving now, especially the ones with kids of their own."

"No wonder Uncle Gene found it so easy to dump the Brennans and their problems on you. You were a natural when it came to taking charge of a family," Kylie observed.

Cade shrugged noncommittally.

Being burdened too early with too many familial responsibilities could also explain his single status at thirty-five, Kylie mused. When it came to family life, he probably had a "been-there, done-that" mentality and was in no rush to take it all on again. Witness his lady dentist friend whose ticking biological clock had sent him on his way.

"Has your immersion in the Austin and Brennan clans made you rule out having a family of your own?" she asked lightly, trying to ignore the peculiar sinking sensation in her chest.

"No, I intend to have kids someday but I admit that so far, it hasn't been my top priority."

"BrenCo tops your priority list," she said knowledgeably and Cade nodded his agreement. "Well, if you want to have a big family you'd better not put it off too much longer," she felt obligated to advise. "After all, that ticking biological clock is—"

"Not quite ready to strike," Cade assured her. "And I have no intention of fathering a whole tribe, two children will suit me just fine." He toyed idly with the salt shaker. "I can still remember watching those two-child families when I was a kid and feeling acute envy."

"Envy?"

"With only two kids, each one could sit by the window in the car." He smiled wryly. "In the Austin family car, we didn't even get our own seat, we had to pile in on top of each other. Try riding cross-country like that. We did, four times. It was literally hell on wheels."

"Our family drove from Virginia to San Diego once, and Dev and I each sat by the window in the back seat," Kylie recalled.

"Which would've been my idea of paradise, no matter how

monotonous the drive." Cade chuckled. "You probably each had your own bedroom, too. Those three-bedroom houses on post or base were great for a family of four, but cramming a family of nine into one of them made for miserably close quarters. It was always the same—our parents in one bedroom, the three boys in another, the four girls in the other. Growing up, I viewed the prospect of having a bedroom all to myself as an inconceivable luxury."

"Which you have now achieved," she reminded him.

"True. But now I don't mind sharing my bed or my room—under certain circumstances." He arched his brows suggestively.

She didn't dare to follow that lead; it conjured up too much internal heat. "Well, as a veteran of one of your idealized two kid families, I always wanted my family to be bigger." Kylie opted for a safer topic. Maybe she really was Born to be Dull? "My cousins had three kids each in their families and I felt cheated there was only Devlin and me in ours. I promised myself that I would have at least three children of my own."

"And do you still want three or has sanity prevailed?"

"I still want three children. They can be all boys or all girls or mixed but I definitely want three."

"Three." Cade considered it. "Okay, I guess I could live with that. But no more after the third baby. If you want something else to mother, I'm sure my sister will be happy to supply a weimaraner puppy."

"Are you proposing to me?" Kylie asked playfully.

Cade choked on his wine.

"I'll take that as a no." She laughed at his expression. "Does this mean our three kids will be born out of wedlock? And what about our dog?"

Cade felt as if his skin were on fire. "This is what happens when you drink Meiers incomparable catawba on an empty stomach. It goes straight to your head." He managed a weak, sheepish smile.

"I'm not trying to get you drunk," Kylie promised. "It's too sleazy and obvious. And don't worry, I have no intention of taking advantage of your diminished capacity, not even if you beg me to."

The waiter arrived with their dinners at that moment, and Cade vowed to double his tip in homage to the impeccable timing. He desperately needed intervention, for try as he may, he couldn't come up with the requisite glib comeback to counter the effects of that three-kids-and-a-dog exchange with Kylie.

He was thoroughly disconcerted. Because for the first time, the prospect of giving up his cherished privacy, of ending the quiet solitude in his house, didn't send a foreboding chill through him. Because the idea of Kylie bearing his children—all *three* of them—seemed exciting and rewarding, not appalling. Even sharing a puppy with her held a certain appeal. He had always liked dogs and kids; he just wasn't in a hurry to live with them again.

Now he felt amenable to the possibility—if Kylie Brennan were a part of it all.

He gripped his fork as he watched her sample her first bite of trout. She tasted it and smiled her approval. Cade wondered if it were possible to implode from the force of unslaked desire. If so, he was in prime danger of it.

He wanted Kylie desperately, and he was experienced enough to know that she wanted him, too, though she was trying hard to fight her attraction. Because she didn't trust him. Her fifty-one percent ownership of BrenCo stock stood between them as solidly as a concrete wall. Whatever decision she made concerning her shares would impact on their relationship, for better or for worse.

Cade consumed his trout, without really tasting it. Worse was not a prospect he cared to consider, but he knew that Better was far from assured. Kylie had that meeting tomorrow with her uncles and their imported nuisance named Axel Dodge. What if they managed to convince her to sell her shares?

"Have you heard from Noah since he and Brenda took off this afternoon?"

Kylie's voice filtered through the fog of gloom that was swiftly encompassing him.

"No." Somewhere out there, his defenseless best friend was at the mercy of Brenda's potent wiles. Cade groaned. "Not a word from him—or her."

"I haven't, either. I guess they're too absorbed in each other to give us a thought," Kylie replied with a bright smile.

Or was it a taunting smile? Cade wasn't sure. Not only were the Brennans deft at backstabbing, but they also enjoyed twisting the knife. Kylie could be doing exactly that. "Absorbed in each other," he repeated cynically. "Is that what they're calling it these days?"

"Why are you so negative? It's possible that Brenda and Noah care deeply for each other."

"I'll grant that landing Noah would be a major coup for Brenda. He's got a nice house, a good job, plenty of money and—"

"He treats her well, they enjoy each other's company." Kylie came to her cousin's defense. "They could be very good for each other."

"Brenda is about as good for him as Delilah was for Samson, and we all know how that turned out," Cade intoned darkly. "And as long as we're on the dismal subject of your cousins, did you find out what else Brent took from Gene's house, besides the two TV sets?"

"Cade, I know you think the U.S. Constitution doesn't apply to my cousin Brent, but he is entitled to be considered innocent until it's proven otherwise."

"I noticed that the piano was still in the living room and the big crystal chandelier was still hanging in the dining room. Brent would need help getting them out so that means he is working alone," Cade speculated, ignoring her concise explanation of criminal law. "What else was missing after your inventory this afternoon?"

Kylie sighed. "It wasn't a very thorough inventory. I had a hard time remembering what was in each room. I know there was an antique tea cart in the living room that isn't there anymore. I remembered a few distinctive pieces, like Grandma's writing desk and a gilded pagoda-shaped mirror, but I truly don't know when I last saw them. It's possible that Uncle Gene could've given them away or sold them after Grandma died."

"I doubt it. More than likely, Brent hauled the stuff to an antiques dealer who paid him a quarter of what it was actually worth. But as long as he got some quick cash in his hands, Brent wouldn't care about the true value. Do you see a correlation here, Kylie? Your uncles want to do the same with—"

"Did Aunt Bobbie call you again about Brent's bail?" Kylie quickly attempted to divert his incipient BrenCo diatribe.

Cade frowned. He was being about as subtle as a thermonuclear weapon. For BrenCo's sake, he *had* to rein himself in. It wasn't easy. "I talked to Bobbie again and we decided that being in a jail cell for a time would give Brent the opportunity to reflect on what he'd done. Maybe even to regret it, although I'm not holding my breath on that one."

"And Aunt Bobbie went along with that?" Kylie asked skeptically, remembering her aunt's earlier reaction to the same plan.

"Yes, with a remarkable lack of hysterics. We ended the conversation on excellent terms, for a change."

"Because you agreed to advance her the cash for Starr Lynn's ice-skating costume!" Kylie exclaimed at once. Her deduction skills had always been first-rate. "You also promised that the money for their trip to the novice competition in Detroit would come out of BrenCo's community athletic fund." She grinned at his look of surprise. "Brenda told me about the fund. She also said you always made sure that Starr Lynn benefited from it, even though Uncle Gene was less than willing to include her."

"Brenda certainly talked a blue streak this afternoon," Cade grumbled.

"I think it's admirable that you took it upon yourself to help Starr Lynn. Brenda and Aunt Bobbie are both appreciative, though you'll probably deny it."

"I probably will."

Kylie laughed. "You try to act like such a gruff curmudgeon but deep down inside, you're—"

"Even gruffer. Ruthless. Autocratic, arrogant and stubborn. Those are only a few of the words that'll be used to describe me in that meeting tomorrow, Kylie."

"Let's not forget to add single-minded to the list," Kylie said dryly. "You turn every conversation back to BrenCo. And right now you're totally fixated on that meeting tomorrow, aren't you?"

"I'd be a fool not to be concerned, Kylie. Think about it. A secret meeting whose sole purpose is to undermine me while I'm given no opportunity to defend myself. Doesn't that strike you as unjust? Criminals, no matter what they've done, are given representation in a hearing but I'm to be shut out of—"

"Cade, tomorrow's meeting isn't a trial," Kylie said earnestly. "It's a—"

"It feels like a trial to me. In a kangaroo court. And here is my crime, Kylie. I've made BrenCo successful enough to stimulate your uncles' greed. You see, the way the company is run, the dividends are reinvested in the business, paying out only a small amount to the shareholders. Your uncle Gene and I agreed on that course of action, to plow most of the profits back into the business. It's one of the reasons why BrenCo is doing so well."

His voice was low and quiet but the intensity of his tone was reflected in his eyes, which held hers in a compelling gaze. Kylie couldn't look away; she didn't even try.

"Artie and Guy and a few other Brennans, Ian and Lauretta in particular, resent the small dividend checks," Cade continued tautly. "Never mind that the continuing growth of the company benefits them and will become even more lucrative for all later on. They would rather sell their shares for a quick, easy profit."

"Then why don't they? After all, nobody is forcing them to hold onto their stock."

"True. But between the two of them, Guy and Artie only own thirty-four percent of the stock. As long as you're the majority holder with me at the helm, our dividend policy holds, which doesn't make that bloodsucker Axel Dodge happy at all. Your uncles will get more money for their stock—substantially more—if you agree to sell, too. That would guarantee Dodge's potential buyer-client total control of BrenCo. They can sell or install new management who will raise the dividend payouts or do whatever they want. Now, do you understand exactly how important your decision is to them?"

"And to you," Kylie reminded him, in the name of fairness.

"They don't care about what effect the fate of the company

will have on the town or even the rest of the Brennan family, Kylie. And I do."

Cade was relentless, Kylie acknowledged. His tenacity and drive both wearied and impressed her. He was strong and powerful and he wouldn't give up. "I'm glad you didn't go into law," she murmured. "You'd have been a terrifying force in the courtroom, whether prosecuting, defending or judging."

"I don't want to terrify you, honey." He reached across the table and took her hand in his. "And I don't want to badger you, either." The pad of his thumb stroked the delicate skin on the inside of her wrist. "I think you know what I do want, Kylie. I want you."

Hot excitement flared through her, and she marveled that he could arouse her so quickly, so wildly with merely a touch, a word, a look... And the promise of what was to come.

By the sexy gleam in his eye and the husky note in his voice, Cade Austin intended to fulfill that promise tonight. *The night before her crucial meeting.*

That nasty little reminder crept into her head, generating a quelling chill. "I know exactly what you want, Cade," she said quietly. If only he didn't view her as an adversary, if only she could believe that the passion he claimed to feel was as real to him as it was for her. If only she could trust him...if only he could trust *her*. If only. "You want complete control of BrenCo. That means controlling me, any way you can."

Cade dropped her hand, scowling his exasperation. "Just when I begin to forget you're a Brennan, you come out with a remark like that!"

"You mean, just when you think you have me duped, I wake up and smell the coffee."

Their waiter happened to be passing by and thought she was making a request. "Coffee, miss? I'll bring it right away."

"Bring it at your own risk," warned Cade. "She drinks tea and perceives any attempt to serve her another beverage as threatening and subversive."

The waiter looked alarmed. "I'll bring your tea right away, ma'am," he promised nervously, taking off.

"Did you have to scare the poor guy?" Kylie complained.

"He looked at me like I'm a maniac in the throes of an attack of PMS."

"Are you? That would certainly explain a lot."

"I won't even dignify that with a response."

The dinner, which had begun on a tentative edgy note, ended the same way. Cade pulled into the driveway of Gene Brennan's house and Kylie flung open the car door and hopped out before he could turn off the engine.

A gust of wind blew a stinging splatter of raindrops in her face. "Stay in the car," she insisted when she saw Cade prepare to get out, presumably to walk her to the front door. "No use both of us getting soaked."

The rain swirled around her as she raced to the porch and into the house.

It wasn't until she was standing in the foyer, shaking the raindrops from her coat, that she realized she'd simply pushed open the front door in her haste to get inside. The door had swung open, meaning it must have been slightly ajar.

She could distinctly remember locking the door when she'd left the house with Cade, and now it was unlocked.

The realization struck at the same moment she heard the sound of water running and splashing loudly within the house. Was the rain pouring in through a major leak in the roof?

Kylie followed the sound into the kitchen and gasped her dismay. The taps had been turned on, and water blasted out of the faucet into the overflowing sink, then spilled onto the floor, turning it into a giant puddle at least an inch deep. She sloshed through it to turn off the taps, only to notice that the water sounds had not ceased, though they were more muted without the torrent from the kitchen faucet.

She hurried into the downstairs powder room, located near the left side of the staircase. Water was gushing from that faucet and had already overflowed the sink to soak the floor. Uttering a particularly salty curse more suited to a sailor than a navy captain's well-brought-up daughter, Kylie quickly turned off the taps. Still, the sound of rushing water did not abate.

Kylie ran upstairs to check the two bathrooms there. After the deluge downstairs, she wasn't really surprised to find the water running in both sinks and both bathtubs, yet the sight dazed her anyway. Both bathrooms were badly flooded. She turned off the water, but it had already begun to seep into the adjoining rooms.

What should she do? Panicked, Kylie ran into her uncle's bedroom and grabbed the phone. Who should she call? The police? A plumber? The dilemma was instantly solved when she heard no dial tone. She would not be calling anyone. The phone was dead, though it had been in working order before she'd left the house to go to dinner with Cade.

Cade! Kylie ran downstairs and threw open the front door, just in time to see the lights of his car heading into the street, away from the house. She could shout but he wouldn't hear her, not from this distance with his car windows shut and the rain making such a racket.

She closed the door and leaned against it, shivering. It occurred to her that it was as cold inside the house as it was on the porch. Which shouldn't be the case. The gas had been turned on this afternoon, and she'd set the thermostat immediately afterward to a toasty seventy degrees. With an ominous foreboding, Kylie walked to the thermostat farther down the hall to find it turned off.

The astonishing yet indisputable facts struck her all over again. Someone had broken inside and in a deliberate act of sabotage, had turned off the heat and turned on every faucet in the house, flooding the place. The phone was dead, too. She would bet the zoning permit to build the new infectious waste autoclave that bit of bad luck wasn't merely coincidental.

Her shock began to lift, giving way to anger. Who had done this? And why? Fear kicked in. What would the perpetrator do next? She was here alone, without a phone to call for help.

Not for long! Her heart thudding, Kylie hurried up the stairs. She would grab the few things she needed for the night and get out of here. She didn't allow herself to consider that her car might have been tampered with. If someone was trying to drive her out of Uncle Gene's house, it wouldn't make sense to sabotage her means of escape. Unless there were other plans for her? Perhaps to get rid of her permanently?

She was in the small guest bedroom she'd always used during

those long ago summer visits with her family, shoving some essentials into her overnight bag, when she heard the front door open. Quietly. Too quietly, as if whoever was opening it didn't want to be heard.

Kylie glanced wildly around her. There was nothing in this little room to use as a weapon. The most obvious choice, the lamp on the bedside table, looked too light and insubstantial to inflict even a bruise. If she'd been in the kitchen, she could've grabbed a knife although the thought of stabbing someone made her knees buckle. Or maybe it was the rampant terror coursing through her. She waited for a bolstering surge of adrenaline, equipping her for flight or fight.

But that particular internal mechanism seemed to be malfunctioning because she could barely stand, ruling out both battling and fleeing. All she wanted to do was to hide.

She heard the footsteps on the stairs. In just a few moments, the intruder would be here on the top floor—looking for her? Kylie reacted instinctively. She sneaked into the small bedroom closet and soundlessly closed the door behind her.

Six

"Kylie?" Cade's voice echoed in the upstairs hallway. "Kylie, where are you?"

Inside the closet, Kylie breathed in the pungent scent of mothballs—there must be hundreds stored in here to produce such an overwhelming odor—and pressed her body closer to the wall. A hanging garment bag swung gently against her and she jumped. Her nerves were truly shot.

She heard Cade calling her name again, his voice louder, his tone more urgent. Kylie remained frozen in the closet, her heart beating at triple time. She'd spent the evening with Cade, she reminded herself. She knew without a doubt he had not been the one who'd broken into the house. For a few tormenting moments, she entertained the notion that he'd hired some goons to do it and was now here to personally finish her off, then decided she was confusing reality with the spate of women-in-jeopardy TV movies she'd watched over the years.

Pride dictated that he not find her cowering in the closet. Kylie slipped out and crept into the hall. Cade was standing at one end, staring into the flooded bathroom.

"The water was running when I came in," she said. "Now I know how the owners of those creekside places feel after a flood."

Cade whirled around, startled. "I've been calling you. Why didn't you answer me? What's going on here?" He sounded as agitated as she felt. "Kylie, are you all right?" He advanced toward her.

"I'm fine. Just a little wet and cold, that's all," she murmured, trying for insouciance. And failing. She was pale and shivering and Cade pulled her into his arms. She was only too glad to let him.

He held her tight and she leaned heavily against him, absorbing the strength and warmth he imparted, feeling protected and inordinately grateful for his strong, solid presence. She buried her face against his chest and closed her eyes as the tension that had gripped her every muscle slowly began to recede.

"I thought you'd gone," she whispered, her voice muffled by his coat. "When I looked out, your car was pulling away."

"I drove one block and turned around." His big hands moved over her back in long gentle strokes. "I didn't like the way the evening ended tonight, Kylie." His lips brushed her shiny dark hair. "I came back to change the ending."

He sniffed suddenly, his brow furrowed. "I think I smell—mothballs?" He took another sniff. "In your hair?"

"Don't worry, it's not the latest scented shampoo on the market." Kylie tried to be flippant.

Cade didn't buy her act. Instead, he deepened his embrace. "Honey, where have you been?"

Kylie thought of the dark acrid closet where she'd taken refuge, and shuddered. "I was scared, Cade," she said softly. She drew back a little and looked up at him. Her hands rested on his chest and he linked his arms around her waist.

He bent his head down and touched his forehead to hers. "Tell me exactly what happened here."

"Someone broke into the house tonight, Cade. Every faucet in the house was turned on and the heat was turned off. I was, uh, packing to spend the night somewhere else when you arrived. How did you get in?"

"The front door is unlocked. I just walked inside."

She'd left the door unlocked? Kylie was horrified by her oversight. Her bulging case file back in Philadelphia offered tragic evidence that one careless mistake was all it took. Of course, she'd carefully locked the door earlier, for all the good that had done. Her bulging case file also offered proof that if someone was intent on committing a crime, precautions were merely a temporary nuisance.

Discouraged, she sagged against Cade. It felt good to let him support her.

"This bathroom is a waterlogged mess," he murmured, staring at the sight. "Are they all like this?"

Kylie nodded. "The kitchen, too. Cleaning up will be—"

"Don't think about a cleanup just yet, Kylie. I'm going to call the police and get them over here to see the damage. It will be useful to have a written police report on file for insurance purposes as well."

"The phone doesn't work," she said wearily. "I think that whoever broke in here did something to it."

"I'll call from my car phone. Come with me."

He took her hand and Kylie compliantly trotted along beside him. Staying inside the house alone, even for a very short while, was not an alternative she cared to consider. Those terror-filled moments in the closet had instilled a fear in her that even her scariest clients had not.

Officers Krajack and Pecoraro arrived and followed Kylie and Cade from one flooded room to another. A further investigation revealed that the phone wires had been cut. As Kylie watched the policemen taking pages of notes, she was struck by the gravity being accorded what actually was a rather minor bit of malicious mischief. She knew she would not have received this sort of attention for a similar incident in a city the size of Philadelphia.

At first she attributed the thoroughness to the dynamics of a small town where crime is rare and every citizen's call was considered important. Then she began to notice the officers' deference to Cade. Every time she supplied an answer to a question, they looked to Cade for confirmation and wrote down what he said. She didn't think any of them noticed when she stopped answering and let Cade do all the talking.

At some other time and place, the closed ranks might have offended her, but at this point she was still too shaken to feel anything but relief that she was safe and not cowering in that closet. Or worse.

"Do you have any ideas who might've done this, Mr. Austin?" asked Krajack.

Cade looked troubled. "Any other time I would swear it was Brent Brennan but I know you have him locked up so that eliminates him as a suspect."

"Brent Brennan isn't in jail," Pecoraro said. "He made bail this afternoon."

"Who posted it?" demanded Cade, and Krajack immediately headed out to the police car to radio for the information.

"Do you really think Brent would do this?" Kylie stared from Cade to Officer Pecoraro, her eyes darkening with apprehension. "Knowing I was here—"

"That would be the precise reason why he would do it." Cade clenched his teeth. "To scare you. To drive you out."

Innocent until proven guilty. Kylie silently repeated her mantra, but when Officer Krajack returned to report that Ian Brennan had posted the bail for his cousin, a wave of anxiety swept through her.

"Ian?" Cade wasn't anxious, he was furious. "Normally, Ian wouldn't give Cousin Brent the time of day, and now suddenly, he bails him out of jail? What's that little weasel doing here in town, anyway? He's supposed to be in law school in Columbus."

"Spring break?" Kylie murmured.

That drew a snicker from Pecoraro. "Sure, why go to some sunny place like Cancún for spring break when you can whoop it up right here in Port McClain?"

Cade's frown grew fiercer. "Would you mind paying a call on both Brent and Ian Brennan tonight?" he asked the officers. "See what either of them knows about what happened here?"

"Sure," Pecoraro agreed. "Krajack and I have our good-cop-bad-cop routine mastered to perfection. We'll get one of them to talk, I can promise you that. Should we call you afterward?"

"Call me in the morning at my office. I'm staying here tonight and you won't be able to reach me since the phone wires are cut," added Cade.

"You're staying here?" Kylie's voice rose in apprehension.

"Good idea." Krajack nodded his approval. "Just in case those little twerps decide to come back to play."

"You don't have to stay here tonight, honey," Cade said soothingly, as he slipped a comforting arm around Kylie's shoulders. "The officers will be glad to escort you to one of the motels out by the interstate exit and stick around till you've checked into a room."

Kylie began to emerge from the lethargy that was engulfing her. She decided that the situation warranted a certain rousing alarm. Cade was clearly directing the police investigation and in her view, the officers seemed to have given him tacit approval to do whatever he chose to "those little twerps" if they were to make another appearance here. Worse, all three believed those little twerps were her cousins!

She forced herself not to jump onto the anti-Brennan bandwagon. Her two years as a public defender had been an exercise in examining the facts of each case rationally and objectively, of not overreacting to circumstantial evidence. And there was not even a shred of that linking her cousins to tonight's antics.

If she were tucked away in some distant motel tonight, there would be no witness to any possible collusion... And collusion among Cade, Krajack and Pecoraro seemed quite possible indeed. "I—I'll stay here tonight," she heard herself say. "I want to start mopping up that water before it does permanent damage to the floors and to the ceiling."

She was prepared to insist on her right to stay, but nobody tried to dissuade her from her decision. The two officers left after a private conversation on the front porch with Cade, one that did not include Kylie. She changed into jeans and a sweatshirt and assembled an assortment of mops, buckets and faded old towels in the kitchen.

It could be worse, she reminded herself, wringing a mopful of water into a bucket. It wasn't as if the place had been flooded with raw sewage or infectious medical waste. The water from the faucets was clean and safe.

But there was so much of it! Too much. Kylie grimaced as water seeped through the leather of her shoes and sloshed over the tops of them, soaking her wool crew socks and the hem of her jeans.

She glanced up in surprise when Cade joined her in the kitchen wearing sneakers, dark blue running shorts and a T-shirt with the BrenCo logo on the front.

"I keep a gym bag in the trunk of my car," he explained his change of clothes as he reached for a mop. "Do you want me to help you here or start on the bathrooms?"

"You don't have to—"

"You'd rather I sit around and watch you work?"

Kylie considered that. "I'd probably end up dumping a bucket of water on you if you did," she admitted.

"I figured. I'll go upstairs and do the bathrooms. When we're finished, we're both going to want to take a shower without having to wade to it. There should be some hot water by then, since the heater is turned on again and working."

"I definitely need to wash the aroma of mothballs out of my hair." Kylie wrinkled her nose in disgust. "I think it's growing stronger rather than fading."

"It only adds to your allure, darling."

Kylie felt anger lash her, even as she tried to reason it away. Cade was kidding, she knew that. He was given to sarcasm, she knew that, too. At times, she admired his gift for the well-timed sardonic crack. But not now. Right now she wanted him to—to what?

She wanted him to cuddle and comfort her, as he'd done earlier. The realization hit her with the force of a raging flood. She wanted him to forget about mops and cleanup, to carry her upstairs and...

Her face flamed. She'd never been passive and dependent in her life and now she seemed to be succumbing to both states, a humiliating first. Brought on by the macho, take-charge domination of Cade Austin. *...that women find irresistible, even femlib types like you.* Brenda's words echoed in her head.

Kylie was appalled. She'd spent years proving to her big brother, Devlin, that anything he could do, she could, too—and maybe even do it better. Only to turn into a simpering wimp at the hands of Cade Austin? A man who wouldn't hesitate to use her weakness to his advantage at BrenCo?

That surge of adrenaline that had remained so elusive earlier, suddenly poured into her system like a blast from an open faucet. With it came some startlingly unexpected developments.

She found herself staring at Cade, at his powerfully muscled arms, bared by the short-sleeve T-shirt, at his long, iron-hard muscular thighs dusted with wiry dark hair. His gym shorts were too skimpy to hide the thick evidence of his virility. Her blood heated in her veins and throbbed in pulsing rhythm. She'd read of studies asserting that danger induced or heightened passion, but she'd never thought to experience the phenomenon personally.

She was definitely experiencing it now, and the unexpected attack of lust struck her hard. No, Kylie vowed. She would not give into it, she would not give in to him!

"We have work to do," she barked out the order.

"Sir, yes, sir!" Cade mimicked a lowly recruit hailing a superior officer, right down to the mock salute. He grabbed a mop and bucket. "I'm off to swab the latrines ASAP."

And though she'd practically demanded that he get to work, Kylie was furious that he was leaving her. Her eyes wild with frustration, she watched him walk out of the kitchen and into the narrow corridor leading to the front hall.

"Do you call all the shots in this town just like you do at BrenCo?" she shouted after him, her tone belligerent and deliberately provoking.

Cade paused and turned to face her. "Meaning?"

"Meaning Port McClain is a police state with you running the show. You don't bother with pesky things like evidence and trials and judges around here. You and your cop buddies have already tried and convicted my cousins. What comes next? The electric chair?"

Cade actually laughed. "Even tyrants like me and my faithful henchmen find that to be excessive punishment for turning on a few faucets. A life sentence without parole will do. Now, any other complaints or can I get started on my job?"

Without waiting for a reply, he headed to the stairs whistling an off-key rendition of "Whistle While You Work." The song playing in Kylie's head was "Town Without Pity."

Cade proved to be an incredibly efficient worker. Kylie was putting the final drying touches on the kitchen when he came back down, having finished both the upstairs bathrooms. He immediately started in on the downstairs powder room.

"Go on upstairs and take your shower," he said when she tried to join him with her mop and bucket a short while later. "It's too small in here for two. I'll take care of it."

Kylie stood on the threshold for a few moments, watching him work. He was as adept with a mop as he was at building a company and running it, she acknowledged silently. She felt the need to make amends for her earlier embarrassing outburst. Nearly ninety minutes worth of slopping cold water around had served to cool her frenzied emotional state.

"Thank you for staying and helping," she murmured. "You wield that mop like a pro."

"One of my many talents." He flashed a mocking grin. "I find manual labor relaxing after a long hard day ruling a police state."

"I admit I was out of line." She lowered her eyes. Playing humble supplicant was difficult. "But you have to admit, you and Officers Krajack and Pecoraro were awfully chummy." She rallied a little. "And they were very willing to do what you—"

"*Suggested* is the word I believe you want to use," Cade interrupted dryly. "Don't say 'commanded' or this paltry attempt at an apology will be all for naught."

She raised her eyes to meet his. "Suggested," she agreed.

"BrenCo contributes to the Port McClain Policemen's Benevolent Fund," Cade explained. "I'm a good friend of the chief's, and I'm personally acquainted with every officer on the force. Some of them have relatives who work at BrenCo. So although I have no authority with the Port McClain PD, I admit I probably do have a certain amount of influence."

"BrenCo maintains a fund for community youth sports programs and contributes to the police department's charity fund. Any other good works I should know about?"

"BrenCo also is an annual contributor to the Volunteer Fire Department, the Port McClain Hospital, and the community Little Theater. There might be a couple others."

"BrenCo is a regular font of benevolence. Your idea or Uncle Gene's? And no false modesty, Cade. Be honest."

"False modesty has never been my strong suit."

"But industrial psychology is. Every aspect of it."

"Let's just say I learned the principles well and applied them." Cade leaned against the doorjamb, his expression thoughtful. "To truly succeed, a company like BrenCo *must* foster goodwill and maintain excellent relations within the community. It took a while to convince Gene—I don't know if he ever really became a true believer—but he gave me a free hand with everything connected with the company, just like he'd promised. Toward the end, I think he came to enjoy the town benefactor reputation that came with BrenCo's pivotal role in Port McClain."

"And the rest of the family?"

"Resented every dime spent on anybody but themselves."

Kylie winced. "I should've seen that one coming."

"You said you wanted honesty."

"Maybe I should've added objectivity, too. You are not objective on the subject of the Brennans, Cade."

"Point taken. Now, go take your shower and get ready for bed. You look ready to collapse and you still reek of mothballs." He eyed her curiously. "You never did say how that happened."

She had no intention of admitting she'd taken terrified refuge in that odoriferous closet. "You can have either Uncle Gene's or my grandparents' bedroom. I'm staying in the little room at the back of the house. I've always used it during my visits here."

"Since I've already sampled Gene's mattress—I think it might've seen torture duty in the Spanish Inquisition—I'll take your grandparents' bedroom. Are you sure you wouldn't rather have it? It's the best room in the house and I don't—"

"No, you can have it. Good night, Cade."

He calmly resumed his mopping. "Good night, Kylie."

* * *

Over two hours later, Kylie lay shivering in the narrow single bed in the back bedroom. Not only was this room the smallest in the house, but she was certain it was also the coldest. Though the radiator made a valiant attempt at hissing out heat, it stood no chance against the force of the wind that blew against the windows. The icy drafts seeping through each ancient window frame defeated any hope of raising the temperature a few more degrees.

Kylie pulled the bedcovers to her neck and curled up on her side in an attempt to conserve body heat, but the blanket and spread were ineffective against the cold. She briefly considered the two woolen blankets stored in the mothball-protected closet, but couldn't bear the thought of using them. Not after she'd finally washed away that throat-closing camphor scent from her hair and skin.

Furthermore, the chill in the room was not the only factor keeping her awake. She was wired and restless, her mind jumbled with images and words, most of them centered on Cade Austin. Who at this moment was lying in bed in a room right down the hall. He was probably sound asleep, Kylie decided resentfully. No doubt he'd conked out the moment his head had hit the pillow while she tossed and turned and grew colder and more wide-awake with each passing second.

The rain, which had let up in the past hour, suddenly intensified again. Kylie groaned. The sound of raindrops pattering against a windowpane was usually benign, even pleasant, but this storm was unlike any other. So were these windows. What were they made of, anyway? It sounded as if someone were tossing handful after handful of marbles against a metal sheet, loud, and thoroughly maddening. After a few minutes of listening to that infernal racket, she was even more keyed up.

And then she became aware of another sound, a peculiar noise that could have been the wind whipping through the bare branches of the trees surrounding the house. Unless it was something else altogether. An otherwordly moan, perhaps? Kylie shuddered. Involuntarily, she recalled some disturbing programs featuring paranormal phenomenon.

There was something about ghosts and cold spots in a room...

Kylie tried to remember what she'd been told about the history of this old house. It had already passed through a few generations of a Port McClain family before coming on the market at a bargain price, at which time Uncle Gene had bought it for himself and his parents. Kylie thought about that long-gone, forgotten family. Had anyone actually died in this house? Maybe in this very room? It was certainly chilly enough to be a ghostly cold spot.

She sat up in bed when an unidentified rattling noise seemed to grow louder. Thinking more practically, she ruled out spirits and considered the possibility of vandals returning to finish what they'd started tonight. Suppose they hadn't actually left the premises? The officers had gone into every room and shone their flashlights into the dark, dank cellar, but they hadn't conducted an exhaustive search of the place. No one had thought to climb through the crawl space to look into the attic. The criminals—perhaps crazed from crack?—could very well be there just waiting to strike!

Kylie hopped out of bed and raced into the hall. She noticed a stream of light coming from beneath the closed door of her grandparents' bedroom and unerringly headed to it.

Propped by pillows in the four-poster bed, Cade was trying to interest himself in a comprehensive biography of Dwight D. Eisenhower. And then he heard the light, tentative knock on the bedroom door. He set the book aside. "Come in."

Kylie opened the door halfway and stood there, barefoot in a long-sleeve plaid nightshirt that reached the tops of her knees. Cade smiled. "Can't sleep, either?"

"My room is too cold. And noisy and—creepy." She nervously tucked a strand of her hair behind her ear. "My imagination has been running riot tonight. I've gone from ghosts to burglars and was on the verge of conjuring up ax-murderers in the attic when I..." Her voice trailed off and she gave a self-mocking laugh. "No, I can't sleep."

In a flash, he'd crossed the room and stood in front of her, clad in white boxer briefs and a T-shirt. Kylie gulped. If he were to ever pose for an underwear ad, it would become an instant collector's item, gracing women's walls from coast to coast.

Cade scooped her up in his arms. "You're shivering and your teeth are chattering," he murmured as he carried her to the bed. "From the cold or from the possibility of a close encounter with clandestine ax-murderers?"

"Who are high on crack," Kylie added wryly. She linked her arms around his neck and held on tight.

"In Port McClain, they'd probably be high on a couple of six-packs." Cade stood beside the bed and laid her down in the middle of it. "You'll be warmer here," he said huskily, climbing in beside her and pulling the covers over them both.

Kylie wasn't sure who moved first, but an instant later, she was back in his arms. She clung to him, admitting the truth to herself at last. The reason she'd stayed in this house tonight had nothing to do with the necessity of mopping the flooded floors or keeping tabs on a possible conspiracy to frame her cousins. She was here because Cade was. Because she, too, wanted to change the ending of their evening.

She wanted the evening to end with the two of them together. Like this.

"Better?" Cade gazed at her through heavy-lidded eyes.

He looked dangerous and sensual, and Kylie had to remind herself to breathe. But she nodded her head. She was exactly where she wanted to be.

His hand cupped her cheek, then moved over her shoulder, his fingers kneading and caressing. He lowered his palms to her breasts, which were taut and swollen against the fabric of her nightshirt. Kylie closed her eyes and uttered a soft moan.

And abruptly, without warning, he withdrew his hand and wrapped his arms around her, holding her tightly against him. "I don't want to take advantage of you," he whispered, his lips brushing the top of her head. "You've had a shock and a scare. You're exhausted and vulnerable and you need to sleep, not to— to—"

"I don't want to go to sleep," Kylie cut in, aware that she sounded slightly whiney. She was beyond caring.

Her arms were pinned to her sides by his. She felt as if she were strapped in a straitjacket, she couldn't free her hands. To caress him. To show him what she really wanted. "And I'm not *vulnerable.* I'm insulted that you think I'm so timid and fragile that I can't handle a little vandalism. You said it yourself—turning on a few faucets is not that big a deal."

"I never meant to imply it wasn't a serious situation," Cade protested. "If you thought that, you're wrong, Kylie. I'm taking this very—"

"Oh, I know. If this were the military our status would be DEFCON One Alert." She wriggled against him, rather experimentally, testing the range of motion allowed to her. Her arms were immobilized but she was able to rub her breasts against his chest, to settle her hips more snugly against him.

Cade groaned. "Lie still or my noble sacrifice will be shot to hell."

Kylie managed to slip her leg between his and press her stomach against the enormous bulge throbbing against the cotton material of his boxers. In the process, her nightshirt slid up, baring her thighs. Their legs tangled, hers smooth and silky, his hard and brushed with wiry-thick hair.

"Your noble sacrifice is to protect me from my own exhausted, vulnerable impulses brought on by my shock and my scare?" She laughed. Taunting him, challenging him. Enticing him.

Cade wondered how she'd managed to convey all those things with a mere laugh. But she had. And now she was using her thigh to apply a gentle rhythmic pressure exactly where he wanted her to.

"I thought you would be tense and uptight," he heard himself say in a thick voice he hardly recognized as his own. "I thought getting you into bed would be as difficult and complicated as planning the North Africa campaign in World War II."

"Is that why you were reading about General Eisenhower, hoping he might offer some tips? He planned the D-Day invasion of Normandy, didn't he?"

Cade closed his eyes. The soft, warm feel of her body caused jolts of sensual lightning to flash through him. Hardly a situation conducive to rational conversation, but he gave it a try. "Kylie, I want you, obviously you know that, but—"

He broke off with a gasp. The fingers of her trapped hand had strayed to the front of his briefs.

"Just wanted to know how obviously you want me, Cade," she said, her eyes gleaming with devilish innocence.

"This is like a bedroom version of Ms. Jekyll and Ms. Hyde." Cade drew in a sharp breath. "As Jekyll, Female Barrister, you look so proper and starchy and you know all the standard rhetoric guaranteed to keep men on guard."

And now she was in bed with him, touching him in a way that heated his blood and scrambled his brains. He tried to remember why he wasn't letting her have free rein with his body, as she so clearly wanted to do.

"I plead guilty, you pegged me correctly, Cade." She stretched her neck to take a light, sexy bite of his earlobe. "I'm usually all those things you said—and maybe worse. I either keep men on guard or send them running."

She kept moving against him, using her body and her legs— he still had full control of her arms—to arouse him. She nibbled sensuously on his neck, along the line of his jaw. "But somehow I'm different with you."

"It's the circumstances that are different, Kylie." Cade laughed grimly, marveling at his own self-control even as he mocked himself for it. He was different with her, too, determined to protect her though the lady did not require or even want his protection.

Give it up and give in, he advised himself. It's what you both want. Definitely what you need.

"You got very little sleep last night in the Port McClain Hotel, you drank too much wine tonight and then came back here to find the place vandalized," he heard himself say instead. "This has not been your usual twenty-four hours, Kylie. It's bound to have had an, uh, unpredictable effect on you."

"You're very modest." She nuzzled her cheek against the raspy stubble on his jaw. "Not giving yourself any credit at all for making me want you."

Still he wouldn't release her arms. He wouldn't kiss her or caress her, either. Kylie might've despaired if she hadn't felt the indisputable proof of his arousal, warm and virile against her belly.

"Credit," he repeated softly. "What if tomorrow it's blame, Kylie?"

She touched her mouth to his, tracing his lips with the tip of her tongue. "I promise to respect you in the morning, darling."

Cade half laughed, half groaned. "I'm giving you one last chance to call this off, baby." His hands began to glide over her back in long, slow circular strokes. Up and down and around until his thumbs grazed the undersides of her breasts.

Kylie's nipples, already pointed and taut, tingled. She whimpered. She wanted him to touch them, with his fingers, with his mouth.

"Speak now or forever hold your peace," Cade drawled. "Or words to that effect." His hands were under her nightshirt, smoothing over the warm bare skin of her midriff. When they slipped inside her panties, Kylie sucked in her breath, contracting her stomach, giving him easier access.

But instead of sliding lower, to touch her where she was hot and achy and swollen, where she most wanted him to touch her, Cade withdrew his hand. He rolled on his back, folding his arms outside the covers.

Kylie shuddered. "I didn't speak," she said raspily. "I didn't call this off." Had she ever felt so frustrated? Or so exasperated? Cade's restraint tonight was propelling her to new heights in both. "I didn't say no, Cade. So what part of *yes* don't you understand?"

"Those chaste, prim cotton panties of yours gave me an attack of conscience." Cade scowled. "They reminded me that you came in here because you were scared and cold, not to get laid. Instead, I hustled you into bed."

He felt like a rat, and he wanted to be the good guy. For her. Cade muttered an oath. Was he becoming unhinged? He'd always been uninhibited and bold, unencumbered by guilt in the bedroom. Except tonight. He was with the woman he wanted more than any other, and he was acting like some kind of idiotic white knight.

Chaste! Prim! Kylie's cheeks were burning. "You were expecting me to wear a—a black satin thong or something?"

"Or nothing at all," Cade amended grimly. "Then we could dispense with any possibility of ambivalence and ambiguity."

"I'm so sorry to disappoint you." Kylie was sarcastic. She sat up in bed and stared at the meticulously sewn pattern on the antique quilt that covered them. The variations of colors and prints seemed to dance before her eyes.

"Going to storm out of here in an outraged huff?" Cade watched her, his gaze hot and intense.

"I'm considering it." She thought of the icy little bedroom that awaited and decided to prolong her consideration a bit.

"Brennans love dramatic exits. I've seen a wide variety over the years." His tone was baiting, his conscience swiftly clearing. He'd given her a choice and an out. Enough time had elapsed for cooler heads to prevail, and she was still here. Not because she was scared and vulnerable, but because she wanted to be. She wanted him. Cade grinned wolfishly.

"Then let's see how my dramatic exit compares to all those others you've seen." Kylie tossed back the covers.

Before she could make another move, Cade's fingers fastened around her wrist.

"I want you to stay." The sound of his voice, deep, husky and excitingly male, affected Kylie viscerally.

Not that she was going to let him know. Not yet. Even though his sexual reticence had been based on concern for her, his determined self-control had made a significant dent in her pride. Now it was time to recoup.

"Does that mean you finally resolved your ambivalence and ambiguity?" She sounded cooler than she felt, which bolstered her confidence. She gave her hand a slight tug but when he didn't release it, she made no further attempt to break free.

"*Mine?* You've got it all wrong, honey. I wasn't bothered by either one, but I wasn't sure about you," Cade retorted. "I wanted you to be clear about your motives before—" He paused to swallow, hard. His eyes were fixed on her and the longer he looked, the more aroused he became. Which amazed him because he was so hot and so hard already that he half expected to implode at any moment.

"Before?" Kylie prompted. The ardent intensity of his gaze was as potent as a caress. Her entire body hummed its response.

Cade's train of thought was as totally derailed as a commuter express that had jumped the tracks. He stared at her beautifully shaped mouth and remembered the taste of her lips. He lowered his eyes to her breasts that were swollen and trembling, the tight crests thrusting against the cloth of her nightshirt. The shirt was twisted to her waist, and he gazed lustily at her long bare legs. The V of her white cotton panties was visible at the tops of her thighs, and he decided that perhaps the garment wasn't as chaste and prim as he'd originally believed.

"Come here." He growled the sexy command.

Kylie managed to hold out long enough to taunt, "Aren't you worried I might hit you with a sexual harassment suit in the morning?"

"I'll countersue." He reached up and pulled her down to him.

Seven

His mouth possessed hers and she responded instantly, urgently to his ardent mastery. She felt his tongue thrust between her parted lips and probe deeply into the warm, moist hollow of her mouth. It was delicious and thrilling and everything she'd been wanting. Coherence and control skidded giddily away as she gave herself up to the wild, sweet pleasure of his lovemaking.

As if to make up for lost time, and his earlier restraint, he stripped her with a swift and dizzying expertise.

"You're so beautiful," he whispered roughly, his eyes taking in every inch of her naked body, which was flushed with desire and with need. For him.

"So are you," Kylie murmured, tugging at the hem of his T-shirt. He was quick to accommodate her and take it off. When she boldly slipped her hands beneath the elastic waistband of his briefs, he obligingly removed them, too.

She ran her hands over the bare muscular length of his body and sighed. He was so strong and powerful and wondrously male. "I've never felt this way before, Cade," she admitted achingly. "What have you done to me?"

"The same thing you've done to me." He cupped her breasts, filling his hands with them, fondling gently. "I'm hungry for you, Kylie," he said hoarsely as his lips closed over her nipple. "Like I've never been before."

Her body arched convulsively as a flash of heat seared her. Kylie surrendered to the intense yearning that pulsated within her. She clung to Cade, caressing him with increasing urgency, wanting to give and give to him. But to take as well. Her hand found him, smooth and hard and throbbing with virility. He moaned his pleasure, and her ability to please him thrilled her.

Cade was equally adept at pleasing and thrilling her. He circled one long finger around the secret bud concealed deep between her thighs, skimming, teasing, applying a gentle pressure yet holding back, until she was twisting helplessly with blind need.

"Oh please, Cade," she cried, tossing her head back and forth on the pillow, enveloped in a white-hot mist of wanting. The erotic tension was driving her out of her mind.

He began to lave her nipple with his tongue, then drew it deeper into his mouth to suck on it. She could feel the sensation spark deeply in her womb, as if a tiny wire were attached, providing an instant connection. Between her legs, his touch became concentrated and intense, and she opened to him as he found her warm wet center.

Kylie cried out, shivering as a fiery shaft of pure pleasure shot through her. Still, it wasn't enough. She wanted him inside her, deep, deep within. She was an empty ache craving to be filled, and only he could give her full completion. "Cade, now," she pleaded.

He raised his head and met her glazed eyes. "Are you okay or am I going to have to delve into my trusty gym bag for something?"

It took a full minute for her to comprehend his question. When she did, she blushed. Precautions had not occurred to her, not once, from the time she'd taken flight to his bedroom until this moment when she'd begged him to take her. For a compulsively careful, ever-cautious woman like her, it was a most telling lapse.

Cade watched her, his green eyes perceptive. She felt as if he were reading her mind, that he knew exactly how unusual her behavior was for her, exactly how powerfully he affected her. But all he said was, "I'll take care of it."

"Quite the Boy Scout, aren't you?" she noted with a touch of asperity as he pulled a foil-wrapped packet from his gym bag. "The living embodiment of their motto Be Prepared."

Once again, her total loss of control sharply contrasted with his ability to think things through, even in the heat of the moment. It seemed a disconcerting replay of their passionate scene earlier in his office. She frowned. "Are you *always* prepared? For *everything?*"

"Always," he agreed wryly, sheathing himself. "For everything."

She had to marvel at his dexterity, at his unshakable reliability but she resented it a little, too. "What else do you keep in that magic bag of yours? Road flares? Tourniquets? A Swiss Army knife? After all, one never knows what emergencies the King of BrenCo and Emperor of Port McClain might encounter in the course of a day."

"You do get irritable when the program isn't moving fast enough for you," Cade observed. He came down on top of her, nuzzling her neck. "I'll keep that in mind for the future."

Her fingers clenched on his shoulders. Whether to hold him or to push him away, she hadn't quite ascertained herself. "Don't patronize me, Cade."

"Uh-oh." Cade heaved a heavy sigh. "This is getting awfully close to the borderline. Why are you upset, honey? Because I didn't cast our fate to the winds and take a big, big chance?"

"I'm not upset!" she snapped, stung. "And I certainly wouldn't be mad about something like that!" Truth be told, he'd really nailed her on that one. It was embarrassing how clearly he read her.

"You think I one-upped you." He trapped her chin with his hand and forced her to meet his too-knowledgeable gaze. "Reconsider, Kylie. This isn't the courtroom and I'm not the prosecuting attorney out to rack up points against you."

He settled his body more fully against her, letting her feel the heavy strength of him. Kylie's muscles relaxed and she accepted the hard, warm weight of him; she savored it. Slowly, sensuously, she began to smooth her hands over his back.

"I guess I can be—competitive," she admitted huskily. Her skin was hot and tingling, every nerve ending jumping with anticipation. "It drives me kind of crazy that I was totally lost and you were completely competent, carefully planning ahead."

"It's something of a character flaw of mine. Don't hold it against me." He nibbled at her lips, his voice deep and raspy with an appealing combination of humor and passion. "That's not to say that my head wasn't spinning, honey. You have that effect on me."

"Is that a compliment or a complaint? From what I've heard, every Brennan makes your head spin. Uncle Gene excepted, of course."

Cade's eyes gleamed. "Consider yourself in a category all your own, Kylie." Before she could say another word, he slanted his mouth over hers, sealing them together in a rapacious and intimate kiss.

Kylie clung to him, running her hands over him, learning the virile textures of his body as he explored her own soft feminine secrets. His big hands cupped her bottom and lifted her, positioning her to receive him.

"Are you ready for me, sweetie?"

"Oh, yes, Cade, I'm ready. I feel as if I've been waiting forever," she added breathlessly.

In a blinding flash of insight she realized how long she really had been waiting; *she'd been waiting for him her entire life!* Waiting and hoping, but never expecting to find a man like him, a man who wasn't intimidated by her strength and her independence, a man who was capable of mastering her when she wanted to be mastered. And right now, in bed, she wanted to be feminine and vulnerable and open, all those things she could never be without the right man. Her heart and soul joined her body in acknowledging that Cade Austin was definitely the right man.

He thrust into her with a sure steady surge, stretching her, filling her, making her cry out his name. Her breathing was shallow and she trembled beneath him as her body softened, accommodating him in a melting flood of sheer pleasure.

Kylie closed her eyes and wrapped herself around him, holding on tight as he began to move in an erotically tantalizing rhythm. Hot ripples of rapture radiated through her body and she matched his pace, her liquid heat enveloping him as their shared pleasure built and grew, stunning them both with its force.

Passion and desire and need combined into a rushing force that swept them both into a vortex of dynamic tension so intense, so electrifying, that it took only moments for both of them to be swept away on wave after wave of pure ecstasy.

Finally, Cade collapsed against her, burying his head in the hollow of her shoulder. Kylie hugged him, feeling incredibly replete—and something much more.

Was she in love? She clung to him, dazed and wondrous. What she felt for Cade was unlike anything else she had ever experienced. And it was not just because he was good in bed—well, fabulous in bed, actually. No, she was too practical to be blinded by sheer sensuality, Kylie assured herself.

What were the lyrics to "I've Never Been in Love Before"? she mused dreamily. Her mother, a show tune fan, often played Broadway soundtracks and Kylie knew the titles and snatches from many a song. If falling in love was this unfamiliar yet enthralling emotional deluge that changed everything, especially herself, then she'd never truly been in love before.

She was in love with Cade Austin. Kylie tried out the words in her head. To her surprise, it didn't sound as strange or self-deluded as she might've thought.

Their bodies still joined, they lay languid and drowsy in the sweet aftermath, kissing and caressing and murmuring soft sexy things to each other. When they finally, reluctantly separated, he tucked her against his side, his arms wrapped around her, keeping her close.

"I have a confession to make." Kylie stretched luxuriously against the length of him. "I've never gone to bed on a first date before." It was important that he realize how much he meant to her, how many of her own rules she'd broken for him.

Cade smiled lazily. "Somehow I knew that. But this didn't feel like a first date, did it? I'm almost grateful to your terminally nitwitted cousins for their part in bringing us together tonight."

His fingers tangled in her dark, thick hair. He felt fantastic, on top of the world. And he'd been taken there by Kylie Brennan who could logically and legitimately qualify as his bona fide nemesis.

Kylie was in no mood to argue about anything with him, not even the alleged guilt or innocence of her cousins. "This was different from any first date I've ever had," she agreed happily. "We skipped that awkward getting-to-know-you stage and really bonded, Cade." She gazed at him, her eyes shining. It was as close to a declaration of love that she dared to make, to herself or to him.

"Oh, yeah!" Cade laughed softly. "We've bonded, baby."

Kylie turned to face him and lifted her mouth to kiss him with all the warmth and tender emotions flowing through her. He quickly took control of the kiss, deepening it into one of intimate possession. His hands moved over her supple curves, savoring their alluring rounded warmth and the creamy smoothness of her skin. Like a spark kindled to flashpoint, a vibrant passion quickly flared between them once more.

Her legs flexed and she lay open and vulnerable to him. Uttering a deep moan, he entered her, losing himself in her velvety softness. The stunning pleasure shredded what little was left of his control. He didn't think anything could be as good as his first time with her but incredibly, this unexpected, impulsive, way-too-soon second time more than equaled it.

He felt her intimate muscles clench him, felt her body suddenly convulse with ecstasy, and her climax triggered his in exquisitely attuned timing. A few moments later, he fell asleep in her arms, too satiated and passion-spent to stay awake and talk.

Kylie didn't mind. Her last coherent thought before she, too, dropped deeply and swiftly off to sleep was that if actions spoke louder than words—as that old tried-and-true adage claimed—they had no need for further conversation, anyway. Tonight, their bodies had told each other everything they needed to know.

Cade and Kylie sat across from each other at a table in The Corner Grill, studying their breakfast menus. Under the table, their legs were comfortably entwined. On top of it, Cade held Kylie's hand, his thumb absently stroking the inside of her wrist.

"I can't concentrate," Kylie admitted, closing her menu in defeat. There were too many new thoughts and images vying for priority and space in her mind to waste brain cells on something as prosaic as breakfast food. "I know the waitress is getting tired of waiting for us to make up our minds. Just order whatever you're having for me, too."

"You want me to order for you? That's more than a little retro, Kylie," Cade used her own quote to rib her.

"Just don't forget that I prefer tea," she added, trying and failing to sound stern.

"Oh, I'm not about to make that mistake again."

Their eyes met and they smiled at each other. They'd been doing a lot of gazing and smiling and touching since awakening earlier that morning. Kylie was amazed at how easy it was to wake up naked in bed with Cade, at how right it felt. She was particularly surprised at the lack of awkwardness and tension that one might assume would occur the morning-after-the-wild-night-before.

But there was no embarrassment or misgivings, no unease. They'd made love again and moved on to shower and dress as if they had done so many times. The intimacy felt natural, their camaraderie unforced.

Since there was no food in Gene's house, Cade suggested breakfast at The Corner Grill before he headed to the office. They'd stopped at his house first, so he could change into his office attire. His CEO power suit, Kylie had teased, watching him dress with admiring, possessive eyes.

She had opted for casual herself: jeans and a close-fitting, gray knit sweater that hugged her firm, rounded breasts and was short enough to reveal a glimpse of her smooth midriff if she moved in certain ways. He devised maneuvers that caused her to move in those ways so he could stare at that tempting band of skin.

Underneath, he knew she wore wine-red bikini panties—that were definitely *not* chaste or prim—and a matching lacy bra that he had personally fastened. Remembering sent frissons of heat through him. The image of her in that sexy lingerie seemed to be seared in his mind's eye and sent his pulses into overdrive everytime he called it up. Cade suppressed a groan. He felt like a sweat-palmed teen slavering over a *Victoria's Secret* catalog.

Their breakfasts arrived—The Corner Room's specialty, blueberry waffles—which Kylie immediately recognized as the supermarket frozen variety. She didn't care. What she ate was irrelevant. Sitting across from Cade, watching him, talking to him, touching him was all that mattered. Her heartbeat raced, her skin tingled. She wanted to be alone with him. The long hours of the day seemed to stretch interminably ahead, and she wanted them to be over so she and Cade could—

Kylie set down her fork in midthought. For the first time since she'd awakened this morning curled in Cade's arms, it occurred to her that he hadn't mentioned seeing her tonight. He'd suggested breakfast, not dinner. She had no idea when they would be together again after leaving The Corner Grill.

Until now, everything had seemed so simple. She was sure they'd skipped all that uncertainty, the does-he-care, how-far-and-how-fast-should-we-go hurdles that tended to plague new relationships. But here she sat, worrying and wondering and not so sure of anything at all.

Her mouth felt dry, her throat seemed to close, and anxiety roiled through her. The symptoms brought back that hideous period in junior high school when she'd been waiting and hoping to be asked to the Spring Dance. Adolescent insecurity was not a place she cared to revisit; for Cade Austin to take her there sent apprehension rippling through her. He had such power over her. It was little consolation that she had willingly granted it.

"Consider our Brennan-free respite officially at an end," Cade's voice intruded on her nervous reverie. "The Terrible Trio has just invaded the premises."

Kylie's gaze followed his to the door where her cousins Brenda, Brent, and Ian were entering the restaurant, already pulling off their coats. Brenda was dressed for work in her waitress uniform, a pink blouse and black slacks, her dark hair pulled high in a ponytail that brushed her collar. Brent wore ripped, faded jeans and a dark sweatshirt cut off at the shoulders, exposing an eye-popping array of tattoos up and down his arms. A ponytail like

Brenda's would've benefited his appearance greatly, but his long unwashed hair hung in scraggly disarray to his shoulders. Ian was preppily clad in khaki trousers, a white oxford cloth shirt and a striped tie, his attire as traditional as his neatly cut hair.

"They're a somewhat, um, eclectic trio but they don't qualify as terrible," Kylie felt obliged to defend them. "Well, except maybe for Brent."

Cade was scowling fiercely at her cousins. If looks could kill, the three Brennans would certainly be headed for the embalming table. "For God's sake, don't make eye contact with any of them," he ordered, but it was too late. Kylie and Brenda had spotted each other, and Kylie gave a hesitant little wave.

Which was all the invitation the trio needed. As the three Brennans approached them, Kylie glanced anxiously from Cade to her cousins, wishing for a court-appointed intermediary to keep the peace, knowing that hapless task could very well fall to her. It was not a pleasant prospect.

The moment the threesome reached the table, Cade stood up, towering over them, his height and his expression intentionally, effectively intimidating. Kylie watched each of her cousins take quick defensive steps away from him.

"Your little trick last night was idiotic beyond imagining," Cade immediately launched his attack, dispensing with even the pretense of a friendly greeting.

"I don't know what you're talking about, Austin." Ian threw back his shoulders and puffed out his chest, presumably to give him greater presence, but he remained short and slim, the runt of the litter yipping at the heels of the pack's alpha male. Cade Austin.

"Yeah, right, Ian." Brenda laughed. "Like any of us are dumb enough to believe that."

"Shut up, Brenda!" Brent flexed his muscles, and shook a threatening fist at his sister. "Or I'll shut your mouth for you."

Kylie's eyes widened. Those tattoos of his did strange things when his skin rippled. Did he actually intend to hit Brenda? He certainly appeared to be capable of it. Automatically, Kylie rose to her feet ready to intervene on the other woman's behalf.

She didn't have to.

"You touch your sister and I'll wipe up the floor with you," Cade promised. He grabbed a fistful of Brent's sweatshirt and lifted him a few inches off the ground. His eyes bored into Brent's until the younger man looked away, sulkily staring at the ground. Only then did Cade speak again.

"Last night's brand of juvenile vandalism is exactly what I'd expect from a witless coward like you, Brent." Cade's tone was filled with such contempt that Kylie cringed.

She watched as Cade abruptly released Brent, dropping him to the floor. Her cousin stumbled backward, his shoulders slumping, his mouth twisting into a pout, but he didn't utter a sound. After his show of belligerence toward Brenda, Kylie was surprised by Brent's passivity. He certainly hadn't flexed a single tattooed muscle against Cade.

Kylie sat back down, feeling superfluous and uneasy. Wishing she'd taken Cade's advice and not made eye contact in the first place.

Cade next turned to Ian, who sidestepped behind a chair in an obvious move to escape Brent's fate.

Brenda noticed, and snickered. "Pick him up and throw him across the room, Cade," she urged gleefully.

"He's not worth the energy." Cade zeroed his laser gaze onto Ian. "I'm fully aware that you're a shortsighted, greedy little weasel, Ian, but I didn't think you were quite *that* stupid as to post Brent's bail so he could vandalize Gene's place. Did you enjoy your visit from the police last night?"

"They have no evidence connecting me to anything," Ian insisted. The fact that he appeared on the verge of panic did not add to his credibility.

Cade's glower heated to nuclear intensity. "That's not what I hear. The charges pending are almost too numerous to mention, but I'll list a few anyway. Burglary, breaking and entering, malicious mischief, for starters. Not to mention conspiracy and risking a catastrophe," he added with barely contained fury.

Kylie's jaw dropped. He had to be kidding, though her cousins didn't seem to get the joke.

"Can you make those charges stick?" Brenda was curious.

Not if the district attorney, defense attorney, or judge had graduated from law school, Kylie thought. She debated whether or not to inform her cousins that Cade was bluffing, that there was no evidence linking either Brent or Ian to the scene, let alone a shred of proof to indict for the more serious crimes Cade had cited.

But Cade answered Brenda's question with one of his own. "Can I make them stick?" he asked coldly. "What do you think?"

By the expressions on the faces of Brenda, Brent and Ian, they clearly thought Cade could and would.

"It wasn't my fault!" Brent exclaimed. Kylie recognized the tone. It was one she heard when a client was about to cut a deal on his own behalf and to hell with his accomplice.

Cade looked bored. "We'll talk about it later. Now get lost."

Brent and Ian left the restaurant, quarreling and nearly tripping over each other in their efforts to make a quick getaway.

Brenda shrugged and sat down in Cade's chair at the table across from Kylie. "Hey, how'd it go last night?" she asked in breezy girlfriend-to-girlfriend fashion, as if the altercation of the past few minutes had not occurred. "You wouldn't believe where Noah and I ended up, Kylie." Her voice lowered. "I have almost ten minutes till my shift starts. Come into the back with me and I'll tell you all—"

Cade slipped his hands under Brenda's armpits and lifted her bodily from the chair. He set her on her feet and glared at her. "I want you to tell me everything you know about the break-in at your uncle Gene's house last night, Brenda. And I mean *everything*. Because if you don't—"

"You'd better stop threatening me and start sweet-talking me into being your ally," Brenda retorted. "You're going to need one, you know."

Cade caught Kylie's eye. "Wasn't that what Stalin said to Roosevelt?"

Kylie almost smiled, but reconsidered and didn't. Cade had already bullied her cousins and seemed intent on continuing the behavior. It was conduct she could not reward, not even subtly, by smiling. Her instincts were to shield and defend the underdog, and right now that was certainly Brenda, not the almighty Cade Austin.

"I'd like to hear about your evening with Noah, Brenda." Kylie turned purposefully to her cousin.

"That's my cue to leave." An impatient Cade glanced at his watch. "I'll talk to you later, Kylie." He leaned down, placed a quick proprietary kiss on her mouth and strode from the restaurant.

"He kissed you!" Brenda gawked after him. "The last time I saw you two together you were yelling at each other on Uncle Gene's front porch. And now—wow! You're a fast worker, Kylie. I want to hear all about *your* night!"

Kylie's cheeks were hot. Her lips tingled and throbbed; it was as if she could actually feel the imprint of Cade's mouth on them. The sensation recurred in her breasts and her nipples tightened. She grew moist and swollen between her thighs, where she still felt evidence of his passionate possession. Kylie drew a sharp, shuddering breath.

"So how good is he in bed?" Brenda asked with real interest. "Four or five stars?"

"Brenda!" Kylie squeaked a protest.

"Should I go higher or lower?" Brenda pressed.

"Brenda, do you plan on working today or are you here as a paying customer?" Another waitress, several years older and at least three sizes bigger, arrived at their table to snarl at Brenda. "Should I take *your* order or will you get moving and wait on the Library Senior Women's committee over there by the window?"

Kylie was relieved at the interruption, despite the older woman's testiness. She simply couldn't confide anything about last night to Brenda or anybody else. What was between herself and Cade was too private, too precious—and too confusing—to share with an outsider. And an outsider was anyone but Cade and herself.

"I'm ready now, Dee." Brenda sighed and rose to her feet. "I'll take the Senior Women's table." She nudged Kylie with her elbow. "To be continued, huh, Kylie?"

Kylie smiled weakly. "I'm glad things worked out well for you and Noah last night, Brenda."

"Obviously, not as well as they did for you and Cade 'cause our date didn't continue through breakfast," Brenda said slyly. Her face softened. "But, yeah, we had a good time. Noah took me, Starr Lynn and my mother to dinner at The Panda House, if you can believe that. I've never had any date invite my mom and my kid to come along with us. Then we went to the rink and watched Starr Lynn practice for a while and ended up at home to watch a video. Noah helped Starr Lynn with her math homework. She actually understood it after he explained it to her.'' Brenda stared into space, in something of a daze. ''He didn't even try to get me into bed, but he kissed me good-night. It *felt* like he wanted me, if you know what I mean, but when he didn't follow up...'' She frowned worriedly. ''What do you think?''

''I think Noah respects you and doesn't want to rush things.'' Kylie's reassurance to Brenda stoked her own anxiety. If not rushing things sexually was a measure of respect, ending her first date with Cade in bed placed her somewhere beyond the pale.

Brenda went to work, and a very preoccupied Kylie left the restaurant to walk to her car parked in the adjacent lot. When a strong hand seized her arm from behind, bringing her to an immediate unwilling halt, red-hot anger streaked through her, combined with an equally potent bolt of fear.

She reacted instinctively, letting the rage take over, knowing that acting afraid around the criminal element was an irrevocable mistake. ''You're in enough trouble without adding assault to the list of charges, Brent!''

''Brent?'' Cade's voice, deep with amusement, echoed in her ears. ''An interesting conclusion, counselor. Whatever happened to your innocent until proven guilty mantra?''

He dropped her arm, and Kylie whirled around to face him. ''Why did you sneak up on me? I thought I was being mugged!''

The relief flowing through her didn't dilute her anger. Instead, it seemed to exponentially increase, abetted by guilt. She'd automatically blamed Brent as her attacker...so much for her lofty proclamations!

''You're not the only one who imagined Brent jumping you out here in a fit of temper.'' Cade's eyebrows drew together. ''Did you really think I'd go off and leave you if there was a possibility that the Dastardly Duo were still lurking around?''

''I thought you'd left for the office—which is what you said.''

''Which is what you assumed,'' he amended. ''I had to escape from listening to the torrid rendition of Brenda's night of passion with poor Noah. I've been waiting out here for you."

Kylie noticed his car parked near hers, exactly where he'd left it earlier when she had followed him in her car to The Corner Grill. Had she been less absorbed in wondering where she stood with Cade, she might've noticed him standing close by.

A cold breeze gusted around them, and she shivered. "There was no torrid rendition or no night of passion. They spent a wholesome family evening together."

"Do I detect an accusatory note in your voice?" Cade was smiling as he reached for her. His gaze fastened on her mouth and he pulled her closer, sliding his hands under her coat to mold her to the hard contours of his body. "Why? For not sticking around to chat with Brenda this morning? Or for bypassing wholesome family fare last night in favor of our adult evening alone?"

"Adult?" Kylie echoed. "That's a bland euphemism for how we spent the night."

Inspired by those sensual memories, her body arched against him, seeking the heat and the satisfaction she'd found with him. They were in a public parking lot, but she felt the hard ridge of his erection pressing insistently against the softness of her belly, her breasts were cushioned provocatively against his chest.

"Bland is not a term that could be used to describe the way we spent last night, honey." His voice reverberated in her ears as he kissed her neck.

Kylie ached with a sweet pain that could not be assuaged here—not unless she wanted to shock the Library Senior Women's committee, seated at their table by the window with an unparalleled view of the parking lot.

Cade, clearly on her wavelength, released her with a sigh of regret. "I'll see you at lunch," he said huskily. "We'll make it a long, long one. Come to my office around noon."

Kylie gave a dreamy nod. He took her keys from her hand and opened her car door. She slipped inside, a syrupy warmth suffusing her. Noon. A glance at the car's clock told her that she had only a few more hours to wait.

And then she gripped the steering wheel, her eyes widening in dismay. "Cade, I can't."

He had closed her door, but opened it again at the sound of her near plaintive wail. "What's the matter, Kylie?"

"I'm meeting my uncles and Axel Dodge for lunch today," Kylie blurted out. "I'm supposed to be at the restaurant by quarter to twelve."

A chill shuddered through her and she averted her eyes, unable to meet his. She felt like a dyed-in-the-wool traitor, the stereotypical backstabbing Brennan. What kind of a woman met with the enemy the very day after a passionate night with her lover?

But before she could formulate an answer, her equitability enabled her to see from her uncles' point of view. Artie and Guy would consider her night with Cade as sleeping with the enemy. To them, her alliance with Cade made her a dyed-in-the-wool traitor.

"I can't cancel, Cade. They're my dad's brothers. I owe them at least an hour for lunch."

Cade stared at her, taking careful note of her distress. "All right," he said after a few long moments. "You have to meet them for lunch."

Kylie was rigid with tension. "I—I did promise."

"Yes, you did."

He was agreeing, he hadn't tried to argue with her, but Kylie felt the barrier between them, as solid and impenetrable as the Berlin Wall once had been. Of course, that had come tumbling down...

"We could have dinner together tonight," she said, hoping she sounded diplomatic, not desperate. "I—I'll cook something at Uncle Gene's."

Cade gave a brief nod. "Call me later," he said briskly and started toward his car.

Kylie leaned out of hers. "Cade, I—you—you do understand why I can't tell you where we're meeting?" Her voice was a plea but she didn't care. "I promised that I'd—"

"Kylie, stop worrying," Cade called over his shoulder. "I understand."

She remembered a judge who'd used that same tone with her in the courtroom. Authoritative. Somewhat patronizing. Dictatorial mixed with a touch of indulgence. The feelings evoked within her were the same then as now, a combination of indignation and relief.

Kylie sat in her car and watched Cade drive away. She had a few hours to kill until that fateful meeting and wondered how to spend them. Returning to Uncle Gene's house where she would be immersed in memories of making love with Cade did not seem like a good idea, not when she needed her thinking to remain clear and impartial.

She began to tally the number of Brennan encounters she'd experienced since arriving in town. It was somewhat similar to comprising a witness list. She had already seen four of her cousins and would see her uncles at lunch. That left her two aunts, Lauretta and Bobbie, unvisited and unseen.

Impulsively, Kylie decided to visit Bobbie. Brenda's pronouncement that Lauretta hated the entire Wayne Brennan branch of the family, whether true or not, made her less than eager to drop in on Uncle Guy's socialite wife.

Bobbie greeted Kylie rather laconically and ushered her into the small frame house she shared with Bridget, Brenda and Starr Lynn in a tidy working-class neighborhood, not far from the BrenCo plant.

There were none of the effusive hugs and kisses Lauretta invariably bestowed, Kylie noted, remembering how thrilled her aunt always claimed to be when Wayne, Connie and the kids came to visit. *And all the while she was hating our guts.* The renegade thought slipped in and Kylie quickly sought to expunge it. Brenda had effectively implanted a subliminal stealth missile in her mind, and awareness of it did not lessen its efficiency.

"What brings you here?" Bobbie asked, seating Kylie at the kitchen table and pouring them each a cup of coffee. Kylie decided to make do and not ask for tea instead. Something about Bobbie, whether it was her dark, vivid blue-black hair—a startling shade that did not occur in nature—her hard unsmiling face, sharply assessing blue eyes, or wiry toughness, precluded special requests.

"I've seen Bridget and Brenda and, uh, Brent and I thought I'd drop by to say hello." Kylie spooned teaspoon after teaspoon of sugar into the dark brew, hoping to make it palatable.

"Before your lunch meeting with Artie and Guy and that slick

Dodge character they dragged down from Cleveland?" Bobbie did not waste time making small talk, she got right to the point. "They want you to sell your shares and sell out BrenCo. They'll lie to you, say anything you want to hear, so you'll do it. Are you going to?"

Stalling, Kylie took a sip of her heavily sweetened coffee. Surprisingly enough, it wasn't bad, as far as coffee went. "I haven't made any decisions," she admitted. "I've heard Cade's side and I feel I should listen to theirs."

"Oh, yeah? And you told Cade that?"

Kylie nodded.

"Bet that went over big." Bobbie gave a snort of laughter.

"He said he understood," Kylie murmured.

"What's to understand? If you go along with those jerks, you're not the whiz kid Gene thought you were. You—hey, wait a minute!" Bobbie interrupted herself. "You said you saw Brent? When? Where? Did you go down to the jail? Who the hell told you to—"

"I saw him this morning at The Corner Grill," Kylie cut in quickly.

"He's out of jail?" Bobbie roared. She began firing questions at Kylie who answered to the best of her ability. None of the answers pleased Bobbie. She began to curse and pound the table and appeared ready to hurl the pot of coffee at some ready target.

Kylie hoped it wouldn't be her. She knew full well that the messenger of bad tidings was often blamed for them, a reaction dating all the way back to antiquity.

"It must've been Guy who gave Ian that money to bail out Brent!" Bobbie raged, after hearing about last night's break-in. "Where else would he have gotten it? That damn Artie never has a spare nickel on hand."

Kylie hadn't intended to tell all, but Bobbie's investigatory techniques—she'd perfected the dual roles of good-cop-bad-cop and played both herself—ferreted out all the facts. Except for one very personal one, that she'd spent the night in bed with Cade.

Kylie drained the rest of the coffee from her cup and poured another, seeking a bolstering jolt of caffeine. "Cade didn't mention

Guy, but he does think Ian deliberately posted bail so Brent could..." Her voice trailed off and she left the obvious unsaid.

Bobbie said it for her. "So Brent could break into Gene's place and damage it. Wait until I see him, I'm going to slap him silly. And that jackass Artie was in on the plan, too, you can count on that!"

Kylie guessed that all four male Brennans were in danger of being slapped silly by Bobbie should they be reckless enough to cross her path.

"I'm calling Bridget right now!" Bobbie grabbed the phone. "When she hears how they used Brent, she'll think twice at letting herself be used! She'd better, or I'll brain her!"

Kylie felt an ominous stirring within her. "Aunt Bobbie, do they want Bridget to—to do something illegal?"

The unknowable, obscure *they*. Usually, Kylie avoided conspiracy theories but this time *they* seemed dishearteningly familiar—her uncles and her cousins Brent and Ian.

"God!" Bobbie seemed to be summoning the Almighty. She replaced the receiver in its cradle, then sank heavily onto the kitchen chair and lit a cigarette. "I can't smoke when Starr Lynn is around," she said, inhaling deeply. "It wouldn't be good for her to breathe smoke, she has to stay in top condition. But at times like this...Damn, why do my kids have to be so stupid? All three of them are idiots who let themselves get jerked around and talked into doing things that anyone with an ounce of common sense would know to run screaming away from."

Kylie studied this calmly pessimistic Bobbie and felt a deep pang of sympathy for her. "What do they want Bridget to do, Aunt Bobbie?" she asked quietly.

"To threaten Cade—and BrenCo—with a sexual harassment suit."

Eight

Kylie went still. "A sexual harassment suit?" The ugly words seemed to reverberate in her head.

"Yeah. Axel Dodge came up with the idea to discredit Cade. Artie and Guy aren't that creative, but they'd go along with any plan to bring down Cade. Bridget is supposed to say she'll file a claim against BrenCo accusing the company of sex discrimination and fostering an atmosphere of pervasive sexual harassment. Those are the exact words they used."

"And what would be the basis of this claim?" Kylie asked tersely.

"She's supposed to say management threatened retaliation against women employees who refused to have sex with them and male workers grabbed their female colleagues' intimate parts," Bobbie recited. "That there were leers and catcalls and dirty jokes and stuff like that happening every day and all of it was reported but nothing was done to stop it."

Kylie felt sick. "Is any of this true?"

"Bridget told me nobody's ever done anything to her. She's never heard any women at BrenCo complain, either, but Axel

Dodge said if Bridget just threatens to file the claim, it'll give them leverage against Cade. Even though there's no proof of anything, he wouldn't want the trouble of a claim like that and to stop it, he'll do whatever they want, like raise the dividend payouts or something. That's what they hope, anyway."

"So the allegations are completely false," Kylie said flatly.

Bobbie nodded. "I tried to tell Bridget it's a dumb plan, but I don't know if she believed me. You can never tell with her."

"It's more than dumb, it constitutes fraud, abuse of process and probably civil conspiracy." Kylie clutched her head in her hands, contemplating the nightmarish case. "Why would Bridget even consider doing such a thing, Aunt Bobbie?"

"Her father doesn't have the time of day for Bridget. Never has." Bobbie sighed. "Brent is Artie's favorite and he tolerates Brenda because of Starr Lynn. He thinks Starr Lynn will be a rich and famous Olympic champion ice skater someday so he treats her nice. Bridget, he totally ignores. Except suddenly this plan comes up and Artie is Mr. Devoted Daddy, taking Bridget out to dinner and giving her money and stuff. Trying to bribe her into cooperating. I warned her about those Brennan men." Bobbie's eyes flashed. "User-slimeball-rats, every last one of them!"

Kylie winced. "I'm sorry for Bridget, Aunt Bobbie, but she can't be allowed to go through with filing a false claim. She'll end up in trouble beyond her wildest dreams." Impulsively, she laid her hand over the older woman's. "The charges I cited are the minimal ones. There are far more serious versions that can be brought against her, and they will be since her claims are patently false."

"You're saying that Cade will fight back?" Bobbie was glum.

Kylie thought of Cade's reaction to such a claim and shuddered. "I think you can safely predict that he will fight any false charges brought against BrenCo with the best attorneys and investigatory team that company money can buy. And since Bridget's claims are untrue, they will be unable to be proved."

She tried to maintain the calm and matter-of-fact demeanor of an unbiased lawyer considering the facts of a hypothetical case. Riling the volatile Bobbie didn't seem to be in anyone's best interest. "Investigators for BrenCo will look for the motive behind the false claims and that will lead to the conspiracy, bringing in Artie and Guy and Axel Dodge."

"So Bridget won't be the only one in trouble?"

To Kylie's alarm, Bobbie seemed enthused by this prospect. "They'll all do jail time," she warned. "They'll also have to pay substantial fines. And after being cleared, BrenCo and Cade himself can sue for damages and libel, just to name a few possibilities. The entire plan is a disaster, Aunt Bobbie, but I think Bridget will be hurt worst of all."

Kylie was relieved to see that her tacked-on warning had its desired effect.

Bobbie's expression turned bleak once more. "Will you try to talk some sense into Bridget? If she won't listen to her mother, maybe she'll pay some mind to you. She thinks you're so pretty and so smart. She kind of admires you."

Kylie doubted that. "I'll talk to Bridget," she promised anyway.

"And if you have any luck getting through to her, you can tackle Brenda next," Bobbie intoned darkly. "She's in way over her head with Noah Wyckoff, that pal of Cade's. Which is exactly what Cade intended. It's part of his plan."

Kylie thought of Cade's reaction to the budding Brenda-Noah romance. "Oh, Aunt Bobbie, I really don't think so."

"It makes perfect sense," insisted Bobbie. "I see Noah using Brenda to get whatever information she hears about Artie and Guy's schemes and then passing it along to Cade. Oh, he's a smooth one, all right!"

Kylie cleared her throat. "Cade or Noah?"

"Both. They know that Noah isn't like the men Brenda's used to. I'm worried sick about her. I even tried some of that retro-psychology, you know, when you say one thing to get somebody to do the exact opposite?"

"You mean reverse psychology."

"Yeah, that's it. I told Brenda to play it cool around Noah, thinking that she'd blow off my advice like she always does and would come on so strong she'd seem like a stalker. I figured, spy mission or not, that would scare him off. He'd tell Cade he couldn't stand it and to infiltrate the Brennans some other way."

"But your plan hasn't worked?"

"No. I can't figure it out. Last night Noah asked me and Starr Lynn to have dinner with them—and we had a great time. Yeah, he's a real slick one."

"Isn't it possible that Noah genuinely cares about Brenda and they don't need manipulation and strategies?" suggested Kylie.

"Oh, sure!" Bobbie gave a cynical snort of laughter. "I bet you think that Cade is just a tame pussycat instead of a man-eating tiger, too. Let me set you straight on that point, sugar. Cade Austin is ruthless. There isn't anything he wouldn't do for BrenCo, and you ought to think about that because you're the one standing in the way of his total control of the company. If he tries to sweet-talk you into bed, keep in mind that what he really wants from you is a helluva lot more than your body."

"You told Brenda that you trusted Cade," Kylie reminded her. Her hand shook a little as she set the coffee cup down, either a reaction from the double ingestion of caffeine or from the nerve Bobbie had so unerringly struck.

"Sure, I trust him not to use Brenda sexually. Cade Austin is too smart to be led around by his—" Bobbie glanced at Kylie and rephrased. "He isn't driven solely by sex. Anyway, he can get it from other women, so why bother to tick me off by messing around with Brenda?" She smiled slightly. "Cade doesn't like it when I get upset."

"But wouldn't that line of reasoning also apply to Noah Wyckoff?"

"Noah is a safe step removed from Cade. They thought I wouldn't catch on because Brenda hasn't. Ha!" Bobbie crushed the stub of her cigarette in a ceramic ashtray shaped like a skate.

"On one of the soaps I watch, somebody said 'being underestimated is a gift.' Well, it's true. I'm underestimated by certain people, but it works for me because they don't know how good I am at figuring things out. And since you're a sweet girl and I always liked you, even though Artie and Guy and Lauretta say you're a phony little nuisance, I'm going to talk to you like I talk to my own girls."

Kylie braced herself for the words of maternal wisdom.

"Watch yourself around Cade Austin." Bobbie lit another cigarette. "He knows that if you get pregnant, your father will insist that you get married. In fact, you'd probably insist on it yourself. Cade is counting on that."

"He's counting on, uh, making me pregnant?" Kylie dared to ask.

"And then making you marry him. That'll put him in the catbird seat once and for all. As your husband, Cade will control BrenCo lock, stock and barrel."

Kylie stared at the swirling stream of smoke. Bobbie had recited a plot straight from daytime television, one she should have found ludicrous, especially after last night. Cade's precautionary actions had thoroughly disputed her aunt's dire predictions. However much he wanted control of BrenCo, there were certain lines Cade wouldn't cross.

Would he? A niggling doubt began to nag at her.

"Look, I don't want BrenCo to be sold," Bobbie continued. "If it is, and Cade is replaced by somebody from some gigantic corporation who doesn't know us, my family loses the most. Cade pays Bridget more than the other receptionists at the company because she's Gene's niece. Starr Lynn gets a chunk of BrenCo community aid money for her training and competition expenses. I know some stranger would never do that for us, and I want Cade to stay in charge. But it's only fair that you have all the facts to protect yourself."

Viewed from Bobbie's dark perspective, Kylie knew that her aunt believed she was helping. Bobbie had nothing to gain and everything to lose if Cade was ousted yet she didn't want to see Kylie duped by him; she didn't want to see Brenda duped, either.

Kylie frowned thoughtfully. In Bobbie's world, obviously someone was always trying to put one over on someone else. It seemed a stressful way to live, remaining hypervigilant, always waiting for the next lie or deceitful trick.

Compassion stirred within her. "I appreciate your concern, Aunt Bobbie," Kylie said softly. "I'll be very careful."

"You really are a smart girl!" Bobbie seemed pleased.

"Brenda and Bridget would yell at me and say I'm paranoid and trying to spoil things for them, but you understand."

She leaned forward in her chair, her eyes blazing with an almost messianic fervor. "I know what it's like to be trapped in a lousy marriage, living with a jerk you hate, watching your kids get more screwed up every day. You don't deserve that, Kylie, even if Gene did leave you all the stock."

The plan was for Kylie to meet her uncles and Axel Dodge at a place called the Peach Tree Inn, halfway between Port McClain and Cleveland. Kylie followed the directions Uncle Guy had given her, exiting the interstate and driving along a seemingly endless two lane road.

Perhaps it was the result of her visit with Aunt Bobbie but suspicion began to gnaw at her. Why had they chosen a place so out of the way? There were certainly enough restaurants in Port McClain without traversing Ohio in search of one. The name of this place raised further distrust. Were there any peach trees in the state of Ohio? What if this so-called Peach Tree Inn didn't exist? Perhaps the idea was to lure her far from town and then...

Kylie felt perspiration bead on her brow. If paranoia was contagious, she'd caught a whopping case of it from Aunt Bobbie.

Doubts that should've occurred to her earlier suddenly struck her now in full force. Aunt Lauretta and Uncle Guy could have hosted this meeting in their house. Certainly, that would've been the easiest course of action, *unless their plans involved disposing a body—hers!* Naturally, they wouldn't want their own home to be the crime scene!

Kylie's heart pounded so ferociously she half expected it to explode from her chest. She was letting her imagination run away with her, she conceded, combining her knowledge of criminal intent and actions with all those programs extolling the despicable deeds family members perpetrate on each other. She was scaring herself silly, which she'd also done last night.

Except last night she had run to Cade and now he had no idea where she was. If only she'd told him! Maybe she should turn around right now and drive back to Port McClain, to BrenCo. It wasn't too late, she could—

A small sign reading Peach Tree Inn, 1 Mile, came into view.

Alone in her car, Kylie actually blushed. There really was a Peach Tree Inn, and she was suddenly quite certain that her uncles had not cooked up some sinister plot to arrange for her untimely demise. She breathed a thankful sigh that no one would ever know about her ridiculous fantasizing. It was the type of thing her supremely confident, never-a-fear brother Devlin would never let her live down!

As for Cade...Kylie grimaced. He would probably tell her she was on the right track, that Brennans were capable of anything.

Cade is ruthless. There isn't anything he wouldn't do for BrenCo, and you ought to think about that because you're the one standing in the way of his total control of the company. Bobbie's voice rang in her ears.

No wonder she was a nervous wreck, she was mired in a swamp of mistrust and suspicions. Cade versus the Brennans; various Brennans versus various others. And all of them versus her?

The Peach Tree Inn was centered in a grove of trees that Kylie supposed could be peach trees. In the bare starkness of mid-March, there were no flowers or fruits on the branches for identity purposes.

A plaque beside the door gave a brief history of the inn. It was a designated historical landmark and had been a working inn since the early 1800s, serving travelers, soldiers and westward-bound pioneers. The brick walls were covered with all sorts of antique memorabilia from old pitchers and pots to yellowed schoolgirl embroidery samplers. The waitresses wore long flowered dresses and aprons, reminiscent of nineteenth-century costumes.

"Kylie, darling!" Lauretta Brennan, wrapped in a fox fur coat, rushed forward to greet her and enveloped her in a hug. She wore a two-piece silk suit and heels, a distinct contrast to Kylie's jeans and sweater.

Kylie well remembered Uncle Guy telling her that "the place we're going is real casual so don't dress up." Was this Aunt Lauretta's casual wear?

"It is just wonderful to see you! Isn't this the most charming place? I do hope you think it was worth the drive," Lauretta chattered on. "The men wanted to meet in Port McClain but I insisted that we have lunch someplace special. Guy and I brought your mother and dad here for dinner a few years ago, during one of their visits to Gene. They absolutely loved it and you'll soon see why. The food is marvelous!"

Taking Kylie's arm, she led the way through a narrow corridor to a dining room far in the back. Kylie made no comments; none were required. Cutting into Lauretta's monologue seemed awkward at best, rude at worst.

Uncles Guy and Artie and a tall gaunt silver-haired man, who had to be Axel Dodge, were seated at a round table in the center of the room, which was otherwise unoccupied. The three men rose when Kylie and Lauretta entered.

Guy introduced Axel Dodge who proceeded to gaze raptly at Kylie. "Guy and Artie told me that their niece was beautiful, but I thought they were merely being loyal doting uncles." He took Kylie's hand between his own. "Now that I've met you, I can see that they didn't exaggerate at all. If anything, they've underestimated your loveliness."

Kylie felt a perverse urge to giggle. Axel Dodge's overblown compliments struck her as hilarious. Surely, he didn't expect to be taken seriously? "Well, as that wise old saying goes, being underestimated is a gift." She managed to keep a straight face, though it took considerable effort.

"Oh, yes, I know that quote. Oliver Wendell Holmes, I believe," Axel said pompously. "Or perhaps it was Oliver Hazard Perry. Yes, it was one or the other."

Bobbie Brennan, quoting a soap opera character, Kylie longed to reply but judiciously refrained from doing so.

"Kylie, you must fill us in on the latest family news!" Lauretta enthused as they all took their seats. She slipped off her fur coat, pausing to stroke the reddish-gold sleeve. "How are your mother and dad enjoying his retirement? And when are they coming to Port McClain for another visit? We miss them! And Devlin, that dear brilliant boy! How is our nephew, the doctor?"

Kylie wondered if she would've bought Lauretta's act, even if Brenda and Bobbie hadn't clued her into the woman's true feelings. Lauretta certainly sounded interested and fond of Wayne, Connie and Devlin. Kylie reflexively returned her aunt's smile. Her uncles were beaming at her, too, though lunching with "the phony little nuisance" must be galling to them all.

As soon as they'd given their orders to the waitress, Axel launched his pitch. He made every single point in favor of Kylie selling her BrenCo stock that Cade predicted he would make. None of them seemed credible to her, and Kylie found herself playing the devil's advocate, tossing out Cade's arguments against a sale.

"I'm concerned about the effects on Port McClain if BrenCo should be sold. Inevitably, there will be some sort of restructuring that will lead to job losses, especially if the headquarters is moved out of town." She glanced from her uncles to Axel Dodge. Only the latter met her gaze.

"There is no reason for a beautiful young woman like you to worry about jobs in Port McClain," Dodge said unctuously. "All you have to do is to think of ways to spend all that money you're going to get from the sale of your shares. You can take great trips, buy a fabulous car and jewelry and all the pretty clothes you want. Wouldn't you just love a fur coat like your aunt Lauretta's?"

Kylie was incredulous. "I'm supposed to go *shopping* after I've helped cripple the economy of an entire town?"

"We did mention that Kylie has a social conscience, Axel," Guy said, chuckling uneasily.

Kylie stared at her uncle. "What about Todd and Polly, Uncle Guy? They've both expressed an interest and a talent for coming to work at BrenCo when they're finished with school, but the company might not be around if it's sold. Don't you want them to have an opportunity to be part of the family business?"

"Dammit, Brent was right! Austin already got to her!" Artie blurted out. "You've been brainwashed and you don't even know it, missy."

"Artie, stop it!" Lauretta snapped a warning.

"Kylie, that particular argument of Cade's—keeping the family business intact for future Brennans—is disingenuous on his part," Axel inserted silkily. "Cade Austin plans to own BrenCo himself, he couldn't care less what any Brennan does or wants in the future."

"That's right," Guy seconded. "As Ian says—"

"Uncle Guy, why did Ian bail Brent out of jail?" Kylie interrupted. Had she been in a courtroom, opposing counsel would've howled an objection, but here at the Peach Tree Inn her question was met with dead silence.

"Ian bailed Brent out of jail?" Lauretta was the first to break it. "When?"

"I believe the more relevant questions are why and how?" Kylie replied quietly.

"Why shouldn't he?" Artie blustered. "Ian and Brent are cousins. Would you let your cousin sit in a jail cell if you could get him out?"

"All right." Kylie gave him that point. "But where did Ian get the money? Most law students don't have twenty-five hundred dollars in ready cash on hand. Unless, things have changed since I was in law school?"

"Guy, where did Ian get twenty-five hundred dollars to bail Brent out of jail?" Lauretta's voice trembled. She stared stonily at her husband, and Kylie was certain that this was the first time her aunt had heard the unwelcome news.

Their meals arrived at that moment, granting Guy a reprieve from having to answer. And while the plates were being set on the table, another guest was escorted into the dining room. The young blond hostess in her sprig muslin gown was flirting with him.

"Cade's here!" Guy gaped at him.

"You told him!" Artie accused, glaring at Kylie. "You promised not to, but you went ahead and did it anyway!"

But Kylie was as stunned as the others by Cade's arrival. She stared at him, watching him chat with the pretty hostess as they walked to a window table. She saw the moment he glanced over at their table for the first time, though Kylie was certain he'd known they were there all along. To Cade's credit, he didn't attempt to act surprised to see them.

Her hands in her lap, Kylie twisted her napkin into a tight coil as Cade ambled over to their table.

"Hello." He smiled laconically, his eyes locking with hers.

"What brings you all the way out here, Cade? The incomparable chicken and dumplings?" Axel Dodge asked caustically.

Cade shrugged. "I got tired of The Corner Grill's tuna on rye. Chicken and dumplings make a nice change."

Lauretta gave a nervous smile. "Won't you join us, Cade? If we push our chairs closer together, we can fit you in."

Kylie gave her aunt full marks for maintaining etiquette under pressure. Or was Lauretta motivated by fear? Until or unless he was dethroned at BrenCo, Cade Austin remained one of the most powerful men in Port McClain.

"Thanks, but I wouldn't dream of crashing your meeting." Cade's gaze remained fixed on Kylie.

"How considerate of you," Kylie said dryly. Even if he hadn't spoken a word to them, the meeting was effectively crashed. His arrival had the effect of a high-speed head-on collision.

She felt all eyes upon her and tried to tamp the surge of excitement that Cade's presence evoked within her. He was so clearly in the wrong, she reminded herself. He'd spied on her, and she did not care to encourage that sort of conduct.

"You followed me here," she said, her tone reproving.

"I didn't personally follow you, but I did arrange to have you followed," Cade admitted coolly, his hazel eyes glittering with challenge. "Pecoraro was off duty this morning and has been tailing you since you left The Corner Grill. He filled me in on your whereabouts."

"You got a cop to tail my niece?" Guy's lips tightened into a thin angry line. "I don't care who you are, Austin, you have no right to intimidate her!"

"Kylie isn't intimidated by me." Cade laughed off the notion. "And you'll have to agree that after last night, she needs protection from certain young goons who might decide that they haven't done enough to—"

"Cade, don't!" Kylie jumped to her feet. "Please," she added urgently.

She didn't want him to launch into a report of last night's misdeeds, she was positive her aunt knew nothing about any of it. Kylie wanted to spare her the knowledge, at least for now.

"What about last night?" Lauretta asked.

Guy, Artie and Axel Dodge remained silent, not even pretending to be curious, thus assuring Kylie that they knew all about last night's break-in. Whether they'd known before or after the fact was the next logical question to ascertain. Had they helped to plan it or been informed by the culprits later on?

"Conspiracy or cover-up?" Cade murmured softly, voicing Kylie's own thoughts aloud. Their mental attunement spooked her a little.

"We don't have to talk about it now," Kylie implored, glancing at her aunt's increasingly anxious face.

Cade followed her gaze and her train of thought. Again.

"No, not now," he agreed. He looked at the five plates of food sitting untouched on the table. "Eat your lunch before it gets cold." He made it sound like an executive order rather than a polite platitude.

After he'd left for his own table, an uncomfortable silence descended. Kylie stared down at the Peach Tree Inn's heralded chicken and dumplings, congealing under a pastelike gravy. She hadn't been very hungry to begin with, and the collective tension surrounding the table killed what little appetite she had. Listlessly, she stirred her fork around the plate.

"Guy, what aren't you telling me about Ian?" Lauretta's voice, shrill with anger and worry, filled the room.

Guy's unoriginal reply, "I don't know what you're talking about," only made his wife press harder.

Kylie knew a full-blown marital battle was brewing and wished for a return of the uncomfortable silence. Apparently Axel Dodge and Uncle Artie did, too.

"Perhaps you two ought to discuss this matter later?" Axel smarmily suggested a moment before Artie snarled, "Just shut up, willya?"

The silence was back.

Kylie made a pretense of eating. Cade caught her surreptitiously glancing at him and acknowledged her by lifting his eyebrows. She quickly looked away. When it happened a second time, then a third, her face flushed scarlet. She was so intensely aware of his presence she couldn't keep her eyes away from him. Worse, he knew it.

She felt restless and on edge. She wanted to march over to Cade's table and challenge him. How dare he have her followed? The more she mulled it over, the more irritated she became. She had been doing quite well at this meeting, holding her own without any trouble at all. Then *he* had arrived...

Kylie's gaze compulsively returned to him and this time when their eyes met, it occurred to her that Cade was experiencing a plight similar to her own. She'd caught *him* staring at *her* each time she'd looked his way. Cade was as aware of her as she was of him. He couldn't keep his eyes off her, and the realization exhilarated her.

While reminding herself that she was still vexed by his interference, another part of her—the romantic, dreamy side that had remained dormant until Cade had awakened those sweet emotions—admitted that she was glad he was here. She longed to bolt from this table and its four dour occupants and join Cade at his.

Her eyes lingered on his hand as she watched him lift his water glass. She studied his long graceful fingers, remembered their wickedly thrilling touch on her skin. Kylie quivered.

"I think Cade Austin's presence here defines the atmosphere you will be living under if you decide not to sell your shares of BrenCo." Axel Dodge's portentous tones finally broke the long silence. "The man is controlling, arrogant, and domineering. Freedom and independence will be nothing but lost concepts to you as long as you possess what Cade Austin wants, Kylie."

"Mr. Dodge, don't insult me with another fallacious argument." Kylie laid down her fork. "It's a waste of time."

"Heh, heh, we did mention that Kylie is an attorney," Uncle Guy gritted through his teeth.

Dodge looked annoyed. "Even if you hadn't, I'd've figured it out for myself by now."

Kylie knew she wasn't being complimented.

"Oh no, here he comes again," a morose Lauretta muttered under her breath. But when Cade reached their table, she flashed a megawatt smile. "I hope you enjoyed your lunch, Cade. Can we persuade you to join us for dessert?"

"Thanks, Lauretta, but I'll pass on dessert," Cade replied perfunctorily before turning his attention to Kylie. "I need a favor, Kylie."

"Anything we can do for you, Cade?" asked the ever-ingratiating Lauretta.

"Thanks, Lauretta, but I need this particular favor from Kylie."

Kylie tilted her head, waiting.

"I'd like a ride back to town, Kylie. Your cousin Bridget drove me out here," Cade paused, to let that register. "She dropped me off so I'm stuck without a car."

"*Bridget* dropped you off?" Artie muttered. He stirred uneasily in his chair and fiddled with his cutlery.

Kylie, an astute interpreter of body language, decided she'd never seen anyone look so guilty in her life. If she'd been defending Uncle Artie in court, she would already be mentally preparing for the appeal, positive that the jury was going to find him guilty on the highest count. Who wouldn't?

She stared at the faces around the table, her stomach churning as she thought of the despicable charges they were trying to talk Bridget into pressing against BrenCo. Her eyes flew to Cade's face. His expression was enigmatic, and she wondered how much he knew about the plot against him. He must know *something*. Mentioning Bridget seemed an obvious clue.

"So Bridget's receptionist duties now include chauffeuring you around?" Axel Dodge gave a tight, false laugh.

Cade made no reply. His face was an unreadable mask that any poker player would envy.

Artie and Guy looked stricken.

"I haven't seen Bridget lately," Lauretta remarked. "Is she growing her hair, I hope? The last time I saw her, it looked like it had been cut with a knife and fork."

Based on her own perception, Kylie again absolved her aunt of any knowledge of Brennan skulduggery. If Lauretta was feeling guilty, she would've been oozing with compliments about Bridget, not mocking her haircut.

"I'll ride back with you, Kylie?" Cade asked. It wasn't really a request, it was a statement of fact, and they all knew it.

"Okay." Kylie shrugged, trying for nonchalance. She wasn't sure if she'd pulled it off.

"Let's go." Cade held out his hand to her.

Kylie casually rose from her chair. Though she couldn't wait to escape, she didn't want to appear too eager. Jumping at Cade's command would boost his male ego into the ionosphere, where *nobody's* ego belonged.

None of them tried to stop her from leaving. Cade's Bridget salvo had served its purpose. The three men were exchanging furtive uncertain glances.

Cade offered no further information. He came around the table and took Kylie by the elbow, rushing her out of the dining room, not bothering to play it cool.

"Did you have to make it so obvious that you were in a hurry to leave?" she whispered as they headed toward the door.

"I wanted to get you out of there before they stuck you with the check," Cade said drolly.

"Oh!" Kylie stopped in her tracks. "I forgot all about the check. I wonder if we were supposed to split it? Maybe I should go back and—"

"Forget it." Cade moved closer to her, so close she could feel his breath rustle her hair. So close she felt the heat radiating from his big, strong frame. "After what they put you through, the least they can do is to pick up the tab for your lunch, which you hardly touched."

"They didn't put me through—"

"Save it, honey," Cade cut in again, pulling her along. "I observed your group luncheon, remember? From where I sat, a bad time was being had by all. And let's not forget last night's water sports."

"Thank you for not telling Aunt Lauretta our suspicions about last night," Kylie said quietly. "I don't know how Uncle Guy is going to explain Ian and the bail money to her, but I'm glad I won't be around for it."

Cade pushed open the front door and wind whipped around them. The sky was gray with the threat of more rain, but her spirits lifted despite the gloomy weather. Cade had been right on target about their *group luncheon*; the tension surrounding their table had been as thick as the chicken gravy on their plates. Being freed from it left her limp with sheer relief.

"I don't want to hurt Lauretta. Her son and her husband are prepared to do that without any help from me." Cade put his arm around Kylie's waist and walked her toward her car, his body deflecting the force of the wind gusts. "I'm not trying to hurt *anyone,* Kylie, but your uncles—"

She held up her hand. "Save the campaign speech. I wanted to hear both sides and meet with all interested parties. Now I have."

"And you've reached a verdict?"

She nodded. "Yes, but I want to talk things over with my dad first. I'll call him tonight."

"Talk it over with me right now," Cade demanded.

"That's a conflict of interest. I want to—"

"This isn't a courtroom, Kylie, and you're not a judge who must remain impartial to both sides." Cade's voice was hard. "You've been playing that little game long enough and I'm tired of indulging you. I know which side you're on, I know you've decided not to sell your shares. I doubt if you ever seriously considered it. Now stop trying to turn a business decision into a melodrama by heightening the suspense. It's very Brennan-like, of course, but most unbecoming."

"I am not one of your employees, and I do not take orders from you!" The built-up tension and anger she'd managed to suppress during today's series of family visits suddenly flared to flashpoint. Kylie shrugged his hand from her waist and moved purposefully away from him. "And stop the anti-Brennan remarks. *I'm* a Brennan."

"Oh, don't I know it." Cade let her go but kept pace with her.

In a more characteristic, contemplative mood, Kylie might have viewed her burst of rage in a positive light. It meant she felt comfortable expressing her anger with Cade, that she dealt with him honestly, in a way she could not deal with her Brennan relatives.

But she was not feeling contemplative. More like combative. "I haven't been playing games and I don't need you to *indulge* me in anything!" she added crossly.

That charge really smarted. Did it mean that everything between them so far had been calculated indulgence on his part, a role he'd played for BrenCo's sake?

They came to a halt in front of her car. Cade leaned against the hood, staring at her with a penetrating intensity.

"What are you going to tell your father, Kylie? That his nephews tried to trash Gene's house? That his brothers are in cahoots with a scoundrel, that they're so unethical and corrupt they've asked Artie's own daughter to file false charges against Gene's company? That they've *all* tried to manipulate you and might've even put you at risk? How do you think your dad will react to that news?"

Kylie knew. "He'd go as ballistic as a missile on a nuclear submarine," she admitted reluctantly.

"Is that what you want, Kylie?"

"Of course not! I—I—" Her voice trailed to a whisper, and she stared bleakly at the thickening storm clouds in the sky.

Cade's point was a legitimate one. If she were to tell her father what was going on in Port McClain, he might well sever his ties with his extended family. And that would hurt her dad, badly. Though Wayne Brennan had little in common with Artie and Guy, she knew he loved his brothers. The Brennans were his family...and hers, too.

"I'm very familiar with the Brennan temper, and your father has a captain's share of it, even if he happens to be retired." Cade watched her intently. "It would be a kindness on your part not to tell him about the—unfortunate revelations of the past day."

"You're right," she said softly. And then it struck her. "You *do* know about the false claims they want Bridget to make against BrenCo!" Just thinking about the treachery chilled her far more deeply than the sudden blast of cold air. "Did she tell you herself?"

Cade shook his head. "Noah did, this morning. Brenda told him about it last night. How did you find out?"

"From Aunt Bobbie. She is aghast. And scared."

And distrustful. *I see Noah using Brenda to get whatever information she hears about Artie and Guy's schemes and then passing it along to Cade.* Kylie recalled her aunt's suspicions and felt an anxious twinge. What if Bobbie was right?

Kylie pictured Brenda's face, aglow as she talked about her unorthodox date with Noah. "It would be terrible if Noah was simply using Brenda, pumping her for information to give to you. Cade, you—you didn't ask him to get close to her for BrenCo's sake, did you?"

Anxiety made her ask. Unfortunately, impatience and sarcasm fueled his reply.

"Yeah, sure I did. I set that plan in motion right after I ordered all the company water coolers to be laced with Agent Orange." Cade heaved an exasperated sigh. "Whose side are you on, Kylie? I thought that after last night, I wouldn't even have to ask."

"Is that why you made love to me?" she asked, the words sticking painfully in her throat. "To get me on your side? So I'll do whatever you want and you won't even have to ask?"

She was confused and vulnerable. Everything was happening so fast, the intimacy between her and Cade was all too new to her. Her feelings for him ran deep, but her confidence was unnervingly, uncharacteristically fragile. She thought she was in love with Cade but had no idea as to his true feelings for her. Sure, he desired her body. He also desired her BrenCo stock, and she didn't know which he wanted more.

She knew she probably sounded as panicky as Aunt Lauretta pressing for information about Ian, as suspicious as Aunt Bobbie speculating on everybody's secret agendas, as insecure as Brenda pondering Noah's desire for her.

She was pathetic! Kylie stared resentfully at Cade. He had reduced her to this!

"You've got things all figured out, don't you?" Instead of being reassuring, Cade was sardonic. "I find it interesting that you apply the innocent until proven guilty principle to everybody but me. You're willing to give your idiotic cousins and hysterical aunts and felonious uncles the benefit of every doubt, but you look for ways to incriminate me. I run a police state, I terrorize your family, I plot with Noah to break Brenda's heart, I trick you into bed for all the wrong reasons. And in addition to all that is your eco-terror that BrenCo is about as good for Port McClain as the oil spill is for wildlife, and you don't want any part of any of it."

"Well, *I* find it interesting that you proudly recite that list but feel no need to—"

"To what? Explain? Apologize? Deny?" He angled closer, his nostrils flared, his eyes sharp with anger. "No, I don't."

"Of course not. You're above all that. Because I'm a Brennan and you're Cade Austin, of a far superior caste," she taunted.

Impulsively, she darted to the driver's side of her car, key in hand, the way she'd been taught in her self-defense course back in Philadelphia. She'd aced her getting-swiftly-and-safely-to-her-car-in-a-dark-lonely-parking-area test.

The unexpectedness of her actions gave her a few crucial moments before Cade sprang to action. By the time his hand was on the door handle, Kylie had already locked herself inside the car.

She opened the window a sliver while the engine roared to life. "Being the human deity you are, I'm sure you'll have no trouble finding a way back to Port McClain," she called through the crack. "You can always command your lackeys at BrenCo to deliver your golden chariot."

"Kylie, stop the car right now," Cade commanded.

As if she were a lackey! Defiantly, Kylie hit the gas pedal instead. Cade wisely released his grip on the door handle before she pulled away.

Through the rearview mirror, she saw Axel Dodge emerging from the Peach Tree Inn with Uncle Artie at his side. Uncle Guy and Aunt Lauretta followed, and it was obvious that the couple were arguing.

"If the chariot doesn't work out, you can catch a ride back with one of them," she suggested and peeled out of the parking lot amidst an impressive squeal of tires.

Nine

An hour later, Kylie parked her car and walked through an icy drizzle to the Rock and Roll Hall of Fame in the heart of downtown Cleveland. The directional signs back at the entrance to the interstate highway had inspired her. She had a choice, to go east or west. To Port McClain or Cleveland?

A return to Port McClain meant waiting for her next run-in with Cade, which would inevitably end either in bed or in an argument. And if that wasn't daunting enough, Port McClain also offered the prospect of yet another encounter with yet another one of her relatives. Or maybe all of them.

An alternative destination did not seem like such a bad idea. Maybe she ought to take advantage of her proximity to Cleveland, where she hadn't been in years, and visit the music museum?

Her brother had driven down from Michigan the summer the Hall of Fame opened and sent her a postcard from there, recommending it. Sight-seeing was something of a family legacy. Wherever they'd lived, their parents had made it a point to take Devlin and Kylie to every local place of interest. Over the years she'd seen scads of arrowheads and suits of medieval armor and mummies. She'd seen battle sites, historic homes and graveyards, and art of every medium.

Kylie decided that now was the ideal time to take a tour of the history of rock. She desperately needed a breather, a diversion, a chance to regain her emotional balance—away from the powerful, provoking, tantalizing presence of Cade Austin. The absence of any Brennans in Cleveland only added appeal.

Approaching the impressive entrance plaza, Kylie entered the building, designed by renowned architect I. M. Pei. She recalled that Devlin claimed his primary site of interest was the Rhythm and Blues section. Being a blues aficionado would be right in keeping with Dev's ultracool image of himself, though Kylie couldn't remember him ever listening to a single blues song when he was not in the presence of his friends.

Lacking witnesses to impress with his hipness, when only his kid sister was around, Devlin Brennan turned on whatever radio station was playing the latest Top 40 hits or watched old sitcom reruns on TV. To Kylie, that was an indicator of his true tastes, which were decidedly mainstream and certainly not cutting-edge entertainment. She smiled with sisterly perception. Dev wouldn't ever want that information revealed!

Suave, detached Devlin. He was never without a girlfriend but none of his relationships became serious. Kylie wondered if he would ever drop his Mr.Cool façade long enough to allow anyone to get close to him. To get to know the real Dev within, the guy who knew all the words to all the verses of the theme songs from "The Facts of Life" and "Silver Spoons." Who mercilessly ribbed his younger sister, yet dropped his guard only with her.

"You'll probably be entranced by the One Hit Wonders, Kylie," Dev had kidded her over the phone shortly after his visit to the Hall of Fame. "Those are the groups who hit it big once and were never heard from again. Fits in with your penchant for society's forgotten."

Inside the main lobby Kylie glanced at the museum store, decided to visit it later, then took the escalator to the ground level and headed straight for the One Hit Wonders. She was pondering the fate of a group called Bob Kuban and the In-men whose one and only hit was a song called "The Cheater" when a voice sounded in her ear.

"I'm warning you in advance so you won't think you're being mugged, I'm right behind you. And I'm going to grab you so you can't run away again."

The advance warning did nothing to lessen her shock at the sound of Cade's voice and the feel of his hands on her shoulders. Kylie gasped and jerked, both audibly and visibly startled.

"Turn around," Cade directed and she did, slowly, gaping at him as if he were an apparition, her eyes round with amazement. He kept his hands on her shoulders anchoring her firmly in front of him.

For one of the few times in her life, Kylie was utterly speechless. Even a simple "hello" was beyond her.

"No opening statement, counselor?" Cade mocked her silence. "You're not going to ask me why I'm here? Or is that too much of a no-brainer?"

Kylie was still too befuddled by his appearance to reply.

"Are you wondering how I got here? Hey, maybe my golden chariot has wings." Those expressive, arched brows of his conveyed his disdain for that particular sally. "Or did I insist that Axel Dodge hand over his car keys to me back at the Peach Tree Inn?"

"You did?" She was awed by the sheer enormity of his colossal nerve. "And he did?"

"Obviously. He had no choice. I drove his car but I did let him ride with me."

"How magnanimous!" Her scattered wits were beginning to regroup. "You're all heart, Cade."

Cade did not disagree. "Dodge and I were both flummoxed when you headed toward Cleveland. He thought you were going to meet with a cabal of attorneys—shows how his mind works, hmm? I had no idea what you were up to. And then you came here."

His fingers dug into the delicate bones of her shoulders. "I still don't know why," he growled. "Are you going to tell me?"

"I didn't know you were following me." Kylie wriggled in

protest, but he didn't relax his grasp. "I never saw you, not once."

"That was intentional. You haven't answered my question. What in the hell are we doing here, Kylie?"

"If you'll loosen your grip, I'll tell you what *I'm* doing here."

"If I do, will you promise not to dash off? I'd hate to have to chase you through this place but I will if you make me. And I'll catch you, Kylie, have no doubts about that."

She had no doubts. His machismo was blazing, he was primed and ready to act. Kylie gulped. She really didn't want to race around the Rock and Roll Hall of Fame with Cade after her in full warrior mode.

"I'm not going to dash anywhere." She lifted her chin, hoping she looked proud and defiant. She was more than a little nervous, but was determined to hold her own. "I came to see everything, all the exhibits and artifacts and films and video clips, and I'm not leaving here until I have. So if you'll let me go, I'll get back to studying the One Hit Wonders."

Cade dropped his hands but stayed directly behind her, poised to capture her should she make a sudden move like the one she'd pulled in the parking lot of the Peach Tree Inn.

The clean fresh scent of her hair, mixed with the spicy allure of her perfume, wafted to his nostrils and his blood stirred in immediate response. As usual, her physical impact on him made him reel and while part of him resented her sensual power, that part kept growing smaller while a very crucial, very male part of him was growing considerably larger.

He glanced at the graceful curve of her neck, the soft, vulnerable nape. His lips had tasted the sweet silky skin there, last night and this morning. He remembered how she had shivered with pleasure and cuddled closer, encouraging him, subtly asking for more. He wanted to do it again, right here, right now.

Cade drew a sharp breath. If he clamped his hands on her shoulders and pulled her back against him, he could kiss her neck and her nape, then turn her in his arms and take her mouth the way he'd been wanting to, from the moment they had left Gene's house this morning.

Instead, the intervening hours had been filled with fury and frustration as he had coped with the latest, most dangerous aggravation that the Brennans had thrown at him. Working separately or jointly, they seemed to have an unlimited arsenal but Kylie Brennan was the most powerful of all...the only one he couldn't control, the only one he couldn't bully, threaten or cajole because she recognized exactly what he was doing and gave it right back in full measure.

And because bullying, threatening and cajoling were not what he wanted to do to her. He and Kylie had their own far more effective, far more satisfying methods of communication. If only they were communicating right now!

Kylie moved along at a leisurely pace with Cade following her, though walking was something of a trial for him. In his current condition, he should be sitting down—preferably with her on his lap, naked. Or perhaps lying down. He closed his eyes to fully appreciate the sequence of erotic pictures that idea conjured up in his mind.

Meanwhile, she seemed fascinated by the display in front of her, totally unaware that he was *burning* for her. Cade clenched his fingers, suppressing the urge to fasten them around her—anywhere. He tried to feign an interest in what she was looking at. And couldn't.

"Who the hell is Joey Powers?" he demanded testily. "I've never heard of the guy."

"Of course you didn't. Neither have I. Because he was a One Hit Wonder from 1963," Kylie explained. "His record was 'Midnight Mary.'"

"Never heard of that, either. Where's Elvis? And the Boss?"

"Not among the One Hit Wonders," Kylie said succinctly.

"No kidding." Cade scowled. "As long as we're stuck in this place, can't we find them? Or at least find someone that anybody's heard of?"

"I take it this is your first visit to the Hall of Fame?" Kylie eyed him knowingly. "Even though you're just an hour away and it opened back in 1995?"

"Thanks to you, this is my first visit."

"Unbelievable." Kylie frowned her disapproval. "If you lived in the Philadelphia area, you're the type who would never bother to go see the Liberty Bell or Independence Hall."

"And I wouldn't feel like I'd missed a thing," Cade admitted, without a twinge of shame. "I bet you've made pilgrimages to both the Liberty Bell and Independence Hall, probably within a month of moving to the city."

"That's true. Oh, look!" She pointed at Good Vibrations: The Making of a Song, an adjacent exhibit examining the creative process of songwriting. "That should be interesting."

Cade rolled his eyes. "I'm already riveted."

Kylie, the inveterate sight-seer, spent the next few hours viewing the exhibits and artifacts and films and video clips in the museum. Cade, whose lifetime record of sight-seeing expeditions could be counted on one hand, grew increasingly restless and bleary-eyed, but he doggedly remained at her side. She didn't allow herself to wonder why.

Her visit here was supposed to be a respite from thinking about Cade, from questioning his motives and weaving fantasies starring the two of them, Kylie reminded herself throughout the afternoon. Even though he was right beside her, never letting her stray more than a few inches away from him—maybe *because* of that—she concentrated fully on the Hall of Fame's sights and sounds.

And she learned a lot about the history of rock and roll. She even stored a few obscure facts about the blues with which she hoped to stump Devlin, that self-proclaimed bogus "Blues Fanatic."

The sky was dark when Kylie and Cade finally emerged from the museum. Fat, wet snowflakes were beginning to fall, lightly coating the street. Cade took Kylie's gloveless hand and tucked it into the pocket of his coat.

"Are you keeping my hand warm or keeping me from taking off?" Kylie quizzed, trying to keep things light and easy.

With nothing around to serve as a buffer, she was faced with all the thoughts, questions and fantasies she'd successfully kept at bay all afternoon. They seemed to engulf her now, the intensity both scaring and exciting her.

"You aren't going anywhere without me." Cade glanced down at her. "We have a date for dinner, remember?"

"Oh! I offered to cook dinner for you tonight at Uncle Gene's!" Kylie exclaimed, remembering her nervous invitation to him earlier that day.

"I won't hold you to that." Cade glanced at his watch. "It's getting late and I'm hungry. By the time we drove back to Port McClain and went grocery shopping I wouldn't be able to wait till the food was cooked. I'd probably end up devouring the stuff raw."

"I'm hungry, too," Kylie admitted. "I didn't eat much lunch at the Peach Tree Inn."

"No wonder. The food was inedible and the company was abominable. And before you take offense, I was specifically referring to Axel Dodge and not any particular Brennan."

He started to walk along the sidewalk and since Kylie's hand was in his pocket, she trotted along with him. "Your drive to Cleveland with Mr. Dodge must have been interesting," she murmured.

"For me it was. For the Not-So-Artful Dodger, it was as hellacious as I could make it. I let him know that I was aware of his plot to use Bridget to file false claims against BrenCo, that she'd already assured me she wouldn't go through with it, and that I fully intend to go after him. It was gratifying to see the sleazy little worm squirm."

"Will you go after him?" She gazed up at him. "Can you?"

"Oh, yeah." His grin was almost feral.

Kylie decided that if Axel Dodge was a little worm metaphorically, then Cade Austin was Bigfoot who'd squashed him during a short stroll.

"I have lots of connections, Kylie. *Legal* ones," Cade added, quirking his brow.

"I wasn't going to accuse you of mobster ties," she mumbled, flushing a little. Considering some of the things she'd said, she understood why he felt the need to clarify. "I'm sure you have *legal* influential friends in high positions."

"Especially in Columbus and Cleveland," Cade confirmed, naming the capital and largest city in the state. "And they will not approve of Dodge's methods of mixing blackmail with business. Be assured we'll find *legal* ways to make his life sheer misery."

"The ultimate misery for him will be having to pay exorbitant defense attorneys' fees." Kylie smiled her approval. "Talk about the punishment fitting the crime!"

"Someone as money-crazed as Axel Dodge deserves nothing less."

"Cade, what about Bridget and my uncles?" she asked quietly.

"Bridget and I had a long talk. She didn't do anything wrong, and after I mentioned what Noah told me, she volunteered information to prevent any wrongdoing from taking place. Which was very unBrennan of her. Ouch!"

Kylie had reached over to smack him with her spare hand. Cade pretended that he'd actually felt the blow through his coat. "Bridget will be rewarded for her honesty. She can choose between a cash bonus or extra paid vacation days," he added.

"Aunt Bobbie will be so relieved." Kylie was glad for her.

"You've heard of the carrot-and-stick style of management, haven't you, Kylie?" A gusty breeze blew snow around them, and they paused to catch their breath. "Well, Bridget got the carrot. Artie and Guy and their sons can expect the stick. That's all I'm going to say about any of them tonight. I'm tired of talking about them, I'm tired of thinking about them."

Cade reached down to smooth her wind-tousled hair away from her face.

The unexpected tender gesture sent glowing frissons through her. When he cupped her cheek, she placed her hand over his. "I feel I ought to apologize for my uncles, being of Brennan blood and all. What they'd planned was unconscionable."

He smiled into her eyes. "Not even the defense lawyer for the truly downtrodden can mount a defense for them, huh?"

"Especially since they wanted to use Bridget to do their dirty work. And most especially since they were motivated by greed. They were willing to turn Bridget into a criminal, just for money!" She was truly appalled.

"*Just* for money isn't the way their petty little minds work, Kylie. Try *anything* for money."

They started walking again. A few minutes later, Cade steered her to the front entrance of a hotel. "Here we are," he announced.

Kylie glanced around. The warmth and light of the lobby beckoned invitingly. It would be wonderful to get out of the cold, away from the wind and the wet snow shower. Her stomach growled, protesting the too-long interval between meals.

"Is their restaurant any good?" she asked conversationally, not caring if it was or wasn't. She was so hungry she could probably polish off a generous serving of the Peach Tree Inn's dubious chicken and dumplings, complete with their version of homemade gravy.

Cade drew her inside, leading her toward the registration desk. "The food here isn't bad, but we're not eating in the restaurant. We'll use room service."

His words hit her like an erotic atomic bomb. Heat exploded in every cell of her body, and suddenly she felt weak. All those feelings and desires she'd managed to suppress all day radiated through her, too powerful and intense to withstand any longer. She stood beside him in a daze, only vaguely aware of the transaction between Cade and the desk clerk as he registered for a room.

The lobby suddenly seemed stifling hot. Her skin felt ultrasensitive, her clothes intolerably irritating against every inch of her body. She took off her coat, seeking some minor relief. Cade automatically reached for it, carrying it for her. His solicitousness pleased her.

"Any luggage, sir?" A bellboy approached them and eyed Kylie speculatively when Cade said no.

Under normal circumstances, she would've been mortified but at this moment it didn't seem to matter that the bellboy thought they'd sneaked into town for a shady tryst. Nothing mattered except being alone with Cade.

They held hands during the ride on the crowded elevator and her heart was thundering in her ears as he led her along the corridor to their room.

"I've never done this before," she admitted as he shoved the electronic key into its slot. "Checked into a hotel without luggage to—spend a few hours in a room."

For a second or two, her confidence faltered and she worried he would think she was cheap and easy—the terms her mother used to describe a woman who would check into a hotel to spend a few hours in a room with a man. No doubt Aunts Bobbie and Lauretta would agree with the description, achieving a rare moment of Brennan harmony.

"We're spending the entire night here, honey," Cade amended. "I already ditched work for most of the day, I might as well take it to the limit and stay out of town tonight. I didn't even leave Donna a number where I can be reached."

His confession bolstered her. "And that's unusual behavior for you?" It was heartening to know that she wasn't the only one acting so out of character.

"Unprecedented." Cade opened the door and pulled her in after him. "Donna might end up filing a missing persons report if I don't check in with her later tonight."

Kylie glided closer to him. All of a sudden, her thighs felt rubbery and she swayed slightly. "I need to eat something. I—I feel a little light-headed."

She assured herself that this was not a modern day mating ritual, a bedroom version of the dainty dropped handkerchief.

But Cade took it that way. He dropped both their coats to the floor. "You need to lie down, sweetheart." His voice was a sexy growl as he swept her off her feet and carried her over to the bed. He laid her down on it then sat on the edge, gazing down at her.

His eyes moved over her face and lowered slowly to her breasts that were already taut and swollen beneath her sweater. Kylie drew shallow breaths through her moistly parted lips. He was only looking at her, but she could feel the effects of his burning gaze every place his eyes lingered.

His palms closed over her breasts and he massaged them, fitting their shape to his hands, playing with them, teasing with his fingers. Kylie moaned. It felt good but it wasn't enough. She wanted more, she needed the exquisitely sensual feel of skin against skin. She knew the thrill of his hands on her bare breasts, the arousing feel of them nestled against the wiry mat of hair on his chest.

Acting on a wild primal instinct, she abruptly pulled off her sweater.

Cade smiled his approval. "Oh, yes, baby." He deftly disposed of her bra and then gathered her to him.

Somehow his shirt had become unbuttoned. His arms were around her and she pressed closer, savoring the male texture of his chest, the hair-roughened skin and hard muscle. The rounded softness of her breasts provided an enticing feminine contrast.

Cade caressed each one, his clever fingers stroking her nipples until she whimpered with pleasure ragged with urgency. Stretching out alongside her, he lifted one rounded breast to his lips and drew the hot pink little bud into his mouth. She felt his tongue swirl around it, then he began to suck.

Desire built and surged through her with each tug of his lips. She felt wilder and even more out of control than she had last night. It was as if her body now demanded the intoxicating release it had only found with Cade, as if she'd been in a constant subconscious state of readiness for him and needed less time, less stimulation to burst into full arousal.

They kissed madly, hungrily, shrugging off garments, pulling off others, until finally both were totally, splendidly naked.

"I want you so much," Cade groaned as he slipped his hand between her legs.

He felt the rich creaminess there, evidence of her desire that was as unmistakable as his own virile arousal. He had the physical proof that she wanted him but he wanted to hear the words from her beautifully shaped mouth.

"Tell me you want me, baby," he rasped, probing her lovingly, intimately, touching her in ways that made her want to scream with sheer ecstasy.

Maybe she did. Kylie was lost in passion, wanting to please him, to give herself to him and take him deep inside her. She saw no reason to be coy, to withhold anything from him, especially not the words he wanted.

"I want you, Cade," she whispered.

Emotional tears filled her eyes. She longed to tell him she loved him, too, because she knew that she did. But she wasn't so far gone not to realize that he hadn't asked that of her, that he might not care to hear a declaration of love.

"I want you so much." She kissed his mouth, his neck, his navel centered deep in the whorl of dark hair. "So much." Her hands caressed him, knowing exactly what excited him most. "So much, Cade."

He rolled her onto her back, handling her as easily as he would a doll, lifting her legs and positioning her to receive him. His hands slid up to join with hers, lacing their fingers as he kissed her with a possessive passion that only she had ever inspired in him.

He'd been wary at first and passed through various stages ranging from alarm to resentment but now, lying here with her, Cade accepted the unfathomable. He'd actually found her. He hadn't thought it possible that there was a woman alive who could interest him, who could engage his attention, who could captivate him as much as his work.

But she existed. She was Kylie Brennan and she wanted him, needed him as much as he wanted and needed her. Which was overwhelmingly. He couldn't wait another second. His body took over, and his mind ceded without a modicum of struggle. It felt fabulous to give up control, to simply give in to the driving force of their passion.

Cade surged into her, felt her welcoming wet heat clasp him. Both moaned, surrendering to the sensations of indescribable, incomparable bliss. Effortlessly, they commenced a frenzied complementing rhythm that sent them spiraling higher, into the realms of rapture. There they soared until both were consumed by spasms of pleasure so fierce that they helplessly exploded into a mind-shattering mutual climax.

Afterward, they lay together, Cade sprawled on his back, his eyes closed, while Kylie curled up next to him, her head nestled in the curve of his shoulder. She felt limp and replete, devoid of tension and energy, unable to do anything but lay quiescently at his side. One of her arms was flung across his middle, the other was tucked beneath her, her legs were splayed over his. She idly caressed him, with her foot, with her fingers, with her lips. She loved touching him, she loved looking at him, she loved *him!*

Minutes might have passed—or maybe hours. Kylie couldn't summon the initiative to raise her wrist and look at her watch. Time seemed irrelevant, the rest of the world didn't exist. There were only she and Cade, together in this moment. She never wanted it to end.

Cade didn't, either. A marvelous sense of rightness filled him. The world was exactly as it should be. Everything had fallen into a kind of cosmic order. As an engineer his precise, meticulously exacting mind revered order.

"It's finally starting to make sense to me," he confided drowsily, speaking his thoughts aloud. His defenses were down, all blocks and barriers eliminated. He wanted to share everything with her, every thought, every insight, merging his mind with hers, just as their bodies had become one.

"Mmm" was all Kylie was capable of replying.

That was enough encouragement for Cade. "All this time, Gene's will simply didn't compute. It didn't fit in with the man I knew so well. I puzzled over it, I raged over it. Nothing drives me crazier than an equation that won't balance and that one was totally out of whack. Until now."

Kylie felt the first ominous stirrings within her. She was lying naked in Cade's arms, dazed by the all-encompassing force of her love for him—and his thoughts were of Gene Brennan's will?

"Until now?" she prompted carefully. She shifted her legs, moving them from his.

"Gene planned for this to happen, Kylie." Suddenly infused with a radiant energy, Cade rolled onto his side, propping his head on his hand. His hazel eyes were bright with exhilaration, inspired by his sudden epiphany. "Gene left you those shares to bring us together. By leaving them to you, he accomplished two things, both vitally important to him. He kept BrenCo family-owned, which is what he'd always dreamed and he kept his promise to me, giving me full control of the company."

"I don't think I understand." Kylie tried to swallow around the thick lump that had lodged in her throat and was growing bigger.

Unfortunately, she was beginning to understand all too well. When she looked at Cade, she saw the man she'd fallen in love with. When he looked at her, he saw her shares of BrenCo stock—and the way to get them. He was all but admitting that to her now.

Her whole body flushed and she was suddenly horribly embarrassed to be lying here nude under his avaricious eyes. She reached for her clothes, her movements slow and subtle. Luckily, they were accessible, laying in a heap on the floor beside the bed.

"Maybe you should explain." She managed to keep her voice steady, which was something of a feat when she felt on the verge of bursting into tears. The optimistic, idealistic part of her urged her to keep an open mind. Maybe she'd absorbed too much of the Brennans collective dark cynicism and was misinterpreting, finding iniquity where there was none.

"Gene wanted me to have BrenCo, he always said so," Cade shared his newfound insight with his newly discovered sexual and emotional soul mate.

For the first time since that wretched will had been read, he felt close to his good friend Gene, connected to his mentor once again. The sense that he'd been betrayed, that Gene had turned out to be yet another lying, backstabbing Brennan had vanished and been replaced with the wonderful glow of understanding.

Cade heaved a contented sigh. "But instead of specifying that in his will, he left the controlling shares to you and now I know why. Gene was matchmaking, Kylie! Nobody knew his brothers better than Eugene Brennan. He'd have calculated they would try something rotten enough to ally you and me against them. And once we were thrown together—well, what Gene wanted to happen, what he knew would happen, actually did. Instant chemistry."

During his rapturous recitation, Kylie had been quietly getting dressed. Now she rose to stand beside the bed, slipping her feet into her loosely laced shoes. Every word seared her, burning her hope into the ashes of heartbreak. The Brennans' dark cynicism was a pale shade of beige in comparison to Cade Austin's own personal brand.

"Instant chemistry," she repeated. "Translation—hot sex. Your theory is that my uncle knew of your prowess with women and with me being one of his moronic nieces—we all know the high opinion Gene had of his brothers' offspring—I would simply fall into your arms. Into your bed. Which I did. Congratulations, Uncle Gene." She lifted her eyes to the ceiling as if in heavenly salute to her departed uncle. "Your scheme worked. I was gullible enough to be swept off my feet by your brilliant, sexually irresistible protégé."

The edge in her voice sliced through Cade's hazy euphoric cloud. He jackknifed to a sitting position, his eyes round and wide as he stared at her. She was fully dressed and standing at the foot of the bed. His breath caught in his chest. "Kylie? Baby, what's wrong?"

She'd meant to simply stalk out of the room—she already had her car keys safely in hand—but the sheer arrogance of his question rooted her to the spot. "You're actually asking me that? Do you really want an answer or just more time to gloat over your temporary triumph? And I do mean *temporary*."

"Kylie, you—I—"

"You just admitted you took me to bed so I'd sign over my BrenCo shares to you. And then you had the gall to insinuate that it's part of some otherworldly plan! To hear you tell it, Uncle Gene is applauding you from the Great Beyond."

Cade ran his hand through his hair. "Sweetie, you've misinterpreted what I—"

"No, you misinterpreted! Your timing was atrocious, Cade. You got careless. You were so full of yourself, so proud of your conquest that you couldn't wait to brag about it to someone— even if that someone was me!"

He felt a sheen of perspiration cover his skin as a sickly apprehension seeped into every pore. He'd been babbling like he had been shot full of truth serum, and thinking back on what he'd said... Cade closed his eyes. It was possible that what he'd said could be interpreted in a way other than he'd intended. Clearly, Kylie had taken his revelation all wrong. He swiftly sought to set the record straight.

"Kylie, I was trying to tell you that we're so right together, that we were made to be together. You affect me like no other woman ever has or ever will. Sweetheart, you make me feel passionate and possessive in a way that I never dreamed I could. It's—"

"Since I'm the only woman who's ever owned controlling interest in the company you want, I believe I do affect you differently," Kylie interjected acidly. "Of course, you want to possess me—along with my BrenCo shares!"

"I'm not talking about BrenCo!" Cade's temper flared. "Will you drop the lawyering and quit arguing with every statement I make? Listen to me, Kylie! When I said you affect me like no other woman, I meant that you—you take me out of myself. Tonight, I completely lost control, I couldn't think of anything but getting inside you. That's never happened to me before and I—" He broke off in a startled gasp. "Kylie, I didn't use anything. This is the first time in my life I didn't stop and remember to use protection."

She couldn't breathe, she couldn't move. Being body-slammed by a professional hockey player wielding a stick must feel similar to this, Kylie thought, dazed. For one terrible second, she feared she might faint but the rallying power of fury revived her, sending a gush of adrenaline surging through her bloodstream.

"Aunt Bobbie was right!" she breathed as her aunt's dire warning blasted through her head. The words resounded in every lobe of her brain. "You plan to get me pregnant and make me marry you so you'll be in the—the catbird seat at BrenCo!"

Cade uttered an expletive that according to the Rock and Roll Hall of Fame was now commonly recorded, but could not be broadcast over the airwaves.

Kylie construed his frustration and anger as further proof of Aunt Bobbie's ghastly theory. She couldn't resist the chance to extol the failure of his loathsome plan.

"It isn't going to work, Cade. For one thing, you fired your ammo at the wrong time of the month and you're not going to get another chance when the target is ripe! You see, *I'm* not as stupid as Uncle Gene thought and *you're* not as smart as he thought. So I guess we can call it a draw and forget—"

"I'm not going to forget anything and neither are you and we both know it," he interrupted tersely. "Now come over here and let me—"

"Make a fool of me again? You really do think I'm an idiot."

"I think you're upset," he tried to soothe her, but even he heard the bark of exasperation in his voice. "You're confused and hurt and I'm sorry about that because the last thing I meant to do was to—"

"Clue me in," she finished for him. "Yes, what a mistake! Sort of like Napoleon at Waterloo. Overconfidence got him, too. My grandmother, Mom's mom, the astrology buff, probably said it best—'When the head swells, the brain stops working.'"

Cade saw her inching toward the door. Now that he was aware of her propensity for speedy getaways, he could predict what she intended to do next. "Don't think of leaving this room, Kylie," he ordered, with far more authority than the situation warranted. She was fully dressed and upright, nearer to the door than he was. He had the added disadvantage of being naked and sitting in bed.

"Don't think your efforts have all been in vain, though." She met his eyes and for a moment the pain was so great, she wanted to crumple to the floor, sobbing. But she didn't. She'd had enough of being weak and foolish.

Holding his eyes, she casually scooped his trousers off the floor. She knew he hadn't seen her action, he was too concerned with maintaining eye contact. "I'm going to sell my BrenCo shares to you, as soon as possible. I want you to have them at the fair market price. That will be best for everybody, the Brennans and Port McClain. And—and me. Our attorneys can work out the terms of sale, although I don't think it'll be difficult."

She didn't stick around to see the smile of ecstasy, which would undoubtedly wreath his face, she didn't wait to hear him thank her profusely and perhaps offer a sporting "No harm done."

Clutching her coat and purse and his pants, she bolted from the hotel room, faster than she'd ever moved before. She heard him roar her name but knew he didn't stand a chance of catching her. After all, he was nude and by the time he managed to pull on the minimum of clothing, she would be in the lobby.

Where she left his pants. Kylie tossed them at the desk as she fled the building, figuring Cade would locate them eventually. Stranding him in Cleveland wasn't completely monstrous. He had his wallet; he could rent a car and drive back to Port McClain.

She had a bit of luck in the capricious weather. The snow had turned back into rain and the wind lessened to little more than a light breeze. Driving would not be a problem tonight. Kylie ran the whole way to her car; she didn't intend to waste a single moment of her head start.

She didn't know what she would do if Cade caught up with her. Would he try to talk his way back into her heart, to charm the panties off her again? Literally!

Or maybe she was flattering herself. Suppose her statement of intent to sell her shares to him precluded any need to rush at all? Maybe Cade was so happy about the turn of events—not only was he getting her BrenCo shares, but he wouldn't be stuck with a Brennan mate in order to have them!—he'd ordered a hearty meal from room service and was breaking into a bottle of champagne right now, celebrating his victory.

Kylie felt tears stain her face and turned the heater on full blast as she rounded the bend to the highway ramp leading out of downtown Cleveland. Once again, the interstate directional signs forced her to make a choice.

Kylie made one.

Ten

A few hours later, she was knocking at the door of her brother's apartment in Ann Arbor, Michigan. She hoped Devlin was home although if he wasn't, she had the option of numerous motels where she could spend the night. But Kylie hadn't come to her big brother for lodging, she'd come for something else, something she'd never sought from him before.

She wasn't exactly sure what it was, but confusion and need and a long shared history with Devlin had caused her to choose the highway sign with arrows pointing to Michigan.

Kylie knocked again and pressed her ear against the door, to hear if there were any sounds of life within. The smoky sounds of a blues singer was vaguely audible. She caught her lower lip between her teeth. Uh-oh.

Moments later, the door opened and Devlin slouched against the door frame wearing only a pair of blue surgical scrub pants, the drawstring loosely tied. He was unshaven, his hair was tousled and his lips were swollen. Sensually swollen. The way lips looked after a marathon kissing session. Kylie remembered how enticing, how sexy Cade's looked when…

"Oh God, I shouldn't have come here!" she blurted out. "My timing is—"

"Incredibly bad, but that's nothing new." Devlin shrugged. It took a great deal to phase him. Obviously, the sight of his younger sister at his door close to midnight wasn't enough. "Come on in," he invited, stepping aside to admit her.

"Dev, who is—oh!" The tanned pretty blonde with enormous breasts and long, long legs sounded petulant. She was nude except for the teensy towel she held in front of her and when she spied Kylie, her eyes narrowed and her mouth thinned into a tight line. "Who are you?" she demanded in something close to a screech.

She sounded like a shrew and she didn't look quite so attractive anymore, Kylie noted, darting a quick glance at her brother.

"Help, she's morphed into a troll before our very eyes," Devlin murmured under his breath. "Looks like you arrived right in the nick of time to save me, Ky." He turned to the blonde. "Shanna, this is my sister, Kylie."

His ironic pronunciation of the word "sister" coupled with his daring bad-boy smile made it inevitable that Shanna would jump to the wrong conclusion. Kylie knew Devlin was counting on it; her brother had already lost interest in his towel-clad companion.

Shanna performed, as if on cue. "You're lying!" she accused in a shriek. "She's your sister like I'm your sister!"

Kylie groaned. Her acquaintance with Shanna had been less than sixty seconds, but that was long enough to know she was yet another one of Devlin's babes-of-the-moment. A Devlin Brennan babe-of-the-moment inevitably had an eye-popping body, which she was happy to show off and share, while her personality skills tended to be nonexistent or limited to histrionics.

Kylie caught herself in the middle of her rote characterization. She sounded disturbingly similar to Cade generalizing about the Brennans!

"I really am his sister." As penance, Kylie made a halfhearted attempt to reassure Shanna. Perhaps if she offered to show her photo driver's license as ID?

She didn't get the chance to suggest it.

"How dumb do you think I am?" Shanna demanded.

Kylie and Devlin exchanged glances. "What a lead-in!" Dev smiled lazily at his sister. "Can I answer it?"

"No," Kylie said severely. She walked toward his tiny kitchen, which also served as a passage between the wide living/dining area and the bedroom/bathroom suite. "I'm going to boil some water for tea. You have tea bags, I hope?"

"I always keep a box on hand, especially for you," Devlin said. "Not that you come to visit much. And while we're on the subject, what brings you here tonight?"

"You're going to let her stay?" Shanna howled while Kylie filled a battered teakettle she'd unearthed from a lower cabinet.

"What kind of a guy would I be if I threw my baby sister out in the street at this time of night?" Devlin asked.

The words were right, but his tone was all wrong. Dev had a gift for subtext; he would say one thing but his voice and his expression conveyed something else entirely.

"I know she's not your sister!" Shanna screamed, deciphering his deliberately false message. Just as Devlin had intended her to do, of course. His babes-of-the-moment were nothing if not predictable. "If you think I'll stay and watch you screw around with another woman, you're—you're—"

"Crazy?" Dev supplied helpfully. "Sick? Yeah, you could be right."

A few minutes later, an outraged Shanna was gone from the apartment, cursing and pulling on a minuscule cotton shirt, miniskirt and heels as she went.

"Whatever." Shrugging, Devlin closed the door behind her.

"You know, Dev, there really are women out there with common sense and brains, who aren't so easily manipulated. Who would actually say something normal like, 'You're Devlin's sister? Nice to meet you,'" Kylie pointed out dryly. "Ever consider dating one of them?"

"Nope. I keep those types as friends. In any other role, they want more than I have to give." He frowned wryly. "Okay, I'll be honest with you. They demand more than I feel like giving. I guess by your earnest, heartfelt standards that makes me shallow, huh?"

"You're not shallow, you just keep yourself so hidden I wonder if anyone will know to look for more." Kylie shook her head. "Meanwhile, you stick to your 'Baywatch' wanna-be types with their flair for bad drama."

"Yeah!" Devlin laughed.

"How did Shanna get so tan in Michigan in the middle of March, anyway? Does she live in a tanning booth? And she must have a few pounds of silicone in those—"

"Don't hold back, Kylie. Let's hear how you really feel about Shanna."

Chuckling, Devlin turned off the blues and switched on his TV set. An ancient episode of "Bewitched" was on and he flopped down in his big, wide BarcaLounger and stared at the screen.

Kylie joined him a few minutes later, setting a cup of tea in front of him. She'd bypassed his trendy assortment of hip, flavored coffees because she knew he liked tea with a teaspoon of sugar and splash of milk, just the way their mom had always fixed it for them.

"Do you still like Original Darren better than Replacement Darren?" Devlin asked, perplexed, his eyes glued to the actors on the screen. "I can't figure out why. To me, the two are interchangeable."

"Just like your girlfriends are interchangeable to you. I see a definite psychological link there." Kylie sipped her tea and settled back against the sofa cushions. "I've been in Port McClain," she murmured, staring sightlessly ahead.

"Ah, the Best Little Toxic Waste Dump Site in Ohio. Uh, sorry, sis. I know you're the current reigning queen of it all, thanks to Uncle Gene's will."

"I've kind of gotten to know the other Brennans better," she said tentatively.

"Is that good or bad? Say, did you ever find out who McClain is? Dad said he didn't exist but where did they come up with the name? There's McClain this and McClain that and there never was a McClain? What, did they just pick some random name out of a hat or something? I don't get it. And why call it *Port*

McClain when it's not a port at all. Who ever heard of a port on a creek? That is one wigged-out place, Ky."

"I—I'm going to sell the BrenCo shares Uncle Gene left me," Kylie tried again. "To Cade Austin."

"Oh, yeah, the company prez. The beloved son Uncle Gene never had. Dad seems to like him okay, though."

"What did Daddy say about Cade, Dev?" Kylie poised on the edge of the sofa, watchful and alert. "Tell me everything."

Devlin waited until a commercial break to reply. "I don't remember Dad saying anything crucial about him. Why? Are you investigating the guy before you sell him those shares? Why not contact the EPA? Maybe they have a Most Wanted List, you know, like the FBI." He guffawed, enjoying his own joke.

Kylie sighed. Her brother had never been emotionally intuitive and he was running true to form tonight. He'd missed every subtle hint she had tried to give him.

"I went to the Rock and Roll Hall of Fame today," she said, giving up her attempts to confide in him. She and Dev were probably never meant to be confidants, anyway.

He was immediately interested and actually looked away from the TV while they discussed the various exhibits and their impressions of them. Kylie wasn't aware of how many times she mentioned Cade's name. He'd been with her at the museum and it was natural for her to quote him, to add his opinions and comments along with her own, especially since she'd found many too funny not to share.

Devlin was not so perceptively challenged that he didn't pick up on those frequent, affectionate references of hers. "Y'know, if I were supposed to guess—out of all the people in Port McClain—who would go with you to the Hall of Fame, Cade Austin is the last person I would've picked. It's easier to imagine Uncle Artie playing hooky from his turnpike tollbooth collector's job to stare at Buddy Holly's high school diploma than to picture Cade Austin paying homage to rock's roots. I thought the guy's interests ran strictly to incinerators and air pollution control."

That was all the encouragement Kylie needed to launch into the full story of her fateful visit to Port McClain—and her dizzying involvement with Cade Austin. She left nothing out, and

Devlin listened attentively. He even switched the television set off, an almost unheard of occurrence as he deemed "background noise" enhanced his concentration.

But he seemed to have no trouble concentrating on his sister's revelations. He rarely interrupted her, letting her talk on and on, until she finally ended her story. Kylie slumped against the cushions, drained of energy and emotion, her blue eyes misty with tears.

"What do you think, Dev?" she asked, her voice quavering. "Doesn't it seem indisputable that Aunt Bobbie was right, after all?"

"Kylie, I don't know Aunt Bobbie all that well but my impression of her is—well, not only does she have both oars out of the water but a lot of time she's missing the rowboat, too. Get what I'm saying?"

Kylie felt a revitalizing flash of temper. She wasn't in the mood for Devlin's glib analogies. "But I told you what Cade did, Dev. And Aunt Bobbie warned me, she predicted it!"

"You couldn't have taken her seriously, Kylie, or you wouldn't have gone to that hotel room with him," Dev countered. "Come on, you admitted he didn't force you, you wanted to go with him."

She blushed, suddenly regretting what she'd confided. She'd said way too much, she decided, her discomfit rapidly increasing. "Never mind, I shouldn't expect you to understand."

Kylie grabbed the remote control and turned on the TV in an attempt to divert him. A rerun of "Charles in Charge" was on. That should do it.

To her surprise, Devlin didn't even glance at the screen.

"I understand pretty much, Kylie. You accused Cade Austin of plotting to knock you up when neither of you were thinking of anything beyond hitting the sheets. You said you were as hot for him as he was for you, so if you honestly forgot about snapping on the latex, the smart money says he forgot all about it, too."

"So you—you think I was wrong?" Kylie swallowed hard.

"Kylie, you left the guy stranded in a hotel room in Cleveland without his pants! Does that strike you as even remotely fair?"

Dev gave his head an incredulous shake. "When it comes to a flair for bad drama, you give my 'Baywatch' wanna-be types some real competition."

Kylie covered her face with her hands. "It seemed like the right thing to do at the time," she murmured glumly. "It seemed like the only thing to do. I—I guess maybe I wasn't thinking very clearly?"

"I guess not," agreed Devlin bluntly. "Kylie, there's just one question I have to ask."

Kylie shivered, dreading it.

"What if you are pregnant? Any chance of that?"

"Well, there's always a chance, but I've always been regular, and it's definitely the wrong time of the month for me to get pregnant."

"Good." Devlin breathed a heartfelt sigh of relief. "Look, if I were you, when you know for sure, I'd let Austin in on the good news. Just drop him a postcard with a couple words to let him know. He must be sweating blood right now. I know I would be."

"You don't think that I—I should attempt to contact him otherwise?" Kylie asked wistfully.

"Definitely not!" Dev was emphatic. "Kylie, you would be setting yourself up for the worst humiliation of your life! I know how I'd feel if a woman did to me what you did to Cade Austin. I'd *never* want to see her again. I'd think she was a raving psycho, and I'd be down on my knees thanking God that I found out the truth about her."

Kylie winced.

"No, do not try to contact the man, little sis," Devlin ranted on. "Take it from me, he'll never forgive you."

"Because you would never forgive a woman who did something like that to you?" she asked dispiritedly.

"Never. A man can forgive certain women some things, like he'll forgive his mother and his sisters and maybe even his grandmother, just about anything. But when it comes to sex—forget about forgiveness. Why bother? There are always other women to treat you right, so why waste time with one who doesn't?"

Kylie stared dully at the TV screen. She felt queasy—the

greasy cheeseburger and fries she'd downed during her drive seemed to have taken permanent residence in her stomach. The tea, now lukewarm, made her feel worse.

"Do you mind if I sack out on your couch tonight, Dev? I'll drive back to Philadelphia in the morning. I have friends there I can stay with while I figure out what to do next."

"Sounds like a plan to me. Although you know you're welcome to stay here for as long as you want."

"Thanks, but this place is too small for both of us. I'd cramp your style."

"So what?" Dev smiled. "I told you a guy can forgive his sister just about anything, even cramping his style."

But Kylie had already moved on in her mind. "I'll call Brenda and ask her to get my things from Uncle Gene's house and mail them to me. And I won't have any contact with Cade," she promised. "Our lawyers will handle the sale."

"Smart girl." Dev patted her shoulder.

Kylie planned to get up the next morning when Devlin did, for an early start on the long drive ahead. But though she awakened as her brother tromped through the apartment getting ready to leave for his shift at the hospital, she was too tired to move from the couch. She decided to rest a little while longer, only a few more minutes, then she would get up and be on her way. She wouldn't have to bother getting dressed because she'd slept in her clothes, a timesaver right there.

Pulling Dev's spare blankets more closely around her, Kylie closed her eyes for just a few more minutes of rest.

Sun was streaming into the apartment through the half-opened blinds the next time she awakened. Kylie sat up at once. She sensed it was late morning, even before a quick glance at her watch confirmed it.

Ten-thirty! So much for her early start to Philadelphia.

Then the pounding on the door started. At first Kylie ignored it, but when the bell began to ring insistently as well, she faced the inevitable. Whoever was at the door had no intention of leaving. Since mail and parcel delivery personnel did not carry on this way, Kylie resigned herself to the probability that the visitor must be Shanna or one of her fellow thwarted clones.

She walked slowly toward the door and attempted to smooth her sleep-mussed hair into some sort of order, using her hand as a makeshift brush. Kylie tried to brace herself for the encounter, fully expecting the door-pounding bell-ringer to accuse her of being a romantic rival for Devlin's attention. She held no hope that the babe would consider listening to reason. Dev didn't go for those types.

Without bothering to glance through the peephole, she pulled open the door while uttering a preemptive, "I'm Dev's sister, visiting from Philadelphia."

"I'm Cade Austin, and I'm going to wring your neck." Cade barged inside.

Kylie gaped at him. He seemed to have a talent for rendering her speechless.

He closed the door and folded his arms in front of his chest. "Well?" he demanded.

Her eyes hungrily drank in the sight of him. He was wearing a blue chambray shirt and jeans, and the vibrant virility of his presence struck her like a physical blow.

"You—you made it out of the hotel," she uttered inanely. Her mind was being bombarded with so many thoughts and feelings she could hardly process them, let alone coherently converse.

"No thanks to you," he said sternly. "You're damn lucky I've had time to cool down because if I'd've caught up with you last night, well, I don't know what I'd've done!"

Kylie rallied. "You come storming in here, threatening me, and you claim you've *cooled down?* As compared to what, an— an incinerator?"

"I'm not threatening you, and you know that, too." Cade fastened his hands around her waist and jerked her toward him. "Or at least you *ought* to know it. I'd better make sure before you go zooming off to God-knows-where because you've assumed I'm going to come after you with a baseball bat. Do you know I'll never hurt you, Kylie?" His voice softened a little, and his fiery hazel eyes met hers. "Do you know that?"

She felt her bones begin to melt, as his fingers began to knead the slender hollow of her waist. Her heart stopped aching and started to jump with mingled excitement and hope. According to her brother's logic, Cade shouldn't even be here. But he was, holding her, looking at her in a way that heated her blood and brightened her lowly spirits.

"Do you honestly believe that I tried to make you pregnant in a premeditated stock grab ploy, Kylie? That I would use you that way?"

"No," she whispered, her voice slightly raw. She'd cried last night as she lay alone on the couch and her throat was still a little sore from the strain. "I—I know that neither of us were thinking of anything beyond hitting the sheets. We both forgot about snapping on the latex."

Devlin's words came out of her mouth because she was too rattled to rephrase.

Cade's lips twitched. "I hadn't quite thought of it in those terms, but you're absolutely right."

"How did you know I was here?" she asked softly. She dared to lay her hands against his chest, her fear of rejection still inhibiting her. Devlin had been so sure that Cade would never want to see her again. It was hard to totally discount that, yet all her feminine instincts were telling her Cade would never not want to see her.

"I called your parents in Florida last night," Cade explained. "I—wondered if you would be heading there. I hoped you might've called them to let them know where you were."

"But I didn't." Kylie was puzzled. "The last time I talked to Mom and Dad was the night I arrived in Port McClain."

"So your mother said. I told her it was imperative that I get in touch with you—I didn't explain why. She suggested you might've gone to see your brother and gave me his address."

"And you made the trip to Ann Arbor, not even knowing if I was here?" Kylie gazed up at him, her blue eyes shining. "Why, Cade?"

"Why do you think, Kylie?"

She tried to move away, but he put his hands over hers and drew her arms around his neck. "Does this help you to come up with the answer?" he asked huskily, bending his head to kiss her neck.

Kylie clung to him, suddenly weak. She leaned her forehead against his chest to hide the sudden swell of tears in her eyes. "Dev said you'd never want to see me again, he said you would never forgive me for what I said and for leaving you at the hotel like that."

"Well, I wasn't happy about it," Cade drawled. "But not once did I consider never seeing you again. All I could think of was when I'd see you next. Kylie, I know this is too soon for you and you'll probably try to talk me out of it, but—" He paused and drew a deep breath. "I love you, Kylie. And BrenCo has nothing to do with how I feel. Give me a chance to prove it to you, sweetheart."

She jerked her head upward and stared at him with wide, startled eyes. "Why would I want to talk you out of it, Cade? I love you so much, I—I—" She felt tears streaming down her cheeks. "Oh, Cade, it's not too soon. I feel as if we've transcended ordinary time and..."

She stared at the ground, her face flushing. "That sounds so banal, doesn't it? If Dev heard it, he'd roll on the floor laughing. Or maybe throw up."

"Well, I'm not laughing or throwing up." Cade lifted her chin, raising her head to meet his eyes. "Will you come back to Port McClain with me, Kylie? We'll take as long as you need to be sure of us, but I'll be upfront and tell you right now that my goal is to marry you. *Not* for your BrenCo shares, let's settle that point, once and for all. Can you believe me, sweetheart? Can we put the suspicions and misinterpretations to rest for good?"

Kylie gazed at him and saw the man she loved, an honest, honorable man who loved her. "I believe you, Cade," she said softly. "I believe *in* you."

He smiled a smile that made her heart sing. "And?" he prompted.

"And I would love to come back to Port McClain with you and marry you as soon as we can plan a real wedding. I'm already sure of us." Kylie snuggled closer to Cade, savoring the warmth and reassurance of his masculine strength. "Do you think

I should have Brenda and Bridget as bridesmaids? Polly, too. To try to achieve some family unity instead of rivalry, for a change." She glanced up to gauge his reaction to that.

He took it well. "If you want, honey. Maybe dealing with the Brennans will be less maddening as a joint endeavor. In some ways, you're already better at it than I am," he acknowledged.

"With certain exceptions. I'll leave the male Brennans to you, to handle as you see fit. And I won't interfere."

"Not much!" Laughing, he lifted her off her feet and swung her around, finally giving in to the relief and joy that seemed to suffuse the very air they breathed.

"I love you, Cade."

"I love you, Kylie." He carried her to the sofa and sat down with her on his lap.

"I think you were right about Uncle Gene and the will, Cade." She searched his face with loving eyes. "He wanted us to get together. If he hadn't died, he would've had to come up with a plan other than the will, of course. Maybe he would've tried to recruit me to work for BrenCo's legal department?"

"Never in a million years." Cade laughed against her lips.

She silenced him with a long and passionate kiss.

When Devlin returned later that day after a long shift at the hospital, he appeared stunned to find the couple sitting at his kitchen table, eating takeout from a nearby Chinese restaurant.

Kylie filled him in on the latest developments.

"You're going to marry her?" Dev gasped, staring at Cade as if he'd just announced he had booked passage on a trip to Mars. "After what she said, after what she did? Hey, I know she's my little sister and I'd forgive her anything, but for *you* to do it... Man, are you insane?"

"No, I'm in love," Cade amended, smiling at Kylie. "You'll find out what it's like yourself someday, Dev."

"Not me!" Devlin proclaimed and turned on his TV set. He lost himself in a rerun episode of "Full House" while Cade and Kylie lost themselves in each other.

* * * * *

Part-Time Wife
SUSAN MALLERY

SILHOUETTE
SPECIAL EDITION

To Tara Gavin—for giving me the opportunity to write books that make me laugh, make me cry, and best of all, books that make me believe anything is possible. My appreciation and my thanks.

Chapter One

At the exact moment the hot water kicked on in the shower, the doorbell rang. Jill Bradford leaned her forehead against the ceramic tile and gritted her teeth. Timing. Life was all about timing and hers was usually bad.

Or maybe it was this house, she thought, grabbing her robe with one hand while she turned off the water with the other. Maybe there was a little light that ran from the bathroom to the front of the building so that every time she tried to take a shower, it went on. People saw the light and knew it was time to come calling. Yesterday it had been young girls selling cookies. Two days ago, someone selling magazine subscriptions.

The bell rang again, and Jill hurried down the hall. She had the fleeting thought that she could not bother with her robe and could simply flash whoever was rude enough to interrupt her shower, but decided against the idea. The way her luck was running, there would be a cop on the other side of the door and she would be arrested.

She reached the front door just as the visitor pressed the bell again. This time the long tone sounded impatient. Jill raised herself up on her toes and stared out the tiny peephole that had obviously been designed by and for the tall people of the world. She stared at the distorted image and gasped.

A cop?

Barely pausing long enough to secure the tie on her robe, she turned the key to release the dead bolt and jerked open the door. "Yes?"

"Ms. Jill Bradford?"

"Yes."

"I'm Craig Haynes."

The police officer paused as if the name was supposed to mean something. Jill stared at him and blinked. It didn't mean a thing to her. She studied the man. He was tall. Too tall for her comfort. She had to crane her head back to see his face. But it was worth the crick in her neck, she decided, taking in curly dark hair, brown eyes and features handsome enough to grace a male model. She inspected the shape of his mouth and the stubborn set of his chin. She didn't have a perfect memory but she was reasonably confident she would have remembered someone who looked as good as he did.

Her gaze slipped down his chest. The black short-sleeved shirt of his uniform outlined his well-muscled body. He had the build of an athlete. Impressive. Very impressive. Even to someone who had sworn off men and relationships.

"I'm sorry, Officer Haynes," she said, returning her attention to his face. "I don't know who you are."

The faint hints of gray at his temples were the only clue he wasn't as young as he appeared. He didn't look thirty, but she would guess he was several years older than that.

He chose that moment to smile. Lines appeared around his eyes and mouth. His teeth flashed white. He should come with a warning label, she thought as her stomach clenched and her knees threatened to buckle. *Do not operate heavy machinery around this man.* If she hadn't been leaning against the doorframe, she would have collapsed in a heap at his feet.

"I should have been more specific," he said. "Your friend Kim gave me your name. She was going to take care of my kids. She said you would be happy to take her place."

Kids? "Oh, now I remember." Jill smiled. "Of course." She pushed the door open wide. "Sorry. Please come in, and we can talk about this."

"Thanks." He stepped past her into the small entryway. The view from the back was pretty impressive, too, she thought as she gave him a quick once-over. Wide shoulders and the kind of butt most women would kill to have. Why was it men had great butts simply by virtue of being men, while women could aerobicize until their hearts were strong enough to power a freight train but the shape was never quite right? Not that Jill spent all that much time on the treadmill. Still, she thought about it a lot and surely that counted for something.

"In here," she said, motioning for Craig to step into the living room.

He moved with an easy long-legged stride. She felt

like a dwarf waddling along behind him. Not that she was heavy. She was just short. And curvy. An unfortunate combination that made her feel like a cuddly kitten in a world full of Barbie dolls.

The perfect creases in his uniform pants, and the carefully trimmed dark hair that stopped just above his collar, made her remember her own disheveled appearance. She touched her short hair and tried to remember how much it had been sticking up the last time she'd looked in a mirror.

"You'll have to excuse me," she said, perching on the edge of the sofa. Craig had chosen the wing chair opposite the fireplace. He leaned forward and placed his uniform cap brim-up on the coffee table. "I've been so busy taking care of things for Kim I haven't had a chance to shower this morning."

She tugged on the hem of her suddenly too-short robe and tried to look mature. She was thirty, but without makeup and tailored clothes, she looked like a teenager. Her mother had told her that in time she would appreciate looking so young, but Jill wasn't sure. She had a bad feeling she was still going to look like a cute, albeit wrinkled, kitten well into her seventies. The tall world did not take short people seriously.

"When did Kim leave?" Craig asked.

"They eloped yesterday." She smiled, remembering her friend's happiness. Kim hadn't been sure it was the right thing to do, but Jill had encouraged her to go. Real love, the forever kind, didn't come around very often. Jill might have had her heart broken more times than any one woman deserved, but she still had faith—for other people, if not for herself.

"It was very romantic," she continued. "Brian

hired a limo to take them to the airport. She'd told a few friends, so they were here to see them off."

She stared out the window, but instead of the front yard and the house across the street, she saw the radiant couple. The love between them had been as tangible as the small bouquet Kim had been holding.

"She called last night from Reno, and they're already married. She should be back in a couple of weeks."

There was a manila folder on top of the glass coffee table. Jill reached for it and flipped it open. There were several sheets of papers covered with careful notes. Lists of people to call, bills to pay, errands to run. She didn't mind. It was the least she could do for a friend. After all, when her life had fallen apart, Kim had offered her a place to stay. Speaking of which, Brian would be moving into Kim's house after the honeymoon. Jill needed to start looking for a place of her own.

Later, she told herself, scanning the list. Craig Haynes. Oh, there he was. Right between canceling a dentist's appointment and checking on the delivery of Kim's new king-size bed.

"Here's the note," she said, then glanced up at Craig.

The police officer had the oddest look on his face. As if he'd never seen anyone like her before. She reached up and fingered the ends of her short hair. Was it sticking up in spikes? Did she still have crumbs from her Pop-Tart toaster pastry around her mouth?

She licked her lips but didn't feel anything. Craig's gaze narrowed and his back stiffened. She almost asked what was wrong, but figured she probably didn't really want to know. She glanced back at the list.

"Jill said you have three boys. Twelve, nine and six. That's really not a problem for me."

She made the statement brightly. Someone who didn't know her wouldn't notice the tightness around the words. No one would be able to feel her heart beating faster. Baby-sitting. There were a thousand other things she would have gladly done for Kim instead, like regrout the shower or put down a tile floor. But she hadn't been given a choice. Still, it was just for a couple of nights. She would survive.

A wave of longing swept over her. She missed her girls. Her fingers tightened on the papers she was holding. They weren't her girls, she reminded herself. She'd just been their stepmother. She must not have been a very good one, either, because ever since the divorce, neither of the girls had wanted to see her. But the pain wasn't enough to stop her from missing them.

"Not so fast," Craig said, leaning forward in the wing chair.

"Hmm? What?" She blinked away the past and focused on the very good-looking man sitting in front of her. "What do you mean?"

"Have you done this sort of thing before?" he asked.

"Taken care of children? Of course. I was a teenager, Officer Haynes. I baby-sat." She thought of mentioning her failed marriage but figured it wasn't his business.

"You're not employed now." It was a statement.

She felt a faint flush on her cheeks. "No. I left my last position a couple of months ago."

"Were you fired?"

"No! Of course not. I just needed to get away. It's

more like a leave of absence. I have an open invitation to return if I want to."

His dark gaze held hers. "The name of the company you worked for?"

"McMillian Insurance in San Clemente. That's Southern California."

"I know where it is." He pulled a small notebook and pen from his shirt pocket and wrote. "Who did you report to there?"

She gave him the name and phone number, then frowned. "Excuse me, Officer Haynes, but I don't understand why you're interrogating me."

"It's Craig, and I'm not going to trust just anyone with my children."

"I appreciate that. I assure you I'm not a convicted felon and—"

"Are you an accused felon?" The corner of his mouth tilted up with a hint of a smile.

"Not that either. I haven't even had a parking ticket in years. My point is, I'm going to be looking after your children for one or two nights. While I appreciate your diligence, I think you're taking it a little too far. I'm hardly going to be an influential force in their lives."

"Is that what you think? Ms. Bradford—"

"Jill," she interrupted.

He nodded. "Jill, I'm not looking for a baby-sitter. Kim had agreed to be a live-in nanny for my three boys. When she decided to elope, she said you'd take the job."

"Well, she was wrong," Jill said without thinking.

A full-time nanny? That was insane. Absolutely the last thing she wanted was to work with someone else's kids. Okay, she didn't have a job right now, but that was because she wasn't sure what she wanted to do with her life. She could go back to San Clemente. Her condo was sublet, but she could rent another one. Her job was waiting. But that didn't feel right. She didn't want to go back to her old life. That was the point of living with Kim for a few weeks.

Craig moved to the edge of the chair. He rested his elbows on his knees and clasped his hands together, clutching the notebook. "Jill, I'm in a bind. I've interviewed literally a dozen women for the position, and Kim was the only one I thought would work. She was young enough to be able to relate to the children and old enough to maintain discipline. She assured me you had experience with children and would be just as suitable. She also said you'd agreed to take her place."

"I said I would baby-sit. She never told me it was a full-time job. My Lord, you probably want me to live with you and your boys."

He nodded. His dark eyebrows drew together. "I'm currently involved in a special investigation. I won't bore you with the details, but it requires me to be gone odd hours. I never know when I'm going to be called away. The boys are too young to be left alone. They need some stability. I've had five nannies in the last four months."

She frowned. "What's wrong with your children?"

He hesitated just long enough for her to suspect there really *was* a problem. "My wife and I divorced several years ago. Although she didn't have much contact with them, her death last year shook them up. The woman who had looked after them left shortly after that. Since then it's been one change after another. With my new assignment and being gone all the time—" He turned his hands palms up and spread his fingers. "They're scared little kids who need someone to look after them. Nothing more."

She rose to her feet and walked to the window. "You're not playing fair," she said slowly, staring at the house across the street. "I have this mental picture of poor starving orphans shivering in the snow."

"Based on the weekly food bill, they're not starving."

Jill grimaced. Damn him, and damn Kim. When her friend returned from her honeymoon, Jill was going to give her a piece of her mind. This wasn't fair. Not to Jill, not to Craig and not to the kids.

She fought against a twinge of guilt. She was partially to blame. When Kim had come to her and talked about eloping, Jill had encouraged her to just go for it. Her life was so upside-down, she wanted someone she cared about to be happy. Kim had worried about the job, and Jill had blithely told her she would step in.

Next time I'll find out the details before agreeing, Jill promised herself. In the meantime, three boys didn't have anyone to look after them.

"I find it difficult to believe that you couldn't find one other nanny you liked," Jill said.

Craig didn't answer. She turned to face him and found him standing only a few feet behind her. She had to tilt her head back to meet his gaze.

"I've taken enough of your time," he said and placed his hat on his head. The black uniform emphasized his dark hair and eyes.

He was leaving. That would be best for both of them. Yet what about the children? She really didn't have a job right now, and she wasn't ready to go back to San Clemente. She might never be ready to do that. Besides, she could use the money. If it wasn't permanent, if she were careful to keep her heart firmly under lock and key, it might not be so bad. She would be a caretaker; she would not get personally involved.

"Spring break is in a few weeks," she said quickly. "Let's give each other a one-week trial. If it works out, I'll stay until break. That will give you time to find someone who wants a permanent position. Agreed?"

He stared down at her. She couldn't read his expression. She wondered how much of that was because he was a cop and how much of it was the man himself. He didn't look like the chatty, outgoing type.

He crossed to her in two long strides and held out his hand. "Agreed."

His smile once again made her knees threaten to buckle. At least she was short enough that if she collapsed it wasn't a real long way down. She extended her hand toward him and tried to give him *her* best smile. He didn't seem the least bit affected. Hmm, she would have to work on it more. She wanted to leave men in a broken heap trailing behind her. Maybe it was—

His skin brushed against hers. Instantly electricity raced between them. His long fingers and broad palm swallowed her hand nearly up to her wrist. Her heart thundered in double time and her breathing choked to a stop. She hoped she didn't look as stunned as she felt. She hoped it was just a quirk of fate, a not-to-be-repeated cosmic thing, because there was no way she was going to get involved with a man. Any man. And certainly not one with children.

Been there, done that, she reminded herself. The

punishing aftermath was still evident in her healing emotional wounds.

"Do you have a car?" Craig asked, apparently unfazed by the sparks leaping between them. Or maybe they were just leaping one way.

"Uh-huh." She withdrew her hand and, before she could stop herself, wiped it on her robe. The soft cotton did nothing to erase the electricity still prickling her skin.

He raised his eyebrows but didn't say anything. She was grateful.

"If you want to pack a few things, we could go right over." He glanced at his watch. "My neighbor could only stay with the boys for an hour."

"They're home today?"

"It's Saturday."

"Oh. I forgot." With the excitement of getting Kim ready to elope, there hadn't been time to keep track of mundane things like days of the week. "No problem." She glanced down at her robe. "Let me take a quick shower and pack enough to last until Monday. I can come back here while they're in school. I still have a few things to take care of for Kim."

She started toward the doorway, then glanced at him. "You can have a seat. Or there's coffee in the kitchen. Whatever."

"I'll wait here," he said.

She stepped into the hallway.

"Jill?"

She turned around. He'd removed his hat and was running his hand through his hair. His self-control slipped a bit, and she saw the worry in his eyes. "I hope Kim knows what a good friend you are. You didn't have to do this. I really appreciate it."

The compliment made her uncomfortable. "No big deal. I'm a sucker for kids and puppies. Be right out."

Even as she hurried up the stairs, she started making a mental list of everything she would have to do. Packing, stopping the paper. She wouldn't worry about the mail today. But Monday she would put it on vacation hold. Kim didn't have any pets, which made that part easy. She would tell Kim's neighbor she was leaving so someone would keep an eye on the house. She would need Craig's phone number, too.

She walked into the guest bathroom and closed the door behind her. As she glanced into the mirror, she stifled a groan. Her hair *was* sticking up in spiky tufts. Her mother had promised her it would darken as she got older, but it was still the color of a rag doll's. She wore it short because otherwise she looked out of proportion. Without makeup, her eyes looked too big and green. That, combined with her small, almost triangular button nose, gave her an uncomfortable resemblance to the kitten so many people likened her to.

"I'll just pencil in some whiskers and be done with it," she muttered under her breath, then turned her back on the image and flipped on the shower. No wonder Craig Haynes had hired her. She looked young enough to be the perfect playmate for his kids.

Craig drew in a deep breath and let it out slowly. Now that Jill had left the room, he was able to ease up on his iron-willed self-control. It was as if the dam burst, as heated blood coursed through his body, settling inappropriately in his groin. He walked to the window and stared out blindly. He hoped his new nanny believed in taking long showers. He was going to need the extra time to get himself back under control.

He could handle the fact that she was an attractive woman, although the petite pixie look had never been his type. Big green eyes and a smile that promised two parts humor and one part sin was okay with him, too. The tousled just-out-of-bed look was a bit more of a problem, but he knew he would have been able to keep it all together...if she hadn't been naked.

He swore under his breath. He'd been so worried about the boys, he hadn't noticed at first. But when she'd settled on the sofa, her full breasts had been evident beneath the thin fabric of her robe. He hadn't had a date in two years. He hadn't been with a woman for even longer. Unfortunately, his body had chosen that moment to surge back to life.

Even with her out of the room and only the faint hint of her perfume lingering in the air, he could feel the need flowing through him. He wanted to go to her and hold her in his arms. He wanted to kiss her and—

"Stop it," he said aloud.

He had to get control. All that mattered was finding someone to take care of the boys. Jill Bradford was only a stopgap. He was going to have to find someone permanent. As if he had the time.

He rubbed the back of his neck. The dull ache that began between his shoulder blades and worked its way up his neck had become a permanent companion. Now it stepped up a degree in intensity. He would start interviewing right away. The agency swore they didn't have anyone else to send him, but there had to be someone. Maybe the perfect nanny was about to leave her job somewhere else. He could only hope.

He heard footsteps overhead. He thought about all

he knew about Jill. Kim had mentioned she was recovering from a messy divorce. He could relate to that. He'd gone through the same thing nearly six years ago. Krystal had wanted out, but she hadn't made it easy. He'd hung on as best he could, trying to be both mother and father to the boys. He'd thought he was doing well, until this last year.

What had gone wrong? Was it the hours he put in? He didn't usually volunteer for special assignments, but this one was different. There wasn't a lot of glory involved. No big drug busts, no fifteen minutes of fame on the local news report. Just directly helping those in need. He'd wanted to give something back. Were his kids paying the price for that?

He knew some of the trouble with the boys was that they'd lost Mrs. Miller. She'd been a part of their lives for nearly five years. Coming on the heels of their mother's death— Craig shook his head. No wonder the boys weren't themselves.

He'd done his best to keep it from happening, but history was repeating itself again. He was gone a lot, as *his* father had been. He was failing his kids, and he wasn't sure how to make it better.

A thunk from the top of the stairs broke through his musings. He walked through the living room and into the hallway. Jill was dragging down a suitcase almost as big as she was.

"I'll get that," he said, taking the stairs two at a time.

"I can manage," she said politely, then stood aside to let him pick up the case. It wasn't very heavy, but she was so tiny, how big could her clothes be?

"Is this it?" he asked when he reached the first floor.

She nodded. "I can come back and get whatever I've forgotten." She had a purse over her shoulder. She shook it once, then frowned. "Keys. I need keys."

While she glanced at the small table in the entryway, then patted her pockets, he studied her. She'd made a quick change. Her short red hair was still damp from her shower. Bangs fell nearly to her delicate eyebrows. The style left her small ears bare. She'd put on some makeup. With it, she looked older, although not anywhere near thirty, which he knew she was. She wore faded jeans that hinted at the curvy legs he'd seen just a few minutes before. The baggy white sweatshirt dwarfed her small frame. She'd pushed up the sleeves, exposing finely boned hands and wrists.

He had the uncomfortable feeling that a man as big as himself could easily crush her if he wasn't careful.

"My keys," she muttered, shaking her purse again. "Come on, Jill, you usually have it together."

"But do you usually talk to yourself?" he asked.

She looked startled, as if she'd forgotten he was there. Then she grinned. "Yeah, I usually do. Sorry. You and the boys will have to get used to it."

"Don't worry. I talk to myself, too. A hazard of the job. Too much time alone." He motioned toward the front door. "Are those your keys in the lock?"

She turned around and stared. "Oh. Thanks."

He pulled them free. "Not a good idea to keep them here. If someone breaks in you want to make it hard, not easy. By leaving the keys in the door, you let him walk out the front, like he belongs here." He shifted the keys until he held the one to her car. "Not to mention giving him a nice late-model vehicle to steal."

"Yeah, yeah, I know. But if I don't keep them in the door, I lose them."

"You lost them anyway."

She stared at him, then reached for her keys. He let them fall in her palm, rather than risk direct contact. Her expression turned thoughtful.

"Craig, do you ever go off duty?"

"Not usually."

"How do the boys feel about that?"

Her green eyes saw too much, he thought grimly. He raised the suitcase slightly. "Do you need anything else?" he asked.

"Nope. I'm ready." She followed him out onto the porch, then locked the door behind them. "What, no patrol car?"

He pointed to his two-year-old Honda. "Sorry, no. There's a utility vehicle at the house so you can cart the boys and their sports equipment around, but I use this to get back and forth to the station."

Her red Mustang convertible was parked in the driveway. She opened the trunk and he set the suitcase inside. "Get many tickets in this?" he asked.

"It looks flashy, but I never drive fast. I know that's disappointing, but at heart I'm pretty boring."

He was about to tell her he wouldn't have used that word to describe her. Cute, maybe. Tempting, probably. Sexy, definitely. But boring? Not in this lifetime. And any man who thought that obviously had his head up his—

He cleared his throat. "I live south of here. In Fern Hill."

"I'm not familiar with the neighborhood."

"It's an independent city. You'll like it. Just follow me. I'll go slow."

Her gaze widened, as if she'd read more into his statement than he'd meant. Before he could explain, she smiled. "Okay, Officer Haynes, I'll be right behind you." She opened the driver's door and slid inside.

As Craig started his car and pulled away from the curb, he thought about what Kim had said when she'd phoned to tell him she couldn't take the job.

"I have a friend who would be perfect for you."

In that moment, on a night when the pressures of the job and raising three kids alone had driven him to the edge of his patience, he'd wanted to believe she referred to more than a baby-sitter.

"Pretty stupid, Haynes," he muttered. He'd given up on relationships a long time ago. There weren't any promises, no sure things. And his ex-wife, Krystal, had taught him the foolishness of trying to believe in love.

So what if he found Jill attractive? All that meant was he wasn't as dead inside as he'd thought. Maybe it was time to think about dating. There was only one problem. He came from a long line of men particularly gifted at screwing up relationships.

Chapter Two

Craig pulled up in front of the house and motioned for Jill to park her car in the driveway. He pushed the button on the garage door opener and got out immediately, but she sat in her red Mustang, staring. He glanced at the two-story home in front of him. It wasn't all that different from his neighbors'. The area was a more recent development, about six years old. He'd bought the house after his divorce, thinking that making a clean break would make it easier for all the boys. Besides, Fern Hill had a great school system with a sports program that was the envy of the state. He'd wanted that for his sons.

He tried to see the house as a stranger would see it. The high peaked roof was Spanish tile, as were most of the others on the street. White stucco with wood accents, tall windows that—he squinted and stared— needed washing pretty badly. The front yard was oversized, mowed but not trimmed. He frowned. Since taking his temporary assignment, he hadn't spent much time at home. The house showed the neglect. He wondered if the boys did, too.

Jill stepped out of her car and gave him a slight smile. "Cops make more money than I thought," she said. "This is nice."

"It's south of the city," he said, "so most people won't make the commute. For me, it's closer to work and closer to Glenwood, where my brothers live."

"Great." But she didn't sound very enthused.

She walked around to the rear of her car and lifted the trunk. Before she could reach for the suitcase, he grabbed it and pulled it out.

This time her smile was genuine. "Thanks. Such nice manners. Your mother must be proud."

Before he had to decide whether to explain that he hadn't seen his mother in years, the front door was flung open and two boys raced down the walkway. Craig grinned when he saw them.

"Is this her?" C.J. asked. His nine-year-old looked like a typical Haynes male, with dark hair and eyes.

"Yes. Jill, this is my middle son, C.J. Short for—"

She looked at the boy and winked. "Let me guess," she said, interrupting. "Craig Junior."

"Yeah." C.J. skittered to a stop in front of her and held out his hand. "Pleased to meet you, Ms. Bradford. I'm very much looking forward to having you as our nanny."

She looked at Craig. "Impressive."

He shrugged. "C.J.'s our charmer."

"And a fine job he does, too." She took the hand the boy offered. "The pleasure is mine, young master C.J."

Craig turned and saw Danny standing by the edge of the driveway. He motioned him closer. His youngest held back a little, then walked toward them. Big eyes took in Jill's appearance, then lingered on the bright red car. Craig put down the suitcase and placed his hand on the boy's shoulder. Danny looked up at him and smiled.

Craig could go weeks without remembering, but sometimes, like now, when Danny smiled, it all came back. Krystal hadn't come home after she'd had their youngest. She'd sent a friend to pack up her clothes, and she'd walked away without looking back. Danny didn't know his mother, although he had some of her features. When the memories returned to force open old wounds, Craig clung to the only sane and constant source of strength in his world: his children.

He bent down and picked up Danny. The child placed one arm around his shoulder and leaned close. "She's pretty. The prettiest of all of them."

"Yes, she is," Craig answered softly. Jill was pretty. And sexy and all kinds of things that most men would enjoy. She was also his employee, and as that, she deserved his respect and nothing more.

C.J. was chattering on about the neighborhood, his friends and what he would really like her to serve for dinner. When his middle son started in on an earnest discussion of why it was important to have dessert with *every* meal, Craig interrupted.

"I'm sure Jill knows what to prepare, C.J."

The boy gave him an unrepentant grin. "Yeah, Dad, but a guy can always hope, can't he?"

"Sure. Hope all you want, then eat your vegetables. Jill, this is my youngest, Danny."

She moved close and touched the boy's arm. Her

green eyes crinkled at the corners as she smiled. "Hi, Danny."

"Do you like little boys?" he asked. "Mrs. Greenway didn't. She said we were more trouble than we were worth."

Craig winced. Mrs. Greenway had stayed for three days before he'd fired her, but she'd made a lasting negative impression on the boys.

Jill nodded. "Of course I like little boys. What's not to like?" She glanced at Craig and rolled her eyes as if to ask what kind of person would take a job watching children if she didn't like them in the first place?

He opened his mouth to reply, then realized he had merely interpreted her look that way. She might have meant something else entirely. He'd barely known Jill Bradford an hour. They couldn't possibly be communicating that well.

But something bright and hot flared to life inside his chest. It wasn't about sex, although he still liked the way she looked in her jeans. It was something more dangerous. A flicker of interest in what and how a woman thought. As if they could be friends. As if he could trust her. Then he reminded himself he didn't trust anyone but family.

"Ben said you should get Mrs. Miller back," Danny said, his hold on Craig's shoulder tightening. "I miss her, too."

"Mrs. Miller was the boys' nanny for several years," Craig explained. "They miss her."

Danny looked at him and bit his bottom lip. "Do you think she misses us?"

"Of course. And now you have Jill."

"Until spring break," she reminded him.

"Until then," he agreed. Danny and C.J. both glanced at him. "Jill is taking the job temporarily. For five weeks. In the meantime, I'll find someone permanent."

Neither boy said anything. Craig fought back a feeling of frustration. How was he supposed to explain and make up for the ongoing turmoil in his children's lives? It would be different if they had the stability of two parents, but there was just him. He was doing the best he could, but sometimes, like now, he had the feeling it wasn't nearly enough.

"We've been alone for ten minutes, Dad," C.J. said. "We didn't burn the house down."

"Congratulations," Craig said. "As I told you before, my neighbor could only stay with them for an hour, so I really appreciate you coming back with me." He glanced at his watch. Damn. He was late already.

"I think your dad has to go to work. Why don't we go inside so he can show me everything, then be on his way?" Jill reached for Danny. Surprisingly, the boy let her lift him down. "You're heavy," she said admiringly. "You must be big for your age."

"He's a shorty," C.J. said, but his tone wasn't unkind.

"Am not!"

Jill bent down so she and Danny were at eye level. "I don't think you're short."

"That's 'coz you're shrimpy, too," he told her.

"Don't you know all the best things come in small packages?" They smiled at each other.

Craig picked up the suitcase again. "Lead the way," he said.

C.J. and Danny took off through the garage. Jill followed more slowly.

"I really appreciate you doing this," he said.

"I'm sure it will be fine." She spoke calmly, but when she glanced at him he could see the panic in her eyes. "It's just been a while since I was around kids."

"It's like riding a bike. You don't forget."

"Are you saying that because you're an expert?"

He paused in the middle of the garage. "No, because I'm a concerned father who's about to leave you alone with his three kids. I'm sort of hoping it's true so that everything will be okay."

"Don't worry. We'll survive."

"C.J. and Danny won't be much of a problem. They're easygoing, although some things still scare Danny."

"He's only six. What would you expect?"

"Exactly," he said, pleased that she was sympathetic. "Ben may not be so easy."

"He's the oldest?"

He nodded. "He's twelve."

"Does he get in a lot of trouble?"

"No. He doesn't do much of anything. He watches TV and plays video games." Craig didn't know what to do for his oldest. He didn't understand the boy's reluctance to participate in anything. Ben was the only one old enough to remember his mother. He didn't like to talk about it, but Craig knew he missed her. Maybe he even felt responsible for her leaving. But he'd never been able to get his son to talk about it.

Nothing had been normal since Krystal left. Not that it was so great before or that he'd ever once wanted her to come back. Hell, he didn't know what *was* normal anymore.

He turned around and pointed to the black sport-utility vehicle. "This is for you. You'll need it to take the boys places. C.J. plays several sports, and Danny is starting Pee-Wee league. The equipment fits in the back easily."

"Groceries, too. I think all boys do is eat."

Craig didn't want to think about that. About Ben and how much weight he'd gained. "Yeah," he said. He walked toward the door leading into the house. "Here's the key." He touched a ring and key hanging from a hook on the wall. "It's an automatic, so you shouldn't have any trouble driving it."

She looked at the large truck-size vehicle. "As long as I don't have to parallel park, I'll be fine."

He opened the door and waited for her to step inside. She did so, then gasped audibly. He looked over her head and saw why.

There was a half bath on the right and the laundry room on the left. Piles of clothing toppled out of both rooms into the small hallway. More clothing was stacked in the family room. There were books, school backpacks, newspapers and toys littering the floor, coffee table and sofa. One end of the big dark blue leather sectional was buried under jackets and a pile of clean clothes he'd managed to run through the washer and dryer the previous evening. He'd asked the boys to sort out their belongings and take them upstairs, but no one had bothered.

Shoes formed an intricate pattern across the rug. Magazines for kids, car lovers, computer buffs and music fans had been tossed everywhere. Stacks of newspapers, more magazines, toys and a few actual books filled the bookcases on either side of the stone fireplace. The entertainment center to the right of the fireplace contained a TV, which was on, a VCR and stereo equipment. Videos had been piled next to the unit. The shelf where they belonged was bare.

Craig shifted her suitcase to his left hand and motioned to the mess. "I don't know what to say," he murmured. "I hadn't realized it had gotten so bad."

Jill turned and looked at him. Her green eyes were wide, her mouth open. "You didn't *realize?* How could you not? This isn't a mess it's a...a..." She closed her mouth. "I don't know what it is."

"I guess I should have gotten in a cleaning service."

He glanced around the room. C.J. and Danny were standing in front of the entrance to the kitchen. He was glad. If Jill saw that, she would turn tail and run. Damn it, he couldn't blame her, either. How had this happened? Why hadn't he been paying attention?

"There are four men living here," he said, by way of an explanation.

"More like four wild animals."

Danny chuckled at her comment. Jill smiled at the boy and the tightness at the base of Craig's neck eased a little. Maybe she wasn't going to leave.

"I'll get a service in," he said.

"I'll arrange it first thing Monday morning," she said, nudging a soccer ball out of her way so she could step farther into the room. "You don't want a nanny, Craig, you want a part-time slave. Anybody around here know what a vacuum looks like?"

"I do!" Danny said brightly. "But I've never used it."

"That seems to be a family trait."

Craig set the suitcase down. "I'm sorry, Jill. I

should have noticed what had happened to this place. We haven't talked about salary yet and I—"

She held up her hand to stop him. "No. I can't be bribed. I agreed to do this for Kim and I will. For exactly what you were going to pay her. Just tell me one thing. Is it worse upstairs?"

"Sure is," C.J. said proudly and grinned. "Wanna see?"

"Not just yet."

Just then something moved on the sofa. Craig saw Ben stretching toward the remote control to change the channel. As always, the sight of his oldest brought on a wave of regret and frustration. He knew he was doing something wrong, but he didn't know what. He tried to encourage the boy to be more active. He practiced sports with him when he could. They'd talked about Ben needing to eat less. Nothing had helped. He could see his oldest was in a lot of pain, but he didn't know how to help.

"Ben, this is Jill Bradford."

Ben didn't bother turning his attention from the television. "I thought her name was Kim."

"I told you yesterday. Kim eloped. Jill is taking her place. Say hello."

"You're leaving us with someone you don't even know? A woman you've just met? Thanks, Dad."

The censure in the twelve-year-old's tone made Craig's hands tighten into fists, but he didn't move. He knew Ben was trying to get to him, but he wasn't going to let it happen. "Ms. Bradford isn't just some woman I found. I've interviewed her and checked on her. She's very—"

The sight of someone on the sofa had startled Jill enough that she was able to focus on something other than the disaster that had once been a very attractive family room. Craig's comment captured her attention. "You checked me out? Behind my back?"

"Yes." He frowned. "I don't know you. I can't trust my children with just anyone."

"I know but it's so yucky. Sneaking around behind my back."

"I did not *sneak*."

His brown eyes darkened with a combination of concern and temper. She understood both. She shouldn't have questioned him, at least not in front of the boys. C.J. and Danny were staring at her, while Ben hadn't taken his attention from the television. The house looked as if it had been overrun by a fraternity, and she was about to be put in charge of three children. She who had sworn she would never get involved with someone else's kids again. She was in over her head and sinking fast. Yet she couldn't walk away. From the look of things, she was needed. Aaron, her ex-husband, had needed a wife and surrogate mother. Any woman would have done. These boys needed a nanny and there was no one else around. She'd always been a sucker for being needed. Only this time she was going to be smart. She was going to keep from getting personally involved. She wasn't the boys' part-time mother, and she wasn't Craig's part-time wife. She was only the hired help. Assuming she survived the first week, when spring break arrived she would be out of here. It was just a job.

Craig glanced at his watch again. He was obviously late. In his well-fitting black uniform, he looked competent and dangerous. An interesting combination. Her body continued to react to this close encounter with a good-looking man. She ignored the sweaty palms and slightly elevated pulse. He would be gone soon. From the looks of the house, he was gone a lot.

"I'll be fine," she said, stepping farther into the room. "You go to work. The boys and I will handle the introductions."

"Are you sure? I hate to leave you but I was due at the station a half hour ago."

"We have lots to do," she said, and smiled brightly. C.J. grinned in return. Danny gave her a shy half smile. Ben ignored everything but the television.

"Okay, boys, be good for Jill. If there's a problem, the station's number is by the phone in the kitchen. See ya." He gave a quick wave and disappeared out the door to the garage.

It was one of those moments when the television went perfectly silent. The sound of the closing door was unnaturally loud in the suddenly still room. Two pairs of eyes focused on her. Jill found herself fighting the urge to run out and tell Craig she'd changed her mind. Instead she glanced around the room, sure it couldn't be as bad as her first impression.

Nope. It was worse. It would take two days to get it picked up enough for the cleaning service to find the dirt. Dear Lord, what had she gotten into?

She thought briefly of Kim's now-empty house and where she was going to go when her roommate returned from her honeymoon. The last couple of nights alone had given her too much time to brood. She was beginning to see that she was coasting through life without any direction. It was time to get moving again. Maybe this challenge was just the jump start she needed.

"Okay, boys," she said. "Let's have a meeting and

get to know each other. I want to hear how you do things, and I want to tell you what I expect in return."

Danny and C.J. were standing in front of the entrance to the kitchen. It was up two steps from the family room. The boys moved toward her. Jill stared at the kitchen and thought she might faint.

There wasn't a square inch of free counter space. Dishes, open boxes of cereal, empty containers of milk, cookies and bags of chips were everywhere. Cupboards were open; most of the shelves were bare. She thought of C.J.'s claim that upstairs was worse. She didn't want to know.

"Where are we going to have our meeting?" Danny asked.

She looked down at him. His light brown eyes were bright with questions and welcome. His shy smile was hard to resist. She glanced around to find a relatively clean spot. Through the kitchen she saw a formal dining room. The table didn't look too overrun with schoolbooks and sports equipment.

"In there," she said, pointing. "Come on, Ben."

The boy ignored her.

She walked over to stand in front of the TV. She was blocking the screen, but he continued to stare as if he could see the program.

"Don't you want to talk?" she asked.

"No. You're not going to stay, so why should I bother?"

"Because it's polite. The world is a nicer place when everyone tries to get along."

"You read that on a bumper sticker?" he asked rudely, still not looking at her.

"Oh, a smartmouth," she said. "Very nice. Very

impressive. You think if you intimidate me, you get your way?"

He shrugged.

Ben had his father's dark hair. She suspected he had his eyes, too, but he wouldn't look at her so she couldn't tell. He was a good-looking kid, although about twenty pounds overweight.

From the corner of her eye, she saw C.J. and Danny watching. She hated being tested her first five minutes on the job and she hated it more that the other two brothers were here to witness the event. If she didn't get Ben's attention, the next five weeks were going to be miserable. She and Craig had given each other an out by agreeing to a one-week trial. If she really hated it here, she wouldn't mind leaving after that time, but she didn't want to be run off by a twelve-year-old with an attitude problem. She had her pride.

More than that, Ben reminded her of a growling but lonely dog. The animal desperately wants petting, but it's afraid to let anyone close enough. So instead, it scares the world away, then whimpers because it's alone.

Of course, she could be reading the situation completely wrong. After all, she'd had stepdaughters for nearly five years and had assumed they cared about her. She'd been proven wrong.

She spun around, then turned off the television. "Please come into the dining room, Ben."

She took a step away. Ben leaned forward and pressed a button on the remote control. The television popped back on. Defiance this soon wasn't good. Jill drew in a deep breath, not sure what to do. She and Craig hadn't discussed discipline. Of course, there hadn't been time to discuss anything.

She thought about physically threatening Ben. There were two problems with that. First, it wasn't really her style. Second, she had a feeling he was taller than her. If only she knew what Craig did in situations like this. Then she looked around at the messy house and the three boys with emotionally hungry eyes. Maybe there wasn't a house rule. Maybe no one had the time or cared enough to lay down the law.

The problem with her trying to do it was that she didn't have a power base.

She could feel C.J. and Danny still watching her, waiting to see what she would do. This showdown with Ben was going to set the tone for her five weeks...or her one week, if she blew it.

Nothing like performing under pressure, she thought, staring at Ben and praying for inspiration. Like a gift from heaven, it arrived.

She smiled, then bent over and swept everything off the right half of the coffee table. Books, magazines, the television remote control, three glasses that were, fortunately, empty and plastic, and a half-eaten sandwich. Ben looked startled. Good. Better to keep him off-balance.

She knelt in front of the coffee table and placed her elbow on the slick wooden surface. She flexed and released her hand. "You ready to back up that smart mouth with some action?" she asked, trying to sound confident and tough. This was all going to blow up in her face if he beat her.

"What are you talking about?"

"You and me. Right here. Right now." She smiled. "Arm wrestling, Ben. If you win, you get to sit here and watch TV until you're old and gray and your bones are dissolving. If I win, you do what I say. Starting with turning off the TV and coming with your brothers for a meeting."

"Cool!" C.J. said. "You can beat him, Jill."

Ben glared at his brother. "This is stupid," he muttered.

But he wasn't looking at the television anymore, Jill thought triumphantly. She shrugged. "Maybe. If you're chicken."

"I'm *not* chicken."

Danny made a clucking noise.

"Shut up, brat."

"I'm not a brat."

"You're a shrimpy brat."

"Boys." Jill spoke firmly. Both of them looked at her. She stared at Ben. "Put up or shut up, young man. Either you're tough, or you're not. Let's find out."

Those dark eyes stared at her. She tried to figure out what he was thinking, but along with his father's good looks, Ben had inherited Craig's ability to keep some of his thoughts to himself.

"If I win, I get to watch TV and I get five bucks."

She thought for a moment, then nodded slowly. "If *I* win, you not only do what I say, but you give up TV for the weekend."

Ben glanced at her right arm, then at her. "Deal." He slid off the sofa and onto the carpet. After placing his elbow on the coffee table, he clasped her hand with his. C.J. and Danny moved closer.

"Come on, Jill, you can do it," Danny said loudly. He ignored Ben's glare.

Jill hoped the boy's confidence in her was going to pay off. Since moving in with Kim, she'd started working out with light weights. She knew she was stronger than she had been, but was it enough? She knew very little about the strength of twelve-year-old boys. She could only hope that Ben's inactive lifestyle gave her an advantage.

Her gaze locked with Ben's. A flicker of uncertainty flashed through his eyes. She thought he might be a little afraid of winning. That would give him more power than most children would find comfortable. At least she liked to think so.

"C.J., you say go," she said, and shifted on the carpet. Ben would probably go for the quick kill. If she could hold on during that, she might have a chance. If she could win, she would make it look hard, so Ben could save face.

Ah, the complications of dealing with a houseful of men, she thought. She leaned forward so she could have the maximum leverage and sucked in a breath.

"Go!" C.J. yelled.

Chapter Three

Jill thought she'd prepared herself for the assault, but when it came, Ben nearly drove her hand into the table. She managed to keep him from slamming it down, but barely. She had to bite her lip to keep from crying out.

She didn't look at him or either of the other boys. She focused all her attention on her arm, willing it to be strong.

She finally managed to get their hands back in an upright position. She pressed hard, and he gave. She risked glancing at him. She saw the panic on his face. He was about to be humiliated in front of his brothers.

Her heart went out to this stubborn, proud, overweight boy who probably endured the taunts of his classmates and the lack of confidence that went with not fitting in. She was torn between wanting to make him feel better and needing to establish a presence in the house. As she'd decided, if she could win, she would. But she wouldn't make it look easy.

Her arm was shaking, but not as badly as Ben's. They knelt there, with their arms perpendicular to the table.

"You gonna beat 'im, Jill?" Danny asked, earning a glare from his oldest brother.

"I'm trying," she said through gritted teeth. She moved slightly to the left, forcing his wrist down.

C.J. laughed. "Come on, Ben. She's just a girl."

"Then you try it," Ben complained. "She's stronger than she looks."

"Lesson number one," Jill said. "Never underestimate the power of a woman."

With that she pressed the back of his hand down onto the wood. Both C.J. and Danny cheered. Ben released her fingers and rubbed his wrist as if it hurt.

"I thought I'd win for sure," he said, then smiled sheepishly. In that moment, he looked exactly like his father. He was going to be a heartbreaker when he grew up, she thought. He leaned over, grabbed the remote control, turned off the television, then handed the clicker to her.

"Haynes men keep their word," he said simply.

He sounded so serious. The words were those of a mature man, not a twelve-year-old boy. But the way he said them, she believed him.

"You're being very gracious," she said. She was surprised. She'd thought he would be a sore loser. One point for him, she thought, deciding that if he really cooperated with her today, she would let him watch a little TV tonight. She'd learned early on it paid to compromise.

"Okay, why don't the three of you give me the nickel tour."

Danny frowned. "We get a nickel if we give you a tour?"

"No, stupid. It's just an expression."

Apparently Ben's magnanimous attitude didn't extend to his brothers. "No name-calling, please." She stood up and placed her hand on Danny's shoulder. "But Ben is right. 'Nickel tour' is just an expression. It means to give someone a quick tour. Not a lot of details."

"Oh, okay."

C.J. looked at her and grinned. "Are you sure you want to see the rest of the house?"

She glanced at the piles of laundry by the door to the garage, then at the dishes in the kitchen. "Sure. How bad can it be?"

The three boys laughed together.

Fifteen minutes later, Jill didn't feel like laughing. She wanted to turn tail and run. She didn't understand how people could live under these conditions. It didn't make sense. Didn't anyone notice that virtually every possession was out of the cupboards, closets and drawers and on the floor?

She stood in the center of the upstairs hall, staring at C.J.'s room. "Doesn't your dad make you pick up your stuff?" she asked.

"Oh, sure," he told her. "All the time. He gets real mad if we don't."

"Then explain this." She motioned to the toys, books, clothes and cassette tapes littering the room.

"He's been gone." C.J. gave her a charming smile. All three brothers were going to cut a swath through the female population when they got older. But for now they were just messy little boys.

There were four bedrooms upstairs. To the left was Craig's. Not wanting to pry, she'd only peeked inside. She'd had a brief impression of large pieces of furniture and a bed that looked big enough to sleep six. Of course, she wasn't even five foot two. To Craig the bed was probably just big enough. His room was relatively tidy, with only a few pieces of clothing tossed on the sofa facing the corner fireplace.

Next to his bedroom was a small alcove. There was a large desk with a computer and printer. Disks had been piled around the keyboard. On the wall was a bulletin board covered with computer-generated graphics.

Each boy had his own bedroom. First Danny's, then C.J.'s, then Ben's. The bathroom they shared was right next to the stairs. Jill glanced in each of the rooms and saw far more than she wanted to. Danny had toys piled everywhere, C.J. had tons of clothes scattered and Ben seemed to be storing half the plates and glasses on his floor. Aside from that, the three rooms were all identical, each with a twin bed, a dresser, a desk and a set of bookshelves attached to the wall.

"You're all slobs," she said, pausing outside their bathroom door. It was closed. She thought about opening it and looking inside, but then decided that some things were best left for professionals.

"We work hard at it," C.J. said.

Danny moved next to her and touched her hand. "I'll help you clean up."

"Thanks, honey."

Ben snorted. "The little shrimp's already sucking up."

"Am not!"

"Are too!"

"Excuse me," Jill said loudly. "You're all going to help me clean up. We're going to do the laundry, pick up everything that doesn't belong on the floor and do the dishes."

There was a collective groan.

"I'm sorry," Jill said. "But it's your fault. If you'd chosen to live like civilized people instead of baboons—"

She knew the word was a mistake as soon as she said it. Instantly all three boys hunched over and started making monkey noises.

"Herds of the Serengeti, return to the family room," she said over the din of their hooting.

They began the awkward shuffle down the stairs. Halfway there, the game changed and became a race. The in-line skates resting on the foyer floor created a hazard, but everyone avoided them.

"Where does the sports equipment go?" she asked.

"There's a closet under the stairs," C.J. told her.

She found the door and opened it. The storage space had a slanted ceiling, but the floor space of a small room. It was empty. "Ah, I see you like to keep it clean in here and not in the rest of the house. It makes perfect sense now. Why didn't someone tell me?"

C.J. grinned, Danny giggled, even Ben forgot to scowl. Together, the four of them walked into the family room. Jill saw her suitcase sitting there. "Where do I sleep?" she asked, realizing she hadn't seen a guest room.

"Here," Danny said, pointing to a door at the far end of the family room.

She walked around him and stuck her head inside

the cheerful bedroom. Big windows looked out onto the backyard. The white wicker furniture looked new. There was a bright yellow bedspread on the double bed, and she could see the entrance to her own private bath.

This was by far the cleanest part of the house.

"Dad says we're not allowed in here," Danny said. "Mrs. Miller lived here before she had to go away. Now you live here."

Jill thought about pointing out the fact that her stay was temporary but figured the boys had been through enough today. Instead, she carried her suitcase into her room, then tried to figure out what should be done first.

"Danny and C.J., you two start sorting laundry."

The boys stared at her blankly, identically confused expressions drawing their mouths into straight lines.

"Clothes," she said, pointing to the piles around the laundry room and flowing into the hallway. "Sort them. By color. One pile for whites. One pile for darks, one for lights and another for jeans."

A lock of medium brown hair fell across Danny's forehead. He was the only one of the Haynes males she'd seen who didn't have dark hair and eyes. "Those piles are going to be huge. They're going to reach the ceiling."

She looked at the mounds of clothing. "Oh, probably, but do the best you can. Ben, I'd like you to help me in the kitchen. We're going to load the dishwasher and try to figure out what color the counters are."

"I know what color they are," C.J. said. "They're white."

She leaned over and wrapped an arm around his neck. Rubbing her knuckles against the top of his head, she said, "I *know* they're white. I was just being funny."

The boy giggled and wiggled, but didn't move away. Her chest tightened in sympathy as she wondered when they had last been hugged by a woman. It couldn't be easy growing up without a mom.

She released C.J. He and Danny went to work on the clothes. Ben followed her into the kitchen, and with only minor grumbling began loading the dishwasher. Jill sorted through cereal boxes, figuring out which were empty and which just needed to be put away. There were piles of food. Bread, chips, jars of salsa. A melted carton of ice cream had spilled on, then stuck to, the counter. She wet a cloth and set it over the mess. Maybe by that night it would have loosened up a little.

From the family room came muffled sounds of a battle being waged. C.J. and Danny were tossing more clothes than they were piling, but the work was getting done. Ben made the flatware dive-bomb the dishwasher. The childish sounds brought back memories of being with her two stepdaughters. She shoved the last box of cereal onto the top pantry shelf and wondered what they were doing now. Did they ever think of her or miss her? She still remembered how hard it had been to lose them. Even after her divorce from Aaron, she'd wanted to see the girls. She'd tried to call them, but their mother said to leave them alone. Jill had quickly found out she didn't have any legal rights to visitation, and when she'd pushed the matter, Patti and Heather had phoned her directly and told her to stop bothering them. They had a mother, they didn't need her.

The words still had the power to wound her. She

hadn't tried to take their mother's place in their lives. She'd just wanted to love them. Was that so bad? It must be a horrible crime because they'd never forgiven her for it.

"You got a husband?" Ben asked.

She spun toward him. He was stacking plates in the bottom of the dishwasher and had his back to her. "No. I'm not married."

"Got any kids?"

"No. Of course not. If I had children, I would be with them."

He looked up at her. "Why?"

"I just would. I wouldn't—" She had started to say, "leave my children," but clamped her mouth shut. Craig had told her that the boys' mother had left them.

Without thinking, she crossed the room to stand next to him. She reached out to touch him, then had second thoughts. Her hand hung awkwardly between them. At the same moment she moved closer, he started to straighten. A lock of dark hair fell onto his forehead. She reached up and brushed it back. Ben stiffened, but didn't move away.

She smiled, then frowned. She was looking *up*. "My word, you *are* taller than me!"

He grinned. Once again, he reminded her of his father. If he could just lose a little weight, he would be a good-looking kid. She wondered what Craig would think if she tried to help Ben with his problem.

By the time Ben had filled the dishwasher and stacked up the dishes for the next load, she'd found out there was no fresh food in the house. Actually there was very little to eat at all. When she commented on the fact, Ben told her that his father had meant to go shopping that day, but he'd been called to work.

"He's on some secret assignment," he said. "He can't talk about it."

"You must be very proud of him. Not many people get to make a difference every time they go to work."

Ben seemed startled by her compliment, then he smiled slowly. "Yeah, I am proud of my dad." Then the smile faded. Was he thinking of all the times his dad was gone?

"I don't suppose he mentioned when he'd be home," she said.

Ben shook his head. "There's phone numbers on the wall." He pointed to a bulletin board stuck above the telephone.

Jill walked over and stared at them. There was the number for the police station, a doctor, then a list of men. Travis, Jordan, Kyle and Austin.

"They're my uncles," Ben offered. "Except Austin. He's not really, but we call him Uncle because we've known him forever."

It must be nice, she thought, thinking of her own scattered family. She'd been an only child and her parents had split up while she was still in grade school. She'd spent the next seven years being shuffled between one household and the other, never really feeling settled or wanted in either.

"We're done!" Danny announced.

She looked into the family room and saw four mountains of laundry. "That's got to be twenty loads," she said in awe.

"It'll take forever," Danny said.

"Maybe not forever. Maybe just until you're in college."

He giggled at the thought.

She made the boys soup and sandwiches for lunch.

There was just enough food to get them through the day. She didn't want to go grocery shopping without talking to Craig and finding out what her budget was. While the boys ate, she put in the first load of whites.

"I can do it loud," C.J. said, then slurped his soup.

"That's nothing," Ben said, and proceeded to prove his point.

There was laughter and more slurping. She bit back a smile. These boys were different from her stepdaughters, but she liked them. They were alive and made her feel the same way. That was something she hadn't enjoyed in a long time.

After a few minutes, the slurping became annoying. She didn't want to tell them to just stop. Better to condition them into following the rules. Easier for everyone in the long run.

"Are you three having a slurping contest?" she asked as she closed the laundry room door behind her.

"I'm winning," Danny said.

"Are you? Oh, that's too bad. Whoever comes in last gets the largest serving of ice cream for dessert."

Silence descended like night at the equator. Instantly and irrevocably. She had to fight back her smile. Ah, the power of dessert. It was a lesson she'd learned well. There was one last carton in the freezer, so she could make good on her promise. She looked at Ben and thought it might be better to get low-fat frozen yogurt next time.

C.J. glanced up at her. "You tricked us, Jill."

"I know." This time she allowed herself to grin. "Being a grown-up is pretty cool."

It was nearly midnight when Craig opened the front door and stepped into the house. Jill's car was still in the driveway. He'd forgotten to give her the garage door opener so she could park her Mustang inside. He'd also forgotten to discuss the details of her salary, give her money for food or talk about days off. He'd left in a hurry because he'd been late. And because he'd been afraid she would change her mind about taking care of the boys. Frankly, he couldn't have blamed her.

He closed the door behind him. There was a nightlight at the top of the stairs, and the house was quiet. Everyone had survived. Relief swept over him, and with it, guilt. Just because he didn't know what to do about his boys didn't mean he could avoid them. He had to take responsibility. Sometimes, though, it was hard being the only one they could depend on.

He glanced at the living room, then did a double take. Where there had been piles of junk sat only furniture. The dining room was the same. He moved to his right, down the small open hall and glanced into the kitchen. The counters were clear, the sink clean, the trash can empty. Beyond, in the family room, most of the toys and sports equipment had been picked up. The videotapes were off the floor and the few piles of laundry left had been sorted by color.

He moved farther into the room. The TV was off, but lights were on. Jill lay curled up asleep at one end of the sofa. All around her were piles of clean, folded laundry. He didn't know whether to wake her up or leave her in peace. He'd never thought of the sofa as particularly comfy, but she was a lot smaller than he.

Before he could decide, she turned her head toward him and opened her eyes. The bright green color surprised him. He'd forgotten the intensity of her gaze. Then she smiled. His body reacted with all the subtlety of a freight train crashing into a brick wall. Blood flowed hot and fast. His breathing increased and an almost unfamiliar pressure swelled in his groin.

"You're home," she said, her voice low and husky. "I wondered if you would be. I almost called the station, but I didn't want to bother you. Is everything okay?"

"Fine." He motioned to the folded laundry. "I'm sorry. I didn't mean to make you do all this work. I really was going to call a service."

"You still are." She sat up and stretched. The hem of her sweatshirt rode up, exposing the barest sliver of bare belly before descending and hiding all from view. "I don't mind doing the laundry and cooking, but I'm scared to go into the boys' bathroom. I think they've invented some new fungus, and I don't want to have to battle it."

"I'll call on Monday," he promised.

She shifted so she was leaning against the arm of the sofa and rested her chin on the back. "I already did. They'll be here at ten. Are you hungry?"

His stomach rumbled at the question. "I guess I am. Come to think of it, I didn't have time to eat today."

She rose to her feet. She must have been asleep for a while. Her hair was all spiky, and it reminded him of their encounter that morning. When she'd been in her robe...and nothing else.

The mental image did nothing to alleviate his now-painful condition. Nor did he want it to. It had been far too long since he'd desired a woman. He didn't have to do anything about it with Jill. In a way it was enough to still be able to feel something.

"Don't be too impressed," she said, leading the way into the kitchen. "It's just pizza. There isn't much here, but I didn't want to go grocery shopping without talking to you first."

"I'm sorry about that, too. I just took off and dumped everything on you. I'd meant to discuss some things, but I had to go in and…" He gave her a half-hearted smile and rubbed the back of his neck. The pain there was pretty constant, the sort of nagging ache brought on by too much stress and too little of everything else.

"Don't worry about it," she said. She opened a box on the counter and slid three slices of thin-crust pizza with everything onto a plate. Then she put it into the microwave oven to heat and opened the refrigerator. "Water, milk, soda or beer?"

"Beer."

She took the bottle and untwisted the cap. "Have a seat," she said, handing him the drink and motioning to the kitchen table. She poured a glass of water for herself.

He stared at it for a moment. "I'm trying to remember the last time I saw this kitchen so clean."

"Judging from the number of dishes we put through the dishwasher, I would say some time last Christmas." She held up her hand before he could speak. "Don't apologize again. I understand. But we do have a few details to work out."

He settled in the seat at the head of the table and gratefully drank his beer. She pulled the pizza out of the oven and gave it to him, then took the chair opposite his. While he ate, they discussed her salary, the grocery budget, the kids' schedules for school and sports.

"Danny and C.J. need to be picked up but Ben takes the bus," he said, then bit into the third piece of pizza.

She sat cross-legged on the kitchen chair. Just looking at her folded legs made his knees throb. She'd run her hands through her hair, but there were still spiky tufts sticking up. Most of the lights in the house were off. Only the lamp in the family room and a small light over the stove illuminated the kitchen. In the dim room, her pupils were huge, nearly covering her irises, and her eyes looked black against her pale skin.

Her small hands fluttered gracefully as she moved. She made notes on a yellow pad, detailing where to pick up whom and what foods made the boys gag.

"I'm not a fancy cook, but pretty much everything I put together is edible," she said.

"That's all we require."

She glanced at him. "This has been hard on you, hasn't it?"

"Yeah." He took a swallow of beer and set the bottle on the table. "Since Mrs. Miller left there's been four different women in here. I guess she spoiled us. I didn't think it would be that difficult to replace her, but I was wrong."

"Well, you've got another five weeks until you have to think about that."

He raised his eyebrows. "What happened to our one-week trial?"

She shrugged. "I spent the day with the boys, and I think I can handle it. Unless they don't like me, I can't think of a reason why I can't stay the agreed time. At least it will save you from having to look for someone instantly."

"I think I've interviewed nearly every nanny in a fifty-mile radius."

He supposed he could have put the boys in some kind of day-care program and then just hired sitters for the weekends, but that never seemed to work out. He had to coordinate meals, cleaning, food shopping. It was easier to find one person to do it all. He was fortunate enough to have the money to pay for outside help. Every day he saw people who survived on much less.

"Now you get a break," Jill said. "Besides, staying here gives me some time, too. When Kim and her husband come home from their honeymoon, the last thing they'll want is a houseguest. I was going to have to look for my own place anyway. I haven't decided if I want to stay here or go back to San Clemente." She looked at him and smiled. "Now I don't have to."

Intellectually he knew his boys were sleeping upstairs. There were neighbors across the street and next door. He and Jill were hardly alone. Yet he couldn't shake the feeling of the world having been reduced to just the two of them. In the brief silences of their conversation he could hear the soft sound of her breathing. Despite his best effort to keep his attention above her shoulders, his gaze was drawn again and again to her chest. Not just to stare at her breasts, although they stirred his imagination, but also to watch her breathe. She wasn't like any woman he'd ever dated. Of course, he was getting old and there was a chance he couldn't remember back that far.

He studied her hands on the glass. Her slender fingers made random patterns in the condensation. Her nails were short and unpainted, but still feminine. He couldn't get over how small she was, every part of her perfectly proportioned, but little. Krystal had been tall, nearly five-nine. Most of the women he'd dated had been tall, as well.

"I didn't know how you wanted to handle discipline with the boys," she said.

"Ben's already been a problem?"

She raised her eyebrows. "Why assume it was him?"

"C.J. is very charming and fun-loving. Like my brother Kyle. He prefers to get his way by cajoling. Danny is going to be shy for the first couple of days, which leaves only Ben."

Ben had also been a problem in the past. Craig grimaced as he remembered the reports from Ben's teachers. The boy was sullen and uncooperative. His grades continued to be good, but he didn't participate in group activities.

"I did convince him to behave," she said, then stared down at the table. "But I'm not sure you'll approve of the method." She glanced up, her gaze sheepish. "I didn't know if you did time-outs or sent the boys to their rooms, and I was afraid if I demanded he do something, he wouldn't. He's even taller than me."

"So what did you do?"

"I challenged him to an arm-wrestling match. If I won, he had to do what I said. If he won, he got to watch TV for the rest of the weekend." She paused and took a sip of water. "I don't know if it's right or not, but when kids get old enough, I like to work out a compromise with them. Time-outs, then removing privileges. I make deals, because that's a part of life. No one gets everything all the time."

He was intrigued. And impressed. "Did you win?"

She smiled slowly. "Yes, but at first I was afraid I wasn't going to. For what it's worth, he was a very gracious loser."

"That's something." The pain at the back of his neck got worse. He rubbed it, wondering when it was going to go away. Probably about the time he got his life together. Like in the next century or so.

"What's wrong?" she asked.

"Nothing. Just stress."

"Do you want some aspirin?"

"That would be great."

She walked across the family room and into her bedroom. When she returned carrying two pills in the palm of her hand, he felt another flash of pain that had nothing to do with the tightness of his muscles. This one involved his soul.

He missed being a part of someone's life. He missed the day-to-day sameness of married life. He didn't miss being married to Krystal, but he missed being emotionally committed to a woman.

He looked at Jill, at her pert features and her bright green eyes. She smiled as she handed over the medication. Their hands barely touched, yet he felt the jolt all the way to his groin.

He'd hired Jill for the boys, to make their lives stable. He hadn't known inviting her into his home was going to cause him to want all the things he knew he could never have.

Chapter Four

"How was your day?" Jill asked as Craig took the aspirin and swallowed.

He hesitated, not sure how to answer her question. A lot of his special project was confidential. Before he could decide what to tell her she settled in the seat opposite him and wrinkled her nose.

"Don't worry about it," she said briskly. "I understand you're involved in something secret. I wasn't asking to get privileged information, I was just being polite. You know. How was your day? My day was fine. That sort of thing."

She tugged on a sleeve of her sweatshirt, pulling the cuff until it was up near her elbow. As she repeated the procedure on her other arm, he noticed how small and delicate her wrists were.

"I'm not used to someone asking," he said at last, mostly because it was the truth. Lately no one had been around enough to bother. He leaned back in his chair and studied the bottle of beer in front of him. "It was...difficult. Every time I think I'm immune to the scum of the world, they manage to surprise me."

She scooted forward and rested her elbows on the table. "What are they doing now?"

"I can't talk about the specifics of the case, but I'll tell you what was reported in the press." He grimaced. "Not on the front page, of course. Someone ripping off the elderly isn't exciting enough."

"Is that what's going on?"

"Yeah. There's a ring of three, maybe four people who get in accidents with senior drivers. They'll stop suddenly so they get rear-ended, or they turn left on a yellow light and drive slow enough to get hit. Anything to make the victims think the accident is their fault. Then they pretend to be concerned, talking about how an aging parent lost his or her license because of an accident. They mention increased insurance rates. It's based on truth, which makes it more frightening for the victims. Often they convince the senior drivers to pay in cash for damages to the car."

"The price of which is several times what it's supposed to be, right?" Jill asked, her green eyes flashing with anger. "How horrible. I don't understand people like that. It's cruel and ugly. I'm glad you're doing something to stop them."

Craig stared at her, surprised by the vehemence of her reaction. Sometimes he talked to his brothers about his work. Except for Jordan, they were cops and they understood. Krystal never had. When he'd tried to talk about his work, she'd gotten bored. In her opinion the fools of the world got what they deserved.

Now, with the perfect vision of hindsight, he wondered what he'd ever seen in her. But he already knew the answer to that question. At twenty-two she'd been stunningly beautiful with a body that could tempt a saint. She knew how to use her best assets to her advantage, and for some reason, she'd set her sights on him. He hadn't been thinking with his head when he'd proposed. The worst of it was, he couldn't even regret what had happened between them. Marrying Krystal had been a mistake, but he would do it all over again if given the choice. The reward of his children wasn't something he could wish away.

"It's slow going," he said, and shrugged. "I'm working with a team of elderly citizens. We're mounting a sting operation."

She grinned. "I bet they're great to work with."

"They are," he agreed. "There's this one woman, Mrs. Hart. She lives alone. She's got to be seventy, but you'd never know it. She's been begging me to let her wear a wire." He glanced at Jill. "A microphone and tape. She keeps cruising around the seniors center and the bingo halls, hoping they'll pick her. I keep telling her she's seen too many movies."

"She sounds terrific."

"Yeah." His smile faded and he hunched over his beer. "I hope they don't get her. A couple of the accidents didn't go as planned. The timing was off, or the jerks doing this stopped too soon. A woman was killed."

"Oh, Craig." She reached across the table and touched his hand with her fingers. The light brush wasn't erotic. Nor was it meant to be. Instead, the caring gesture offered comfort and he accepted it.

"We'll get 'em. I don't usually do this kind of work, but the detectives needed some assistance and I volunteered. When the hours keep me away from the kids, I try to justify it by telling myself I'm doing the right thing."

"You are," she assured him. She pulled her hand away and laced her fingers together on the edge of the table. "Why a cop?"

"That's easy. I come from a long line of cops. Four generations on my dad's side. All my uncles—my dad was one of six. Two of my brothers. Jordan's the only holdout. He's a fire fighter. We tease him about it." Craig took a sip of beer. "If you ask me, anyone voluntarily going into a burning building day after day is crazy."

"Some people would say that about what you do."

"Maybe."

The corners of her mouth tilted up. "So you're one of four boys, you have five uncles and three boys of your own. There aren't many girls in your family, are there?"

"There hadn't been one born in four generations. My brother Travis had a girl, though."

"Oh, progress for the female gender."

"Jordan has a theory that Haynes men only have girls when they're in love. If it's true, it doesn't say much about the last four generations of husbands. Or my marriage. Elizabeth—that's Travis's wife—says it's more about the female being predisposed to accept male or female sperm. She pointed out that she's one of three girls, and she comes from a family that mostly has daughters. I guess when Kyle and Sandy have their baby we'll know who's right."

Jill was staring at him as if he'd grown a second head. "You look lost," he said.

"I am. All these names. How big is your family?"

"I have three brothers and Austin. He's family, but not by blood."

"Where are your folks?"

He didn't like talking about that, but it was a reasonable question. "My mom took off about fifteen years ago. My dad hadn't been much of a husband. He fooled around constantly. She took it for as long as she could, then one day she walked out. She didn't bother packing a bag or leaving a note. She just left. We never saw her again."

"If she didn't take any luggage, how do you know—" She bit on her lower lip.

"How do we know something didn't happen to her?"

She nodded.

"Jordan saw her leave. She told him she'd had it and wasn't coming back. He was only seventeen and didn't know what to do. He came to me. I was already out of college and living on my own. I told him to keep what he heard to himself. It was hard on all of us. Probably hardest on Kyle, because he's the youngest."

Her green eyes were wide and dark with emotion. It wasn't pity. Maybe concern. "I'm sorry."

"Thanks. My brothers and I were always close, but after that we pulled together more. My dad remarried a couple of times, then moved to Florida. I haven't seen him since before Ben was born." And he didn't want to. He would never forgive his father for what he'd done to the family.

"You'll meet my brothers while you're here," he said. "We get together a lot."

"It sounds nice, but a little overwhelming. I'm an only child. As it is, I'm going to have my hands full adjusting to living with a houseful of men." She grinned. "I'm thrilled to have my own bathroom so I won't have to fight to keep the toilet seat down."

"I trained them better than that. It shouldn't be a problem anywhere."

She looked at the table, then at him. Her full mouth straightened. "You know, Craig, despite how you're beating yourself up right now, you've done a good job with the boys."

"I don't think I want to know how you read my mind."

"It wasn't hard. I think most single parents worry that they're not doing enough. Add to that the pressures that go with your job and it doesn't take a rocket scientist to figure it out. But from what I saw today, they're good kids."

"I can't take credit for that," he said. "Everything is so messed up." Ben. What was he going to do about his oldest?

"Divorce has a way of doing that to families."

He took a swallow of beer. "So what's your story?"

"It's not very interesting." She leaned back in her chair and raised her hands, palms up. "I met a man I loved and who I thought loved me. It was a whirlwind courtship. I married him, and his two daughters came to live with us." She smiled, but there was sadness in her eyes.

"Patti and Heather were so sweet. I adored them. I wanted to be their mother. I did everything I could for them. I was working, so I didn't have a lot of time." She paused, as if thinking. "I was working extra hours. Aaron had high alimony payments so I supported the household. I really didn't mind. Looking back, I suppose I should have."

"How long has it been?"

"Eighteen months. I know what you're thinking. That I should be over it by now. In a way I am. It's just that I tried too hard not to think about it, and then one day I couldn't think about anything else."

"I'm surprised Aaron allowed you to support his two kids." He shook his head. "I guess I shouldn't be. My ex-wife used to tell me that I was old-fashioned. According to her, my philosophies about men and women went out with hoopskirts."

"We never really talked about it," she said. "I sort of offered and he accepted. It was an unspoken rule in our family. He didn't have to say what he wanted or needed. I just knew."

Craig understood about that kind of selfishness. He'd grown up watching his father expect the same from his mother. "But he never bothered figuring out what you wanted."

She shook her head. "The really sad part is, until a few months ago, I had convinced myself I didn't want anything at all. That just being part of the family was enough."

He and Krystal had been the same way, except in his case, he'd been the one anticipating her needs. She'd taken easily, without once feeling the need to give back. As a point of honor, he'd done the opposite of his father. He'd sworn fidelity. Foolishly, he'd expected the same. But Krystal had never agreed with him about that. In fact, they'd agreed on very little.

Jill drew in a slow breath. "Eventually I figured out Aaron married me to get custody of the children. It hurt, but I got over it. Then one day we ended up in court."

She drew her knees to her chest and wrapped her

arms around her calves. He wanted to move around the table and comfort her. The impulse surprised him. He'd known this woman less than twenty-four hours. Yet there was something about the night. Something about the moment and the confessions that made it seem that they'd known each other for much longer. Maybe it was the shared pain. Like wounded warriors, they talked about their injuries and knew what the other had endured.

"His ex-wife won back custody of her daughters and just like that the girls were gone." She blinked several times. "Then Aaron didn't need me anymore."

Everything about her—the way her shoulders hunched forward, the set of her mouth, her fingers locked so tightly together that her knuckles turned white—told him there was more to the story. But he didn't ask.

She looked up and forced a shaky smile. "I tell myself it's Aaron's loss. I doubt I was the best wife in the world, but I tried hard, and I make a dynamite meat loaf. How many people can claim that kind of f-fame?" Her voice cracked on the last word.

She cleared her throat and continued. "I could have handled it," she said softly. "If only someone had told me it was just temporary. I wouldn't have felt like such a fool. I would have made sure it wouldn't hurt so bad."

"Your ex-husband and my ex-wife should be locked up together. They deserve each other."

She glanced at him. "I thought you said Krystal was, ah, you know."

"Dead?"

She nodded.

"She is. But they still deserve each other. Aaron sounds like a jerk."

"Don't expect me to defend him," she said. "I'm done with that. And while I appreciate the words of support, I'd like to remind you that you've known me a day. You've only heard my side of this story. His is probably completely different."

"Maybe, but I'll take your word for what really happened. I'm sure Aaron regrets the loss. You've got a lot going for you."

She chuckled. "Oh, sure. I have a temporary job, after which I'll be unemployed again. I'm divorced and just turned thirty. Men are lining up for miles."

He wanted to tell her he would line up, but that would lead them in a direction neither of them wanted to go. Even as he held back the words, he noticed how the soft light cast shadows on her face, highlighting her cheekbones. In his mind, she *did* have a lot going for her. She was bright, funny and sexy as hell. And small. Concern mixed with desire as he wondered if he would physically hurt her if they ever…

He cut off that line of thought. They weren't ever going to do anything. They'd both learned their lessons.

"You've probably been wondering why I'm living with Kim," she said. "I do plan to get back to my life. I did fine for just over a year. I grieved, I got angry, I did all the things those self-help books say you're supposed to. I moved on. Then one day I couldn't do anything but feel the pain. The thought of going to my job overwhelmed me. I realized that instead of actually going through the steps, I'd been talking about them and thinking about them, but not being in them, if that makes sense. Circling around them like a caged lion. I needed to get away and start over. Kim had lost her roommate so moving in with her seemed like the perfect thing to do. I leased out my condo and drove up."

She rested her chin on her knees. "You know what hurts the most?"

"No."

"I don't miss Aaron so much. I miss those girls. That was the worst. Finding out they'd been using me, too. Apparently they'd been calling their mother all the time and I never knew. She was telling them things about me. Mean things. I thought they cared about me and they didn't." Her voice got thick. She swallowed.

"In court—" She cleared her throat, obviously fighting tears. "In court, when we lost custody, I asked if I could see them sometime. The judge told me I had no legal rights. Then he asked the girls what they wanted. They laughed at me and made fun of me. I had no idea. I—"

He hadn't meant to go to her, but he couldn't watch her in pain anymore. He rose from his chair and circled the table. Before she could protest, he picked her up in his arms. She didn't weigh as much as Ben, he thought, surprised. She murmured a protest, but he ignored her and settled on her seat, with her on his lap.

She was as tiny as he'd imagined she would be, with slim arms, slender legs and small hands. She tried to push away.

"Damn it, Jill, I'm not making a pass at you," he said. "I'm giving you a hug."

"I know, but this—" Then a tear escaped from her right eye. She brushed it away and buried her face in his shoulder.

She didn't cry. She just huddled against him, shaking with misery. Her ragged breathing fanned his neck. He told himself it wasn't about sex, and despite the arousal pressing against his fly, it wasn't. She needed holding, and he needed to hold.

Craig tried to remember the last time he'd been this close to a woman. He tried to remember the last time he'd wanted to be.

He inhaled the sweet fragrance of Jill's body. He stroked his hands up and down her back. Bits of what she'd told him floated through his mind. He wanted to find her ex-husband and beat him into a bloody pulp. He wanted to talk some sense into those two girls. He worked with the worst type of humanity every day, but he hated to see others tainted and hurt by contamination.

"Damn," she said, and straightened. Her face was dry, her mouth pulled into a straight line. "This is horribly unprofessional behavior. I swear, I don't usually fall apart like this."

"It's okay."

"No, it's not. But thanks for pretending. You're a nice man."

She sniffed once, then slid off his lap. He let her go, because he had no excuse to keep her, and trying to make one up would be dangerous for both of them. At this moment, with his groin swollen and aching and his blood pounding through his heated body, he didn't feel very nice.

She brushed her cheek with the back of her hand, then smiled. If the corners trembled a little, he wasn't going to mention it.

"Bet you're sorry you asked about *my* life," she said.

"Actually, I'm not."

"It's probably better that you know. I'll do a good job with your kids, but I won't get personally involved. In five weeks I'm going to walk away. I can't risk getting hurt again."

"I understand."

"Thanks for everything. Good night."

She gave him a brief wave, then walked down the two stairs into the family room, and across to her bedroom. She closed the door behind her.

He watched her go, then stood alone in silence. He couldn't risk getting hurt, either. Krystal had taught him about the exquisite torture of a marriage gone bad. Night after night, he'd waited for her, wondering who she'd been with, and what he was doing wrong. He kept thinking if he was more...*something*— though he didn't know what—she wouldn't stray. But she had. And he'd been left to pick up the pieces of their broken family.

He knew what he wanted the next time around. He wanted a sure thing. He wasn't going to take any more chances on something as nebulous as love.

Chapter Five

"I feel like I'm feeding an army," Jill muttered as she grabbed another armful of grocery bags and started through the short hallway that led into the family room.

She'd filled nearly two carts with food and spent more money in an hour than she'd spent on herself in the past four months. She set the bags on the counter and went back for the last couple. While she appreciated that some young man had helped her load the groceries into the car, it would have been a lot more helpful if he could have followed her home and helped her carry them inside.

She slammed the rear door of the utility vehicle, then kicked the door to the garage shut behind her. When she put the last two bags down, she counted.

"...fifteen, sixteen, *seventeen* bags? These boys know how to eat."

Before starting to unload everything, she tossed another load of laundry into the washer. She'd barely gotten the frozen food into the freezer when the phone rang.

She juggled bags of apples in one hand and reached for the receiver with the other.

"Hello, Haynes residence," she said, tucking the phone between her head and shoulder and trying to remember what she'd planned for dinner that night. Did she need to make a salad?

"Jill, it's Kim. Are you still speaking to me?"

Jill set the apples on the counter and bumped the refrigerator door closed. She leaned against the kitchen wall by the phone and sighed. "Kim. I wondered when I'd hear from you."

"Are you mad?"

"Not exactly." She sank onto the sparkling floor. The service she'd hired had sent four cleaning people over. They'd gone through the house like a plague of locusts and had finished in three hours. It would have taken her two, maybe three days.

As she closed her eyes and drew in a breath, she inhaled the scent of pine cleaner and lemon furniture polish.

Her friend sighed. "I'm really sorry. I should have told you the truth, but I knew if I did, you'd say no and then I couldn't go get married and, Jill, I feel so bad."

Amazingly, Kim got that out in one long breath.

"Not bad enough," Jill said.

"So you *are* mad."

"No, but I would have liked to have known what I was getting into. Mr. Haynes thought he was hiring a full-time nanny, and I thought I was baby-sitting for a couple of nights."

"But it can't be too awful. You took the job."

"You didn't leave me a lot of choice. The poor man was desperate."

"I'm sorry."

"Don't keep apologizing. I'm not upset." She glanced around at the piles of laundry yet to be folded and the groceries she had to put away. Her gaze strayed to the clock and she realized she had to leave in less than an hour to pick up Danny and C.J. at school.

"This job might be good for me," she said slowly. "At least I don't have to worry about finding a place when you come home from your honeymoon. This job will give me time to think."

"So you don't hate me?"

"No, I don't. How was the wedding?"

"Wonderful. And the honeymoon is even better. Oh, Jill, Brian is everything I dreamed he would be. I can't believe I put off getting married to him for so long. Every day is better than the one before. He's thoughtful and tender. My heart beats faster when he comes into the room. And the sex—"

"Spare me the details," Jill said quickly. "I'll use my imagination."

Kim laughed. "Then you'd better have a good one because—"

"Kim!"

"Okay, I won't tease you anymore." Her friend was silent for a moment. "I do appreciate all you've done. Without you reminding me what was really important, I wouldn't have married Brian."

"You were there for me. When I realized I couldn't

stand it anymore, you gave me a place to run to," Jill said. "I owed you. Now we're even."

"How are the boys?"

"Interesting. Very different from Patti and Heather. But I like them."

Over the phone line she heard the sound of a door opening. Kim called her husband over. There was a breath of silence, then a soft giggle.

"Sounds like you two have plans," Jill said. "I'll talk to you when you get back."

"Definitely. We want to have you over for dinner."

"Sounds great. Bye." She hung up the receiver.

Despite the bags of groceries that needed to be emptied, she sat on the floor a little longer. She envied Kim her happiness. Jill tried to remember the last time she'd been excited about a man. She had been married to Aaron for five years, but the thrill wore off very quickly. Had she expected too much, or had she sensed that he was holding back something of himself?

Funny that she never thought about leaving him. Of course, he'd gone out of his way to make her feel obligated to the girls. Maybe that was his way of making sure she was around. Sometimes she felt as if Aaron had played her the way an experienced fisherman plays with a prize bass. Reeling her in slowly, teasing her with just enough line so that the hook sank in deep.

She stood up and put away the rest of the groceries. She glanced at the clock, then made a batch of quick bread. The timer on the oven would turn the heat off at the right time, so it wouldn't overcook. Then she grabbed her purse and keys and headed out to the garage.

Five minutes later she pulled up in front of the

school. She joined a long line of cars filled with mothers waiting for their children.

She watched the smiling kids run toward their parents. There hadn't been a lot of laughter in her house when she was growing up. Before the divorce, her parents had fought constantly. After the divorce, they'd spent their time thinking up ways to torment each other. Usually she was the preferred method, each parent playing her against the other. Once she'd grown up and escaped, she'd been willing to do anything to belong to a family, even turn a blind eye to Aaron's real motive for marrying her.

Before she could question her gullibility, she glanced up and saw two boys racing toward the vehicle. They were laughing, and she couldn't help but smile back. She unlocked the car and they tumbled inside. Danny took the front seat. C.J. had had it that morning.

"How was your day?" she asked and waited until they'd put on their seat belts before starting the engine.

"Great," C.J. said. "I've got to do a science project."

"Wonderful," she thought, fighting back a groan. She had a mental picture of a pudding-filled volcano exploding in her freshly cleaned kitchen.

"What about you, Danny?"

Craig's youngest frowned. "I wanna play Pee-Wee ball, but Daddy won't practice with me. He said he would this weekend, but he was gone."

"Your father is working on something special right now. It's important for him to be gone. But he thinks about you and misses you. As soon as he can, he'll start spending more time at home." She paused, wondering if either boy would ask how she knew this bit of information. She didn't, exactly. She was assuming. Because Craig was a decent guy and he genuinely seemed to care about his kids.

"You don't have to practice," C.J. said. "Everyone gets on a team."

"I know." Danny blew his bangs out of his eyes. "But I don't want to be on a *baby* team. I wanna be good."

"Not a problem," Jill said, glancing at him. "We'll help you."

Danny made a face that said he wasn't impressed with the offer.

"I'll have you know that I'm a very good Pee-Wee ball player," she said.

C.J. looked at her and grinned. "You're lying. You've never played Pee-Wee ball."

"Well, I could if I wanted to."

Danny laughed. "You're too big."

"There's a first," she said. "Okay, maybe I haven't played Pee-Wee ball, but I can still help. Your brothers can, too. You'll see, Danny. You'll do great."

"I'll help the kid out," C.J. said. "But Ben won't. He just watches TV or plays video games after school."

Jill didn't like the sound of that. Children needed to get outside and run around. When she'd been a child, she'd often escaped outside to get away from her parents. There, in a tree house, she'd been able to pretend she was somewhere else—in a place where people cared about each other.

She turned the corner and stopped behind the school bus. It turned on its flashing red lights as children began to step down. Ben was one of the last ones off.

None of the other children spoke to him as they walked away in groups of twos and threes.

Jill stared at the boy. He had his father's good looks, but he needed to lose weight. His whole body shook when he walked. She frowned, wondering if she was qualified to deal with this problem. Then she realized Ben didn't have anyone else right now. She was going to have to do her best and pray that it was enough.

When he was in the car, she signaled and pulled away from the curb.

"How was your day?" she asked brightly, glancing at him in the rearview mirror.

He looked out the side window and didn't meet her gaze. "Dumb."

"Okay." She thought for a moment, trying to plan the afternoon. It was staying lighter longer so there would be plenty of time. "What's the homework situation for everyone?"

"I don't have any," C.J. said quickly.

"Me, either," Danny piped in.

Ben didn't bother answering.

"No one has homework?" They all shook their heads. "Interesting. No homework on a Monday night. Gee, I'm very surprised. I thought everyone would have *some* homework. But if you say you don't have any, no problem."

They were all lying, she thought, fighting a grin. But she knew how to fix them. She turned on the radio and found one of those stations playing elevator music. The kind with twenty-year-old songs sung by a no-name group. She turned the radio up just loud enough to be annoying, then joined in.

Her natural inclination was to sing off-key and this

time she didn't fight it. She sang right along, loudly, making up words if she didn't know them.

The boys stared at each other in disbelief. C.J. clasped his hands around his neck and made a choking sound.

"Jill?" Danny said. "Why are you singing like that?"

"Because I want to. If you don't have homework, then there's plenty of time to listen to my singing. I'm going to take the long way home."

"I've got word lists and a math page," Danny said quickly.

"Really?" she said, sounding surprised.

"I've got Spanish and history," Ben said.

She looked at C.J. in the mirror. He smiled. "Okay, maybe some math and spelling."

She clicked off the radio. "Ah, the truth at last. Okay, here's the plan. We're going to have a snack and do homework for a half hour, then we'll help Danny with his Pee-Wee tryouts. Then, if there's any homework left, it can be done after dinner."

"I don't want to," Ben said.

Jill raised her eyebrows. "Which part doesn't appeal to you?"

"Helping the pip-squeak. I'm gonna watch TV."

"But, Ben, you're the oldest. I would have thought you would want to help your brother out. Don't you play Little League?"

"Not anymore," C.J. said and puffed up his cheeks. "Lard-o is too fat."

Before she could say anything, Ben launched himself at his younger brother. C.J. grabbed him and they started wrestling together. Jill glanced at the street signs. They were only about three blocks from home, but she wanted to prove a point. She pulled to the side of the road and put the car in park.

Danny stared at her. She gave him a wink. In the back seat the boys were grunting and squirming. After a couple of minutes, Ben looked up.

"Aren't you gonna stop us?"

Jill shrugged.

C.J. looked around. "Why'd you pull over here?"

"Because you're acting like animals. It's not safe to drive with loose animals in the car. If you want to settle down, we'll go home. If not, we'll sit here. Oh, look at that girl," she said, pointing to a pretty blonde who was about ten years old. Jill rolled down the window and waved.

"Don't do that," C.J. said from the back of the car. "She'll see you."

"That's the point," Jill said, still smiling and waving. The girl waved back uncertainly.

C.J. groaned and slunk down in his seat. "Please stop."

"Are you two done?" she asked. "If so, then you can apologize, promise not to do it again and we'll leave."

"I'm sorry," C.J. said quickly. "Real sorry. I'll never wrestle with Ben in the car again. I swear!"

She glanced over her shoulder at Ben and raised her eyebrows. "How long do you think it will be until someone you know comes along?"

"I'm sorry, too," he said. "I won't do it again."

"Perfect."

Jill rolled up the window, put the car in drive and headed for home. The last quarter mile was blissfully silent.

After she'd parked in the garage, the boys climbed

out. C.J. paused in front of her. "You're not like our other nannies," he said.

"I'm not surprised. Is that a good thing or a bad thing?"

He grinned. "I'll get back to you."

"I want one more slice," Danny whined, inching closer to the counter.

"Me, too," Ben said, stacking his books on top of each other. The boys had been doing their homework at the kitchen table.

"After we practice and have dinner," Jill said. "You've had your snack already."

Danny eyed the sliced loaf on the counter. "But it was good."

"I'm glad you liked the prune bread. I—"

She stopped talking when she realized all three boys were staring at her. Their eyes widened and their mouths opened.

C.J. recovered first. "*Prune* bread?"

"Yes."

He fell to his knees and started choking. "I'm dying, I'm dying."

Ben followed his lead and dropped to the floor. He writhed in agony. "Prunes. Yuck. She's poisoning us."

Danny stared at his brothers, then her. He wasn't certain who he wanted to side with. Jill ignored his older brothers.

"Don't worry about it," she said. "It was delicious before you knew what it was. It's still delicious. Let's go outside and practice."

She held out her hand. Danny grabbed her fingers. They started for the door. "I know how many slices there were," she called over her shoulder. "So don't even think about sneaking any."

It was warmer today, but still sweatshirt weather. The sky was a brilliant California blue. Tall trees reached for the heavens. The green leaves seemed brighter in the afternoon light, or maybe it was her mood. There was nothing like taking care of three boys to give her something other than herself to think about. Jill wondered if that was part of her problem. She'd had too much free mental time on her hands.

By the time she'd dug out a couple of mitts and a bat, the other two boys had joined them. She didn't comment on Ben's appearance, not wanting to make a big deal of it, but in her heart, she was pleased he wanted to participate.

She tossed them mitts, then found a couple of big plastic balls that wouldn't go far, and wouldn't do any damage if they hit something. Ben came over and took them from her. "I'll pitch," he said.

He'd pulled on a baseball cap. It hid most of his dark hair from view. He wore a loose sweatshirt and jeans. Her heart ached for him. She'd been out of place at home, but at least she'd been able to fit in at school. Ben carried his pain with him everywhere.

She gave him a quick smile and gently touched his cheek. He stiffened at the contact but didn't pull away. His dark gaze met hers. Some emotion flickered there. She couldn't read it, but she knew it was hurting him. She wanted to pull him close and hug him until he felt better, but she didn't have the right. Even if she did, Ben wouldn't let her. He was as prickly as a porcupine.

"Batter up," he called, moving to the center of the yard.

There was more room in the front than in the back, so that was where they played. Jill stayed in the background, filling in where she was needed. C.J. was fast and talented, with the grace of a natural athlete. Ben had the same raw ability, but his weight slowed him down. He could pitch with perfect precision, but he got winded if he tried to run the bases. Even six-year-old Danny could catch him.

Jill stared at the youngest of Craig Haynes's boys. Danny stood hunched over his bat, his face scrunched up in concentration. Ben released the ball. Danny swung and missed.

"Keep your eyes open," C.J. called from the outfield.

"I am."

"Then hit the dumb ball."

"I'm tryin'." Frustration filled Danny's voice, but he didn't give up. He tossed the ball back to Ben and hunched over again.

"Is he standing right?" she asked, coming up to stand behind him. "Maybe it's his shoulders."

Danny looked at her and grimaced. "It's not my shoulders. Ben and C.J. are better than me."

"They're also older and have had more practice. You're going to make it. You're determined, and sometimes that's more important than raw talent."

He beamed, then hunched over. Jill moved back and studied him. He didn't have his brothers' dark hair or eyes. He must take after his mother. Despite having checked on the cleaning crew while they worked and going into all the bedrooms to put clean laundry on the beds, she hadn't seen a picture of the boys' mother. While she was curious about Krystal Haynes, she wasn't comfortable with snooping.

Ben pitched again.

"Keep your eyes open," Jill called.

Danny swung hard. The bat cracked against the plastic ball and sent it sailing toward the heavens.

"You did it!" she said and clapped her hands. Danny tossed off his hat in celebration.

Ben jumped to snag the ball, but he missed.

"Jeez, fatty, can't you do anything?" C.J. said as he raced toward it. He caught the ball in his glove, went down on one knee, rolled onto his back and came up, still holding the ball in his glove. "Craig Haynes, Jr., wins the national championship." He bowed to an imaginary crowd.

Ben threw off his glove and started for the house.

"Ben," she called.

The boy kept walking. He stalked through the garage. She ran after him. "Ben, wait. I know C.J. is being a pain, but you're doing great. Please don't leave."

In the background, she heard a car pull up at the curb.

Ben turned to look at her. Tears swam in his eyes, but he blinked them back. "Go back where you came from. We don't need you here. We don't like you." With that, he opened the door to the family room and stepped into the house. The door slammed shut behind him.

"Daddy, Daddy!"

She turned and saw C.J. and Danny running toward their father. She hadn't seen Craig since Saturday night. He was gone when she woke up Sunday morning and didn't come home until after she went to bed.

He wore his uniform, but he'd left his hat inside his car. The sunlight caught the dark wavy hair. He was tall and broad, and for some reason, her heart began fluttering foolishly in her chest. She told herself it was just the uniform, or the strangeness of the situation. Maybe it was a bit of indigestion. Maybe she'd eaten her slice of prune bread too quickly.

The two boys embraced their father. He squatted down and hugged them. She liked the way he touched them so easily. Some fathers had trouble showing affection. A hug went a long way toward making many problems right. After all, Craig had made her feel better, just by holding her in his arms.

She didn't want to remember that. Nor did she want to remember how good she'd felt sitting on his lap. It hadn't seemed to matter that they were practically strangers. It wasn't like her to expose her emotions like that. She wasn't sure what had happened. Better that it be the late hour of the night and not the man. She knew the danger of getting involved.

"How's everything going?" Craig asked as she approached.

"It was going fine until a couple of minutes ago. We're helping Danny so he'll make a good Pee-Wee team."

"I don't want to be with the babies," his youngest said loudly.

"You won't be," Craig said. He glanced around. "Where's Ben?"

"He went inside," Danny said. "He got mad when he couldn't catch a ball."

"That's not exactly what happened," Jill reminded him.

C.J. stepped away from his father and shuffled his feet. "He *is* fat."

Jill dropped to her knees and took C.J.'s hands in

hers. He had his father's eyes and hair, too. Both the older boys definitely took after their dad.

She stared at the boy. "Ben knows he's overweight. I think it bothers him. What do you think?"

C.J. shrugged uncomfortably. "Why does he have to be like that? It's gross."

"Don't you think he wants to change? But it's hard. When you make fun of him, he feels bad. When he feels bad, he eats. I'm not saying this is your fault, because it isn't. But you're not helping."

C.J. drew in a deep breath. "I'm sorry."

"Maybe you should apologize to your brother instead of me."

"Jeez, do I have to?"

She smiled. "Yeah, you do."

"Bummer." He gave her a quick grin and started for the house.

Jill sank onto the grass and buried her face in her hands. "Maybe we should have kept that one-week trial," she said. "After all this, you're going to be the one wanting me to leave."

"Don't go, Jill," Danny said and flung himself at her.

She caught the young boy and pulled him onto her lap. His sturdy arms wrapped around her back and he hugged her close.

"Don't go," he repeated. "I like having you here."

She brushed his light brown hair from his eyes and smiled. "I'm glad someone likes me."

She held him tight. It had been a long time since she'd hugged a child. After the divorce, she'd been cut off from the girls. A cruel and unusual punishment, but there hadn't been anyone to take her side. Her heart filled with an achy kind of joy and she wondered if this was going to cost her later.

She released Danny. "Up with you, young man. We've got work to do."

Danny slid onto the grass, then sprang to his feet. Craig held out his hand to her. She took it reluctantly. As she'd expected, the second their fingers touched, hot, fluttery sensations raced down her arm to settle in her breasts and between her thighs. She allowed him to pull her to her feet, hoping madly that it really was indigestion and not something more deadly, like attraction.

When she was on her feet, Craig didn't release her hand. He glanced at her fingers, then returned his gaze to her face. "Thanks for what you said about Ben. I don't know what to do about him."

"Have you talked to anyone?"

"A counselor, you mean?"

She nodded.

"No, but maybe I should. I don't want him to be so unhappy, and I worry about his health. He's just a kid. This should be a fun time for him. But it isn't."

The father shared the son's pain, but this hurt couldn't be hugged away. "I wish I had the answers," she said. "I've got a few ideas. Maybe we can talk about them later."

"I'd like that."

He released her hand and bent over to pick up Danny. The boy looped his arms around his father's neck. Craig placed his hand at the small of her back and urged her toward the house. She fought against the heat spiraling through her middle. She didn't like that this house of males was getting to her.

"Are you in for the evening?" she asked, hoping

he would be leaving soon so she could get her heart rate back to normal.

"I've got a late meeting, but I'll be here until nine. I thought I could help with dinner."

"I will, too," Danny said, giving her his best smile.

"Great." So much for regaining her equilibrium.

"Jill made prune bread," the boy told his father.

"Good."

"You like it?"

"Of course. Anything homemade is a treat."

"Oh. Okay. I like it, too."

Jill glanced at them. The ache in her chest intensified. Craig Haynes had everything she'd ever wanted. With every word he spoke, with every action, he and his sons invited her into their lives. Staying disconnected—*not* getting involved—was going to be harder than she'd thought.

Chapter Six

Craig shut Danny's door. C.J.'s light was already out. That left only Ben. He hesitated outside his oldest's room. Ben had been unusually quiet during dinner. Not belligerent, just thoughtful. Was he thinking about how unhappy he was? Was he wishing his father hadn't let him down?

Craig remembered all the times *his* father had let him down. In the end, he'd hated his old man. Would Ben grow up to feel the same way? Craig didn't want to think about that. He didn't want to know that he'd failed his son so badly. He wanted to believe it wasn't too late, but he didn't know what to do to bridge the chasm already between them.

He crossed the hallway and tapped on Ben's door. At the muffled "Come in," he entered.

He glanced around, surprised. All the boys had cleaned their rooms. When the service had come through that morning, everything had been dusted and vacuumed. It made a big difference. He should have done it months ago.

Ben sat up in bed playing a hand-held video game. He didn't bother glancing up as his father entered. Craig settled on the chair by the desk and waited.

For a few minutes there was only the faint sound of a battle being fought on the tiny screen. Then there was an explosion. Ben grimaced and looked up. "Yeah, Dad?"

"I just came to say good-night."

Ben looked away, as if to say he knew there had to be more. There was.

"How was your day at school?"

"Fine."

"Classes going okay?"

"I guess."

The boy stared at his video game but didn't turn it on. Craig couldn't believe he felt this awkward. This was his kid. They should at least be friends. He grimaced. At one time they had been. But things had changed. Ben had been hit the hardest by the divorce, and later by Krystal's death. He had been old enough to really remember his mother.

He cleared his throat. "Jill seems to be working out."

"I guess."

One "fine" and two "I guesses." They sure were bonding now. "I really appreciate you taking the time to help Danny today. He wants to do well for Pee-Wee tryouts."

"They don't turn anyone away."

"I know, but if he's halfway decent, he'll get on a better team. Anyway, thanks for doing that."

Ben didn't answer. Craig wondered if the boy felt as uncomfortable as he did. But, damn it, he was the adult. He had to try.

He leaned forward and rested his elbows on his knees, then laced his fingers together. There was a time when he and Ben had had plenty to say to each other. Years ago they'd been buddies. C.J. and Danny had been babies, but Ben had been his friend. He hated to see that change.

"You going out for Little League?" he asked, hoping to spark some interest.

Something close to pain flashed across Ben's face. "It's dumb," he said, and turned toward the wall. He put the video game on the nightstand, then settled down on the mattress. Craig knew he'd been dismissed.

He rose to his feet and crossed to the bed. He bent over and touched his son's arm. "I love you, Ben. If you want to talk or anything..." His voice trailed off. "I'll always make time for you, son." His throat tightened and he walked out of the room.

He paused at the top of the stairs. He was doing a poor job as a father, and he had no one to blame but himself. When had he stopped being a friend as well as a parent? When had he first been afraid that they would want more than he had to give?

He couldn't point his finger to a particular day, or hour, but he knew it involved Krystal. She'd rattled his confidence and changed the shape of his world. He'd been stripped of his pride and left bleeding. The boys were the true casualties of that particular war.

He had to stop avoiding his kids, he told himself. It wasn't making anything better. It only accentuated the problem. As soon as this assignment was over he would—

The phone rang. He thought about getting it but knew Jill would pick it up. It was probably just the station asking him to come in earlier.

As he started down the stairs, he realized he didn't have to wait for the assignment to be over before making changes. He could start now with small things. He didn't want his kids becoming strangers.

When he walked into the kitchen, Jill was just hanging up the receiver. She scribbled something on a small pad of paper.

"Was that the station?" he asked.

She glanced up. Color stained her cheeks. "Um, not exactly." She looked at the floor, then at the note and the refrigerator, before settling her gaze on the center of his chest.

"Someone named Austin just called. He said to tell you that it's been so long since he's seen you that he's forgotten what you and the boys look like. Call him and set up a date for a barbecue or suffer the consequences."

Jill's blush deepened. Craig leaned against the doorframe and folded his arms over his chest. He fought back a smile. "What else did he say?"

"Well, he said that—" She cleared her throat. "He said if I'm the reason you've been laying low, then it's about time and I'm welcome too."

He had the fleeting thought that life would be pretty damn pleasant if Jill *was* the reason he hadn't spent time with his family. "What did you tell him?"

"That I'm just the new nanny. I tried to convince him I was old and matronly, but he won't believe me. Who is that guy?"

"A friend of the family, but we all think of him as a Haynes. Austin's got a research company. He does work with heat-resistant polymers and other substances. Very high-tech stuff. It's used in the space shuttle and for certain manufacturing processes."

"He didn't sound like a scientist."

"He doesn't look like one either," he said, remembering how all the women in Glenwood had sighed over his friend's good looks. He figured it was the earring that got to the women. Glenwood wasn't an earring sort of town.

She motioned to the full coffeepot on the counter. "I thought you might like some before you went back to the station."

"Sure. Thanks."

He walked to the table and pulled out one of the chairs. After turning it neatly, he sat, straddling it and resting his forearms on the back. She poured coffee into a mug and brought it over black.

He smiled his thanks. "Travis and Austin became friends first. Then he was just part of the family." He frowned, trying to remember all that had happened. "He was gone for a while. He stole a car and was sent to a juvenile facility. It ended up being the best thing for him. He met a man who taught him about chemistry and manufacturing. The old guy got him a scholarship, and Austin never looked back. His company has grown. It's privately owned." He grinned. "Just the five of us."

Jill took the seat opposite. "Five of you?"

"Austin, of course, and me and my three brothers."

She shook her head. "I'm confused. You guys are all partners?"

"Yes." He took a sip of coffee.

She brushed her bangs off her forehead and frowned. "If the company is doing well, why aren't you rich?"

"I can afford a full-time nanny, can't I?"

"How much is the company worth?"

He shrugged. "Millions."

"And you work as a cop?"

"I want to."

"But you don't have to?"

He thought about the last financial statement. "No, I don't have to." None of his brothers did. But money wasn't important. It never had been. They hadn't grown up lacking things; they'd grown up lacking love.

"You are too weird," Jill said, pushing to her feet. "You want some prune bread?"

"Sure. And why am I weird? Lots of people enjoy their work."

"I guess. Although when I was at the insurance company, if someone had offered me a large income, I think I would have quit that very day."

"You have to do something with your time. All of us work."

"Your brothers?" She sliced the rest of the loaf onto a plate and set it in front of him. Then she got a diet soda from the refrigerator and returned to her seat. "Maybe it's a faulty gene pool," she said. "You all have an unnatural desire to be employed."

"You could be right." He snagged a slice and took a bite. "I've thought about quitting, but I couldn't figure out what I'd do with myself. Besides, I like making a difference. Like on this case. If we can nail the bastards preying on the elderly, then a whole bunch of people will be saved a lot of heartache."

Her full lips curved up at the corners. "An honest-to-God hero. I thought you guys only existed in the movies."

Her praise made him uncomfortable. "I'm no hero. Just look at my kids."

"You mean Ben, don't you?"

He nodded and pushed away the plate. "I don't know where I went wrong with him. I guess I've been working too much. I don't know him anymore. We don't have anything to talk about."

"He's unhappy about his weight," Jill said.

"I know. Maybe I should hook him up with a counselor. Or one of those camps over the summer. But I hate to separate the boys. What do you think?"

"I understand your concerns. Has he been on a diet before?"

"No. We talked about it, but Mrs. Miller never thought there was a problem. She said he would outgrow it. But then she was a large woman herself. Since she left, no one has been around long enough to do anything."

"He needs to lose the weight, but if he's never been on a diet, then maybe we could try that before sending him away to a camp."

Craig liked the sound of the word "we" on her lips. It made him feel that he wasn't in this alone.

She waved her diet soda in the air. "After the divorce, I gained about fifteen pounds. It doesn't sound like much, but at five-one and three-quarters—"

He laughed. "Can't you just say five-two?"

She straightened in her chair. "Number one, we aren't all blessed by being tall, and number two, I'm not going to exaggerate. Five-one and three-quarters is a very nice height."

He was willing to admit it looked pretty fine on her. He held up his hands in a gesture of surrender. "You're right. Sorry for interrupting."

She sniffed, then continued. "On me, fifteen pounds is about two dress sizes. I had the body tone of a water balloon. Anyway, I took it off with a low-fat diet and exercise. Now I'm a walking fiend. Maybe we could try the same with Ben. I think the key is to not let him get hungry or feel deprived. I know kids need a certain amount of fat for growth and energy. Let me talk to Ben and do some research in the library. Maybe we can work out a program he can live with."

"Thanks," he said, knowing he owed her a lot more. "You didn't sign up for this when you agreed to look after my kids."

"Maybe not, but I'm having a good time. It's nice to think about someone other than myself."

He glanced at his watch. "I've got to go. Bingo gets out soon and I want to be there. Several of the accidents have occurred at this time of night and on the same street."

He rose to his feet and Jill did the same. She circled around the table and placed her hand on his forearm. The top of her head barely came to his shoulder, but her spine was pure steel, and her touch, while gentle, offered strength.

"You're doing a good thing," she said.

"At the expense of what? My kids?"

"They understand, and they're proud of you."

"It's not enough."

She gave him a half smile. "Maybe not, but it's a start."

Their gazes locked. The pure green of her irises reminded him of cat eyes. Her expression was just as enigmatic. He didn't know what she was thinking. With any luck, she couldn't read his mind, either. Because he wasn't busy being grateful for her advice, or planning low-fat meals for his kid. Instead he was wondering what her mouth would taste like against his and how she would feel in his arms. The memory of holding her on his lap was enough to fuel his already-active imagination. He wanted to bury himself inside her, touching her, kissing her until she was wild with passion, then drained by fulfillment.

His arousal made itself known against the fly of his uniform trousers. He ignored the throbbing.

"Thanks for talking with me tonight," he said. "And thanks for the advice." It had been a long time since he'd been able to talk with anyone.

"My pleasure." An emotion flickered in her cat eyes. He almost convinced himself she wanted him to kiss her, but he knew it was just wishful thinking.

He walked out of the room and toward the garage. He was a damn fool if he started projecting his desires onto Jill. She'd made it clear this was nothing but a temporary job for her, and he knew better than to get involved in something that wasn't a sure thing.

It was barely six when Jill knocked on Ben's door. She was a little nervous, not sure what her reception would be. Would he be mad that she was trying to help?

She opened the door and stepped into the dark room. The sun was just up and little light shone through the space between the shade and the edge of the window.

As her eyes adjusted to the darkness she could make out Ben sleeping on his side, facing the door. Lying down, tucked under the covers, he didn't seem as grown-up. There was a sweetness about him that made her heart ache with longing for a child of her own.

She sat on the edge of the mattress and shook his arm. "Ben, it's Jill."

"Huh?" He raised his head and blinked, then stared at the clock. A scowl pulled his eyebrows together. "It's an hour early. It's only six. Can't you tell time?"

So much for the warm welcome. "I'm going for a walk. I thought you might want to come with me."

He rolled away from her. "You thought wrong. I don't want to take a walk."

"I like to walk in the morning. It's good exercise and helps keep my weight down. But the best part is no one has to know. I'll be back before C.J. and Danny wake up."

She waited, counting her heartbeats. At ten, Ben turned toward her. Distrust and hope warred in his eyes. "Yeah?"

"Yeah." She stood up. "I'll wait for you downstairs. Put on something comfortable and athletic shoes."

Five minutes later, he met her by the front door. When they walked outside, she inhaled the sweet smell of morning. It was still early enough to need a jacket, even with the walking, but it was going to be another warm, perfect California spring day.

They walked in silence to the end of the block. Ben seemed to keep up with her easily, so she increased her pace. After another few minutes of quiet, she pointed out a budding flower. He didn't say anything. She tried to console herself with the fact that if he didn't talk, he couldn't be sarcastic.

A neighbor's dog trotted out to greet them. She

paused long enough to pat it. Ben scratched its ears, too, and when she glanced at him, she caught a faint smile. Maybe, she thought, casually crossing her fingers for luck. Just maybe this was going to work.

When they'd been walking for nearly twenty minutes, she said, "I think I'd like to make your lunch for a while. Can you bring food from home or would all your friends laugh at you?"

He shrugged. "About half the kids bring their lunches. It's not so bad. But in a bag, okay? The real nerds still use lunch boxes."

"No lunch boxes, I swear." She smiled. "I'll give you lots of food. You won't be hungry. You can eat it all or just eat some of it. If you don't like something I make, then tell me and I'll change it. All I ask in return is that you don't trade it for junk food. Do you drink milk at school?"

"Nah. It's not cold enough. There's a soda machine, or I get juice."

"Both of those are fine." She knew she was treading on delicate ground here. She didn't know Ben very well and he didn't trust her yet. If she said the wrong thing, he might never respond to her. "It's not about how much you eat, but what you eat. There's lots of fun things to have. Cookies, frozen yogurt. It won't be hard."

He didn't say anything. They turned around and started for the house.

"I want to help you, Ben," she said, not looking at him. "If you want me to. No one would have to know. It could be our secret."

Silence. Jill drew in a deep breath. She'd tried. The rest was up to him.

When they reached their house, she stopped by the

porch and stretched out her legs. Ben watched her for a moment, then did the same. He finished before her and pushed open the front door, then paused.

"Can you make my lunch today?" he asked, staring at his shoes.

Happiness filled her and she had to fight back a smile. "Sure. I'd be happy to."

"Thanks, Jill." He raced inside.

Jill turned her head toward the faint breeze rustling the leaves on the trees and told herself the burning in her eyes was just from the dryness of the wind.

"Come on, batter, batter, batter," Jill called and clapped her hands together. "Hit it clean over the house."

Danny glanced over his shoulder at her. "Ji-ill, it's just a plastic ball. It's not gonna go that far."

"How do you know until you try?"

He grinned, then hunched over the imaginary plate. Ben pitched perfectly. The ball came sailing straight and true. Danny struck with all his might, dropped the bat and started running.

Jill leaned back against the tree and watched the three boys at play. It had been a week since she'd arrived at the Haynes household. In some ways, it felt as if she'd always been here. They'd settled into a routine, and she was getting to know the boys.

She and Ben had walked together for the past four mornings. Slowly, he was opening up to her, telling her about school and his few friends. He was self-conscious about his appearance, but when he forgot about it, he was funny and bright and a pleasure to be with. So far, he'd taken the lunches she made and given her enough feedback on the food to convince her he was actually eating it. She'd made a few low-fat changes in the evening meals, so he didn't have to have a different menu. He followed her lead, taking more of what she took more of, less of the dishes she ignored.

She turned her attention to the youngest of the Haynes boys. Danny was a sweetheart. He gave everything a hundred percent and wore his heart on his sleeve. He would never be the athlete his brothers were, but it wasn't for lack of trying. Even as C.J. caught the ball and started toward their makeshift third base, Danny kept on running. It didn't matter that his brother was bigger or faster. Danny was the little engine that could. One day that trait would help make him successful.

Then there was C.J. Jill studied the middle of the three boys. Craig Junior had his father's good looks and smooth delivery. He had that innate ability to say the right thing at the right time. He had enough charm to be a gigolo in his next life, although she hoped he chose something more stable for this one.

All in all, she was pretty happy with how her job was going. It wasn't tough duty and she was well paid.

"It's C.J.'s turn to hit," Ben said.

"But I wanna try again," Danny whined.

"You got tagged out. It's not your turn."

"Yes, it is!" Danny stamped his foot.

"If you're gonna act like a baby, you can't play," Ben said.

C.J. strolled over to join his brothers, but he didn't take sides.

"I'm not a baby."

"Are too."

Danny dropped his bat and curled his hands into fists. "Am not. And you're just a fat old mobyhead."

C.J. started to laugh. Jill straightened up. Mobyhead?

"Boys," she started, but it was too late. Ben tore off his glove and dropped it on the ground.

"This is stupid," he said, and headed for the house.

"You come back here," Danny said. "You help me. Ben, you have to help me."

His big brother ignored him and kept on going.

Danny ran to Jill. Tears streamed down his cheeks. "He has to help me. I want to do better."

"Maybe you should have thought about that before you called him names."

"He called me names, too."

Danny had a point. "Okay, that was wrong. However, did you do anything to make him think you were acting like a baby?"

C.J. strolled over. "I don't mind missing my turn."

Danny sniffed. "I didn't mean to," he said softly. The sun caught his light brown hair and turned it the color of gold.

"I'm not the one you have to apologize to. And while we're on the subject, what's a mobyhead?"

Danny flushed, but C.J. laughed. "Danny doesn't want to say a bad word. You know."

She shook her head. She didn't know.

"Moby. Like that whale book."

"*Moby Dick?*" She frowned, then said, "Oh, I get it." She glared at Danny. "You were calling your brother a dickhead? Danny, I'm ashamed of you."

He dropped his chin to his chest and sniffed. "Sorry."

"You already said that. Once again, I'm not the

person you need to apologize to. But before you go in, I want to remind you, we do not use that kind of language."

"But he called me a baby."

"He's worked with you every single afternoon this week. He's pitched to you and has given you advice on how to get better. Did you ever thank him? Did you ever tell him you appreciated his efforts? No, you got mad and called him names."

By now Danny's tears were flowing fast and furious. He glared at her. "I hate you," he said and ran inside.

Jill sighed. So much for things going well. C.J. picked up the mitts, the bat and the ball. She glanced at him. "I believe it's now your turn to be mad at me."

"Nah. You're okay. For a girl."

They looked at each other and smiled. She rose to her feet and ruffled his hair. "You're not so bad yourself."

As they walked to the house, C.J. took hold of her hand. She was surprised, but didn't pull back. In that moment she realized she hadn't expected him to be the first one to steal her heart. But a piece had just been magically removed. How much more damage would this family do, before she had the chance to get away?

Chapter Seven

Everyone slept in on Saturday. Jill got up around seven, showered and put on jeans and a sweatshirt. She had to admit that this job was really easy to dress for. She sure didn't miss having to put on a suit and panty hose every day.

She made a detour on her way to the kitchen and peeked out the window. Craig's car was parked in front of the house. It was strange to never know if he was home or not. Worse, once she realized he was in the house—sleeping upstairs—her stomach gave a little flutter. She wondered what he slept in.... She pressed her palm to her belly and willed herself to stay calm. It didn't matter if he was home. It didn't matter if he wasn't. She wasn't interested. He was her employer, nothing else. She wasn't going to get involved.

And pigs landed regularly at the airport just outside town.

She turned around and headed for the kitchen, trying to justify her attraction to Craig. He was a handsome man. She hadn't been with a man in a couple of years. The last few months of her marriage had been during the custody trial for the girls and she and Aaron hadn't been intimate much. She hadn't dated at all since then, so she was simply reacting to the proximity of an available male. It would have been the same with anyone. This wasn't specifically about Craig.

As she collected the ingredients to make pancakes, she thought it was pretty stupid to lie to herself. After all, she knew the truth. She might not like it, but she knew it.

In the two weeks she'd been a member of the Haynes household, she'd had several late-night or early-morning talks with her employer. If he wasn't home for dinner, she left something out for him. Usually she heard him in the kitchen and came out to see how he was. At first she'd been a little self-conscious, but then she reminded herself that he'd already seen her in a skimpy robe that first day he showed up at Kim's house. So seeing her in a terry-cloth one that brushed the floor was hardly exciting.

In the silent hours of night, he talked about his work, and she brought him up-to-date on the children. They talked about who was angry with whom, who was doing homework and who had broken what. In the time since her divorce, she'd forgotten how volatile childish tempers could be. One minute there were screams of hatred and the next they were playing together. She figured as long as everyone got along in the end, she didn't mind.

She hadn't heard Craig come in the previous night. Idly, she wondered if he was home for the weekend.

He hadn't had a day off since she arrived two weeks ago. The boys told her that he usually worked regular hours, but this special assignment demanded more. They weren't sure what he was doing, but they knew it was something they could be proud of.

They worried about their dad, and he worried about them. She poured milk into the pancake batter and stirred it vigorously. Aaron had always been concerned with how things looked, while Craig worried about how things really were. Too bad she hadn't seen her ex was a jerk before she married him.

When the batter was finished, she rinsed off the first strawberries of the season, cut them up and put them in a bowl. Then she started coffee. When the pot was dripping steadily, she went upstairs to wake the boys.

C.J. was already sitting up and reading. He gave her a smile and said he would be right down.

Danny stirred sleepily. "What's for breakfast, Jill?" he asked.

She bent over and brushed his hair from his eyes. "Pancakes."

He smiled. "Good. I love pancakes. I can eat a hundred."

She bent over and kissed his cheek. "Then that's how many I'm going to make for you."

She stood up and moved into Ben's room. When she opened the door, he opened his eyes and glanced at her, then at the clock.

"It's late."

"I know. Breakfast is ready."

Dark eyes met hers. "What about our walk?"

"Everyone gets to take a day off. Instead of walking, you can play outside with your brothers today. I don't know if your dad is going to stay home or not, but maybe we can do something as a group. The zoo, or a park. Don't worry, I'll make sure you get exercise."

He didn't return her smile. Instead, his big dark eyes widened. He flushed slightly. "Thanks, Jill."

"You're welcome." Her throat was uncomfortably tight as she backed out of the room.

She paused by Craig's room but didn't knock. She wasn't sure what time he'd come home, and he probably needed his sleep. He'd been working impossible hours since she arrived and for who knew how long before that.

Involuntarily, she brushed her fingers against the smooth surface of the door. Images sprang into her mind. Images of what Craig might look like on the other side of this door. She didn't want to think about it, but she couldn't help herself. Was he lying there in a tangle of sheets, his long, lean, athletic body bare? She knew he was alone. Craig wasn't the type to bring a woman home. She wondered what he did for sex. Was there a discreet lady friend somewhere? Did he have a type, and if he did, what was it?

"None of my business," she said softly, and turned toward the stairs.

Ten minutes later she slipped the first four pancakes off the electric griddle and put them on a warming plate. Ten minutes after that, all three boys sat around the table drinking juice and laughing. Jill served them. Ben stared at the pancakes uncertainly.

She leaned over his shoulder and set down the bowl of berries. "Have all the fruit and syrup you want," she said quietly. "Stay away from the butter."

He gave her a grateful smile.

"What are we going to do today?" Danny asked. "I finished my homework yesterday."

"Me, too," C.J. said, then stuck a piece of pancake in his mouth. "Is Dad home?" he mumbled.

"Yes," she said. "Don't talk with your mouth full."

"Yes'm." He barely moved his lips as he spoke the word. She had to turn away to hide a grin.

"Do you think Daddy will stay with us today?" Danny asked.

"Nah, he's gonna be too busy," Ben answered for her.

Jill didn't like his answer, but she didn't have a better one. Craig hadn't told her his plans. Maybe she should tell him that his sons assumed he wouldn't have time for them.

She got up to pour herself more coffee. There was a creak on the stairs. She set the pot down, turned and was instantly pleased she wasn't holding anything as fragile as a glass coffeepot.

Craig walked into the kitchen. There was nothing extraordinary about the action. She'd seen him walk into the kitchen before. But she'd never seen him out of uniform, and, frankly, he took her breath away.

He was dressed simply. Bare feet, worn jeans, a sweatshirt. Thousands, maybe millions of men wore the same casual clothes on the weekend. But other men weren't Craig.

His dark hair was still damp from the shower and smoothed away from his face. One stubborn lock brushed against his forehead. His jaw was clean-shaven, his smile easy. The university logo on the sweatshirt had seen several dozen washings. The once dark blue fabric had faded. But it looked soft, and it highlighted the width of his shoulders. His jeans hung loosely on his legs, the denim lighter at the seams, knees and, intriguingly, at the crotch.

Nothing about his clothing was overtly erotic, yet she couldn't stop the ripple of need that coursed through her. Her heart pounded hard and loud in her chest and her palms were suddenly sweaty.

Their eyes met. She sent up a quick prayer that he couldn't read what she'd been thinking. It would be too humiliating.

"Morning," he said.

The three boys turned as one. "Dad!" They tumbled from their seats and into his arms. In the confusion of hugs and questions, Jill tried to draw in a steadying breath.

"How many pancakes would you like?" she asked, and was pleased when her voice sounded normal.

"A plateful. I'm starved. I didn't get dinner." He glanced at the table, then at her. "This looks great. Thanks, Jill."

He'd said her name a hundred times before, but this time was different. This time the sound skittered across her skin, making the hairs on the back of her neck stand up.

"My pleasure." She poured more batter on the griddle.

"Are you going to work today?" Danny asked as he stepped back and stared at his father.

Craig leaned over and ruffled his hair. "Nope. I'm off for the whole weekend."

"Wow! Can we practice baseball?"

"Sure. Whatever you want."

The three boys grabbed him again and held on tight.

Craig turned away from the table, dragging them along. C.J. laughed. Even Ben giggled.

"You boys going to let me go?" Craig asked.

"No!" they answered as one.

With that, Craig dropped to his knees, taking the boys with him. They swarmed over him, like bees on a flower. They were one mass of tickling, wrestling, hugging bodies.

"I've got you now."

"I'll get you back."

"Let's tickle Dad."

"Let's not."

Bits of conversation overlapped. Jill turned the pancakes and stared at the Haynes males enjoying themselves. She felt as if she were on the outside of the inner circle. The familiarity of the emotion startled her. In that moment, she realized she'd spent much of her marriage on the outside looking in. She'd fooled herself into believing that she belonged, but it wasn't true. It had never been true.

She set the cooked pancakes on the warming tray.

"You boys planning to finish your breakfast anytime soon?" she asked.

"No!" Danny said. He was tugging on his father's leg. Ben had wrestled one of Craig's arms to the ground and was trying to pin it there. C.J. lunged for her.

She tried to jump back, but she wasn't fast enough. He tugged on her leg. Her knee gave, and she started to fall. She didn't know what to brace herself on. She didn't want to hurt any of the boys.

Before she could figure out what to do, Craig twisted free and grabbed her. He spun her as she fell, so she landed across his lap. Her bottom connected with his rock-hard thighs.

She barely had time to absorb the feeling of his body so close to hers when Danny flung himself on top of them both. His bony legs splayed over her hips and he leaned down to press his nose against hers.

"I'm the winner," he said.

She smiled. "You are?"

"Yep."

Craig laughed. She felt the vibration of sound against her arm, which was pinned against his chest. C.J. came up behind her and started tickling her. She shrieked.

"Stop that," she demanded between gasps.

"She's real ticklish," C.J. crowed in delight.

Ben started to attack, too.

Jill tried to slip away, but she was trapped. Craig leaned over, trying to shield her with his body. As his weight shifted, they all tumbled together, a wild assortment of arms and tangled legs.

She laughed until her sides ached and she couldn't catch her breath. For that moment, she was a part of the family. She knew it was temporary, but she didn't care. The warmth and happiness thawed the ice around her soul.

"Okay, boys, get up," Craig said. "While we finish breakfast, we'll decide what we're going to do this weekend. But whatever it is, we're going to do it together."

"Everything?" Danny asked as he stood up. "Even go to the bathroom?"

"You are so weird," Ben said and lunged for his brother. Danny shrieked and took off around the table.

In a matter of seconds, all three of them were racing around the room.

Craig shook his head. "I think my brothers and I were worse. I don't know how my mother stood it."

"I'm sure she loved you all."

Jill stood up and brushed off her behind. Without thinking, she offered her hand to Craig. He took it and rose to his feet. Once there, he towered over her. Six feet of sexually enticing male.

"What do *you* want to do this weekend?" Craig asked her.

"I get a vote?"

"Sure, you're part of the family."

C.J. stopped running and leaned against her. "Let's go bike riding."

Danny flopped into his seat. His light brown hair fell into his eyes. "I wanna play baseball."

"I want to go to the movies," Ben said.

All four males stared at her. Jill was torn between wanting to belong and reminding them that she was just the temporary help. She would only be here for another three weeks. Not that she'd seen Craig interviewing anyone else for her job.

If she were smart, she would ask for the day off. Craig was home; he could handle the kids by himself. She opened her mouth to say just that.

"I'd like to not have to cook dinner tonight," she said, then wondered where that had come from.

"Done," Craig said, pulling out the chair at the head of the table. "Everyone gets his or her wish."

There was a collective cheer.

Jill walked to the counter and put four pancakes on a plate. If she'd known Craig was going to be granting wishes so easily, she might have asked for something more intriguing.

They stopped to rest in the park. Craig sat on the ground with his back against a tree, while Danny flopped next to him. Ben, C.J. and Jill sprawled across a picnic table, using the attached bench seats as footrests.

Overhead the sun was bright, and the temperature was just warm enough not to be cool. As his boys chattered, Craig tried to remember the last time he'd taken the day off and done nothing except have fun. Usually there were errands to run and the boys had activities. But today everyone seemed to be content to be together.

"We can take the short way home," he said, then stretched. "Of course the long way goes right by the ice-cream shop."

C.J. grinned down at him. "Gee, Dad, let's go the long way."

Jill leaned over and bumped C.J.'s shoulder. "And people say you're not too smart."

He laughed. "I'm very smart."

"So smart you've got Krissie Nelson doing your math homework for you. Don't think I haven't caught on."

C.J.'s eyes widened and he looked as startled as a mouse facing down a tiger. "How'd you know that?" he asked, then clamped his hand over his mouth.

Ben laughed. "You blew it, bozo. Now you're dead meat."

C.J. looked at Jill. "She just did it at recess a couple times. How'd you find out?"

Jill arched her eyebrows. "I know everything." She

touched his face. "You left your homework out on the kitchen table yesterday morning and Krissie had written a note on the paper. Cheating is stupid and you're not. Okay?"

C.J. flushed. "Yeah. Sorry." He glanced at his father. "Dad?"

Craig was torn between wanting to ground C.J. for the next fifteen years and being impressed with how Jill had handled the situation. He fought down the flicker of annoyance that she hadn't discussed it with him, then realized that in the past four days he'd only been home to sleep for a couple of hours.

"I expect better of you," he said quietly.

C.J. sucked in a breath as if he'd been mortally wounded. "Dad—" He broke off and stared at the trees for a moment. "I won't do it again."

Jill stood up and jumped to the ground. "Let's go get some ice cream," she said and headed for her bike. Everyone followed.

When C.J. walked by, Craig snagged his arm. Father and son looked at each other for a moment, then C.J. mumbled, "I'm sorry," and ducked into his embrace. Craig held him tightly for a moment.

"I know," he said and smoothed the boy's hair.

When he released him, C.J. smiled and reached for his bike. Order had been restored.

A bike path wound through the large park. Ben led the way. Craig glanced at Jill's bike. He'd borrowed it from a neighbor. She caught him staring.

"What's so interesting about my bike?" she asked.

"I didn't know the seat went down that far." It was as far down as it would go and she still had to stretch to reach the pedals.

"We aren't all descendants of Amazons," she said

tartly. "Besides, you're just jealous. Short people are superior and you tall people know it."

He laughed. "How do you figure?"

"We're ecologically superior. We take up less space, use less oxygen and don't need as much food or clothing. All that and we're just as smart and productive. There's really no reason for tall people to exist at all, but as a group, short people are very kind to those less fortunate souls." She smiled sweetly, then raised her chin, obviously proud of the way she talked herself out of that one.

This afternoon she wore a short-sleeved shirt tucked into stone-washed jeans. A baseball cap covered her bright red hair and sunglasses shielded her eyes.

"You don't expect anyone to believe that, do you?" Ben asked from the front of the group.

"Yes," she shot back. "You especially!"

He laughed.

Craig tried to remember the last time he'd been out like this with the boys. Recently there hadn't been a lot of fun in their lives. He had no one to blame but himself. He'd been afraid of his children and right now he couldn't figure out why.

Some of it, he admitted, was Krystal. She'd had the unique ability to make him feel inadequate. He should have recovered from her betrayals a long time ago. Maybe he had and just hadn't realized it. Maybe he was hiding behind her memory because it was easier than facing the real world.

They came out of the park at the west end. Across the street was the ice-cream store. They waited for the light, then rode across together. After leaving their bikes outside, they entered the small establishment.

There were tiny tables and chairs with round seats

pushed up against the plate glass window. In the center of the store was a long refrigerator case. C.J. and Danny raced toward it and pressed their faces close, as if they had to see the contents rather than read the labels.

"I want two scoops," Danny said.

"Me, too." C.J. licked his lips. "Rocky Road and something else."

"Peanut butter!"

"Gross," C.J. said good-naturedly.

Craig glanced over and saw Ben and Jill having a whispered conversation. She was pointing to the display of toppings. Ben listened intently, then nodded.

Craig strolled over to join them. "What are you going to have?" he asked Jill.

"Just some yogurt," she said. "Ice cream is too rich for me."

Ten minutes later they were all seated on the benches outside. Danny had settled on a single scoop of peanut butter. C.J. had two scoops of Rocky Road topped with hot fudge. Craig had chosen strawberry ice cream, plain, while Jill was eating yogurt out of a cone. Ben came out of the store last. He had a large dish of yogurt covered with fruit and multicolored sprinkles.

"What was the secret conference about?" Craig asked.

Jill glanced at him, then at the three boys sitting on the next bench. There was a steady flow of traffic in the middle of the afternoon, and the sound of the cars kept their conversation from carrying. Even so, she lowered her voice.

"Ben wanted to know what he should have. He's sort of on a diet." She looked at her cone, then at him.

While in the ice-cream shop she'd pulled off her sunglasses. Now he could see the bright green of her irises. "We've been walking every day." She laughed. "Actually, I've been walking. He's starting to run and jump and complain about how slow I am. He's taking a lunch to school and avoiding junk food. It's only been a week, but I can already see a difference."

Craig looked at his oldest, hoping she was right. Damn it, the boy deserved better than an unhappy childhood because of something as preventable as his weight. He knew it wasn't going to be an easy change, but it was possible.

"If nothing else, he seems happier," Craig said. "He's out bike riding with us. He never used to do that."

"I think he's afraid," she said. "Of being laughed at. Of being different. He wants to change but doesn't know how. He also doesn't want a fuss made." She smiled. "We have these very indirect conversations. I suppose at some point someone will have to discuss his weight with him, but so far, this plan seems to be working."

He reached out and touched her arm. "You've been good for all of us, Jill. I don't know how to thank you."

Something hot and smoky flared to life in her eyes. He told himself it was just a reflection of sunlight, but that didn't stop his sudden rush of desire. Then she blinked and her expression changed. For a moment, he thought she was going to remind him this was only temporary. He didn't want to hear that right now. He didn't want to do anything but sit here and eat his ice cream. He wanted to listen to the boys' chatter and feel that he was finally doing something right.

She gave him a quick smile. "You don't have to thank me," she said. "I'm having fun."

He leaned back on the bench and realized that for the first time in weeks, maybe months, the pain in his upper back and neck was gone. He shifted slightly, until their thighs brushed. Need spiraled up to his groin. The aching was a pleasant change from feeling nothing. He could want her without doing anything about the desire. He could admire her without making her a part of his life. He could like her and still be able to let her go.

At least that's what he was going to keep telling himself...for as long as it took, until the lie became truth.

Chapter Eight

Jill could hear the baseball announcer on the television. It was about three-thirty Sunday afternoon, but despite the perfect weather, all three boys were inside, watching the game.

She paused beside the sofa. "You guys okay?" she asked.

C.J. gave her a halfhearted smile. Danny shrugged. Ben didn't bother looking at her. Craig was at the far end of the sofa, sitting on the built-in recliner, reading the Sunday paper.

"Craig?"

He glanced up at her. "Yes?"

"Do you want some popcorn or something?"

His dark eyes gave nothing away. "Sure." He returned his attention to the article he was reading.

She stood in the center of the room not sure what was going on. Yesterday had been wonderful. The five of them had spent the day together. They'd worked with Danny, gone bike riding, to the movies, then out to dinner. Afterward, they'd played cards until an hour past the boys' bedtime, because they were having such a good time. Today she felt like an unwelcome intruder spying on a secret society meeting. Signals and messages were being passed around, but she didn't know what they were. Had she done something wrong? Was everyone mad at her?

Jill tried to remember if she'd said or done something offensive the previous day, or even that morning, but she couldn't think of anything. Everyone had been fine yesterday but moody this morning.

Craig stood up and dropped the newspaper on the floor. Before she could ask him what was wrong, he brushed past her and walked up the stairs. Ben also rose to his feet and headed for the kitchen. He opened the pantry and pulled out the bag of miniature candy bars she kept for Danny and C.J.'s lunches, grabbed a handful and returned to his seat. Not once did he look at her or acknowledge her presence in the room.

"Ben, can I fix you a snack?" she asked, bewildered by his behavior. He'd been doing so well. Why was he suddenly eating candy?

He glared at her. "You're not my mother, you're just the dumb nanny. You won't even be here much longer. Quit acting like you belong and leave me alone."

Jill felt as if she'd been slapped. She didn't know whether to reprimand him or hide out in her bedroom. She settled on stunned silence. The other two boys stared at the television as if their lives depended on the outcome of the game. Ben tore off the candy wrappers and devoured the treats, one after the other. When he was done, he got up and marched past her without saying a word.

Craig passed him on the way downstairs and entered the family room. Jill stared at him. He'd changed from jeans and a T-shirt into a dark suit and cream-colored shirt. His silk tie was dark blue with flecks of gold.

"You're going out," she said. Obviously.

Craig focused his attention on some point over her left shoulder. "I don't know when I'll be back."

"What about dinner?" she asked, feeling oddly betrayed by his behavior.

He hesitated. "I don't know when I'll be back," he repeated, and then he was gone.

What on earth was going on? Had everyone been given a script but her? She sat on the sofa and stared unseeingly at the television. What was it...all-males-act-like-a-jerk day? Yesterday they'd almost been a family and today she was the enemy. It wasn't fair.

Danny crawled next to her. His big eyes were filled with a questioning pain. She wanted to ask what the problem was but suddenly she didn't have the words. When he shimmied closer, she pulled him onto her lap and wrapped her arms around him. He huddled next to her like a hurt animal seeking warmth.

A few minutes later C.J. leaned against her. She settled one arm around his shoulders. Silently, they watched the rest of the game. She didn't ask what was wrong, and they didn't offer the information. When she mentioned dinner, both boys claimed not to be hungry. They went up to their rooms and closed the doors, shutting her out.

Jill approached Ben's door and tapped softly. There was no answer. She turned the handle and pushed it open. Ben was asleep on his bed. She moved closer. The light on the nightstand was on, illuminating his face. She saw the tracks of tears on his skin. Her heart tightened inside her chest. She didn't know why he was hurting so she couldn't fix it.

She sat on the side of the bed and stroked his arm. He woke gradually. When he saw her, he bit his lower lip.

"I'm sorry," he mumbled, and flung himself at her.

She embraced him, feeling the awkward bones and angles of his adolescent body. He cried as if he'd lost everything dear to him. She rocked him gently, murmuring words of comfort, then sat with him until he slept again.

It was nearly nine when she made her way downstairs. Most of the lights were off. She didn't bother checking for Craig's car, so she was surprised to see him sitting in the family room. He leaned back against the sofa, his eyes closed, a drink in one hand.

He'd taken off his suit jacket and his tie. His shirt was open at the neck and the sleeves were rolled up to his elbows. She was used to seeing him in his uniform, and yesterday she'd finally convinced her heart not to flutter at the sight of him in jeans. Now she had to adjust to a completely different Craig. The successful entrepreneur. The expensive cut and material of the suit reminded her that he'd made a fortune on investments and that they really had nothing in common.

"I see you found your way back," she said. "Is everything all right?"

"You probably think we're all behaving like jerks," he said, not answering the question.

"The thought crossed my mind."

"Krystal died a year ago today."

The simple sentence caused everything to click into place. Jill sank onto the sofa and released the breath she hadn't known she'd been holding. "I'm so sorry."

"No need to be," he said, not looking at her. "I don't give a damn. But it's hard on the boys."

It was hard on him, too. She could see it in the lines on his face and the way his fingers gripped the glass, but she didn't say that.

He leaned forward and pulled open a slim drawer in the front of the end table. Under some papers was a framed photograph. He handed it to her. Jill turned it toward the light and stared at the stunning woman who had once been Craig's wife.

The photograph was several years old. Craig looked younger and there wasn't any gray at his temples. He was wearing shorts and nothing else. The woman standing next to him on the beach was tall, slender and beautiful enough to be a fashion model. Dark eyes, dark hair and a smile that promised the world. She was laughing. Involuntarily, Jill found herself wanting to smile back.

Yet, as she looked closer, she saw something cruel in the expression on Krystal's face. The set of her mouth was selfish. She didn't look like the kind of woman who would be more interested in her children than herself.

"She's very beautiful," she said carefully, handing back the picture.

Craig studied it for a moment. "Being admired was Krystal's goal in life." He set the photograph face-down on the table.

"Did you go to visit her grave?" she asked.

He nodded. "It's been a year. I started out just going for a drive, but that's where I ended up." He took a sip of his drink. "I didn't feel anything different standing there. I guess I wanted to see if there were still any ghosts. Seems like the only ones left are the ones I carry with me."

It took her a moment to realize that the bitterness on her tongue came from envy. She was envious of a dead woman. Of the power she still had over her family and the way she still possessed Craig's mind.

None of this matters, she reminded herself. Craig wasn't her man, the boys weren't her children. She was here very temporarily. But telling herself the obvious did nothing about the emotion.

"This must be very difficult for you," she said. "A year isn't all that long. You need to give yourself time to move from loving to remembering."

He turned his head and stared at her. "I haven't loved Krystal in years. If ever." He raised his glass as if toasting the photograph. "One didn't *love* Krystal, one admired and adored her. She was more interested in how things looked rather than how they really were. A tough attitude to teach children, but by God, she tried her best." His gaze narrowed. "To you, my sweet wife. May you be in the hell you deserve."

He drained his glass with one long swallow, set it next to the picture and leaned against the sofa.

"I'm sorry," Jill whispered.

"Me, too. Every damn day. That's the irony of it. I was so determined not to be like my dad." His smile was bitter. "I wasn't. Not even for a moment. It was Krystal. She could have been his twin."

"I don't understand," Jill said, before she could stop herself. She wasn't sure she wanted to hear this, but she couldn't seem to force herself to leave. Part of it was that Craig was in pain and she was at her best when someone needed her. Part of it was the man himself. She wanted to know all about him, especially his past.

"The Haynes family curse," he said. "I have five uncles and not one of them has ever been faithful to a woman. My father believed if he slept in his bed at night, he could do what he wanted the rest of the time. I swore I wouldn't be like him. I was going to be different. I wanted a wife and kids, like the old man, but I was going to be there for them. I swore fidelity, to honor and love. What a joke."

His pain was a tangible beast in the room. She could hear it breathing, clawing at him, draining his life force. She wanted to go to him and comfort him, but he wasn't Danny or C.J. He was a man, and she didn't have the right.

"I can't see you acting dishonorably," she said quietly.

"Is it honorable to be a fool?" He didn't wait for an answer, but instead continued to speak. "She was a sable-haired beauty. Now I see I wasn't thinking with my head when I met her. I was taken in by the big eyes and ready smile. I thought she was sweet and innocent. I couldn't have been more wrong. I found out later that she screwed the chauffeur who drove her to the church. They got it on right there in the back seat of the limo. After the wedding she and I drove off in the same car. And I didn't know."

Jill didn't know what to say. It was all too much to take in. Was it possible that someone could behave that horribly? She remembered what Aaron had done to her and she knew it was.

"It took me years to figure out the truth," he said, rising to his feet and crossing to the small wet bar in the far corner. "Maybe I didn't want to know what was going on. The minute I admitted it to myself, I would have had to have thrown her out. I worried about the boys and what that would do to them. I wanted so much more for them."

He uncapped a bottle of Scotch and poured about an inch into his glass. "You want some?" he asked.

"No thanks."

He leaned against the bar and stared at the empty fireplace. "In the end, she left on her own. I didn't even have the balls to throw her out. Once she was gone, she never bothered with her children. She saw them occasionally, but it was just for a few minutes at a time." He took a drink of the Scotch. "I didn't know what was right. Should I have refused to let them see her at all? Were the short visits better than nothing? Did it all confuse them?" He shrugged. "I guess I'll never know."

Dark hair fell across his forehead. She wanted to go to him and brush it away. She wanted to hold him until the pain faded and he could forget. How could Krystal have behaved like that? Didn't she know how lucky she was to have Craig? If Jill had met a man like him she would have—

She slammed the door hard on that train of thought. It was dangerous and unproductive. Krystal or no Krystal, Craig was off-limits. Jill wasn't going to get involved. This was a part-time situation.

Craig downed the last of his drink and set the glass on the bar. He swore.

"Are you more angry with her or at yourself?" she asked.

He looked at her. "Both. I hate her for what she was, and I hate myself for being such a wimp. I should have thrown her out of our lives years ago. Except then—" He shook his head. "Hell. Relationships. Do any of them work out?"

She didn't have an answer for that. She wanted them to. She believed in love—for others, if not for herself. "Some people have happy marriages," she said at last.

"Yeah. My brother Travis and his wife. And Kyle has Sandy. Austin's happy with Rebecca and if he can do it…" He walked over to the sofa and sat down. He rested his elbows on his knees and laced his hands together. "I used to think it was a family curse, but now I think it might just be me."

"Do you date much?"

He looked at her and tried to smile. The corners of his mouth tilted up, but the smile never reached his eyes. He was a beautiful, wounded male. Her heart went out to him. She wanted to touch him…heal him. Instead, she kept herself firmly in her seat.

"I don't have a lot of time. Between the boys and work." He shrugged. "Besides, I don't want to introduce them to someone until I know there's a chance that the relationship might work out. I think it would confuse them more. Sometimes it's easier to just stay home. Do you?"

"Date?" Her laugh was genuine. "No. I'm not really the dating type. And since leaving San Clemente, I haven't run into a lot of single men."

"Why do people get married?" he asked.

"Because they're in love."

"Do you believe in love?"

"Of course. Don't you?"

He drew in a breath and let it out slowly. "I'm not so sure anymore. Nothing's for sure."

"There are no guarantees, if that's what you mean, but that's not an excuse to stop trying. Eventually, there's someone out there who believes the same way and wants the same things."

"Is that love?"

"It's a part of it."

"Did you love Aaron?"

"I—" She hesitated. "I thought I did. Looking back I see that I just wanted to belong to someone, to be a part of a family. I think maybe I took the easy way out. I should have asked questions, but I didn't want to know the truth."

"Like me," he said softly.

"Yes."

The single word hung in the air and she wondered what else she'd just agreed to. Her gaze riveted on the open V of his shirt and the few dark hairs she saw. Her fingers curled toward her palms as she thought about touching him there. What would it be like?

A flush climbed her cheeks, and she looked away. The clock came into view. "Oh, it's nearly eleven," she said, shocked at how quickly the time had gone by.

Craig stood up. "I've got to be in early tomorrow. I think we're getting close on this case. Mrs. Hart is wearing a wire. A car seems to be following her, but so far no one's made a move."

"I hope it works out," she said. Before she could stand on her own, he offered his hand. She rested her fingers on his and let him pull her to her feet.

Heat radiated from him. She wanted to warm herself against him until the ice around her heart thawed. She wanted to be held in his strong arms until her strength returned.

He released her hand and smiled at her. "I always forget you're so short."

"I am not. I'm perfectly proportioned."

His smile faded. The heat moved from his body to his eyes, where she saw *and* felt the flames.

"I couldn't agree more," he said and reached for her.

She went into his embrace because the act of refusing required more strength than she possessed. His large hands spanned her back, drawing her next to him. Her fingers brushed his chest. She felt the solid muscles ripple beneath her touch.

He loomed above her, tall, powerful, masculine. Her lips trembled slightly as she anticipated what his kiss was going to feel like.

But instead of kissing her, he chuckled. "This will never work," he said.

She stiffened, prepared to pull away. "I'm sure it wasn't my idea."

Rather than releasing her, he tugged her along until he reached the end of the sofa. There he sat on the arm and spread his legs. He settled her against the apex of his thighs. They were nearly at eye level.

"Much better," he said, then covered her mouth with his.

She didn't have time to resist or think or relax or question him about anything. One moment she was wondering if she'd been insulted, the next she was being consumed by fire.

The gentle brush of his lips belied the inherent strength of his passion. She could feel it vibrating through his skin, she could smell it in the scent of his body. Inside, her heart pounded frantically. Her blood rushed, making her ears ring and her hands tremble.

He held her at her waist, his fingers brushing near her spine, his thumbs resting on her belly. Their thighs touched but not intimately. She wasn't flush against his crotch, although the thought of being there made her woman's place flare with heat.

Her hands clung to his shoulders, holding on as if she was in danger of being swept away. Just from an innocent kiss.

That's all it was. Firm lips exploring hers. He murmured her name, then kissed her again, making no effort to deepen the caress. From top to bottom, corner to corner, he discovered her lips. Then, without warning, he stroked her with his tongue.

It was as if she'd been doused by a bucket of liquid desire. From the top of her head, down to her curling toes, need swept across her skin. Her breasts swelled until her bra became an uncomfortable confinement. Her nipples hardened, then ached. Her hips arched forward, finding nothing, and her panties dampened with a sudden rush of moisture as her body prepared itself for his wondrous assault.

She parted instantly for him, admitting him into her mouth. He touched her tongue delicately with his, as if asking permission to continue. Overwhelmed by unexpected need, she clamped her lips around him and sucked.

The results were instantaneous. The hands at her waist dropped to her behind and cupped the curves, hauling her hard against him. He shifted until she was flush against him, her hot, damp need resting against the hard ridge of his arousal.

Her breasts flattened against his chest. He tilted his head and stroked his tongue against hers. She clung to him, first holding on to his shoulders, then sliding her hands down his back. Sinewy muscles rippled as if her touch could bring this large man to his knees. She arched against him, wanting it to be true, wanting more.

In response, he slipped one hand between them. His long fingers brushed against her belly, then lower, teasing her through the layers of panties and jeans. His thumb found her point of desire and he pressed there, making her whimper.

He raised his head slightly and kissed her jaw, then lower, down her neck to the collar of her shirt.

"You're incredible," he murmured against her skin. "I want to take you right here."

His words thrilled her. The hoarseness of his voice and the way his hands shook left her weak with desire.

She wanted to make love more than she'd wanted anything, but… "Craig?"

"Yeah, I know." He moved his hands back to her waist, then set her away from him. Fire still burned in his eyes, but it had been banked.

His gaze met hers. "I'm not going to apologize because I'm not sorry that happened." His smile was sheepish. "I just want you to know I don't go around seducing the boys' nannies. You're the first woman—" He cleared his throat. "No one's made me feel like this since my divorce."

"Me, either," she said, and was shocked her voice was still so breathless. Every part of her hummed with desire. She wanted him more than she wanted to be sensible. Thank goodness one of them was thinking straight.

He shifted on the sofa arm and grimaced. "You didn't sign on for this. I guess I'm saying—"

She touched her fingers to his mouth. "I know what you're saying."

Actually she didn't, but she didn't want to hear any more. If he said that this was a mistake and would never be repeated, she would be crushed. If he said it was the start of something else, she would be terrified. Better to be confused.

He bent forward and kissed her forehead. "Thanks for understanding, Jill."

Understanding what? But she didn't ask. She just stood there in the family room, long after he'd disappeared upstairs. She listened to her blood race and felt the aching need in her body. Just a couple more weeks, she told herself. Then she could walk away without looking back.

Craig was back in uniform the next morning. He joined the boys for breakfast. That was unusual, but Jill tried not to let it get to her. She ignored the way the black shirt emphasized his strength and the firm line of his freshly shaved jaw. She didn't acknowledge the secret half smile he gave her as he said, "Good morning."

"Hey, Dad," C.J. said, and handed over a box of cereal.

The boys seemed to have recovered from yesterday's upset. Except Ben. When Jill went to put a load of laundry in the washer, he followed her.

She measured in the detergent, then tossed in the whites. Socks and underwear quickly filled the machine. She set it, but didn't pull out the knob to start the cycle.

"What's wrong?" she asked, her back to the boy.

She thought it would be easier for both of them to speak without actually looking at each other.

"Yesterday—"

"You've already apologized. Your dad told me about your mom. It's okay."

"I know. I just—" He moved closer. "I didn't want to eat that candy. I don't know why I did. I thought I was mad at you, and I wanted to hurt you."

She turned toward him. "Ben, that only hurts you."

He nodded, obviously miserable.

She held out her arms. He slammed against her, nearly knocking her off her feet. She leaned against the washer and absorbed his misery.

"It was just a mistake," she said as she smoothed his hair. "You'll do better today."

"But we didn't go for a walk."

"I didn't know if you'd want to."

He raised his head. Tears swam in his eyes. "I did."

"We'll go tomorrow. I promise."

He swiped at his face with the back of his hand. "Okay."

"Let's go get some breakfast."

He walked with her to the table. Craig glanced at her, but she smiled to tell him everything was fine.

"I thought I'd take you boys to school today."

"Cool," Danny said. "Dibs on front."

"It's my turn," C.J. said.

Danny stuck out his lower lip but didn't argue.

Jill started making Ben's lunch.

The conversation flowed behind her. She liked mornings with the boys. As long as they weren't fighting, they were great fun to be with. Craig's voice traveled across the kitchen and set her nerves to quivering. She worked quickly so she didn't have to think about what had happened—and not happened—between them last night.

"Jill, are you leaving soon?" Danny asked.

She looked at the boy. "What do you mean?"

"Yesterday Ben said you were gonna be going. Are you leaving us?"

All three boys stared accusingly at her.

"When I started, I told you I was just staying until spring break."

"But that was before," Ben said. "You can't go."

"Jill has her own life to think of," Craig said. "Leave her alone. Which reminds me. I've got to start interviewing nannies."

Another nanny? The thought should have thrilled her, but instead she felt vaguely unsettled. She wasn't ready to move on.

C.J. pushed his cereal bowl away. "It's too soon, Jill."

"Stay," Ben said.

"I have a job," she said. "My condo is only sublet until September. I really can't...." But she didn't know what she couldn't do.

"Then stay until then," C.J. said. "Until September. We can spend the summer together."

"We'll have the best time!" Danny promised. He scrunched up his nose. "Please?"

Her throat tightened, making it difficult to swallow. It wasn't supposed to be like this. She wasn't supposed to get involved.

She glanced at Craig. "I haven't set up any interviews," he said. "I'd love for you to stay. But it's your decision."

Staying was risky. Not just because Craig reduced

her to putty in his arms, but because of the boys. She was foolish to think she could hold her heart at bay.

September. That was over five months away. Five months was a long time. She could figure out what she wanted to do with her life. So far she hadn't given that a thought. Staying here would allow her to finish healing and then plan things out.

Could she take the chance? She stared at the three boys. Could she walk away from them now, when they were just figuring out how to live together?

"All right," she said. "I'll stay until September."

There was a collective cheer. C.J. and Danny raced over and hugged her. Craig stood up. "Thanks, Jill. I really appreciate this." He glanced at his children. "We'd better get going."

The boys started for the door. Ben came back and reached for the lunch sack she was holding out. He hesitated, then bent down and kissed her cheek.

"Way cool," he said.

She watched him walk away and knew she'd just given up another chunk of her heart. How long until Danny and Craig took the rest?

Chapter Nine

"You can't go on the teacups. You'll throw up," Ben said with the superiority of the older brother who has experienced life.

Danny's lower lip quivered. "I can too go on the ride, and I won't throw up. You're just a fat old mobyhead!"

Ben lunged for Danny. C.J. stuck out a foot and nearly tripped him. Danny started to cry.

"Boys, it looks to me as if everyone is a little tired," Jill said. "Maybe we should all go back to the room and take a nap."

"No way!" Ben said.

"Jill, come on, *I* wasn't doing anything wrong," C.J. told her.

"I don't want to take a nap." Danny wiped his face with the back of his hand.

Craig put his arm around her shoulders and grinned.

"I'd like to take this moment to remind you that I did offer you the week off. You're the one who got excited and declared that you hadn't been to Disneyland in years."

She laughed as she glanced up at him. "Everyone gets to make one mistake."

As he winked, her stomach tightened slightly and she had to fight to keep her toes from curling inside her athletic shoes. "Okay, here's how it goes. Ben, you and C.J. get one of the cups and your dad, Danny and I will take another." She glanced at the youngest Haynes. "Danny, if you throw up, I'm going to be very unhappy."

"I won't," he promised and leaned against her. The line moved forward as the brightly colored teacups the size of large dining-room tables twirled and spun on a rapidly spinning base.

She'd agreed to come with the boys and their father to Disneyland for the reason she'd told Craig. She *hadn't* been here in years. In addition, she was concerned about Ben. He'd been on his low-fat, more-exercise program for a month and was doing great. However, a week at an amusement park could be a lot of temptation for a twelve-year-old boy. The last reason, the one she admitted only to herself, and only in the privacy of her hotel room late at night when she couldn't sleep, was that she wanted to know what Craig was like when he wasn't so caught up in work.

It was a delicious form of torture. He was far too good-looking for a mere mortal man. Her heart was in a constant state of excitement; her palms sweated on an alarmingly regular basis. If she didn't know better, she would think she was coming down with some deadly tropical disease. But it wasn't anything that interesting. Only attraction to her boss. A condition so common, it was a cliché.

Not that anything had happened between them. There had been that one kiss, then nothing. It was as if by agreeing to stay with the boys through the end of summer, she'd reminded him of her position in his house. He hadn't made another move. No matter how often she'd silently willed him to.

The line moved forward again. The boys talked with one another. This was their second day at the park. They'd driven down in two easy days, stopping at several places along the way. They'd spent the night in a resort just north of Santa Barbara. For the first time, she'd seen proof of Craig's financial resources. He'd put himself and the boys up in a two-bedroom suite, complete with a stunning view of the mountains and a whirlpool bath that could float a battalion. Her room across the hall had been equally lovely, with a king-size bed, a sitting area and a pretty impressive tub of its own. She'd protested the expense, but Craig had just laughed.

Now they were staying at the Disneyland Hotel. The sleeping arrangements were repeated. She had a mini-suite across the hall. After a long day of rides and adventures, it was nice to stretch out in the quiet. Occasionally, she wished for something more—someone to turn to, someone to hold her. If she made the mistake of closing her eyes and visualizing herself with someone, he always looked exactly like Craig.

"We're next!" Ben shouted. The young man monitoring the ride motioned him to a cup on the far side. Ben and C.J. took off running.

"We're together," Craig said, pointing at Danny, then at her.

"Right over here, sir," the attendant said.

The three of them walked toward the cup. Danny danced around them. "Can we go really fast? Can we spin so fast we fly away? Can we spin faster than Ben and C.J.? You think I'm gonna throw up?"

Jill ruffled his hair. "Yes, we'll go fast, and, no, you're not going to throw up."

She slipped into the cup and sat. Danny was next to her, Craig across from her. The area was tight. Their knees bumped.

"What do we do?" Danny asked.

Craig placed the boy's hands on the plate-size disk sticking up from the center of the cup. "Once the ride starts, turn this as fast as you can. We'll spin around."

Danny bounced in his seat. "How do you know when the ride starts?"

Jill leaned close and grinned. "The floor starts moving."

"Really?"

Faint freckles stretched across his nose. She'd had the boys' hair cut before they left, so his bangs didn't fall all the way to his eyes. Like Craig and herself, he was dressed in jeans and a short-sleeved shirt. The Southern California spring weather was perfect. Clear skies, balmy days, cool nights. It was the stuff travel videos were made of.

Suddenly the cup began to move.

"Now!" Craig said and reached for the control in the center of the cup. Jill grabbed it, too. They turned together, pulling their teacup around.

Danny forgot to help. He was too busy staring at everything. He spotted his brothers and screamed with delight. "We're going faster!"

Ben and C.J. were hunched over, working frantically to turn their cup. Others around them swirled and spun until the area was a mass of wildly rotating teacups.

Jill laughed. She looked up and saw the beautiful merry-go-round spinning out of sight. She had a view of other rides and blurry people before her attention focused on Craig.

In an effort to keep the cup turning, they both spun the control. Their hands constantly brushed and overlapped. His skin was dry and warm, his fingers strong. Since arriving at the park, there had been a lot of touching. He often draped his arm around her while they were standing in line for rides. She'd held hands with him as they'd made their way through the crowd after the parade the previous night. Bodies had brushed on various rides.

If she was foolish, she would allow herself to believe this was all real. She might even start to picture herself staying in Craig's home. But that wasn't going to happen. This wasn't her family, he wasn't her man. She was still on the outside, looking in.

The ride slowed. When it stopped, Danny scrambled out and raced to his brothers. "I didn't throw up once, and we went faster than you."

"Brat," Ben said good-naturedly and spun Danny around. The boy shrieked with laughter.

Craig glanced at his watch. "I'm starving. Where should we go for lunch? I'd say fast food, but I don't want to do that to Ben." He stared at his oldest. "I can't believe the change in him. It's only been a month, but he looks like a different kid."

Jill followed his gaze. The weight was falling off the boy. Between the low-fat food and his increased activities, he was becoming a new person.

"I know what you mean," she said. "All his clothes were hanging on him. We had to buy new jeans for this trip."

"It's not just how he looks. He seems to be enjoying life more. He's always running and jumping, and he's a hell of a lot more fun to be around. He looks happy."

"Yeah." She smiled. "A few more pounds, and he'll be nearly as good-looking as his father."

The words came out of her mouth without warning. She wanted to call them back, but it was too late. They hung there between them, loud and obvious.

Jill clamped her hand over her mouth and blushed. She could feel the heat climbing her cheeks to her hairline.

She risked glancing at Craig. He raised his eyebrows. "What I meant," she said, then cleared her throat. "That is—"

He silenced her with a quick shake of his head. "I don't want to hear what you meant, lady. I like what you said just fine."

"I bet," she grumbled.

"For what it's worth, you're not half-bad yourself."

"Gee, thanks. Not half-bad. I live for compliments like that."

He smiled at her, but the fire in his eyes spoke of something else. Something tempting and potentially dangerous. She didn't dare indulge, but if he asked, it was going to be hard to say no.

She searched her mind for a safe topic that would change the subject. "C.J. looks a lot like you, too," she said brightly. "Only Danny is different. He must take after his mother."

Instead of answering, Craig called for the boys, then

returned his attention to her. "Let's head back to the hotel," he said. "We can use the rest, and there will be more choices, food-wise."

"Good idea." She glanced at him out of the corner of her eye. If she wasn't mistaken, she'd upset Craig. But how? By saying Danny looked like his mother? She squeezed her eyes shut and fought back a groan. After all Craig had told her about Krystal, it wasn't surprising that he didn't want to be reminded of her. Dumb, Bradford, really dumb.

She touched his arm. "Sorry," she said softly.

He stared at her for a moment, then dropped his arm around her shoulders and pulled her close. "Don't apologize," he said, brushing his lips against the top of her head. "You didn't do anything wrong. Let's go eat."

They headed for the monorail that would take them back to the hotel. Craig kept his arm around her shoulders, although Danny ducked between them. C.J. took his father's other hand, and Ben surprised her by grabbing her arm and hanging on. It was a perfect moment and she wanted it to last forever.

"More wine?" Craig asked, holding up the bottle.

Jill glanced at him, then shyly averted her eyes. "Sure," she said, holding out her glass.

He poured the pale liquid, then set the bottle back into the portable ice bucket next to the table. Candlelight flickered from all the tables. In the corner, a small four-piece combo provided soft music, and several couples filled the small square of dance floor next to them.

He drew in a deep breath and raised his glass. "To the peace and quiet."

She smiled. "Without the boys around, I'm not sure I'll know what to do with myself."

He wanted to tell her he would think of something. Just staring at her brought several suggestions to mind. But he didn't voice them. They hadn't even had the salad yet. However, the lack of food didn't keep him from wanting her.

Women's ability to transform themselves had always amazed him, and Jill was no exception. This afternoon she'd been funny and charming in jeans and a white shirt that shouldn't have been sexy but was. She'd worn athletic shoes and a Goofy hat, complete with floppy ears. She'd eaten cotton candy with Ben, ridden the scariest rides without flinching and had generally been one of the guys.

Tonight, just a couple of hours later, she was every man's fantasy. Her hair looked casually tousled, with a few wisps falling on her forehead. Makeup deepened her green irises until they glowed like emeralds. She wore a dress that matched her eyes. The silky green fabric clung to her curves in a way that made his mouth water. The deep scoop neck gave him a glimpse of creamy breasts. Except for a delicate gold chain around her wrist, her arms were bare. She swayed in time with the music and he was mesmerized.

If only she wasn't so damn small. As he studied her, he couldn't help but picture her naked...in bed...wanting him. But that's as far as his imagination went. Would he hurt her? If he forgot himself in the heat of the moment, could his weight crush her? He'd had his share of lovers when he'd been in college, and they'd all been tall women, with long legs and torsos. Feminine, but not fragile. And *fragile* was the word he used when he thought of Jill.

It's not going to be a problem because you're not going to do anything, he reminded himself. He was taking her out for a nice dinner to thank her for all she'd done on this trip. Also, because he liked being alone with her. But it wasn't a romantic rendezvous, no matter how much he wanted it to be.

She took a sip of wine and sighed.

"What's wrong?" he asked.

"I'm just worried about the boys. Do you think they're all right?"

He laughed. "They're in a huge suite with unlimited junk food, cable TV and a baby-sitter who was pretty enough to play Cinderella in the parade. I think they're really happy."

"Well, if you put it like that." She glanced up at him. "I'm having a wonderful time, Craig. Thanks for inviting me."

"Thank you for coming with us. It wasn't part of your job description."

"I know, but what would I have done if I'd stayed behind? With you and the boys gone, I would have had too much time on my hands."

The waiter approached and set their salads in front of them. Craig thanked him and picked up his fork. "So what do you think of the Magic Kingdom?"

"It's wonderful. No matter how old I get, I always have a wonderful time at Disneyland."

"Good. I thought we'd spend most of tomorrow on Tom Sawyer's Island."

"Do I get to be an Indian?" she asked, her eyes glowing with amusement.

Heat seared through him, sparking an arousal that threatened his composure. "You get to be anything you want."

They ate in silence for a few minutes. The quiet wasn't uncomfortable. In addition to finding her damned attractive, Craig thought Jill was easy to be around. She didn't expect a lot of chatter or mind if the conversation strayed from her interests. In fact, he thought, frowning, she rarely talked about herself. He didn't know very much about her at all.

"I never thought to ask," he said. "Is being here bringing up memories of your stepchildren?"

She glanced up, obviously startled. "No. I never thought about it. I'm sure Aaron and I brought the girls here, but I don't remember much about our visit. I guess it wasn't very memorable."

"He has two girls?"

She nodded.

"Are they really different from boys?"

She grinned. "Let's put it this way. Patti and Heather never had a farting contest in the car, or anywhere else for that matter."

The waiter returned and cleared their plates. The combo started another song—a slow and sultry number that made him long to be close to her.

"Dance?" he asked, rising to his feet and holding out his hand.

She hesitated. "I'm not very good."

"Neither am I."

She took his hand and allowed him to lead her to the tiny floor. Several other couples were already there, swaying to the music. There wasn't room to do anything fancy, and he was grateful. He just wanted to hold Jill in his arms and torture himself into mindlessness.

She was wearing high heels and her head nearly cleared his shoulders. He placed one hand on the small of her back and linked his other with hers. Three inches separated them. He waited until they'd found their rhythm together before drawing her closer.

He'd thought she might resist the contact, but she flowed against him like water over stone, molding herself to his body. Her curves teased him. Through his suit jacket and shirt, he felt the soft imprint of her breasts. Her breath heated his skin and her legs brushed against his.

They took small steps, circling with the other dancers, not talking but absorbing the sounds and sensations. Without thinking, he released her fingers and pressed both his hands against her back. She was fine-boned and all woman. Need rocketed through him. She fanned the desire when she slipped her hands under his jacket and hugged his waist.

Their breathing became synchronized, their steps, smaller. With the slightest hint from her, he would have carried her back to her hotel room and made love with her until they were both too exhausted to do more than cling to each other. But she didn't hint and he didn't offer. So when the song ended, they parted, clapping politely, and he led her toward their table.

They passed an elderly couple. The woman smiled at him. "You and your wife are very lovely together. Are you celebrating an anniversary?"

"No," he said, thinking it would be too much trouble to correct their false impression.

She winked. "Maybe not tonight, but my guess is you'll be celebrating many, many more."

"Thank you." He nodded and placed his hand on Jill's back. She moved forward, then slipped into her chair before he could pull it out for her.

She was quiet for the rest of the meal. She didn't

meet his gaze, and when the main course came, she only ate a small amount.

"Did you like your dinner?" he asked when the waiter took away her nearly full plate.

"It was delicious. I just wasn't hungry."

"Why?"

She glanced around. "Can we leave, please?"

"Sure." He signaled for the check.

In a matter of moments, he'd charged the meal to the room and followed her outside. A dull ache began at the base of his neck and worked its way down to his shoulder blades.

"Jill, what's wrong?" he asked.

There were several couples standing outside the restaurant. She shook her head and started walking. Just past the dancing fountains was a small wooden bench, partially hidden by the lush foliage. She sank down onto the seat.

"Jill?"

She stared up at him, her eyes twin pools of confusion. Without thinking, he settled next to her, gathered her in his arms and kissed her.

Her mouth was as soft and sweet as he remembered. Her lips parted instantly and he touched the delicate surface of her tongue. She responded by clinging to him. Their breathing increased. The steady throbbing between his legs quickened to an unbearable cadence of pulsing pressure.

He moved his hands over her back, tracing a line from her spine to her derriere, then cupping her hips. Before he moved higher and touched her breasts, she broke away.

"Stop," she said hoarsely. "You must stop."

"Why?"

Her laughter had a sharp edge. "Because I'm not doing this again."

"What are you talking about?"

She moved back on the bench until they weren't touching at all. Her face was in shadows; only her eyes were lit by the lights along the path in front of them. She rested her hands on her lap. She seemed calm, even relaxed. Only her fingers betrayed her as they twisted together.

"This isn't right. At least it's not right for me." She cleared her throat. "I can't do this again."

"Do what?"

"Be used. All my life men have used me."

He stiffened. He wanted to protest that he hadn't used her, but sensed this wasn't really about him. "What do you mean?"

"Men have used me to get what they want. They've never cared about me. My father used me to upset my mother, before and after the divorce. My stepfather pretended to be my friend in front of other people, but when we were alone, he told me I was stupid and ugly and that he didn't like me at all."

"Bastard," Craig growled, wishing he could find the man and beat him into a whining, bleeding pulp.

"Then Aaron used me in the biggest way possible. We had mutual friends, and he knew that my goal in life was to be a part of a family. When we started dating, he used that against me. He talked about the girls and how much they needed a mother in their lives. I was too ignorant to realize they already had one. I bought his story, married him, moved in and proceeded to support the entire family."

She closed her eyes and drew in a deep breath. "After a couple of years I wanted a baby of my own.

Aaron was against the idea. He already had two children, he didn't want any more.''

"I'm sorry," he said softly. Bitterness filled his mouth. All three of his boys had been accidents. Krystal hadn't wanted children, either. Aaron was a complete jerk if he didn't know what a treasure he'd had in Jill.

"I kept after him about a baby, and he finally agreed. We tried for six months, but nothing happened." She looked at him. Her mouth trembled, but she spoke clearly. "I wanted to go to a doctor, but he said we should keep trying. Then his ex-wife sued for custody of the girls."

"You don't have to tell me this," he said.

"Yes, I do. I want you to know why I feel the way I do." She shifted on the seat, turning toward him. "Once the court proceedings started, we both agreed it would be silly for me to get pregnant now. I went back on the Pill. When we lost the custody battle, Aaron was furious. I tried to comfort him."

Her hands twisted together frantically. He leaned forward and covered her fingers with his. She clutched his hand as if it were a lifeline. Her dark gaze locked on his. His heart ached for her. No one should have to suffer this much for anyone, least of all a creep like Aaron.

"We were still in the courtroom," she continued. "His ex-wife was laughing and hugging the girls. I tried to hold him, but he pushed me away. I remember crying. I was devastated. I told Aaron we could still have a baby of our o-own." Her voice cracked.

"She looked at me, then—Aaron's ex-wife. She stared at me with pity and called me a fool. There in front of the judge and everyone, she told me that

Aaron had had a vasectomy years ago. Right after Heather was born. So unless he'd had it reversed, there wasn't going to be another baby."

Craig swore loudly. The urge to violence nearly overwhelmed him. That piece of— He swore again. Jill didn't seem to hear him. She kept on talking.

"Aaron just looked away. He didn't say a word. When I asked him if it was true, he just shrugged, like it didn't matter. The girls ignored me, too. As if I'd never existed for them. All those years had meant nothing. That week Aaron told me he would have his attorney draw up the divorce papers."

She started to shake. Craig didn't know whether to pull her close or leave her alone. She settled the matter by releasing her hands and folding her arms over her chest.

"I never saw him again. I never spoke to him. I don't know if I would have wanted to save the marriage or not, but I didn't get the chance to decide. I gave him and his daughters everything I had, and they never gave anything back. I suppose I'm a fool for taking it all those years. But I just wanted to belong. For once in my life, I wanted to be a part of a family."

Her story stunned him. It was too much to absorb. He knew there were bastards in the world; his father was one of the biggest. How had Jill hooked up with so many? She deserved more.

"Jill, I'm not Aaron."

"I know, but even if you were, it doesn't matter. I'm not going to be used again. I'm not going to be taken advantage of just because I'm convenient. I'm here to look after your children, and that's all I want to do. I can't afford to get involved with you. It's too much like what just happened to me. It would be too easy to fall for you. I don't want to get hurt again.''

He wanted to protest. It wouldn't have to be like that. He and Jill had a powerful attraction between them. Maybe—

Maybe what? He, of all people, should understand her concerns. He was a little gun-shy himself. He was only interested in a sure thing and life didn't come with guarantees. Was he willing to promise her exactly what she needed? He already knew the answer to that. They were both too wounded for a relationship between them to work.

''You're right,'' he said. ''I'm sorry.''

''Don't apologize. This was all pretty wonderful. I'm not ungrateful or angry. I just finally figured this out, and I wanted to be honest with you.'' Her smile trembled a little at the corners, but he wasn't going to comment on the fact.

''I appreciate that,'' he said.

He wanted more, though. He wanted it all. Damn the consequences, there was something about Jill that appealed to him. But he couldn't force it. Besides, he was forgetting who was important here. It wasn't him, it was the boys. They'd been through so much. They deserved better. Right now, Jill was the best part of their lives. They didn't need him messing that up for them.

''I still want to apologize,'' he told her. ''Frankly, I want to find Aaron and your stepfather and beat them both up.''

''Thank you for that. I wouldn't mind watching.''

They stared at each other. He wondered if she felt as awkward as he did. Even if he couldn't have a relationship with her, he wanted her to stay for the boys. How did he tell her that?

"Friends?" he said at last, holding out his hand.

She hesitated for a moment, then took it in hers. "Friends," she agreed.

Friends, he thought. Why did the word sound so empty?

Chapter Ten

On the way to Disneyland, the miles had seemed to fly by, but on the way home, they crawled. Jill caught herself staring at the speedometer for the third time that hour. The needle was still set at sixty-five. She supposed they must really be going that fast, but it didn't feel like it. She just wanted to get back to the house so she could escape to her room.

The radio played softly but the sad country music didn't do anything to improve her mood. There wasn't even arguing from the boys to distract her. They'd gotten an early start so they could make the drive back in one day. The boys were dozing in the back seat. Danny had barely stirred enough to eat breakfast.

Jill stared out the side window and fought down a sigh. She wanted to offer to drive, but she and Craig had traded off less than a half hour ago. She closed her eyes and willed herself to be anywhere but here.

It was her own fault. She knew better, but she'd done it anyway. She'd withdrawn from Craig and the boys, and now they all knew something was wrong.

She'd caught Craig studying her when he thought she didn't see. The boys had all stared at her with their soulful eyes full of pain and questions. She'd thought about explaining, but what was there to say?

She should never have let Craig take her to dinner. She should never have agreed to that dance, or responded to his kiss. She should never have told him the truth.

Every time she thought about what she'd said, embarrassment flooded her body. Her face got hot, her palms dampened, and she felt like the world's biggest fool. How could she have let Aaron treat her like that? How could she have willingly admitted it to Craig? Thinking about the past didn't make her angry, it made her feel worthless.

It had been the night, she told herself. When he'd kissed her, she'd wanted him so much. She'd wanted it to be real. All of it. Not just his affection, but the boys' feelings, too. She liked taking care of them. She liked being the one they confessed their secrets to, the one they ran to when they were hurt. She even liked that they felt secure enough to get mad at her. After years of being lonely, her heart responded to the love between the boys and their father. She wanted a piece of that for herself. Was that so wrong?

She knew the answer. Of course it wasn't wrong. It also wasn't real. She was just the hired help. Craig was doing exactly what Aaron did, only Craig was being honest. He paid her for her services, gave her a title and time off if she wanted it. She'd known the risks when she'd taken the job. She shifted on her seat.

That wasn't completely true. There was one risk she hadn't considered.

Craig.

What was she going to do about him? When he held her in his arms, she wanted to surrender all to him. She wanted to be with him, touch him, feel him against her, in her. He made her feel safe and cared for. He was the kind of man a woman dreamed about marrying. He was a fantasy come to life. Good-looking, honest, intelligent, funny, loving and sexy enough to melt pure steel, let alone her lonely woman's heart.

That made it worse—being so close to what she could never have. She still believed in love, just not for herself. Somehow, she always came out on the losing end of her romantic relationships.

For some people, things just sort of worked out. Kim had found Brian. They were deeply in love. It hadn't worked out for Craig, she reminded herself. Krystal had nearly destroyed him. They were two wounded souls. What did that mean? Should they try to find comfort together, or should they run like hell before they got hurt again?

Her first instinct was to run. She wanted to open the car door, jump out and run as fast and as far away as possible. She glanced over her shoulder at the boys. They were all dozing. She couldn't abandon them unexpectedly. They'd already been through so much. She would have to find her way to make peace with her feelings about Craig. How hard could that be? After her confession a few days ago, she'd made it clear she wasn't interested in a personal relationship. Craig was too much of a gentleman not to honor her request.

The realization should have made her happy. It

should have made her able to relax. It didn't. Instead, she found herself counting the mile markers and wishing she had the courage to try again.

They returned home to a musty house and a flashing answering machine. Jill instructed the boys to carry their bags upstairs. Ben and C.J. hauled their stuff up immediately. Danny sat at the bottom of the stairs and stared listlessly at her.

"I don't feel good," he said.

Jill frowned. He'd been quiet the whole way home. Too quiet. She touched his face. It was warm. "You might have a fever. Where's the thermometer?"

He shrugged. His light brown hair stuck to his forehead in sweaty patches.

Craig brought in another load of luggage. He paused. "What's the problem?"

"I think Danny's sick," she said.

He came over and looked at his son. "He's got a fever. How long have you felt bad?" he asked.

Danny shrugged again. "Last night, maybe."

Craig took the stairs two at a time. He returned with a thermometer, which he rinsed at the sink before sticking it into Danny's mouth. The boy obligingly clamped his tongue over it and leaned against the railing.

C.J. came downstairs and looked at him. "What's wrong with him?"

"I'm not sure," Jill said, bending over and touching Danny's face again. "Maybe it's just from the trip."

C.J. walked into the family room and stopped in front of the answering machine. "There's a message, Dad."

"Go ahead and play it."

Jill expected it to be someone from the station, but instead a woman identified herself as a teacher from Danny's school. "Mr. Haynes, one of Danny's classmates has come down with chicken pox. The incubation on that is about fourteen to twenty-one days, so he will probably get sick sometime during the spring break. I'm sorry to be the bearer of such bad news." There was a pause and the sound of ruffling papers. The voice continued.

"I see here you have two other boys. If they haven't been exposed, you're going to have to expect the worst. Call me if you need any more information." She left her number, then hung up.

Jill stared at Craig. "Tell me C.J. and Ben have already been exposed."

"They haven't."

She looked down at Danny. Chicken pox times three. The teacher had been right about expecting the worst. She removed the thermometer and studied it. "Just a hair over a hundred. You have a fever, my man. Can you make it up the stairs to your bed?"

Before he could answer, Craig picked him up and carried him. Jill glanced at C.J. "Enjoy your last few days of health."

"I won't get 'em," he said confidently.

"Uh-huh. No one asks you your opinion. This stuff is very contagious. Look at it this way. You'll miss school, lay around and watch TV all day, and I'll try to tempt you to eat with pudding and ice cream."

C.J. grinned. "All right!"

"We'll see how you like it when it happens," she said, and moved into the kitchen. She put a call into the children's pediatrician to find out if there was anything she needed to be aware of, then sat at the table and wrote out a shopping list. She was preparing for a siege. About the time Danny was feeling better, C.J. and Ben would start getting sick. She figured it was going to be about three weeks of hell.

Craig came into the kitchen. "I put Danny in bed. He says he just wants to sleep."

She looked up from her list. "It's probably the best thing for him. I've put a call in to the doctor. There's some children's medication on the top shelf. That should help his fever."

"I'll take it up to him." He ran his hand through his hair. "They've been inoculated against just about everything else. I'm sorry this had to happen while you were here. I can see if the station will let me extend my vacation."

She shook her head. "Don't be silly. You had enough trouble getting the days off to take the boys to Disneyland. If you hadn't arranged it months ago, you couldn't have done it at all. We'll be fine. Danny will be up and feeling better before C.J. or Ben gets it. By then, I'll be an expert."

"And exhausted."

"Maybe, but I can always sleep later." She gave him a half smile. "Can you take care of things here while I run to the grocery store? I want to lay in supplies."

"Sure." He followed her out to the garage. "The timing is really bad on this."

"There's no good time for kids to be sick."

"I know, but—"

She paused and glanced at him. Despite the long drive, the lines of weariness by his eyes and the stubble darkening his jaw, he was still good-looking enough to make her heart pound as if she'd just endured an advanced step-aerobics class. Worse, she knew what he was thinking.

"I'm not leaving," she said softly.

He shoved his hands in his front jeans pockets. "You've thought about it."

He had her there. "Yes, it crossed my mind. But I agreed to take this job, and I don't turn my back on my responsibilities."

"I don't want you to stay if you don't want to be here."

"I know." She stared at the concrete floor of the garage, then glanced back at him. "It's not that simple, Craig. You know that. Part of me is scared. I like the boys, being with them, with you. Being part of this family. It's all I've ever wanted. But it's temporary. I can't let myself get emotionally involved."

"If it's that complicated, maybe you should leave. I don't want you getting hurt."

His concern was bittersweet. There was a part of her that appreciated his willingness to sacrifice for her, while the rest of her was wounded that he would consider letting her go without a fight. Her conflict only proved how terribly confused she was by the situation.

"I think I need to stay," she said. "Not just because I gave my word, but because I have something to prove to myself. I need to be able to do this and then walk away."

"What if we don't want you to go?"

We. What we? The boys? Him and the boys? Or just him?

"I don't have an answer for that," she said. "I'm sorry about what happened when we were away. I shouldn't have sent out such mixed signals."

"It's my fault," he said quickly.

"Stop being such a nice guy. It wasn't your fault. Or maybe we're equally to blame. I knew going to dinner was a mistake, but I wanted to do it anyway be-cause—" She ducked her head, fighting a heat flaring on her cheeks.

"Because there's an obvious attraction between us." His voice was low and husky.

"Something like that."

"Exactly like that." He moved closer and touched his forefinger to her chin, forcing her to look at him. His dark eyes blazed with fire again. The heat warmed her from the inside out. Her breasts swelled, and her thighs began to tremble.

"What makes it scary for both of us is that it's more than just sexual attraction," he said. "We happen to like each other, too."

The blush on her cheeks deepened. "How can you even talk about it?"

"How can we not? Silence won't make it go away. If I can't trust you with this conversation, Jill, what's the point of having the feelings?"

He terrified her. The urge to run was stronger than any passionate fire. She wanted to bolt for freedom and safety. Craig was everything she'd ever wanted in a man. He was honest enough to make her squirm.

He brushed his thumb across her mouth. She wanted to taste his skin. She wanted to pull him close and kiss him. She needed to get away.

"Let it go," he said. "Stop thinking about it. We're both carrying around a lot of misery from our pasts. We don't have to make any decisions today."

That sounded simple enough, but how was she supposed to shut down her brain?

"I have to get to the grocery store," she said. "And you should check on Danny."

This time she gave in to the urge to run. She half jogged to the car, then backed out of the driveway quickly. Stop thinking about it, she thought, grimacing. Yeah, right. How was she supposed to do that?

Two weeks and six days later Jill had her answer. Exhaustion. A person could forget anything if she was exhausted enough. She sank into the kitchen chair and listened to the blissful silence. Danny and Ben were at school and C.J. was upstairs, playing video games and listening to his radio.

She'd barely finished nursing Danny through the fever and itchy rash when Ben had come down with chicken pox. Two days later, C.J. had a fever and the first hint of red on his back. She'd played board games, rented videos, made enough Jell-O and pudding to float a small armada. She'd tempted their appetites with homemade bread, an assortment of soups, rice pudding and Popsicles. She'd forced liquids down their throats, held them when they cried, was patient when they whined and generally used up every single bit of strength she had.

C.J. would probably go back to school tomorrow, then she could get on with her regular routine. The first thing she wanted to do was catch up on her sleep.

Jill rubbed her eyes. They were gritty from long nights up with the boys. Craig had helped out as much as he could, but they'd had a break in the case and he'd had to go help make three arrests. That last guy was still at large, but the elderly citizens were no longer in danger of being hurt or swindled. Last night,

Mrs. Hart had sent over a large chocolate cake to say thank you. Everyone had enjoyed a slice of it except Jill. She glanced at it now, sitting on the counter. It didn't tempt her at all, which was odd. She loved chocolate.

She rose to her feet and walked to the bottom of the stairs. Everything hurt. Her legs, her arms, her head, even her hair was throbbing in time with her pulse.

"C.J.," she called.

"Yeah?"

"I'm going to take a nap. Wake me up when you want lunch."

"Okay, Jill."

She thought about going into her bedroom, but suddenly it was just too far away. The sofa was closer. The plump cushions looked inviting. She would just lay her head down for a moment.

The next thing she knew, strong arms were lifting her up in the air. Everything was very surreal, fading in and out. Sounds gurgled, as if she were underwater. She blinked and focused on a familiar face.

"Craig?" she asked. Her voice was a whisper. She cleared her throat to speak louder, but it didn't help.

"Hush," he told her. "I've got you. I'm putting you to bed." His arms tightened slightly. "Why the hell didn't you tell me you hadn't been exposed to chicken pox?"

"Huh?" She tried to raise her head, but it was too much effort. "Chicken pox? Didn't I have them when I was little? I don't remember."

"No, you didn't, because you've got them now." He placed her on the bed.

The sheets felt cool against her heated skin, especially when he pulled off her T-shirt and jeans. His strong hands reached behind her and unfastened her bra.

"I'm naked," she whispered in wonder.

"Just about." He stuck her hands into the short sleeves of the oversized T-shirt she wore to bed, then pulled it down to her waist.

"Did you look?"

He chuckled. "You're delirious with fever, if you have to ask. Of course I looked. I'm a guy. Put this under your tongue."

She opened her mouth obediently as he placed the thermometer in her mouth. She watched him fold her clothes. The edges of the room seemed to be blurring.

"I called the doctor," he said. "We have to watch you. The big concern is fever. We have to keep that down. You're going to have to drink a lot of liquids. Can you do that?"

She thought about nodding, but it took too much effort. She fluttered her fingers instead.

He pulled the thermometer out of her mouth. "A hundred and one. Damn." He eased her down on the mattress. "Try to sleep, Jill. I'm going to be right here."

She closed her eyes, then opened them again. "Danny, Ben. I have to pick them up."

"I'll take care of it. You just concentrate on getting well."

He squeezed her hand, then bent over and kissed her forehead. "I'm really sorry about this, Jill."

"S'okay." She wanted to ask him to kiss her again. She'd liked the feel of his lips on hers. She would tell him. Just as soon as she opened her eyes.

Although the thought stayed in her mind, she never got around to mentioning it. When she next surfaced, the room was dark, and Craig was dozing in a chair beside her bed. He must have heard her stirring. He came awake instantly and smiled.

"Feel like drinking something?"

"Sure."

Her throat was dry, and she could barely talk. She made a move to sit up. The second her legs brushed against the sheets, she realized her skin was one hot, burning itch.

"Oh, my Lord," she said and threw back the sheets.

A rash covered her from the tips of her toes to the tops of her thighs. She stared at it in the dim light. She could make out tiny bumps. She had to curl her fingers into her palms to keep from scratching.

Craig sucked in his breath. "It looks bad."

She realized it was on her back, her belly, her arms. "It's everywhere," she said miserably, desperately wanting to rub against the sheets but knowing she shouldn't. Tears sprang to her eyes.

"Oh, honey, don't," Craig said, sliding off the chair and onto the floor. He knelt beside her and held out his arms. She threw herself against him and whimpered.

"Hush," he murmured. "We'll use ice and lotion. The doctor gave you a prescription to help with the itching, too. You'll be okay."

She realized he wasn't holding her. Because she was hideous looking, she thought, even as a rational part of her whispered that he was probably concerned about making it worse.

She drew back and stared at him. "Is it on my face?"

He cupped her chin in his hands and kissed the tip of her nose. "You're as pretty as ever," he said.

She sniffed.

He got her the medication, then served her soup and water. By the time she'd gotten the food down, the itching had subsided. She wanted to stay awake and talk, but she was exhausted. Her eyes drifted closed. The last thing she remembered was Craig sitting on the bed, stroking the back of her hand. She fell asleep to the thought that Krystal Haynes had been the stupidest woman on the face of the planet.

It was light the next time she woke up. Instead of Craig sitting in the chair by her bed, she saw a familiar dark-haired brunette with laughing brown eyes and an impish smile.

"Kim?"

"Hey, you're alive," her friend said and leaned forward in the chair. "How are you feeling?"

"Everything hurts and itches." She shifted uncomfortably. "What are you doing here?"

"I called yesterday to say hi, and Craig told me what had happened. I volunteered to come look after you." Kim's smile faded. "Jeez, I feel so bad. I can't believe you got the chicken pox."

"Don't remind me."

"This is all my fault."

Was it just her imagination, or was everyone in her life suddenly willing to take the blame for her misfortunes? "It's nobody's fault. It just happened."

"But if I hadn't run off with Brian—"

"You wouldn't be happily married now." She reached for the glass of water on the nightstand, but it was just out of reach. Kim grabbed it and handed it to her, hovering near the bed in case Jill couldn't hold it herself.

"Thanks," Jill said, and took a sip. The cool water eased the dryness in her throat. She still felt hot and slightly out of focus. "Do I have a fever?"

"Last time I checked, it was around a hundred. It's come down a little, so we think you'll live."

"Oh, thanks." She raised the glass and held it against her forehead. "How is everyone holding up?"

"Fine. These boys are a handful. How do you manage?"

"It's not so bad."

Kim settled in the chair. She pulled her legs up close to her chest and wrapped her arms around her calves. Her blue-black hair gleamed in the sunlight filtering through the curtains.

"That's easy for you to say," Kim told her. "Every fifteen minutes at least one of them asks if you're going to be okay. The youngest—" She hesitated, as if trying to remember his name.

"Danny."

"Yeah, Danny. He thinks it's his fault because he got sick first."

"I hope you told him it wasn't."

"Of course. But I think he needs to hear it from you. Maybe you could tell him when he gets home from school."

"Hmm, I will." Her eyelids felt heavy. She set the glass on the nightstand.

Kim stood up. "I better get some soup into you before you fall asleep again." She walked to the door, then turned back. "I owe you big-time, Jill."

"Just be happy with Brian."

"I am."

"And name your firstborn after me."

Kim laughed. "Even if it's a boy?"

"Especially if it's a boy."

Five days later Jill was so bored she wanted to scream. The rash was gone, as was Kim. She'd convinced Danny that her getting sick wasn't his fault. They'd had a long discussion about germs, and now he wanted to be a doctor so he could kill them all. Kim had returned to her new husband and job, the boys were in school and Craig was at the station. The only reason Jill was still in bed was that she'd promised to stay in her room for one more day.

"But I'm bored!" she said loudly. There was no one to hear her complaint, although she felt better voicing it out loud.

Craig had brought in a portable television and set it up on the dresser. It didn't help. She didn't know enough about the story lines on the soaps to be interested and talk shows made her squirm. How could those people confess all those personal things in public?

She tried reading, but she was too restless. She'd been stuck in bed for a week. Her muscles had probably atrophied to the consistency of taffy. The only saving grace was that she hadn't been very interested in food, so she'd lost a couple of pounds.

She glanced around the room, searching for something to do. Her gaze settled on the open bathroom door. She would kill for a shower. She threw back the covers and rose to her feet. The room circled around once before settling in one place. As she walked slowly toward the bathroom, she consoled herself with the thought that she wasn't actually breaking her word. She was still staying in her room. Sort of.

She glanced in the mirror and grimaced. Her hair was matted, her face pale. Her eyes were huge and dark. She looked like a refugee from a war zone.

She splashed water on her face, then brushed her teeth. After turning on the shower, she pulled off her nightshirt and tossed it in the dirty clothes hamper. Her underwear followed. Then she stepped into the steamy spray.

The warm water was heaven. She washed her hair twice, then used a deep conditioner. Although the activity drained her, she didn't leave the stall. It felt too good to be up and moving around. Besides, when she felt shaky, she simply leaned against the tile walls.

After ten minutes, she gave her hair a final rinse and quickly washed the rest of her. She was weak but focused. Thank goodness the fever was gone. She hated that half-here, half-somewhere-else feeling.

She pushed open the glass door and stepped onto the floor mat. As she reached for her towel, her fingers brushed against the bare towel rack. She'd forgotten to put one out.

Suddenly the bathroom door flew open, and Craig stepped inside.

"What the hell are you doing?" he asked, his tone furious. He took in her appearance, turned quickly and opened the cabinet above the toilet. Not looking at her, he grabbed a towel and thrust it toward her. So much for dazzling him with her naked self.

She clutched the towel loosely around herself. He was in uniform. As always, he took her breath away. Of course, in her weakened condition, that was easier than usual. His brows pulled together in a frown, giving him the appearance of an angry deity. He radiated strength and male passion. Desire made her tremble. The weakness in her knees wasn't all from her illness. She wanted him.

"Well?" he demanded, reminding her he'd asked what she'd been doing.

Wasn't it obvious? "Taking a shower."

"Damn it, Jill, I came home to check on you, and you weren't in bed. I called and called, and you didn't answer." He still wasn't looking at her. Okay, she was a little weak and pale, but she wasn't hideous-looking, was she?

"I was in the shower. I couldn't hear you." She was dripping and starting to feel a little cold. Not to mention a little naked. If only she could get him to notice. She eyed the bathroom floor, trying to figure out exactly how long it was. Would he fit there? It might be uncomfortable, but she was starting not to mind the thought. She giggled softly. Insane thoughts. Maybe the fever wasn't all gone. Maybe it had burned away her second thoughts.

"You promised not to get out of bed."

"No, I promised not to leave my room. Technically, this is still part of my room."

He swore under his breath, then just stood there, not looking at her. Almost as if he didn't notice that she was naked. But she noticed. Water dripped from her hair and cooled her skin, while her lascivious thoughts heated it. The combination made her break out in tiny goose bumps. Her breasts strained toward him. She knew that if she looked down, her nipples would be hard. When the hell was he going to notice she was wearing nothing but a towel?

"I'm really sorry, Craig. I didn't mean to worry

you. I just wanted to take a shower." She gave up. He *wasn't* going to notice. "If you're done yelling at me, could you please leave so I can get dressed?"

As soon as she said the words, he sucked in a breath. His gaze raked her body. She felt it as strongly as a touch, as if he'd slipped his hands from her breasts down her belly to the apex of her thighs. Desire filled her, making her most feminine place swell and dampen. She moistened her lips in anticipation of his kiss.

Without saying a word, he turned on his heel and left the room.

"Are you even going to say goodbye?" she asked softly, as the door slammed behind him. Her cheeks burned as if he'd slapped her. In a way he had.

There she was, seminaked before him, and he hadn't even bothered with a come-on. She buried her face in the towel, then raised her head and glanced at the mirror.

Her moan was involuntary. Her wet hair hung down. Water collected on the pointy ends and dripped steadily. Her nose was red, her eyes wide. She looked like a drowned kitten. No wonder he hadn't wanted her.

"I should be h-happy," she said, her voice cracking on the last word. But she wasn't. He didn't want her. Aaron hadn't wanted her. No one wanted her.

She knew she was behaving irrationally. It was just her weakened condition. That didn't stop the tears from spilling onto her cheeks, or a sob from breaking free.

Craig must have been waiting for her right outside the door because he was at her side in an instant.

"Jill? What's wrong?"

"N-nothing," she said. "N-nothing at a-all. I look like a drowned k-kitten. No one wants me."

He made comforting noises deep in his throat as he wrapped the towel securely around her. She wanted to tell him not to treat her like a child, but she liked the way she felt when he lifted her up in his arms.

He sat on the edge of the bed and settled her on his lap. "I want you," he said.

She sniffed loudly and brushed her wet hair off her forehead. "No you don't. You're just saying that to be polite."

His dark gaze met hers. "I'm not that nice."

He'd wrapped the towel around her tightly, but she was sitting on the corner. When she shifted, it loosened. It started to slip down, but she didn't do anything to stop it. Instead, she placed her hands on his shoulders.

"Are you sure?" she asked.

He pulled her closer. She felt the hardness of his arousal press against her hip. "Very sure." He reached up and grabbed her wrists, lifting her hands away. "Jill, you're the one who keeps putting the brakes on a personal relationship. Are you saying you've changed your mind?"

"I—" She didn't have an answer to that. Nothing made sense. She studied his face, his familiar features. She trusted him. She liked him. She wanted him. Maybe it was a reaction to being sick. She didn't know. "I'm just so tired of being alone," she said.

He nodded slowly. "Me, too." He put her hands back on his shoulders and wrapped his arms around her. Then his mouth found hers and she didn't feel alone anymore.

Chapter Eleven

She responded instantly. When Craig tightened his arms around her, she drew him into her mouth, as if she were starving and he her only hope of survival.

He angled his head, dipping his tongue inside, tasting her sweetness mingling with the mint of toothpaste. She smelled fresh and clean, her body was warm. He wanted to strip her towel off her and take her right there, that minute. The need inside him had flared to life with a painful intensity that sucked the air from his lungs. But instead of giving in, he hung on, because he needed this to be magic for her. His pleasure depended as much on chasing her to paradise and making her lose control as it did on finding a place of refuge between her silky thighs.

So instead of tilting her back and burying himself inside her, he kept his hands on her arms. He had to get control before he risked touching her anywhere else.

He brushed his tongue over hers, circling her, discovering the sweet secrets of her mouth. His lips pressed harder, demanding more, and she gave all she had to him. She leaned toward him, arching her body against him. Her towel slipped lower. He sensed it, more than felt it. When he could bear it no longer, he raised his head and looked at her.

The soft yellow terry cloth pooled at her waist, exposing her torso. Her hair was still damp and rumpled, her face pale, her eyes wide and unfocused. She smiled at him, a "come love me" kind of smile that upped the pressure in his groin about fifty percent.

He could see her collarbone, the faint dusting of freckles on her creamy skin. His gaze dipped lower to her breasts. His breath caught in his throat. Without conscious thought, he raised his hands and cupped her perfect round flesh.

She was large for her petite frame and the lush curves filled his palms. She responded instantly to his embrace, moaning his name and leaning forward to press a kiss to his throat. Her hot breath and warm lips taunted him, as did the feel of her in his hands.

She was warm, living satin. Supple, soft, sensual. He traced her curves, then ran his thumbs over the taut points of her coral-tipped nipples. A ripple shot through her and she exhaled his name.

With one easy movement, he kicked off his shoes, then stretched out on the bed. She tumbled next to him. He caught her, cushioning her fall. The fluffy towel tangled around her. He left it in place, liking the peekaboo effect. He saw one breast, a bit of her right thigh, her belly and the lower part of her legs. One arm was trapped by the terry cloth.

He turned and supported himself on one elbow. With his free hand, he touched her face.

"You're so beautiful," he murmured.

She smiled. "Hardly."

"You are. Your eyes were the first thing I noticed about you."

She wrinkled her nose. "I look like a kitten. It's not a comparison most people aspire to."

"I saw the likeness at first," he admitted, "but now I just see you."

He stroked her cheek, then her nose. He followed the path down to her mouth. She parted her lips. Her tongue darted out and licked the tip of his finger. Instantly fire shot through him.

He swore under his breath.

She smiled. "Did you like that?"

"Let's just say I'd like anything you did right now." He circled her mouth with his finger.

She leaned her head forward, opened her mouth and captured his finger. She drew him in deeply, then suckled him, circling his sensitized skin with her tongue.

The movement mimicked what they would do later, the completion of their act of love. It was as if someone had hooked up a direct circuit from his index finger to his groin. Sensation raced down, engorging him, making him flex painfully against the fly of his trousers. His skin heated to the point of burning.

He pulled his finger free and kissed her. Passion caught him in its grip until he feared for his control. In the back of his mind was the constant worry that she was so small. He didn't want to hurt her.

He plunged his tongue inside, as if daring her to do

with that what she'd done with his finger. She obliged him until he thought he might explode. He retreated and she followed. While she touched and tasted his mouth, he clamped his lips around her and tormented her in return. She writhed beneath him.

He stroked her bare arm, then her midriff. Brushing the towel aside, he cupped the curve of her hip, then traced her thighs. She was all woman, all curves, in a compact package. He reversed his steps until he cupped her breast. While his fingers teased her already tight nipple, he broke the kiss and trailed down her throat. She arched her head back, urging him on.

He tasted her skin and explored her smooth chest, before dipping lower. A quick jerk freed her of the towel. He tossed it over his shoulder and she was bare to his gaze.

He stared at her full breasts, then at her narrow waist and the sweep of her hips. At the apex of her thighs, her curls were only a shade or two darker than the hair on her head. He placed his hand on her belly. His little finger nestled in her curls, his thumb nearly touched her breasts. She was too small.

If he'd been any kind of gentleman, he would have stopped. Instead, his mind raced to find a dozen different ways to make it work. It had to be possible. If he didn't make love with her, he would die.

He tried to remember how long it had been since he'd touched a woman intimately. Months. Years. He'd begun to think he would never experience that particular pleasure again. After a while, his body had ceased wanting the release and he'd put that part of his life on hold. He'd always equated lovemaking with love, having given up mindless sex shortly after his teens. He didn't love Jill—at least he assumed he didn't. But this intimacy felt right. Maybe it was what she'd said. They were both tired of being alone. He trusted her. That was more than what he could have said about Krystal.

"What are you thinking?" she asked, reaching for the first button on his uniform shirt.

"That I'm going to hurt you. You're too small."

She laughed and her breasts bounced in time with her amusement. He wanted to beg her to do it again, but his mouth was dry and he couldn't speak. He lowered his head and took one of her nipples in his mouth.

She grabbed his head as if to hold him in place. He wanted to tell her he had no plans to go anywhere, but that would have meant stopping. Instead, he rolled the tight point between his lips. He circled her with his tongue, then lifted his mouth slightly and blew on the damp flesh.

Her hips tilted toward him, her grip on his hair tightened. He moved to her other breast and repeated his ministrations. Her arms fell to her sides as she rocked her head from side to side. With each breath, she moaned.

He placed his hand flat on her belly, then slid it lower until his fingers encountered her curls. He could feel the softness of her, the dampness. Lower and lower until her waiting warmth enveloped him. The temptation of slick heat was more than he could resist. He eased one finger inside of her.

Instantly, she parted her thighs. He tested the tight circle that would milk him to ecstasy. Her muscles clenched around him and he groaned.

Even as his tongue traced a tight circle over her nipple, his fingers found a matching taut peak between her legs. He circled that place, too, moving around and around before stroking over it. Once. Quickly.

Her hips flexed toward him. Her breathing rate increased, as did the temperature of her skin. He brushed the spot, inciting the same response. As he drew his head down her body, pausing to lick her belly and nip at her side, he moved his fingers rhythmically. He picked up speed to match her breathing. She clawed at the sheets and called his name. He nibbled on her hipbone, then traced a line through her curls and finally bent low so he could replace his hand with his mouth.

At the first touch of his tongue, she screamed, though it wasn't especially loud. The sound had a half-embarrassed quality to it that made him smile.

His body was doing some screaming of its own. The fire between his legs had reached the point of being unbearable, but he didn't stop what he was doing. He'd always enjoyed touching a woman everywhere, tasting her, bringing her to pleasure first. If he waited until they climaxed together, he didn't get to watch her, or listen to her breathing, or see the flush on her skin. It took away from the experience. So even as his erection throbbed and flexed, and his muscles tightened in anticipation, he slowed the cadence of his tongue against her most feminine place.

He circled her, sweeping around, but not touching the vibrating place of need. He dipped inside her, then returned to the tiny place. Only when her breath came in pants and her bent legs trembled did he move faster, bringing her quickly to the point of release.

She hung there for a heartbeat, her body unbelievably tight. He flicked his tongue quickly, then slipped a finger inside her and pressed upward, as if to caress the spot from both sides.

She convulsed around him. She trembled and shook. Powerful contractions squeezed his finger as he felt and watched her experience perfection. As he continued to touch her gently, lightly, she rode the crest of fulfillment until at last it slowed and she was still.

He sat up and stared at her. Her irises were huge. A flush covered her chest. She blinked several times as if the world was just now coming into focus.

"I think the earth moved," she said, her voice sounding stunned.

He smiled.

"I'm not kidding. I think I've been doing it wrong all these years. It's never been—" She exhaled. "You should teach a class. Trust me, you could make a fortune."

He bent over and kissed her. She locked her arms around him, holding him close.

"Thank you," she whispered.

"You're welco—"

She slipped her tongue into his ear. Instantly, his body stiffened. Delicious tingles raced through him. She nipped his lobe, then moved lower and sucked on his neck. Her teeth grated erotically.

He braced his weight on his arms, determined to let her have her way with him. She reached for the buttons on his shirt and began unfastening them. By the time she'd pulled the cloth free from his trousers, he'd begun to shake.

She raised herself up slightly and, as she drew the shirt apart, placed her mouth against his chest. She trailed kisses from his throat to his waistband. She circled her tongue through the hair until she found his nipples, then teased him into mindlessness.

When he couldn't stand it anymore, he pushed himself into a sitting position and ripped off his shirt. She sat up, completely naked and apparently unselfconscious.

Her hands followed the path the shirt had taken. She touched his shoulders, then stroked down his arms. She knelt before him, her breasts swaying free. He reached for them, cupping her gently. She tilted her head back.

"I can't believe how that makes me feel," she said.

"It does a lot for me, too." His voice was hoarse.

Keeping her head back, she leaned toward him so that her breasts brushed against his chest. The faint touch of her taut nipples was a pleasing form of torture. She swayed back and forth, keeping her balance by resting her hands on his shoulders. Suddenly she stopped and stared at him. Her green eyes widened.

"Oh, Craig, I'm not on the Pill anymore."

Birth control. Protection. He should have thought of it before. He grinned. Who'd had the time?

"I've got some condoms upstairs," he said, sliding off the bed.

She stood up and shook her head. "You stay right here. I'll get them. Where are they?"

"My nightstand. On the left side, top drawer."

She started out of the room, then glanced over her shoulder at him. "While I'm gone, feel free to take off the rest of your clothes."

He watched her leave, then did as she requested, quickly pulling off his socks, then stepping out of his trousers and briefs. Once that was done, he didn't know whether he should sit on the side of the bed or lie down.

He glanced at himself and frowned. His arousal was so *obvious*. He didn't want to scare her off. He was still worried about the size problem. His finger had slipped inside her easily enough, but this was a little…larger.

Before he could figure out what to do, she'd returned with a small box of condoms. She touched the top. "Unopened."

"I just bought them."

She moved to the side of the bed. "I'm glad."

He'd settled on a sitting position. When she stepped in front of him, he was glad. He took the box from her and set it on the nightstand, then grabbed her hips and lifted her onto his lap. She straddled him, his arousal trapped between their bellies. She wiggled and he almost lost his control right there.

"Damn it, woman!" he growled.

She giggled. "I love it when you talk dirty."

He stared at her. "Are you feeling all right?"

"Fishing for more compliments?"

"No. You just spent a week in bed. I don't want to overdo it."

"I'm a little tired, but I think I can stay awake for another five or ten minutes."

"It'll take longer than that," he said.

She smiled. "Not if I do my job right."

He raised his hand and touched her cheek. "I didn't think you'd be like this."

"Like what?"

"So comfortable with yourself and me. You don't mind being naked."

She surprised him by blushing. "I'm not normally

like this. You make me feel comfortable." She shrugged. "Maybe comfortable isn't the right word. I can see that you want me. The way you watch me makes me feel very attractive and feminine."

"You are."

"Shut up and kiss me."

He obliged her. He tilted his head and pressed his mouth against her. She opened for him immediately and took him with a passion that sent his control into the next dimension. Suddenly he had to touch her everywhere, be with her, in her. Damn it, she was already wet and naked. What more did he want?

He touched her back, her thighs, her breasts, then fumbled for the box of protection. Even as he was sliding back on the bed, he ripped the box open and pulled out a condom. He was shaking so badly he could barely open the package.

Once he was stretched out on the mattress, she rained kisses on his chest.

"You're not helping," he said, trying to smooth the latex sheath over himself.

She wiggled against his thighs and licked a damp circle around his belly button. "I'm not trying to."

At last it was in place. He looked at her. "I want you on top. You'll have more control."

She nodded, then raised herself up on her knees. He reached his hand between them and placed the other on her hip. Inch by inch, she lowered herself on him.

He watched her face, trying to judge if he was hurting her. She closed her eyes and smiled. If her look of pleasure was anything to go by, he fit just fine. He let go of his worries as he guided her down. Every part of him focused on the damp heat surrounding him.

Her body stretched to accommodate him, sliding slowly, caressing him like a benediction.

When she would have rocked her hips, he stilled her with his hands. "Not yet," he groaned, between clenched teeth.

"I told you it wouldn't take but five minutes," she murmured, her tone teasing.

He told himself it was because it had been so long, but he knew it was also about Jill. As his gaze focused on her face, then dropped lower to her breasts, he knew it was specifically about her.

The thought should have scared him to death, but strangely, it didn't.

He released his hold on her hips and she began to move. He helped her find the rhythm. As they rocked together, her body continued to stretch around him, allowing him to go deeper. He arched up, filling her until she took all of him.

"Do it," she said.

Her permission was all he needed. His mind cleared of everything but the need for release. He thrust against her quickly, moving up and down. She matched his movements, adding friction that would send him over the edge.

He tried to focus on her, on her head tilted back, on the sleek, pure lines of her neck, on the way her breasts swayed and bounced, on her hands splaying and releasing. He could feel her muscles tightening as she took pleasure in their joining. The pressure built inside him. He wouldn't be able to hold back.

He reached his hand between them, then slipped his thumb into her damp curls. He touched her most sensitive spot and pressed, allowing her to find the rhythm that would please her most. She caught her breath. He pressed harder. Instantly her body began to ripple and clench. It was all he needed. The world disappeared into a rush of pleasure so intense he lost contact with everything but the feel of her body around him and the sound of his name on her lips.

When he finally focused again, Jill sagged against him in contentment. "I could die a happy person right now," she said.

"I know what you mean."

She snuggled against him like the kitten she compared herself to. "Hmm, I can hear the vibration of your voice through your chest. Say something again."

He stroked her short hair. "What do you want me to say?"

There was no answer. He raised his head. Jill was stretched out on his chest, her eyes closed, her breathing even. Exhaustion had caught up with her.

He half rose into a sitting position so he could snag the covers. She didn't stir. He pulled the sheet and light blanket over both of them, then glanced at the clock. They had a couple of hours until the boys had to be picked up at school. He wrapped his arms around her and listened to her heart beating in time with his.

When she awoke it was night. Jill blinked in the darkness. She distinctly remembered it being daylight when she'd last been awake. She'd taken a shower and then—

She froze, terrified of the memories crashing in on her. She'd behaved like a wanton, throwing herself at Craig. Oh, Lord, what must he think of her?

She lay very still, trying to figure out if she was alone or not. This bedroom was at the back of the house, so there wasn't any streetlight filtering through the drapes to help. She listened for breathing, but didn't hear any but her own. Finally she shifted to see the clock and bumped into something very warm and very naked in her bed. She winced.

"It's nearly midnight," he said.

"Oh, my. How long have I been asleep?"

"About eight hours. I guess I tired you out."

She didn't have to see him to know he was smiling. She could hear it in his voice. A blush flared on her cheeks. "Oh, Craig, I'm sorry."

He reached for her and pulled her against him. Arms and legs tangled together until he settled back with her head on his shoulder and his arms around her.

"What are you sorry about?" he asked.

"I—" She could lie and say she was sorry for falling asleep like that, but somehow she didn't think he would buy it.

"Are you feeling okay?" he asked.

"Yes. I feel great. Renewed, in fact." She drew in a deep breath and let it out slowly. "I didn't mean to do that."

"Make love?"

She nodded, rubbing her cheek against his bare skin. "I threw myself at you. I don't even want to think about it."

He chuckled. "I do. In fact, I can't seem to think about anything else."

She buried her face in his side and moaned. "I can't believe I used you the same way everyone has used me. Just to get what I wanted. I'm slime. I'm lower than slime. I'm silt sludge that aspires to be slime."

He drew away from her for a second and clicked on the bedside light. Then he fluffed up the pillows and pushed them behind him so he was sitting up.

"Number one," he said, looking at her. "No one did anything they didn't want to do, least of all me. I'm glad we made love, Jill, and I'd like it better if you didn't have any regrets, either."

"But, I—"

"No. You didn't. You didn't throw yourself at me or coerce me. I haven't been with a woman in a long time. I thought that part of me was dead. I'm glad to know it's not."

"But—"

He smiled. "You worry too much. Can't you just be happy it felt so good?"

"But isn't it going to be awkward now? What will we say to each other? How will we act in front of the boys? Doesn't this change everything?"

"No."

She waited but he didn't say anything else. "That's it? Just 'no'?"

He winked.

"Damn it, Craig."

Without warning, he slipped down the mattress and grabbed her, hauling her close. "I love it when you talk dirty," he said.

She wanted to resist. She wanted to have a rational conversation. They couldn't just ignore what had happened. Then his fingers trailed across her breasts and she thought that maybe they could.

"I don't want to hurt you if you're sore," he murmured against her breast.

"I'm fine." She ran her fingers across his chest, savoring the contrast of cool hair and warm skin. She lingered over his heart and felt the rapid pounding.

"You're sure?"

She reached her hand down and touched his arousal. As she'd hoped, that shut him up.

They moved together in a dance of desire, taking what they'd already learned about each other and applying it to make the sensations more intense, the pleasure more incredible. When he moved to shift her on top of him, she shook her head.

"I want you on top," she said.

"I'm afraid I'll hurt you."

"I'll be fine," she said. "I trust you."

As he knelt between her thighs and slowly entered her, she wondered how long it had been since she'd trusted anyone, let alone a man. Then he withdrew, only to thrust inside her again, and the question was forgotten in the magic of the moment.

Craig was gone when she woke up. She vaguely remembered a quick goodbye kiss before he left for the station. She rolled over and stared at the clock. It was going to ring in ten minutes, then she would go wake up the boys. Ben was probably already up. He'd told her that he was walking without her. She was proud of him. He'd lost most of the weight and he looked terrific.

She sat up and turned off the alarm, then reached for her robe. Before she could stagger into the bathroom, the phone rang. She had an extension in her room. She reached for it, smiling in anticipation, knowing Craig had called to say good-morning.

"Hello?" she said.

"Hi, uh, it's Jill, right?" The unfamiliar voice sounded panicked.

"Yes, this is Jill Bradford."

"Great. I'm Kyle. Craig's youngest brother. Is he there?"

"No, he's left for the station."

"Oh, God. Okay. Damn. Um, could you tell him—" Kyle drew in an audible breath. "Oh, God. It's Sandy. She's having the baby. Now. Soon. We're leaving for the hospital now and if you could tell him." He swore again. "She's had three, so this is no big deal for her, but I don't think I can go through this. Anyway, tell Craig to hurry."

He hung up without saying goodbye.

She stared at the phone for a moment, then dialed the station. She was put through to Craig immediately.

"I already know," he said. "Travis called. Look, I don't want to take the boys out of school. They missed too many days being sick. Pack enough for everyone for the weekend, then after you pick them up, swing by the station and get me. I'm glad we've nearly wrapped up that case with the elderly drivers so I can take the weekend off."

"Weekend off? I'm confused. What's going on?"

He chuckled. "Sorry, Jill. This is all new to you, isn't it? Sandy's having her baby. We all have to be there. It's a Haynes brothers tradition. We're *always* there for each other."

"Which means?"

"We're going to Glenwood."

Chapter Twelve

Tiny babies slept on, unaware of the fuss being made over them by the group of people staring at them from the other side of the glass. Craig had done this three times with Krystal, and also with Travis and Austin. He supposed he should be jaded by now, but he wasn't. The sight of the infants' innocent, scrunched-up faces always got him right in the center of his chest.

Jill pointed to one baby in a little pink stocking cap. "That's her."

He stared, amazed. "It must be true."

"What?"

"The Haynes family curse is really broken. After four generations of only boys, Kyle just had the second girl."

Jill frowned, as if in thought. "Now who had the first one?"

"Travis."

"Okay, Travis is married to Sandy?"

He smiled and dropped his arm over her shoulder. "No. Travis is married to Elizabeth."

"I'll never get this straight."

He led her to a bench on the other side of the wide corridor. This might be a hospital, but close to the nursery it didn't feel too antiseptic. When they were seated, he shifted so he was facing her.

"It's very simple," he said.

"For you. I'm an only child, and I'm not even married. Keeping track of my family is a snap."

The color had returned to Jill's face after her illness. She still tired easily—she'd slept the whole way in the car—but the fever was gone and she claimed to have most of her energy back. She wore a simple shirt tucked into black jeans. The shirt was the exact color of her eyes. Makeup emphasized their shape. Her mouth was kissably pink. Delicate gold earrings glittered in the overhead lights.

She was beautiful, and not just because of how she looked. They hadn't had a moment to talk about what had happened yesterday and last night. They'd become lovers, then their world had been turned upside down by the birth of Kyle's daughter. Most women would have been clinging, or whining, wanting to know where things stood. Not that he had an answer for that. They'd gone from friendly to intimate without much in the way of a warning. For all he knew, Jill would want to back off for a while to catch her breath. He didn't know what he wanted, yet. There hadn't been time to think. Whatever their decision, Jill wasn't pressuring him right now and he was grateful.

Their lovemaking had been more than he'd imagined, and he'd imagined a lot. But the thought of committing to anyone, even her, gave him a bad feeling in the pit of his stomach. The risk was too great. He only wanted a sure thing. Even Jill couldn't guarantee that.

While they couldn't talk about themselves in this public setting, he could explain the intricacies of his family.

"I'm one of four brothers," he said. "I'm the oldest. I have three boys."

She smiled. "That part I knew."

"Next comes Travis. He's the sheriff here in Glenwood. He's married to Elizabeth. They have two children, both girls. The oldest, Mandy, is Elizabeth's by a previous marriage."

Jill nodded. "Travis and Elizabeth, two girls. Got it."

"Next is Jordan. He's the black sheep of the family. A fire fighter instead of a cop. He's not married."

"Thank goodness! Less for me to keep track of."

"Then Kyle. He's the youngest and a deputy here in Glenwood. He married Sandy, who had three children from a previous marriage. Two girls, one boy. She's the one who just had the baby. Finally, our friend Austin is married to Rebecca. They adopted a boy and had a boy together. He owns the company we all invested in." He leaned back. "See, very simple."

She stared at him for a moment and then started laughing. "Oh, yeah. Really simple. Why did I ever think it was a problem?"

"Once you meet everyone, you'll be able to put faces with the names."

She shook her head. "Now I know why that house looked like a day-care center when we dropped off the boys."

"Between us, we do have a lot of kids." He started to say more, then heard someone call his name. He glanced up and saw his brothers approaching. Austin was with them.

Craig rose to his feet. Kyle reached him first and gave him a hug that about cracked his ribs. Travis and Jordan joined the pair and added their strength to the embrace. Soon all four brothers were slapping each other on the back. As always, Austin hung just a little outside the circle. Kyle and Jordan parted for him and he stepped inside.

"Who's the redhead?" Jordan asked.

"Who wants to know?" Craig countered, grinning with pride.

The men laughed and separated. Craig held out his hand to Jill. She accepted it and rose slowly to her feet. Her mouth was hanging open slightly. She closed it, looking a little shell-shocked.

"These are my brothers," he said proudly. "And this is Jill. She's the boys' nanny."

Travis and Jordan glanced significantly at his and Jill's clasped hands, then at each other. Eyebrows rose. He knew what they were thinking. Let 'em, he told himself. Maybe he would get lucky and it would be true.

He moved behind Jill and placed his hands on her shoulders. "Starting from left to right. Kyle, Austin, Jordan and Travis."

She shook hands with each of them in turn. "I'm never going to keep you straight."

"It's easy," Kyle told her. "I'm the best looking and the smartest. Austin's wearing an earring. Travis is maybe an inch taller than me, and Jordan doesn't talk much."

Travis leaned behind the other two men and cuffed Kyle. "I'm better looking."

"I'm smarter," Jordan said.

"I won't argue with the earring," Austin said.

"Oh, my." Jill sounded uncertain.

"You okay?" Craig asked.

"It's a little overwhelming." She craned her neck. "You didn't tell me everyone was so tall. This is some gene pool."

Austin looked down at her. "The Haynes brothers are short, but we put up with them."

"Short?" Jill laughed. "Maybe to you and your friends." She rotated her shoulders. "My neck already hurts from looking up."

Travis elbowed his way between Craig and Jill. "Don't monopolize the lady, brother." Travis took Jill's arm and led her down the corridor. "I'm sure my brother hasn't told you everything about the family. There are a couple of things I'd like to clarify and maybe one or two stories you'd like to hear."

Jill gave Craig a helpless look over her shoulder, but Travis insisted.

"You'll be fine," Craig told her, watching them go. He wasn't concerned. Travis might tease him, but he would never do anything mean-spirited. He turned his attention to the youngest of the Haynes brothers. "How are you feeling?"

Kyle shrugged. "I keep telling myself Sandy did all the hard work, but jeez, Craig, I'm still shaking."

Craig patted his brother on the back. "It gets worse for a while, but then it gets better. At least Sandy's had babies in the house. She'll know what to do."

"What if—" Kyle cleared his throat. "What if I'm not a good father?"

Craig glanced at him, then at Jordan. They all had the famous Haynes good looks. Dark hair and eyes, muscular bodies. They were intelligent, funny and caring. And they were all scared to death of screwing up the way their father had.

Travis had been through a divorce before he found Elizabeth. Before falling for Sandy, Kyle had made a practice of dumping women before they could dump him. Jordan seemed to go through his life avoiding emotional commitments of any kind, and no one knew why. He, Craig, had married Krystal. Enough said.

"You can do your best," he told his brother. "That's the only advice I can give you. Every day, try to do your best. Anyway, you already know how to be a dad. You're father to Sandy's three kids."

Kyle hunched his shoulders. Like Jordan and Austin, he was wearing jeans and a shirt. Only Craig and Travis were in uniform. "This is different. Sandy's kids were already grown-up enough to have personalities. I didn't think there was much I could do wrong. But this is a baby."

"A girl," Craig said. "Two miracles."

"The curse is broken," Jordan said.

Craig didn't want to think about that. "Speaking of Sandy's kids, Jill and I can take them for a few days if you'd like. We talked about it on the way down."

"Thanks." Kyle punched him in the arm. "Austin and Rebecca have already offered. They've got the most room, and we won't have to take anyone out of school. It'll be easier staying local."

"They want to stay with us because of the upstairs playroom," Austin said.

"No problem," Craig said. "Just thought I'd offer."

Kyle nodded. "I appreciate it. Everyone is pitching in. That's one of the things I like best about this family. Even Louise is going to come stay with Sandy and me for the first month."

"She's a big help," Craig said. At the mention of Louise, Jordan got the oddest look on his face. Anger and something else. Betrayal maybe? From Louise? That didn't make sense. The older woman had been working for Travis for several years. Since the brothers had started marrying and having children, she'd been helping out. Everyone liked her.

Kyle stared at the tight circle of friends. "You guys ever think it would turn out like this?"

"No," Craig said easily. "I didn't think we'd get this lucky." He was talking about them all staying friends, but Kyle meant something else.

"I never thought I would be this happy," he said, then shrugged. "I know that sounds lame."

"No, it doesn't," Jordan said. "Not after what we went through."

"I never thought I'd get this lucky," Austin said quietly.

Craig remembered his friend's past. Austin had been abandoned by his mother when he was just a kid. It was during his time at the Glenwood orphanage that he'd met and made friends with the Haynes brothers. He'd grown from a skinny, hostile kid into a successful entrepreneur. After years of holding himself apart, he'd finally found his way into a circle of love. All because of a woman named Rebecca and her unwillingness to give up on the man she loved.

Thinking about the past kept Craig from dealing with the present. He had to fight down feelings of envy as he stared at his brothers and Austin. They'd found something wonderful with someone special. They'd found love.

He glanced at Jordan and saw the same conflicting emotions reflected in his brother's gaze. What had the two of them done wrong? Krystal had been mistake number one for him. What was the name of Jordan's mistake?

Damn it, nothing was easy. He wanted what Travis, Kyle and Austin had. He wanted to believe in someone again, but it was hard. Krystal had scarred him and he wasn't sure he would ever recover. What about Jill? Was he already involved with her and just fooling himself that he wasn't? She was so different from his ex-wife. His feelings were different, too. There was less lightning and a lot more caring.

Krystal had been very high maintenance, but Jill was more concerned about taking care of others. That made him want to take care of her. He admired her, appreciated the way she looked after the boys. She was a dynamo in bed and just thinking about it made his body throb. Was that…love?

Even as he asked the question, a voice in his head reminded him that he wasn't going to do this again. Not unless there were guarantees. Besides, more than once Jill had made it clear that she wasn't interested in anything permanent. When her time was up, she would be gone.

The huge table sat twenty, and nearly every chair had been used. Jill stood up with the other two women and helped clear the table. The men made a half-hearted attempt to offer assistance. Elizabeth brushed them off with a good-natured, "Oh, please, we know you're lying!"

The sound of laughter accompanied Jill into the kitchen. Once there, she paused to admire the spacious room. A huge greenhouse window offered a view of the rolling grass and the forest beyond. At least that's what she'd been told. It had been dusk when they'd arrived at Rebecca and Austin's house.

Bleached cabinets hugged the walls. The tile was white, the appliances black, and the floor was the same bleached wood as the cabinets. Blue-and-white wallpaper added color to the large room.

"Impressive," Jill said softly as she put the dishes down on the counter.

"I like it."

She spun toward the sound and saw Rebecca walking toward her carrying an armful of plates and silverware. Austin's wife was taller than Jill, but most people were. She had long, curly dark hair and the kind of face that would make a perfect cameo. She wore a flowing dress that stopped midway between her knees and ankles, and Jill had the impression that Rebecca Lucas belonged in a gentler time. She wondered what this delicate-looking woman was doing with a husband who looked like a dark pirate and even had the earring.

Rebecca approached and put down the plates. "I'm sure you're still feeling overwhelmed."

"A little."

"You'll get used to everyone. I had the advantage of getting to know Travis first, then his brothers. By the time Austin and I—" She paused and a faint blush stained her cheeks.

"Dated?" Jill offered helpfully.

The blush deepened. "Austin and I never really dated. We just sort of got married. I had a crush on him for years, then one night..." She waved her hand. "It's a long story. I'll tell it to you sometime. Anyway, I already knew everyone. Elizabeth also met the brothers a few at a time. And Sandy had known them from when she lived here in Glenwood and had gone to school with them. I can't imagine what it must be like for you, coming in cold like this."

"Sandy's easy," Jill said and grinned. "She's still in the hospital, so I don't have to worry about her. Everyone else is confusing. It's not just the adults, it's the kids."

Rebecca tilted her head toward the noise coming from the living room. "There are a bunch." Rebecca lifted the cover off a large chocolate cake. "Could you get the plates, please? We'll need..." She counted on her fingers. "Kyle left for the hospital so that's seven adults and ten kids. Is that right?"

Jill laughed. "You're asking the wrong person. You'd better cut up the whole cake. I'm sure there won't be leftovers."

"Good idea."

As Rebecca filled the plates, Jill carried them into the dining room. The children returned to their seats. She put a piece in front of Ben. He looked at her questioningly. She bent close to his ear.

"It's up to you," she murmured. "If you want to eat it, then go ahead. You're doing great. If you think it's going to make you feel bad, then don't."

He nodded. "I'll just have half," he said, reaching for a knife and carefully cutting the cake into two pieces.

She dropped a quick kiss on the top of his head before returning to the kitchen. By the time everyone had been served, Elizabeth announced that the coffee was done. Cups were poured and passed around the table. There was a lull in the conversation. Elizabeth raised her cup.

"I'd like to propose a toast. To the infamous Haynes brothers and their friends."

Jill took a sip of coffee, then leaned toward Craig. "Why are you infamous?"

Austin heard the question. "You haven't told her?" the dark-eyed pirate asked.

Craig groaned. "Don't start on this. It was a long time ago. We've all grown up and matured."

"What was a long time ago?" Jill wanted to know.

Elizabeth leaned forward and grinned. "Honey, the stories we could tell you about these boys. They would make your hair curl."

"Like what?"

"Can I please be excused?" a girl about C.J.'s age asked.

"Me, too," Danny said. "You guys are just gonna talk about the olden days."

Craig looked at Travis, then shrugged. "All children are excused. Go to the playroom and try to get along."

The kids cheered as they raced from the room. Within seconds, footsteps thundered on the stairs as the horde ascended to what Jill supposed was a huge playroom. The Lucas family didn't seem to do anything by halves.

Rebecca glanced at her husband. "The Haynes brothers and Austin turned dating into an art form. From what I understand, there wasn't a girl in a twenty-mile radius who was safe from them."

"Cheerleaders," Elizabeth said. "Brainy types, flirts, shy ones. It didn't matter. No one was immune to their charm."

"Really?" Jill glanced at Craig, who was squirming in his chair. Travis and Jordan didn't look any more comfortable. Even Austin seemed to find the silverware on the table fascinating.

"None of us do that anymore," Craig said.

"I don't understand," Jill said. "You're saying that all the brothers were—"

"Heartbreakers," Rebecca said. "They loved 'em and left 'em. Tempting them with promises, then—"

"I never made promises," Craig said heatedly.

"I was up-front from the beginning," Travis added.

Elizabeth leaned over and kissed her husband on the mouth. For that second, their love was as tangible as the table itself. Jill felt a flicker of envy.

"We know that," Elizabeth said. "We're just teasing you because we love you."

"That's right," Rebecca added. "After all, look at how you've changed."

"Jordan hasn't," Travis said, obviously pleased to have the attention on someone else. "He's holding out and needs a woman."

Jordan shook his head. "Don't forget Craig. He needs a woman, too."

Austin lifted his eyebrows. "Maybe not."

Now it was Jill's turn to blush.

"You didn't answer the question, Jordan," Craig said. "Anyone special in your life?"

"I've sworn off women."

Rebecca laughed. "We'll find you someone." She rose to her feet and began collecting dessert plates. "Didn't we just clear this table?"

"Yes, you did, and now it's our turn." Austin stood and shooed her toward the living room. "You ladies go talk about us while we finish."

"You don't have to ask me twice." Elizabeth linked arms with Rebecca. The two of them came around and collected Jill. Together they walked into the living room.

The huge space had been designed for comfort. There was a rock fireplace in one corner, with three sofas scattered around. A few wing chairs completed the conversation grouping. Tables were bare except for a couple of floral arrangements. Paintings of outdoor scenes, women with children and one seascape hung on the walls. The predominant colors were rose and cream, with colonial blue accents. The effect was that of space and comfort. Children would be welcome here. There was nothing for them to break or ruin. The room would easily seat twenty, yet gave the impression of being welcoming and intimate.

"I'm impressed," Jill said. "Who did the decorating?"

"I did," Rebecca answered. "Austin helped. We preplanned the room on his computer. After that, it was pretty easy. I assume I got lucky because I don't have an artistic bone in my body."

"You can't tell," Jill said.

Elizabeth sat in a wing chair next to a rose-and-cream-striped sofa. Jill sank down onto the couch and Rebecca joined her. She felt them staring at her.

"What do you want to know?" she asked.

Rebecca laughed. "Elizabeth, something is wrong. We used to be subtle."

"I guess we're out of practice. I suppose it's because we haven't had anyone to interrogate in so long. Not since Kyle started dating Sandy. Craig brought a couple of women around, but they obviously didn't mean anything to him."

Jill wondered if Elizabeth was implying that Craig was interested in her. She didn't know what to say to that. She and Craig were lovers. No, they'd made love. But they hadn't talked about it. In a way, she was glad. She didn't know what she wanted from him. The thought of a relationship terrified her. The situation was too close to what had happened with Aaron. A single father with kids in need of help. She refused to be used again. She reminded herself Craig was nothing like Aaron, and she believed that with all her heart. Yet she'd been wrong before. She wasn't willing to be wrong again.

"I like Craig," she admitted at last. "We're friends. But I'm really there to look after his boys. Nothing else."

"Too bad," Elizabeth said. "He's a great guy. All the brothers are. It's a shame about their family."

"I know a little about what happened with his father," she said.

Elizabeth grimaced. "That man is a bastard. I get so angry when I think about what he did to his sons." She glanced at Jill. "We tease them about their dating habits when they were young, but the truth is they're all wonderful men."

"They seem very close," Jill said.

"They had to be. I can't imagine what it was like for their mother. I don't blame the poor woman. I just wish she'd been stronger. She should have thrown her husband out."

"I agree." Rebecca sighed. "The past tainted them all. Austin lived a different kind of hell when he was growing up. It still affects him."

Jill had to consciously keep her mouth closed. Rebecca looked as innocent as a nun. She couldn't believe the other woman had actually used a bad word.

"I swear, these men are all walking around with wounded souls," Rebecca continued. "They don't want anybody inside, but they desperately need the loving. I just want to hug them all until they're healed."

"If only it were that simple," Elizabeth said. She glanced up at Jill and smiled guiltily. "Sorry. I didn't mean for this to get so serious."

"I understand," Jill said.

Rebecca leaned forward. "Be kind to Craig, Jill. He deserves that. He's one of the good guys."

Before she could continue, the men strolled into the living room. Elizabeth and Rebecca rose to their feet and walked to their husbands. There was that moment of silent communications. Hands touched, eyes met, half smiles were shared. Austin sat in one of the large chairs and pulled Rebecca onto his lap. She went easily, as if they'd performed this ritual a thousand times before. A young boy of maybe eight or nine raced into the room and joined them, squirming for a place on his father's lap.

Jill stared at the three of them. That must be their adopted boy. Both Austin and Rebecca had dark hair, while the child was blond. Elizabeth sat on a sofa. Travis stretched out and rested his head on her lap. Several more children came into the room.

Craig made his way to where Jill was seated. She held her breath as he paused, then released it when he took the place in the middle, leaving the other side for Danny, who climbed up next to him. He put his arm around the boy, then glanced at her and smiled. Their shoulders brushed. She could inhale the scent of him. For that moment, it was enough.

Be kind to Craig... He's one of the good guys. Rebecca's advice repeated over and over in her head. She knew he was a good man. She'd been touched by his kindness.

Lazy conversation filled the room, punctuated by laughter. This was a collection of people who enjoyed being together. Even the children participated. Only Jordan sat alone on the fringes of the room.

As she studied him, she realized he was single and didn't have a child. He should be exactly what she was looking for. Yet she didn't feel even a flicker of interest. She didn't want to go talk to him; she wanted to be next to Craig.

Dumb, Bradford, she told herself, but she didn't move. For this moment, she was a part of what she'd always wanted. The Haynes family circle widened enough to admit her. The fantasy of being loved for herself had finally come true. And for tonight, she was going to live it for all she could.

Chapter Thirteen

The women cooed like doves. Craig watched from the doorway of the nursery as Elizabeth, Rebecca, Sandy and Jill hovered over the bassinet.

"She's beautiful," Jill said, touching her finger to the infant's tiny hand.

"Just like her mother," Rebecca said.

"Better." Sandy straightened and winced. "She looks just like her dad." She shifted her weight. "I'd forgotten how much this hurt. I'm too old for this giving-birth stuff. Next time Kyle can do it."

"Next time?" Elizabeth raised her eyebrows. "You're thinking of having another one?"

Sandy smiled. "I think Kyle would like to, but I'm not so sure. This makes four kids. We're going to talk about it."

Jill glanced up and saw Craig in the doorway. "You want to come see?" she asked.

He shook his head. "You go ahead."

He'd already spent the better part of an hour holding the perfect little girl. Staring down at her red, wrinkled face had given him an odd feeling. He wanted a daughter.

Of course he loved his boys and he wouldn't trade them for anything, but a girl would have been great. He frowned. Although he wouldn't want one like Krystal.

"What are you so serious about?" Jordan asked, coming across the second-story landing and pausing beside him.

Craig shrugged. "Just thinking."

Jordan glanced into the nursery. "You'd think with all the kids running around here, they'd get tired of new ones being born."

"Sorry, it doesn't work that way. Every kid is special."

Jordan looked skeptical. "You've got three already. Are you trying to tell me you want another one?"

"Maybe," he said, watching Jill.

She smiled down at the baby. He read the longing in her eyes, although he doubted anyone else saw it. "You think it's true?" he asked.

"What?" Jordan wanted to know.

"The curse. You think the real reason we had four generations of boys is none of the men loved their wives?"

"I don't know. What do you think?"

Craig pushed off the door and walked over to the railing. From here he could see Louise climbing the stairs, and beyond her to the first floor. Travis and Kyle were downstairs, playing some kind of tag game with several of the children. Shouts of laughter and snatches of conversation drifted up to the second floor.

"If the curse is true," Craig said, "it doesn't say much about my marriage to Krystal."

"You got a divorce. What did you expect? You don't divorce someone you're in love with."

"Are they still gawkin' at that child? I swear, a body would think they'd never seen a baby before." Louise reached the top of the stairs, then crossed to the nursery. She placed her hands on her hips. "You women need to let the poor thing sleep. She's not going anywhere. You can look at her later."

Craig stared after her and grinned. Louise was a force of nature. She was in her mid-forties, with short blond hair and a smile that invited the world to share her joke. Her clothing was a little eccentric, with mismatching colors that somehow managed to look right. She dressed to emphasize her impressive hourglass figure and didn't look like anyone's idea of a mother, but she'd helped out Travis and Elizabeth for nearly two years. When Austin and Rebecca had their baby, she'd gone to stay with them for several weeks. Now she was going to help Sandy and Kyle.

"Go on with you now," she said, flapping her arms.

Elizabeth, Rebecca and Jill slowly walked into the hallway and started down the stairs. Sandy lingered by the bassinet.

"How you feelin'?" Louise asked, touching Sandy's arm. "Everything hurt?"

"Just about." Sandy's smile trembled at the corners. "I'm way too old for this."

"Nonsense. You're just the right age. You've done yourself proud." Louise pulled her close and held her.

Craig turned away, suddenly embarrassed for intruding on an obviously personal moment. He glanced at his brother and saw Jordan scowling at the two women.

"What's wrong?" he asked.

Jordan shrugged and shifted so he was leaning against the railing. "Don't you find it odd that Louise is a part of the family?"

"I hadn't really thought about it. Travis hired her years ago, while he was still a bachelor."

"I know. But she's always around at family events. We don't know that much about her. We don't know who she really is."

"She's just Louise. What's the problem?" Craig frowned. Jordan didn't usually take a dislike to someone without good reason.

Jordan glanced over his shoulder. Louise looked up. Their gazes locked. An emotion that looked very much like pain crossed the older woman's face. Then Sandy spoke, drawing Louise's attention to herself.

"What's going on?" Craig asked quietly.

"Nothing. It's old news. It doesn't matter anymore. If it ever did."

"Damn it, Jordan, just tell me—"

"Hey, you two wanna play football?" Kyle called from the first floor.

"Sure." Jordan headed for the stairs.

"You're not going to tell me, are you?" Craig asked, following him.

"It doesn't matter anymore. I shouldn't have said anything."

There was a secret between Jordan and Louise. But what could those two possibly have in common? Before Craig could try to figure it out, he was hustled outside.

Travis and Kyle were acting as team captains. All the children were standing in front of them, obviously willing themselves to be picked first.

"Danny," Travis said.

Danny whooped loudly and jumped next to his team captain. "Look, Daddy, I got picked first!"

Craig smiled. "I see. Good for you."

Kyle picked Michael, Austin's adoptive son. The boy called on Rebecca, but she threw up her hands and said she wasn't going to play so he picked Austin instead.

Danny yelled, "Jill!"

She thought for a moment. "All right. I'll play."

Craig moved toward her. "The games sometimes get rough."

Travis nudged him with his elbow. "Don't worry, Craig, I'll take care of her."

"Me, too," Danny said, grinning.

He wanted to protest, but he didn't have the right. Jill gave him a "see there" look and went to stand next to Danny. She chose C.J., Austin chose Jonathan, and so it went until everyone had a team. Elizabeth and Jill were the only women playing. The kids varied in age and skill level, but none of that mattered. They were out here to have fun. It was warm in the sunny afternoon. Everyone was in shorts and T-shirts, except, of course, for Rebecca, who wore a sundress.

Travis hiked the ball to Jordan, who threw it long. Craig kept back, trying to make sure no one got hurt. Especially not Jill.

She was so tiny. She wore a bright blue T-shirt tucked into white shorts, so she was easy to spot in the shifting mass of players. She darted and ran. At one point, she nearly caught the ball. C.J. dove for her legs and knocked her down. They tumbled together like puppies, Ben and Danny joining the fun. Jill came up laughing. She ruffled Ben's hair, then tickled C.J. until he begged for mercy. Danny stood up and tugged her to her feet. Still smiling, she rejoined the game.

She touched Craig's arm as she jogged past. "What I lack in size, I make up for in speed and agility."

"I see that," he said.

Eventually he relaxed. He went out for a pass and caught it, giving his team the first score.

As he walked back for the kickoff, Jill fell into step with him. "You didn't tell me you'd made all-American in high school. I'm very impressed."

He wanted to puff out his chest with pride. "Yeah, well, it was a great time in my life, but I don't use it as an introduction."

"Did you play football in college?"

"Some. But six feet isn't all that big there."

Jordan called her over to hike the ball. She waved and darted away. Craig slowed as he watched her have a whispered conversation with his brother. Jordan bent low and placed his hand on her shoulder. She stared intently, nodding every few seconds. Craig felt his fingers bend into fists, even as he told himself Jordan would never make a move on Jill.

"You're falling hard, buddy," Austin said, reading his mind.

Craig forced himself to smile. "You fell first."

Austin looked at his wife. "Thank God. She's the best thing that ever happened to me."

Craig had spent countless weekends with his family, but this was the first time he remembered having to fight constant waves of envy. He envied Kyle and Sandy their beautiful daughter. He envied both his married brothers and Austin their happiness. He didn't begrudge them what they had, he just wanted to know how he could do it, too. And this protective jealousy Jill inspired. What did that mean? Was he starting to really care about her, or just turning into a jerk?

"Ready?" Jordan called to the team.

Jill bent over the ball. Jordan stood right behind her, his hands brushing the inside of her thighs. Craig took a step toward them.

"Thirty-two, thirty-two, hut, hut, hut!"

Instead of snapping the ball, Jill picked it up and started to run. Michael and Kyle got her first and grabbed her around the legs. One of the kids slipped and went careening into the pile, pushing everyone off-balance. They tumbled together. The tackle got bigger. Craig started toward them. Jill was on the bottom.

Jordan reached her first. He moved people aside until he finally pulled her out. She was dazed, but still smiling.

"I guess you're too little to play with the big boys," he said, lifting her up in his arms.

"It's the story of my life."

Before Craig could do something stupid like challenge Jordan to a fight, Jordan walked toward him, then Craig lifted Jill onto his shoulders. "You'd better keep her out of trouble."

Craig reached up and grabbed her thighs to hold her in place. "You okay up there?" he asked.

"I like the view. Am I too heavy?"

He chuckled. "Hardly. Did you get hurt in the tackle?"

"No, I'm fine."

Jill shifted to keep her balance. She'd never been

on a man's shoulders before, but she liked it. She wasn't kidding about the view. She could see everything.

She rested a hand on Craig's head. His hair was soft and springy beneath her fingers. He held on to her thighs, and the feel of his fingers brushing against her bare legs sent tingles all through her body.

They moved to the sidelines to watch the game.

"What do you think of all this?" he asked as Danny was handed the ball and started to run.

"You have a wonderful family. I've never known brothers who are as close as you four. It's terrific."

"We got lucky about some things, although we fought like hell when we were growing up."

"I think all kids do. The question is, are you there for each other when you're needed? And that answer is yes. I know your three boys watch you and their uncles. They're learning a good lesson."

They concentrated on the game for a few minutes. She enjoyed the way Craig's boys played with the other kids. And seeing the Haynes men in action, she was starting to see the similarities and differences. C.J. was very much like his youngest uncle, Kyle. An easygoing charmer. Ben was a little bit more like a cross between his dad and Travis. And Danny... She frowned. Danny was going to be his own man.

Craig tried hard to treat the boys equally and not show favoritism, but if he were to admit any at all, she suspected Danny would be his favorite. He always took extra time with the boy. Maybe because Danny had grown up with no memory of his mother, he'd bonded more with his father.

The other team made a touchdown, tying the score.

Jill tapped Craig on the shoulder. "I must be getting too heavy. Please put me down."

"You don't weigh anything," he said as he swung her to the ground. She sat under the shade of an oak tree. Craig settled next to her.

"This is great for the boys," she said, watching Ben catch a ball and run several feet before being tackled.

"Yeah." Craig leaned against the base of the tree. "It's been too long between visits. I get so caught up in work, I forget how good it feels to come back to Glenwood. The boys and I need this connection with family."

She glanced over her shoulder at him and smiled. "In a couple of weeks I'll remind you it's time to come back."

He touched her back with his hand, his fingers lingering as they slid down her spine. "You do that."

Warmth curled in her belly. The heat had very little to do with sexual desire and almost everything to do with the comfort of belonging. She'd thought she'd found something special with Aaron and his girls, but comparing that to this group of caring people was like comparing a single raisin to a gourmet banquet.

She was starving for their love and caring. Every part of her called out to join in. To be part of the circle. Funny, she'd been married to Aaron and she'd never felt as if she fit in. Maybe, in her heart, she had sensed he didn't love her. She knew that she'd never fully trusted him, although she'd spent years trying to convince herself she did.

With Craig, she didn't have to do any convincing. She trusted him implicitly because he was a kind, decent man. His incredible body and knee-weakening good looks were just a bonus to the real treasure of the man himself.

"Everyone has noticed that Ben's lost weight," Craig said. "He's real proud. I can see it in the way he walks. It's like he's a different person. He's more friendly, more outgoing. He's also more patient with the younger kids."

"I think he was always outgoing, but the weight made him self-conscious." She scooted back to lean against the tree. Craig put his arm around her and pulled her against him. She rested her head on his chest.

"I noticed C.J. isn't so much of a smartmouth these days. Danny has more confidence."

"They're growing up," she said.

"Maybe. But I think it's because of you."

Pleasure filled her. "Really?"

"Yeah." He drew in a deep breath. "You've had an effect on me, too, Jill."

The grass was soft under her bare legs. Above them, the sky was a brilliant blue. The sounds of shouts and laughter from the football game carried to them. She absorbed them all, saving them to remember later.

His arm was like a warm band of protection. She continued to rest her cheek on his chest, not only to listen to his heart, but also to avoid his gaze. She wasn't sure she wanted to have this conversation.

"We can't pretend it didn't happen," he said. "Maybe I should say— I can't. Making love with you meant something. To me, at least."

That got her attention. She tilted her head so she could look at his face. "Of course it meant something to me, too. I don't give myself lightly. You're the first man I've been with since my divorce."

"I wasn't saying that. We have to deal with what we did. There are ramifications of making love."

Making love. Lovers. Lovely words, but did they apply to this situation? Hadn't she and Craig both admitted to just reacting?

"A temporary romantic relationship will upset and confuse the boys," she said. "I don't want to be responsible for that. They've been through enough."

Craig stiffened and dropped his arm from her shoulders. "A temporary romantic relationship?"

"It couldn't be anything else," she blurted out.

"Why not?"

"Because..."

Because anything else was too terrifying to consider. If the sex became lovemaking, then her heart would be at risk. She would care more. She would fall for him. Once again she would be admitted because she was convenient, not because *she* was loved. This time, being used would destroy her.

"Because you don't really care about me," she said. "You're just reacting to the situation."

"You sound very sure of yourself."

"I am."

"How do you know it's not more than that?" She'd been able to read his expression for quite some time, but now his dark eyes and firm mouth gave nothing away.

She fumbled for words. "Because... That is..." She cleared her throat. "You can't expect me to believe anything else. What are you trying to say? That you've been single all these years, suddenly I show up and poof, you're healed? After hating Krystal and not trusting women, you want to make a commitment? I don't think so."

Her temper flared and she shifted until she was kneeling next to him. "It's all so convenient. That's what I resent the most. You're hinting at a relationship just about the time that everything is settling into place at home. The boys like me, you like me, so what better way to keep me where you want me than with terrific sex and the promise of something permanent in the not-to-be-named future?"

Suddenly she *could* read his expression, and he was damned angry.

"I'm not your ex-husband," he said, his voice low and cold. "If you think I am, you don't know me at all."

She twisted her fingers together. "I know, Craig. I'm sorry. You're not Aaron. You're also right about me not knowing you. We don't know each other very well. That's part of the problem. I thought I knew him and I was wrong. What if I'm wrong about you, too?"

"No," he said. "This isn't about me, it's about you. You want me to be a jerk. You want to believe I'm just like him because then you don't have to risk anything. You want me to be willing to make a commitment, but what do you have to put on the line?"

"That's not fair," she said hotly.

"Isn't it? Doesn't this truth thing go both ways?"

"I would never do anything to hurt you."

"How do I know that? My ex-wife was the most dishonest person I'd ever met, yet I'm willing to give you a chance. Why can't you do the same?"

He made it sound so reasonable. She didn't want to think she was being unfair. She'd never meant to be. "I don't know what to say."

He rose to his feet and towered over her. "I don't know what we could have had between us, but I was willing to give it a shot. I know it's hard to believe that after all this time you're the first woman who's turned me on, but it's true. And I don't just mean about sex. I mean about everything. Being with you—"

He broke off and shoved his hands in his pockets. "Hell, it doesn't matter."

She wanted to tell him that it did, but he wasn't listening to her anymore. She'd taken care of that.

"You say you don't want to confuse the children, but I think the person you're really afraid for is yourself," he said. "You're the one who's confused. Maybe you picked Aaron on purpose. Maybe you wanted someone who would use you so you wouldn't have to deal with the consequences of a real relationship."

She stood up and glared at him. "How dare you? You have no right to say that to me."

"Tell me one thing, Jill. You're a bright woman. You held a responsible job. Why couldn't you see what a jerk Aaron was? Why did you stay with him? It was easy, wasn't it? Life is always easier when you get to hold a piece of yourself back. It's giving everything away that gets so damn messy."

He turned on his heel and started for the house. She wanted to go after him, but she didn't know what she was going to say. Accuse him of being a selfish jerk? Hard words to speak when there was a very good chance that he was right...about everything.

Chapter Fourteen

Jill added the eggs, oil and the prune mixture to the dry ingredients, then stirred until everything had blended together. Last she dumped in the nuts. After spooning the quick bread into the pan, she popped it in the oven and set the timer. As much as the boys complained about prune bread, they managed to devour nearly the whole loaf in one sitting every time she made it.

She glanced at the clock and saw she had a few minutes before she had to leave to pick up Danny at school. C.J. and Ben were both spending the afternoon with friends.

Jill walked through the family room, pausing to straighten a pile of magazines. The house was never in perfect order, but she didn't mind. Better for everyone to be happy than the edges of the books lined up with the front of the shelf. Craig had wanted to keep the cleaning service, so she didn't have to worry about scrubbing the bathrooms, but with five people in one house, there was plenty of other work to keep her busy. Especially now that Craig was home most evenings.

The last man who had been trying to cheat the elderly drivers had finally been arrested, and Craig was back on a regular schedule. He was home for dinner more often than not. At first it had been odd having him around, but she'd grown used to talking to him at the dinner table. They spent time with the boys, helping with homework, reading or playing games. She felt like a necessary part of a team. Which was odd because she and Craig were barely speaking to each other if they happened to be alone.

Other people made it safe. When the final arrest had been made, several of the senior citizens Craig had been trying to protect had invited him and his boys over for dinner. He'd brought Jill along. She'd loved the evening. She and Craig had sat next to each other and chatted. But as soon as they returned home and the boys went to bed, there was nothing to say.

She grabbed her purse from her bedroom and walked out into the garage. After pushing the garage door button, she waited for it to finish opening, then put the sport-utility vehicle into reverse and backed out.

The tension had started after their weekend in Glenwood three weeks ago. Neither of them wanted to talk about it. So they avoided the subject and each other. It was easier than facing the truth.

As she pulled up to the stop sign, she knew she had only herself to blame. Craig had wanted to talk about it. He'd wanted to consider the possibility that they might have a chance at a relationship, but Jill couldn't do that. She couldn't risk the pain. But even as she hid behind her fears, she wondered if Craig was right.

Had she chosen Aaron deliberately, knowing that it probably wouldn't work? Had she kept a piece of herself back from him and the girls? Had it been easier to live in the pretend world than to risk finding and possibly losing real love?

She didn't want to think that about herself. Everyone had failings, but no one liked to think about them. And to have Craig be the one pointing them out to her... She pressed on the gas and shuddered. Yet there was a part of her that knew he was right.

She *was* a smart woman. She had hidden the truth from herself. She'd gone into the marriage because it was easy and she'd stayed because it gave her an excuse not to try again.

She glanced in the rearview mirror, but instead of the car behind her, she saw only ugly truths. She gave so much to Aaron and the girls, but she gave because of what she wanted back, not because of what they needed. Oh, she cared about them. There were nights when missing the girls kept her up. But she rarely thought about Aaron.

The divorce had been painful to her pride, but losing her husband hadn't touched her heart.

She pulled into the line of cars already waiting in front of the school. The children had just been let out and most came running toward the vehicles. A few paused to chat with friends until sharp honks reminded them that someone was waiting. Jill scanned the children, looking for Danny. She finally spotted the little boy walking slowly across the grass.

She frowned. Danny usually ran, skipped or jumped

when he was going somewhere. Walking was too boring. As he approached, she opened the car door, then took his books and set them in the back seat. He reached for the seat belt without saying anything.

"Danny, do you feel all right?" she asked.

"I guess."

She touched his forehead, then his cheeks. He didn't feel warm. "Are you tired? Do you think you're coming down with something?"

He shook his head.

She stared at him. He hadn't really been himself for several days. Now that she was thinking about it, she'd been noticing odd things on and off for about a week.

"Is there a problem with your Pee-Wee team?"

"No. I'm doing good. I might get to play third base." For a moment he smiled, and the Danny she knew returned. Then, just as quickly, his smile faded and he was gone.

"Your brothers are visiting friends this afternoon. It's just going to be the two of us. What would you like to do?"

He shrugged. "Nothing."

"I'll help you with your hitting if you want," she offered.

"No thanks." He stared out the side window.

Not knowing what else to say, she started the car and drove home. Once there, Danny ate half a piece of still-warm prune bread, then completed his math sheet. He didn't have any more homework, so he excused himself and went to his room.

Fifteen minutes later, Jill couldn't stand it. She climbed the stairs, went to his closed door and knocked. "Danny, may I come in?"

"Okay."

She opened the door and stepped inside. He was sitting in the center of his bed, hugging a ragged teddy bear. One of the animal's ears was missing and the fur had been rubbed off its paws. Danny looked so alone and sad. She sank down next to him and gently drew him into her arms.

"Tell me what's wrong," she said.

He didn't speak.

She rocked back and forth, holding him. He was small and slight. He continued to clutch at his bear. The sound of slow, steady breathing filled the room. She stroked his soft hair and waited.

Finally he sighed. "I'm not big enough," he said softly.

"For what?"

"For everything."

"You're big enough to get dressed on your own. Big enough to eat. Big enough to go to school, to play ball, to watch TV. You're big enough to get into trouble."

He raised his head and looked at her. He wasn't smiling. His light brown eyes were wide and filled with misery. "I'm not as big as C.J. and Ben."

"But they're older than you. You won't be as big as them until you're all grown up."

He shook his head. "I'm smaller than they were."

He slipped out of her embrace and started for the door. She followed. In the hallway, on a narrow section of wall next to the computer, were several horizontal lines with names next to them. She hadn't noticed them before. They showed the boys' heights at different ages.

"See," he said, pointing. "There's Ben when he was seven. C.J. was even taller." He leaned against the wall. He was definitely a couple of inches shorter. "I'm going to be seven next month. I won't grow enough in time to be as tall as them."

Jill knelt on the carpet and pulled Danny close to her. "Honey, people grow at different rates. Look at your uncles and your dad. You'll catch up. If not this year, then soon. Even if you don't, it's still all right. You don't have to be tall. You're wonderful just the way you are. Besides, didn't we decide that the best things come in small packages?"

But Danny didn't smile at her joke. He clung to her, sobbing as if his heart was broken. She held on, murmuring words of comfort, wondering why she ever thought she would be able to take this job and not get involved.

That night, after the boys were in bed, Jill asked Craig if she could speak with him. Evenings were the worst for the two of them. As soon as they were alone, the tension in the room climbed to an unbearable pitch. Usually they compensated by ignoring it. They were painfully polite in choosing television shows or movies to watch. Sometimes they just read, but that, too, was fraught with pitfalls. There was the choice of music, the volume, who used which lamp, the problem of chuckling at a funny part, then deciding whether or not to explain the humor.

Often, Jill sat staring unseeingly at the pages of her book, willing herself to find the courage to talk about what had happened between them. She kept thinking that if they could discuss the intimacy they'd shared, they would be able to find a new level of understanding. If they couldn't be lovers, they could at least be friends.

The problem was, she wanted to be lovers. She hadn't been able to think of anything else since they'd returned from Glenwood. Night after night she relived those wonderful hours with Craig. He was the kind of lover most women only dreamed about. Gentle, considerate, patient, and as much concerned about her pleasure as his own.

She kept remembering him telling her they could give the relationship a chance. Her fear got in the way of that one. So where did that leave them?

It would have been easier to forget everything if they hadn't gotten along so well in the other areas of their lives. If they'd disagreed over how to discipline the boys, or if he'd hated her cooking or was dating someone. But none of that was true, which made pretending to be immune to him even more difficult.

"I need to talk to you about Danny," she said, standing in the center of the family room. "If this is a good time?"

"Sure." He put down the book he was reading and motioned for her to take a seat on the sofa.

She sat a couple of cushions away and angled toward him. The overhead light illuminated him clearly. She could see the faint gray at his temples, the stubble darkening his cheeks. His expression was politely interested. Not by even a flicker of a lash did he give away what he was really thinking.

Now that he was on a regular schedule, he changed out of his uniform when he got home from work. She'd finally grown used to seeing him in jeans and a shirt, although the sight of worn denim caressing his thighs still had the ability to make her heart race.

Tonight she ignored the soft, faded material *and* the

way it hugged his muscles. She kept her attention on her hands.

"What about Danny?" he asked, prompting her.

"He hasn't been himself for the past week or so."

"I thought I noticed something. I asked him about it a couple of days ago, but he said he was fine."

She glanced at him. "I didn't realize you'd seen it, too."

"I was going to mention it, but there wasn't anything to say. I thought maybe I was imagining things. Obviously I'm not."

"No. This afternoon he didn't want to do anything. He just went in his room, sat on his bed and hugged his bear."

Craig frowned. "I don't like the sound of that. He'd practically relegated that to the closet. So what's the problem?"

She smiled. "Actually it's nothing to worry about. He showed me the wall by the computer where you keep track of the boys' heights at different ages. He's concerned that he's shorter than both Ben and C.J. were when they turned seven. His birthday is only a few weeks away, and he knows he can't catch up. I told him that everyone grows at different rates of speed. He'll catch up eventually. I think he feels better now. He was more cheerful at dinner. But maybe you could talk to him and tell him he's perfect the way he is. Maybe..." She trailed off.

Craig wasn't paying attention to what she was saying anymore. He stared past her, eyebrows drawn together as if he were wrestling with a difficult problem. A muscle twitched in his cheek. Something dark and painful passed through his eyes.

"Damn," he said softly. "I didn't want it to come up like this."

Cold fear rippled down Jill's spine. "Like what? Craig, what's wrong? Is he sick? Oh, God, he doesn't have something wrong with him, does he?"

When he didn't speak, she leaned forward and grasped his forearm. "Answer me, damn it. What's wrong with Danny?"

Craig drew in a deep breath. "Nothing. He's not sick. At least not that I know of. He's fine." He glanced down at her hand and touched the backs of her fingers. "I swear to you, Jill. It's not that."

Slowly she released him. Worry had formed a knot in the pit of her stomach. At his reassurance, it loosened a little, but didn't go away. "Then what is it?"

"Can we please not talk about this?" he asked.

She stared at him, not sure how to answer. "If you prefer, but I'd like to help."

"No one can help.... Hell, you might as well know the truth."

He pulled free of her touch and looked straight ahead. He braced his elbows on his knees and rested his head in his hands. "I don't know how tall Danny is going to be when he grows up. I don't know what he's going to look like or what he's going to want to be. I don't know anything about him."

"I don't understand."

"Danny's not my son."

Jill stared at him, uncomprehending. Not his son? Danny? Little Danny with the big eyes and the smile that— The smile that didn't look anything like his father's.

"Wait a minute," she said, half to herself. "That's crazy. Sure he doesn't look as much like you as the other two, but he has some of Krystal's features. The shape of his eyes. If you adopted him—"

He straightened and shook his head. "We didn't adopt him. He's Krystal's. He's just not mine."

She opened her mouth, but didn't know what to say. Not his? That was crazy. "Then how did you get him?"

"I didn't plan it, that's for damn sure." He leaned back against the sofa. If his hands hadn't been curled into tight fists, she might have thought the telling didn't affect him. But the white knuckles and straining tendons gave him away. She ached for him.

"Krystal and I had been separated, but still in the same house," he said. "Not the best way to live or bring up kids. Ben was five, C.J. barely two. She didn't bring her men home. I used to tell myself that was something. God, I was a fool."

"I'm sorry," she said softly.

"Me, too." He closed his eyes. "I told you before she'd been unfaithful from the beginning."

"Yes."

"Once we'd finally started talking about getting a divorce, she went wild. Coming in at all hours of the night, usually drunk. Men started calling here. I hated it and her. Then one night, she came on to me. I was immune by then, and she was furious. She finally blurted out she was pregnant and had planned to pass the kid off as mine. But when I wouldn't cooperate, she was forced to tell me the truth."

Jill shuddered. Craig's pain filled the room. She wanted to comfort him the same way she'd comforted Danny earlier that afternoon. But Craig wasn't a six-year-old boy. She drew her knees up to her chest and wrapped her arms around her legs.

"At first I thought she was going to have an abortion," he continued, opening his eyes, but not looking at her. "She didn't. I don't know why, and I never bothered to ask. As her pregnancy started to show, she became less active, sexually, although she still went out at night."

"You never asked who the father was?"

"No. I told her I didn't care. In my heart, I was curious, and hurt, but I didn't want her to know. She asked to stay until the baby was born, then she'd move out. She'd decided to give it up for adoption. I agreed. Ben and C.J. didn't really understand what was going on. I tried to shield them from her as much as possible."

He glanced at her and grimaced. "I couldn't disconnect from her, though. When her time came, I drove her to the hospital, but instead of leaving I stayed. What a sucker I was. I hated her, but even she deserved someone there. Then they brought me this tiny baby and placed him in my arms. Krystal hadn't bothered to make any arrangements. I saw her staring at me and then I knew. She'd planned it all along. She'd known I would take in her child. I never despised her more than I did at that moment. But I couldn't blame the kid for what his mother had done."

"You did the right thing," she whispered, too stunned to do more than take in all that he was telling her. Danny wasn't his. She couldn't believe it. He'd never even given a hint. Of course, being Craig, he wouldn't ever slight the boy. He'd had her convinced Danny was his favorite.

"I couldn't let him go to strangers," he said. "Besides, by then Krystal had explained her pregnancy to the boys. They were expecting a baby brother or sister.

After she left the hospital, she got her things and that was it."

Craig shifted uneasily on the sofa. He already regretted his confession. Jill was staring at him as if he'd just rescued an entire classroom of children from a burning building.

"I'm not a hero," he said harshly. "Don't start thinking I am."

"What would you call it then?"

"Making the best of a bad situation. I did what any decent person would have done. Keeping Danny was the right decision. I didn't trust Krystal to actually give him up. Do you know what that kid's life would have been like with only her as a parent?"

"He would never have survived."

"Exactly."

The room was silent for a moment. Jill looked at him, studying him as if they'd just met. The lamp behind her made her red hair glow, as if touched by moonlight. Her delicate features were so different from Krystal's obvious and flashy beauty. Why couldn't he have fallen for someone like her instead of Krystal? Then he remembered the boys, and he knew that whatever his ex-wife had cost him, it was worth every payment because he had them.

"Are you going to tell Danny?" she asked.

"Maybe when he's older. I know he already feels a little different. I don't want that information weighing on him, as well. Besides, as far as I'm concerned, Danny is as much mine as Ben and C.J."

"Do you know who—" She paused and shrugged. "You know."

"No, I don't know who his father is. Krystal said she didn't know, either. I don't know if she was lying, but it doesn't matter now. When Danny was born, I had him tested for drug addiction and AIDS.'' He swore. ''I had myself tested, too. Just to be safe. Hell of a thing for a husband to have to do because his wife is a slut. Everything came back negative. I know we got lucky. The way Krystal was living her life, who knows what could have happened. But that's over now.''

He was ashamed of his past and talking about it brought everything back. He just wanted to get away.

He rose to his feet. Jill stood up and moved close. ''I'm so sorry,'' she murmured.

''Don't be. It's done. We survived.''

''You did better than that.'' She stared up at him. Tears clung to her lower lashes.

''Stop,'' he said, touching his finger to the single tear that escaped. ''It's not that bad.''

''I can't believe she did that to you. And her children. To walk away from them like that. Didn't she know what a precious gift they are?''

''Appreciation was never one of Krystal's best qualities. Besides, it's over now. The boys are fine and I am, too. I'm going to make damn sure I'm never in that situation again.''

''Life doesn't come with guarantees.''

''Maybe not, but next time I'm not taking any chances.''

Chapter Fifteen

Craig heard soft voices in the hallway, followed by muffled footsteps in the hall. He finished fastening his belt, then opened his bedroom door. Ben and Jill had already reached the front door and were heading outside for their morning walk. He followed after them and arrived at the front door just as they started stretching. He pushed aside the front-window drapes to watch.

It was a perfect late-spring morning. The sky was clear, the air still with just a hint of coolness. Dew coated the lawn, making the individual blades of grass glisten. Pansies and marigolds provided bright color along the walkway.

Ben waited impatiently by the sidewalk. He shifted his weight from foot to foot and motioned for them to get going. Jill laughed. She shook out each leg, then moved toward him.

They were both wearing shorts and T-shirts. His once-pudgy son had slimmed down. According to Jill he'd already lost fifteen of the extra twenty pounds he carried. With his new eating habits and increased activity, the rest would be gone by the end of summer.

Ben had lost more than weight. He'd changed from a sullen boy who never wanted to participate in anything to a funny, outspoken charmer. He would never match C.J.'s natural ability, but he was a close second.

As Jill and Ben walked down the sidewalk, she wrapped her arm around his neck and dropped a quick kiss on his head. The boy responded by giving her a fierce hug.

Craig felt a sharp pain in the center of his chest. Why hadn't he seen the potential danger? It should have been obvious from the beginning. Everything about Jill's personality screamed that she was someone who gave fully. She could no more hold back than she could stop breathing. He'd hired her to take care of his sons and she'd done so completely, without thought of her feelings. He wondered if she knew she'd given away her heart.

He let the drapes fall back in place. He would have expected her to be won over by C.J.'s charm, or Danny's sweetness, but it was his oldest she related to the most. Maybe it was because they were both wounded. Maybe it was because a person most appreciated that which she had worked to achieve. Whatever the reason, at the end of summer, Jill Bradford was going to find it difficult to walk away.

He should have been pleased. Thoughts of keeping Jill around occupied most of his day. She'd made a place for herself in all their hearts. If he searched the world, he doubted he would find a woman more different from Krystal. Whereas his late wife had only taken, Jill preferred to give. Krystal thought of herself, Jill thought of others. Even in bed, they were nothing alike. Krystal had orchestrated those times as if they were a staged event. She'd been interested in drama, experimentation and results. Cuddling to be close, touching for the sake of simply touching had been as foreign to her as fidelity.

Jill gave her body with the same easy selflessness as she gave her heart. She savored the heat and passion of lovemaking, yet lingered over the softer, gentler pursuits.

He wanted her. He needed her. He couldn't imagine life without her. He'd sworn next time he wasn't taking any chances, yet he wanted to take this one. Was that love?

He wanted it to be, yet it seemed too easy. He'd lived six years of hell with Krystal and six years of being alone. After all that time was he supposed to believe he would find someone just like that? Meeting Jill had been a quirk of fate. If her friend Kim hadn't eloped after agreeing to take care of the boys, he and Jill wouldn't have met. Was it possible that some cosmic force in charge of love had arranged things so poorly? If by chance she'd been gone that morning, or had refused the job, then he would have spent the rest of his life searching for what he'd already lost.

He didn't want to think about that. He crossed the living room and entered the kitchen. Jill had put on coffee. He poured himself a mug and sipped the steaming liquid.

There were no easy answers to their situation. They'd both been burned. He regretted telling her the truth about Danny. If they were to take a chance on a relationship, he didn't want it to be because she thought he was some kind of hero. He wasn't. He was just a man and father trying to do the best he could. He wasn't trying to prove anything.

He wanted her to love him for himself. He leaned against the counter and took another sip. Ironically, that's exactly what Jill wanted, too. She wanted to be loved for *her*self.

They were both afraid, both hurting, both terrified of and desperate for love. Who was going to risk it all first?

He put down the coffee. He already knew the answer to that. The hard part would be convincing Jill that his feelings were about her and not just about finding a substitute mother for his children.

"We're doing better," Jill said when she finished counting. "Only fifteen bags for this trip to the grocery store."

Groceries covered the countertop. Her biweekly shopping trips still left her stunned by the amount of food this family consumed. She knew it was going to get worse. When the boys were teenagers, they would eat nearly twice as much. She sure hoped Craig's stock in Austin's company continued to perform well. He was going to need the extra income.

Ben strolled into the kitchen and eyed the bags. "Did you buy low-fat cookies?" he asked.

"Of course."

"Thanks." He grinned.

Although the boys came with her to the market, they hung out by the hot-rod magazines or played video games. She'd quickly found it was easier if they stayed busy and away from her. If they followed her through the store, they were constantly adding things to her cart and she was constantly pulling them out.

"There were some new fat-free hot dogs, so I thought we could try those," she said.

Ben frowned. "What's in them?"

"Turkey and—" She thought for a moment. "Maybe it's better if we don't ask too many questions."

He grabbed the grocery bag on the end of the counter and put it on the kitchen table. Then he reached inside and pulled out a huge bunch of bananas. He put them in the fruit bowl.

"Jill, there's this, uh, dance at school next week. I sort of have to go. It's part of my P.E. grade."

She glanced at him. Color stained his cheeks. He focused on emptying the bag and didn't look at her. Her heart went out to him. Growing up was tough.

"I'm sure you'll have fun," she said.

"I don't know how to dance."

"I'm not the greatest, but I'd be happy to help."

He cleared his throat, then shrugged. "Okay. Thanks." He dug out a bag of apples and walked them over to the fridge. "Um, do you think—" He cleared his throat again.

"What?"

He shrugged.

She carried cans of tomato sauce to the pantry and stacked them on the shelves. Then she paused by the refrigerator and rested her hand on Ben's shoulder.

"You have done a wonderful thing these last couple of months. You've changed the way you eat and how you treat your body. You're active and that's the key to maintaining your weight. This has been a hard lesson for you, but you've learned and you're going to be fine."

He looked at her. His dark eyes were cloudy with confusion. "Yeah?"

"I promise. Do you know what your friends are wearing to the dance?"

"A shirt maybe. No tie, though."

"Do you want to get something new? I'm sure your dad would agree."

"Okay. I don't think any of my good trousers fit me anymore." He closed the fridge door and leaned against it. "Will girls want to dance with me?" he asked, his words coming out in a rush.

She wrapped her arms around him and pulled him close. She could feel his spine and shoulder blades. She glanced up.

"Darn it, anyway, Ben, stop growing. I swear you're another half inch taller."

He smiled. "You're just short."

His smile reminded her so much of his father that her heart nearly stopped. She touched his cheek. "Ben, you're going to be a heartbreaker, just like your daddy. Be kind to those little girls at the dance. Be sweet to them, tell them they're pretty and treat them with respect. If you do that, they'll follow you anywhere."

"Yeah?"

"I swear."

"Thanks, Jill, I—" He broke off and hugged her tight. He was getting stronger and practically squeezed out all her air.

When he released her, she coughed a little. "In another couple of years you'll be able to pick me up."

"I already can." He approached. She ducked away.

"I don't think so," she said. "And let's not test your theory."

He grinned. A lock of dark hair tumbled across his forehead. She brushed it away, then pointed at the grocery bag still on the table. "Fold."

"Yes, ma'am."

She continued unpacking food and laundry supplies while Ben talked about his day. As she listened, her mind raced. What was Craig going to say when he found out that Ben was going to his first dance? It was a rite of passage, the first sign that his oldest was on the road to becoming a man.

Jill was glad she was going to be here to see it. She would have to remember to check the camera for film. She wanted to get plenty of pictures. In fact, she should take pictures of all of them. Children changed so quickly. Especially at Danny's age.

Danny. She paused, a bag of frozen vegetables in one hand and a half gallon of ice cream in the other. She'd barely seen Craig since he'd told her the truth about his youngest. It had been a couple of days, but the information still astounded her.

Danny wasn't his son. She didn't know which shocked her more—the fact that Krystal had intended to trick Craig into thinking it was his, that she'd been willing to give up her child for adoption or that Craig had taken the boy in and treated him like one of his own.

"Jill?" Ben held open the freezer door.

She looked at the frozen food she held. "Oh, thanks. I was just thinking."

"I guess."

She gave him a quick smile. "You can go outside with your brothers."

"I don't mind helping."

She tossed him the empty bag and reached for the next one. Cereal. These boys went through more cereal than any ten normal people could eat. She pulled out the boxes.

What astonished her the most was that she'd assumed Danny was his favorite. There was something special about Craig's relationship with his youngest. Now she knew what it was. Craig was an honorable man. He would do his best by the boy and that meant making sure he never had a hint that he was different. In time, he would need to be told, but only when he was old enough to handle the information. In the meantime he was growing up surrounded by love.

"What's in here?" Ben asked, pulling out a white plastic bag.

Jill turned toward him and bit back a gasp. How could she have forgotten? "Just girl stuff," she said, trying to sound calm.

He shuddered as if he'd touched bug guts, then tossed her the bag. It circled lazily thought the air. A square pink-and-white box slipped free and tumbled to the ground. She and Ben reached for it at the same time. She tried to cover the lettering with her fingers, but he got there first. He handed her the box.

The front door opened. "Ben, are you comin' or what?" C.J. called.

"Go ahead," Jill told him and sank into one of the kitchen chairs.

When he left without a backward glance, she told herself he hadn't seen anything. She hoped she was right.

After tossing the box on the table, she read the front panel: Accurate Home Pregnancy Test.

It was unlikely, she told herself as the familiar panic welled up inside. They'd used protection. Which sometimes fails, a little voice whispered. The odds were against her being pregnant, she silently argued. Except she was late. Very late.

She should have started her period about ten days ago. There hadn't even been a hint of anything. Which meant the stress of everything had affected her, or she was going to have a child.

A baby. She leaned back in the chair and closed her eyes. If she was, what would she do? What would Craig say? Would he think she had tried to trap him, much as Krystal had? After all, she'd been the one coming on to him.

As always, the thought of her wanton behavior made her blush. She buried her face in her hands. She hadn't planned for them to do anything. Of course, she'd thought about making love with Craig. How could she live with him day after day and *not* think about it? But thinking and doing weren't the same thing. Still, when he'd walked in on her in the bathroom, it had seemed so right.

It hadn't even been about finding love. Instead, she'd suddenly gotten tired of feeling lonely. Was that so bad? Did she deserve to be punished for one night of comfort?

Since returning from Glenwood, she and Craig had been involved in an elaborate dance of avoidance. Except for that night when he'd confessed the truth about Danny, they hadn't had a single personal conversation. She was still reeling from his accusations. In the past week, she'd tried not to think about them, but she couldn't think about anything else.

Had she deliberately chosen Aaron so she could

hold some part of herself back? Did she find it easier to exist in impossible situations because she secretly wanted to be disappointed? Was she so afraid of giving and receiving genuine love?

And what about Craig? He came from a long line of failed marriages. The Haynes family didn't have a great record when it came to relationships. Yet look at what was happening now. Travis and his wife. Kyle and Sandy. Was it Craig's turn? Was it hers? How did she feel about him?

She picked up the box and stared at it for a moment. If she didn't love him, was she strong enough to walk away even if she was carrying his child?

A baby. She smiled as tears sprang to her eyes. A child of her own. It was a dream come true.

She brushed her eyes with the back of her hand. A baby wasn't her whole dream, she admitted to herself. She'd also wanted a husband. Someone she loved and respected. Someone she could trust and admire. Someone who would cherish her. Had she already found that?

If only... If only she could know his feelings. She stood up and grabbed the pregnancy kit. As she headed into her bedroom, she knew it didn't matter. Even if Craig admitted he cared about her, how was she going to trust him? How would she know that he wasn't just interested in having a mother for his children? She'd already been burned like that before.

She placed the pregnancy kit inside the medicine chest. She knew there wasn't an easy solution to the problem. There was no way Craig could prove that he wanted her and not just the convenience of having her around. She would have to take a step of faith. She wasn't sure she could.

Summer was fast approaching, then it would be September. Her condo lease would be up, her job would be waiting. Would she stay or would she go? Could she walk away from Craig and the boys? Could she risk being used once again?

How much of her confusion was fear of the past repeating itself and how much of it fear of love? Until she answered that question, she knew she wouldn't be able to decide.

"Dad?"

Craig looked up from the book he was reading. It was nearly ten. "What's wrong, Ben? Don't you feel well?"

His oldest stepped into the bedroom and shrugged. "I'm fine. I just can't sleep."

Craig patted the cushion next to him on the small sofa in front of the fireplace in his bedroom. He placed a bookmark in his book and set it on the table. "Are you worried about your dance next week?"

"A little, but I think it's gonna be okay." Ben plopped down. He pushed up the long sleeves of his pajama top and sat cross-legged in the corner. "I think I saw something, and I don't know if I should say anything or not."

"Okay. What did you see?"

Ben looked at him, then ducked his head. "It's about Jill."

Craig's stomach clenched. Was something wrong with her? Was she ill? Was she leaving? "What about Jill?"

"We were putting away groceries a couple of days ago. I was helping, and she had this plastic bag. She didn't want me to touch it. She didn't say that, but I could tell.'' He paused. Color stole up his face.

What had he seen? Birth control? The thought gave Craig a jolt of hope. Maybe Jill was willing to admit she had feelings for him. "Then what happened?"

"I sorta tossed it to her and this box fell out. I swear it just fell on its own. I wasn't trying to do anything wrong."

Craig leaned over and placed his hand on his son's shoulder. "I know you weren't. It's all right. What did you see?"

Ben stared at him. "I'm not sure. It said Home Pregnancy Test on the label. Is Jill gonna have a baby?"

Even as conflicting emotions raced through him, Craig forced himself not to react. He didn't want to frighten or confuse Ben and he didn't want to get either of their hopes up. He knew the boys wanted Jill to stay permanently.

"I don't know if Jill's pregnant," he said. Could she be? They'd used a condom. Of course, condoms occasionally failed. Pregnant? A baby.

"Are you going to say anything?" Ben asked. "I don't want her to think I was prying."

"She knows you wouldn't do that, son. I'll talk to her."

Ben nodded, then rose to his feet. "If she has a baby will she have to leave?"

"No. She won't. She can stay right here."

Ben nodded. Craig wasn't sure if the boy knew who the father might be. They'd talked about sex several times over the past couple of years. Ben had a clear understanding of the conception process. Craig thought about reassuring him that there wasn't a strange man in Jill's life, but then he figured he'd better talk to her first. If she was pregnant—

Ben closed the door quietly behind himself. Craig sagged back against the sofa. A baby. He grinned. Hot damn. He hadn't seriously thought about having another child, but at that moment he realized how much he wanted one with Jill. A girl, just like her mother.

A girl. He sobered quickly. Would it be a girl? Had the curse been broken by love?

He'd spent the past six years hiding, waiting for something certain. Instead, life had given him the gift of Jill Bradford. Given a choice between his precious sure thing and her, he knew what he would choose. Jill. Always Jill.

He was finally willing to take a chance. All he had to do was convince her this was about her and not the children.

He stood up and started for the door. As he reached for the handle, he froze in place and swore. If she was pregnant, she would never be able to accept his love. She would assume any declaration by him was about the baby and his feelings of responsibility. After what he'd told her about Danny, she would be even more cautious about getting involved with him.

She wanted to know it was about her and not the children or the pregnancy. Somehow he would have to find the words. Now that he'd finally figured out he'd been given a second chance, he didn't plan to blow it.

Chapter Sixteen

Craig headed for the stairs. He wasn't sure what he was going to say to her, but he prayed he would find the words once he got there.

He crossed the dark family room. There was a light shining under her door. He knocked softly.

"Come in," she called.

He opened the door and stepped into her bedroom.

She sat on top of her bed, with the small television tuned to an old movie. When she saw him, she reached for the remote control and flipped off the set. Her eyes were wide and green, their expression questioning. She gave him a half smile.

"What can I do for you?" she asked.

Words failed him. He knew he wouldn't be able to find the right ones, anyway. How could he explain love and caring when he'd just figured it out for himself? How could he make her understand the emptiness he'd felt inside and how she'd managed to find her way in to fill every crevice of need? How could he tell her that she was the most loving, giving person he'd ever met?

He crossed to the bed and stared down at her. Without conscious thought, he reached for the hem of his T-shirt and pulled it over his head. Then he waited for her reaction.

He braced himself for her rejection or for her to calmly tell him they had to talk about this first. He even told himself she might slap him for being so presumptuous. Instead, she rose on her knees and pressed her mouth against the center of his chest.

Jill knew this was a mistake. She even knew why Craig was here. But she could no more have turned him away than she could have turned back time. They needed to talk and try to figure out what they were going to do. The logical part of her brain told her they should talk *first*. The rest of her body, on fire from the moment he'd walked into her room, slammed the door on logic and begged her just to feel.

She complied. She touched his warm skin, running her fingers across his shoulders and down his arms. She kissed his chest, his flat nipples, his belly. The waistband of his jeans rested just below his belly button. She dipped her tongue inside and teased with a quick flick of dampness.

He groaned. "Do you know what you do to me?"

"If it's anything like what you do to me, we're both in trouble," she said.

He reached for her, tugging on her arms until she

rose to her feet. With her on the bed, she was taller. She grinned and wrapped her arms around his neck. "Now I've got you where I want you."

"And I've got you."

He gripped her around the waist and stepped away from the bed. She caught her breath and wrapped her legs around his hips. Instantly her damp, hot center came in contact with his arousal.

She clung to him as he spun them both around in the room. When she was too dizzy to do more than hang on, he slowed and pressed his mouth against hers.

Their lips brushed together, moving slowly in a dance of sensation so sweet, she wanted to weep. She parted and he swept inside. Fiery need cascaded through her, sensitizing every part of her body, making her tremble in his embrace. If he hadn't been supporting her, she would have slipped to the ground.

He sat on the edge of the bed. Her legs hugged his thighs. As she traced the rippling muscles in his back, he unfastened the buttons down the front of her shirt. When he'd tugged the garment free, he flipped open her bra with a quick flick of his fingers.

He cupped her curves, then sank back on the mattress, taking her with him. She landed on her hands and knees, her head slightly higher than his. He took advantage of the situation and reached up to suckle her. At the first moist touch of his mouth on her sensitized taut peaks, her arms began to tremble. She had to hold in a moan.

"Don't," he murmured against her skin. "Don't be quiet. The boys can't hear us from here."

"They can if I start screaming," she said in a gasp as his thumb and forefinger teased her other nipple.

He chuckled. His warm breath fanned her flesh. He moved his free hand between them and rubbed her damp heat. She was frozen in place, caught between two pleasures so intense, she thought she might perish.

He tilted his head slightly so he could reach her other nipple. His fingers caressed her breasts, stroking the soft undersides. Between her legs, he continued to slip back and forth, bringing her closer to her moment of release.

She rocked in rhythm with him, urging him to do more, but frustrated by the layers of clothing between them. When she couldn't stand it anymore, she straightened and reached for the button at the waistband of her jeans. Craig raised his eyebrows, then stretched out lazily, lacing his hands behind his head.

"Don't look so damn smug," she muttered as she crawled over him and pulled off the rest of her clothes.

"I can't help it. You're cute when you're turned on."

"Gee, thanks."

He released one hand and patted his belly. "Come on back."

She knelt next to him and started to lift her leg over his waist. He grabbed her hips. "Not there."

He urged her up until she was beside his shoulders. She stared down at him. "Here?"

"Yes." He reached for the pillows and pulled them out from under the bedspread. After slipping two under his head, he drew her over him, so she straddled his neck. He reached up and parted the damp curls, then touched his tongue to her most sensitive place.

Jill closed her eyes and fought back a scream of pure pleasure. She'd never done it exactly like this before. The new position made her feel exposed and vulnerable, but at the same time heightened her pleasure. She felt as if Craig could see all of her.

She braced her hands on her thighs and began to rock in counterpoint to the quick flicking of his tongue. Every fiber of her being focused on that tiny point of pleasure. She could feel herself collecting, tensing, readying for the moment of ecstasy.

He grabbed her hands and pulled them down so she could hold herself apart for him. She continued to thrust back and forth, urging him faster, deeper, harder. The passion grew. She was caught up in the intensity and barely noticed him shifting beneath her. The bed rocked as if he was moving.

Just as she came within a heartbeat of her release, he stopped. With a quick, fluid movement, he turned her on her back and kicked off his jeans. He'd already worked them halfway down his thighs. Before she could protest or even lose her passion, he plunged deeply inside her, filling her until she thought she would explode.

She opened her eyes and found him watching her. Passion filled his dark eyes, passion and something else. Something warm and wonderfully tempting. If she'd been able to think or do anything but remind herself to keep breathing, she might have called it love.

But she couldn't do anything else right now. She

could only react. He braced his hands on either side of her shoulders. His powerful legs and hips thrust him inside her, then he withdrew in a rhythm designed to drive her over the edge of sanity. Within seconds, she was as close as she'd been before.

Even as the ripples of ecstasy swept through her and her body convulsed around his, she felt him achieve his release. She forced herself to continue to hold his gaze, staring in wonder at the pleasure tightening his features, at the way he exposed all of himself to her. As she wrapped her arms around his shoulders and her legs around his hips, holding him tight, she felt the first prickle of tears.

He held her while she cried. "I'm s-sorry," she said shakily. "It's j-just—"

"You don't have to explain," he said. "I understand."

She was glad someone did. It didn't make sense to her.

Gradually, his murmured words and the slow stroking of his hands against her skin comforted her. She pulled back and stared at him.

"It's never been like this before," she said.

"I know. For me, too." He shifted so he was lying next to her, then pulled her on top of him. He ran his fingers through her hair and traced the length of her spine. "I remember the first time I saw you. At Kim's."

"Hmm, me, too."

"You were naked."

She tried to sit up, but he held her against him. "I was not."

"You were naked under your robe."

"Oh." She felt her cheeks heat. "That."

"Yes, that. You made it very difficult for me to hold a rational conversation. How was I supposed to talk to you about my children when your breasts were swaying back and forth like that? Don't ever answer the door like that again."

She giggled. She'd thought the robe covered her fine. Apparently, she'd been wrong. "I haven't flashed anyone else that I know of."

"Good."

He sighed. She felt the rise and fall of his chest, then she closed her eyes and listened to the sound of his heartbeat. Images sprang to mind. Bits of conversation, time they'd spent together. A shiver raced through her.

"You cold?" he asked, reaching for the bedspread.

"No. Just an aftershock." She bent her knee and ran her foot up and down his calf. "Craig, we have to talk."

"I know."

She hadn't thought it would hurt this much, but it did. The exquisite pain filled her until she didn't want to breathe. But she had to. And she had to say the words. "Ben told you about what he saw."

"Yes."

So he knew about the pregnancy test. That was why he'd come to her. Damn. Of course that was the reason, but she'd really hoped it was something else. Something he'd thought of on his own.

"I like you, Jill," he said slowly. "I respect you."

"I feel the same way." But liking and respecting

weren't loving. Her heart tightened a little. She kept her eyes closed, wanting to pull away, but knowing he wouldn't let her.

"You make me feel alive," he went on. "I'd forgotten what that felt like. I've been going through the motions for years. I've been lonely. Until I met you."

Oh, God, she wanted it to be true. She hadn't known how much until this moment. She curled her fingers into her palm and bit down on her knuckle.

He continued to stroke her hair. His other hand cupped her buttocks and squeezed gently. "I guess I don't have to tell you that you turn me on."

If her answering laugh sounded a little like a sob, he didn't seem to notice.

"I've been scared," he said. "That's not something I'm proud to admit, but it's true. You've helped me change that. I've seen that I've been hiding from the boys and that's wrong for them and for me. They need me around almost as much as I need to be around them. I was looking for a sure thing, with them and with love. But life doesn't work that way. Sometimes you have to be willing to take chances. I'm willing, Jill. I love you. I want to marry you."

She raised her head and glanced down at him. If only he knew how much she wanted that to be true. Just hearing the words...believing them even for a second. It was a million times more wonderful than she thought it would be.

His dark eyes were bright with emotion. If only she could believe.

"I love you, too," she whispered. When he started to speak, she covered his mouth with her hand.

"Let me finish," she said, then paused. "I—I guess I've loved you for a long time. Maybe from the first time I saw you with the boys. It would be easy to accept your proposal, but I can't."

"Jill—"

"No. It's my turn. I can't do this again, Craig. I can't do the right thing for the wrong reason. I can't afford to be second-best."

"You wouldn't be. This isn't about you being pregnant."

"But if Ben hadn't told you about the test you wouldn't be here right now."

"Maybe not at this minute, but soon."

She slid off him and sat on the edge of the bed. "I don't believe you."

"I want you in my life," he said. "The boys want you. It's not about the things you do. Hell, if it makes you feel better, I'll hire a housekeeper and a nanny. We just want you. I want you."

"I can't spend the rest of my life wondering if it's real."

He sat up and grabbed her shoulders, then turned her toward him. "I knew you were going to be difficult about this. How can one small woman be so damned stubborn?"

"Just lucky, I guess." But she couldn't make herself smile.

"Jill, I love you. Please believe me."

"I want to," she said. "If you only knew how much." He had no idea how much. But it wasn't to be. She needed to know they were talking about an honest affection and not simply obligation.

"I want to marry you," he insisted.

"You don't have to. I'm not pregnant."

She wanted to be a coward and look away, but she forced herself to stare at his face. She searched carefully for the flicker of relief and the verbal backpedaling as he tried to withdraw his proposal.

But Craig didn't look relieved. Instead, something amazingly like disappointment crossed his features. "Are you sure?" he asked, his mouth turning down at the corners. "Couldn't the test be wrong?"

"You sound like you *want* me to be pregnant."

"Of course I do," he said forcefully, shaking her gently. "What did you think this whole damn conversation was about? I want to marry you and be with you. I want to break the Haynes curse and have a daughter who looks just like her mother. I want it all, Jill, but only if I can have it with you."

The shaking started from the inside. She blinked several times, sure he must have misunderstood. "I'm not pregnant," she repeated.

"I got that."

"And you still want to marry me?"

"Of course. I love you."

"Even without the baby?"

"There is no getting through to you," he said with exasperation, then hauled her close and kissed her.

She hung limply in his arms as his lips pressed against hers. Thoughts raced through her mind. He knew she wasn't pregnant. He still wanted to marry her. He wanted to marry *her!*

She surged against him, knocking him off-balance.

They tumbled back on the bed, a tangle of arms and legs.

"You mean it?" she asked.

He took her hand in his and stared into her eyes. "Jill Bradford, I love you more than life itself. I want to make love with you until we're both so old our bones are threatening to crack. I want to wake up next to you, I want to see you grow round with my child. Will you marry me? For better or for worse, for richer or poorer, as long as we both shall live?"

She grabbed him by the back of his head and pulled him closer. "Yes," she said, and kissed him. "Yes, yes, yes."

He laughed. "The boys are going to be thrilled. They love you very much."

"I know. I love them, too."

He touched her face, then ran his thumb across her lips. "I meant what I said about the baby, Jill. I'd love to have a child with you."

"I want that, too."

"Maybe we can get started on it right now."

She smiled. "Maybe we already did."

At his frown, she giggled. "I'm not pregnant, Craig. We didn't use any protection."

He drew his eyebrows together, then relaxed as the realization dawned. "I didn't think about it because I thought you already were pregnant. Why didn't you stop me?"

"I'm not sure. I wasn't paying attention. Maybe I wanted it to be true."

"If not this time, then next time," he promised.

"Or the time after that," she said.

He moved his hand over her breasts and grinned as her breath caught. "As many times as it takes," he agreed. "It's not as if it's hard work or anything."

He reached between her thighs and touched her quivering skin, then entered her.

She wrapped her legs around his hips and drew him closer. "I love you," she whispered. "For always."

"For always," he echoed, then led them on a journey that would seal that love forever.

* * * *

Susan Mallery currently has a new series out in Silhouette Special Edition™. It starts in January with The Rancher Next Door.

SILHOUETTE®

NORA ROBERTS
NIGHT MOVES

TWO ROMANTIC THRILLERS IN ONE BOOK

From dusk till dawn,
the hours of darkness are
filled with mystery, danger
...and desire.

Available from 18th January

*Available at most branches of WH Smith,
Tesco, Martins, Borders, Eason, Sainsbury's
and most good paperback bookshops.*

SUPERROMANCE™

Enjoy the drama, explore the emotions, experience the relationship

Superromance is a fantastic new Silhouette® series.

Longer than other Silhouette books, Superromance offers you emotionally involving, exciting stories, with a touch of the unexpected.

4 GREAT NEW TITLES A MONTH

Available at most branches of WH Smith, Tesco, Martins, Borders, Eason, Sainsbury's, and most good paperback bookshops.

SILHOUETTE SUPERROMANCE

is proud to present

nine months later

Friends... Lovers... Strangers...
These couples' lives are about to change
radically as they become parents-to-be

HER BEST FRIEND'S BABY
CJ Carmichael
January

THE PULL OF THE MOON
Darlene Graham
February

EXPECTATIONS
Brenda Novak
March

THE FOURTH CHILD
CJ Carmichael
April

Join us every month throughout the whole of 2002 for one of these dramatic, involving, emotional books.